Published by:

I0692824

PUBLISHING

please visit us on the web at:
www.cafepress.com/manning
http://shermanmanning.blogspot.com/

or contact us at:
hallopeter@freesurf.ch

© Copyright 2005 A&M Publishing and Sherman D. Manning
Honoring HarperCollins

ISBN 0-9743260-4-6

Other Books by **Sherman Manning:**

Reach Beyond the Break and Hold On
Dream and Grow Rich
If It Doesn't Fit, You Must Acquit
Through the Valley of the Shadow of Death (Columbine High School)
Teens Are Dying/Parents Are Crying: Where Do We Go From Here?
American Dream, A Search for Justice Vol. 1
American Dream, A Search for Justice Vol. 2
Creating Monsters
From Palace to Prison

HarperCollins books may be purchased at local bookstores or over the Internet. The author encourages readers to purchase books in bulk by writing to: Special Markets Department, HarperCollins Publishers, Inc., 10 East 53rd Street, New York, NY 10022.

DISCLAIMER

Warning: High school hotties, college studs, jocks, nerds, geeks and freaks may be featured in this book. *Harper Collins*, A&M and this author clearly understand the temptation by *some* teachers and parents to keep this book away from grade schools. This author actually concurs with that assessment. This book should be read by those sixteen years old and older...

Contributions to this book have been made by many high school and college students as well as professors across the world. We challenge you (the person holding this book right now... Y-o-u...) to go online and find Brian Glover (Santa Barbara, CA), Tim Tidaback, Jason Shapiro (Duke), Dr. Cory Floyd, Orville Schell, Abby Goodnough, Grant Gordon, Kyle (Los Altos), Tompone, Josh Glenny, Odessa Bethea, Eugene Redmond, Jeff Moss, Mike Lynn and Tyler Hudson. I want you to tinker, blog, message, text and e-mail til you inundate the Web with this book. The salacious details that are often covered in this book are things we're not supposed to *write* about.

As you enter into this forbidden land of sex, sex, sex, drugs, rock and roll, roll with the punches and let the saga unfold for you.

We salute the *Summer Bridge*, Jake Weary, Zach Roerig, Agim Kaba, Ryan Weston (Cheshire High School), Joel Corona (St. Helena, CA), Brandon and Brian Kniffen, Denver Dunn, Bret Ratner (Beverly Hill, CA), Judge Richard A. Howard, Dan Cummings, Barbara Hinkle, Chris McClendon, Boys and Girl Scouts of America, YMCA, Youth to Youth, Push America.org, Junior Achievement and Eric Bulrice.

We also salute Mr. Ralph White of Stockton, California and Oilman David Perez of San Diego. Ralph White went down to New Orleans and brought a bus load of Hurricane Katrina victims back to Stockton, CA. He owns the *Whitehouse* Hotels and is a millionaire. Mr. Perez brought a plane load back to San Diego. Hector Hoyos, Eli Manning, Kanye West, Matt Damon and Warrick Dunn... We salute Caron Butler, Stephen Marbury and Cindy Sheehan. We need **you** to use Craigslists, Nola.com, podcasting and texting to tell all of the aforementioned folks that this book is out! Tell somebody, tell somebody... And pray for the Gulf Coast victims. Pray that this horrible tragedy will forge new allies and bring people together. Maybe, perhaps I hope, churches will *open* the doors of the *church* and take these families in...

We celebrate creative writers sitting undiscovered in high schools and college dorms all across America. We invite the writings, essays, ideas and comments of writers. We invite writers, teachers and students concerned about justice to comment on our blog at http://DashCash.Blogspot.com. Those who want to comment and get involved on issues pertaining to stopping child abuse and preventing child molestation should go to the blog http://SaveShastaGroene.Blogspot.com today. Those Boston Legal, Ally McBeal and The Practice fans should go to http://TheLawFirmTV.Blogspot.com and those interested in fighting wrongful convictions, getting innocent folks out of prisons, etc., should go to www.Cafepress.com/Manning and get "From the Palace to the Prison" and then go to http://SwissWishFoundation.Blogspot.com...

We encourage you to download these blogs and send copies to pastors, professors, frats, judges, lawyers and libraries. If you are a student and you need a scholarship, tuition money or a *stipend*, etc., there is immediate money available. A. Read every page of this book and you will discover many offers for book and tuition money. B. Go to *DashCash.Blogspot*.com. We cannot overemphasize the fact that high school students such as Daniel Asare (John F. Kennedy High...Sacto), Joshua Walker (Temecula, CA), Joel Corona, Ryan Weston, Kevin Shelton, Daniel Browning Smith (Santa Monica), law student Morgan Nelson, Jeff Cavaliere, Adam and Sean Seratilli, A. Lidogoster (Brooklyn), Bill Hall (Rancho Cordova), Jamie Miller (podcaster in Rancho Cordova), staff and students at the Wind Youth Center, Eric Haynes, Reuben Martinez (Libros Pana Ninos), Mike Bonanno (NY), Heidi Fugames (L.A.), Luke and Kyle Abbott (Santa Cruz), Luke Sears, Damascus High School students, Bad Ass Café, John Parrish (Imperial, MO), Peter Beinart, John Lechner, Kenny Wayne Shephard, Jeff Tweiten (Seattle), Carla K. Johnson, Rancho Buena Vista High School students in San Diego, Joe Schlosser at Christian Brothers High School, Zack Foote (Sacto), Coosa Valley Technical College in Rome, Georgia and Jay Baruchel in Hollywood... Reach out to these people and inform them that *Blue-Eyed Blonde* is on the (press) **run**.

We want Adrian Holovaty, Tyler Farrar, Kip Conner, Conrad Rupp, Steven Drozd and Tina Paymaster to know this tome is out. Many of them wrote us over and over asking, "When is the tome coming out?" And now that it is out, we can't reach them all. We have no idea where our interns, i.e., Casey Gray, Elias Ravin, Ryan Sheehy, Alex Hurst, Jack Rosenfeld, Austin Cregg, Aaron Richter are... You can find them. We want Wade Lagrone, Craig Newmark, Davis (The Scholar), Daniel Yoder, Daniel Cummings (Bait and Tackle shop in Florida), Carly Simon, Sequib Keval (Elk Grove), Doug

Pieper (Folsom), Seamus Farrow, Michael Colen, Luke Klipp, Aaron Peckham to know this thing has hit the freaking streets.

If you have a blog, podcast, e-mail, text, messaging or any device, tool, outlet, trinket, gadget, etc., etc., which can be used to *alert others* (seriously)... Please, please alert Corbin Dahl (J.F.K. High), Bryan Lemieux, Riley Evans, James Henderson (Davis High School), Bruce Mai (Sheldon High School), Brian Hawn (Atlanta, GA), Matthew Putrino-Mamola (Chris. Bros. H.S.), Brian Martin, Jimmy Wong, Shayan Vaghefi, Jimmy Wong, Shad Selby, Joe Schumacher (River City High). We believe this kind of national recognition encourages creativity among college and high school students and teachers. We want Jonathan Meyer and Jill Meyer (Skyhawk Communications, Sacto), Sacactors.com, Evan Nossorf, Amber Kloss, Rachael Devlin, Nicole Townsend, Tony Kwong, Julee Fessender, Rhett Snider and Johnny Weir...

We salute companies offering training programs for students i.e., Sacactors.com... We salute Jerry Saetern of World of Good Tastes of Sacramento, Larry Moss (Creative Director of Runyan, Saltzman & Einhorn). This is the time for *Breanna Mastropoalo* to shine! Michael Scott Sellers? Adrianna Ver de Franco? Neal Carlson, Fatima Hoang, Zach Weary? Christopher Hillerman? FaceBook.com? Mozilla Foundation? Chaz Wolcott? Wil Seabrook? Joshua Dick? Josh Helfgott? Kari and Patrick Andal? Clark Domae? Ken Holliday? B. J. Hickman? Dominic Sophia? Cody Alcott? Jeremy Elan? Marc Zuckerberg? Tai Matthews, Joshua Bruce, Wade Robson, Zach Smilovitz, Joshua Frey, Ryan Carlson, Matt Maloney (Green Bay, Wisc.), Ken Jacobson, Kevin Mahaffey, Nate Berkus. Casey Ryle (Rancho Cordova, CA).

We want them to know this thing is out! Jody Carlin, Chris Redden (St. Helena, CA) won't discover this tome unless you tell them about it. I want America to continue to pray for the Boy Scouts of America. They mean so much to so many! I salute Scoutmaster Steve McCullagh and little Ryan Collins. Salute Mr. Bitzer and all of their family members. Go on to Scout Websites and post prayers and messages of encouragement.

This book is a reminder to all technocrats, nerds, geeks, rebels and freaks that the mainstream media has already forgotten the scouts. Let us not forget! Get every Scout this book. This is a book for Scouts even if the media does not tell us it is...

I need thousands of my readers to contact Fort Hays State University student Ryan Leiker, Yulia Tymoschenko, Tracy Lamourie (The Canadian Coalition Against the Death Penalty), Mario

3

Voorhemes (Vienna, Austria... Can *you* find Mario?), Juan David Ramirez, Pete McCloskey, Eva M. Martinez, Eva Sandoval, Fred and Joan Baker (Golden State Steel Co.), Elias Reyes, Anthony Contreras (Manhattan Beach), Tayde Polomardes, lest they not know.

Do not ever forget Michael J. Shibe, Mike Lacroix, Ronald H. Bitzer, Scott Edward Powell... We pray (consistently) for their families, friends, kids and scouts. Blake Stimson (U. C. Davis Art History Professor), Blake Ross (Stanford) and all Girl Scouts gotta know this book is out. Go to their message and discussion boards and let them know. We want Steve Swenson (Trek Bicycle Corp...Waterloo, Wis.), John Burke, Jules Helms (NY), Chad Kramer, Jeff Gordon, Sean (who appeared on Larry Elder TV on 7/29/05), Lovesac Furniture Company, Jeff Love (Burlingame, CA), Mr. Vincent (reporter for ITN), Kyle Tompane, Greg Afani and Wes Kovarik... I want all y'all to call 916-340-0505 and help them. Get involved *today* with these great geeks, freaks, nerds, etc. Again 916-340-0505 or wsww www.*CALyouth.*org...

Blog, Tinker, E-mail and Text these folks today!!
Danke Schon... *Now* enjoy *Blue-Eyed Blonde*

PRAISE AND CRITICISM

"Shackelford and *Sherman* put it down in this book. It's tight." - *Eminem*

"I enjoyed this book immensely." - *Scott Turow*

"I think Sherman stole my style and mastered it." - *John Grisham*

"One of the biggest crocks of liberal crap I've read." - *Rush Limbaugh*

"Every lawyer should read this book." - *Gerry Spence*

"I enjoyed this thing called *Blue-Eyed Blonde*." - *P. Diddy*

"This was a fast and terrific read." - *Paris Hilton*

"It don't get no better than this." - *Snoop Dogg*

"This was thought provoking and well researched." - *Po Bronson* - Wired Magazine

"I think this book should win a Pulitzer." - *Professor Dylan Rodriguez*

"Sherman has his finger on the pulse of the youth." - President of *Myspace.com*

"I found this to be a great read." - *Marcus Pinkus* - Tribe.net

"I read this book and laughed. It's B.S." - *Sean Hannity*

"A fabulous book that we need." - *Chris Purvis* - Sacramento

"I hope the frat kids will read this." - *Mel Gibson*

"I read it three times. I got something new every time." - *Michael Moore*

"I really, really enjoyed this book." - *Jonathan Crier*
"I hope politicians read it and weep." - *Trent Reznor*

"I tell lawyers not to try another case involving juveniles til they read this book."
- *Attorney Richard Ben Viniste*

"This will rock the world." - *Shavo Odadjian*
"Hollywood is calling for the *Blue-Eyed Blonde*" - *Jerry Bruckheimer*

"I give it five stars and twenty codes." - *Steve Johnston* - Storycode.com

"It's a great read." - *Derrick Ontai* - Surfing the Nations

"I thought he'd never write it." - *Daven Yamada*

"America Idol fans - read up." - *Anthony Fedorov*

"It's one of the best books out." - *Val Litwin* - *Extreme Kindness*

"Teens - make your parents read this." - *Marcos Garza*

"Hilarious, brutal and candid." - *Josh Johns* - Friendster.com

"I don't read much but this was worth it." - *Joshua Walker* - Myspace.com

"Right to the point and right on time." - *R. Mihaldko* - Cuddleparty.com

"I can't believe this guy wrote this." - *Nathan Craft*

"Gothics will love this." - *Kyle Love*

"Don't blink or you'll miss the point." - *Joe Klein* - West Hollywood

"My group of buddies love this book." - *Mike Ciompi* - Hollywood

"Nerds will get it." - *Wes Kovarik* - Antioch
"A terrible book that I hate." - *Tanvir Robinson*

"This book should be required reading." - *Brad Pitt*

"My senior class is reading this in groups." - *Riley Evans* - Davis Senior High

"It was great." - *John Peters* - A. I. Contestant

"What are you waiting on? Read it." - *Mario Vazquez*

"It's quite touching." - *Judd Harris* - A. I. Contestant

"A moving read." - *Johnny Weir* - skater

"I loved the book." - *Rosie O'Donnell*

"Amazing read." - *Lisa Ling*

"This book is tight. It kept me up for hours. Sherman Manning knows how to keep the pages turning."
- *Eminem*

"Every college student must get this book." - *Heath Ledger*

"Barrett Lyon and Ero Carrera both sent me this book. It's awesome."
- *Jake Phelps, Thrasher Magazine*
-
"Matthew Feeley and Sam Neuman told me about this book; I read it and read it again."
- *Billy McNair – Peerflix*

"Our web site crashed the first day *Blue-Eyed Blonde* came out. Teenagers from all over the world are talking about it."
- *Taek Kwon, CEO Friendster.com*

In this sensational book, *Jeremy Shackelford* is a stud, a jock and a fraternity leader. He graduates Magna Cum Laude from U. C. Davis in California . . . He interned at the State Capitol for the *Terminator*. Jeff Bezos, Bill Gates, Terry Semel and Marc Cuban all gave Jeremy lucrative job offers. But *Jeremy Shackelford* is a podcaster, a blogger, an iPodder and the Editor of the Sacramento Bee Newspaper. He kicks it with Marcus Pinkus, Victor Rasuk, Brad Pitt, Angelina Jolie, Adam Curry, Josh Davis, Dennis Lloyd and Trent Reznor. In the process of wining, dining, sex, drugs, rock and roll, Jeremy stumbles upon some information . . . A powerful secret. His journalistic discovery; could be deadly . . .

PREFACE: ASHTON KUTCHER

Some people believe that youngsters don't give a damn about politics, crime and punishment. That's bunk. We actually do care. Our problem has been the lies and hypocrisy disguising themselves as democracy . . . We can certainly relate to the *Blue-Eyed Blonde* . . . I received this book in manuscript form in June 2005. I read it while on a flight to the Bahamas. It is an awesome read. It's sexual, sensual, funny and enlightening. It was written for the pod casting, iPod, gaming and the Internet generation. This book is Sirius satellite writing. My only criticism is that *Harper Collins* names *Sherman D. Manning* as the author. I think *Jeremy* and *Paul Shackelford* ought to be the authors and Sherman is the editor. Nevertheless, publishers will be publishers and just because I *punk* people and produce *Beauty and the Geek,* doesn't mean I can tell a publisher what to do. I think that if we all will go online and e-mail the different people who are named in this book and tell them, "You are not being *punk'd;* **you** are really, really mentioned in a brand new book called *Blue-Eyed Blonde.*" This thing will explode across the globe.

I hope that Russell Simmons, Marc Emery, Mel Gibson, Bill Gates, George Soros, Quincy Jones, Jeff Bezos, Larry and Sergey and all of Hollywood will buy thousands of copies of this book and load them into high schools, colleges, libraries, group homes, churches and prisons. The temptation is to read this book and rob it. Rob it of its humor, excitement, inspiration and its authenticity and then to leave it. But our challenge as young people is to wave this book in the face of our politicians - from the President of the United States of America, down to the local city councilman or the warden at the juvenile. We need to put this book **in their face** and say, "What about the *Blue-Eyed Blonde?*"

I care about the war in Iraq. I care about our young men and women losing their lives everyday on foreign soil. I care about the abuse of prisoners in Guantanimo Bay. But I also care about the terrorism taking place on street corners in L.A., Atlanta, Chicago and Detroit. I care about the abuse of men, women and children in prisons right here in America. And charity begins at home . . .

I don't even need to try to inspire people in their teens and twenties to read this book. I know you will. And you'll pass it around the frats, sororities, clubs and football teams. And the guys in jail will be all over this book. My strong suggestion (again) is that we the youth do to our parents what they did to us. Demand that **they read it**. And when they read *this book* we will see a change.

9

Don't get lost in the sex, drugs, and rock and roll in this book. Don't get lost in the action, mystery and the spellbinding plots of the story; read it all with an open mind and you'll get it . . .

When you finish reading this preface; *before* you read the book, I want you to e-mail or text message at *least* two friends and tell them to go to Amazon.com, the local B. Dalton, Borders, etc. or www.cafepress.com/Manning and get a copy of this book **today**.

You also must read "*From the Palace To the Prison*" by Sherman Manning. If your local bookstore does not have this book yet tell them to get it. If they don't get it, *punk* them. Some people will say there is too much sex or violence in this book, etc. *Punk* em! Bishop T. D. Jakes will like this book. It's real life and it deals with real issues.

Now turn on that P.C. and e-mail your friends. Catch me, Simon Cowell, P. Diddy, Clay Aiken, Michael Phelps and Angelina Jolie in chat rooms (Yahoo!) and discussion groups as we'll talk about it and give our opinions. It's a great, fast and spellbinding read.

Ashton Kutcher

ACKNOWLEDGEMENTS

When I read great books by John Grisham, Tom Clancy, Al Franken and William Bernhardt, I skim the acknowledgements. I hope you won't do that. This book is incomplete and does not make sense without the acknowledgements. **Please read closely.**

I want to offer praise and honor to James and Dollie Manning. I thank Brenda Smith, Shanteeka, Shateecia, First Lady Sabine, Jr., Kimberly, Peter and Katrin Andrist, the late Johnnie Cochran, Michael Moore and George Soros. I thank all of my stealth supporters as well as Jodie Evans, (*Code Pink* Women for Peace) Bev Smith, Randi Rhodes, Attorney Thomas Mesereau, Willie Gary, all the folks at *Wired* Magazine, *Tribe*.net, Fortune Magazine, Gayle King, Montel Williams, Rubin "Hurricane" Carter, Barry Scheck, Professors Mike Vitiello and Dylan Rodriguez, Chris Abani and all of the many (many) professors from around the nation for their support.

This tome would not have been possible without the support, research, encouragement and inspiration of Angelina Jolie, Brad Pitt, Jamie Foxx, Denzel Washington, Bruce Springsteen, Anthony Fedorov, Clay Aiken, Timothy Goebel, Johnny Weir, Mike Ciompi, Dianne Sawyer, Jennifer Anniston, Sergey Brin, Larry Page, Yahoo!, Dr. Phil McGraw, Marshall Mathers, Murray J. Janus, Chris Purvis, Jesus Maldonado, Myspace.com, Buddypics.com, Friendster.com, Alex Benzer, U. C. Davis Law School, the Innocence Projects in San Diego and New York and the folks at the America Urban Radio Network.

I salute John Elsmore, Bishop T. D. Jakes, Andrew Young, Ashton Kutcher, Val Litwin, Marc Emery, Rene Boje, Harvey Levin, Gerry Spence, Hayden Christensen, Matt Damon, Tony Danza, Craig Newman, Sandra Bullock, Drew Barrymore, Matt Matteucci, President Nelson Mandela and Bill Gates.

I need to let you know that writing this book was monumental and a task of titanic proportions. This book pulled things out of me, which I didn't even know that I had within me. I think one can learn while, through and by teaching others. Likewise the more you write about a thing, situation or problem, the more you learn about it. I know I learned a lot in this book. And one of the things I learned was how America has failed her *children*. The parents have absolutely failed the teens. I'm concerned about this tendency to *blame victims*. We have talked about our kids joining gangs, using meth, cheating and going to jail, etc. But all of the problems our kids face are problems we introduced them to. We smoke up cigarettes while telling them *not* to smoke. It reminds me of the anti-smoking commercials which are sponsored by *Phillip Morris Tobacco Company* . . . Teens see this B.S. and hypocrisy and they get livid. They watch us go to church Sunday after Sunday and come home with greed, hatred and malice in **our** hearts. When they pick up the Bible and read Matthew, Chapter 25 they wonder why they have not seen *us* feeding the hungry or clothing the naked or visiting those in prisons.

This hypocrisy and *do as I say* and not as I do is killing us. It is *Creating Monsters*. It is making teens bitter, jaded and angry. And there are those **right now** who won't want **this book** in grade schools because the word "ass" is in it. There are *some* who will go off due to the sex, drugs or rock and roll in this book. But it ain't for **you** anyway. This book is for seniors at Davis Senior High School, Franklin High School, Northside High School, Folsom High, U. C. Davis College, Harvard, Carnegie Mellon, Morehouse, Howard, Spelman, U.C.L.A. and Boston College. This book entertains, wines, dines and inspires guys who are die-hard frat brothers, gals in sororities, juveniles, jails, thugs, geeks, freaks, nerds and athletes.

This book is for the dreamers, guys and gals who are still struggling their way through school and college, etc. This book is for those who are stuck at the bottom of the mountain of success but still struggling to make it to the top. **We** wrote this for *you*.

And I did say **we** because this book absolutely *ain't* possible without all that I got, learned and gained from my co-authors - *Mr. Jeremy Shackelford* and *Paul Shackelford.* I really, really, really want to thank *Jeremy* and *Paul* for all of their efforts, data, resources, connections, suggestions, contributions, contacts and advice. I would have never met Benjamin McKenzie, Zach Braff, Mr. Roerig, Mike Cardelle, Adam Brody, Anthony Fedorov, Mike Phelps, Taylor Hackford or Mel Gibson had it not been for *Jeremy Shackelford.* So I dare not take the contributions, support, concern and efforts of *Jeremy* and *Paul* for granted. "Thank You!"

I thank all the staff at *Harper Collins*, *A&M Publishing*, Cafepress, CraigsLists, Amazon.com, Google, Yahoo!, AskJeeves.com, www.43things.com, Bezos, Buffet and Donald Trump. I couldn't do what I do if some of these people didn't do what they do. I hope every White college and high school student will share this book with their friends. I hope my dear White brothers and friends, i.e. Jeremy Shackelford, Scott Coffman and Paul Shackelford have told their story effectively. I hope that Taek Kwon, Scott Sassa, Antonio Pontarelli, Robert Butler (Casa Robles), Ronald King (surgical technician at Western Career College), Attorney David Pollack, Maja

Szalavitz, Derrick Flowers (Charlotte, NC), Robert Freeman (Minneapolis, MN), Alex Ochoa, Riley Evans, Tim Vincent, Kurt Basa (Dallas, TX), Grant and Janice (The Coffee Shop), Jamie Kennedy and Kermin Flemming will get a hold of *this* book. I hope *you* will tell them about it. I hope those working with youth at Boys and Girls Clubs, YMCAs, Boy Scouts and Girl Scouts, JROTC and ROTC members will receive e-mails, texts, telephone calls and podcasts about this book. I hope you all will call radio stations, e-mail and snail mail letters to the editors, etc. and discuss the *Blue-Eyed Blonde* with them.

Call and e-mail the National Lawyer's Guild, Amnesty International, the Associated Press, *Michael* Shackelford (Sand Springs, Oklahoma), Cornerstone Baptist Church, Doug Banks, Rappers, Rockers, Rene Hinojosa (San Bernardino), Bill Cosby, Kris Anaya, your principle, your student leaders and *your* pals about this book. I hope you'll meet up in Internet cafes, libraries, sports bars, Luna's Café, Starbucks, etc. etc. and critique this book. And since I know that eighty percent of the first ten thousand readers of this book will be between the ages of seventeen through thirty years of age, I must tell you to *use your computer*. Inundate the blogs, pod-casts, web chat rooms and discussion groups with *Blue-Eyed Blonde*. **You** are the computer geniuses and you know what to do. Do your thing and I'll just watch you. We are rushing to press. I won't delay this power by worrying about *typographical* errors or punctuation problems, etc. We'll fix it all in the second printing. For now we are going *up* with this book. Again I can't thank Jeremy and Paul enough for all that they have done to make this book a **hit** . . .

Sherman D. Manning
August 2005

DAMON DASH

My name is Jeremy Shackelford. I'm not sure exactly what I'm doing at the moment. Today is February third. I'm writing this because I feel like writing it. Perhaps it will be used in a story, column or maybe even a tome. I want the world to know that White people such as myself are also moved, touched and inspired by African American success stories. One such story is that of a young man from Harlem named *Damon Dash*. Damon is not only a hero to Blacks in America, but people who look like *me* in Europe and around the world are learning the tale of Damon's success. He lost his mother at a young age. He was not born with a silver spoon in his mouth nor golden slippers, but he had hopes, goals, dreams and visions. Damon checked himself into a boarding school because he felt he was letting himself down. Damon began to read everything he got his hands on. Damon knew that knowledge, information and studying led to power. Damon knew there were *no free rides* in America. *Damon* knew he could be as big, as powerful, as great and as rich as his dreams could be.

"If you can think or imagine it, you can be it or do it," Damon says.

(Publisher's Note: *Sherman Manning* writes more specifics on *Damon Dash* in this book. We hope Mr. Dash will sponsor five thousand copies of this book so we can provide them to inner city youth. We believe Bill Gates, Chris Gardner and perhaps Mr. Soros will match him.)

I initially read Damon's story as I learned about the break up of *Jay Z* and *Damon*. I was impressed with and by the fact that Damon did not speak ill of Jay Z. Damon Dash is a *man*. He empowers people. He now owns the Damon Dash Music Group along with tons of other businesses. He is blazing a trail, which will be a roadmap for others to follow.

As I contemplate how, why and *if* I will involve my credibility, efforts and resources into the issues raised to me by *Sherman Manning*, I simply could not close out this day without writing about *Damon*. I am a writer. I hope one day, some way that kids around the country will stumble upon these words in a diary, journal or article. And I hope those young people in high schools, colleges, churches, jails and juveniles will be inspired to read, study and dream big dreams like Damon did. I hope they will know that *all things are possible to him that believeth*. Damon Dash is a living witness to that.

Jeremy Shackelford

BLUE EYED BLONDE

Jeremy Shackelford had blue eyes, blonde hair and he was roughly 5 feet 10 ½ inches tall. Jeremy weighed 169 pounds. He had the chest of *Michael Phelps*, the shoulders of *Anthony Fedorov* and a big, juicy butt like his pal, *Timothy Goebel*. He played basketball, football and volleyball. *Jeremy* was a Casanova of sorts dating more than a dozen girls during his junior year at *U. C. Davis* College. He was extremely mature and confident in public. Yet secretly he was still, at times, a kid. He often went online to www.Myspace.com and kept in touch with his former high school pals across the country. He chatted with Joshua Walker in Temecula, CA, Wes Kovarik in Antioch, CA and his buddy, Scott at uncrowned.com. Jeremy also e-mailed Timothy Goebel and Johnny Weir quite regularly. His buddy, Gabriel Afani was now at Cal State Bernadino and *Gabe* would ask, "Why do you waste your time online with skaters? You need to go to Serena Williams' blog and post a comment - send her a picture and try to hook up a date, dude."

Jeremy hailed from Oklahoma City, Oklahoma. He grew up in a neighborhood called Rancho Cordova. Rancho Cordova was about eighty-five percent White, ten percent Mexican and five percent Black. As far as Jeremy knew, Rancho Cordova did not have a race problem. He had White buddies who were as mesmerized by the brilliance and philanthropy of *Damon Dash* as they were of the music and presence of the band, *My Chemical Romance*. Everybody in Rancho Cordova knew the real life rags-to-riches story of Damon Dash.

"He makes it cool to be smart, to be a C.E.O. and he empowers people. Damon Dash is addicted to **money**," Jeremy's pal *Brian Hawn* from Atlanta once told Jeremy. Brian visited every summer along with his mom, Michelle . . . *Eminem* was also a household name in Rancho Cordova. Jeremy was so fascinated by the lyrics of *Slim Shady's* music that he began writing him and Eminem replied. "When I come to Oklahoma on tour, you can come backstage and meet me. Bring some babes with you so we all can get busy," Shady had e-mailed him.

"You're a freaking liar dude. You're making this up. Why would *Slim Shady* respond to *you*? You're a square. You're just trying to outdo *me* because I got an e-mail from Gerard Way," Jeremy's brother had said.

His little brother, that is, Paul Shackelford was two years younger than Jeremy. "Dude, you did get an e-mail from Clay Aiken and Aron Carter sent you one because you sent so many e-mails you blew up his computer. But you never got a reply from G. Way," Jeremy said while punching his kid brother.

Truth be told, both Jeremy and Paul were *World Wide Web thespians*. These guys would tinker and tweak on the web until they were able to get replies from all kinds of rock bands, actors, athletes and celebrities of every stripe. But Jeremy was now one up because he had a real life, authentic reply from the one and only *Eminem* . . .

In one of the few conversations with their mom about their dad, their mom said, "Your dad is ten percent Indian but you could not tell by looking at him."

Back when Jeremy was only twelve years old he asked his mom, "Where is our dad, Mom?"

She replied, "Last I heard, he was in prison for armed robbery and attempted murder. Don't ever think about him. If he cared about us, he would call or write. So since he forgot us you should forget him!"

Jeremy had read where *Tyler Perry* was abused by his father and had turned pain into power by *writing*. Tyler had watched *Oprah* one day and got a flame sparked when Oprah said, "All y'all should keep a diary." That flame led to Tyler Perry's fame. Tyler had gone from a destitute and homeless man to the writer and producer of "Diaries of a Mad Black Woman".

Reading Tyler Perry's story had inspired Jeremy to write a missive to Michael Moore right after he produced his first documentary. To Jeremy's surprise, Michael Moore wrote back. It was a powerful inspiration to get a snail mail missive from Michael . . .

It was now 2002 and Jeremy was a senior at U. C. Davis. He was a big man on campus. Good looking, in all the right cliques and clubs and quarterback of the football team. Jeremy wrote columns for *The Aggie* newspaper and he had numerous blogs online. Marcus Pinkus at Tribe.net, Meg Whitman at E-Bay, and even Craig Newmark, owner of CraigsLists.com all expressed an interest in Jeremy. He had ample job offers waiting for him the minute his college days were over. But right now he was enjoying every minute of his college days and nights . . . Jeremy was a member of the Pi Kappa Phi Fraternity and involved with *Push America's Journey of Hope*. It was the Internet, which had been responsible for Jeremy getting with Chris Vomund. "Other than sex, drugs, rock and roll, what are you and my frat brothers up to down at the University of Missouri - Columbia?" Jeremy asked Chris.

"Journey of Hope . . . Push America . . . You should look at our site at www.PushAmerica.org. We believe in teaching teamwork, empathy and service. We party, get our groove on, hang out with a lot of females, etc. But for a few hours each week and a month every summer we give back. Some guys volunteer their entire summer doing community service.   We mentor teens, teach literacy and visit juveniles. I'm gonna give your info to Chris Kozak, Walter Pape (Colorado State University Junior) and Bryan Eichler, dude."

And the rest is history. Jeremy did a lot of work with Push America and he always brought electricity, energy and excitement to his efforts . . . He was a stud, a jock, an intelligent and gregarious youngster. In spite of all odds, Jeremy pushed himself to excel at all that he did. He was majoring in journalism and had several other job offers outside the numerous ones which involved the Internet. In fact, he had a job lined up at *Sinclair Broadcasting* in Baltimore.

Jeremy was dating Lisa, a cheerleader on the *Aggie* squad. Lisa was articulate, fine, had blonde hair, hazel eyes, nice breasts, chunky but shapely buns, nice legs and even pretty feet. "If you lick my toes and suck on em, I'll toss your salad when I go down on you," Lisa once joked to him.

Life was good. Jeremy would wake up every morning excited, refreshed and energetic about his future. He was taking it all in. He even enjoyed his weekend job as a delivery boy for Domino's Pizza. He'd applied for an internship at the Sacramento Bee newspaper, but was told by Rick Rodriguez, "The only position open now is for a minority."

Delivering pizza was not a plush weekend job and often collided with his Push America gig, but Jeremy enjoyed doing it. He met lots of unique, interesting and sometimes powerful folks while delivering those pizzas. "Even the governor eats pizza," he once quipped to his little brother, Paul over the telephone.

And it was on a pizza delivery in Sacramento, at the Radisson Hotel that Jeremy would begin the Genesis of his comprehension of power; political power. He was met at the door of Suite 6600 by the *Governator* himself.   "Does that pizza have extra cheese und pepperoni?" Arnold asked.

"Yes sir, Herr Schwarzenegger," came his reply.

Jeremy was star struck, mesmerized and spellbound. Nothing, he felt, had ever happened to him like this. Yes, he knew Eminem, Adam Levine, Mickey Madden, Todd Solondz and Johnny Weir. Yes, he corresponded with Michael Moore, Dave Lieberman and others. But to meet the *Terminator* turned *Governator* at his hotel, on a pizza delivery, was way cool. Damn, I love my job. I'm glad I didn't think I was too good to tote pizzas, Jeremy thought as he stood there . . . He kept the receipt signed by Arnold.

"This receipt will be worth a hella lotta money on E-Bay," he told Lisa later. "Don't you have to turn in receipts at work?" Lisa asked.

"I paid cash for the sale from my tips. Management could care less about receipts as long as they get their money, honey."

Jeremy talked about meeting Arnold to everybody who would listen. For weeks on end it was all about Arnold. He e-mailed Clay Aiken, Kevin Shelton, Kevin Olivero and Justin Daley and told them all about the meeting. About a month later, Jeremy got the breakthrough he hoped for. Jeremy got another delivery to the Radisson Hotel, same suite. The door opened slowly and Jeremy could see the end of the unlit cigar before he saw much else. "Hello *Jedemy*," Arnold stated. "You are best delivery boy in *Caleefornia*," Arnold said.

"Danke schon, Herr Arnold," Jeremy said sheepishly. "I was wondering if I could ever see what your office looks like at the Capitol, sir," Jeremy blurted out. He surprised himself. He'd known for weeks that he wanted to ask this question. He had debated over and over in his mind whether or not asking this would be appropriate. But Jeremy dreamed big dreams. He wanted to see Donald Trump's estate, Bill Gate's mansion and the White House. Jeremy wanted to shake hands with Marc Cuban, Matt Damon, Bono, Damon Dash, Oprah and Paris Hilton. He thought success might rub off on him. He wanted to see it all. "You only live once," he told himself and yes, he would not miss this chance to ask Arnold. He felt he'd gotten this call again for a reason . . . He second-guessed himself over and over. Why didn't I strike up a conversation when I made that first delivery, he'd thought that *first* time. But here he was again at the door of opportunity and he would not leave til he asked. *Jeremy Shackelford* had popped the question.

"Sure young man, when will you like to come by?" Arnold asked.

"Anytime you're available, sir." Jeremy said.

"Oh, you want me to serve as your tour guide, huh? I tell you what, *Jedemy*, call my office tomorrow at 10:00 a.m. and work out a time with my assistant, Margita Thompson."

The Capitol tour had come and gone. In fact, Jeremy had so impressed Arnold that Arnold offered him a summer job. His job would be writing press releases for Arnold's administration. The job paid fifty dollars an hour and retired Jeremy from the delivering of pizzas . . . Jeremy continued to grow, dream, imagine and to visualize. He believed in the power of the mind. "If you can see it in your mind, you can be it in reality," he'd heard Damon Dash say one time on TV. "Nothing can stop a youngster from achieving success if he or she has a dream and works to make it so," he'd heard L. A. Reid say. Jeff Bezos, Craig Newmark, Marcus Pincus and Steven Spielberg all seemed to concur with that statement.

And Jeremy was also inspired by things he read which showed people giving back to society. He loved a story telling true-life tales of philanthropy and altruism. He connected on the Web with volunteermatch.org and *gave* even though he had not yet *arrived.* He contacted Jaron Henrie-McCrea who had just won a young filmmaker's Oscar, Josh Schwartz and Benjamin at the O. C. via e-mail and motivated them to write comments of inspiration on his blog. He e-mailed *Friendster.com,* C.E.O. Taek Kwon and inspired him to carry his blog blurbs and to send every Friendster member an announcement about the blog. He contacted acclaimed pianists Gideon Rubin, Peter Serkin and Christopher O'Riley and got them to agree to tutor kids for free one day a month. He convinced Idyllwild Arts Academy instructors to allow their creative writing students to contribute to his blogs. He got Michael Noble and Eric Bulrice to write essays for other teens to see called "What I Like About Music".

He got Marissa Mayer at Google to give free sponsored links to Push America.org and his other projects - Danielle Hutchings was a gal pal with whom Jeremy had once had a one night stand. But even though their relationship never continued, she kept reading his blogs and she got Ryan Stauffer and Douglas Wahl to write blogs for high school seniors who wanted to become designers. They got civil engineering Professor Robert Bea involved - Kris Anaya and Angel Deradoorian wrote blogs on indie-rock . . . Nick Viskovich wrote on why frats should stop binge drinking and creative ways to have a blast without getting smashed. Kappa Alpha Psi, Sigma Chi, Tau Gamma Theta, Pi Kappa Phi and other Greek, African American and Latino frats from across the U.S. connected with Jeremy on Yahoo, Myspace.com and other sites to blog, chat and advise. Isaak Brown, his dad, Dr. Donald Brown and William Lowman contributed to Jeremy's online chats. Jaret Cellmer did a blog and so did Jabe Robinson. Jonathan Saffran Foer did an odd blog.

Jeremy worked telephonically and electronically with Rock the Vote, Hans Riemer, Eli Pariser, and the Youth Policy Action Center at www.youthpolicyaction

center.org and David Smith. He helped Thaddeus Ferber launch the site www.mobilize.org. . .

It is now January 2005 and Jeremy Shackelford is the Editor in Chief of the Sacramento Bee. It's strange how life can work out sometimes. Few years ago this same paper had rejected Jeremy. Their rejection led Jeremy to Domino's Pizza. The Domino's delivery job had led Jeremy to the Radisson. The Radisson had led to Arnold and Arnold led to a prestigious job writing press releases and the powerful press releases had caught the eye of the publisher of the Bee. The Bee's offer led to Jeremy forgetting Sinclair Broadcasting. Jeremy was hip to the fact that it wasn't all just coincidence. He knew *luck* was when *preparation* meets *opportunity*. He knew he'd prepared his entire life. He was ready for this job and this day.

Jeremy had read everything he could get his hands on his whole life. He'd studied Lee Iaccoca, David Boies, Tom Mesereau, Dennis Kimbro, Tony Robbins, Zig Zigler and Russell Simmons. He'd studied communication, persuasion, leadership and psychology. That reading and preparation got him ready to meet Arnold. And because he communicated effectively, he had impressed Arnold to give him a job. And his reading, college and studying had led to his ability to write the hell out of a press release. Those press releases led to Jeremy becoming the youngest Chief Editor of the Sacramento Bee.

Now he had the job, the looks, the gifts and the connections. He'd graduated Magna Cum Laude in 2002 from U. C. Davis with that Journalism Degree. He'd left Lisa in 2003 for an affair with Margita Thompson. He dropped Margita after only two weeks and got hooked up with Mary Hanlon Stone. Mary was sexy, smart and kinky with a capital **K**. Whips and chains were her tools of intimacy. She likes threesomes. She wanted a threesome with Jeremy and his brother. Just from a photo of Paul, she decided she wanted to whip and screw the two. She wanted a threesome with Jeremy and Scott Parsely. She saw Scott's blog from Shrewsbury, Pennsylvania and decided she wanted it. Josh Paul in San Diego? She saw Josh getting a makeover on K.C.R.A. Channel 3 and fantasized about spanking the buns of Josh and Jeremy for fun. She wanted to do Timothy Goebel, Clay Aiken, Johnny Weir and Eminem, all *with* Jeremy. She was weird. She was way out there. Mary Hanlon also likes crank. The crank, it would turn out, would lead to the demise of their relationship. Jeremy would not do drugs. In the corridors of power at the State Capitol, he had heard tales of great men with talent and promise who destroyed their careers, families and lives by using drugs. Other than an occasional martini, Jeremy did not even drink.

So he stood in his downtown apartment on Century Street, just off J. Boulevard, one foggy morning looking out of the window. His mind traveled back in time to Oklahoma. He wondered aloud what his mom thought of him. "Did she think he was a success? Was she proud of him? And by the way, what should he get for her birthday coming on

January 24th.". . . . Life was marvelous. Jeremy had drive, determination, charisma and pizzazz. He inspired those around him and made them want to be better and do more. He thought like a revolutionary. He wanted to *change* the *world*. He planned to use the Bee as a vehicle to lift his voice above the mountains of mediocrity and tell the world what he thought. He wanted to be seen and heard. He had a lot of inner turmoil and contradictions. At times, he felt like a preacher who would rid the world of hatred, poverty and racism. At other times, he just wanted to get rich and run to the hills. He always felt like an odd ball. "How many twenty-three or twenty-four year olds still blog on Myspace.com, Xanga.com and spend a lot of time trying to help high school seniors get ready for college?" Jeremy asked himself. "Especially when you've now got the job as *Editor in Chief* of a newspaper." . . . Kevin Mahaffey, Ero Carrera and Adam Brody all clowned Jeremy in e-mails - i.e. "Dear Editor Elect . . . How much are you being paid for your Kiddie Blog on myspace.com?" wrote the O. C.'s Adam Brody. "But it's really cool (on a serious note) that you care enough to spend time reaching teens. If more folks like **you** would go to these teen sites, we could keep perverts and molesters *off line*," Adam wrote to Jeremy.

Josh Davis of Wired Magazine wrote about Jeremy in his column. Matt Damon read the column and texted a long, long message to Jeremy. It was rambling, complimentary and had a lot of questions. Jeremy wrote back, "Dear Matt, thank you so very much for your concern, interest and your curiosity. Only *Nate Berkus* (smile) writes longer messages than you do. But I enjoyed reading it and will save it. Not to worry, you won't see it on E-Bay or Inside Edition . . .

Today I read about a Black woman in Washington State, from Sacramento who chopped off the head of her own daughter. She drowned her own baby girl in the bathtub and then decided to decapitate her. She says her daughter was a demon child. She is in a cult.

I also read about Mr. Schwartzmiller. He is turning out to be the most prolific sexual predator of children. He allegedly has thousands of victims on all coasts and even in Brazil. I tried to imagine what could possibly drive a grown man to stoop low enough to date rape and steal the innocence of children. I almost cried thinking about it, Matt. Then I read about L. Dennis Kozlowski and Mark H. Swartz. These tycoons and CEO's of *Tyco* were convicted of looting Tyco of more than $600 million in corporate loans and bonuses. They were found guilty on twenty-two of twenty-three counts of grand larceny, conspiracy, securities fraud and falsifying business records. L. Dennis

Kozlowski had an eighteen million dollar Manhattan apartment, a six thousand dollar shower curtain and an infamous $2.5 million birthday party on the Mediterranean Island of Sardinia. Matt, Swartz, the Chief Financial Officer in cahoots with Dennis - stole millions of dollars in loan and bonus scams. These cons financed lavish life styles with money they pillaged from Tyco . . . Matt, it has taken nearly four years to try these guys in criminal court. And Ken Lay has yet to go to trial. It is indicative of the fact that justice can be bought. And there is no equal justice under the law. Even when Swartz and Kozlowski go to prison, they'll go to country clubs, I assure you. But if you're poor, minority or middle class in America, it is very, very difficult to obtain justice in the criminal justice system.

Matt, my stomach absolutely turned when I read about these high-class thugs in suits and ties who pilfer the savings of their poor employees and squander corporate resources like it's water. My blood boils and I tremble when I see corruption and fraud on the highest level of government politics and corporations. Matt, Representative Randy (Duke) Cunningham is involved in *Masiongate* for his vote selling and for living off the corrupted money of Mitchell Wade, Tom Delay, Mr. Deal, etc. So much corruption turning the corridors of power into the corridors of corruption. And usually the public looks the other way. Even *George Bush* is as crooked as tricky Dick Nixon was and . . . I am sick of it . . . It will take students, young people your age and mine, to clean this mess up. I think we're ready. We are blamed by our elders. They say we smoke too much and drink too much while they choke us with their cigars and sicken us in their drunken stupor. All the evil, wrong and perversions we know, we learned from them. Matt, I am no saint. I have sex. I have sex. I do have sex. Good sex! I love women. I love their bodies, tits, buns and their feet. I love rock music as well as some of the rap lyrics. But I am not a crook. I believe it is just wrong to steal - period. But our C student president and draft dodging V*eep* sees nothing wrong with Cheney getting money from Halliburton while they overcharge the government for meals for the troops in Iraq.

Mentioning Iraq? Matt, it is a total and complete mess. It is a cesspool of wickedness. It is blood for oil. It is a quagmire. It is a war for profits only. We should not have our young, patriotic men dying in Iraq for a *Bush Lie* . . ."

Jeremy laid it all on the line for Matt in his text. When Matt read it he was mesmerized and transfixed . . .

Jeremy called his pal Chris Fan who was about to graduate from U. C. Davis. "How is Jennifer Grutzius, Mr. Fan?" Jeremy asked.

"She's fine." Chris told him.

"How good is the sex, dude? Is she good in bed?" Jeremy asked.

"Are you coming to my graduation?" Chris stated.

Jeremy had a secret desire to fight racism, which was born out of a speech by *Martin Luther King, Jr.* The speech had been played for Jeremy by visiting U. C. Davis Professor Dylan Rodriguez. This speech spellbound, befuddled and mesmerized Jeremy. In King's eloquent voice, Jeremy heard love, power and conviction. He contrasted the conviction he heard in King's voice to the empty and shallow rhetoric he heard in today's microwave-like speeches. Damn, we could use a Dr. King right now, Jeremy thought as he listened to the scripted, uneventful speech Bush gave at his inauguration. Jeremy was not a liberal or a democrat. He was a self-described pragmatist. Although he voted for Kerry, to him, even Kerry was lacking. "These guys have no passion, no conviction and no integrity," Jeremy had said to his brother in a telephone call in November of 2004.

"Where are the politicians willing to go out on a limb and speak truth to power? Where are the public servants willing to take a stand, which is unpopular, and say, 'Bring me your tired and huddled masses yearning to breathe free?' I'm sick of snake oil salesmen and even *Bush* Lite democrats. Look at the way we went to war on a lie and traded *blood* for *oil,* little brother. Bush is a warmonger and wants to be a dictator," Jeremy told Paul.

"Hey, calm down, big brother. You're just a bleeding heart liberal. We needed to get rid of Saddam. The intelligence was bad but the ends justify the means. The world is better off without Saddam. You know that, Jeremy," Paul spoke into the telephone.

"Well, what about Osama *Benforgotten* Laden? When will we locate the bastard who knocked those buildings down on 9/11 and killed over three thousand people? Don't you remember how nervous, numbed and fearful we all felt when we saw people jumping out of windows choosing death by dive instead of being burned alive? Paul, Osama did that - not Hussein. I want the culprit who broke America's heart - caught. I want the man caught who methodically and strategically orchestrated a plot, which brought us to our knees. Osama made thousands of kids grow up in fatherless or motherless homes. He wrecked the lives of an entire generation of children. But we lost him at Tora Bora and camouflaged our inability to catch him by sending the troops to look for non-existent weapons of mass destruction."

"Jeremy, did you call me just for a diatribe? Are you gonna tell me about your job? Better yet, Mary Hanlon Stone, the dominatrix and kink master. Did you let her strap on and dig into your butt yet? Has she tossed your salad?" Paul asked.

"You've lost your freaking mind. I will never, ever allow anyone, not even Paris Hilton or Angelina Jolie put anything inside of me. My butt hole has a permanent tattoo, which says, *exit* only on it. Only yours says *enter* in the *center*, dude," Jeremy retorted.

"What about the Castro district? Mom says she saw you on the news holding hands with Mayor Gavin Newsome and declaring it marriage day, a few weeks ago. And he is leaving his wife, Jeremy. This is not going to turn out to be another New Jersey Governor story, is it?"

Jeremy said, "Gavin is not gay, bro. And I am as straight as an arrow. I don't even like kidding around like that. I won't discuss kinky Mary with you . . . But I do want to know about Big Butt Beth whom Mom said you're dating. How fat is she?"

"Don't call her Big Butt and I'm not dating her. She looks a little like Lyndsey Colip or Alison Terry. She's not exactly Jennifer Armiento but she's nice. But we're only good friends, Jeremy. Anyway, send me a copy of your new paper. What is it called the *Queen Bee*?"

Jeremy chuckled, "Okay kid, I'll let you go now. Gotta go meet Craig *Dog-faced* Bone at 98 Rock. He's a D.J. and I'm selling him my old truck."

"Take it easy," Paul said as he hung up the telephone.

Jeremy wanted to travel. He wanted to go meet up with Timothy Goebels, Johnny Weir etc. etc. and try to get them to hook him up with some of the female skaters. He wanted to meet up with Adrian Holovaty and other geeks and tinkerers. He wanted to go hook up with Chad Kramer, Jeff Gordon, Chad Harper (private investigator who read the Push America Blogs . . .) and Paul Rademacher. He wanted to meet Tara Calishain, Editor of Research Buzz and co-author of *Google* Hacks. He wanted to travel and see the world. Jeremy enjoyed meeting new people. He loved music. He loved swimming, surfing, wakeboarding, skateboarding and volleyball. He also wanted to go meet Andy Roddick who texted him numerous messages.

Jeremy cashed in on his job signing bonus and decided to take a trip around the world alone. He would fly from Sacramento to Atlanta, Georgia. In Atlanta, he would rent a car. He'd stay in Atlanta for a few days and then drive back to the West Coast making a lot of stops. He planned for the trek across the states to last for thirty-nine days. . . He flew the redeye into Atlanta and arrived at Hartsfield Jackson Memorial Airport at 7:12 a.m. on a Saturday. The airport was humongous. Jeremy walked through the terminal to Starbucks. At Starbucks he ordered an Espresso and balked at the $7.50 cost. He took his coffee and got a newspaper and sat down. Guess I'll see what's going on in America today, he thought. "DEATH SOUGHT FOR MASTER MANIPULATOR", read the headline. Jeremy continued reading it . . .

"The only fitting punishment for Marcus Wesson's slaughter of his children - some of them children he had with his own daughters - is death," the prosecution argued during Friday's sentencing. Prosecutor Lisa Gamoian called Wesson a "Master Manipulator" whose sexual, emotional and financial exploitation of his children culminated in their slaughter and execution.

Jeremy read where this was the most gruesome murder case seen in Fresno. The sight of the nine bodies piled and tangled with bloody clothes in a corner of the Wesson home shocked even the veteran law officers who found them on March 12, 2004. He read about the arrest of Marion P. "Mollie" Fry, 49 and Attorney Dale C. Schafer, 51 of El Dorado County, California . . .

This physician and her attorney husband have been indicted by a federal grand jury in Sacramento on charges of conspiracy to distribute and manufacture marijuana and manufacturing at least one hundred marijuana plants.

The story read: "You'd think cops would have something better to do than arrest people for growing medical marijuana," Attorney Laurence Jeffrey Lichter stated.

Lichter, Lichter, Jeremy wondered. The name rings a bell. I think he works with Ruiz and the famed Attorney Tony Serra. "Oh shit," Jeremy said as he stared at the next headline - "BEE PUBLISHES RESULTS OF PAMELA GRACE".

Jeremy thought, here we go, the paper I'm about to take over and scandal breaks out. My new boss elect writes a missive of apology due to the firing of one of the best columnist at the Bee.

"An internal investigation into the published work of former Bee columnist, Pamela Grace found forty-three cases in which individuals named by the writer could not be authenticated as real people." - it read.

"Pamela Grace, sister of court TV's Nancy Grace . . . Whose column ran three days a week on the Bee's metro page, resigned after she failed to substantiate details from several recent columns. She has denied fabricating any information." The story read: "She wrote 171 columns for the Bee. The interrogation found thirty names in twenty-seven separate columns which could not be verified . . . Many of the columns in question fit a template: essays, often with a surprising O. Henry Twist, about singular persons who face a challenge(s), and surmounts it. Their stories frequently reflect a theme taken from current headlines - wildfires, for example, or prison brutality, school shootings, murderous road rage or a high profile trial". It read . . ."Pamela Grace provided intimate details about the individuals and their lives, from the creases in their faces to the names of their pets".

Jeremy said, "Shit, guess I should call Stuart Drown, Anita Creamer or R. E. Graswich to see how things are going on the morale side since this story broke." He thought, Pete Basofin didn't tell me it would happen so soon. Jeremy wondered to himself how could Grace's work have escaped editorial scrutiny for so long? Probably because of Pamela's elevated status as a columnist, her journalistic credentials and her sister, Attorney Nancy Grace. At age twenty-five, Pamela won a 1986 Pulitzer Prize at the Denver Post. Pam got other prestigious awards as well, including a George Polk Award and the 1990 commentary prize from the American Society of Newspaper Editors. He thought, with credentials like hers, being a high profile writer, etc., it is first nature even to trust her. Columnists are given broad latitude in their writing style. It's more personalized. They share their voice and their views with the community. Jeremy thought about how much the community gets misled by lying reporters' editors who embellish and fabricate. He thought most politicians, i.e. George Bush are able to distort the truth and hoodwink the public by giving access and granting interviews to only government-friendly reporters. This is not the kind of journalism I'll allow at the Bee, he thought. How many times have we overlooked great writers, great stories and great authors simply because they didn't have the right credentials or they didn't go to the right schools? Jeremy thought, with this kind of bullshit, scandal and fabrication, it's gonna come a time when only the Internet, independent press or alternative media outlets will be trusted. Over and over major publishers, major news media organizations, etc. are failing to report the facts. We won't touch certain stories and we are selling out. It is as if editors are becoming more like republican politicians, he thought. He then read a story in which *McClatchy* News was being sued for fabricating the number of its subscribers. *McClatchy* News. The *McClatchy* News Company. "Damn." . . .

Let's check out the business scams of the day, he thought. "SCRUSHY ACQUITTED ON ALL 36 CHARGES", the bold black headline read. You're shitting me, Jeremy thought. Wait, I've got to call Marcus Pinkus on this one . . . With his cell phone in hand, he dialed

Marcus in San Francisco . . . No answer . . . He tried Craig Newmark and got an answer. "Did you read the Scrushy news?" Jeremy asked.

"Indeed I did. I just told Blake Ross out at Stanford that I hope I can afford a lawyer like Donald Watkins if I ever get into trouble," Craig said.

"How could he walk away a free man being cleared on all charges? He inflated the earnings of HealthSouth Corp. by $2.7 billion. All five former HealthSouth Chief Financial Officers pleaded guilty and testified that Richard Scrushy led this massive scheme of corruption. Craig, courtroom observers viewed this case as stronger than in most fraud trials, but the jury deliberated twenty-one days and acquitted this guy in Birmingham, Alabama of all thirty-six counts of fraud, false corporate reporting and making false statements to regulators."

Newmark replied, "But you're innocent til proven guilty beyond a reasonable doubt. And this was not a civil trial. The burden of proof is on the prosecution, Jeremy and quite frankly, being a multi-millionaire will often buy you an enormous amount of reasonable doubt. I'm not saying Scrushy was innocent. I don't know the man one way or another. But I am saying you're innocent til proven *indigent*. And Scrushy was not indigent. If he had been a poor White guy with a public defender with half the evidence against him, he'd be in prison *now*. But the jury has spoken. Now let's see if all of that crying, church going and praising God, Scrushy was doing, will continue now that his ass is off the hook," Craig said.

Jeremy chimed in, "Yeah, to get that close to becoming an inmate in the prison system ought to be enough to frighten anybody into charity work. I'm gonna look for Scrushy on the Internet, blogs, pod-casts and the A. P. ninety days from now. Let's see if he helps some poor guy accused of a crime to buy a Donald Watkins, Gerry Spence or a Bruce Cutler. I'm not hating on Scrushy, man but every time I read the paper I see a pattern . . . Poor, Black, Brown, indigent and accused. Guilty, guilty, guilty. Rich, prominent or politician. . Not guilty or a slap on the wrist. Hey, maybe I'll do a story on the guy when I take over the Bee. Anyway, how's CraigsLists.com going, pal?"

"We are doing fantastic! We are really reaching across the world with our service. Now we're strategizing to try to steal or at least share some of the high school crowd, which uses Friendster and Myspace.com a lot. I'm consulting with Gabriel out at Atomi and Wes Kovarick on that. We've surveyed Daniel Asare and all the kids out at John F. Kennedy High School. Jeremy, you got any suggestions on how we can use our site to attract younger users?"

Jeremy said, "I'm looking at my resources now . . . I get a lot of comments from high schoolers on my blogs . . . Okay - Soroptimist International awards scholarships to students. You should check with them as well as some of their recipients, i.e. Justin Cardinale, Jeffrey Bramell and Kevin Olivero all in Amador County. Look up Rodrigo Ojeda-Beck, Riley Evans, Tanvir Kapoor who just completed a film called, "The Face of Hate" at Davis Senior High School. Students who normally don't come out to discussions or events focusing on community issues are going to see that film during airings. Tap into them. Get Kyle Love out at Auburn High School. Justin Daly in Tracey, California. Look up *Scouting For All* in Petaluma and find The Youth Pastor of *The Rock Church* in Sacramento. Craig, all juniors and seniors in high schools have strong political opinions. They want to be seen and heard. But you gotta suck them in with entertainment like the right rock bands, the right awards, etc. Give them the chance to be heard via setting up blogs and *safe* dating sites. Keep the predators and protesters off the sites and I guarantee you'll get em . . . Gotta go, dude."

Craig said, "Thanks so much, stud. Stay safe and don't forget about Scrushy."

"No chance!"

They hung up. Jeremy pressed re-dial. "Craig, also you wanna get in touch with Russell Simmons, L.A. Reid and perhaps John Bartleson out at Def Jam. The hip-hop crowd is young, interracial and active. And don't underestimate the potency, reach and connectedness of those Michael Jackson fans. Gregory Stork heads up the Jackson Fan Club in Germany. Dude has diehard fans in China, Japan, South Africa and even India. You want Lacey R. and Cynthia D'Huart in Murieta, California. These youngsters are connected. The web brings them together. I'd look up Steven Cozza and Josh Walker in Temecula, California if I were you. And try to interest a designer named Esteban in Miami. Jules Helms (dance instructor in NY) and Cyclist Tyler Farrar. Contract every GLSA in California. I'm telling ya, if you tap into the student clubs, they will spread the word about your new features on your site."

Craig was taking notes. "Thank you very much, dude. You should write a book. You could use your new job and newspaper to promote it."

Jeremy replied, "As a journalist of course writing, a book is not entirely out of the question. But I'm not sure America is ready for **my** kind of book. I would mix humor, blood, happiness, trauma, sex, drugs, rock and roll all in one book. I would have to write like life is.

I wouldn't know whether to call it a novel, non-fiction or partial fiction, dude. Reading a book I wrote would be an interactive process. I'd ask my readers to market the freaking book. I'd tell them to use voter registration rolls, property records, telephone books, identity data basis, people finder and accurint, court records, newspaper archives and Google to locate each and every person named in my book (good or bad) and tell them they were in my book. I would want every single person whom I named or referred to (in my book) to know they were in my book. And the only way to be certain they knew would be to ask the Daniel Asare's, Kevin Olivero's, Riley Evan's, etc. (in the book) to log on, find em and e-mail them.

Then the biggest problem I'd have would be with the publisher. I would want to cut into their profits by using *some* of the profits to help kids go to college, teach creative writing and journalism classes and clinics. I am not so sure Harper Collins, St. Martins Press or Doubleday would go for that. Craig, I would want to be the freaking *Damon Dash* of book writers. I'd want to do what no other author is doing; *create other authors*. I'd want to empower kids in junior high, college and alternative schools to *write* and publish them. If we had to develop street teams to sell their books at car washes and bake sells, I'd do it. If I had to dress them up as Eagle Scouts and send them door-to-door to *sell,* I would. Dave Matthews sold his tapes and CD's out of his trunk. So did Damon Dash when he signed Jay Z. Ivanla Vanzant sold her booklets out of her trunk . . . Dude, I don't know. See there is a book called *Rainbow Party* that parents are raising hell about. On the one hand, my book(s) would definitely appeal to the sixteen through thirty-five year olds. And college kids would probably be down with it. But *some* closed-minded parents would hate the profanity or the sex. A book by me would be like watching a soap opera like *As the World Turns*. Just a variety of issues, subjects and situations. There is a nut named Barbara Ryan on *As the World Turns* who tries to **control** her kid's lives. She is out there. And so many moms are like that. That crowd would protest my book."

Craig interrupted, "Are you watching *Soaps* now, Jeremy?"

"Hell, no! My mom watched them and I'd see them in passing. But my point is, I would probably stir up major controversy in schools with my book, if I wrote one. You'd have the cafeteria Christians who would blackball my book. You know the Karl Rove, George Bush type Christians who claim to *love God* but hate peace and hate the poor. Craig, the biggest mistake any publisher would or could make would be to let something I write see the light of day in *tome* form. See those teenagers and kids my age are extremely intelligent and awesomely energetic. Kids are savvy. And if just one connected teen sat their ass down and started reading a book *I* wrote, it would be *on*. I'd tell them the freaking truth. And truth is like music. It's a magnet for galvanizing people. I'd send my book to folks like Jacob Tuthill or Stephon Simmons in Sacramento. I'd send it to the frat brothers, Eagle Scouts, Justin Daley, Junior Achievement participants and skateboarders. I'd get my book in the hands of my pals like Tim Goebels, Clay Aiken, Natalie Portman, Marshall Mathers, Johnny Weir, Bo Bice and Mike Ciompi in Hollywood and they would push it and plug it. And this would make the Christian Rights angrier and angrier. Hell, they might try to sue me if I tried to write a book, Craig."

Craig replied, "I'll be watching you, Jeremy. It sounds like you have given the idea of writing a book a lot of thought, kid. Hell, you keep mentioning this *Damon Cash* dude. Who's he?"

Jeremy laughed. "It's *Dash* not Cash but the D-Dash does have a lot of cash. Damon is a young, brilliant, altruistic, C.E.O. and founder of the Damon Dash Music Group. He's a hip-hop impresario. Had there been no Damon Dash, there would be no Jay Z. You heard of Jay Z?"

Craig said, "A rapper, right?"

"Yes," Jeremy said.

Craig replied, "I'm not a big rap fan other than a bit of Eminem occasionally but I've heard of Jay Z."

"Jay Z couldn't get signed when he started out and D-Dash developed a marketing plan to sell CD's out of the trunk of their cars. Wow! Dude, Damon has a rags-to-riches story. He is a modern day Howard Hughes, a Black Bill Gates or Jeff Bezos. This third grade teacher is a White sister named Joanne Goldberg. When Mrs. Goldberg did a fundraiser to raise money for a new school library, D-Dash decided to pay for it. He's a reader, a thinker, an innovator and he's unselfish. He believes in bringing people up with him. He's not selfish. I'm not a big rap fan either, but I'm addicted to success. And the Damon Dash story is a true-life success story. It needs to be told over and over and over again. Black kids, White kids, people in juveniles, etc., all over the world need to read about how Damon got his start. How he *read* everything he could get his hands on. How his mother taught him to learn about other cultures, business and history. How his mother taught him that your money may be short but your *vision* can be long. His mother taught him to dream bigger than his neighborhood. She taught him to dream bigger than one side of town. She taught Damon that if he could see it with his mind, he could be it in time. I think about Oprah's "Never in Your Wildest Dreams" bus tour when I think about Damon. He is an icon who can be held up as an example for all the youth to see."

Craig interrupted, "Then why don't you get off your White posterior and write a book and get D-Dash to help you market it. Get him to donate five thousand copies or so to Oprah's Angel Network and if he did that, the rest would be history. You'd get all the O. C. fans reading your book. You'd get the American Idol fans. Send it to Bo Bice, Constantine Maroulis, Paula and Anthony Fedorov to review . . .".

Jeremy said, "You know Fiona Apple? Her new albums was not *released*, it *escaped*. Go to a fan site called Freefiona.com and you'll see that her album was given to her label, Sony/Epic in May 2003. It was the first album she'd released in four years. According to the fan site and other Internet sources, Epic didn't hear a radio friendly hit single on the album and refused to release it. Like a modern rearrangement of a long forgotten show tune. 'Extraordinary Machines' seemed a bit out of context. Apple's lyrics and singing were just as knowing and self-aware as her previous work but with an *unexpected pinch*, of *humor*. But nothing happened; no tour, no press, nothing, until a couple of weeks ago. The complete eleven song album appeared on one fan site, then several, in nearly CD quality MP3 files or download, which it promptly - and repeatedly - was . . . Wilco's 'Yankee Hotel Foxtrot' rejected by reprise, then released on the Internet before its subsequent release by another record company.

Craig, other albums appear on peer-to-peer networks and fan sites prior to official release (and until cease and desist notices arrive from the RIAA), despite (or possibly because of) the best efforts of their record companies and managers, most recently, the current U2 album, 'How to Dismantle an Atomic Bomb', was in fans' hands (and on their iPods and hard drives) a week before it hit the stores. But Fiona's 'Extraordinary' marks the first time a possibly unfinished album by a popular artist was released on the Internet. Its release has not gone unnoticed. 'A Free Fiona' Website arranged for fans to picket the Epic's New York offices . . . Craig, I'd get my book to Adam Levine, Don Cheadle and Brad Pitt. I'd get it to Bruce Springsteen, Bono, Bon Jovi and Bob Geldof. I'd tell my readers to text, e-mail and blog Hollywood over and over til Steven Spielberg, David E. Kelly, Adam Brody and Frank Darabont read it. I'd do some controversial stuff like use several pictures or unauthorized data, etc. til Hollywood notices. Natalie Portman, Brad Pitt, Morgan Freeman, Jamie Foxx and the fellas in *System of a Down* would be down with a book by me. But the

Christian Rights, the Falwells and James Dobsons would despise it. Craig, I'd write a book like I love my life. Some parts would be so exciting that you'd feel like you were at a *Green Day* concert. You'd get that adrenaline rush that comes when you activate that gland at the base of the skull. Kids would get a *rush* reading my stuff. Then all of a sudden, without warning I'd interrupt, break the thought or subject train with a fact, i.e. *every three seconds* a child dies in Africa or I'd interrupt the Rush, the high, etc. with an appeal to my readers to go *online* and find the folks mentioned in this book. E-mail them and tell them to get this book cause they're in it. Craig, you think I'm an idiot, right?"

Craig replied, "Jeremy, I'm telling you the God's honest truth, kid - if you write a book and do the stuff you are talking about. . .the interactive sort of Reality TV type tome, kid *you will* write your name in **history**. You will cause a lot of young writers to write, publish, think, dream and to get involved. Jeremy, write man. Write Jeremy, write. If you write, get the book to that one Michael Jackson fan you've been telling me about. Get the book to that one nerd at John F. Kennedy, Davis or Independence High School. Get it to Rachel Scott's brother Craig Scott. Get the book to that one geek, freak or Internet chatter, blogger or tinkerer and they will put it out there. Hell, you'll even be good for my business. Folks will be all on my lists posting 'Heidi Fugames you are in a new book. Send me an e-mail if you got this message.' Write it and get it to Matthew Read, Jacob Tuthill, Lauryn Hill, Simmons and Dash and you will make history! You'll give away a lot of books. Give poor kids gratis E-books, etc. and call on Bill Gates, me, Jeff Bezos, Oprah, Gayle King, Quincy Jones and Bill Cosby to fund or sponsor books for schools and colleges. Johnathon Nelson, Tammy Young and all of my site users would love your type book. Jeremy, write a freaking book, dude. Get it to Modesto Realtor Jerry Roberts, Sacramento resident, June Reiner, ninety-year-old Marxist Leon Lefson and to Reachmedia Owner Tom Joyner in Dallas. Just sit down and put it down and put it out there. I believe with every fiber of my being that *this is the time* for the kind of interactive tome you've mentioned here. Just get it to Jamie Derummond, Will Smith or D-Dash/Cash and it will rocket. Jeremy, I'm talking about an innovative, hyperactive, motivational, situational book that will skyrocket through the schools and frats and chats, to brats and . . . Dude, write a book!" Craig said.

Jeremy said, "Darn . . . Alex Benzer, Tom Rundle, Private Eye Chad Harper and many others who text me and reply to my blogs would perhaps be into my writing, but . . . Wow - wooh dude, I have not even started my new job yet and I'm sitting at a freaking Starbucks in Atlanta, talking long distance with you about some far-fetched idea of me writing a book.

Craig interjected, "I didn't know you were in Atlanta, dude, but don't contradict yourself. You keep telling me about how Damon Dash was the least likely and how he's doing the almighty. I've heard you mention Tyler Perry, Chris Gardner, Jeff Bezos, Pat Croce, Tony Robbins and Brad Pitt, etc. I heard you mention Zach Roerig and Michael Cardele and all those folks who started with zero. How dare you not believe you can do the impossible and see the invisible? Six years ago, I was just a two-bit engineer at IBM. Look at me now. Look at Maheesh out at Cafepress and Tiffany Chiles out at Don Diva. **You** can do it, kid. But don't only go for the big guys. You wanna find Amber Deahn who is a Denny's waitress out in South Dakota, Ricky Mitchell and Gary in Summerville, Georgia, Eddie and Ralph Cannon in Dublin, Georgia, Telfair County, etc. Put the names of those country boys like David Joiner and James Nesmith in Wrightsville, Georgia, Gary Browning, Brian Foskuhl and Daniel Clay Hollifield all in Richmond, Virginia. Put their names in a book. They would love to be able to walk into Billiards, Starbucks, Ace Hardware Store or Books A Million and tell the store clerk, cashier or the help at Wal-Mart, 'Hey you see here in this book - that's me.' You'll have kids all over Myspace.com and Friendster posting messages and bulletins about your book. And you could send me some of those customers. I want the teens on Buddypics.com, LiveJournal and Ratemyprofessor.com to come to CraigsLists.com. Jeremy - I don't know what the hell you are doing in Atlanta, Georgia but I know what you ought to be doing - writing a book. Tyler Perry was watching Oprah when she said people should write down their feelings, thoughts, ideas, dreams and goals, etc. And the rest for Tyler is history. He has a mansion right in the city where you are. What are you waiting on?"

Jeremy took another swig of Espresso and said, "I'll think about it but I've got other shit to do right now. I'm getting ready to ride across America. But I do keep a lot of notes and I journal, dude. . . Craig? Honestly, do you really, really believe that if I wrote the kind of shit we've been talking about, all of my rambling idea and ideals, my opinions, my curiosities, my interests, etc., you really believe people would read it? No shit?"

Craig replied, "I would stake my company on it, Jeremy. *You* could use any theme, subject or subjects, etc. Whatever the hell *you* write about would be the written *O. C.*, an American Idol like book.

You could rant, rave and speak *truth* to *power*. You would be the *Michael Moore* of writers if not the D-Dash/Cash. It would work. And if you really offer teens online the opportunity to get their music, lyrics, poetry and essays *published* you'll *blow up* bigger than any writer I've ever known. I really believe if you do this and do it quickly, you will succeed in publishing the way Gerry Spence succeeds in *lawyering*. Kevin Henkes, Kevin Mahaffey, David Craeighton and Nate Berkus would love it. Go for it, dude. Go! Go! Go!"

Jeremy smiled, "Okay Craig. I'll let you go, bro."

Craig replied, "Thanks for the pick me up, dude. I'll see ya."

Jeremy just sat there a moment. He checked his e-mails. Sean McNulty, Ashley Wilder, Kevin Shelton, Mrs. Pamzich, Paul Ruditis, Jamie Kennedy, Omar Reece, Daniel Asare, Karen Mutasa, Fariba Garmani, Kelly Schoolmeester, BizarreBids.com, Contagiousmedia.com, Jonah Peratti, Carlos Smith and Susan Yu . . . Jeremy wondered, who is Mutasa, Garmani and Mrs. Pamzich? I don't recognize them . . . I'll read em later. Jeremy was spinning. The conversation with Craig really had him thinking. He knew what he thought and he said to himself, I'm probably foolish if I don't write a damn book. I meet people all the time in person and over the Internet who think like I think. I meet many who have read, are reading or have just bought a new book just cause: cause somebody *told* them it was cool. Cause somebody told them *not* to read it. Cause somebody told them it was sexual, sensual or inspirational. He met people all the time who bought a book cause they liked the picture on the cover or bought it just so they could dispute it on their blogs or on their iPods etc. How many times had he heard Howard Stern, Sean Hannity, etc. discussing books which they thought were terrible, rambling, dull or boring? Jeremy said to himself, I could actually be one of a kind.

I probably could do for publishing what D-Dash has done for the music industry. I could find any subject, which I felt a passion about and write about it. Use it as my theme or subject. And sporadically crossover into other subjects, which I care about. I would write with my heart not my head. I would write how I feel. I'd be a writer youngsters would identify with. Maybe I can get an older, wiser co-writer. But my book would be uncensored. I would not P.G. or sanitize it. I'd come raw, real and uncut. Maybe I'd get it to *Straight Edge* in Reno and San Francisco. *Straight Edge* is a unique crew. Some of them are fanatics and violent. Maybe something in my book would click inside one or two of them and they'll decide to stop the violence and focus on the positive aspects of *Straight Edge*. Maybe I could feature student scholars in schools and colleges. I could do this.

I could do this. Damn, I could do this. I guess the question I should be asking myself is, what am I waiting on? I feel like this can happen . . . But I can't put the wheels before the wagon. I have to enjoy my trip. I have to relax, see the city, eat some good food, eat some pussy, think, live, play and have fun. Then I must get ready to take over the Sacramento Bee. I must make damn sure there are no more Pamela Graces at the Bee. I don't want lying, fabricating and biased writers like her working for me. I'm certain Nancy Grace, that prejudiced, cunning and right-winged bitch was feeding these lies to her sister. Nancy Grace is a disgrace. What happened to Geraldo Rivera, Dan Rather and Randall Pinkston? I want people bold like Geraldo who will ask tough questions and cover all angles of a story . . . He ordered him another Espresso in the Starbucks. He took his coffee and walked out to the baggage claim area. After he got his bags, a blue suitcase, a brown garment bag and a green gym bag. He walked out to hail a taxi. Out on the curb of the airport a bell cap yelled, "May I help you, sir?"

Jeremy said, "No. I'm fine." He hopped in the first cab and asked to be taken to the best rental car company in the city. Along the thirty-five minute ride, Jeremy second-guessed his own request. We probably passed ten car rentals already, he thought to himself. Finally they arrived at Hertz. There he saw it, a golden Lincoln Town Car.

"I want that one," he told the agent. "Long distance, insurance, turn it in, in California. Here's my credit card."

He pulled out of Hertz with GPS on and a city map in hand. Let's go see Atlanta, he thought. Let's see the *city too busy to hate*.

Jeremy felt that lump in his throat, butterflies in his stomach and that little (unnoticeable) nervous twitch he got when he was really excited . . .

"You won't have no problems in this here city. You is a *Blue-Eyed Blonde*, White boy. Atlanta loves blue-eyed blondes. Hell, America loves y'all! Look at FHM, Stuff, Maxim, Playboy, Hustler, The New Yorker, GQ and any other magazine in America. All you see is blonde hair and blue eyes. It's your ticket to success. You are blessed," the cabbie had told Jeremy.

He does not know me, Jeremy thought to himself as he got on to Interstate 285 headed to the *Marriott Marquis Hotel*. I get sick and tired of people judging *me* on stereotypes. Because of the color of my hair, eyes, etc., they automatically assume that they know me. They act like I didn't study, work, achieve and strive to be *who* I am, *how* I am and *where* I am in my life. They don't know me . . . Who am I? Jeremy questioned himself after his silent litany and monologue. I want the world to know who I am. I want to be a *mover* and *shaker*, a

35

power broker, and a man about the town. I want to be so successful, so powerful, so on top of life that everybody will have to take note. Jeremy always had a problem with being *defined* by looks alone. He wanted people to know who he was on the inside. He felt that he deserved to be heard and he had so much to say . . . He flipped on the radio and tuned in V-103 Rock. Edmond Patterson was on claiming it was Kid Rock day. Edmond was a nut but he could play some rock music. Jeremy drove on down 285 and exited off to I-75 until he got to Marietta Street. As he passed by cars he wondered who were all the people in those cars. What were they thinking? What were their lives about? How old is she? What weight is he? Who is in that car? At times, Jeremy was full of questions. Who am I? Why am I here? How long will I live? When will I marry? How many kids will I have - were questions he often asked himself? Jeremy often wondered did the average White college male ask the same questions. For that matter, he wondered does the average White college kid (period) ask themselves these *questions*. Sometimes Jeremy felt like a man in a *straight jacket*. He wanted to do so many things in life. He'd get a rush and felt as if there were not enough hours in the day to do all he wanted to do. Am I manic-depressive? He considered it as he finally pulled up in front of the Marriott Marquis Hotel.

The hotel was fabulous! From his car, he could see hanging chandeliers on the inside of all the glass revolving doors. Jeremy opened the car door almost at the same time in which the parking attendant or valet pulled open the car door. The attendant gave him a numbered card as he explained with a southern drawl that Jeremy should bring the card to the parking desk whenever he wanted his car. "Or you can call from your room and your car will be waiting on you out front," he said.

The valet or bell cap (or whatever the hell you call them) came and began helping Jeremy carry his luggage into the towering downtown hotel. "Won't me to help ya all the way to ya room?" the guy asked Jeremy.

He wants a big tip, Jeremy thought. About an hour later Jeremy was in his suite sprawled across his bed, face down, fully clothed when he picked up the telephone to call Blockbuster videos. "Do you have a movie on 'Malcolm' by Spike Lee?" he asked.

The answer was, "Yes".

"What about '*Mr. Hurricane*' with Denzel Washington?" Jeremy asked.

"Yes." Again.

Finally, "Do you have 'Shawshank Redemption' with Morgan Freeman?"

"Yes." Again was the answer.

Nine hours later, Jeremy lay awake in bed realizing that he'd not seen any of the city of Atlanta. Hell, he even had a concierge to fetch the videos for him. He'd had room service to bring him his (favorite) scrambled eggs, six slices of bacon and toast. He had eaten midway through the "Mr. Hurricane" movie, which he'd watched after the "Malcolm" movie. It's only Hollywood - this stuff is not real. None of this is real. It's exaggerated and embellished, Jeremy thought. But Wow, he pondered. Did my government really, really keep a man locked away in prison for crimes he did not commit for twenty-one years? That was the question, the idea that haunted this young man throughout the movie. "Shit," he mumbled. And now at almost 2:30 a.m. Morgan Freeman, Tim Robbins, Denzel Washington, Spike Lee and a stack of mail were literally and spiritually in the room with Jeremy. He opened up a letter from (this writer) me. He read:

Dear Jeremy, this is *Sherman D. Manning*. As you may recall from my previous epistle (*if* you perused it . . .), I am a wrongly convicted author. I did not receive a reply to my previous missive to you. Yet, prison has taught me *patience*. And my business taught me *persistence*. So I'm writing again to congratulate you on your recent appointment as Chief Editor of the Sacramento Bee Newspaper. I have written various reporters over the years at the Bee, i.e. Andy Furillo, etc. and received no reply. Many media persons have no interest in replying to prisoners. I would hope that perhaps your appointment presents a window of opportunity for those of us who reside in *gated communities* to be heard. I don't need you for *me*. But what I need is for you to see, the need for persons in the press to expose, cover and probe the judicial systems across North America.

Jeremy, you are a special young man. All of the doors of America's opportunities are wide open to you. In America, they say if you're White, you're just right. I saw your photo in the Bee and I recognize that not only do you have White skin but also you've been blessed with blonde hair and blue eyes. You can utilize your blonde hair and blue eyes to go anywhere in the world and be accepted, heard and taken seriously. I don't suggest that your skin color, etc. are a curse. I say they are a blessing if you use them wisely. I would hope you took the time to buy Malcolm's autobiography, "The Miraculous Journey of Rubin 'Hurricane' Carter" and to watch the DVD of *Shawshank Redemption* by Frank Darabont. These books and/or films will touch you in unique ways.

37

I wish you would at least send an e-mail to my wife at Hallopeter@freesurf.ch and verify that you received my missives. I also hope you will check me out on Amazon.com, go to Walden Bookstore and/or visit www.cafepress.com/Manning and get my books. Jeremy, I don't need money. I don't need sympathy! I don't need you to wish me well or to congratulate me on using my time constructively. Without arrogance, I tell you I know who I am. I know what I'm about. I'm okay. But I do need you to *use your* power, use your creativity, your muscle, use your newspaper to tell the truth for our youth. I want the world to know that our prisons are *Creating Monsters*. I want the world to know that our system neglects, fails to protect and disrespects our boys and girls everyday. I want you to utilize your press credentials to go inside LA County Jail. When you go in there, I want you to visit five jail inmates randomly selected. I only want you to be certain that the five inmates you visit have blonde hair and blue eyes. And if three out of the five have not been sexually abused and raped in LA County Jail, I'll give you ten thousand dollars. Ten grand if I'm embellishing or exaggerating this. Perhaps you may wonder why Oprah, Montel or Tavis Smiley, etc., have not covered the rapes of blue-eyed blondes which transpire *each and every* day of the week in our nations juveniles, jails and prisons. The answer is complex pragmatically and simplistic on an authentic level. To be concise, they don't know. To be true, they don't care.

On one level, if White people really, really knew how many White kids are sadistically molested in Chesterfield County Jail (Virginia), Fulton and Dekalb County Jails (Atlanta), Rikers Island (NY), Sacramento County Jail, Los Angeles City Jail (in LA County), Reidsville State Prison, Angola, Lorton, Corcoran, Folsom, Salinas Valley, Pelican Bay, California Youth Authority, etc. and in every (yes, I do mean **every**) jail and juvenile and prison all across America, if White people *knew,* I know they would use the senate, the congress, the full house of representatives and even the president to shut down the system. They couldn't take it. I know what I'm talking about, Jeremy. I've been dealing with and intimately involved with White people all of my life. I attended many White schools; I live next door to a White brain surgeon. My neighbor on the right is a Jewish Civil Lawyer and my neighbor across the street is (Dr. Zweig) a White plastic surgeon. My wife is White . . . All 33 ½ years of my life I have been a lover of good, God-fearing, unbiased and non-racist White folks. And I have found many, i.e. the late Dr. Fred Allman, Jr. who was a brilliant orthopedic surgeon who always taught me sports medicine in the summertime, Milton Friedman, an entrepreneur, Dr.

Milton Frank and his wife, Cookie. Terry Randolph who was the secretary of the late Rev. Hosea Williams . . .

All of the aforementioned White people (and probably a hundred more) were and are White people whom I know well. I've eaten in their homes; they've come to my luncheons, private parties at my office, funerals of my loved ones, etc. I know them and they know me. Nobody can talk to me about Ronald Frances Wright, Gary Browning, Brian Foschul, Attorney Murray J. Janus, Clay Hollifield or Alexander Dugdale all of whom are from Richmond, Virginia. You can't tell me about Eddie and Ralph Cannon, Curtis Sykes (or Sikes?) David Joiner or Sam Fuick of Atlanta, GA. I know these folks as personal friends, colleagues and advisors . . .

Jeremy, *if* these people and just one hundred other White Americans, i.e. politicians, pastors and entrepreneurs, knew how often their White brothers were raped in prisons, I assure you they would demand an urgent state of emergency be called in the Department of U.S. Justice. They don't know. Do you? If not, why not? There are a number of reasons, including the fact that Professor Terry Kupers points out that seventy percent of the male prison molestations in U.S. juveniles, jails and prisons go unreported. Most young fifteen through twenty-five-year old blue-eyed boys and men don't want to admit, confess or announce that their manhood was *taken* by some Black, Indian or Brown dude or a big ole White dude in prison. The prison predator banks on the embarrassment factor and uses it to his advantage. He knows most guys in prison will never report rape. He also banks on the fact that most prison guards *don't care* about rape and the prison predators manipulates public apathy. He knows that most civilians subconsciously know rape happens in prison. But A. They have no idea that the majority of the victims are White. B. They have absolutely no idea that statistics prove that every sixty-two seconds a White inmate is raped everyday in America's jails, juveniles and prisons. The prison predator also knows that the few who know about *some* of it sort of justify it, by thinking, well he shouldn't have gone to prison in the first place. Ipso facto, Jeremy, nobody connects the dots and considers that pragmatically every time a guy has his anus taken in prison, the blood dripping from his anus represents and contributes to the blood which flows and will continue to flow down the streets, on the playgrounds, in the schools and neighborhoods all over America everyday. The big secret is this: ninety-nine percent of the guys held in county jails and juveniles today will be out in the streets in less than eighteen months. And more than eighty-five percent of the two million men held in prisons today will be out of prison in less than five years. Ipso facto, about 725 thousand inmates get released and become *out*-mates every year.

And it does not take a rocket scientist to figure out that boys, males and men who were abused, beat, mistreated, molested, maimed, branded, raped and left for dead in prison *will get out* and take their hurt, sorrow, fear, anger and madness (not to mention their diseases) to the playgrounds, day care, nurseries, churches, barrios, ghettos, suburbs and homes with them.

Jeremy, go online and access child molesters. Count the child molesters just for the Sacramento, California area and you will see that White child predators outnumber Black and Brown molesters ten to one. Per capita, there are far, far more White molesters than there are Black and Brown combined. You can't convince me that this does not have something to do with the fact that *most* of the *victims* of rapes in juveniles, jails and prisons are White. I don't buy pedophilia being innate. And I'd like to see you investigate scientifically the *roots* of molestation. If you go back far enough, I assure you that prisons will be a major part of the contributing factor. You will find that many of the *victims* of child crimes were victimized by White men who were themselves victimized in group homes, foster homes, juveniles, jails and shelters. And if the victimizers have never personally been arrested, I guarantee you that somewhere along the way, you'll find a victimizer involved in the chain of abuse who was in prison. And *that* victimizer was victimized in prison.

America refuses to adequately deal with child molestation. We thump at it. We throw rhetoric at it. We overlook it. We act like it is normal or under control, etc.

Do you understand the horror, the tragedy, travesty and sadistic nature of the epidemic problems we have with molestation in Catholic Churches? Most victims of Catholic Priest molestations are White. And for years, priests benefited from the same shame by boys to admit being victims, which the prison predator banks on. Priests knew most boys wouldn't tell. And when a few of the boys mustered up the nerves to tell it - as you may recall - America **reacted** immediately. Priests were jailed, fined and sentenced to prisons. Many churches were bankrupted because White juries rendered verdicts to the tunes of tens of millions of dollars in favor of the blonde-haired, blue-eyed victims of rape . . . Jeremy, tell the story to America. Tell them the truth. Tell them about *your* brothers who are being traumatized, victimized and savagely raped in prisons.

If you wonder what **I'll** get out of your telling it? Revenge! I will get the satisfaction of knowing that the system which arrested, tried, convicted and sentenced me for *crimes* which I did *not*, would *not* and could not have committed, that system is being exposed for at least some of its crime, rage and senselessness. I'll enjoy the process of watching the same folks who ignored my letters proclaiming my innocence and begging for attention, etc. I'll get a climax out of watching them defend this criminal enterprise, which they're running in the name of justice, law and order. Jeremy, if you want, you can do an expose and just call it *Blue-Eyed Blonde* . . . Tell me, did you ever get those films and that book? I'm about to become *redundant* so I'll close for now . . . I remain *Sherman D. Manning*, J98796 - Mule Creek State Prison . . . **Keep Hope Alive . . .**

Jeremy, put down the letter. He pondered and thought . . . "Sherman Diahric Manning," he mumbled. He remembered the very first time he heard the name Sherman Manning. It was Craig Dog Face or "Dog Face Bone" as Sherman called him. He had been listening to 98 Rock in Sacramento when Dog Face interviewed this prison author over the telephone. "What are you in prison for?" Craig asked me.

"I'm wrongly convicted of attempted murder," was the reply as Jeremy recalled. And Jeremy remembered Craig asking this writer, "You mean you have a book out and *I'm* in it. If I go to www.cafepress.com/Palace2Prison, I'll see the book?" stated Craig. Upon hearing that, Jeremy had gone online and ordered "From The Palace to the Prison". He utilized the links and also ordered "American Dream/A Search for Justice" as well as "Creating Monsters". Reading all three of these books had stirred up something in Jeremy's belly. This stirring or pulling, which Jeremy felt, was unusual and subconscious. He didn't see it coming. I think I'll write this guy back, Jeremy thought to himself as he whipped out his PC . . .

Dear Mr. Manning, the missive began . . . I'm in Atlanta, Georgia. It is now 3:10 a.m. I've watched "Shawshank Redemption", "Mr. Hurricane" as well as the "Malcolm" movie. Not necessarily per your suggestion. But I'd always wanted to see these movies anyway. Sherman, at this very moment, Alicia Keyes is blasting from the radio in my room. "Some people want it all", she's singing. And that is my problem with you, sir. I think you want it all. You want me to write about you and your issues. You *want me* to utilize the Sacramento Bee as a bully pulpit for your issues. I won't be manipulated by you or any other prisoner. Now perhaps your intentions are genuine. I don't know. But what I do know is, I don't have time for this. And I don't have time for you, sir. So with all due respect, I'd ask you not to pen me another missive. It's not personal, Mr. Manning. I'm just a busy person. Thanks for your time. I wish you well. You're in my thoughts and prayers . . . Jeremy.

As Jeremy finished this missive, he began to feel a little knot in the pit of his belly. He thought about his own dad who was allegedly, supposedly, somewhere in prison. I don't reach out to try to find my own dad and help him, so why should I try to help some dude I don't even know, Jeremy thought to himself. He was trying to justify the harsh letter he had just written, which was basically a kiss-off letter. He tried to forget about it. But the what ifs and the why's started haunting him. Why did I not tell this guy that I bought and read *his* books? Why did I choose to come to Sherman's *hometown* to begin my trek across America, he thought. *Just a coincidence*, he convinced himself. Sherman just wanted publicity for "himself" Jeremy convinced himself. But wait, this guy is *not* in prison for child molestation. Nor does he claim to be a *victim* of child rape. So what if he's right about the *Blue-Eyed Blonde Syndrome* in the prisons. *If*, just *if* I exposed the roots of molestation in our juvenile and jail system and even if I admitted that Sherman was the guy who introduced me to this issue, it would only benefit Sherman in a residual way. And *if it* is this epidemic, I'll get a Pulitzer Prize and even more importantly, I can shine a much-needed light on child predators and save lives in the process.

He thought . . .there it was again - the twins . . . the contradictions within himself. The secret desire to **make a difference**. That part of him which really, really *cared* about people. That place inside him, which was touched and stoked when he heard that famous preacher, Dr. Martin Luther King, Jr. speak on tape. That place inside him which was moved when he watched Denzel as Rubin "Hurricane" Carter tell his lawyers, "Get me out! You've got to get me out of this prison. I can't stay here much longer because I'm innocent." That thing, source or spot inside Jeremy which was moved when he read of Malcolm transforming from a racist to a man who believed Whites and Blacks should work together to solve racism in America. That place would rise to the surface when he heard, "Get busy living or get busy dying". Jeremy was in denial about that place.

"Why did I not tell Sherman that I also read, "Long Walk to Freedom" by Nelson Mandela and it held me spellbound? What if . . . Jeremy contrasted that with what he considered his own "selfish" thoughts of the possibilities for a Pulitzer Prize . . . notoriety, fame and . . . there came that word again . . . "power" . . .

Jeremy showered, thought about Mary Hanlon Stone and went to sleep. . . Late morning, Jeremy froze as he felt the snub nose end of the

357 Magnum at his right temple. The gloved hand, which held the pistol, was attached to a Black man's body. "I want all of your money, White boy," came the command.

"Damn!" Jeremy reached inside his right pants pocket.

"Slowly, White boy. Don't move too fast or I'll splatter your brains all over this place. I promise you, I will blow your brains out."

"I'm not gonna try anything. Please don't shoot me. Please," Jeremy said as he handed over his wallet. "Please, please, I beg you - don't shoot me. Please," Jeremy cried.

The big Black guy looked like Chyle Lebuff's roommate or Forest Whittaker. Jeremy trembled, turned red and tears flowed ever so softly down his cheeks. Damn. The wallet did not suffice.

"Gimme yo watch, ring, chain and everything," the Black guy said.

"I don't have a ring, sir," Jeremy stated as he pulled off his watch and the gold chain his mom had given him for his sixteenth birthday.

"You ain't got no ring? You ain't married?" the Black guy inquired with disdain in his voice.

"No, sir. I'm not married," Jeremy replied sheepishly.

"Oh, you must be a faggot," stated the Black dude.

"No, I'm straight, sir. I'm just young and not married yet."

The Black dude grinned as if it were music to his ears. "Well, you'll be a faggot by the time I'm finished with you. Turn around and get on your knees, Blondie," he told Jeremy.

"Please mister, don't rape me. I'll give you anything. We can go to my ATM machine and I'll give you five thousand dollars. Anything, but please don't rape me, sir," Jeremy pleaded as he trembled.

The Black dude was stoic, unmoved and seemed like a rock. "Get down on your knees and suck my (expletive) cock right now or you are dead. Do what the (expletive) I tell you to do and you can keep yo (expletive) life, Blondie. Diss me one mo time and I put this (expletive) bullet right between your pretty blue eyes."

Jeremy turned around, kneeled down and lost his oral virginity. Awful, horrible, sick, wicked and terrible were not even adequate enough to describe how Jeremy felt. He didn't hate or despise gays or lesbians but to be forced to have sex with anybody was a horrible and tragic thing. It was even sicker to be forced to have sex with a person of the same sex when you are straight. Forced sex with a member of the opposite sex, if you are lesbian or gay was just as bad. Jeremy sucked and cried. Cried and sucked. Damn, this is too sick to tell.

"Suck me til I cum and swallow it," the Black monster said as he laughed. "Suck it." This big, nasty Black dude exploded in Jeremy's mouth. Jeremy gagged and nearly regurgitated.

"Pull your pants down and lay on your (expletive) face, Blondie."

Jeremy had lost his will, fight and all courage. He submitted. He didn't even look to see where the gun was. He'd seen it enough. Jeremy pulled down his blue jeans and boxers to his ankles and lay there with his eyes tightly closed. He was foaming about the mouth. The Black rapist spit on Jeremy's anus and rammed it in. He pushed, pulled, in and out. Over and over again for what felt like hours . . . Finally, he speedily pulled it out and Jeremy lay there with a bloody anus, crying, trembling, traumatized, terrified and horrified and then he heard a telephone ring . . . He woke up and realized it was only a dream. In fact, a nightmare unlike any nightmare he had ever had. A nightmare he would never forget!

The ring was a wakeup telephone call. It was this ring, which reminded Jeremy that yes, "it's time to get up." Jeremy pulled himself from underneath the covers and began his day.

Day 2

It was 6:30 p.m. and Jeremy had transferred all the data from his meticulous note taking onto his computer. His habit of journaling at the beginning and ending of each day had been a religious practice for him since he was a twelve-year-old kid. He refused absolutely to call it a diary. That sounded too feminine. He could live with the word journal but he preferred to call it simply "note taking". Jeremy put *everything* and I do mean everything in his notes. From the first time he had masturbated to the time he caught crabs - was in his notes. His high school prom was prominently featured in his notes. His hidden hurt, pain and struggle trying to figure out where his dad was and whether or not he'd ever actually search for him - was in his notes. His eighth grade homeroom teacher and her flaming red hair was profiled in his journal. Margarette Barraicua, the teacher who had licked her tongue at him and seemingly wanted to screw him while he was only fifteen years old was in his notes. That time when he had first heard a recording of a King speech was in his notes. Love, hate, good, evil, race, class, status, the pursuit driven life, etc. were all in his notes. Jeremy had enough damn notes to write a tome or two. He was a writer. . .

9:00 p.m. he stepped into the *Cotton Club*. The club was nice, women were hot and drugs were aplenty. Within only ten minutes, he had been offered everything from weed to speed. There were a lot of Georgia Tech students at the club. It was cool . . .

11:35 p.m. Jeremy went inside of Club 51 on West Peachtree Street in Midtown. It was not happening in Club 51. It's now midnight and Jeremy finds himself spell bound at a strip club called *The Purple Onion*. He reached into his pocket and pulled out a five spot and placed it on the bar. She danced, she moved, touched herself, licked her lips slowly from right to left . . . "Want a private dance?" she asked Jeremy.

"How much?" he inquired.

"Depends on what you want. Suck and (expletive) is a C-note. Just a blowjob is fifty. If you want to go in the back door that's $150.00."

Jeremy couldn't believe it . . . He pulled out a one hundred dollar bill . . . 3:30 a.m. and Jeremy is back at the Marriott reading his mail. He read mail from me. He actually had a stack of it, "Damn this Sherman, dude. Six letters and all of them are seven, eight and nine pages long. I should have left this garbage in California. But hell, since I brought it with me, I'll at least read it all." Jeremy thought . . .

Day 7

Jeremy is in the Waffle House in Raleigh, North Carolina, hundreds of miles away from Atlanta, Georgia. As he sipped upon his stale coffee he thought back on what Dollie Manning had told him in Atlanta, Georgia. He had actually gone to her house before he left the city. It started with a telephone call. "Ma'am, I'm Jeremy Shackelford and I'm the Editor in Chief of the Sacramento Bee newspaper. Your son inundates me with mail."

She laughed, "That's lil Sherman for you."

"I am really on vacation. I kinda wish I could meet you and talk with you about Sherman. He's been asking me to write about him in my newspaper when I take over as Editor in a few weeks. I'm *not* saying I will and there is always a possibility that if I do, I might not write the story he would want me to write. He doesn't even know I'm in Atlanta, ma'am but since I'm in your city could I meet you?"

He had gone to 2547 Abner Place in Buckhead and was surprised when he pulled up to the large gated house. There at mom's gate was a security guard who checked Jeremy's driver's license and asked him to "State your business, sir," before he pressed the button which opened the gates. Jeremy had pulled up and saw a beautiful house. Just beautiful. Not what I expected. Sherman didn't tell me his family was rich, he thought. Once he was inside mom's house and the ice had been broken, etc. Jeremy sat in the home of James and Dollie Manning. The housekeeper served tea and cookies and mom laid it on him. "My son is innocent. He might not be perfect. He is a long way from a saint, but Sherman is a special young man. I *know my son.* And I'm not the kind of mother who lives in denial. If I had a son who committed murder, rape or whatever, I'd not accept it. And to be candid I might not *discuss* it. But I can tell you one thing, I would not lie for him or defend him if he did it. They have my son in prison in California and he won't even let us come see him. I miss my baby so much. What kind of a system will keep an innocent man in prison?"

    * * *

    . . . That meeting at my mom's house had lasted nearly four hours. Jeremy had left there impressed, touched, humbled and angry. Angry about the injustice of my incarceration? Angry at the harsh kiss-off letter he'd sent me a few days before? Hell no. He was mad at himself for going to see my mother. The spell of a mother's love is enough to touch any man.

    * * *

    It was unprofessional and unrealistic for me to visit the family of a prisoner who writes to me in my capacity as a journalist. This kind of emotional involvement, personal connection, etc. leads to bias, favoritism and cheap journalism. I don't know this man. But I must admit he has a great mom. I've got to get out of Atlanta, Georgia as fast as I can. No more social calls, Jeremy had scribed in his journal . . .

    He checked his e-mails at the Waffle House as he downed a glass of milk. His mom, Paul, Mike, Lisa, Becky and Joseph had all e-mailed him. Joseph? Jeremy hadn't heard from Joseph in months. They were inseparable as kids and even best friends in high school. But since high school, they had only sporadically called and e-mailed each other. Joseph had gone on to Floyd, Illinois and started an Internet company with their high school buddy Scott Coffman. Coffman, it turns out had an uncle who lived in Floyd. Scott's Uncle Bill was a venture capitalist and had always liked Scott. From the first time Uncle Bill visited Scott's family back in Rancho Cordova he had told Scott's mom, "Since Ella and I can't have children, Scott is my son. He can come to Floyd when he grows up and I'll teach him how to make money."

    Scott cashed in on the invitation and took the first train to Floyd, Illinois after high school and boot camp. He talked Joseph into coming and they started S.J.I. Dynamics, which was a Website design company. The money was good. Well, Scott Coffman knew *me.* In a ranting conversation, Jeremy had mentioned my name to Joseph and my letter writing campaign. And Joseph mentioned me over beer one night to Scott. Scott went online and found out I was the Sherman

Manning from Atlanta, Georgia. The Sherman Manning who did boot camp with Scott Coffman years before at RTCC Command, in San Diego, CA. In boot camp, I was the Recruit Chief Petty Officer. Scott was seven years younger than me but we were buddies. Although I'd pulled his demerit chits twice, he liked me. "Why did you wait so long to decide to join the navy?" he once asked me. To make a long story short, Scott and I both got knocked out of boot camp. Ipso facto, we both received RE4 discharges . . .

Jeremy stared at the e-mail:

" . . .Dude, Scott knows your pen pal (smile) Sherman Diahric Manning. Bad news and good news. Bad news 1st. He's stalking U. Sherm is an undercover racist and is actually suspected of killing a White child predator in Tennessee years ago. Good news 4 U, he's in prison. Scott suspects he's fixated on U cause he wants to kill U. Dude U need to call me ASAP . . . J."

Wow. Was the truth on me finally coming out? Had my cover been blown? Jeremy used his cell to call the U.S. Navy RTCC in San Diego. Fifty-one minutes and four cups of Waffle House coffee later, Jeremy was on the telephone with Senior Chief Petty Officer (Ret.) Franklin. "Yeah, I remember Ensign Manning, son. He was a horrible guy. He was aggressive, rebellious and he hated authority. I helped get him kicked out the navy."

Jeremy said, "Senior Chief, do you think Manning is capable of murder?"

Senior Chief Franklin replied, "He's probably capable of anything. It's been a long time but all I can tell you is he was not navy material. I thought he joined out of some type of rebellion against his family. I heard that he came from money and apparently his father wanted him to follow in his footsteps and Manning rebelled by joining the navy. But I thought when we kicked him out he went on and attended Morehouse College in Atlanta. Probably got kicked out of Morehouse also, you know."

Jeremy thanked him and hung up. What he did know was the Morehouse speculation was a leap and that it was an incorrect leap. Jeremy had verified that "Sherman Manning graduated Morehouse, Magna Cum Laude" according to University Records. "Damn, I've got to call Joseph and get to the bottom of this Manning matter. One could argue that he possibly fits the profile of a killer. But a racist killer? That really doesn't add up. His wife is White. Hell, he grew up in a gated White community. But wait . . . could he have been molested by a White guy and kept it secret? And wouldn't that explain why he seems consumed with exposing child predators? Would that explain why Sherman Manning was called by sex crimes except Dr. Terry Kupers, "One of the most well read theorists on sexual conduct I've ever spoken with."

"Hi Joseph, it's Jeremy."

Joseph yelled out in riotous laughter. "Dude, What's up?" He was tickled to death. "I can't believe it took you so long to check in, bro. Figured after that e-mail, you'd call right away. What's wrong? Is Mary Hanlon Stone with you? Does she have you tied up with whips and chains?"

Jeremy took a swig of coffee and breathed deeply. He slowly and methodically spoke into the cell, "Joseph, I'm not in a laughing mood. I've spent no less than three hours calling around the damned country checking out Scott's theory on Sherman Manning. I . . ."

Joseph interrupted, "Dude it was a (expletive) joke. It's all good. I was kidding about all of that. Scott said Sherman was one of the coolest Black guys he knew in boot camp. I was just pulling your chain a little, Jeremy. Lighten up."

This perturbed Jeremy a lot. "You mean to tell me that I've interrupted my day, my life, wasting my money, time and brain power calling around the country tracking down retired company commanders and you were joking? I could kick your ass."

Scott grabbed the telephone . . . "Tell me what you know about Sherman Manning," Jeremy asked him.

Scott replied, "Dude, it's been more than a decade. All I can tell you are two things: A. Joseph completely made that stalking stuff up in the e-mail. We were just jerking your chain. B. The *Sherman Manning* I knew was gregarious, affable, articulate, extremely intelligent and pretty much nonviolent. And he liked White women. He was peculiar in that he was not the O. J. Simpson or Clarence Thomas type. He was indeed a *Black man.* Proud of Black accomplishments and civil rights. Keenly aware of the existence of racism, even in the military. And he was not the type who liked *only* White women. After we were kicked out of the Navy, we spent a weekend screwing chicks off base. He screwed three chicks, one White, one Black and one Chinese. So he was a biracial type guy," Scott chuckled . . . "but I couldn't believe he was or is in prison for attempted murder. I wonder does he even remember me. Maybe I should drop dude a line."

Jeremy yelled, "No! Please don't. The last thing I want Sherman Manning to know is that you know me. He'll try to manipulate you to get to me. No, absolutely do not write this guy a letter."

Scott replied, "Wait a (expletive) minute here, bro. I'm a man. I write who I want to write. I mean with all due respect, what's really going on here? Have you written him?"

Jeremy said, "Yes, but I . . ."

"So who are *you* to tell *me* not to write to a guy that *I know*? That's bullshit. *You* have something going on that's not really my concern, Jeremy but there is something going on here. It's plausible that the guy reached out to you because he's in prison and he reads a lot and he wants you to help him with your newspaper! Do a story or something. I don't know all the details, but Jeremy you are in *Atlanta, Georgia*. And that is Sherman's hometown."

Although Jeremy knew he was no longer in Atlanta, he didn't interrupt Scott.

"So it is not plausible, coincidence or realistic to me that you think nothing of this man and you don't believe anything he has to say. But you happen to trot down to *Atlanta* to begin your vacation. Either consciously or subconsciously, you were driven or led to Atlanta. Now why, I don't know unless you tell me. I think you went there to investigate and dig into his past and that's okay. But what's not okay is your denial about the *why* of your trip. And you're so disinterested in this guy that when you happen to get a fake e-mail from us, you spend three or four hours on the telephone calling around the world to check him out. And now you tell me 'don't write him because he may try to use *you* to get to *me*'. Who is being unrealistic here, Jeremy?"

Day 13

Jeremy is now in Richmond, Virginia. In Richmond, he'd checked into the Radisson Hotel on Grace Street. In one of my epistles, I'd written:

Jeremy, you can call Attorney Murray J. Janus in Richmond, Virginia. Murray Janus is the best, most pre-eminent trial lawyer in the Commonwealth of Virginia. Murray employed Attorney David Hicks when Hicks was fresh out of law school. They tried the famed Beverly Ann Monroe case together. The case was featured on *Hard Copy* and *Inside Edition*. One of the very few murder trials in which Barrister Janus lost. I remember it as if it were yesterday - "With *everything* that is inside me, I ask you to please find Beverly Ann Monroe not guilty of murder. She did not kill her boyfriend, Roger De La Buerde. She loved him. Thank you," Janus said in his closing argument. It was one of the best closing arguments I'd ever heard. As Janus walked outside of the courthouse the lights shine, cameras rolled and a bank of microphones were shoved in Mr. Janus' face . . . "I tried the case as best I could and now it's in the hands of the jury," he said as he climbed into his silver Mercedes. Yet the jury convicted Beverly. Years later *Dateline* did a story on the Monroe case. After her verdict was overturned . . . they found tapes, which proved prosecutorial misconduct and witness tampering. Detectives and the D.A had fixed Beverly's trial . . .. Janus knows about wrongful convictions and he knows **me**. He knows Russell Camosky lied on me in Virginia and *tried* to file a claim that I drew a gun on him. Murray got a call from D.A. David Hicks at 1:00 a.m. one morning telling him that Chesterfield County had a warrant for the arrest of "your friend Sherman Manning by some guy claiming Manning tried to rob him. Mr. Janus, Manning is the richest brother I know. And you know him better than I do. I think you ought to call Aubrey Davis (the prosecutor in Chesterfield, VA) and try to prevent an embarrassment to Mr. Manning." Mr. Janus took care of it. There was an arrest. But it was Mr. Camosky who was arrested on filing false charges and harassment. He'd tried to sell me drugs. It was a long story but there was nothing to it. When I went on trial in Santa Monica - Judge Robert Altman allowed Russell Camosky to fly in to California and testify *against me*. We called the Chesterfield D.A. in open court, "Judge Altman I would not trust Russell Camosky on a stack of Bibles! Russell is out of jail on bail for rape and sodomy. He's in violation of bail by being in California now. He has a long criminal record for robbery, assault, extortion, drugs and sex crimes. I would not trust him." In spite of all of this, Judge Altman allowed Russell to sit in front of the *all White* jury and say, "Manning is violent. He tried to shoot me in Virginia because I looked at his lady." His story was ridiculous, incredible and riddled with inconsistency, but apparently the jury bought his story. And Jeremy, if you were to call Mr. Janus, he could tell you about me and how they *set me up* - 804/643-1400. Jeremy, just call him.

. . . Jeremy had *met* with Mr. Janus earlier in the day. He thought, since I had to stop in Richmond and my hotel is only a few blocks away from Janus' office, it's not unreasonable for me to stop by his office. Since Mr. Janus is a famous lawyer I could actually do a story on him one day. Perhaps a human interest story or something. And if the name Sherman Manning comes up during our chat, oh well. But Janus had exploded during their interview. "You bullshit your way into my town and my office claiming you want to do a story on *me!* Now I find out why you're really here. Why the hell didn't you tell Jackie what you really wanted? (Jackie is Janus' secretary). I would have talked to you, son but we could have done this over the telephone in three minutes. Sherman Manning is innocent! They lied on him and set him up. And if I could get him out of jail in California I would. I wish I could help him. And he's not the only one; there are thousands of innocent, wrongly convicted men caged like animals in our prisons. There are also tens of thousands who are not innocent but are sitting in prison due to drug addictions, embellished charges or they fit certain profiles, etc. But don't ever bullshit me about why you wanna see me. I bill $750.00 per hour for my time. Now get out! Go see Attorney Barry Scheck if you wanna talk about wrongful convictions . . ."

That's the arrogant powerful, tough, candid but caring Murray J. Janus that I know.

At the Radisson Hotel, Jeremy began looking on the Internet. He was about to do a search on Barry Scheck and the Innocence Project. He wanted to know everything he could about Barry Scheck. But . . . it would have to *wait*. Instead, he *searched* for nightclubs, bars and restaurants in the Richmond area. He was preparing for a night out on the town . . . He went to the Pyramid near downtown Richmond. Wrong club. After paying the ten-dollar cover charge and looking around the place, he left. Jeremy traveled on over to the East side of Grace Street and stopped at Christopher's Club and Grill, wrong night . . . Jeremy was glad he started early because thus far he was having a bad, boring night. He went to a club and restaurant on Chesapeake called *The Tobacco Company*. This place is fabulous, he thought. "Wow, look at all the ladies in bikini-type uniforms, carrying silver trays with cigars," he said to himself. "I could fall in love in here."

A smooth brunette who was a Brooke Shields look alike trotted over to Jeremy and said, "Would you like a table, the bar or will you be going to the dance floor, sir?" Jeremy settled for the bar. And then a petite little red head who was scantily clad in a short, real short blackish sort of see-through skirt and a tight net halter top came to the bar with a silver tray. "Would you like a cigar, sir?" she said.

Although smoking was not Jeremy's thing he could not resist the cute little lady who appeared to be no more than eighteen. "Yes, top of the line, please," he said.

She picked up a cigar quite gracefully and lady like from the sparkling tray, which hung from the string, which was strung around her neck and attached to either side of the tray. "Open wide," she said to Jeremy as she held the cigar up to his lips. He smells her sweet perfume. Looks at her lips, breasts, eyes and then notices the light blue fingernail polish on her fingertips. The fingernail polish does not match her outfit but she's sexy, he thinks. He opens his mouth and she softly inserts the tip of the cigar into his mouth. "Would you like a light, sir?"

Jeremy was lost, lost in her grace, class and sexiness and also wondering *why* would he be buying a cigar if he didn't want a light. Jeremy didn't understand that most people who bought the cigars at *The Tobacco Company* bought them not to smoke but basically for the exact, same reason(s) he had bought one - for the status, power, attention and because it seemed to be the thing to do. Perhaps Rush Limbaugh, Arnold Schwarzenegger or William Shatner had influenced him. In fact, he once met Mr. Shatner while working for the Governor. Jeremy had been embarrassed when he walked up to shake his hand . . . "Nice to meet you, young man," Mr. Shatner had greeted him.

"My pleasure, *Denny Crane*," Jeremy had replied. Everybody laughed . . .

After giving the hostess a twenty spot and telling her to keep the change, Jeremy thought about Arnold. It had been a while since he thought about the Governor. A puzzling man. A vague, ambiguous and meandering man. I don't know any more about Arnold's political beliefs now than I did before I ever even worked for him, Jeremy thought. Was Arnold just another con, crook, liar, game player, cold, ruthless, go along to get along type guy? Who is Arnold Schwarzenegger, Jeremy said to himself. Why the hell am I thinking about Arnold? Must be the cigar. I do know Arnold is not the worst of the worst. I disagree with his cutting funding for education. I think our children are the most important people in the world. We should do everything we can to feed, clothe, protect, educate and inspire our children. Why would any good man not see or agree with this? And I really think it's foolish to put all of those billions of dollars into prisons. I want violent offenders locked up! I want predators off the streets. I want violent offenders punished severely. But I don't want weed smokers, credit card scammers, burglars and petty thieves in prisons being exposed to murderers and rapists. This association leads to assimilation. The viciousness rubs off! The predatory behavior, characteristics and traits are indeed contagious. Why can't my former boss see this? One problem is the people he surrounds himself with. The Pete Wilsons, etc., etc.

Arnold needs to bring in fresh new blood. New ideas, new mindsets and some innovative strategists who can pragmatically show him how to correct corrections. But I must remember that even though I think Arnold has a lot of good in him, he is politically ambitious. And unfortunately compromise, deception, gamesmanship, showmanship and charisma all go hand in hand with the desire for higher office, Jeremy said to himself.

It seemed as if hours had passed since he'd choked on that cigar after getting a light and giving the hostess a twenty spot. Jeremy was hungry. He went to the outer courts of *The Tobacco Company*, found a table, ordered a steak and dined . . .

Back at the hotel, Jeremy watched about an hour of a cheesy x-rated movie. Mary Hanlon Stone, he thought. Wonder what Mary is doing? He thought to himself. His silent dialogue or monologue went wild as he said, "Mary, I want to marry you. I want to spend every single day of the rest of my life with you. You are beautiful, sexy, bright and extremely intelligent. But you've got to get over the whips and chains, Mary. And that other strap on stuff you're into; where did you learn that? What makes you want that? I just can't and won't even consider that. Do you want a man or do you want Clay Aiken? Do you want a real authentic relationship or do you want a fling? I'm not a freak. This is not *West* Hollywood. I'm not Simon Cowell or Randy. They are both undercover gays. I am a *man*. A real man through and through. I want to marry you. I'm not in Scissor Sisters. I'm not Jimmy Kimmel or Conan O'Brien. I'm not the undercover gay guy who became *Mr. Star Jones*. I am Jeremy Shackelford. I'm a man. Mary Hanlon Stone, can you hear me?" He laughed out loud, of course she couldn't hear him. And fortunately, she would never see this (he thought) as he scribbled rapidly in his journal.

After the adult video, thoughts of Ms. Stone and note taking, Jeremy went online, as it was time to search the World Wide Web for Attorney Barry Scheck and the Innocence Project. As he googled the name Barry Scheck, he thought, why do I give a damn about Barry Scheck? He thought back on what Scott had asked him, "What's really going on here?"

* * *

. . . She was sixteen years old when Donald Ezzard promised to love faithfully. Donald was good looking, charming and had charisma. He was also extremely intelligent. So was his identical twin brother Ronald. It has been said that the rift or distance that came between us was perhaps due to the fact that Donald abandoned her after I was born. I looked just like him. He carried the seed, which impregnated Brenda Smith with her only son. Brenda loved me. Brenda was a good mother. But as I began to grow from, say about five years old, I took on all of Donald's physical and facial features. Brenda moved further and further away from me. It hurt me. I was a kid. I didn't understand. Nobody knew my secret pain and hurt. I would be thirteen years old before I even laid my eyes on the man who carried the seed of *me*. Recently I heard from Eddie Long that "God trusted

53

your daddy to *carry* the seed. But God didn't trust your daddy to *nurture* the seed. You're hurting and crying because your daddy wasn't in your life. But *if* he had been in your life, you would have been messed up and screwed up." I read where God told Jeremiah that before I formed thee in thy mother's womb, I knew thee. I'd come to realize God never makes a mistake. And some things we don't understand but if we press forward much will be revealed in *time*. I had already learned that Jeremy also had a drop out dad. He had no idea where his father was. I wondered did he know *all* of my story . . .

Thousands of miles away, this woman is struggling to make ends meet. She is a bit down on her luck. Seems to her that life is rough, tough and cold. She, like Brenda, also made a lot of mistakes as a young mother. But this woman, Leslie Rau was still a good human being. And her son, James Emslander should not be in prison. She knew this. I knew this. It was funny to me how life brings certain people together at certain times for certain seasons and certain reasons. If I had not met her son in prison, she would not be a part of my *story*. If Leslie had not made the mistakes, which she made, her son would not have come to prison and met me. If Brenda had not made her mistakes, I would not be where I am. I neither blame Leslie for James coming to prison, nor Brenda for my coming to prison. I simply mean they had to do or not do what they did, in order for us to do or not do what we did. Leslie and James have resolved their issues. They love each other. Brenda and I resolved our differences, we love each other. James knows where his father *is* in California. I know where my father *was* in Georgia. I honestly, sincerely wonder, will Jeremy ever know where to find his father.

Day 14

Jeremy got up late planning to leave Richmond, Virginia. He had been up very late analyzing the voluminous data on the Innocence Projects Website. Barry Scheck, Peter Neufeld, Benjamin Cardoza Law School, etc. The stuff he saw, read and perused absolutely held him spellbound for hours. Jeremy had wondered how this stuff could be. He took a lot of notes and downloaded a lot of data from the site. On the suggested reading list, he saw "Actual Innocence" by Barry Scheck and to his utter surprise, "From the Palace to the Prison" by me . . .

It's 10:00 a.m. and the e-mails are many. Joseph, Scott, Paul, Andy Furillo, Lisa, etc., etc. The e-mail from Joseph read . . . "Are you still in Atlanta, Georgia home of your notorious pen pal, Sherman Manning? Come clean, bro. Are you doing a story on the dude or what? If you are, that's cool but don't lie about it. How are the chicks in hot-Atlanta? Drop me a line to let me know you're cool." . . . Joe.

Scott's e-mail read, "Mr. Shackelford, how are ya, pal? My bad for getting upset the other day. I guess I can try to understand what you meant about not writing Sherman. Obviously he could be guilty of attempted murder. Obviously I don't know what kind of man he became after boot camp. Besides, I'm not a lawyer, social worker and I'm not a priest. So I decided you have a valid point. He definitely would want me to try to encourage you to use your position to help him. So to save us all a conflict, I'll leave it alone. I'm not gonna write him. In fact, if I may offer an opinion, I'd suggest you forget all about him. He's got three hots and a cot. He'll be okay. And on our little blow up, pal never forget that we are both Kappa Alpha order men! U R legitimately N I am in spirit. Stay safe." . . . Scott.

"He knows I'm not *Kappa Alpha*," Jeremy said to himself.

. . . 3:26 p.m. and Jeremy has already checked into the Dupont Plaza Hotel in Washington D.C. a mile away from the White House, two blocks away from the Dupont Circle Park. The hotel was quite fabulous Jeremy thought. I wonder if he knew when he checked in that my father was part owner of that hotel. I wonder if he knew that the massage parlor on the eighth floor of that hotel was also owned by my dad.

Jeremy enjoyed the view from his suite. Standing on the terrace at about 4:15 p.m. he spotted her. She was what the Black guys would call *bootylicious*. But Jeremy described her as "Gorgeously Attractive". She walked along the sidewalk a rocks throw away from Jeremy on the terrace. If I yell, it will seem discourteous and tacky. But how else can I stop her. Shit - I want this woman, now! Time was running out. If he didn't do or say something quick, she'd be gone.

"Ma'am," he yelled. She actually stopped and looked in his direction. "Excuse me, I don't mean to yell but I need to talk with you. Can you please meet me in the hotel lobby?"

Bad call, he thought. Too suspicious. He could be a killer for all she knew. Why did he say that? And on the fat chance that she actually did meet him, *what the hell* would he say to her? Hello, I'm a blue-eyed blonde, can we screw? He tried to recover as he yelled, "Never mind, just wait there and I'll come out."

She did wait. She gave him a chance to prove himself. Sarah was a lovely young lady. By 7:30 p.m. they were having drinks at Mr. P's on P. Street in downtown D.C. "I really like you, Jeremy but I've got to get home. I only live a few blocks from your hotel. I took the day off from my firm and I was just taking a walk when you stalked me earlier."

Jeremy laughed. "Well, Attorney Sarah Abrams, may I escort you home?" he asked.

"Why certainly," she replied.

As they walked arm in arm, he couldn't help it - this will be the first pussy I've gotten in D.C., first pussy in days and the first lawyer pussy ever - a lot of firsts, he thought. During their stroll Sarah talked about her job. "I've only been with this firm for three years. I joined fresh out of law school. It's called Bremner, Janus, Cook and Levin. I . . ."

Jeremy interrupted, "Janus? What Janus? What's Janus' first name?"

"*The Janus* . . . Murray J. Janus," Sarah laughed.

"I thought he was in Richmond, Virginia," Jeremy replied.

"And your Bee is in Sacramento, but you're owned by McClatchy News, which is here in D.C." Sarah said.

"How did you know about McClatchy?" Jeremy said.

"Well, A. I'm a lawyer and we try to be well informed. B. Their office is on the third floor of our building. We have the entire twelfth floor of the National Press Building."

"Shit," Jeremy said out loud.

"What do you mean, shit?" Sarah exclaimed.

Should I tell her? And if I don't, will Murray Janus tell her? Does Janus ever even come to D.C.? A large firm, several offices. The Richmond office has a corporate law division, civil, as well as personal injury practice. Perhaps Sarah works in civil or corporate and has no reason to ever have a detailed knowledge of criminal law and no reason to have ever had a discussion with Janus or anybody about Sherman Manning. Besides, Sherman has been in prison more than eight years. So when Sherman was hanging around in D.C. and Virginia, Sarah was not even in law school yet. She probably was not even in college, he thought.

"Hold on and calm down counselor. I'll explain," as he spoke, Jeremy, was calculating and deciding exactly what he was gonna explain and how. But certainly it would all depend upon what she knew, would or would not likely discover and on whether or not he'd ever see this woman again. After all, D.C. was a couple thousand miles from California and long distance relationships rarely ever lasted. "Do you practice criminal law like Mr. Janus?"

Sarah laughed, "Hell no, Jeremy." He breathed a sigh of relief as she continued. "Very few criminal lawyers make good money and it takes a certain stomach to represent child predators, murderers and the dregs of society. I.e., I could not have represented Jeffrey Dahmer, Richard Ramirez, O. J. Simpson or these little bastards who kill their parents and *blame it on the rain*. I am a corporate lawyer, Jeremy. But let's get back to you. Janus? Richmond! Your 'Shit' comment. Did you all of a sudden smell a bad odor or do you need to do some explaining?"

Jeremy decided to tell a part of the truth. Play it safe. Just in case. As they passed by the circled park at Dupont, Jeremy looked at the wooden benches and noticed a man curled up on the bench asleep. Obviously a homeless man. A few feet away sat a gentleman on the very same bench who appeared to be wearing a three thousand dollar suit. A middle aged White man working frantically on his computer. Cell phone in one hand, other hand on the mouse. Strange town, Jeremy thought. Only a couple of miles away from the White House and you have homeless people, White people at that, sleeping on the streets. The man sitting next to the homeless man is obviously oblivious to the plight of his homeless brother sleeping next to him. How could he sit there, Jeremy thought to himself, and do nothing, absolutely nothing to aid, assist or care for the homeless guy next to him? That's pretty cold. Jeremy reckoned silently.

He answered Sarah. "I was in Richmond on a potential story involving lawyers, criminal defense, etc. You know, sort of like the Beverly Ann Monroe case and how she was set up. So I interviewed Attorney Janus at his office," he said.

"Fantastic," Sarah replied with gleeful ebullience. "I know a lot about Beverly's case and I know a lot about wrongful convictions, Jeremy. Mr. Janus requires *all* attorneys in his firm, civil, corporate, no matter; he requires that we take on one pro bono criminal case per year. And last year, the case I took on and won by the way, led me to the famous Mr. Barry Scheck and the Innocence Project. In fact, I still keep up with the Innocence Projects as they are sprouting up all over the country. I love what Scheck does and what he represents. This man frees the innocent who have been hauled off to prisons for stuff they didn't do. I'm excited! You've got to come inside and tell me all about your story, Jeremy. And when we have our weekly firm teleconference, I'll tell Mr. Janus that I know you!"

Shit, again Jeremy said. This time the shit was silent. I'm in way over my head, he thought. Some way, some how I've got to get off of this subject. What if she knows of Manning? She knows of Monroe and Monroe was convicted way back in 1994. Jeremy continued his racing thoughts as Sarah placed the key inside the golden doorknob of her apartment in Georgetown.

"Nice place," he said after walking in behind Sarah and being invited to take a seat. Sarah washed her hands in the kitchen and brought Jeremy a Coca Cola.

If I can overcome this Janus, Manning bullshit and steer back to a neutral subject, I'll bang her and leave. By the time she speaks to Janus and finds out all the other B.S., I'll be out of town. She's young, I'm young. She's horny, single, intelligent and totally not a virgin. It won't be the end of the damned world. I'll meet many other women and she'll certainly meet many, many more men. She's well grounded, attractive and obviously she earns a good income. More than I'll be earning ever. So let me just do this Pi Kappa Phi style and get outta here. I'll just act like we did at U. C. Davis. Find em, (expletive) em and forget em. Like the binge drinking, pledges, dares, orgies and all the other stuff that takes place in institutions of higher learning across the good ole U.S. of A. What would Paul do? How about Joseph or Scott? They would remind me that I'm too uptight. I'm taking this shit way too seriously.

I should just lie, lie, lie. I should know how to lie with ease by now. After all the lying I saw up close and personal at the State Capitol. I watched state senators, assemblymen and a virtual garden variety of politicians sell their votes, sell their support and look straight at their constituents and lie about it. They lied about life and death issues, lied about electricity, public health, education, doctored and fixed legislation. Democrats were weak kneed and afraid to be called liberals. Republicans manipulated religion and pretended to love God while appearing to hate their brothers. What the hell am I worried about? Why not lie, he thought?

"Do you want to have sex?" he actually did it. The old college stud rose to the occasion. Maybe Zig Zigler, Les Brown, Tony Robbins and all the self-help gurus were right. Ask for what you want.

"Yes, I'd like that. Do you have a condom?" she asked.

Shit, he thought. He tried not to appear too excited but the lump between his legs deceived him. He needed to appear cool, calm and collected like this sort of thing happened to *him* all the time. But what if it also happened to *her* all the time, he thought. Glad I do have a condom cause she could have anything, he thought. Oh, no! I hope she's not into that S&M, wanna tie me up and whip me like Mary - had a little strap on - Hanlon Stone stuff. No way. Too easy . . . Manning? Sherman Manning. What if all of this was a set up? Sherman is brilliant. Murray Janus is brilliant. What if they're in on this? Like

Sherman has a camera in this place and I'll be videotaped banging Sarah. And she'll say it was rape and I'll go to jail. Or they'll just blackmail me into doing a series of front-page stories on Sherman. You cannot put anything pass lawyers. And she is a *lawyer*. And I am an idiot for dreaming up this bullshit that's so unrealistic. I'm a nut case for even letting Manning dominate my thoughts. This man is in prison. Safely tucked away in California. I'm a fool, Jeremy chuckled.

"What's funny, Mr. Shackelford? Do you find it amusing that I want to (expletive) your brains out?"

He got another rise. "No, I'm only thinking of how we met, how exciting and fabulous this is about to be." He was ready.

"And it will be," Sarah said as she got up out of her chair and moved gracefully over to the couch. She sat up close to him and continued, "After we talk about your story. After you promise me that there will be a story, after you promise to mention Janus and our firm in the story and after you swear to me that you will stay in town at least three more days and let me give you a personal workshop or clinic of sorts on wrongful convictions and the American Judicial System."

Jeremy still had a lump but some kind of way the lump had traveled from his groin area all the way up to his esophagus. His cell rang and after saying, "Excuse me, counselor," he answered. Saved by the bell, he thought. What Jeremy needed was a pattern interrupt time. He needed a little time to decide how to handle this mess. Keep the goal in mind. The goal is sex. I wanna do her before I exit the Nation's Capital, he thought. "J," he spoke into the telephone.

"Man, don't you read your e-mails. I know you're on your *Amazing Race* and journey across America, but life still goes on back here in California. You have a newspaper to run in less than a month, dude. And I am your best reporter. And you see no need to check in with old Andy to find out what's going on at the Bee," Furillo spoke rapidly.

"Furillo, what's going on, man? How are ya? Long time no speak."

"Where are you?" Andy asked.

About to get laid was Jeremy's thought. Sarah had trotted off to another room to find files, paperwork, her briefcase, etc. Jeremy was tempted to tell Andy all about her and what he was planning. Andy would be proud of his new boss. By the way it wouldn't hurt to start developing the stud reputation at the Bee as he had at U.C.D. There were assorted whispers and rumors about favoritism and the power of the *Governator*. Folks were gossiping around the water cooler

59

claiming that a graduate in journalism whose only real job experience was delivering pizza and being a press aide did not deserve the top job at a well-respected newspaper. Upon the untimely departure of Rick Rodriguez, many surmised that Gary Delsohn, Andy Furillo, Dan Walters or Dianna Griego would get the top job. But no, someway somehow, Jeremy had been anointed and appointed. Most believed without question that Arnold Schwarzenegger had something to do with Jeremy acquiring this job . . . Jeremy decided not to chance it. Sarah was a lawyer - she could be standing nearby listening. "I'm in the Nation's Capital," he said.

Andy immediately knew that Jeremy had done the right thing and gone to D.C. to check out the home office of the McClatchy News Company. The parent company to the Bee. "That's good, dude. We've got a stack of mail here for you. You have mail from all around the country including seven or eight missives from Mule Creek State Prison - Sherman."

Jeremy interrupted. "Listen, I've got to go but Fed Ex all that mail to me here in D.C. Send it to the Dupont Plaza Hotel. I'll read it all on the road. Can you get it here tomorrow?"

Andy said, "Sure and I'll just *File 13* this mail from Manning. Any other mail you want me to throw away?"

Jeremy was slightly perturbed, "Mr. Furillo, I'll discard the mail, which I don't want. But for now, please forward *all* the mail to me. Every bit of it. Thanks. Gotta go, pal." Jeremy hung up.

He wondered about some of his old buddies. Jeffrey Klein in Hollywood, CA. The gothic, freaky-looking dude with the make up, black fingernails and goatee. Jeffrey must have had twenty piercing all over his thin framed body. Jeff is a nut. Wonder if he has a job yet. What about Matthew Miller in Stockton? Wes Kovarik in Antioch, Stephon Simmons in SAC, Kyle and Belinda Love in Auburn, Dr. Chris Kallakin in Malibu? I wonder what is Anthony Fedorov doing in Tremont, Pennsylvania? Bo Bice, Greg Sieman, Owen LaFave in Riverview, Florida, Jason Shapiro in Coral Springs, Florida? Is Jason still at Duke studying mathematics and economics? How are Mike and Jacob Bruer out at Hofstra? Is Mike still aspiring to become a Chippendale dancer? Is Lisa dating? Is Mary Hanlon Stone still whipping and chaining? Life, he said to himself . . .

Queen Sarah stepped back into the room. Sex was obviously not on her mind. At least not yet. She was definitely not alone. Sarah was packing! She had folders, news clippings, legal journals, a brief case and three tomes. He saw them clearly . . . "The Perpetual Prisoner Machine" by Joel Dyer, "Actual Innocence" by Scheck and . . .

"American Dream/A Search for Justice" . . . Unreal, he thought. It's worse than I thought. She actually knows Sherman D. Manning. He told me all about how he and Harper Collins gave away five hundred copies of **that** book. More than one hundred copies went to lawyers. And after he sent her his book, he probably wrote to her. I know how Sherman operates. And since they have Janus and Scheck in common, I know she wrote him back. Is it even worth it? Should I cut my losses, invent an emergency and leave now? Get out while I can. What the hell, he thought.

Day 16

Jeremy has been in D.C. for two days now. Thus far, he's spent only about four hours total at his suite at the Dupont Plaza Hotel. It had been nearly 2:30 a.m. that first night before he and Sarah had stripped, showered and screwed. It had been awesome. So awesome that the condom had torn during their third time around the mountain. Kissing, touching, moaning, groaning, sucking and, of course, the other stuff. They did it all. And I do mean all. It was awesome, splendid and perhaps the best Jeremy had ever had. Good enough to bust the condom. And Mary Hanlon Stone did have one thing in common with Sarah. One kinky idiosyncrasy . . .

Jeremy had been impressed; a better word might be *stunned* by all the data, which Sarah had shared with him. Sarah was thorough, detailed and specific. She provided empirical evidence, documented and indisputable, uncontested research which proved her points conclusively. But, believe it or not Sarah didn't have time to talk about "American Dream/A Search for Justice" nor did she mention my name at all.

She wrapped up her impromptu workshop for Jeremy with Barry Scheck. She finished as if she were giving a closing argument in a live courtroom. She must have watched *The Practice* . . . She must watch *Boston Legal*, Jeremy thought. She was good. Articulate, witty, quick on her feet, fluent, strong and even eloquent. "You're good," he had told her.

"Better than Johnnie Cochran?" she asked.

"Much better than Johnnie Cochran." With that said, the session had come to an end and their shower and sex was to begin . . .

7:30 a.m. and Jeremy and Sarah were having breakfast on the patio of Crown Books and Café in Dupont. The waiter came over and took their orders. The waiter was a funny-looking White dude with a long ponytail. Jeremy wondered was this guy an undercover gothic who put on all black at night . . . Breakfast was going well when the twins within Jeremy began that inner struggle. This time the good guy won. "I need to tell you something, Sarah," Jeremy stated with all the authority and journalistic command he could muster.

After all, he was a man now. And he was about to take over a large newspaper and there would be many times when he'd need to talk man to man, man to woman and employer to employee with reporters and the public, etc. So now was the time to put it all out there. "Sarah, I did not tell you everything about my meeting with Mr. Janus. I actually went to see him with an ulterior motive. Sherman Diahric Manning. I should have explained all of this the first day. I know, I know, I know. And when you showed me a copy of one of his books in your condo that was also a perfect segue, which I failed to utilize. Sorry. I'm really, really sorry. Gumption tells me that you've probably communicated with Mr. Manning via the mail. You probably heard about him through Janus. And you definitely know much more about the guy than I do. But let me tell you the story of how I came to know of Mr. Manning and then you can interrogate or berate me."

* * *

Jeremy told her everything including his suspicion that I was just another run of the mill prisoner trying to manipulate the press. But he left the door open and made it quite obvious to Sarah in his thirteen-minute monologue that the moment she dotted the I's or crossed a few T's for him, he was perhaps ready to entertain the idea that perhaps he was too skeptical of me. The moment Sarah confirmed how well she knew me or knew of me, Jeremy was ready. Just a few solid statements concerning Janus' belief in me and perhaps some inside data on conversations about me with Janus would have been enough to finally give Jeremy the ammunition which he needed. To tell himself it was okay to care. Okay to give a damn and yes, okay to get involved. By that time, I had indeed received the kiss off missive from Jeremy but had continued to write him day after day and epistle after epistle. I guess I kinda felt deep within that there was something to this Shackelford guy. Or maybe I thought he was naïve and uncorrupted. Or perhaps I thought . . . I think it was a combination of all of the above and more. Be nice to claim I'd received a divine mandate from God or that some angel had told me Jeremy was the right guy for the job. But that would not be true. Truth is, I wrote a lot of people. Usually I asked them not to reply via missive to me in the prison. I usually asked for e-mails. Only about forty to fifty percent of them ever even replied. And one can only imagine that if a well-established author with his own money could only get a bit less than half of the folks he wrote to send an e-mail back, then the prospect for unknown prisoners with little or no money, getting snail mail replies was slim to none. It was actually quite sad and shameful . . .

    * * *

Well Jeremy finished his spiel and took a swig of orange juice as he prepared to listen.

Sarah began sternly and methodically. "Mr. Shackelford," she began, which was a bad sign. "I really do like you a lot."

Prepare for kiss off, he knew. It's over. I blew it, he thought.

Sarah continued, "I like you in a very special way. And I actually understand what you are going through. Actually, I've never met Mr. Manning. I know nothing about Mr. Manning. And to be frank, Mr. Janus has never mentioned him to me. In fact, the reason I did not comment or elaborate on Mr. Manning the other night when I had his book was because I have not read it yet."

Jeremy felt like a damned fool. This honesty stuff is way overrated, he thought. "I plan to read it soon, Jeremy. I think it's probably a good book. I saw it up front in this (Crown) store about two weeks ago and the clerk said it sells well so I will get to it. Most especially, after all you've told me now, I **must** read it. I forgive you. You didn't actually *lie* to me. But I must make this observation if I can. You seemed to have glossed over the fact that according to your own words, this guy is asking you to publicize and expose the tragedy of the raping of basically *Blue-Eyed Blondes* in prison. And so, if this is the case and this is what he is asking you to expose, for the life of me I cannot comprehend why you cannot conduct your own independent survey or engage in investigative journalism on your own and if you become convinced that this is an epidemic in the prisons and juveniles, then do the story. You are not obligated to even mention Mr. Manning *if* you do the story. So unless I missed something or my lawyerly listening skills are dulling, I would be led to surmise that you have a hunch that Mr. Manning himself deserves some play, do you not?"

Jeremy chuckled. "Damn, I see why they sent you to law school," he told her.

It is now 3:25 p.m. as Jeremy steps into the suite of his hotel at the Dupont Plaza Hotel. He's feeling good. In fact, very good. He closes the door, drops his briefcase and begins walking toward the terrace and then he sees him. "What the (expletive) are *you* doing in my hotel, man? Why are *you* here? How did *you* get inside? How did *you* know I was here? Man, you'd better start talking fast."

Jeremy was startled, angry and very, very confused. But the coy laughter he heard and the wide grin he observed made him more angry than anything. He's actually mocking me as if the joke's on me, he thought.

"Dude, come on lighten up and relax. I promise you, I swear to you that I will not hurt you. I mean you no harm. This was meant to be. This was supposed to happen. I had to come here. I actually had no choice," he stated.

"*Sherman Manning* . . ." Jeremy yelled as he stood angrily, defiantly and hesitantly, ". . .could have gotten into my room just as you did. Paul, I know you're my brother, but man, come on. I didn't even know that you knew I was here."

Paul chuckled. "I'm your little brother, Jerry," Paul said knowing Jeremy *hated* it when people confused his name with Jerry. But brothers will be brothers. "And I hack computers, bro. I'm down with Defcon, Caleb Sima and Kevin Mahaffey. So you know that I know how to defeat a computerized door to a hotel room that requires a cheap security card. I used this," Paul stated as he held up a funny-looking plastic card, which was strikingly similar to Jeremy's door card. I called Furillo and he told me you were at this hotel. So since I have to be in D.C. for two days, unless you're leaving town tonight, I figured I'd surprise you and yes, crash with you too."

"Okay, slow down, Paulie." There he got him back as Paul hated the name Paulie. "What do you mean you *have* to be in D.C. for two days, dude?"

Paul decided to explain with no sarcasm. "I lost a (expletive) bet, man. You're gonna think I'm crazy or weird or way out, but I had a bet with a friend of mine. You don't know him. He's a Black guy. Anyway, he bet me back during the World Series and it's time to pay up. I'm not religious but I won't play with *God*. I gave my word. I bet him . . . If I won, I got five hundred dollars. If he won, I had to meet him here in D.C. at *Manpower*."

Jeremy said, "What the hell is *Manpower*?"

"The opposite of woman power, fool. No Manpower is a darker version of the *Promise Keepers*. I shouldn't say it that way but what I'm trying to say is more Blacks attend Manpower than Whites. But there are Whites at Manpower too. So we won't be the only Whites there."

"We? I thought you said your friend was Black," Jeremy said.

Paul goes, "He is Black, but you're White."

"I knew *I* was . . . or *am White*, but you said *we* won't be the only Whites there. What other White person are you hauling off to a stadium for Manpower, little brother?"

Paul laughed, "Why *you*, of course. I promised I'd get *you* to go with us."

There went the peace. "No way. You had absolutely no way of knowing I would ever even be in Washington, D.C. and no idea what my agenda would be at this time of year so how in the hell could you promise to wrap me up and deliver me to Manpower?"

"Calm down, big brother. You're right, I didn't know where you'd be or what you'd be doing so I promised I'd come and promised to try to get you to go also. You're here; I'm here. Never mind why we are here. We are here. In this time and in this place and we're going - tonight."

Jeremy was livid. What about his date with Sarah? How would she feel about being stood up for a Promise Keepers convention or Manpower or whatever the hell it was? But how often would Jeremy be in D.C. and have his little brother with him. It had after all been a very long time since they did anything together. Paul told Jeremy all the details about his bet, the flight to D.C., taxi ride to his hotel, etc. Jeremy told Paul about Sarah, Sarah and more about Sarah. Paul was well aware of the e-mail from Joseph and Scott.

* * *

He knew that Scott knew me. He also knew about Jeremy's *no contact* decree with Scott concerning me. Actually Paul was a little disappointed with Jeremy in that regard. After all their own father was perhaps somewhere in a prison and, some kind of way, while a kid, Paul has convinced himself that the only reason his father had abandoned them was because he was somewhere in prison. So then the prison authorities, whoever they were and wherever that was, they were the enemy. The big bad guys with guns and badges had come and got their dad. This was the only reason Paul and Jeremy had been denied a father. And one day he'd get out and come get his two sons. This was Paul's childhood fantasy and although Jeremy never thought of their dad as the good guy, they never discussed it. Not since that time when they were kids and Paul shared this idea with Jeremy. And Jeremy had replied, "He could write us if he wanted to find us. He abandoned Mom before he was arrested. He knows our telephone number."

Paul had teared up and since that time, they barely even mentioned their dad. But Paul, even now as a young man, still subconsciously held on to the residue of the fantasy, which had helped him cope with being a fatherless son. And the anger at a system, which had apparently taken their dad away, made me or any other guy in jail the good guy and the system which held us the bad guys. Paul didn't tell anyone this foolishness. He rarely ever even thought about law and order or justice and jail. But deep within, he held on to the belief or desperate hope that the prisons were bad and his daddy was good. And so in private moments, after hearing of how livid and adamant Jeremy was about Scott not writing me - *That's not cool*, Paul had thought to himself.

So as they talked and wrestled and pillow fought in D.C., Jeremy purposely avoided any serious discussion of *me*. He glossed over the Janus/Manning factor and certainly withheld any details about going to my family's home in Atlanta. In fact, it turns out that while Jeremy was in Atlanta after he'd visited with my parents, he'd actually gone to my house. Hell, had my wife not been in Switzerland, he may have even interviewed her. But he drove up to my estate and parked outside the gate and just stared at my house. Could a potential killer, a mad man or crook have actually lived in that house, he'd asked himself as he stared through the black gates? Seems like Jeremy was as tied up and as confused as I was at that juncture. I still recall how angry, livid and disappointed I was when I got that kiss-off letter from Jeremy.

I could not understand why this man didn't even mention going to or having gone to visit my family in Atlanta in that letter. I had no way of timing it or figuring out whether he'd written the letter before he visited my mom. My mind told me it had to have been written *after* his Atlanta visit. But my heart told me it could not be. My mind and heart were in conflict. I knew my mother. Integrity, honor and love emanates out of her very being. She is a woman of dignity. And nobody would have been able to convince me that this man was not affected by a conversation with my mother. And my mother was never wrong. "That young man does not believe you tried to kill anybody, Sherman," Mom had told me. "Do you really think he came all the way to Atlanta for nothing? My mind does not fool me. I sat with him and saw him, Sherman, live and in the flesh. That blonde-headed blued-eyed guy felt something when we talked. The good Lord moves in mysterious ways. He wonders, we can't perceive," Mom had told me.

Damn, I had been extremely excited. In fact, I was bouncing off the walls when I got the incredible, unbelievable news that *Shackelford came* to see me - *Sherman*!

But when the kiss-off letter came I . . . . California prisons absolutely abuse, delay, sabotage and tamper with inmates' mail. They commit federal crimes routinely with mail. At various times we get mail, which is thirty days old. And sometimes it only takes four or five days. So unless a person dates the letter, if the postage date or stamp is unclear, one has no way of knowing *when* a letter was sent, written or mailed. So I hoped against hope that another letter was forthcoming. Any day now I'll get a letter explaining it all. Jeremy will clear it all up. And I know that this man will help me to expose one of the best-kept secrets of America; *the* best kept secret of our Nation's prisons. The time has come to blow the damned whistle on this madness.

If Jeremy doesn't mention **my** name . . . If I don't even get a footnote of a mention, it's okay. If there is a God (and I know there is), *He* will bless *me* for reaching outside of my own box, getting out of my own comfort zone and speaking up on an issue that does not benefit *me*. I know about slavery, racism and all of that. But that bullshit does not justify what I saw in L.A. County Jail. White kids being forcefully sodomized with brooms. White boys being train raped by seven and eight guys. I could live with the fact that predators took their jewelry, shoes and clothes. I could even turn a deaf ear to the fact that White guys were routinely forced to give up their bunks and sleep on the concrete floors in 2500 and other parts of the jail. That was wrong and bad enough. But to force any human being to have sex was too much to bear. I can't see this wickedness and not speak out.

And I know it's a White thing. I know by and large, it's mostly Whites being raped. Not because they are weaker and not because they're cowards, but because in ninety percent of the juveniles, jails and prisons in America, they are outnumbered. And society thinks without thinking . . . They hear the numbers and ambiguous numerical statistics and it leads them to think that perhaps there are only a couple of thousand White guys in prison. But if they knew that there are well over four hundred thousand Caucasian males in jails, juveniles and prisons and according to Professor James Liebman, at least forty percent of them have been raped. Quite frankly, I think that's a conservative estimate but even with that . . . Forty percent of four hundred thousand? If America finds out that one hundred and eighty thousand White, mostly young, blue-eyed and mostly blonde . . . men are raped every single year in prison . . . America will go crazy. Little old White women, who have not even spoken the word prison in there lifetime, will call the U.S. Senate, college students who binge drink every weekend and cram think during the week, will rise up and demand a change.

I know White folks. I know that had somebody told the late Senator Strom Thurmond that perhaps a quarter million White kids were being forcefully sodomized in prisons by darkies, him and Senator Robert Byrd would have kicked ass and taken names later. I know damn well I'm right. The force of righteousness is on my side.

This sadistic raping, torture and the *sodomization* of White guys in prisons is like the *sodomization* of little White altar boys by priests, which has been for decades; *hidden in plain sight*! The White church couldn't *see* it, rarely thought about it and subconsciously lived in a state of denial. And there is something about situations in which men feel helpless and we struggle with denial and abandonment. There seems to be this inner struggle that says, "It's probably not happening" and if it's happening, it's an aberration and not the norm". And if our illusions or delusions or our fantasy, which we develop to keep us shielded from helplessness; if that bubble is burst, we often abandon even the people that we love. So then the victims of rape, abuse and torture often are re-victimized when the ones who love them, leave them.

Lisa Ling exposed the torture and rape of women in the Congo. On the Oprah show, Lisa interviewed Black men who watched their wives get raped. The women would be forced to endure train rapes. Often they'd force one of the women's children to spread their own mother's legs. One son would have to tie the leg or foot of his mother to one tree. And another son or daughter would be forced at gunpoint to tie his mother's other leg or foot to another tree. And the entire family would be forced to watch their mother, wife and children get trained raped. In many instances, the vicious rebels and rapists also force the mother's own sons to "Rape you mother". And Lisa found that, after all the women went through, very often their own husband would *leave them.* It is sick and shameful and there is no defense for these men abandoning their wives. It's inexcusable. And I believe the reason the men would leave is because deep within, they felt ashamed and hurt that they could not protect their own Kith and Kin. They felt their children would not respect them and . . . in the process they re-victimized their wives by abandoning them when they needed them most. And Oprah asked Lisa, "Why America did not know about what was going on in the Congo." America is still a racist country. Let's fact it, these people are dark-skinned. Mr. Bush's administration considers them savages. They don't matter. If they were White, our military would be inside the Congo kicking butt and taking names later. You can't rape White women and get away with it. . .

I know when Shackelford looks into my claims, he will tell the world about what is happening *right this minute,* this very second, to White men and boys in prison. That's what I thought, prayed for and hoped for.

* * *

68

. . . Jeremy and Paul were now at Manpower. They had met Paul's Black buddy, Leroy one hour before they were due to arrive at the stadium. Jeremy had called Sarah and explained his predicament although he left out the fact that Paul had hacked his way into his hotel room. Sarah had actually been supportive cause she believed in God and she believed that although she was Catholic, any connection with God was better than none at all.

Leroy had explained to Jeremy and Paul that Bishop T. D. Jakes had been called by *Time Magazine* the Black Billy Graham. Leroy told them that once every year, T. D. Jakes has a convention for men only. He also does one called, "Woman Thou Art Loosed" for women only. Jakes got the *Woman Thou Art Loosed* name for the women's convention based on St. Luke, Chapter 13 verses 11 & 12. And behold there was a woman which had a spirit of infirmity for eighteen years and had been bent over, bowed down, tied up and crippled and could not lift herself up. And in Verse 12, Jesus saw her and he *called* her to him. And said unto this woman, "Woman *thou art loosed* from thine infirmity." Leroy went on to explain to Paul and Jeremy that Bishop Jakes started Woman Thou Art Loosed and Manpower in a storefront church in Charleston, West Virginia. Jeremy interrupted, "What is a storefront church?"

And Leroy said, "They call it a store front church because it is a small little building that sometimes is a store during the week and doubles as a church on the weekend. It has little fold up aluminum chairs and can usually seat only about forty-five or fifty people comfortably. Anyway, over the years, they outgrew the storefront and moved to the Potter's House in Dallas, Texas. Woman Thou Art Loosed now has about fifty to sixty thousand attendees. It's so big that they have to book stadiums to accommodate the crowds and in Manpower while Manpower is going on, they beam it live via satellite into more than four hundred prisons all across America. Jakes has a special calling and ministry for men in prison. And in Manpower, he brings in Bishop Noel Jones, Bishop Eddie Long and Kirk Franklin."

Paul and Jeremy interrupted simultaneously, "Oh yeah. I know Kirk Franklin."

Leroy said, "And my mother believes Jakes might be a money hungry crook."

Jeremy chimed in, "Then why would you take us to see a crook?"

"Well, I look at it this way," Leroy replied. "It's not about Jakes, the man. It is about the ministry. I personally believe he is a man of God with an anointing on his life unlike anything I've ever seen. But if I knew for a fact that he was a complete crook, I'd still go to

Manpower. The reason I'd go is because unlike Benny Hinn and I mean Benny no disrespect - maybe Benny is for real, but I don't think so, but when you go to a Benny crusade, it's all about the healing, the miracles or the hope that you'll get physical healing for your body. And Benny does not really say anything. But when you go to Manpower, this big ole brother preaches self-help, healing, emotional breakthrough, spiritual deliverance and psychological deliverance is there for you. Jakes can preach. His messages are so unique, so filled with wisdom, encouragement and advice that an atheist or agnostic could enjoy Manpower. And his messages lead *you*, back to you, back to the Bible and back to God. He is not the star of the show. God is the star and Jakes is just the mailman dropping a letter in your mailbox."

Leroy talked about twenty minutes basically explaining what they would experience. They were there in the Jack Kent Cook Stadium in Landover, Maryland. They were joined by nearly thirty-five thousand other men. Black men, White men, and Mexican men. The place was jam-packed. Cameras were everywhere. Big screens, musical instruments, etc. and to Jeremy's surprise there were a lot of young men in their twenties there.

How do you get this many men together in one city, one stadium all in the name of God, Jeremy asked himself? As Jeremy looked up on the stage, the only two men he recognized were Deion Sanders and Michael Irving, Jr.

"Is that Deion and Michael from the Dallas Cowboys?" Jeremy asked Leroy.

Paul hurriedly jumped in with the answer, "Yes!"

Paul and Jeremy had never witnessed anything like this before in their lives. Jeremy had heard of the Black colleges Spring break called *Freaknick*. Jeremy had personally gone to two White Spring breaks down in Florida. But to be in a football stadium with no game and to have this many men bussed in, trained in, flown in from all around the world with not a woman in sight was new to Jeremy . . . And there he stood. He was tall, big, baldheaded and Black. Bishop Thomas Dexter Jakes stood there with the microphone held in his hand.

"I want to thank God for all of you men who have come here to this stadium to lift up the name of Jesus Christ. I am excited. I have a word from the Lord for you brothers. I didn't come to play any games. I didn't come with any milk and cookies. I came to bring you some real meat that you can chew on til we meet again. I don't believe that you have come here for a game . . . As people pass by this stadium and look at us shouting, cheering and clapping, they don't understand how we could get so many men together without a game. They can't understand why we are here. But God has brought us together at this particular time for a reason. Destiny is inside of each one of you. There is a prophecy over your life. There is a reason you are here. After all you've gone through. You're here tonight for a reason. I want to preach tonight from the subject: *Bad Boys; Bad Boys* and the **God** who loves them."

Jakes went on to talk about Joseph in the book of Genesis. He explained how Joseph had been set up and falsely accused of a sex crime. Jakes told how Joseph had been convicted with an "R" in his jacket and went to prison for 13 ½ years - *But* **God** had a plan for Joseph. And that's why we are in the prisons. There is not a lot of money in the prisons. There is a lot of hatred, hopelessness and helplessness in the prisons. Prison is a dank, dark and dirty place. But the God of Abraham, Isaac and Jacob, the God of my grandmamma and granddaddy Nem, the God that woke me up this morning and started me on my way, that God can reach down in low down, dark and dirty places. He specializes in reaching you right where you are . . . God does not choose and select his leaders and preachers like we do. We look for the Harvard, Moorehouse and Yale graduates. But God went out to an old sheep stall and found a little shepherd boy who stank and was dirty and said, I know you are smelly with your stinky self, but David I want **you**! Yes, God chooses Bad Boys who have been down and out. He'll step into a hog pen and find him a prodigal son and say *I want you*. He stepped into a dirty, filthy and dark gated community. He looked inside Pelican Bay, Lorton Penitentiary, Rikers Island or Reidsville State Prison and said, I *want Joseph*. I know he don't look like it, it may not seem like it, he's got a rape on his record, don't nobody want to deal with you, but I want *you*! I want you all over here in this stadium, I want you men who are watching us in prisons all over this country right now to grab another brother by the hand and say, "Bad Boy, Bad Boy, what you gonna do when *He comes for you*". Look em back square in their face and yell to him to the top of your lungs and say, "Bad Boy, Get Ready, Get Ready, Get Ready; *God is coming for you*!"

. . . God, God, God! He chooses who He uses and tonight He chose you! There were a lot of men more qualified than Jacob to carry the seed of Joseph. The name Jacob literally means *trickster*. Jacob was a trickster, a conman and a crook. But when he wrestled all night with the Angel, God asked him, "What is your name?" Jacob said, "My name is trickster. My name is a conman. I am what they named me." But God told Jacob, "*Your name is not Jacob*. Your name is

71

Israel. And Israel means *prince*. And yet if you keep reading the Bible, you'll find that God himself would vacillate from calling him Jacob and Israel. One moment God would call him Prince and a few chapters later he'd call him Trickster. You see God knew Jacob as a prince but he also knew that the prince still had some trickster inside him. And some of you men that are in this stadium, some of you watching in the prison; the enemy wants you to think that because you're a Bad Boy, God can't use you. The enemy named you a thug, a rapist, a con, a robber or a crook, but there is a *prince inside you*.

You might be down today, but you can get back up again. All of us got twins within us wrestling and trying to hinder us from our destiny. All of us got some wounds, some hurts, some trauma and some mess. But don't let your mess stop you from moving. You've got to believe that it's not over just because you got in trouble. You've got to know that God still loves you. Even when your family changes their telephone number or puts a block on the telephone. Even when they forget about you and won't write to you in the prison. You've got to remember that they also forgot about Joseph! Many of them forgot about Malcolm, they forgot about Rubin "Hurricane" Carter, and yes they forgot Mandela, but God. God! God! God reached down and pulled Joseph up out of that prison and said, I still remember you. Joseph I got your back. I loved you when I formed you in your mother's womb! I loved you when I first gave you that dream. I loved you when Jacob, your daddy, gave you that coat of many colors. I loved you when your own brothers plotted to kill you. I loved you when your own brothers decided to throw you into a pit. I loved you when you were sold into slavery. I loved you, Joseph when you were working in Potiphar's house and his wife lied on you and called you a rapist. I loved you all the while you've been in this prison trying to get out of trouble.

I loved you when you helped the Chief Baker and the Butler while you were doing time even though you committed no crime. I loved you Joseph when the Butler and the Baker got out of jail and they forgot about you. But Joseph, I am God and I change not! All the while you've been in the *prison*, I was getting you ready for the *palace*. Arise out of the ashes of defeat, shake off the prison mentality, take off the prison uniform. I'm about to make you the Prince of Egypt.

And men - listen to me; the Lord sent me here to tell you - you in this stadium, you in that prison, you in that juvenile or jail cell; God still remembers you. And God can come and get you. Help is on the way. I don't care how bad it looks and how late it looks; God can do the Almighty through the least likely. God has not *forgotten* you. I know you are a Bad Boy. I know you smoke dope, you drink liquor and you've lain with some of everybody, but God can raise you up . . .

You must stop waiting on a leader. I'll say it again, stop waiting on a leader . . . Dr. Martin Luther King, Jr. was a great man and he served his purpose. Rev. Hosea Williams was a great man and he served his purpose. It's your turn now! It's your time to be blessed . . .

When that woman met Jesus at the well she was going to get water. She had her little water pots or buckets with her. And the minute she found out that Jesus was in town, she dropped her water pots.

I need **you** right in that prison, I need **you** right in this stadium to drop your buckets where you are. God has a plan for **you**. There is something God wants you to do. If it's cutting grass, sweeping streets, chopping meat, leading a march, writing a poem, a play, a book or a song. You have got to *find your* place. You must find *your passion* and once you find it, hone it.

. . . Even though you're having to eat *dirt in the* prison, God will sprinkle gold into the dust. You can rise up and find your place. You can rise up and find your passion, your place and your element. David used a slingshot and a rock to kill a giant. There are some giant killers right in this stadium. There are some *giant* killers right in that prison. There are princes, men of greatness all over this place. But you gotta get up. Don't lose your focus, your goals and your dreams. . ."

Jakes preached that stadium crazy. Men were jumping, shouting, clapping and crying. Jeremy and Paul had never seen so many men crying like that. And near the end of his message, Jakes told the crowd that, "I want every man in here and even those watching in prison to grab the hand of the man next to you; look him in the eye and tell him, 'I got your back'. Look right in his eyes and tell that brother, 'I'll be your keeper. I'll keep you covered in prayer. I won't forget you. God has not forgotten you!'" And Jakes told the men in that stadium, "I want every man in this stadium to look at the closest camera to your seat. Look straight in that camera and tell all the brothers in the prisons that I'm here for you. I'll pray for you. I'll write you back. I'll take your call. I won't forget you. God has not forgotten you!"

(Author's Note . . . Jeremy wants every person perusing this tome to go to *www.were not afraid.com* . . . We send our deepest regards and heartfelt condolences to all of the victims of 7/7 in London. We hope our readers will make certain the *Benton* sisters in Tennessee as well as their pal, *Tai Matthews* get copies of this tome. *Jeremy* sends a shout out to Jose Nachles, (cancer treatment therapist) Clay Ellis and

Michael Pugliesce. We hope *Ripley's Believe It Or Not* winner (world's most *Flexible Man. . .*) Daniel will get a copy of this book. Daniel is a flexible role model. If you all contact Daniel and he writes us, we'll use a photo in the revised edition of this book ...)

     * * *

...Eric Bulrice, Jake Weary, Kevin Olivers and Justin Cardinale are awesome young men...we hope Eric, Mr. Noble, Scott Reed, Chaz Wolcott, Clark Domae, Michael Goldfine and Professor Adam Wassen get a hold of the *Blue-Eyed Blonde*. When Shawn Abbott (Ivy League Admissions), Max (Oakland, CA), Scot Parsley and Davis (The Scholar...Political Activist...) get this book, it's on and cracking...

We want all of the youngsters who are reading this book to go to www.urbandictionary.com and make submissions. We want folks like Scott Reed and Chaz Wolcott (Nevada) to get involved with our writing. We have heard all the folks who say young people don't read and are not involved politically, etc. But we don't buy that. We, therefore, are all calling on Bonnie Evans, Maranda Klemens, Genevieve Reinhart, Riley Evans and James Henderson (all of Davis Senior High in Davis, CA) and Daniel Asare (John F. Kennedy High in Sacto...) to blog, message, text and post your pals and spark the debate about Blue-Eyed Blonde. Don't even wait or procrastinate... Do it now. Go to www.DashCash. Blogspot.com and post a message. Go to Myspace.com, Friendship.com and Buddypics.com and Livejournal.com and organize book reading clubs, discussions, etc. Jeremy Shackelford (as well as Michael Shackelford...actually Michael is from Sand Spring...) as well as this writer, etc. have total faith in our youth. When we get Nathan Craft, www.PushAmerica.org, Mr. Bulrice and all the student nerds, geeks and freaks hooked up online discussing the issues covered in this tome, we will revolutionize America. If you'll go to www.wavesofterror.com and ask how to reach Jordan and bring Jordan into the discussion, we are on the move. This writer wants Charlie Wildman (Wildman-C. in Prattville, Alabama), Matthew Wetherington, Mark Delgado (and Jeana Cook in El Paso, Texas), Caleb Kerby and folks at Casey's Coffee Plaza in Chester, New Jersey, etc. to push the envelope. Get involved with our scholarship offers and contests, etc. If you know of a high school senior, college freshman, etc. who needs help with tuition, books, room and board, let us know. We will help pay stipends and grant scholarships. But *you* gotta get online and tell others about the offer. You must call, write, text message your fellow students, frat brothers, etc. Jeffrey Frieders (Sacramento), Chris Austad (Bellflower, CA), Derrick Flowers (Charlotte, NC), Richard Rubin, Freekey Zeekey,

Tony Yayo, Kenneth Depagter, Gloria Sherman, Andrew Glassman and Ron Corning (ABC News) and tell them the book is out. I.e. Peter Grammatas owns a flower shop somewhere in New York. Riley Evans and *you* can find Mr. Grammatas. You all can find Dr. Kaliakan (Malibu), Aaron Shansky, Kurt Fielding (U.S.C. student) and tell them to go to Cafepress and get the book. Kanaan Sartain, Clayson Whitney, Martin Stock (Germany) Ryan Janousek and Joshua Walker (Temecula, CA) will not know this book is out til *you* tell them. You gotta tell Karen Mutasa, Cynthia D'Huart, Zach Weary and Craig Newmark it's out.

I want all the folks at *Straight Edge* in San Francisco and Nevada, Jake Thiel, Steve York, Nathan Sweeton and Chris Dawes to know. Sherry, Dimitri Hamlin, Michael Grillone, Dan Cummings and his son, Daniel, Vincent Kartheiser, Lori Grub, Adam Morgan (Heber Springs, AK) Ryne DeGrave, Jared Yates, Russ Stratfull, Robert Baron (U. C. Davis), Lenny Krayzelburg, Bobby Ginepri, Michael Braun (Silver Spring, Maryland) Wes Kovarik (Antioch, CA), Cornerstone Church (Sand Springs, Oklahoma) and Michael Todd (LA, CA) need to know this tome is out. This book is interactive and designed to spark controversy. We offer five hundred dollars to the first youth who locates and e-mails seventy-five people in this book and let's them know the book is out and they're in it... when you do it - e-mail proof to Hallopeter@freesurf.ch and snail mail a copy of the data to this writer... We share our profits. You should go to *cafepress.com/Manning* and get a copy of "From the Palace to the Prison" and enter those contests.

For the top *five* students who design the top five blogs on *Blue-Eyed Blonde*, you get one thousand dollars. If your blog gets more than two thousand hits per day, you'll receive fifteen hundred dollars. Get involved *today*. If you are seventeen or older, you should start a *NAPS* Chapter in your area today. Steve Cozza (Petaluma, CA), Joshua Walker (Temecula), Lacey (Murrietta), Mike Noble, school newspapers, college journalism departments, etc., let us hear from you. *Your* comments may appear in the revised copy of this book...

* * *

It was very late when Paul, Leroy and Jeremy left the stadium. In the parking lot they saw grown men still crying, trembling, shaking and speaking in unknown tongues. As they got into Jeremy's rented Town Car, Jeremy looked at Paul and said, "Amazing." Paul said to both Jeremy and Leroy, "Awesome."

Leroy said, "I told you, White boys." Everybody laughed...

"Where to gentlemen?" Paul asked.

"The Waffle House."

They went to three different waffle houses and all three were filled to capacity... They decided to go to Jeremy's hotel and see if room service would whip up some breakfast for them.

Day 20

Jeremy got up early and showered. Paul and Leroy had both left town the day before. Jeremy sat at his journal and I should say note pad and began writing notes, which he would be transferring to his P.C. in a little while... He still had this habit of putting his days, nights, exploits and sights on paper in a sort of long hand and then retyping them with additional data onto his computer...

"I'm going to ask Sarah to become Attorney *Sarah Abrams Shackelford*. I will no longer deceive myself in any way, shape, form or fashion. I love Sarah. I am totally *in* love with Sarah. I want to marry her. It's not just the sex... First time we made love... Wow! Those pink bikini panties... I could see the very lips of her vagina curled outside the black trim of those pink panties. Her bra didn't match. It was red for some reason. One day I'll ask her why her undergarments were mismatched that first night. But she has this splendid body. Yes, gorgeously attractive. A class act. Leroy would say she's *bootylicious*! Leroy told me that Sarah was stacked like dirty clothes and he wished he was the laundry boy, when he met her. Her feet are pretty. Her toes are perfect. The nipples are hard, erect and pink... She is witty, intelligent, argumentative, kind, she thinks in a multidimensional manner; always analyzing things from diverse, unique and un-thought of perspectives. She's a woman of class, integrity, grace and substance.

I never, ever planned to marry this young. But I'm going to ask Sarah to marry me. I have no idea what she'll say. And if she says yes, then what. She lives here in D.C. and I live in Sacramento. There's very little chance she'll give up a six-figure income at a prestigious law firm to uproot herself and move to Sacramento. All of her family and friends live right here in Hyattsville, Maryland... Am I willing to sacrifice *my* job??? I will need this job in order to accomplish my next mission... Perhaps I can transfer to the McClatchy News office here in D.C. But I would have to give up my new job as Editor in Chief. But someway, somehow Sarah and I will figure it out, if she says *yes*...

Jeremy wrote: The other night at Manpower, I did not get saved! It wasn't lightning and thunder or some mystical experience for me. I did no shouting, jumping or dancing in the aisles. I did not speak with those funny sounding tongues like a lot of guys did. But in my own unusual way, I had the time of my life. That preacher knows how to move a crowd. And I was moved. I sat there and thought about the time when Sarah and I walked through Dupont Circle and I criticized the other White man who sat next to a sleeping homeless White brother man and was oblivious to the homeless man's plight. I was eager and enthusiastic in my willingness to silently criticize and ridicule the man in the Italian suit. I had all the inner arguments about what the man with the computer and cell phone should do. In a sense, I was saying he should drop his cell and computer and reach out and help a man in need... I know a little bit about the Bible. And I know that when Christ met the woman who had an issue of blood, she touched the hem of his garment and Jesus made her whole. He didn't care what color she was. He didn't care *how* or *why* she got sick. He just healed her...

I began to ask myself in Manpower why didn't I drop my water pots and cast my bucket in the sand or grass in Dupont Circle? Why didn't I do something to help this homeless man? It didn't matter how he got dirty or when he got in trouble. It shouldn't matter if he was White, Black, dark or light... Why didn't I do something *other* than point my finger at another man and criticize him for not dropping his cell phone?

I am going to do this... I will do a story; a major story on *Sherman D. Manning*! I will utilize my paper, my presses and my staff to bust the prison system wide open. I will drop my water pots and let the chips fall where they may. I can no longer fool the man in the mirror... This week, I will write to Sherman and tell him, "I'm in...I won't forget you! I've got your back."

I will operationalize every contact at our disposal at the Sacramento Bee to front page the story, which is hidden in plain sight. The story of the forceful enslavement, rape and torture of the *Blue-Eyed Blondes* (male and female) in juveniles, jails and prisons. I'll expose and publicize it in a five story, Sunday feature series. And I will also begin working behind the scenes to get Arnold Schwarzenegger to give Sherman Manning his freedom. Arnold has the power, with the stroke of his ink pen to exonerate and liberate Sherman. I'm cognizant of the fact that Sherman is not doing life in prison and I also know that he, like me, is a Bad Boy. But I'm coming for him. He's been caged long enough. He has been trapped three thousand miles away from his family long enough.

I will not ask Jesse Jackson or anybody else why they've not championed his cause. I won't wait or hesitate on explanations or discussions. I'll cast my bucket in the sand and go to work behind the scenes to get him home. I know Arnold better than most people will ever know him. Arnold is big; Arnold is bad. He is the ultimate *Bad Boy*. And I do not agree with all of his politics, posturing and some of the people who are around him. But at the end of the day, if California ever had a Governor with the gall, the nuts, the courage and guts to get Sherman out of prison, it is Arnold. I'm coming for him...

Sherman is quite intelligent, brilliant in a sense and also manipulative. I usually associate the word manipulative with a negative connotation as most of us do. Yet, authentic manipulation is not bad. He knew I'd be impressed with his desire to expose sexual rapes against White guys in prisons. He knew that if I took the story, it would be because of him. And he also knew I'd check **him** out. And he knew exactly what I would find... A wrongful conviction. Tomes written *by* him that deserved to be read. So that is manipulation. I have no problem with it. If I were in prison wrongly, I'd want to tell the world about it also. And I'm not as smart as Sherman is. He has methodically, systematically obtained and researched empirical data, which conclusively proves his points concerning the rapes in prisons. I still recall reading this from Sherman:

Jeremy, my light brother, please understand that the notion of being sexually assaulted conjures up a repugnant vision for us. And I suspect the reality of these rapes is more psychologically and mentally damaging than we can ever fathom. In Philadelphia, in 1968 in a twenty-four month time span, two thousand male rapes were documented on fifteen hundred victims by thirty-five hundred aggressors. That report concluded that, "virtually every slightly built young man committed to jail by the courts - many of them merely to await trial - is sexually approached within hours of his admission to jail. Many young men are overwhelmed and repeatedly raped by gangs of inmate aggressors".

Jeremy, incredibly, I sent you that antiquated data because, it is one of the *only sources* in existence concerning the frequency of sexual assaults on prisoners. Neither State today, nor the Justice Department even bothers to keep statistics on prison rapes. Jeremy, ask yourself why? One of the few reports on such torture was produced in 1996 by Human Rights Watch. It found "sexual abuse is endemic to prisons across the nation".

Jeremy, get the book by James Gilligan, "Violence". Dr. Gilligan estimated in 1996 that *eighteen rapes per minute* occur in prisons. Re-read that sentence. That's 168,000 rapes in gated communities every week. Jeremy almost *nine million* rapes per year. Dr. Terry Kupers of San Francisco estimated in 2003 that twenty-five rapes per minute take place in California's prisons, jails and juveniles and that seventy percent of the victims were White. *You do the numbers.* Kupers was speaking of California alone! This is sick! This is an epidemic. This is horrible. And when you tell White America about this, I promise you, they will rise up."

That's indicative and reflective of the kind of data Sherman routinely sends me in the mail. And yet, he received a letter from me asking him not to write me back... But his letters keep coming. I am convinced that even if I never mentioned Sherman by name, he would still desire me to tell this story to America...

I became a journalist because I wanted to tell true stories. I wanted to educate, inspire, uplift and to enlighten. I would be remiss to not tell this story...

I must figure out, in the next few days exactly *when* to send Sherman the news. More importantly I've got to figure out exactly when to propose to Sarah. Perhaps the most important decision of my life is the decision to ask her to marry me. A part of me does not want to be tied down. I still have a lot of living to do. I want to see everything, try everything, meet everybody and go everywhere. But I also want inner happiness. And a part of my happiness comes from knowing I have someone to share it with. I want to share my success, failure, joys and even my sorrows with someone else who gives a damn.

I'm at a crossroads, a turning point and at a juncture in my life when things are transitioning. I guess I'm growing up, moving forward and maturing...

I must also decide if I really do want to find and meet my father. It is easy for those on the outside looking in to say they *know* I want to know him. But I'm *me* and nobody knows me like me. And since I don't yet fully know all of me. There is no way anyone else can really know me.

I did learn, experience and absorb a lot at Manpower. I'm still feeling the after affects or the residue of that powerful message which was spoken by Tom D. Jakes even now. I hear the preaching in my ears and I see it in my mind. I know I felt something special in that stadium. *But to thine ownself be true...* I'm not there yet. I hope to one day arrive.

In the meantime, I want to live life to the fullest... By the way, if Sarah says yes, I will reward myself with a nice shot of pussy. I cannot lie to me. I want to go out with a bang. I will go out and screw somebody to death. Maybe teacher Kim Alexander. Maybe I can screw a Paris Hilton look-a-like. I'm not certain who she will be, but I will find somebody who just wants to bang, one last time before I get hitched. Bet on that...

I'll get my brother, Paul to be the best man. I love my little brother. There are a lot of special qualities trapped inside of Paul. Our cousin, Michael Shackelford in Sand Springs, Oklahoma used to kid that Paul would become a minister. Our buddy, Jai Breisch says Paul will become a lawyer. Beth Nimmo and her son, Craig Scott loves Paul a lot. I remember when Paul was fourteen and we spent the summer in Salt Lake City, Utah. All our friends like Michael Snyder, Ryan Salgado, Ryan Hanretty, Devin Gordon and Sean Farmer thought Paul would become a comedian.

Paul is big on playing practical jokes on people. I remember Kurtis Parks, Timothy Sauer, Trevor Loflin, Patrick Knill and a few of us got together and formed a basketball team for our neighborhood. We played against the fat boys like Steve Peak, Kevin Henkes, Kevin Mahaffey, John and Kelsey Peters, Gary and Larry Lane and the *grandson* of Dave Walker and Lois Hart. We played at the YMCA and went undefeated for an entire season. I averaged fourteen points a game! Those were the good old days.

I think I'd like to start some kind of in-door skate park. I love to skateboard. I'm actually very good at it. I don't own a hog, I've never parachuted but I can skateboard.

I think I can bring Sean Farmer down to Sacramento to run the skate park for me. Sean is awesome. And Sean is a personal friend of Andy McDonald's as well as Tony Hawks. Maybe I can get them to come to the grand opening in Sacramento!

I would use skateboarding as a metaphor for teaching life skills to teens. I'd have soda, chips and pizzas for the kids. We'd let them free for all a lot but we'd also teach little short clinics and workshops on leadership, success and motivation. In skateboarding, you fall down a lot, but you pick yourself up, brush yourself off and keep going. At Manpower, Donnie McClurkin sang, "We fall down but we get up. A saint is just a sinner who fell, but got back up again." I want to teach kids this in a very non preachy, a cool, hip and a down to earth kind of way. I'm excited!

Look at me; I'm sounding like a preacher. Funny...Jakes talked about Joshua. He said Joshua was a *do it* man. A warrior and a fighter... Moses died and Joshua had to carry on. And in my life, whether or not I ever meet my father, I've got to carry on. I can't procrastinate. I can't just talk about it. I've got to do all I can to live a successful life and make a little time to help a stranger along the road. Mom will be proud of me. I'd probably never admit to David

Craeighton, Frankie Muniz, Matthew Falber, Bob Klein, Aron Goldin, Victor Mercado or Mike Milke that I still strive to make my mother proud of me. I love my mother. She means the world to me. She means the world to me... I wonder did she ever find any of my Playboy Magazines underneath my mattress? Wonder how many of my little boyhood secrets she knows about. I remember when she caught me behind the house inside the damn doghouse with Tiffany. We had our underwear on. We thought the way to *do* it was just to roll around on each other. We were stupid...

I wonder about a lot of things these days. I think, I pray, I dream and I hope.

I think about poverty and wealth, success and failure. I love America. I think this is the greatest country in the world. I also understand clearly that some people are just lazy. Some folks don't want to work. They want handouts and free lunches. I don't support that notion. Able-bodied men and women ought to want to work. Pride, self-esteem and self-respect are fertilized by working, building and creating. But America is not without blame or blemish either. I've seen a lot of poverty, which is not the fault of the victims. No child is responsible for the failures or the sins of their fathers or mothers. We have homeless children sleeping outside on the streets of D.C. a mile away from the White House. We have retarded and disabled people who are homeless, hungry and in need of help.

And our politicos ignore them. Our people ignore them. The poor and retarded are one of our best-kept secrets. I'll figure out a way to do something with my writing to help feed the hungry and clothe the naked...

Foster homes and group homes are also on my agenda. I'm coming for them with my pen. This pen is mightier than any sword. And Sherman did not focus a *lot* on this issue in his many epistles, but my own research has proven to me that we must take a closer look at foster homes.

There are abuse, torture and child molestations taking place every day of the week in these group and foster homes. There is no national tracking system, which keeps any statistics on the sexual assaults in orphanages or foster homes. It's not important enough for us to care; you'd think. But I want to know how many babies, boys and teens are being legally taken in by families and illegally raped. And I want to deal with the psychological and emotional affects of kids having to grow up in foster families.

Many are lucky enough to get good or half way decent foster parents. I salute them. But what does it do mentally to a child to lose

81

or to be pulled away from his or her biological parents? We need to analyze it and address it. I plan to expose it.

I did not get into journalism just to write tabloid stories. My stories must have substance. They must anger, perturb, disturb and embarrass. I must be bold, I must be scathing and at times, I must manipulate for the greater good...

I've already done a lot of homework and investigation independently on some of the issues Sherman is passionate about exposing. Using a contact, which Sarah has, I was able to conduct twenty interviews with ex-cons. There were juvenile offenders ranging in age from fourteen through seventeen years old. Of the twenty, sixteen said they knew of someone being raped in juvenile. Nine of those sixteen said they were approached sexually. Six of those nine were raped. Only two of the six reported being raped to staff. That is thirty percent being raped in this unscientific survey, which I took. And my reporter's observation led me to believe that *four* other guys whom I interviewed may have been raped but were way too embarrassed to admit to me this kind of assault. If I'm only *half* correct, that would bring the total to eight out of twenty. I also interviewed counselors at two juveniles in Maryland and found that even they were extremely reluctant to discuss male rapes in juvenile. Neither of them would agree to speak on the record! I also contacted three counselors working in the California Youth Authority. Two hung up on me and one spoke on the condition of anonymity. Thus far, of the counselor working in juvies in Maryland and the one who spoke anonymously in California, I gathered that rape is common, consistent, expected and too often condoned by staff.

I was also warned by the California counselor to "Watch the CCPOA. If you allege that any of their guards are at fault in these sex assaults, they will try to destroy you!" I called Andy Furillo and asked him what he knew about the CCPOA and Andy replied, "Are you nuts? They are the most powerful, corrupted and destructive group of thugs in the State of California. Even your daddy, Arnold won't touch the CCPOA!" I'm pragmatic and I'm also cunning. I think I'm sharp enough to focus the attention in a way that even the arrogance and swagger of the CCPOA can't blow away... Andy spoke for nearly twenty minutes about the CCPOA.

He also told me, "Those guys are so organized that when or if they discover an inmate trying to reach outside the prison, they will pay inmates to lie and accuse that inmate to undermine his plea for help." Andy continued, "Three years ago a guy wrote me about official C.D.C. corruption and a week after he wrote me I got a Rap

Sheet from C.D.C., sender unknown... The Rap Sheet indicated this guy raped boys and girls. They even showed a conviction on him for raping an eighty-seven-year-old woman. I'm not exaggerating, Jeremy. They sent me what they call kites."

I interrupted, "I know what a *kite* is Andy."

Andy retorted, "Oh yeah, I forgot about your pen pal Manning. That's what all this shit is about, right? You're trying to do a story on Manning!!"

I replied, "I'm not *thinking* about *Manning*. I'm thinking about the CCPOA." Andy said, "Whatever you say, Jeremy, but anyway they sent me *kites* from other prisoners, written about my *source*. He was a drug addict, pervert, a thief and a predator! According to their kites. It took me five months to verify they were lying. The CCPOA actually changed the guy's instant offense as well as his Rap Sheet in the computer to corroborate and reflect him being a rapist. They are methodical, sophisticated and ruthless. Jeremy, I won't divulge, over the telephone, everything I had to do to get his authentic Rap Sheet. But I'll say this, he was in prison for armed robbery and assault, period. Jeremy, a word to the wise, leave the CCPOA off of your radar..."

I'm not as concerned about the CCPOA as I am about sodomy and rape in prisons. And my focus will be on all prisons as well as jails and juveniles. But if in the process, the CCPOA wants to take me on, I'll say let's get it on. I'll fight the good fight with every ounce of power, knowledge and skill I have. They can't pay me off. They can't bribe me. I'm not one of these wards. They can't arbitrarily and capriciously transfer me to another prison...

Andy also stated he'd e-mail me a recent article which mentions the CCPOA.

Late last night, I spoke via teleconference with David Figler, Attorney Bob Shore, Beverly Smith, Nate Coffin, Chris Salgado, Lisa Ling and Amanda Lewis. We had a private strategy session. I was totally impressed with all of them. Hope they were impressed with me.

Yiani at Boink Magazine called the other day. I also spoke with Felix Dennis out at Stuff. Wes Kovarik, Christopher Quick, Jake McKay and photographer Mark Brown are all advising me on some things I could do to publicize the skate park I wanna open. Perhaps I'm putting the wheels before the wagon but *prior planning prevents poor performance*. Matt Dalio, Beau Levejquo and Jim Griffin all have pledged their support. I've got to try to locate Jamey Townsend; I think he still lives in Cornelius, North Carolina. I'm not certain. I've spoken with Roy Johansen a/k/a Iris. Roy is actually from Kennesaw,

Georgia. Roy's house is bigger than even the Manning estate. Roy was quite interested in perhaps doing a fictional tome on my findings. "Let me know when you're finished, Jeremy. Be certain you give me a *first call*. I believe Spielberg, John Ketchum and even Michael Moore will be interested in this. I wanna have a shot at turning it into a novel before they can get any movies or documentary interests."

I was excited about that. Timothy Sauer is still in community college. Dude should be trying to get a job at A&M or for Casablanca or something. Some people just fart their way through life never, ever reaching any higher than self-imposed limitations. This is one of the reasons why I am excited, motivated and hyped up about my life in general.

High schools, colleges and even middle schools and churches are now sending me invitations to speak about journalism. I'm clicked up now I guess. Perhaps because of the spread on me announcing my new job and also perhaps because of the Registration Card I filled out at Manpower. Macarena Hernandez, Jason Blair, Andrew Ross Sorkin, Chris Hedges, Tavis Smiley and Charlie Rose have all e-mailed me. I love speaking, debating, oratory and seminars, etc.

I'm glad, very glad that I was on the debating team in high school and in college. "The power to communicate your ideas, thoughts, visions and dreams effectively are the single most important power you can develop. You must hone, sharpen, polish and develop your ability to speak daily," my debate coach taught us in college. I'm glad I started early. It appears I'm journeying to the microphone at a rapid pace. My future seems bright. My focus is clear. I know exactly where I'm going and I'm figuring out *how to get there...*

Sometimes life seems so complicated and perplexing. Sometimes we don't know which way is up or which way to turn. But I'm coming to believe that life is not as complicated as we often think it is. I know sometimes we utilize a series of old sayings and clichés or adages. But many of those old sayings have power. They seem like bullshit, but think about it. My buddy, Mike Emslander, used to always say, "Do unto others as you'd have them do unto you." Now having heard it so many times, as a college stud, I barely paid it any attention. But Emslander was right. I thought about it, if I actually tried to treat other people in a manner in which I wished to be treated, I couldn't be sexist, racist, *classist* or arrogant. I can't think of a single time that I wanted to be mistreated. Who wants anybody to steal from them? Back to Michael Albert Emslander's motto to do unto others... now I can't think of a time I wanted to be *stolen* from. I withdraw that statement. When Michael Albert (he hates me calling him Albert) and I were in our freshman year at U. C. Davis, we both had nice little sports cars. But one day we went to Berkeley to pick up Dave Walker and Lois Hart's grandson and we saw a Gremlin for sale. We decided to start an impromptu car dealership. We bought the Gremlin for six hundred dollars. We were gonna fix it up and sell it to Doris Matsui's son. We knew he was looking for a car. Albert said we could sell it for two grand. We'd split the profits.

Well, Albert drove my sports car back to our campus. And unfortunately I allowed him to drive ahead of me. Albert drives like a bat out of hell. He was pushing 95 mph easily. I did not have my cell phone. That old Gremlin was perhaps twenty years old. The owner said he was the sole owner and he gave us this cockamamie story about the car having fifty thousand more good miles left on it. I was able to get it up to 45 miles per hour. It started smoking, then shaking and then clunk... That day I would have paid somebody to *steal that car from me*!

Nevertheless, we all want to be respected, cared for and loved. We cannot change who we are. We can improve on ourselves and work to break bad habits and stuff. But at the end of the day, we can't change our color, (except *Michael Jackson*), we can't change our height, (unless you wear lifts like my old boss) and we are *who we are*. And if we'd just consider others, we'd be a kinder and gentler *race* of people. The only race, which would matter, would be the *human* race. We would do justice, have mercy and walk humbly with the Creator.

Quite frankly, it would be impossible to even lie to another person if we took Albert's slogan to heart. Who wants to be lied to? Who wants to be cheated and deceived? None of us do. So why do we do it? I'm beginning to sound like a philosopher now. A sage of the age. Perhaps a guru. Blame it on Paul! Blame Leroy! Hell, blame the right Reverend T. D. Jakes and Manpower. I gotta admit, I'll probably go to another Manpower or what Jakes called the *Megafest*. Jakes is doing a *cruise* to Jamaica for couples! It would be nice to take Sarah on that cruise. But could we screw on the cruise? I wouldn't want to fornicate on a cruise of Christians. But hell, who are they anyway? Why hide from men what can't be hidden from the man maker? God sees it all. And I worship no *man*. Not even the *Pope*! I wish the pontiff well! I hope he's okay. *If* he's sincere, he's probably a good man. But I see people worshiping him. It's ridiculous and preposterous to worship any *man*. I don't need to go through Jakes, the Pope or Reverend so and so, to reach Almighty God. If that were the case, then remove the Bible and give me the Pope. You can respect a man and appreciate their position without elevating them to a status, which is angelic. That smacks of idolatry.

So if I wanna screw Sarah on the cruise, I'll screw her. But wait - the marriage? I still have not even popped the big question. *If* she says yes - maybe we could marry on the cruise. Maybe Jakes could perform the wedding... As a matter of fact, it's time for me to stop being nervous, anxious and to stop trying to avoid it, I've got to go ask Sarah to marry me. Maybe I'll reserve us a table at Ruth Chris Steakhouse on Connecticut and right after dessert, get on one knee and say, "Sarah, it would be my proud, pleasing privilege to take your hand in marriage." Nah, that sounds stupid - "Sarah, will you please be my wife?" Nope, sounds like I'm begging - "Sarah, what do you think about me asking you to marry me?" That's ridiculous. Hell, I don't know how I'll ask her, but it's time to get started.

... Jeremy was acting like a kid in a candy store. Jeremy called Paul and expected Paul to advise against it. To his utter surprise, Paul replied, "J, that's hella cool, man. Wait til I tell Moms you're getting hitched."

Jeremy told Paul, "No way! You're it! Seal your lips! Don't tell anybody because A. I don't know what she's gonna say. B. Hell, I don't know what B. is yet, but don't tell anybody."

Paul replied, "On my skin, on Kappa Alpha order, I swear I won't."

"Your skin! Where did you get that lame talk from? You sound like Lyle Kundert, Jr. or some other madman. If it's on your skin it might roll off those pimples! And you're not a Kappa man so forget that crap. Just don't say a word and I'll call you back tonight." Jeremy said.

"Okay and you'd better call me back," Paul said.

At 7:56 p.m. Jeremy arrived at Ruth Chris Steakhouse. He was absolutely dressed to kill. Jeremy had on a silk python print shirt, a pair of linen classic pants, a python belt and python loafers. He had on a Bulova watch and was wearing a tad of Aramis cologne. Sarah arrived at 7:59 p.m. and joined Jeremy who was already seated at their window table, which he'd reserved.

After ordering martinis, soda and water, Jeremy began. He started telling Sarah about some of his dreams, visions and hopes. Sarah soaked it all up. She was stunning in her soft, red silky, stylish dress. Jeremy had no idea what name brand her clothing was. He knew very little about women's clothing, but he did know she wore hers well. She was hot, hot, hot!...

After dinner, they moved on to their second round of drinks. It happened. After all of the thoughts, hopes, fantasies, nervousness and anxiety, etc., Jeremy Shackelford, from Rancho Cordova, Oklahoma, the buddy of Joseph, Scott, Albert and Tim. Jeremy, the same guy who beat out Jamie Cordis, Tony Cummings, Jeremy Wagner, Jared Broughton, Shannon Mullaney, Jared Watsabaugh, David Lucchett and Dan Parkinson for senior class best groomed and most likely to succeed. Jeremy got down on one knee in that fine restaurant and popped the question. He licked his lips, cleared his throat and said, "Sarah, will you be my wife? I love you so much."

Sarah touched his shoulders with her hands and she had a kind of nervous look on her face. "I also love you, Jeremy. You are so special to me. I think about you all the time. You are a stud and a jock. You're so - man! But I'm not *in love* with you. I love the sex! I love your intellect and you have a beautiful heart. But it's too early. Your career has not even begun. You've not lived yet. My career is just beginning to thrive. I can't leave D.C. I would not ask you to leave Sacramento. I..."

Jeremy was lost in her words. All of the explanations about careers and geographical locations, etc. were irrelevant. He focused on those six crushing words, "*I'm not in love with you.*" Damn.

...At 11:23 p.m. Jeremy was actually in his hotel room, in his own suite - alone. "Glad u did not tell Mom. She said no!" He e-mailed to Paul. Jeremy didn't want to breathe. He was actually sick to his stomach. He undressed himself, climbed into bed and went to sleep. The dreams and nightmares went on and on and on.

He dreamed senseless dreams. He had an affair with Caroline Ketcham. He was shot and killed by John Ketcham. He opened a car lot with psychic Sylvia Brown. He spoke at Kyle Love's wedding. In those wild dreams all throughout the night, Jeremy always pictured himself with a wedding ring on his finger. It made no sense...

Day 21

Jeremy got up and showered. This was the longest shower he had taken in D.C. It took him about thirty-five minutes to get out of it. He felt safe in the shower. He didn't have to face the world in the shower. There was no stress, anger or hurt in the shower. "Damn I wish I could just stay in this shower forever," he said to himself. But finally he got out, dried off and blow-dried his hair. He pictured Paris Hilton, Britney Spears and... lots of women...then here comes Sarah back into his head again. Shit. Jeremy had a tough agenda for today. Lots of calls to make. Lots of e-mails and snail mails to peruse. He thought about his father. I wonder where in the hell is my so-called father. He got back in bed and fell asleep again. At 10:02 a.m. he was awakened to the ringing of his hotel phone. He rolled over and answered.

"Jeremy, good morning, honey. I'm sorry," she spoke into his ear. It was Sarah. She tried to explain her position and in a sense reassure him of his manhood. "You are a good, decent man. I'm just not ready for marriage," Sarah said.

Jeremy was cordial but told her he was busy for lunch and didn't know what he was doing for dinner. "I've got a lot to deal with," he told her. "You can understand that I've got to process all of this and so perhaps it would be better if I just called you tomorrow."

After the call, Jeremy got up, ordered room service and checked his voluminous e-mails. Brian Greene, Columbia University, Tolerance.org, Nicholas Ficarra, Nate Smith, Jesse James, Mike Walker, Morgan Hamm, Kurt Niehoff, Mark Barondess, John Parrish, Nate Berkus and Kevin Henkes. Thus far, Jeremy only recognized three of the names which had e-mailed him. He continued looking - more names: Kevin Mahaffey, Heidi Fugames, Mark Brown, Jason Jones, Brad Warren, Seth Meyers, Anthony Fedorov, Channing Hartelius, Grayson Holmes, Nathan Sweetin, Herb Vest, Wes Kovarik, Stephon Simmons, Alan Nierob, Marc Forster, Greg Sieman, Chris Zeleny, Trevor Gordan, Karl Roberts. "Is any of this shit Spam?" Jeremy asked himself. Actually some of the names were vaguely recognizable but Jeremy had not gotten this much e-mail from strangers since the big article naming him as the new head of the Sacramento Bee. Chris Kaliakin, Janne Dewitt, Bo Bice, Kelsey Peters, Brad Warner, George Lowe, Sr., Luke Wood, Roy Johansen, Timothy Sauer, Leone Lebuff, Joanne Muller, Zack Roerig, Meko Huges, Danny Pintauro, Michael Cardale, Jared Watsabaugh, Kyle Brownell, John and Caroline Ketcham, Jose Tickell, Jeremy Wagner, Tony Cummings, Les Brown, Dan Parkinson and Mina and Gregory Leierwood.

"Where do I begin?" Jeremy quizzed himself. "Let me begin with Leierwood... the last shall be first." - Mr. Shackelford: I'm Dan Parkinson, son of Mina and Greg Leierwood. I'm a pacifist and I work with Steve and Virginia Pearcy as well as Jodie Evans of Codepink Women for Peace. I live in Minneapolis and... - J. deleted the e-mail. - Dear Mr. Shackelford, I'm John Ketcham. I produced the movie "Mr. Hurricane" with Denzel Washington. I heard from a source that you were interested in selling film rights to a molestation expose you're doing... - Saved! - Dear Mr. Shackelford, I am Mark Brown and I'm a photographer. I was on Oprah when I gave free photos to

South African indigents…" Save, Jeremy pressed. "Heidi Fugames rings a bell," Jeremy mumbled…

After spending nearly two hours online, Jeremy decided to go through some of his stacks of snail mail. Mail, which had now (twice) been Fed Ex'd to him by Andy Furillo. From the desk of Heidi Fugames… He also opened a missive from Shemar Moore… He opened another missive from Actor David Lee Gallagher…one from Spike Lee… a missive from Shemm. He got a letter from Tyler Perry. Tyler wrote "Diaries of a Mad Black Woman" and Tyler lives a block away from my family's estate in Atlanta… Jeremy had twelve letters from *Sherman Manning*. He decided to open my letters later that evening. Jeremy got himself dressed and went for a walk. He walked out to Dupont Circle and just sat on one of the park benches. He wondered if he would see that same homeless White brother that day. He did not. But a homeless guy who was Black came over. "How you doing, Mr. White man. I'm tryin to git me some food. Can you spare five dollars so I can go get me a sandwich?"

Jeremy said, "What's your name, sir?"

The guy replied, "My name Tommy. Why you asked?"

Jeremy said, "I wanted to know your name. Listen, I know you just want to buy some alcohol. And I'm not a fool enough to think I can say or do something in the next few minutes that's gonna stop you from drinking, but before you drink you ought to *eat* something. Hold on, Tommy."

Jeremy reached inside his blazer for his cell phone and Tommy balled up his fist and snapped. "What the (expletive) you doin, man?"

Jeremy said, "Calm down, man. I'm just getting my phone."

Tommy said, "For what? Calling the *Po Ho*?"

"What is Po Ho?" Jeremy asked.

"The Five O," Tommy said.

Jeremy said, "What would I call the police for?" He called Dominos Pizza and ordered four extra large pizzas and twenty-four sodas. "Go get all your buddies together, Mr. Tommy. We're gonna throw a pizza party right here in Dupont Circle and then we can all get drunk." Tommy trotted off in the direction of Massachusetts Street. He was gone about ten minutes and returned with seven homeless people. One of them was a loud White woman who was disheveled and appeared to be about forty years old. Peggy was a loud, funny and gregarious person. "My White Knight. My shining White prince has come to git his princess. I'm here! I'm Peggy! I'm yours," she said to Jeremy.

The pizza showed up and Peggy reached into her bag and pulled out a bottle of rubbing alcohol.

"Do you drink that stuff," Jeremy asked.

"Hell, nah. It ain't that serious. I keeps me some rubbing alcohol to wash my hands and face so I don't catch nothing out here sleeping on these street," she told him.

They ate, laughed, told war stories and Jeremy had more fun than he'd ever had with his frat brothers. After the food and laughter, it was getting to be around 2:00 p.m. and Tommy said, "Y'all ready to git drunk?"

They all said, "Yes."

"Gimme five dollars and I'm a git us some Wild Irish Rose," Tommy said.

"What's that?" Jeremy asked.

"Just gimme the money," Tommy said.

Jeremy gave him ten dollars. An hour later they were all drunk. The Wild Irish Rose tasted like Kool-Aid to Jeremy but it hit him all at once and he passed out cold. At about 4:30 p.m. he woke up and said, "Shit, I know they robbed me." But to Jeremy's surprise, Tommy was sitting on one side of him and Peggy was on the other side as if bodyguards. His watch, wallet, credit cards and even his cell phone were all in tact. But Peggy was on his cell phone yakking away. "Well, my prince is awake now so I got to go." She gave Jeremy his cell phone back.

"I love y'all," Jeremy said. "But I gotta go. I'll come back tomorrow."

Tommy smiled and looked Jeremy directly in those blue eyes and said, "You somebody special young man and I just wanna say, *thank you.*"

"You're welcome, sir. I'll come back tomorrow." Jeremy walked out of the park with the stench of alcohol on his breath. He thought about Sarah. He thought about Peggy, life, Paris Hilton, Shia Lebeouf, Omar Rojas, Ramon Rendon, Chris Drouin, Ric Campo (Temecula, CA), Jeff Beisel, Larry Lane, Paul Kim, Martha Stewart, Vanessa G. at New York Magazine, Laura Cohen at the Wall Street Journal, Gloria Sherman and Mary Hanlon Stone... "Wonder what Murray Janus is doing?" Jeremy said thinking out loud. Jeremy thought about life.

He went back into the hotel and up to his suite. He walked over to the couch and randomly opened an epistle from me...

Dear Jeremy, I'm willing to write when no one is *looking.* I'll write when no one is *reading.* I'll write when nobody is *paying.* I am a writer all the way down to my core. One day, Jeremy, someway, someone will read what I write and learn. Even if you never *read this*, still I *write*. If you never decide to join me or assist me on this *journey* to *justice,* still I fight. I fight because what I see around me is not *right*. The hurt, the pain, the trauma, the rapes, the threats and the evils, which I see, bother me. This is not normal. I see caged loneliness. I see boys trying to imitate men. And I also see sports stars celebrated as heroes and role models who are void, empty shells. They earn multi-millions of dollars and some won't give a dime to try to help lift the boats, which are stuck at the bottom. And the few who do give, do so for publicity only. Some of them will write a check to the hood for a couple of thousand dollars. But they'll pay twenty million dollars to settle sex cases. When their ass is on the line or their reputation is threatened, they'll pay millions to make their cases go away. But call them up and ask them to donate a million to Headstart, daycare, junior achievement or upward bound, ask them to give ten or twenty thousand dollars to the neighborhood library and they'll hang up on you.

Americans are obese on comfort and the trappings of success. We act like we can take our riches to heaven or hell with us. But Tyler Perry said it right, Jeremy. When you are thirty-five thousand feet in the air on a plane and things go wrong, you'll realize how little you really *own* or possess... After September 11th, 2001, we all took a look within ourselves. We thought about family, life, love and giving. But we now have amnesia and have fallen back into our selfishness. I want the prison systems and the juveniles revolutionized. I want the *monster* creating, rapes, stickings and the killings to stop. I will write. I will write! I will write! I fight when I write...

Jeremy read the final paragraph of my letter to him and he sat back and closed his eyes. He could hear the words ringing in his ears. Would I write when no one is looking, reading or paying me? "That's a real *writer*," he said to himself. Jeremy knew that *passion* is what you are driven to do when no one is looking and no one is interested. Passion is - are *you* willing to do what you do even if it *cost you your life*...

After reading three of my missives, Jeremy called Love Limousine Company to see if they would take him to Richmond, Virginia and bring him back. I don't feel like driving and there is a concert at *Twisters* in Richmond. *Capital Years* and *Cake* are performing. I feel like rocking out tonight. Jeremy arrived at Twisters in Richmond, Virginia at 11:17 p.m. The driver came around to the right rear of the silver Mercedes Limousine to open the door for

Jeremy. He stepped out of the limousine and people were staring through the dark glass windowed front of Twisters.

Jeremy was sharply dressed. He had on a blackberry compact velvet double-breasted suit, quarry double-circle print shirt, pink silver cufflinks, Aldo Faux-skin loafers and Donald Trump, the fragrance. He walked inside the club and the music was loud, the air was thick with smoke and the people were crammed and packed inside. *Capital Years* were done. Cake was on stage doing their thing. It was cool.

Jeremy met a nice-looking strawberry blonde named Robin. He bought her a drink and they found their way over to a little makeshift food court or café area near the rear of the club. Jeremy had always thought it strange that Twisters would locate the only table area for food consumption in the back directly across from the restrooms. They sat, chatted, exchanged telephone numbers, etc. Jeremy was shocked to learn that Robin was the sister of his pal, Greg Pugh whom Jeremy had met at Twisters the first time he'd gone there. "Shall we dance?" Jeremy eventually asked Robin. People were diving into the dance floor. Jeremy always found it funny that people would literally get up on stage and dive on top of the heads and shoulders of the crowd. He never did. One Long Island Ice Tea and a Screwdriver later Jeremy left the club alone. "Get me back to D.C., please," he said to the driver. Robin had been nice. She was pretty and affable enough to screw. But Jeremy was still stuck on Sarah.

He arrived at his hotel at 3:10 a.m. In the lobby, he was greeted with, "Good morning, sir," by a blonde bombshell. She was the hotel clerk, Patricia. He made his way up to his suite, sat by the telephone and picked up the receiver. He dialed zero. "Patricia," he said. "This is Jeremy Shackelford. Would you like to have sex right now?"

Jeremy was a bit tipsy, but he was coherent. Silence from Patricia and then a tad bit of nervous laughter. "I want to kiss you, run my fingers slowly through your hair. I want to kiss your inner thighs, the top of your vagina while I slowly finger you, kiss your belly button, lick, kiss and suck your nipples and then stick my..." She hung up!

Jeremy felt embarrassed. He would call later and apologize to her - say he was inebriated and intoxicated. He decided to take a long, cold shower. He began taking off his clothes when he heard a knock on his door. "Didn't order room service. Shit, I hope she didn't call hotel security or the police and say I sexually harassed her."

He went to the door and looked through the peephole. When he made visual contact, he said, "Shit." as he opened the door. "Please try to understand. I'm not a pervert. I don't need to go to jail or get kicked out of the hotel. I don't need a pair of handcuffs on my wrists. I just think you're hot," he said to Patricia.

She brushed past him and stepped into the room.

"I hope you can make me cum in fifteen minutes or less," she said.

"Damn!!" Twenty-two minutes later, Patricia was back at the front desk smiling and Jeremy was showering.

Since it was nearly five o'clock a.m., Jeremy decided not to even go to sleep. He called his mom. "I love you so much," he said to her.

"I love you, too. What's wrong, Jeremy?"

He told her, "Nothing. I just wanted to remind you that I love you."

She was touched. They engaged in idle chatter for nearly thirty minutes and then hung up. He called Paul's number and left a message on the machine. "Love ya, lil brother. Just called to tell you that I'm okay. Says she's not ready. Gotta go, brother."

He called Joseph. And also got a machine. "Joseph, I'm checking up on you, pal. Give me a call before I leave D.C. Say hello to Scott. You guys be good. Keep the faith."

Jeremy ordered breakfast and a pot of coffee. "It's time now to get busy and get ready for Sacramento. I've got to put together my plan. I've got to get busy for this story, which will rock the nation. I'm gonna tell my White brothers and sisters about the shocking plight of the White guy in prison. It's time to prepare for lift off. I'll go visit Sherman when I get to Sacramento. It's better not to write him that letter. I'll go see him," he said. He read more mail.

He read a news story, which had been forwarded by Andy Furillo - "*Ruling Threatens Segregation Policy*", the headline read. And the under-headline was "State Defends Separating New Inmates by Race". Jeremy mumbled, "Sherman told me about this bull crap. He told me C.D.C. blatantly deceived the court by claiming that they only segregated by race during the first sixty days. He told me that the race issue was complex but that C.D.C. has a *vested interest* in segregating inmates because as long as the *kept* were fighting each other over race, drugs and gangs, C.D.C. didn't have to worry about inmates fighting the keepers." Jeremy recounted one of my missives, which stated, "Jeremy, they mistreat us, set us up, abuse us and totally disrespect us. I.e. they are taking tobacco from us yet refusing to treat the addictions. No nicotine patches, gum, etc. And this will lead to extortion, bribery and violence. Staff will continue to smoke. I promise you. I watched staff smuggle and sell tobacco to inmates at New Folsom State Prison when they took tobacco... They are taking more and more from us everyday. They took weights from us years ago. They feed us like animals. I fed my dogs better than they feed us. And they make getting books and educational materials into prisons more and more difficult. My point is, Jeremy, they treat us terribly and *some* of the new guys are serving *life* in prison. And they are ticking time bombs ready to kill. And C.D.C. keeps them distracted and basically keeps them occupied with prison wars. And whom the gods would destroy, they first of all divided. Many States, including Georgia do *not* use *race* to house their inmates."

Jeremy went back to the news article. ... The U.S. Supreme Court ruled that California prisons could *no longer* segregate *new* inmates by race, except under extraordinary circumstances. Civil Rights Advocates around the nation, along with the U.S. Attorney General's office hailed the ruling as long overdue... C.D.C. staff says, "Integration will lead to extreme violence in the racially charged atmosphere behind prison walls." Jeremy questioned himself, "What do they mean racially charged atmosphere? Prisons are merely a *microcosm* of society at large. Prisoners come from our neighborhoods. And we claim America has done so well on the race issue that even I am opposed to some of the affirmative action programs I see. So why would prisons be so racially charged? Does staff provide the stimulus for this racism? What's really going on?"

He read on... "It's impossible to predict what is going to happen. Integration in the prison systems can be very much like trying to integrate the Deep South forty years ago," stated Martin Aroilan, the officer's CCPOA President at Chino Prison.

Jeremy stopped and called the Georgia Department of Corrections. He finally got a hold of Leland Linahan, Warden at Valdosta State Prison in Valdosta, Georgia. Mr. Linahan responded to Jeremy's query by saying, "I can't critique California and their prisons. I will tell you that in thirty years of corrections, I've had California inmates transfer here to our system and by and large they *kiss the ground* when they find out we *don't segregate* by race. We have White boys and Blacks who were segregated up there but they come here and fit right in. So this could lead a person to assume it must be something *staff* is doing or condoning up there to keep inmates segregated. Here in Georgia, the Deep South, we integrated our prisons in the 70s. When we first did it there were riots. Hell on earth. But we followed the law. And a few years later it became the norm. If you are a racist and don't want to live with a darkie or a White boy - *don't come* to *prison*. If you come to prison, you will follow the rules.

And the rules say we can't segregate. Don't follow the rules and you will live in the hole."

Jeremy thanked Mr. Linahan for his insight and hung up. "Those California bastards are playing a game," Jeremy said. "And voters don't know because, we don't pay attention. I've been reading about their segregation in Sherman's tomes and epistles for a good while now." Jeremy read on... "The inmates are the ones that insist on segregation," stated a prison official.

"I think it's the death kneel for racial segregation in California prisons. It's a continuation of a long line of cases beginning with Brown vs. The Board of Education in which the courts have determined that American society, inside and outside of prison should not be segregated based on race," states Bert H. Deixler, Attorney for the Black inmate who filed the case after being segregated at several prisons, including CIM.

Jeremy read on and came to the conclusion that C.D.C. has no plans to follow the court's order and instead will utilize loopholes and technicalities to defend their Jim Crow practices. Jeremy read where officials in the CCPOA basically blamed it all on inmates and gangs. It was interesting to Jeremy that when officials decided to *take* things from inmates they found a way to do it. I.e., they are removing all tobacco even though it is legal and more addictive than heroin. Nobody is worried about inmates or gangs rioting, stabbing or killing staff behind their addictions! They took *weights* although gang members loved the weights and used them to stay in shape. They took most family and conjugal visits and nobody was worried about how gang members would react.

They took all girly magazines. No frontal nudity is allowed i.e. Hustler, Playboy, etc. After allowing them in prisons for decades, staff didn't worry about inmates attacking them. But when it comes to integration, "Oh, we can't control them. Inmates run the prisons," staff says.

Jeremy read about the Mexican Mafia: Hispanic inmates connected to organized crime based in Mexico... *Nortenos*: Nortenos are Hispanics from the North of Bakersfield. *Surenos*: Hispanics from South of Bakersfield. *Crips*: A predominately Black Street Gang. *Bloods*: A predominantly Black street gang. *Black Guerrilla Family*: aka *BGF*: Islamic Blacks. *Nazi Low Rider*/aka *N.L.R.*: White inmates. *Aryan Brotherhood*/aka *A.B.*: White inmates. All of the above gangs who could not keep their weights...could **not** keep their family visits... could **not** keep Playboy Magazine, could **not** keep staff from taking tobacco... but they **can force** staff to *segregate*?

Jeremy read that, "Racial segregation and classifications raise special fears that they are motivated by an invidious purpose...", written by the majority of the Supreme Court. Of course, Clarence (Ward Connerly) Thomas dissented. Jeremy read that, "The U. S. Justice Department backed the inmate in the case, noting America's *uniquely pernicious history* of racial discrimination in prisons that needed remedy. No other State or the Federal Bureau of Prisons *has found it necessary* to **segregate** *prisoners by race*, it said."

Why only California? Jeremy thought... The lawsuit was filed in 1987 by Garrison Johnson. Jeremy also read where several C.D.C. staff *whistle blowers* admitted that C.D.C. lied, deceived and blatantly mislead the U.S. Supreme Court by *claiming* they *only* segregate by race during the first sixty days. Jeremy read where Senator Gloria Romero sent a letter to Schwarzenegger calling for him to end the segregation *without wasting more taxpayer money*, trying to fight the inevitable. "The California Department of Corrections is licking its wounds, but this is clearly over," Romero said. "The message from the Supreme Court is very clear that California needs to move into the post Civil Rights era. You do not judge a person on the basis of their skin color even when they are in prison."

Jeremy finished the article and made a note to call Gloria Romero. He then opened another missive from me. It read:

"My White brother in Christ. I greet you in peace and with the love of God. Tonight, Jeremy, I'm writing to Andrew Ross Sorkin, Tavis Smiley, Tom Joyner, Bev Smith, Randi Rhodes, Christine Craft, Mel Bacon, George Soros, Martha Stewart and Chris Hedges. I'm asking all of them as well as you to please, please, please tell America about her prisons. Jeremy, I appeal to the human part of you. I reach out to your spirit. I need you to do this. I've written you over and over to no avail. But I cannot give up. I won't quit. I told you, *I must write* when nobody is paying attention. I've got to write when they're not looking. I'm gonna write even if they don't read. I must write, if they don't pay. I'm a man on a mission. I seek justice for the tens of thousands of rape victims trapped in these juveniles, jails, prisons and group homes. Most of whom will get out and become victimizers. If you *hate* them, it's okay. If you refuse to celebrate them, it's okay. But if you don't save them, *we will pay.* Our children, our parents, friends and family members will pay. We will pay when these guys come out of prisons tougher, rougher, meaner, sicker, slicker and when they get out they kill or molest quicker. Jeremy, what we are doing ain't working. The national judicial system is broken. It is a shame before God. It costs taxpayers hundreds of billions of dollars. The California

Prison System alone costs more than seven billion dollars. Yet the seven billion is pumped into a crooked cesspool of sin, hatred and wickedness.

I tell you again, Jeremy, I don't care if you don't mention *my name*. Forget *me*. This is for the *Blue-Eyed Blonde* victims and boys or male victims as well as female victims who are being viciously and sadistically raped over and over in prisons everyday! This is to stop the madness. This is to help them get the *America Dream*, which is (to them) a *Search For Justice*. This is to stop the system from *Creating Monsters*. This is to transform the lives of those who went *From the Palace to the Prison* and get them back to the Palace. I write to you with my heart and soul. I write you with everything that is inside me and ask you to tell America about her prisons. I write you telling you the *bloodstained underwear* of our boys, girls, men and women in prisons are on our hands. Ipso facto, the bloodstained underwear and panties of every child victim of molestation at the hands of an ex-prisoner is *on our hands*. Jeremy, the system must be changed. We must be bold! We must be innovative and creative. We must turn cell blocks into classrooms. We must hold prison staff accountable. We must hold prisoners accountable. We must punish lawbreakers and deal with the underlying causes of crime. We must pour billions of dollars into preventing crime. We must call on Anthony Forte at CSUS, Steve York at U. C. San Diego, Constantine Maroulis, Clay Aiken, Bo Bice, Tom Trundle, Jai Breisch, Shemm, Kid Rock, Bruce Springsteen, Eli Pariser, David Banneker, and Akon and ally them with churches, politicians and schools…

We must form this (NAPS) *National Association of Public Safety*, which I've been writing about. And NAPS can serve as an umbrella for other groups, i.e. *Critical Resistance, Justice For All*, Prison Projects, etc. and we must bring Russell Simmons, Eminen, Anthony Fedorov, Martha Stewart, George Soros, Peter B. Lewis, Jerry Keenan, The ABA, the NACDL, NAACP, White churches, Black churches and mothers and fathers together. And together, we must all look higher than the fence posts of our own individual or even group agendas. We must get out of our boxes and put it all on the line to establish *peace on earth* and good will toward men. It's not about *me*, Jeremy. It is actually not about *us*. It is more about the children. What kind of planet will we leave for the little ones? At the rate we're going, by *policing the world* and sending our teenage boys off to die for oil. With the way we refuse to pay for their college educations, refuse to feed our hungry, clothe our naked…with the way we refuse to spread democracy in the hoods, in the ghettos and barrios. With the way we refuse to protect White boys in juveniles, jails and prisons. With the way we hoodwink, bamboozle and hypnotize our citizens into believing that the rapes in the prisons are unrelated to the rapes outside the prisons. We are gonna leave a cold, bitter, mad and sad place for our children to live.

We systematically deceive the public into the erroneous belief that the way we should deal with molesters is to protest against them moving into our neighborhoods once they get out of prison. We are psychologically hoodwinked into thinking we are doing something to protect our children or fight crime when we hold up some sign saying, "A Molester Is In our Midst" and put it in the ex-con's yard. But I see nobody putting up signs in the Catholic churches saying, "The Priest is a Molester". I see nobody picketing or protesting outside police precincts when a molesting cop is arrested.

What we need to do is get proactive and creative. We need to really get a handle on this peculiar, unusual, perverted and devastating criminal behavior. It takes a filthy, sick, dwarfed person to want sex with a child. This is sick. So we must identify the sickness and begin to treat it before it is acted upon. We need to bring in Dr. Phil and every psychologist in our nation and hold a summit meeting on the profiles of a child molester. And as we begin to understand this criminal disease, we can head it off and *save the children*. No, we don't need to be *soft on crime*. I'm writing now about catching the traits and signs of a potential child *predator* before he or she commits a crime, and treating it. And when a person does *rape a child*, we must punish severely. And we have to treat them for their sickness while we punish them for their crime.

Jeremy, can you hear me? I'm calling on you to expose this travesty. If you want to ignore my voice, okay. But you can't ignore the cries and screams of the children. They are calling you! They can't get Mr. Bush to listen because he's too busy policing the world and fighting for oil. They can't get help from the Catholic Church because a lot of them are covering for molesting priests. But they're *calling* on you to protect them. Jeremy, we need you to be a real reporter, journalist and writer. You understand the media. You know the media can make or break a person, a cause or a struggle. You see them deceive us everyday with generalities, misinformation, disinformation and propaganda. You know the media will ignore the good a man does today, but remember the bad he was accused of doing thirty years ago. We need you to rise up and be unique. Rise up and share the Armstrong Williams, Rush *Hush* Limbaughs and zealots like Sean Hannity. *You can* and will be heard if you tell this story.

Tell it, Jeremy. We need you to tell this story. This very moment as I write this missive... *This very moment* - as you read this missive, there are **Children!!**... **Children** being fondled, raped, sodomized, violated and penetrated by adult ex-cons who learned abnormal, confusing and criminal behavior while they were being raped in juveniles, jails and prisons. In a sense, every baby being raped right now is a victim of a failed, corrupted, torturous and cruel prison system. It is a system busting at its seams, boiling over with hate, violence and wickedness. You **must tell** America what is going on inside their walls. Remind them that 725 thousand inmates this year will be out-mates next year... *Sherman Manning*.

Jeremy closed his eyes and thought about Sarah. He thought about the first time they met and the first time they had sex. "Do I really love her? Am I just in lust? Should I call her or perhaps take her out before I leave this city?" He quizzed himself. The inner dialogue or self talk proceeded... "I'm gonna turn in the rental car in a couple of days, fly to New York and just club to death. I'll go to *Rounds*, The Lime Light, Club Magic and Club Retro. She says I need to live? I'll live all right. . ."

Day 23

Jeremy got up, showered, ate and dressed himself for work. He read two e-mails from Paul. Paul was still a bit lost. A good guy. Highly intelligent and witty. But Paul had been moving from job to job lately, i.e. a bartender, gas station attendant, construction worker, etc. He definitely has not yet found himself but he was cool. Jeremy sporadically thought about things Paul used to do and say and Jeremy would laugh out loud.

"Maybe I need to call *Tyler Perry* and tell him to write a script called 'Diaries of a Mad White Boy'," Jeremy told himself. Jeremy spent about two hours journalizing, meticulously describing his master plan for his debut expose at the Bee. He wrote down all of his impressions, feelings, thoughts and plans. I'm gonna ask Paul to move out there to Sacramento with me. I will not *preach* to him. I will not lecture him. I'll just let him watch me live and it may influence him to find himself. I love my little brother. Jeremy put on a tie and grabbed his briefcase and called for the Town Car. Today, he was meeting with a member of the Innocence Project at 1:00 p.m. and he had a meeting on his itinerary for 4:00 p.m. with (SPR) a group called *Stop Prisoner Rape*...

At 12:22 Jeremy was at a traffic light on Lee Highway. It was one of those dreary, rainy days outside D.C. The meeting with the law professor was at a Chinese restaurant in Alexandria, Virginia. During the drive Jeremy blasted the CD player. He'd bought some CD's the day before during that do nothing day. In the car, he listened to Shemm, U2, Eminem (believe it or not), Velvet Revolver and Marilyn Manson.

Now as he sat at the traffic light, he flipped in a Les Brown CD. Les was a motivational speaker. Les is pretty good, Jeremy thought. The CD was called "Live Your Dreams". Later, Jeremy figured he'd listen to Zig Zigler and Tony Robbins. The light turned green and Jeremy stepped on the accelerator. Live Your Dreams was over and Jeremy decided to put in "It's Not Over Til You Win" also by Les. Even better, Jeremy thought. Damn I should have listened to this type shit in high school, he thought. The problem is packaging. My frat brothers would have never listened to this type CD because it's not cool. But if they knew about all of the nuggets, the anecdotes and chicken soup for young people's souls contained in these type CD's, they'd listen. Getting pussy, binge drinking, pledging, hazing and all that shit have their place, but none of that shit helps you when you're trying to get a job. How much pussy I got is the last thing on my mind when I'm going to a job interview. Young people need Les Brown and Tony Robbins. But somebody has got to figure out a way to present it to kids in a way they can relate to. I guess Sherman calls it *edertaining* or *eductaining*. Whatever the hell he calls it, the fact is, you educate kids while entertaining them, he thought as *Mamie Brown's* baby boy Les boomed in the Town Car speakers.

Jeremy pulled into the left turning lane at the stop light. He was at the busy intersection of Lee Highway and Turner Blvd. He stopped at the red light and put on his left turning signal. He pulled Les out and put Manson back in. The left turning arrow turned green and Jeremy stepped on the accelerator. About halfway through the turn, an eighteen-wheeler crashed into the passenger's side of the Town Car. The Mack truck pushed that Town Car eight feet before it stopped. Blood, glass and smoke were everywhere. Fortunately, the Mack truck driver was unharmed. Other than being drunk while driving on wet streets, he was fine. Passersby came to screeching halts as they whipped out cell phones to call for fire trucks, police, ambulances, etc. The Town Car looked bad. Really bad. The Mack truck driver climbed out of the truck and ran over to Jeremy's car. He snatched open the door and yelled, "Are you okay?"...

Paul was at his new apartment right outside Rancho Cordova watching Steve Harvey Big Time. "Look at these idiots," Paul yelled to the tube. "Jenna Cook and Mark Delgado are actually switching underwear on TV. Let me turn this . . . way out," Paul said. Paul actually cut off the TV and turned on a CD. He played Shemm. Paul grabbed a beer from the refrigerator and sat down to chill out. He thought about his pal, David Hankins who had also just moved out of his parents' house. David moved to Minneapolis, Minnesota. Paul thought, wonder how old David likes Minneapolis? David and Paul had actually gotten into a fistfight a few months ago over Samantha Cooley. Samantha was not all that, but she was okay. "I should have stayed with Beth," Paul said. He pulled out the Shemm CD and jammed, "American Idiot" by Green Day. That's what I am, an *America* (expletive) *Idiot* for leaving Beth, Paul thought. He began to think of Belinda Love. Belinda was bad. Her son, Kyle (who was suing E.V. Cain Middle School for their bias and discrimination against him) was cool but he was a momma's boy and stayed on his mom's leg. Ipso facto, Paul couldn't get the time he wanted to *make his move*. "Gabe Teague? Casey Finch? Emmett Brown? What the hell are they doing, Paul wondered. He hit repeat on American Idiot and thought about *George* Bush. Bush is a liar and a cheater. Liar, liar, pants on fire, Paul thought. "But I'd screw his daughters any day. They look like freaks. Mary Hanlon Stone type freaks," he said. Paul was feeling pretty good. Life was okay. In fact, Paul was beginning a new job tomorrow. A job which paid well and a job he was told could catapult him to opulence.

Back in D.C., the trucker checked Jeremy's pulse. He breathed deeply as if relieved. Damn, I'm drunk, roads are slick, it's raining and I slam into a damn car. I could have killed this kid, the trucker thought as he heard sirens in the background.

The paramedics from unit 101 arrived. Two female EMT's hopped out of the ambulance and ran toward the Town Car. "Is everybody okay?" one female yelled as the other one checked Jeremy's pulse. He's a kid, she thought as she waited for the beat of his pulse…

The telephone rang in Rancho Cordova. The house was empty. Only Jeremy's mom was home. "Hello-o-o," Mrs. Shackelford almost sang into the telephone. At the end of the call, she dialed Paul's number to give him the news…

In D. C., the paramedic said to the trucker, "He's dead." She had tears in her eyes… Due to blunt trauma force to the head and severe bleeding internally, just like that; Jeremy Shackelford was no more. What would become of his dreams, his visions and his hopes? Why does God allow horrible, tragic and horrendous things to happen to good people? Why Jeremy? Why now? Why? Why? Why? Could Romans 8:28 actually be correct when it says, "All things worketh together for good, for those who love God and are called according to his purpose." What could be good about a good young man having his life cut down, halted and ended with a massive car wreck? What would Sarah think? Would anybody try to find Jeremy's father to tell him his oldest son was killed on impact on the wet, slick and dangerous streets of our Nations Capital... Damn!...

"Paul, Jeremy is dead! Jeremy is dead! He was killed in a car accident. He's dead, Paul, dead!" About fifteen minutes after that traumatizing telephone call, Paul was at his mom's house hugging her. Paul felt a tightening in his chest and stomach. His breathing was shallow and he had a headache. And he knew he had to be strong for his mom. He was all she had left. "If those bastards hadn't taken my father, he would be here," Paul said to himself. For a while he just held his mother. She sobbed and wept uncontrollably. Paul finally asked her did she think anybody knew how to contact or notify his dad. "No," she said through the tears.

Paul went into the kitchen and made his mom a cup of hot tea. He then began calling the family, friends, the newspaper in Sacramento and Margita Thompson at Schwarzenegger's office... About an hour later Arnold himself called to offer his condolences. "Please let me know when the funeral will be held. I'll clear out my schedule and come. I'd like to say something about Jeremy," he told Paul.

Paul flew out that evening on a 9:30 p.m. flight to D.C. He went to the morgue and held his breath as he identified his brother's body. He went to Jeremy's hotel and cleared it out. Clothing, mail, papers, computer, disks, etc., etc. He went to the towing company and got Jeremy's briefcase and cell, etc., etc. He was out running around in D.C. until nearly 5:00 a.m. He went back to Jeremy's hotel room and just lay across his brother's bed. He felt closer in that bed. No crying, just silence... He called Sarah. She promised to come to the funeral. He called Joseph at 11:30 a.m. He went to the airport and flew out at 1:30 p.m. Later Jeremy's body was flown home and picked up by Rucker's Morticians.

Five days after that horrible crash, Jeremy was laid to rest. At the funeral, Father Jim Elmslander delivered a prayer. Arnold Schwarzenegger actually performed the eulogy. Arnold talked fondly about Jeremy's first pizza delivery to him. Arnold said he had been impressed with Jeremy and that Jeremy had big dreams and great plans. "Jeremy Shackelford cared about people. He was matured way beyond his age. He was fun, loving and exciting to be around. America will miss him, *Caleefornia* will miss him; I'll miss him," Arnold said.

There was not a dry eye in the room, except perhaps Paul. He had this need to be strong for his mom. He appeared stoic, sullen and a bit detached. It was, however, the saddest, darkest and longest day of Paul's entire life...

Three weeks after Jeremy's death and funeral, Paul finally began going through Jeremy's computer. Unfortunately, he didn't have Jeremy's password, etc. It was actually a tough nut to crack. He called Joseph, Scott and even Kevin Mahaffey at Flexis to find out how to hack it. Paul was a brilliant hacker, but for this job it took the combined suggestions of Joe, Scott and Kevin to get in. He did get in. He meticulously read each and every word of his brother's journal. He also read the manual notebook written out in long hand. He read about Jeremy's sexual escapades. He read about Jeremy's first, second and third time having sex. He read about Jeremy's puppy love, infatuation and how he'd masturbate thinking of his eighth grade homeroom teacher. He read about U. C. Davis, the nerds, geeks, freaks, gothics, gays, lesbians, football team and the cheerleaders. He read about the party girls who made themselves sexually available to football, baseball and basketball players. He read about the pizza deliveries. There were strange deliveries. There were sexual deliveries. On these deliveries, Jeremy was hit on by gays, lesbians, little old ladies, priests as well as politicians. There were frightening times, challenging times, times Jeremy declined the offers for sex, jewelry and unusual gifts, etc. But there were many times when Jeremy said, "Yes."

Yes, to a *desperate housewife* who was married to a congressman. She'd ordered an extra large pepperoni with extra cheese. By the time they finished screwing, the pizza was cold. She sucked him and screwed his brains out. She called him once after that night but Jeremy decided it was unhealthy to continue an illicit affair with a married woman.

Then there were tons of notes on Jeremy's job at the Capitol. His working with Margita, Stuzman and even Arnold. There were notes about assemblymen and state senators. Jeremy was very impressed with Jackie Goldberg, Gloria Romero, Jackie Speier and Mr. Perata. There were a lot of senators Jeremy described as flakes, out of touch, liars and greedy, etc. There were notes about the call he got offering the new job with the great salary. There were notes on his desire to journey across America. Notes on Atlanta, *my* mom, their meeting. "Wait a minute," Paul said. "He met with Manning's mom?" There were notes on the impression and feelings he got while parked outside *my* house in Buckhead. Notes on his meeting with Murray J. Janus, notes on *my* letters, notes on *me*...

"Sherman D. Manning may not be innocent. I am unsure at this juncture. Yet there are three things about which I am certain. A. He touched a lot of lives before he went to prison. With his epistles and tomes, he continues (even now) to reach out and touch people on the four corners of the planet. B. He is brilliant. Perhaps his brilliance in some way helped lead to his incarceration. C. He is passionate about trying to do something about the rapes and assaults, which are taking place in juveniles, jails and prisons. He is without a doubt, sincerely concerned about this matter."

Paul stopped reading and called Scott. He told Scott, "Jeremy must have thirty letters from Sherman Manning. And, and I think he was gonna do a story on the dude. He met his mom! Went to his house! Dude, I just really started on this Manning stuff, but there's tons of stuff on him. I wish you were here to help sort through it all."

Scott replied, "I *knew* something was going on. I just couldn't put my finger on it. But I was a fool for letting him convince me not to write to Sherman. Are you gonna write him?"

"Write him to say what?" Paul asked.

"Well, you can begin with telling him Jeremy died in a car crash," Scott said.

"He probably read it in the paper already. There was a very big story on it. But I'm not gonna *do anything*. I've got to dig in this ton of stuff and find out exactly what Jeremy had planned here. I'm not far enough into it to know where he was going. Let me read some more and I'll call you tomorrow or the day after."

* * *

They hung up and Scott wrote me. I was jubilant and excited to receive his missive. I immediately remembered him from Boot Camp; Company 048. He basically told me about the car crash. Of course, I'd already followed the news story closely. The news had floored me! I was torn up, hurt, let down and discombobulated. But I had no idea Jeremy had decided to write me, then not to write me, but instead to visit me! It's probably best I didn't know. Had I known this man had been moved to join me in exposing juvenile rapes, prison sexual assaults, etc. then all of a sudden, he was dead, it would have been an indescribable let down. For the time, I just grieved that a young man was dead. And certainly a part of me felt that since he was a good young man; eventually he would come around and perhaps do a story on the issues which I inundated him concerning… Scott didn't *know* either. All he told me was that Jeremy said a few nice things about me, i.e. I was brilliant. I did not need to have my ego stroked! Stroking me would not bring Jeremy back to life. Stroking me would not stop prison, juvenile and jail rapes... Scott signed off by saying, I could *write* anytime and could *call him*.

* * *

Paul continued to read Jeremy's journal. He vacillated from reading the computer journal, missives from me to Jeremy and Jeremy's impressions of me. Paul spent a total of 4 ½ hours reading about me that day alone. At 11:25 Paul called Britney Snowden and told her he'd like to come over.

"No, my parents are in town and they're staying with me. What about tomorrow night?" Brittany said.

Paul said, "Okay." But he was let down. He was horny. His hormones were going crazy. He'd been to D.C., spent nights sleeping at his mom's house, to be sure she was okay, planned and attended the funeral. He was hurting, tired, horny, lonely and confused. Still trying to figure out why bad, tragic and horrible things happen to good people. It crushed him. He was also angry.

Paul grabbed a Playboy Magazine and...was not satisfied. He turned on the Internet and opted to beat off to Paris Hilton! It was quite intense. Paul finished up, cleaned up and went to sleep. He dreamed about Jeremy. And he dreamed about Jeremy and he dreamed about Jeremy...

* * *

Back in the gated community, I took a day off and just rested. I took a whole day of just doing nothing. I stayed in bed and slept underneath the fan. And taking a day off was a big deal for me in the prison. I worked vigorously to never become a statistic. When the prison was awake, I tried to sleep. When they were asleep, I tried to wake. I wanted nothing to do with prison. I read, I studied, I wrote, I visualized, I prayed, I used my mind, my hopes and my ambitions to keep me free. I couldn't and wouldn't die there. Some thought I was lucky but I was blessed. I never gave up. I would not quit. I could not quit. Quitting was not an option. Giving up was not in my makeup. I had to fight; I had to write.

Andrew Young, the late Rev. Hosea Williams, my mother, my father, my African, Swiss and my American ancestors had taught me that if you holler loud enough, long enough and strong enough; someway, someday, somebody would hear you. I had to cast my buckets where I was and do *everything* I could to keep my mind occupied. I would not let *time do me*. I hoped Martha Stewart, P. Diddy, Nathan McCall, Jimmy Kimmel and many others would hear the call and help sound the alarm. But I knew God. And the God that I worshipped deposited into my spirit the fervent belief that I would be okay no matter who did or did not help.

My duty and responsibility was to use my mind, my spirit, my pen and my money to help somebody else. There were a lot of losers in prisons. There were some, whom I knew, should never, ever be free...but there were also boys being molested and programmed to molest. There were also fifteen, sixteen and seventeen year olds being thrown into the den of thieves and the havens of despair and schooled in how to commit more severe crimes. I had to speak out. I couldn't keep quiet. Quitting was not an option. Jeremy was gone. I couldn't bring him back.

But there had to be a way to *put it out there* for all the world to see. I would not quit until I found a way...

* * *

Paul awakened after six hours of sleep. He was groggy. His breath stank and he needed to take a crap. He looked almost as bad as he felt. While he was brushing his teeth, he thought about Manpower. He could literally see that big old, bald-headed sweating T. D. Jakes on his mind's eye. He heard the words... "Just when you think you can't take anymore. Just when you think you can't take anymore... I got my kick back!" He recalled Jakes talking about marathon runners and how many times they're about to quit. But they get a kick, a surge or a *second wind.* Paul thought, maybe it's time for my second wind. For twenty-one years, I've just been farting in the wind. I've been eating, showering, shitting, shaving and screwing. I feel about as useless as Jimmy Kimmel. "I feel like Henry on *As The World Turns*," Paul said as he chuckled. "But seriously, maybe it's time for my second act, my second wind."

Paul sat down in front of Jeremy's note book. He decided to delay reading anything on me til later. He wanted to dig into another area for now. He found a section describing people to whom Jeremy had looked up to, i.e. Jeremy wrote, "The toughest reporter on TV is Dan Rather. He's candid, courageous and an authentic reporter. Most journalism or reporting is watered down and weak now-a-days. I'm not a big fan of soft interviews. I want real reporters willing to tackle real issues with determination. I also look up to the work ethic, style and writing skills of Hunter S. Thompson and Leonard Pitts, Jr.".

"I want to bring candor, integrity, passion and skill to my profession. I desire to leave a legacy and to have my work evidence my passion. I want to use the Sacramento Bee to enlighten, educate, inspire and to entertain. I don't wanna be a Regular Joe," he wrote.

Paul took a break after reading for two hours and decided to call Alex Benzer. Alex Benzer is the inventor of software which teaches people to set up blogs. Paul asked Alex how he could start a blog and then how could he publicize it. Alex explained blogging and mentioned www.livejournal.com, www.Myspace.com and www.TheFaceBook.com. Alex told Paul that his company (Webligo Developments) would help him. "Perhaps you should advertise it on Craig's Links etc.," Alex said. "But what do you want to blog about? Justice, politics, dating or what?"

Paul explained that he was not certain yet. "I'm just finding my way, pal. I'm lost without my brother. But there were some issues which he held close to his heart, and I wanna blog about em."

They chatted for fifteen minutes and then hung up. Paul then called his mom. Mom said all was well and she'd like Paul to come *home* for dinner. Paul looked at e-mails from filmmaker John Ketcham, Taylor Hackford, Michael Moore and Spike Lee. He was mesmerized by these important people writing to his brother. A movie? Film? Documentary?…

Brenton from Studio Oliver in Atlanta called. Anthony at Ambush Makeover called. Sam Neuman called. All short conversations. Modeling was now the last thing on Paul's mind. He'd gotten the job offer on a fluke anyway. He didn't think he really had the looks to model anyway. But…

Paul went back to what he called, "The *Manning* Factor". He said, "Let me read more notes on Mr. Manning, journaling about the dude, and see where Jeremy as going with this and maybe I can find out why."

Paul thought, concentrated, read, pondered and poured almost three hours into figuring out the *Manning* Factor.

"It seems like Jeremy didn't think Manning should be in prison. And it's extremely clear to me that Jeremy believed this prison rape issue was serious and should be exposed," Paul mumbled to himself.

* * *

Meanwhile, Scott read another missive from me.

"I want you to know C.D.C. may contact you. They've been known to call folks that I write and to discourage them from writing to me. And sporadically somebody will call and say they got a letter and they don't want prisoners writing them. That's music to their ears. And they will punish us for exercising our constitutional rights. I blame the public also. If a guy's already in prison, why not ignore the letter if you don't want it? Or why not write back and say don't *write* me! But calling the keepers is dramatic."

"How can I visit you Sherman? I'd like to see you, pal", Scott wrote to me.

* * *

Paul was consumed with the journal. It was interesting, amazing and really unique. Reading it was like climbing into another man's mind. It was like talking or listening to Jeremy say, "This is who I am. This is what I think! This is what I know. This is what I'm about. These things matter to me."

Paul read where Jeremy believed most of the U.S. Senate was filled with rock stars, guys drunk with power and sold out to big businesses. And Paul had a bad taste in his mouth for politicians. "Who do these people think they are? They control the very purse strings of our entire nation and they act like it's their damned money. They are sick", Jeremy wrote.

Paul stopped reading and went to take a crap. He sat on the commode for twenty minutes. He texted a message to Andy Furillo. "Dear Andy: What do you think about helping me to tell a story which was extremely important to my brother? I'm nowhere near finished perusing my brother's diary, but from what I'm gathering, it appears Jeremy intended to use his position at the Bee to do a series of explosive stories on juvenile, jail and prison rapes nationwide. Seemingly Jeremy intended to also publicize some analysis by *Sherman D. Manning* and quote him verbatim a lot. I have absolutely no journalism training and I was not interested in these issues at all. But Jeremy and his prison pen pal (*S.M.*) have sold me. I give a damn! I'm in! I don't know what to do but I do know *why*. And I don't know who - *you*? I need somebody to sponsor, guide or shepherd me as I embark upon telling my brother's story. Will you help me? Paul Shackelford".

Less than an hour later, Paul received this: "Hi Paul, Andy here. Your brother was a smart young man. And I send my condolences to you and your family. I'm sorry he died. I'm an old fashioned reporter and I have no love for prison guards, directors or the prison system. But I'm not interested in doing any exposés on Manning or prisons, etc. I'd advise you to do something *else* to honor your great brother's life. The best thing to do would probably be just to live your life, remember him and move on... Andy Furillo".

Paul was absolutely livid. His blood boiled! Just a few months earlier, given the same circumstances, Paul would have literally gone to Q. Street in Sacramento and kicked Furillo's ass! But Paul was growing up, maturing and developing. He decided the best revenge would be to succeed! I'll make that bastard wish he'd helped me. I will put this story out there for all to see. I know for a fact that when people read about prison rapes and discover the statistics, etc., they'll make the connection and shit will happen. I don't need Andy Furillo. I'll call Dan Rather, Peter Jennings, Ted Koppell, Chris Hedges, Andy Ross Sorkins, George Soros, Mel Bacon, Peter B. Lewis, John Sperling or Jeffrey Coffman. Somebody will help me to tell this story, Paul thought.

Hours later, Brittany came over. They hugged, kissed, rubbed, broke out a condom and made love. The sex was great! Brittany liked it slow, hot, passionately and boisterously. Brittany would yell loud enough for neighbors to hear. She was a trickster in bed. By trickster, I mean she'd get you there and stop! Her timing was awesome! She knew just when to pull you out of her or pull away from you. She'd grab it, squeeze it tightly and cause you not to cum. "Not yet," she'd say and laugh. She'd wait a minute or two and then insert you back into her vagina.

Brittany was also a master at the art of performing fellatio. She knew how to do it. She would kiss it, lick it...

Brittany didn't stay all night. She screwed, showered and left. Paul slept late. When he did get up, he called Alex Benzer... Paul called tons of other folks including: Karl Roberts (Fairfax, VA), Luke Sears, Luke Woods (Santa Cruz), Beau Levojnuo (Sacto), Peter Grossman, Brian Hedenberg, James Sooy, Mark Delgado (El Paso), Kevin Henkes, David Gallager, Ryan Salgado (Salt Lake City, Utah, Kelsey Peters (Oceanside), Jenna Cook, Sammy Miller and the principal of Manteca High School, Jeannette Walls, John Taylor, Ken Wheaton, B. J. Sigesmund, Gilbert Willie, Jr. and Tavis Smiley. Lots of them were *not* in or unavailable. He left messages and spent almost two hours telling those folks how and why they would or could play a role in helping him to tell Jeremy's story and informing them that a major part of Jeremy's story was Sherman Manning and "We can't tell Sherman or Jeremy's story without telling the story of juvenile and jail rapes," Paul (i.e.) told Tavis Smiley.

Tavis had been one of the many callers who was not in but did return Paul's call. At the end of their chat, Tavis said, "You need to also call Roberta Franklin, Bev Smith, Tom Joyner and Earl Graves... America needs to hear this story. And I agree that those rapes and molestations by Catholic priests have been swept under the rug for decades. And there could really be a connection between molestations in church, juveniles, jails, prisons and the molestations we read about taking place on playgrounds. I'm in Paul. Just let me know when, where and what you need me to do. I'll be down with you." Paul had his spirits lifted after the Tavis call. Screw Furillo! Who needs him, Paul thought. Paul called Scott. Upon telling Scott where he was mentally, Scott was *in* and later Joseph...

Forty days after Jeremy's untimely death, Paul was in Washington, D.C. He had checked in at the Omni Hotel on P. Street.

　　　* * *

Paul still had not written me but Scott had corresponded with me numerous times. Scott and I had even talked over the telephone. And the cat was out of the bag. Scott had made it quite clear to me that Jeremy was about to tell the story and had he not died in a car crash, he would have told it. Close but no cigar, I had thought. Sometimes in life and especially in places of confinement, it seems you get so close, so many times, but nothing ever happens. You feel like you're farting in the wind and you become cynical. But Scott had enough enthusiasm for both of us. "Some way, somehow, Paul is going to get this story out there to the world. I *know* he will Sherman," Scott had told me.

　　　* * *

In D. C. Paul had a meeting with Sarah at 7:00 p.m. that Thursday evening. Sarah had insisted they meet at her place because she had tons of documents to show him on prisons, wrongful convictions and rapes in prison. *Some* of which she had gotten for Jeremy, but not turned over to him before he died... 7:04 Paul rang the doorbell. Sarah let him in and shook his hand. "Come in, have a seat, Paul. So good to see you. You remind me of your brother."

Paul went over and sat on the couch.

"Would you like a soda?" she asked.

"Yes, a Sprite if you have it."

Sarah brought the Sprite and handed Paul an empty glass. She began to meticulously pour the Sprite into his glass quite lady like. Suddenly she spilled lots of the Sprite all over his lap. "Oh my God. I'm sorry," she said. She ran and got a towel and began wiping his lap. "You need to take these off, so I can dry them," she told him as she unzipped his pants.

"No, it's okay," Paul said slowly, but by this time she had his pants down to his ankles. He kicked off his shoes and pulled his feet out of the pants. Sarah got on her knees and began wiping his groin area. She pulled down his boxers and stuck his penis in her mouth. He didn't stop her. She was all over him. She pulled it out and lifted her skirt up and got on top of him. She rode him. They screwed. They hugged, they kissed. Damn. What the hell were they thinking???

After sex, "How could you do this to my brother?" Paul asked Sarah.

"How could *you* do this to *your* brother?" Sarah stated. "And unfortunately, your brother is dead."

"Are you just a slut?" Paul asked.

"How dare you? I could ask you have you no loyalty?" Sarah replied.

"Slow down. The bottom line is, we were wrong." Paul said. "And we both know this. You started it but I could have stopped it. I didn't. You're hot. It happened but that's that. I say, never again," Paul said.

"I second the motion," Sarah said. And slowly they began making love again. And again... By midnight they lay there in the silence of the night. "Wonder if Jeremy is looking down on us," Paul asked.

"I hope not," said Sarah.

"Just give me all the documents, tomes, volumes and data and I'll shower and take it with me," Paul said.

"Are you leaving town?"

"I have to pick up where my brother left off. And doing his ex-girl won't help me to do it. By the way, did you love him? Why did you say no?"

Sarah turned red. "I don't want to do this. Not here. Not now," Sarah said.

"Did you love him?"

Sarah was visibly shaking. "I was not totally *in* love with him but I did love him. I am not ready to marry anyone. Not yet."

Paul got up and went to the shower. Sarah brought towels to the shower for him and placed his dry pants inside the bathroom. Turns out the Sprite dried naturally but a small stain - looked like sperm... Paul finished, dried off, got dressed, got the papers, etc. and left. No hug, no kiss, barely a good bye. As he left, he knew he would never, ever be returning to this condo. He had a mission to accomplish.

Back at the Omni Hotel, he had lots of e-mails including one from Matt and his boys. One was a transportation and logistics management student, one was a dance major, one was a music major, etc. All were students at the University of Arkansas at Fayetteville. Their claim to fame was an appearance on *Steve Harvey Big Time*. They'd heard from friends of Scott's about Jeremy...Ipso facto, they heard about Paul and one of them had a friend who was the victim of a Catholic priest. They just wanted to encourage Paul to get the story out there. So did Charlie Wildman and Kelsey Peters. After reading the various e-mails, Paul switched on the TV and actually went to the Christian channel. There he saw *The Potters House* featuring Bishop

T. D. Jakes. Jakes was in high gear. "God brought Joseph outta prison. And God brought Paul out of prison. And God can bring you out of prison. God can do the almighty, through the least likely. God can bring you from the background to the forefront," Jakes was saying. "There is life after this and life after that. There is life after dope and life after crack. You need to take your life to Jesus. You need to take your case to Jesus. You can't get away from him. You can run but you can't hide," Jakes said.

I need to get right, Paul thought. But I wanna have fun. I don't want to be a holy roller. I don't want to be rigid or strange. I'd like to live right, be a good person but have fun also. I want to be able to help lil Jai Breisch, Dr. Stu and Dr. Sally Breisch (www.4kali.org) to honor the memory of Kali Breisch who had her life cut down in the Tsunami. I need to figure out a way to get Alex at Webligo, Kevin Mahaffey, John Herring at Flexilis in Los Angeles and Jeff Moss at Defcon to help me make *service* a cool and hip thing to do. These guys can put it out there. They can hack, quack, blog, text and flex the power of the information superhighway and tell the world a message.

"I don't even know yet what *all* the message will entail. But there is a message. There is a reason my brother lived. I can't let his legacy die. I can't allow my life to be as complicated and frustrated as his was. I can't spend a year deciding whether or not I'm gonna do something. I gotta be in it to win it. I gotta announce it and publicize it. I know the what, now I just need the how," Paul said...

"You gotta get back in the fight. Don't quit. Don't give up," Jakes was saying on the telecast. "It gets dark and it gets lonely, but God is trying to tell you something. God has a plan for your life. Destiny is inside you. Eyes have not seen and ears have not heard and neither has it entered into the heart of man the things *God* has in store for those that love Him. *Do you love God*? I wanna know do you love Him? I know you told some lies. I know you cheated and fornicated. I know you smoked dope and you're still drinking. But, do you at least love the Lord **God**? Do you love him enough to let him use *you*? Will you let him lead you and guide you? God has something for you to do." Paul took a deep breath, turned off the TV and just sat there in his room...

Few days later, Paul was still in D.C. He had been reading, analyzing, scrutinizing and strategizing. He had contacted Murray J. Janus, Barry Scheck, Attorney John Elmore, Rubin "Hurricane" Carter and Clara Boggs of Justice Denied Magazine. He also had teleconferenced with *Stop Prisoner Rape* in D.C. and had obtained an enormous amount of data on rapes in juveniles, jails and prisons.

Sarah had called him twice and each time he *truly* told her, "I have *no* time. None. I'm inundated with my work. Buried!"

Paul had his day entirely interrupted with a big story, which mesmerized him... Brian Nichols was in court at the Fulton County Courthouse in Atlanta, Georgia. Brian was on trial for raping his ex-girlfriend. Mr. Nichols wrestled the gun away from a female deputy and went into the court and shot the Judge, stenographer and one deputy. All three were killed. Brian escaped the courthouse and found a photographer for the Atlanta Constitution Newspaper and said, "Give me your car keys or I'll kill you."

The photographer handed over his keys.

"Get in the trunk," Brian ordered and the photographer ran. He got away. Brian drove his car down a few levels in the courthouse parking lot and left it there. He somehow ended up attacking and killing an armed U.S. Immigration Officer. Brian took this guy's gun, badge and truck. Brian was a madman, a monster, a beast. Thus far, four human beings were dead at the hands of Brian Nichols. Brian was not your typical killer. He grew up in a gated community. He went to college and was a computer technician. He was a proud Black man who says he was set up by his ex-girlfriend.

Brian went to an apartment complex in Gwinnett County. This is a predominantly White area outside Atlanta. At this apartment complex, Brian seemed to be hunting more prey. He sat in the truck of his last murder victim, in the parking lot in Gwinnett County. A twenty-six-year-old White waitress came out to her car to go buy a pack of smokes. She spotted Brian sitting in the truck and had an eerie feeling. Nevertheless, she got in her car and drove to the store. Five minutes later, she returned and saw the same truck occupied by the lone Black man. But he had moved to another parking spot. This young woman thought it odd that this man had moved, but was still sitting in the truck in the parking lot. Still, she got out of her car with cigarettes in hand and when she closed her car door, she also heard his truck door close. As she nervously took her steps toward her apartment, she felt a gun to the back of her neck. "I have a gun. If you scream I'll kill you," Brian said to her. "Don't scream! Go into your apartment and just do what I tell you. Do you know who I am?"

Her name was Ashley Smith. Whey they got in the apartment, she recognized him from the news. He was Brian Nichols, the most wanted man in America. The subject of the biggest manhunt in the history of the State of Georgia.

A day after Brian Nichols had put the gun to Ashley's neck; she was *alive* and well and he was in custody. He was a cop killer, a judge and woman killer. He had killed a judge and a stenographer in open court. He had commandeered his way out of the courthouse. He'd out-foxed, outwitted and out-maneuvered the Atlanta Police Department, Fulton County Sheriff's, Georgia State Police, U.S. Marshall and the Federal Bureau of Investigations, killing everybody who got in his way… The news reported this woman, "somehow escaped and called 911". Paul thought the *story* was - how a single White female had been able to out-slick a killer. The speculation was that perhaps he had fallen asleep and given Ashley the opportunity to get away. Many speculated he had raped her. Why not? Allegedly, he raped his girlfriend. Ashley was pretty, petite and young. A man who has killed four people knows his time is limited. He'll commit suicide or be the victim of homicide. He knew if he got lucky enough not to be killed he'd face the death penalty. So with nothing to lose, why wouldn't an accused rapist rape a pretty young White girl?

Paul was absolutely obsessed with this story. "What is the media not telling us," he asked himself. The answer came in the form of a blog by Jai Breisch of the 4kai organization in Salt Lake City, Utah. On his blog, Jai wrote… I am appalled by the way the media refuses to tell a full story. It is sad when I have to get my data from a prisoner… *Sherman D. Manning* called me today and told me the real inside story. Captain Raleigh Rucker is a pastor/mortician/Deputy Sheriff. Apparently Sherman is a buddy of Captain Rucker's - not to mention the fact that former Atlanta Mayor Andrew Young, Former Chief of Police Eldrin Bell and Atlanta Police Lieutenant T. J. Sciplio, all chat (daily) with Sherman on the telephone. *Sherman* told me (Jai Breisch) today. "Jai, Brian Nichols held Ashley Smith as a prisoner for 7 ½ hours. Seven is the number of *rest*. Ashley did not escape. Brian let her go. He had to tell her, *woman thou art loosed.* Once inside the apartment, he told her to get in the bathtub. He looked around and found some things to tie her up with. He came back and asked her could she get up. Her feet had fallen asleep. He helped her. He picked her up and got her out of the tub. Ashley told him he needed to stop. 'I'm a widow. My husband was murdered four years ago and died (literally) in my arms. You have killed four people. Those are fathers, sons, mothers and daughters. Their families are hurting. Brian you need to stop the killing… Do you mind if I read to you from this book I'm reading called, *The Purpose Driven Life*?' she asked him.

Sherman reports to me (Jai) that she read to him from this book and from her Bible. He asked her to re-read a chapter, which talked about every life having a purpose. She told him, "If you don't stop, they're gonna kill you."

Brian replied, "I'm *already* dead."

She said, "No! You are standing right in front of me. Do you believe in miracles?" Ashley asked him. "It is a miracle that you *found me*. You are standing here in my apartment and that is a miracle. It was a miracle you got out of that court with every single law enforcement agency in the entire state looking for you, but you're still here. Maybe God spared your life so you can turn yourself in and go into the prisons and *transform* them," she told Brian. She cooked him bacon and pancakes. "Real pancakes," Brian had said.

"Jai," Sherman told me, "this woman tamed the beast inside Brian. She prayed with him, read to him, ministered to him and then fed him.

"Each one of us has the capacity and even the propensity to kill. Given certain circumstances, we can all kill," Sherman explained. "It's like Beauty and the Beast. We all have a beast inside of us, but Ashley looked into the eyes of the beast and found a speck of beauty. She tamed the beast and ministered the good news of God. The Bible said, the Lion and the Lamb will lay down together. Daniel was thrown into a lion's den, but God sent an angel to transform lions into lambs. Daniel lullaby'd himself to sleep singing all day, and then all night. *Angel*s and Lions keep watching over me my Lord... God sent this man to Ashley. Ashley is the only woman in the entire State of Georgia who could have dealt with Brian. Sherman explained that tragedy prepares you for triumph. Sherman says that God had hardened her and softened her to deal with this man.

When he went into her apartment, he went in a *dead man walking* and came out alive. He had been dead to the beauty. The spirit man and the light of Jesus. Sherman says, the steps of a righteous man are *ordered* by the Lord. They are not suggested, advised or requested. They are *ordered*. This woman was a widow and she could not have gotten back into her car and drove away. The first miracle was her getting out of the car against her better instincts. God had been behind the scenes like a puppet master, orchestrating and manipulating all the invisible spiritual forces in order to bring this widow to this place and spot Brian sitting in a parking space."

Sherman said, "Jai, you always hear, God allows horrible things to happen; so you will never let it happen to somebody else. Ashley watched her husband die and she never let it happen again. She stopped a beast from murdering again. Jai, we hear that there is some good to come out of even the worst of situations. There was good to come out of Ashley watching her husband die... She learned how to handle pain, sorrow and grief. And in describing this to the beast, he

115

too saw her beauty. In causing him to see her beauty, she was able to convince him that, 'If you kill me, my daughter won't have a mommy or a daddy.'"

Sherman said to me, "Jai, had not God allowed her to watch her husband die and to enter into a *prison of suffering*, she would not have been able to relate to Brian and describe to him the *Palace* of Salvation. The other good that came out of it was preventing her own child from losing her mother. God knows what's best for us." Sherman explained that the Battle was not Ashley's but God's. He ordered her steps and led Brian to her doorstep. All things work together for good for those that love God and are called according to his purpose. Back when her husband died in her arms, it didn't look good. When she had to cry herself to sleep at night wondering why God allowed her daughter to lose her daddy it didn't *seem* good. It didn't feel good. But God had already scheduled an appointment for Brian to meet Ashley. He used her pain to increase her power.

Sherman explained that God says in Habukkah that you must write the vision and make it plain, though it tarry before the end it shall speak and not lie. God explained to Eve in Genesis that her vision was for an appointed time... Ashley had an appointment. Before her daddy even met her mother. Before her father even had a gleam in his eyes on a cold night which led him to her mother. God knew Ashley before he had even ever formed her in her mother's womb. Ashley had a date with destiny and she had to go through all that she went through in order to make it to the place which God was sending her to. Brian Nichols saw Jesus in Ashley. She saw some beauty in the Beast. She tamed that Beast with the love of God and cooked for him. She prayed with him and read to him. The Lion and Lamb laid down together. She knew that the beauty must be found in the beast before the beast devours people.   Religion can cause the beast and rage to go undetected. But the Beast needs to be dealt with. Sherman reiterated the fact that all of us have a beast inside. All of us have the ability to snap, kill and maim. Many American soldiers are pastors, saints and ministers at home.   But they find the capacity to drop bombs, assassinate, kill and destroy when they just up and fight wars for the U. S. Military. If the capacity to kill were an aberration or limited to only a few, the military would be filled with pacifists unable to carry out their mission.

Jai went on to explain that Sherman believed that when Ashley explained to Brian, "It is a miracle that you made it out of that courthouse, through all those roadblocks and a city which is on lockdown. God wanted you here to meet up with me." Brian came back to *life*. Brian told her she was an angel sent from God... Her beauty had connected with his spirit. And the man who entered her apartment as a monster had now transformed and come alive. The same man who met her with a gun to her neck and a threat was now pulling hope out of her heart and identifying the prophetic moment. He said that he was lost and that God led him right to her. This widow woman was hardened and softened by her own tragedy and selected to anoint his feet, give him hope, feed him and send him back into his destiny.

If I had been in that parking lot, I'd be dead according to Sherman's theory. If Sherman had been there he'd be dead. Some folks would have attempted to cry their way out. Some would have tried to scream or shout their way out. He would have killed them. Some folks would have never thought to read to him. And had they read to him, it would have been the wrong book. No Black woman was right for this appointment. Some would have appealed to a racial or ethnic connection. Some White women would have been too intimidated by the big Black man with those guns... but this widow was supposed to meet Brian. This widow served God's purpose. And in the process, she saved his life. Sherman explained again that without question, the police wanted Brian dead. He was an armed man. He was a cop killer. He was a judge killer. Had there been no Ashley, no cameras and no nation watching, they would have killed this man, Sherman told me (Jai). But God had a plan for Brian. There are some brothers in prison who would never listen to a Billy Graham or Carlton Pearson. There are some brothers in Jackson, Reidsville State Penitentiary and Alto, etc. They will only listen to a cop killer. They only identify with a beast, a thug and a murderer. And when Brian speaks to them and explains how God transformed him on his road to the pen, they will understand clearly how God transformed Paul when he was still Saul on the road to Damascus. Sherman explained that even church folks who claim to love God but subconsciously hate their brethren. They think the Bible is the word of God. But they are *cafeteria Christians* and they pick and choose which chapters and verses they'll use for life. They ignore the verses, which make them uncomfortable. They brush over Saul and his murderous, killing and savage state. They prefer to talk about Saul after he became Paul the Chief Apostle. Sherman said, "Jai, do you understand Saul was a murderer, a torturer, a beast and a killer? He killed church people. He was a hit man, a crook, a cop killer and a mafia member. And on the road to Damascus, God changed him and transformed him. Brian was a killer and a Beast. And on the road to hell in Gwinnett

County, he had to ask this widow woman what must I do to be saved. And his belief in God can transmogrify him forever. People will call for the death penalty. They wanted us to assume she escaped. But they won't mention the fact that there was no rape. Since they say he raped his ex-girlfriend why did he not rape Ashley? She is a pretty young lady and she's fine.

"The press won't deal with the fact that maybe Brian was wrongly accused of that rape. And the church won't deal with maybe Brian pre-Ashley was Saul. But Brian post-Ashley is Paul. The church likes to select and elect *princes* from high and exalted places. We look for a college graduate. We want you to come from the right lineage, heritage and the right family. We look for a prince and a king in all of the high places. But God goes out and finds him a boy who cleans up the dung or the manure of sheep. And God says, I see you in the low place and I know you smell because you're dealing in all of that stinky stuff. But David, I see a king inside of you. Joseph, I see you trapped in Rikers Island, in Reidsville, in San Quentin or in Mule Creek Prison. Joseph, I know you were convicted of rape. I see you all down in the prison doing time even though you committed no crime. I see that 'R' in your jacket and all of the propaganda in your C-file. But Joseph, you are a *prince*. And I'm moving you out of the prison and into the palace."

Sherman said, "Jai, Jesus said, 'I was hungry and you fed me not. I was in prison and you visited me not.'" And a prison is not just a physical place. Brian was in the prison of his anger and his killing spree. And Ashley visited him. *Visit* in Hebrew means to restore and to rehabilitate. Ashley did what prison guards won't do. She looked into his eyes and visited (restored) him. He was hungry and she fed him pancakes and bacon. Jai, can you imagine cooking for a wanted man? Cooking for a killer. But Ashley understood the story about the woman who had cleaned her house because Jesus was coming to visit her at 6:00 p.m. on a Friday. She pulled out her best china and lit up her candles. She disconnected her telephone and put on Christian music in the background. And at 6:00 p.m. a cat scratched her screen door, crying meow, meow... She told that cat to scat because Jesus was coming. An hour later a drunk knocked on her door and begged for coffee. She slammed the door in his face because Jesus was coming to her house. A little while later a naked man appeared on her doorstep and she called the police. Finally Jesus showed up in a fleshly form at midnight and she immediately recognized him. 'Master, why are you late? You are God in the flesh and you can't lie,' she said.

118

"'I was on time just like I said I would be. I was that cat and you turned me away. I was in that drunkard and you refused to let me inside. I was that homeless man. Sister, I was hungry and you fed me not. I was naked and you clothed me not.'

"Jai, Ashley saw Jesus in that brother with the three guns and she knew he was lost and God sent him to her. God does the almighty, through the least likely. God chooses Jumping Jimmy, Dirty Dancing Daniel and Freaking Freddy and says, I *want* you! She served her purpose."

Jai closed his blog by saying that, "In the meantime maybe God is trying to tell us something."

Paul sat there shaking. He literally felt something inside him pulling, tugging at his heart strings. It was the same feeling that he had at Manpower in the stadium… It felt like an angel. Paul cleared the blog, from his computer and typed this, "Dear Sherman Manning. I am Jeremy's brother. I think I was supposed to meet you. I feel like I already know you. I have read so much about you. I want to help you to tell the story of the tragic, horrible and evil crimes, taking place in the prisons. I believe we have a divine appointment. I am convinced there are no coincidences in life.

By the way, I just finished reading a blog by Jai Breisch in which he described a telephone call he had with you. His description of your chat was powerful, moving and inspiring. I want you to call me at (telephone no. deleted) as soon as you receive this. I plan to remain here in D. C. for eight to ten more days. If this letter is delayed getting to you then call me at my home in Oklahoma at (deleted no.) as soon as you can. I will accept the collect call. We need a plan and a strategy to get this mess into the press… respectfully, Paul Shackelford."

He called for a concierge and immediately had the letter sent via express mail, registered, certified, return receipt requested. I got the missive three days later and immediately called the Omni Hotel. They *refused* my call and I panicked! I called Scott and he called Paul. Scott gave me a cell phone number and I reached Paul at 2:17 p.m. Our greeting was cordial, careful and intense. I sort of felt like I was speaking to Jeremy. It was surreal. We spoke for fifteen minutes and Paul joked about the recording, which comes over the telephone every five minutes reminding him that I'm in prison. By the time we really got into our chat, the sixty second warning, "Your call will be terminated in sixty seconds", came on. "Call me right back," Paul told me.

119

I called back and Paul and I began talking about what Jeremy had planned to do. "I'm in this to win it, Sherm. I won't let Jeremy's work, his mission and goals go unfulfilled," he told me. We exchanged pleasantries and I promised to call Paul the next day.

Paul began to search the Internet for organizations dealing with prisons. He found many of them but most were small and indigent. He looked for churches, which had prison outreach programs, and all he could find was Bible correspondence ministries. "Where are the church social justice groups? The one's which help get justice for prisoners?" Paul asked himself as he moved his mouse. It's almost like these prisoners don't even exist. Who can they call on, write to or depend upon if/when they are abused, mistreated and neglected in prison? He thought. Maybe that's why my dad has not contacted us. Maybe he is being beat, mistreated or perhaps he's even dead, Paul thought.

Paul then sent an e-mail to Derrick Flowers in Charlotte, North Carolina. He also e-mailed Tyler Perry, Jai Breisch, Oprah, Spike Lee, Bev Smith, Dawn Hill, Tom Joyner, Roland Watts, Michael Cardelle, Ryan Hanretty and Professor Robert Cling... Paul decided also to e-mail Norman Mailer, Chris Hedges, Andy Ross Sorkin and the Nation News. Paul said, "I've got to get a top reporter with clout to agree to do this story. It can't be a one-time story. It must be a series. I've got to find my man in the press."

Paul thought about Brian Nichols again. "Maybe this guy will go teach others in prison how not to do what he did. Maybe he'll turn cellblocks into classrooms. Maybe he'll get Rick Warren, Les Brown, John Elmore, Gilbert Willie and Mel Bacon to sponsor books, Bibles, newspapers and study materials for guys in prisons," Paul said.

Sherman came into Jeremy's life for a reason. And now it is my goal, my challenge, my purpose and mission to tell the world about the vicious cycle of the raping and tortures of the *Blue-Eyed Blonde* in juveniles, jails and prisons. I won't stop til I get it done.

Benny Hinn ain't gonna help tell it. James Dobson won't stand with me. Even most local churches are so tied up in their own religiosity and doctrines that they have no time to do *justice*, love, mercy and walk humbly with their God. They do more talking than walking. Their rhetoric is their strategy. But we gotta tap my age group. We must get Nathan Craft, Steve York, Paul Ortiz (American River College), Tim Goebbels, Craig Scott, Jail Breisch, Jordan and Belinda of (*waves of terror.com*), Ricky Martin, Lisa Ling, Nate Berkus and all the frats to help us. We must tap into that rock, rebel, hip-hop crowd on college campuses and in high schools across the country. We must meet the youth at the pizza parlor, at Papa Johns, Dominos, the high school football games and pep rallies. Get Tony Danza, Russell Simmons, Rilo Kiley, Baron Davis, *Dogface*, Mr. LeBeouf, Mr. Roerig, Bev Smith and Tom Rundle behind us. We can do this, Paul was thinking...

...And then she called. "Hello, Paul. How are you, stud? I miss you," she spoke into the telephone.

"Respectfully, I must tell you I'm extremely busy. I'm just inundated with this research," Paul told Sarah.

"I wanna screw," she retorted. "I want to get down on my hands and knees doggy style and I want you to pull up behind me..."

Paul actually laughed. "I heard you were screwing Jai Breisch, the Rock Star, jock/blogger. And Floyd Abrams and Murray J. Janus. How could you find time to *squeeze me in*, Sarah?" Paul stated.

They chatted for ten minutes and Paul brushed her off by claiming he'd call later. He checked his e-mail: David Lee Gallagher, Rilo Evans, James Henderson, Tanvir Kapoor and Scott. Scott forwarded him an e-email attachment containing an article: *Church Offers Inmates Guidance*. (Garden Path Ministries...Garden path@scal.net...www.gardenpath.org). There was a White woman, Lou Ann Carl, visiting a Black woman, inmate Robin Goodall. They met through Garden Path, according to the article, written by Paige Austin of The Press-Enterprise. The moment Robin Goodall and Lou Ann Carl first saw each other, their eyes began leaking tears. "I was wondering if I was ever going to meet you," Robin whispered through her trembling lips. "I will carry this picture of you in my heart for life."

Robin, a forty-six-year-old native of Carson, CA sat underneath the fluorescent lights of a hallway at the California Institution for Women intermittently wringing her hands and clasping them to her bosom. The rules prohibited hugging. It was difficult not to hug because these two women had bared their hearts to each other in a series of epistles through this Wildomar Church based program in which *volunteers offer spiritual guidance to inmates*. Lou Ann had guided Robin through numerous spiritual exercises to help Robin overcome an avalanche of hurt, shame, self-doubt and guilt, which tied her to a life of drug addiction and prostitution. Now the day had come in March that they finally met, face to face.

"You just want to hug but you're not allowed to" Mrs. Carl said. "It's harder than I thought it would be." They had to settle for a long handshake and heartfelt words. "I'm so proud of you," Mrs. Carl told Robin.

Paul read on and discovered that when the two of them began corresponding, Goodall was uncertain what she expected to get from the program and she was very reluctant to share her personal history. "I thought, Lord, these people want to know all about my past," she recalled. "With twenty-five years of drug bondage, I was guilty of almost every sin you can think of."

But Lou Ann continued to write from her Corona Christian home. She probed, inspired and encouraged Robin. Robin began to feel stronger and she started releasing the pain. Her faith in the universe began to grow. "It was," she said, "a long and challenging journey." Her neck and wrists bare the jagged self-inflicted scars of her tragic past. "Her letters meant so much to me. I felt like I wasn't alone anymore. I began to wonder about her and I would picture her walking to her mailbox to get my letter and I couldn't wait for her letters to come," Robin said.

For Mrs. Carl, this exchange was also mesmerizing and life altering. She is a trained volunteer with Garden Path and she corresponds with a group of inmates, most of whom she will never meet. She says, "It's hard for me because I get very close. I love these girls and I want what's best for them, but you just have to pray for them and let them go. No matter what, I will never give up on them."

This is emotionally intense volunteer work according to Rosalie Campbell, Founder of Garden Path, based out of Cornerstone Church in Wildomar, CA. The program utilizes principles of the twelve-step addiction program with personal exploration and Christian faith using *gardening metaphors of growth and rebirth.*

As Paul read this, he thought about Jeremy's journal in which he mentioned the thought of starting a skating park and utilizing metaphors of skateboarding concerning perseverance and self-confidence. "This skating park idea could work similar to Garden Path. Yet, Skateboarding Path would be more geared toward the youth. We could get high school and college volunteers perhaps trained and advised by Rosalie. And then do workshops once a month and get students to write to prisoners. This could revolutionize the prisons, Paul thought. He finished up the article and learned that more inmates are asking to join the program, yet there is a shortage of volunteers. "Why did Scott send me this?" Paul chuckled. "Does he think I'm some sort of bleeding heart liberal?"

Paul went back to e-mails again. He had an e-mail from Brian Lane of the Neon Fields, Brent Fewkes of the Mourning After and several others including Shemm, etc. Brent and Brian were both offering to do benefit concerts to help Paul start a prison rights group.

Paul was trying to figure out who in the hell got the idea that he was starting a prisoner help type group. Tanvir Kapoor, Riley Evans and James Henderson were all recent graduates of Davis High School and they e-mailed to inform Paul that their blog on www.Myspace.com mentioned his prison journalism course, which he'd be teaching. I don't have a degree in journalism, Paul thought. And even if people are confusing my lack of credentials with Jeremy's credentials, who is behind this lie that I'm starting a journalism class?

Hoops For Hope in Colorado e-mailed him. Bo Bice, Judd Harris, Jared Yates, Constantine Maroulis, Anthony Fedorov, Timothy Goebels, Cleto, Tony Cummings, Nathan Craft, Josh Walker and Maneesh Sethi e-mailed… They all volunteered to work with him to raise money for "whatever type prison group you are starting in memory of your brother", they basically said.

Josh Goldin, Balreet Kaur, Kyle Love, Ramon Rendon, Wes Kovarik, Tim Cordis and Zach Roerig wrote. Jeremy Wagner, Douglas Watsabaugh, Dan Broughton, Steve the sailor, SRC Records, Josh Tickell, Michael Cardale, Steve York, John Herring, Christopher Paolini, Kevin Henkes, Dave Sticher, Missionaries from Freedom Road Baptist Church, Josh Quirin, Shane Kangas and Dr. William Pollack wrote to him. This is too much, Paul thought. He decided to drink a beer.

A Month Later

Paul was home. He had read every single document written by his late brother. He had now meticulously examined every entry, note and sentence written by his brother. He'd combed and re-combed. He had read every letter, which I sent to Jeremy. He felt like he knew Jeremy Shackelford better than any person alive. He knew that Jeremy had literally figured out a way to translate or interpret the vile and sickening happening inside America's juveniles and jails to America. Jeremy had figured out how to make it cool enough for youth, relevant enough for seniors and salacious enough for publishers. Jeremy had a methodical and systematic approach, which would be pragmatic, authentic, raw and entertaining. Jeremy was on to a story which would open up a dialogue, a set of actions and even student protests all across this nation. Jeremy had investigated, analyzed, scrutinized and calculated his approach. He had his shit together. The T's had been crossed and the I's were dotted. Damn, Paul thought. My brother was a genius.

And so Paul was now preparing to finally go see *Sherman Manning*. He said, "I can't finish this til I meet the man who reached all the way from behind the walls of a prison cell and sparked a fire in the belly of my brother. I gotta go see Sherman, he had decided and he would soon reveal to *me* that he was ready to see **me**."

Paul wanted to brush up on three more issues exhaustively prior to visiting me and prior to deciding exactly how to honor Jeremy. What he did know was that he would not rest until this story of molestation and madness was told the way his brother wanted it told. And he was narrowing down the avenues, which he would be taking to get the story told!

Now he wanted to focus on empirical data, which would prove a *line* and connection between the raping of men and women in the prisons and the assaults on the innocence of our children in the streets. He knew that America is very uncomfortable talking about child molestation. He also knew Americans needed an enemy. He knew that when we rarely do discuss child molestation we must make it a "they" and "them" issue. We must also subconsciously make child molestation a *thing* or *things* rather than an issue about a *person* or *persons*. We run away from the truth! We think *we can't handle the truth*. If we were true, Paul knew, we'd have to admit that our children, our boys and our girls are being accosted, assaulted, raped, molested and hurt by *people* (not things) and that more often than not, it's not the lone Black man in dark sunglasses and a trench coat raping kids. It is the familiar White face of the Catholic priest the coach, the ballet instructor, the fireman, police officer, judges and even family members who are victimizing our children.

And *if* or *when* we admitted that it was *our* children being molested by our priests, our families, our friends, etc., then we'd have to begin to admit liability. And taking responsibility for our own failures as a family, a community, a race, a nation or a people was/is too painful for most of us. How can you get an arrogant president like George Bush to admit that his indifference to all those letters from guys in prisons in Texas stating, "Dear Governor Bush, I'm being raped, etc." is directly responsible for and connected to the child being molested in the streets by an ex-con? It is unthinkable to assume our senators, congress members, pastors and parents are willing to admit that, "Because I failed to insist upon rehabilitation, fair and humane treatment in juveniles, jails and prisons... guys get out of prison more deadly, dastardly and perverted than they were when they went in and this failure to intervene as a society is directly responsible for the rapes, molestations, killings and kidnappings in the streets." Jeremy had written, Paul had read and now clearly understood.

Paul now knew that if America was ever going to leave no child behind and protect all of our children, we would have to come to the table as senators, congress persons, governors, mayors, professors, teachers, parents, psychologists, students, cons, ex-cons, molesters and ex-molesters and we would have to identify the traits of a molester. We'd need to profile the characteristics of the monster. We'd need to *treat* the *roots* of *rape*. We'd need to develop methodologies to intervene and confront those traits early on and thereby begin to *prevent* molestations from occurring.

We can't accomplish monumental success such as this as long as we are denying the problem, treating symptoms and not illness, dealing with affects and not causes. What makes a grown man want to sleep with a child? What makes a forty-year-old female teacher want to get down and dirty with an eleven or twelve-year-old boy? What is different about the mental apparatus and stimuli of a pedophile versus a normal adult who is attracted to other adults? What is normal? Is there a line between eccentricity and perversion? Should we rethink how we punish sexual predators? Should there be a distinction between how society punishes the twenty-three-year-old adult who has consensual sex with a fifteen-year-young child and how we punish a thirty-three year old who has forceful sex with a fifteen year old? Must we examine psychologically what it is which causes some men to desire intimacy with younger women? Must we create a difference in how we approach the punishment of different types of sexual offenses?

Paul was beginning to clearly see how unclear the issues were. They were unique, complex and often confusing... What Paul still knew beyond all doubt was that forceful rape must be punished severely. And anyone who entered into intimacy with a *child* must be dealt with sternly, severely and swiftly.

He needed to clearly understand a pragmatic approach to truth in sentencing and various ways of dealing with the various kinds of sex crimes, conduct and eccentricities. Paul read a study by prominent Attorney Roy Black which said that "Rape is easy to allege, difficult to prove and easy to convict. Juries convict innocent men of rape every hour of every day of every week."

And so the question (again) in Paul's mind was how do you get a summit meeting of sorts in which psychologists, victims, victimizers, pastors, teachers and students come together and re-think how we punish sexual predators and who we *label* as sexual predators...

Next, Paul thought, I must find a way to bring all of these loosely knitted organizations together to expose, assault and attack wrongful convictions. The cat is out of the bag. We all know that folks are convicted for crimes they did not commit. We are cognizant of cases, i.e. Anthony Porter, Rubin "Hurricane" Carter, Rolando Cruz, David

Quindt, Greg Wilhoit and Geronimo Pratt. We know that juries get it wrong. We know some judges are biased, gung ho and out for injustice. We know about corrupted prosecutors. We know that Joe Paulus in Green Bay, Wisconsin was a stoic prosecutor, a liar, a racketeer, and an overzealous fraud on the justice system. We know Joe Paulus was dubbed *Hollywood Joe* as he took on high profile cases such as a so-called police officer who allegedly murdered his own wife. We know that at the very time that John Maloney was being prosecuted for murdering his ex-wife by Joe Paulus, this same Joe Paulus was taking bribes to fix and dismiss other criminal cases. Out of respect for Matt, Sean and Aaron Maloney, we can't ignore the fact that their dad, John probably did not get a fair trial. Jennifer, John's sister, deserves justice! Little Aaron and Sean Maloney deserve justice. I can hear Aaron and Sean calling out to America saying, *our dad is innocent*. And Joe Paulus is not the only prosecutor who is/was corrupted.

In Richmond, VA, Henrico, Atlanta, GA, Dekalb, Los Angeles, CA, Santa Monica, New York, Chicago, Cook County, etc., prosecutors, judges and police very often take bribes and manipulate evidence in trials, etc. We know that there are wrongful convictions and innocent men in prison. I need to get as much empirical and statistical data as I can from Sheila Barry who is a part time novelist, investigator and head of Truth in Justice. I need Barry Scheck, Peter Neufeld, Linda Starr and every Innocence Project across this nation to give me names and cases of egregious wrongful convictions.

I need to dramatize these travesties. I need a town hall meeting in which these police officers, detectives, prosecutors, judges and juries are brought face to face with their victims. I want David Quindt, Anthony Porter, Rolando Cruz and Mr. Wilhoit to sit face to face with all of the players in the judicial system and tell them *what* going to prison for crimes, which they did not commit, did to their lives. I want Aaron and Sean Maloney to tell them how it feels to grow up with a father in prison for something he didn't do. I want Greg Sieman to be there. I want Chris Ochoa, Kenny Waters and Johnnie Cochran to be there. I want a truth and reconciliation summit in which we approach all these insulated and isolated judges who rule with iron fists and destroy families at the stroke of their pens. I want them to be at this meeting.

And I also want to read some of the hundreds of letters of these people who write to *The Bev Smith Show* at American Urban Radio Network and Rolando Watts at Lie Detector, pleading for help because they say they're innocent! I want to check out these stories and separate the wheat from the chaff. I want real reporters at this meeting, not the bull shitters, Uncle Toms, conservatives or even the knee-jerk liberals. I want real journalists there who want the facts, just the facts. I gotta get a centralized system for organizing, filing and featuring these cases of wrongful convictions.

(...Lee Henry Vollick (Murrieta, CA) is a dynamite young man. His mom (B. Vollick) raised him well... Lee Vollick is a marvelous example of why a *tome* like this is so successful. Lee is nineteen years old and simply wants the world to know he loves the troops but he hates war. "I wanted a catalyst for my protest and burning the flag got people's attention," Lee Henry stated.

When *Sherman D. Manning* read of how cops beat and abused Lee Henry, Sherman called the Vollick residence from his prison cell. Mrs. Vollick initially refused the collect call. Never one to give up easily, *Sherman* called back and Mrs. Vollick accepted. "Who are you? What do you want with my son? He made a mistake. *You're* in *jail*!" she yelled.

"Actually, I'm in prison and I'm wrongly convicted," Sherman stated. "You remind me of *my* mom..."

Mrs. Vollick melted. "Well, I accepted because *curiosity* got the best of me."

Sherman then told her she should tell Lee Henry about *Code Pink Women For Peace* and his dear friend, *Jodie Evans*. He praised Jodie and talked about how she was his *shero*.

"That may be exactly what Lee Henry needs, a *constructive* way to protest and I'm glad you called," she said.

* * *

Paul would come to learn how difficult it was *to reach* from behind prison walls and get people to respond. Paul was impressed by the perseverance of Sherman. It reminded him of guys like "Hurricane" Carter, John Artis and Rolando Cruz. Ipso facto, there are millions of frustrated, angry, brilliant and energetic eighteen and nineteen-year-old young men and women in this country. If we podcast, blog, do E-books and print books, we can get them to the Lee Henry's of our nation and world and they can literally take the books to the hoods and sell them. That's what happened with Teri Woods (anybody reading can e-mail Teri Woods and let her know Jeremy, Paul and Sherman were not selfish. Let her know, she's in this book).

Teri Woods was a crack addict. Her man went to prison on a three-strikes drug case. Teri was rebellious and didn't like being told what to do. She moved out of her momma's house and got emancipated at sixteen. She wanted to do her thing! Now her man was in prison and she was still hooked on a crack pipe. She turned her friend Adrienne on to the pipe and watched her almost die. By 1991, Teri looked around and noticed all of her friends and loved one's were dead or in jail. "I gotta do something. I gotta get out of this prison of drugs," Teri said.

She went to paralegal school and went to work in a law office. "You mean to tell me *they* tell me when I can go to lunch, take a break, etc.," Teri said to herself. This *job* is just *another* form of a prison cell, Terri thought. So Teri wrote a book and titled it, "Live to the Game". She sent it from publisher to publisher and all the big houses turned her down. She put her manuscript up in her closet and forgot about it. A friend of hers named Tracey, worked in a bookstore and said, "Let me read it."

Tracy read it and loved it. A woman named Noveline crazy-glued five hundred books together for Teri. Teri took all five hundred books to the hood and sold them for twenty dollars each. The first day, she sold three hundred and fifty copies. Another friend showed her how to get bar codes for the book, etc., etc.

Teri now owns the *Hip Hop Fiction Publishing Company* and has signed five authors. Her company is worth about ten million dollars. She **owns** it. From a crack pipe to a best-selling author, to the president and founder of her own publishing company.

How many Lee Henry's, Jeff Mattenleys, Will Fry, Riley Evans, James Hendersons, Josh Goldins and Tanvir Kapoors reading now had a book, an idea, a dream or a vision and you gave up on it? You put it up on a shelf in your closet? You need to pull that idea, that dream, that vision or hope down off the shelf and get back in the game and stay *true to the game*. Start you a blog, podcast, write a book, song, rap or a poem and tell us about it. E-mail Hallopeter@freesurf.ch and we may help you. Be creative. Utilize Myspace.com, Yahoo! Chat rooms, blogs and school newspapers to write essays to tell others to pull their ideas out of that closet and off that shelf. Link your essay up to our websites, blogs and e-mails and we will use our resources to help tell others about it...

Tina was a teenaged *mother*. She was on welfare. Tina went from being on welfare to being a millionaire. Tina wrote *Ellora's Cave* (go to www.Ellora's Cave.com). She's written thirty E-books and is starting a magazine called *Lady Jaided*.

You, reading this right now can pull your idea off the shelf and out of the closet. Contact Charlotte Gibson, Judy Tate, our pal, Jamie Kennedy (yes, the actor/comedian) and put your ideas out there. Don't give up on your dream. You need not be a one-dimensional person.

Get active. Get online. Put *your* fingers to working on your mouse, keyboard, telephone, etc. *We* wanna hear what you have to say. We'll *represent* and *tell* the world about **you**. You don't need to support *Sherman Manning*

personally in order to get our interests, our efforts, our backing and even our support. Don't wait; e-mail us *today* so we can announce, expose and support *your* dream.

Paul continued, "I need to interview activist law students who utilize DNA and other evidence to exonerate the wrongly convicted. Often times the guys who have been freed get out and never look back. It's not necessarily that they don't care about the guys who are left behind, but their lives and minds are so screwed up by the system that they are often afraid to look back.

"I.e., Peter Rose bolted through an emergency side door to shake reporters and camera crews, fed up with their demands to tell his story, over and over. How did it feel, they asked, to be wrongly convicted of the lowest of crimes? Did he hold a grudge for the ten years he'd been branded a child rapist?

"Peter jumped a rope barrier and was out the door to join his family, as he yelled about the *silence*, which had met his claims of innocence for nearly a decade while he was in prison. Silence from the press, the police, even his court-appointed lawyer. 'I believe lunch was more important to him than my trial,' Rose said."

Paul continued... "Once the Northern California Innocence Project took up his case, Peter was being believed by the most persistent of advocates - a succession of law students working under a pair of seasoned defense lawyers. After two years of work, they were able to upset his conviction and get him freed from prison. They then cleared his name. I wonder how Peter felt when he got his first piece of pussy. When he first cummed and nutted in some real pussy and not that hand job he'd been giving himself for ten years. I know I shouldn't be thinking like this but damn, ten years with no p-hole is a very long time."

Paul continued, "Do you really expect to trap men like animals in a zoo with no *women*, no education, no counseling, etc. for years on end and expect them to exit prisons in better condition than they were when they entered? This is absolutely a system, which is seemingly designed to fail miserably. Society is supposed to modernize, improve with time as the knowledge pool expands, etc. But as it pertains to issues of youth crime and punishment and law and order, it seems our prisons and the methodology we employ inside them are frozen in time. We are dealing with 2005 problems with a 1975 mentality or strategy. Why would Pete Rose need to sit dehumanized, animalized in prison for ten years for crimes he did not commit with all the billions of dollars we spend arresting, detaining and imprisoning them; why do we spend so little analyzing and counseling them? And why can't we utilize our awesome power, wealth, technology and science to free the innocent? Why did it take twenty-seven years, twenty-seven years to free Geronimo Pratt? Fifteen years for Kenny Waters?

"Oprah, Bev Smith, Tony Danza, Tavis Smiley, Air America, All America needs to demand a change! It should not take *miracles* to release, exonerate, vindicate and expose a wrongful conviction. We've got to care. And the strategy must be to *reiterate* to the American people that any time the wrong man goes into prison, the right man remains out of prison to continue his raping, stealing, killing and molesting. We must sound a trumpet..."

Paul continued... "What about the cut and dried cases? I.e. in one Los Angeles robbery case a surveillance tape showed the six-foot-six robber walking past a ruler that had been painted on the frame of the Office Depot entry door. The man convicted of the crime, Jason Kindle, was a foot shorter."

Paul mesmerized himself as he continued to reflect upon the voluminous data, which had been provided to him by Golden State University law student Dan Taylor. Dan had written in the notes on the Rose, Kindle and Quindt case - "Mr. Shackelford, you'll find that overturning a wrongful conviction is much like pulling teeth with no anesthesia. Only it's much slower and more painful."

Paul mumbled, "I must get back to this wrongful conviction stuff later. It's freaking pissin me off! Let me read this e-mail from Davis Senior High School student Tanvir Kapoor."

The e-mail from Tanvir stated, "I'm Tanvir Kapoor and I'm mad as hell! I am angry about a series of things including a recent incident at my high school in which two White kids spread racist graffiti. Riley Evans and James Henderson are both pals of mine. Riley, James and many of us came together and led three hundred students on a peace march to protest this racism.

"I heard about your brother from Sherman Manning. Sherman enjoys rock star status on our campus. He helped galvanize us by writing to, for, about and with us. Many parents were opposed to us communicating with a convict, but we are pragmatic rebels. We know a person can be falsely accused and wrongly convicted. We are cognizant of the fact that the best method to shut up a leader, diminish his worth and silence his voice is to put him in prison for a sick crime. And when they hoodwink us and convince us he is a rapist (Joseph) or murderer (Hurricane, Porter, Quindt, Wilhoit, etc.) then we abandon, ignore and alienate him. Riley, James and I will not go for it! We are mobilizing teens in high schools, shelters, juveniles, colleges and churches across this nation. We are promoting peace, diversity, conscientiousness and love. We won't be stopped! If teens in the 60s could build bonfires in the streets, we can and will build our movement. And when one of ours does fail, screw up or gets in trouble, we won't abandon them.

"We will prevent crime with NAPS (National Association of Public Safety) through peer to peer counseling, workshops, seminars and book parties. And we will write to, listen to and send books to guys in juveniles and prisons. If we send them books by Tony Robbins, Zig Zigler, Sherman Manning and Walter Dean Meyers, it can change them. We'll send them data on Clayton Lillard, Dr. Phil, Oprah and Prison Fellowship. We will protect public safety by providing a net to catch ex-offenders before their behaviors spiral out of control.

"We have waited for presidents, senators, governors, etc. to protect our schools and neighborhoods. But all too often, all we are, are knee jerk reactionaries. It takes Columbine or Montana to get the cameras and politicians to focus on schools, violence and bullying. And that attention is short lived. After a few ratings blitzes the media, the focus and the reporters develop amnesia. But *we* are committed to hanging around and consistently working even behind the scenes to address the social issues, which lead to violence, drug abuse, crime, molestations and racism. We are casting our buckets in the grass, sand, water, hoods, barrios, churches and schools right where we are. And *we will change the world*! Maybe you can mention us in whatever it is you and *Sherman* are doing. Travis Taylor, Betty Ragsdale, Bertha Hurd, Robinson Moore, Garrett Goll and Sean Maloney are all working with us.

"And we're building our own publishing company. We are sending Sherman's books (which include poems, essays, lyrics and comments by *us*) into prisons, juveniles, jails, colleges and schools all over this world. We will change the planet. Russ Stratfull, Jacob Tuthill and Tony Cummings have all just signed on today! We are crazy! I.e. we have mock trials, debate teams, leadership development teams and even our own P.R. team. We have ten students at each school who only deal with publicity. They read each book and they google *each* and *every name* in the book. And they locate, e-mail or telephone each person (I.e. Tuthill, Sacramento, Josh Treadway, Escondido, Kyern Bennett, Davis, CA, etc., etc.) and tell them

"You're in the book. You gotta go to cafepress.com/palace2prison and get it..."

Paul finished up Tanvir's lengthy e-mail and went back to his thoughts, notes and other data on wrongful convictions. Paul was sort of in a foggy focus... Okay, what were the three things I said I needed to pinpoint or get a clear cut strategy on before I go to Mule Creek Prison and meet *Manning,* Paul silently inquired of himself. Damn, I don't even remember. I think A. was - understanding and defining the correlation between sex crimes in prisons and sex crimes in civilian life. I think B. was - to gather enough empirical data to prove conclusively that wrongful convictions in America are not an aberration or an anomaly but that they take place everyday. I think C. Shit, what was C? I'm not even sure but I think it should be a solution. I need a strategy. I need some specific steps, which I can lay out for citizens to take in order to *protect public safety.*

Paul went back to Dan Taylor's notes. Dan was a good-looking young man who planned to go on and practice criminal law after law school. Paul had absolutely no idea that Dan Taylor, George Derieg and Chris Ochoa were what the ladies termed "fine". Arguably they were the *studliest* three young men in their class. Chris was the most passionate of the three. Chris was passionate because to him the *law* was *personal.* Justice was urgent and wrongful convictions were intimate to him. Chris himself had sat in prison in Texas, wrongly convicted of murders he did not commit.

Missives to (then) Governor George W. Bush had proven useless. Letters to the media went unanswered. It had taken Barry Scheck, Johnnie Cochran and the Innocence Project to eventually exonerate and vindicate Chris Ochoa. Upon being released, Chris had told Dan Rather and Geraldo Rivera, "I will not forget the others left behind. There are tens of thousands of people behind bars who should not be there." Chris decided his options were to preach or argue. So he settled on the idea of going to law school. "A lawyer argues and he can also preach. But a great pastor can't practice law without a law degree," he rationalized. Chris transferred to Golden Gate from the University of Wisconsin. There was an Innocence Project at the California Western School of Law in San Diego and there was an Innocence Project at the Northern California Innocence Project based out of Santa Clara Law School. Chris was getting his feet wet at the satellite office in Golden Gate University in San Francisco. "It is horrible, tragic and very, very scary to be trapped in prison when you know you're innocent. Trust me, I know. I've been there," Chris had said to Dan upon meeting him. "The only person standing between a falsely accused client and his jail cell is the lawyer. We must care about our clients," Chris said.

Former Golden Gate student, Marilyn Underwood - "Pushed and pushed and pushed," she said, "until the State DNA lab confirmed it still had the evidence and, yes there was enough to do a DNA test which would prove the semen from the rape evidence was not Pete Rose's." Two other students with two supervising lawyers wrote the petition which persuaded the judge to order the test.

Again, "Why in the hell do students have to free an innocent man from a vicious prison? How can students know more than district attorneys, detectives and judges?" Paul asked himself.

In this age of technology, the information superhighway, voice prints, faxes, spam, digital equipment, cell phone cameras, space technology and polygraphs - why and how can this happen in America? I don't understand. Is this why I've not seen my father since I was a boy? Is he sitting somewhere in a prison cell for a crime he did not commit? Do I need Kathleen Ridolfi, Susan Rutberg, Barry Scheck, Dan Taylor or Floyd Abrams to find him and get him out?

Ken Marsh was freed last summer after twenty-one years in prison for the death of his girlfriend's toddler. DNA and Cal Western law students came to his rescue. What could twenty-one years in prison for a vicious and horrendous crime of which you're innocent do to your mind? What could that feel like?...

John Stoll...Wow - Stoll! Bakersfield! Ed Jagels the infamous D.A. Jagels buried John Stoll in the California prison system for child molestation in an alleged sex ring targeting youngsters in Kern County. Forty people went to prison. All were eventually released except Stoll. He was abandoned by his family and left for dead by his friends...

Finally, an exonerated friend persuaded his lawyer to *do something for Stoll*. The lawyer contacted the Innocence Project. Cal Western and Santa Clara students and lawyers worked on the case. Soon, Stoll said, "People started to visit. I started getting hope."

Two law students - of the dozen who worked for Stoll, along with seven lawyers and an investigator - stayed with the case through their summer vacations and a year past their project courses. The defense team tracked down Stoll's now grown accusers. Ridolfi personally paid to fly in witnesses for hearings. They recanted...Stoll was released after more than fourteen years, nearly penniless. Ridolfi and her partner, Innocence Project Legal Director, Linda Starr, invited him to live in their guest cottage for a year to get his bearings.

They ought to make a movie about this case and these great lawyers. Where is Spielberg, David E. Kelly, Spike Lee and Mel

Gibson? Hell, where is Michael Moore? Kathleen Ridolfi, Janice Brickley, Rutburg and Scheck should all have a documentary made about them. It would motivate Gerry Spence, Floyd Abrams and Dick Scruggs to get involved. Hell, they can all afford it.

All the big lawyers like Bruce Cutler and David Boies should spend three months per year *freeing* the innocent. If we don't get wrongly convicted men out of prisons, we should bow our heads in shame as Americans.

John Stoll still lives in Starr and Ridolfi's cottage. On a balmy winter day, an investigator drops off a used motorcycle for him. His new neighbors wave. He smiles back, showing a set of teeth donated by a team of local dentists who saw him on television. Stoll is sixty-one and says, "When they turn you loose, there's nothing there for you. Not even a letter to potential employers explaining the twenty year gap in your job history."

Stoll applied for State compensation that's available to innocent people who were wrongly convicted. It can amount to one hundred dollars for each day of loss, but it's rarely granted and never yet to someone exonerated by the Innocence Project. Reading all of this and reflecting on it turned Paul's stomach. And now I must decide what is the best avenue for exposing this bullshit to the world, Paul thought. I gotta make it raw and dramatize it. I must put it before the nation and embarrass us all. Maybe I can get Peter Brant, Sandra J. Brant and Victor Fuller to serialize my findings in *Interview Magazine*. I gotta put it out there in a hip publication. I gotta appeal to the MTV crowd. I gotta get Eminem, Clay Aiken, Michael Moore, Bruce Springsteen, Scissors Sisters, Brad Pitt, Steve Madden and Mel Gibson interested. We need to get celebrities behind this.

I must convince little old church-going ladies that our prisons house innocent as well as non-violent men. I must convince them that prisons are universities for advanced degrees in how to commit more crimes. I must convince the world that youngsters are being forcefully raped everyday in juveniles, jails and prisons. And these victims are coming out of prison humiliated, angry, confused and depressed. And these victims get out and become victimizers. I must convince college professors, students, pastors and fraternities, etc., to *save our streets* and *save our children*. And the way to save the children and prevent molestations, rapes and the victimization of our innocent citizens, is to punish, **treat** and rehabilitate those who are in our prisons. Ipso facto, the system must be forced to protect those serving time for minor crimes. Ipso facto, union bosses cannot be allowed to run the prisons and to abuse inmates. The unions have a right to fight for good wages, proper equipment and better working conditions for its officers. There is nothing wrong with the CCPOA fighting for justice for its officers. But the CCPOA cannot be allowed to control the governor, dictate policy and/or to protect renegade cops. The CCPOA must respect the *will of the people* who pay their salaries. And the salary paying citizens deserve to know what's going on in their prisons. This layer of secrecy, which protects the criminal and unethical behavior of bad prison guards must be exposed. Taxpaying citizens are *employers* and an employer deserves to know what's going on with its *employees*. Prison guards' records must be transparent. We should reward good guards, discipline, punish and fire the bad ones.

Paul decided - It's time for me to take a break. He decided to read one more e-mail. This one was from Gregory Seaman in Detroit, Michigan. Greg's e-mail stated: "Mr. Shackelford, how are you? I am an engineer in Detroit, Michigan. My mother is wrongly convicted of murdering my abusive father. I love my family dearly. My family has been torn asunder. My estranged brother, Jeff, would blame it on my mom, Nancy. I blame it on the root of the problem; abuse. My mom was definitely abused by my dad. It is tragic. But my mom should not be in prison. Also, it's tragic that prior to my mom's wrongful conviction I didn't *think* about prisons and I didn't think about prisoners. I was a rich White kid. And most rich kids never even contemplate the existence of prisons and much less the possibility of going to prison. I heard through Todd and Lawrence Kaluzny that you were contemplating doing a drama, play or movie about prisons. I would hope you'd contemplate mentioning wrongful convictions and women in prisons. I hope you point out also the failures of our jury system and how often they get it wrong... Point out also the fact that White people go to prison also. So prisons affect us all..."

As Paul read the final paragraph of Mr. Seaman's e-mail, Paul mumbled, "Everybody wants to push their agenda on to me. I'm going to do a news story at minimum, an expose or series of stories at best; primarily focusing on the sexual rapes, enslavement and mistreatment of the average White kid who ends up in juvenile, jail or prison. And a Black man is responsible for me being led to do this work. Yet, everybody thinks I'm doing a movie, a video or something *other* than what I'm doing. I feel for them all. But I cannot be all things to all people.

"I will pray for Greg Seaman. I literally feel he loves his mother. And I wish he and his brother would make up. But I'm not so sure his mother is wrongly convicted. She *hatcheted* her husband to death. She seemed as guilty as hell to me from what I saw and read. But maybe she was freaked out. I don't know. I do know that it's funny how long most of us live on this planet without ever giving prisons or prisoners a second thought.

"We smoke our pot, drink our beer, live our lives and don't think about these places, which house human beings unless we happen to know somebody in jail. But the minute someone we know or love is arrested, we become concerned about law and order. We get courts, judges, juries and justice on our minds. We - the White people. And those who are Black and Mexicans should have their asses kicked. I'm sorry to say it but fortunately I'm talking to myself. I would never say this to a Black or Brown person because they would consider me a racist. All of a sudden, nothing else I've done up until this point in my life would mean anything. Whether I have a Black girlfriend or a Brown best friend would be irrelevant. Even if I were a paying member of the NAACP, it would be irrelevant to *them*. The moment they heard me put any blame on them, I'd be racist in their eyes. But the fact of the matter is that with the way Blacks and Browns are arrested for the same things, I would get a warning for. With the way minorities go to prison for the same stuff I would receive a *fine* for. With the irrefutable empirical data, which proves conclusively, that Blacks get the death penalty sixty-four percent more often than Whites. And with all of the evidence we have about media bias against minorities, crack being pumped into predominantly Black neighborhoods and so forth and so on, I believe that there is absolutely no excuse for the divisions and lack of togetherness in Black and Brown people in this country.

"All the Black celebrities and sports stars, etc. - Where are they on issues of law and order and prisons in America? MIA! Shaq, Kobe, Michael Jordan and most of them are missing in action. Michael Jackson had never done anything to help a brother in prison or said a word about so-called false accusations or wrongful prosecutions until he got charged with child molestation, and even the guys who have literally been in prison with a conviction, etc. Once they get out they develop amnesia.

"Mike Tyson got out after serving time for rape and instead of giving some money to Barry Scheck or hiring lawyers for poor defendants, he blew a three hundred million dollar fortune. O. J. was acquitted due to the brilliance, dedication and commitment to justice of Johnnie Cochran and his pal, Barry Scheck. But O. J. hasn't said a word about the ones he left in LA County Jail. To him they can go to hell. They are the no J's.

"Where is Geronimo Pratt? Where are the Black pastors! There are 123,000 Black pastors in America and Black churches raise fifty-seven billion dollars per year. And they put all of their money into our White banks. They buy Cadillacs, Lincolns and Armani's with their fifty-seven billion Black dollars.

"With the way they are routinely railroaded, mistreated and set up by a White judicial system, you would think that by now they would have a national organization which specifically fights wrongful convictions, abuse of prisoners and reaches out to guys behind walls. But instead, Black pastors don't even write letters of reply to Black, Brown or White prisoners who write to them seeking help."

Paul continued, "They are obviously asleep. And I say they should be ashamed as well as Whites such as me should be ashamed that a growing number of White kids are filling up the prisons for petty crimes, drug offenses and other non-violent offenses. And they are being raped, beat or pressured into hate groups or gangs for protection and our White leaders are also silent.

"Furthermore, we should all be ashamed that we have not come **together** in a bipartisan relationship to do justice, have mercy and walk humbly with God. After all the authentic fact is that Red, Yellow, Black and White we are all the same in God's sight. We ought to stand together as people, all people, one nation, indivisible under God.

"It should not be about Black or White, dark or light, it should be about wrong and right. A Black pastor who would hear about the rape of a White prisoner and not fight for his protection is a Black pastor I don't want to hear preach. A White pastor who could know an innocent Black man is in prison or a guilty Brown man is being beat by prison guards and yet dismiss it by saying, 'He shouldn't have gone to prison.' That's a White pastor who can't preach to me.

"We need some Rick Warrens, T. D. Jakes, Noel Jones, Paula Whites and Eddie Longs to come together. Not just to preach but to raise tens of millions of dollars to do for the prison movement what Karl Rowe did for republicans. We need Alex Benzer, Craig Newmark, Nick Lamar (Folsom, CA), Lance Chin (Sacto, CA), David Luong (Sacto), Lance Carlson (Winona, Minnesota), Andrew Kenney and Eli Pariser… These people need to come together and organize."

Paul was exhausted. He shut down and drank a beer. "I definitely need some pussy. It's my outlet. I need to hit one. Paris Hilton? No!! She wouldn't screw me. Britney? Nope, she's pregnant. Maybe Paula Abdul. She'll give it to anybody." Paul laughed. "Paula can never say no to anybody. She loves Bo Bice. She's the queen of nice. She loves Fedorov, Michael Phelps,

Constantine. She can't be mean. I need to do her. I guess I'll just stroke and think of Paula. But sex can wait. Let me read the latest snail missive from *Sherman*."

Paul didn't notice he'd begun referring to me by my first name rather than his standard *Mr. Manning*. Paul opened a thick ass envelope with the infamous *Mule Creek State Prison* stamped on it.

"Dear Paul: How are you, pal? (My missive to him (Paul) began.) I'm holding on by the grace of God. I am a bit perturbed due to some recent developments including the case of Christopher Frank Pittman. This twelve-year-old boy killed his grandparents with a shotgun and then burned the house down. He says Zoloft made him do it. Texas Civil Lawyer Andy Vickery tried the case pro bono. The jury convicted the kid and the judge sentenced the kid to two concurrent thirty-year sentences. Chris will be forty-two years old when he gets released from the prison.

"During the trial, the judge offered to resolve the case with a plea deal. Andy rejected the deal in which the judge could have sentenced Chris to as little as two years. Unfortunately, I believe Chris does deserve to be punished. I also believe Zoloft had something to do with this. And it is always troubling when we try kids as adults. This boy was twelve years old. How do we try fifth and sixth graders as adults in America? Paul, the law is important. But law must be tempered with mercy in order to obtain justice! I don't believe this kid totally blacked out. I don't believe this boy should walk away Scot-free. I also do not believe we should try a twelve year old as a man. Where do we draw the line? Everything is not *black and white*. There are special circumstances. This kid could have been punished by keeping him in juvenile til he was twenty-one. That would have been a nine or ten-year sentence. Not for warehousing, but for intervention, treatment, counseling and for transformation. I just don't believe *that* jury did the right thing. I also think Andy Vickery should be applauded. Andy feels bad for not taking the deal. But Andy did his best for Chris. And Andy tried one helluva case!

"I hope he will continue to fight drug companies and hold them accountable with our legal system. I hope he continues to make a lot of money and to give back by taking on two or three pro bono criminal cases per year to fight for the underdog. That's what a real lawyer does, Paul...

"That's really why I like Tom Mesereau so much. It's not because Tom is representing Michael Jackson. I could care less about Michael. If Michael molested children, he should go to prison - period! If Michael Jackson is a child predator those kids are victims and they deserve punishment for there victimizer! But no matter how bad it looks, the law should be followed. He is presumed innocent and a jury should not convict him (I kind of believe they will) on hearsay, conjecture, bias or eccentricity. A jury should *only* convict him *if* the case is proven by evidence, in a court of law, beyond a reasonable doubt to a moral certainty!!

"Tom is the hero though, Paul. I know Tom personally. I remember him going down to Alabama to represent a poor Black guy in a death penalty case pro bono! I know he has a poor people's law clinic at Fame Church in LA. That's why I love Tom because he loves **justice!**"

Paul could tell from perusing my missive that I was angry. I'd learned how to channel my anger into my writing. I wrote in a manic and scathing manner. To write was therapeutic and helpful for me. I wrote to survive, to live, to help and to hope. Writing was my *way out of* the misery, the pain, the hurt, the sorrow and the madness of the prison. Writing was my *way out of no way...* Paul continued my missive...

"It ain't about Mr. Jackson, Paul. It's the concern, the love for justice and the righteous indignation, which moves and motivates Mr. Mesereau that I love. I'm not concerned about Michael or O. J. I want to help the no J's. Paul, Andy Vickery of Houston, Texas, Howard Mims, Barry Scheck and Gloria Killian are the heroes. I need you to help me to connect Jason Kwock, Timothy Goebel, Johnny Weir, Eminem, Bo Bice, Paris Hilton, Nicole Ritchie and Lisa Ling with Betty Waters and Peter Neufeld. I need you to find a way to help me get justice for the poor, the lonely and the downtrodden. Paul, I want the world to know there are some Mel Bacons, Ari Ackermans (www.Bunk1.com), Galens, Shelia Barrys and some David Protesses who do give a damn about justice and wrongful convictions and the innocent who are trapped in prison...

"But Paul, let us never forget our *main mission.* Our chief mission is to *tell the world*, the *nation*, the citizens of this great country about the rapes and vicious molestations, which are transpiring and occurring in every jail, juvenile and prison in America **right now**! We must *tell them* about it. We gotta let them know! We gotta let them know!!"

Paul continued but he coughed and said, "Sherman is long-winded but the shit is good; he's never boring." Continuing on - he read:

"Paul, I am sick and tired of being sick and tired. Tired of the ignorance, the hurt, the anger and the pain that I see all around me.

And perhaps you assume that the persons I am speaking of are the persons in prisons. Not *this* time. At this juncture, Paul, I'm speaking of the media and our politicians. Political pundits i.e. Rush Limbaugh, Sean Hannity and O'Reilly. World News organizations, senators, those at the White House, etc., they are absolutely ignorant, careless and angry.

"Some of the angriest folks I've ever encountered in my lifetime are *some* of these so-called conservatives! I'm not speaking of fiscal conservatives. Nor am I writing of *all* republicans. I am talking about folks who hate the poor, despise lesbians and have total disdain for anyone who does not agree with their political beliefs. They are like zealots and fanatics. And unfortunately too many of them are in power. They control the money, the media and the government. And they strategically, systematically and methodically manipulate the news, movies, soap operas and even sitcoms. And this manipulation of the information molds, shapes and affects public opinions.

"These images, which we see on the television, help us shape our beliefs. I.e. beliefs about law and order, justice, the police, prisons and our court system. By and large, most of us believe that *most* of the folks in prisons are there for violent and vicious crimes. Wrong! There are more non-violent offenders in prisons nationwide than there are violent ones. There are petty thieves, credit card scammers, burglars, drug addicts and drug salesmen than there are molesters, rapists and murderers in our prisons.

"Most of us think prisoners are coddled and they eat good food, get paid good money and learn a lot of trades in prisons. Wrong. There are more lockdown type warehouses than there are working prisons in the U.S.A. and of the few, which do employ its prisoners, they mostly produce goods or provide services *for* the States which saves the taxpayers' money!

"Most of us believe that there are very few instances of guard abuse or disrespect in our prisons. According to Professor Heaphy, forty-seven percent of California prison guards are corrupt and abuse prisoners. According to Professor Zimring, thirty-eight percent of prison guards across the country are racist, violent or abusive. And eighty-two percent of the guys in prisons today will be out of prison within less than five years. And we *house* burglars with rapists. We house eighteen year olds with fifty-eight year olds. We put guys with five-year sentences right along side the guys with *life without* parole sentences... Paul, this is a recipe for madness, riots, rapes and killings. The ingredients for how to make monsters are in the hands of wardens all across America. It is as if prison authorities are crazed and mad

140

scientists who have mastered the recipes for the systematic, methodical and scientific creation of failed, crippled and vicious humans.

"Paul, I still believe in human beings. I can't give up on us. I love us. We gotta lot of problems, bro. And we still face the difficulties of today and tomorrow. And it's easy to become cynical. But, man, when you look back at where we've come from, you can find reasons to continue to believe in **us**. Look back at slavery, Jim Crow, Whites only and Black folks not being able to vote right here in America. We've come a long way. Look back at AIDS, syphilis, cancer, leukemia and look at polio. Look at all the racial gains and scientific treatments and cures that we've come up with. Look at the Martin Luther King, Jr., John F. Kennedy, Dr. Keith Black and Dr. Ben Carson that America created. We have come a long way.

"And so I still believe that *if* little old White women, Black women, Mexicans and Indians are given the *truth* about wrongful convictions, crime and punishment, rapes and violence in prisons, *we,* America, will rise up and demand a change in how we do justice in America.

"Our nation will perhaps remain divided on some issues such as gay marriage, abortion and welfare. We may remain largely divided and partisan on some issues, but I'm convinced that we can all agree that we ought to feed our hungry, clothe our naked and yes, even protect the bodies of *boys* in juveniles, jails and prisons. As sick, unethical and deceptive as many people believe Mr. Bush is, I even believe that *Bush* would not want fifteen, sixteen, seventeen and eighteen-year-old Caucasians (and Black or Brown) kids molested, bullied and terrorized in prisons. But to be honest, I don't think Bush really knows about the Abu Ghraibs right here in Tennessee, Georgia, California, Arizona, Texas and New York. The information, which he receives about prisons is filtered screened and sanitized. The folks reporting to the president don't even know what's going on in here.

"Paul, it is my job, my duty, my responsibility, aim and vision to tell *the truth*. I must put the facts out there. The facts, just the *facts* and let the chips fall where they may.

"I can't do it alone. I will continue to ask great men such as Mel Bacon of Coronado Stone Products in Fontana, California, George Soros of the Open Society Institute, Peter B. Lewis of Progressive Insurance Company, Don King, Bill Gates and Jeff Bezos to help us put **this tome** (as well as '*From the Palace to the Prison*' and '*Creating Monsters*') into the hands of juveniles, jail and prison inmates and the family members of inmates.

"Folks, i.e. David Inocencio and Mike Kroll (of *The Beat Within*...telephone # 415/503-4170, www.TheBeatWithin.org) and Roberta Franklin of the *Family Members of Inmates* in Montgomery, Alabama, etc., would love for Mr. Soros, Mr. Bacon or Mr. Gates to log on to www.Cafepress.com/*Blonde* and order two thousand (or so) copies of *this book* and send them directly to these organizations so they can get this book to people who need it. Many churches and pastors, i.e. Bishop T. D. Jakes, Bishop Noel Jones (in LA) or Eddie Long (in Atlanta) would love to receive a thousand copies of this book to give away to their youth. And the information in this book *will* cause some folks to turn their lives around, Paul."

Paul stopped and said, "Book? What the hell is Sherman Manning writing about? Book? This is a missive to me but it appears he's (Sherman) writing about a *book*. Did I miss something? Did he send me a book? Am I smoking too much bud or what?"

Paul then wrote me a letter to ask, "What *book* are you talking about?"

I wrote back:

"The book that I'm writing now, bro. That was a test missive to see if you had been binge drinking, were high or if you were paying attention to my letters. Anyway, *I* confess, I am writing *another* book. I can't wait on your White ass to do something. I must fight! I must write. *Write or die*!

"Paul, Catholic Seminary students like Uriel Ojeda, rappers like Eminem, Clay Aiken, Anthony Fedorov, Timothy Goebel, Johnny Weir, Craig Scott, Ashton Kutcher, Paris Hilton, Lisa Ling and Bo Bice had all written to me and told me that they will support a book on this subject... I gotta write, man.

"Neither Mr. Bush, nor John Kerry ever mentioned homelessness, mental illness or American public safety in any of the debates. They talked about flip-flopping, Iraq, Osama *Been Forgotten* and Saddam. But we heard nothing about our homeless and mentally disabled. And most of the homeless and mentally ill in America are veterans! "Kerry is a veteran and as he announced, he was *reporting for duty*, he said nothing about the thousands of wounded, crippled, crazed and diseased veterans who reported for duty and served in Iraq and Afghanistan and are now living on the streets. Many came back to America physically and remained in war zones mentally. Due to poverty, mental illness or war torn minds, many of them committed crimes and went to prisons. Bush didn't mention them. They are humans too. They matter. We all matter. And so since I can't depend on ya'll White folks to put it out there, Paul, I gotta write a book, man.

142

"Come on, lighten up, Paul. I know *you care*. And I know millions of White and Black folks who do care. And I'm *not* doing another book yet. But just as Jeremy (rest in peace) did, I do journal on a daily basis. And I encourage **you** to journal, Paul. Everyday you ought to write notes, situations and essays to yourself, etc., because you never know when that stuff might come in handy.

"Mark Winer, Harper Collins, St. Martin's Press, etc., could come calling and perhaps we can consider doing a book someday. But for now, Paul get off your White ass and get this story out. There is a paralysis which can come from too much analysis. We have talked the talk now let's walk the walk. We must get up and do this. As Dr. Phil says, '*We can do this*!' Paul, I am ready to do *it now*. You must be bold, courageous and you must move forward now. Put it out there. I'm waiting to see some action.

"I don't care if the story is in *The Washington Post*, *The Nation*, The New York Times, The Sacramento Bee or even a free community paper. Get it out there. Now let's go... Keep the faith, bro. Sherm."

Paul was really thinking...transfixed, spellbound and quite frankly mesmerized. Michael Moore wrote another e-mail to Paul. We redacted some of the e-mail.

From Michael Moore to Paul Shackelford... "The lies of the Bush Administration are tied to the war in Iraq, Abu Ghraib, Dick Cheney and Halliburton's crooked monopoly, as well as Karl Rove who did out Ambassador Joe Wilson's wife... And *Sherman* can link the abuse at Abu Ghraib to the abuses in American jails, juveniles and prisons - you'll start a revolution. High school juniors and seniors are rebellious. They are a unique group. If you bring a song, poem or book before them, they will read it. Go to any American high school and you'll find gay, lesbian and straight alliances, debate teams, student government clubs and little politicians in the making. *If* you guys do a book and get it to these youth groups, they will push it! They will blog it, podcast it, blurb it and link it. You want youth scholars, nerds, gothics and any standout kids to get a copy.

"Lesra Martin was only sixteen years old when he read Rubin "Hurricane" Carter's tome, "The 16th Round" and Lesra was so moved, touched and spellbound that he went to visit Big Rube... *Sherman* does not seek youth visits or even senior citizen visitors, I know. But the point is Lesra was only sixteen and willing to believe in a man who was convicted of a triple murder. When young people are presented with powerful, credible and interesting artistic *expression*, they respond. They don't give a damn what jaded, biased and (sometimes)

143

prejudiced adults say or think. They're gonna touch the damned fire anyway to see if it burns."

Mr. Moore continued… "Paul, if you all do a book on these rape, molestation, injustice and abuse in juveniles type issues that *Sherman* keeps writing *me* about, all you need to do is get *ten copies* to ten high school students. I promise you, they'll read twenty or thirty pages, stop - go online, chat, blog, link and tinker. They'll read some more and text their pals, etc., etc., and within ten or fifteen days, your book will bust through the roof, dude. You'll have critics, skeptics and parents. You'll have the same parents who don't go to P.T.A. meetings, don't tutor their kids, don't go to the high school basket ball games to see Christian play, etc. You'll have the same parents who don't know the story of Joseph in the Bible, which they claim to believe in. Paul, they don't know the Bible was written by ex-murderers, thugs and accused convicts, etc. They forgot Paul used to be a murderer named Saul. These same parents are out of touch with their teens and kids and they are just jaded… Well, these parents will rise up and attack *Sherman* cause he's in prison and attack you too.

"But don't despair. The more parents that tell kids **not** to read the book (*if* you all do a book and I damn sure think you should) the more kids **will** read the book. And *if* you all maintain the same level of responsible writing as *Sherman* did in 'Creating Monsters' and in 'From the Palace to the Prison' then teens will be better off after reading it.

"At sixteen, Bush will let them sign up for the U. S. Marines. At seventeen, we trust them to be responsible enough to go over to Iraq and handle Uzi's, M-16's and bombs. But *if* they make it back home at eighteen or nineteen or even twenty years old as decorated vets, we don't trust them to buy a freaking beer. *WE* the adults. *WE* the politicians. *WE* the parents… We think a youngster is old enough to fight, kill and die at seventeen or eighteen, but not old enough to decide whether or not to buy a beer. Hell, we'll send them off to college i.e., U. C. Davis, CSU, Carnegie Mellon, Boston University at sixteen or seventeen. They can live in the dorms away from home, but we won't trust them to decide whether or not to buy a beer. And we wonder why they lash out, disobey, join gangs, cliques or become outcasts, etc.

"Kids want their own identity. And I assure you, the same thing about the power of Rubin 'Hurricane' Carter's writing which sparked flames in the spirit of sixteen-year-old Lesra Martin - that *power* is evident in the writing of *Sherman D. Manning*. He does not tell kids *what* to think or even *how* to think; he just asks them to *think*. Paul,

144

Sherman does not tell high school and college youth how, when or even where to *express* themselves. He (Sherman) just suggests that they express themselves.

"Dude - Adults keep telling us kids don't care and kids can't think, etc. When I read Sherman's blog, I got the feeling that kids can do anything if we get our asses out of the way. Give them some structure, guidance and get out of the way..." (redacted paragraphs...)

Mr. Moore concluded his e-mail with this... "Paul, you are *young* and why do *you* care? That's the same reason teens in high schools, freshmen, seniors, frat members and sorority sisters will care. Dude, get the damned book written. Let *Sherman* edit it and do a lot of the writing and send *five* copies to high school seniors and *five* copies to college students - then sit back. The teens will spread the word. Just watch. I *know* what youngsters can do. Get the freaking book out there. Tell Sherman to call me at 212... (redacted no.) ... Respectfully, *Michael Moore* - Filmmaker."

Well, Mr. Moore has spoken. Paul was quite interested in what Mr. Moore had to say. We hope each of you reading this book at this very moment will (indeed) call a pal, text a stud, geek, freak, nerd, honey, hot momma or whoever and tell them about this book. Inundate blogs, message boards and websites with the title of **this** book as well as a link to www.*Cafepress.com/Manning* so they can get their copy. If you want to use this book as a fundraising tool, let us know now.

Wanna volunteer as an adviser, critic, tutor, writer, photographer, etc., let us know now. Snail mail Sherman at *Sherman D. Manning, J98796* - M.C.S.P., A-2-240, P.O. Box 409020, Ione, CA 95640 *today*!

Want your photo in the next book? - Snail mail it. No *nudity* allowed! *No* nudity accepted! Want your band, club, group, squad, etc. in the next book? - Snail mail it to Mr. Manning today! And if you want to volunteer, write, get published etc., e-mail our team at *Hallopeter@freesurf.ch*. If you are sixteen or younger, please get *parental* permission. No person under sixteen should write a prisoner *without parental* supervision...That's our opinion. Know Alexander Dugdale? Clay Hollifield? Davis on The Scholar? Chaz Wolcott? E-mail, Google, text or Myspace.com them and tell them *they are in this book...*

...Paul took a deep breath and picked up the telephone. He called his pal, Scott Coffman. By the time he and Scott were finished chatting, Paul had been fully briefed on an interest in his story by an executive with the Los Angeles Times. Four days later, Paul was in Los Angeles staying at *the* Bonaventure Hotel waiting to meet with

Mr. Reid Collins. He'd arrived in L.A. on the red-eye late Thursday evening. After checking into his suite, Paul flopped down into one of the two large chairs, which were located on either side of an expensive coffee table. Paul was exhausted. He had spent most of the six-hour flight going over Jeremy's journal, notes from me, notes from networks and cramming statistics into his head. He believed that prior planning prevents poor performance. He wanted to be *ready*.

As Paul sat in the suite of his hotel room, he felt ready but tired. The phone rang and it was Reid. *Mrs*. Reid Collins. Reid could hear the surprise in Paul's voice. "You thought I was a man didn't you?" she asked.

"Well, ma'am since I'd never spoken with *you* and your assistants didn't say, I kinda expected a *man*."

Reid exclaimed, "You men are so stereotypical. This is 2005, Mr. Shackelford. Why would you assume that every publisher must be White, male and balding? I earn $815,000 per year. I'm Latino and under forty. Does this bother you? Are you racist as well as sexist?"

Damn, Paul thought, a *sensitive* one. Shit, I'm getting off on the wrong foot here, Paul thought. "I apologize. I am neither sexist nor racist. I'm just impressed and exhausted."

Reid accepted his apology and agreed to meet him at "The Palm" restaurant the next day to discuss his story over lunch.

At 12:01 Friday, Paul had a window seat as he noticed the tall brunette, with the nice Tina Turner legs, in heels stepping out of a Mercedes Benz limousine. The stretch was golden in color. Could *that* be Reid, he thought. It was.

They ate filet mignon and engaged in idle chatter, pleasantries and general dialogue as Paul tried to think of a way to get down to business.

* * *

A few hundred miles away at Catholic Central High School, a young teacher, Matt Yonker discussed, "Creating Monsters" with students Zack Burkes, Bridgewater, Joe Filke and pals, Uriel Ojeda and Nate Solov. "What can we, as Catholic youth, do to get involved with social justice in America?" Matt asked his students.

Mr. Burkes raised his hand. "Maybe we could start an organization or start a youth chapter of Sherman's NAPS (National Association for Public Safety). We could canvass the neighborhoods and get petitions signed to restore rehabilitation in prisons. Obviously our senators, congress and president don't know what they are doing. They are locking up more and more people. But crime is going up. And more and more get out and tear up our cities before they go back.

146

And we need to change what is taking place in the prisons. We have spent four hundred billion dollars on the wars in Iraq and Afghanistan. Why can't we spend whatever it takes to change men in prisons and teach them how to *live* when they get out? But if someone asked the White House for *half* of that - two hundred billion dollars - to transform our prisons, I assure you, excuses would be made about how/why we can't afford it.

"If we ask for one hundred billion dollars to make our schools safer, pay teachers more, etc., our government would cry indigent. But we will pay for wars!

"So I think we need to educate our elders about justice to counter that garbage they get fed by the media!"

Matt said, "That sounds good, but how would you propose to implement it? Talk is easy but would you really be able to influence your pals to get out, put feet in the streets and do this?"

    * * *

Back at *The Palm*, Reid told Paul, "Let's go back to your suite and talk business."

Paul considered it a bit odd that this powerful, attractive and sexy woman, who was supposed to discuss his potential story over lunch, wanted to go back to his suite to talk. What's really going on here, Paul thought. Yet, he paid the tab and they left The Palm. Paul had not rented a car so he had no problem hopping in the back seat of the triple stretch limousine to make the journey back to his hotel suite. The minute the chauffeur closed the door of the limo, Reid poured herself a gin and tonic. Paul declined her offer for a drink. Reid picked up the car phone and told the driver, "Drive around for about thirty-five minutes and then take us to the Bonaventure Hotel, John."

When she hung up, Paul said, "Why are we driving around for thirty-five minutes? Are we sightseeing? Are you going to show me the city or something?"

Reid turned around and looked directly into Paul's eyes and asked, "Are you gay?"

Paul wrinkled his forehead and tightened his eyelids and said, "Hell no."

Smiling and slowly moving her tongue across her lips, right to left, Reid said softly, "Then prove it. Screw my brains out. Have you ever had pussy in the back of a limo?"

Paul was excited and he showed it by immediately pulling Reid on top of him. As they kissed, she moaned, groaned and she struggled to pull off her panties. They were pink, wet and smelled like a mixture of strawberries and watermelon. *Strange*, Paul thought as Reid rubbed her wet panties across his nose. She then threw the panties on the floor of the limo and unzipped his pants...

They pulled up in front of the Bonaventure Hotel exactly two nutts and thirty-nine minutes later. "Damn, you're wild," Paul said to Reid as the driver opened the door for them to exit the limo.

As they stepped inside the lobby of the Bonaventure, Reid took control and said, "Let's sit at this table over here and you can tell me all about your story. It should be easier now that you don't have to lust after me anymore. You need not wonder what color panties I'm wearing, how my pussy smells and all the other things men wonder about when they meet rich, powerful women. I figured we'd get the bullshit out of the way and all of the small talk, etc., etc., out of the way. You cummed twice, I got one fabulous orgasm and now here we are. Let me go to the Ladies Room and freshen up. You go to the Boy's Room, wash the pussy off your face and meet me back here in five minutes."

* * *

Zach Burkes had e-mailed Craig Kielburger, the twenty-year-old Canadian who founded *Free The Children* at age thirteen. Zach's initial e-mail asked Craig how he started *Free The Children*. He also requested tactics and strategies for motivating others. "How were you able to influence peers to actually get involved and do something? I would appreciate your reply. I'm trying to get students in my class at *Catholic Central* here in Modesto, California to do the unthinkable. I want us to *Free the Prisoners*! Ipso facto, protect public safety!"

Zach was surprised to receive a reply from Craig via e-mail nearly twenty minutes after his first e-mail. Craig wanted more specifics. "Exactly what do you plan to do?" Craig had asked.

Zach had to admit that he had not finalized or crystallized his plans. "But I want *justice* in America! And from my viewpoint, when we put innocent people in prison, we risk public safety. And we waste time, talent and energy in so many foolish ways, i.e., we hold up signs protesting when we discover a child molester or rapist is being released into our community. I want to *know* where they *live*. I know who to watch and where to watch. But - we overlook the fact that most child molesters work in schools, churches and in positions of power. They are our uncles, brothers, fathers, firemen, police and judges. I.e., three weeks ago a top official with the Boy Scouts of America pled guilty to selling child porn. This predator was in charge of a Boy Scout program, which was supposed to protect children from child predators. He was the last person we would suspect.

"I.e., again: Michael R. Woodbury! *Attorney* Mike Woodbury! *Pastor* Mike Woodbury? Youth Leader Mike Woodbury, Director of the Young Men's Leadership Development Program for the *Church of Jesus Christ Latter Day Saints* of Sacramento. Arrested and charged two weeks ago with thirty-one counts of child molestation! Nobody would have even suspected this prestigious lawyer and leader to be a molester!

"So Craig, it would appear to me that our nation fails miserably at identifying child molesters among us; especially when they wear priestly robes, suits, ties and even black robes. Cloaked in position of authority, class and officialdom, they deceive us and often go undetected.

"The fact that we get out in the streets and wave banners saying we don't want that molester moving to our neighborhood, etc., our protests and demonstrations are a good indicator of the fact that we do care. We are angry and hurt that our children are being harmed.

"And very often anger can lead to a crisis in the emotions; thereby causing irrational behavior and misplaced energy. I think we are wasting our time, Craig, protesting against people who are released from prison and yelling that we don't want them living in our neighborhood. Pragmatically, it makes no sense.

"It only scratches at the surface. We would be better off debunking the myths of the laws which often allow a convicted child predator to get off with probation, but punishes burglars and folks convicted of DUI with twenty-five to life. We need to go back to the basics and start from scratch. Step one: Develop more skills at identifying the tendencies, characteristics and traits of potential child molesters. And when we identify a person who is potentially en-route to becoming a molester, let's pay the money to intervene, treat, counsel and help him or her! Step Two: When a person does commit child molestation, etc., we must punish them severely and treat them while we punish them. We need equal justice and protection under the law. We must stop allowing people to get off with slaps on the wrists when they rape children. When we look at *who* commits these heinous molestations, we may better understand how and why they so often get away with it.

"Craig, there are so many back room, under the carpet, in the closet and *in chambers* deals reached for child molesters that *don't get* reported. The news media barely reports five percent of the child rape cases, which are pled out in closed chambers.

"Day after day the C.E.O.s of large corporations, pastors, teachers, firemen, physicians and engineers plead *no contest* or the

Alford plea to raping babies, infants, boys and girls. And these sickos get probation!!

"Craig, our citizens think if it ain't in the newspaper or on the evening news, it didn't happen. But tell the tens of thousands of little boys who have been groomed, molested, injured, harmed and abused by their priest, teachers and other professionals, that *it* didn't *happen*. They know it did! And the reason many of the victims and their families don't raise hell when the media doesn't report their cases, etc., is because they usually *don't want* publicity. Craig, most boys don't want the world to know them in their *fifteen minutes* as the victim of a sex crime! And so forth and so on. Craig, we are lost! In the midst of all of this, we have police officers and prosecutors who don't like bad P.R. and they want to be seen as being *tough on crime*. And they love to chase the limelight and claim, 'We've solved this crime.' And very often, these people in law enforcement are willing to lock up the *wrong man* for the right crime and give them a lot of prison time just to say they have a *conviction*.

"And when they send these innocent persons to prisons, this opens up a large can of worms. I.e., innocent persons go to prison and are victimized, assaulted and raped by other prisoners. These assaults, rapes and this scandalization leads to ultimate devastation. And when these devastated men get out of prisons, they are monsters.

"Also - the absolute worst thing that happens in a case of a wrongful conviction is we leave a predator, a monster or a molester free to roam the streets and continue to molest, rape and even kill before we catch them.

"Craig, I want to *protect public safety*. I want to be tough on crime by being *pragmatic* on crime. I want to energize and galvanize all those people who are willing to canvass the neighborhoods and announce the *release* of an offender from prison. I want to *redirect* their efforts into canvassing the neighborhoods and identifying the rapists who are among us. I want them to join with us and demand that prosecutors and judges release, exonerate and vindicate the guys who are in prison but did not do it. I want them to join with me and demand that in cases of wrongful conviction, we also demand a *rightful* prosecution. I also want them to join us in demanding treatment for those in prisons who did do it.

"Craig, I want the Catholic church and all churches to get off their high horses and care for those in our prisons. They are coming out. And if we abandoned, mistreated, abused or ignored them in prisons they will rape, rob, molest, steal or kill when they get out of prison.

150

"Craig, I've attached a copy of an interview I read in a newspaper called *The Beat Within* out of San Francisco (www.TheBeatWithin.org., volume 10.13). This was written by a twenty-three-year-old prison journalist. I think you'll find that this twenty-three year old makes a lot of sense. I plan to write to him. I just want to bring as many people together as I can to fight for the safety of our public. We have waited on politicians and they've failed us. We've looked to our priests and they've molested us.

"We can wait no longer! We kids are gonna lead the way. We'll ask Bill Gates, Mel Bacon, George Soros and Jeff Bezos to help us educate the public and protect our kids. I need your advice on how to *operationalize* and fine-tune my plan. How do I bring people together? Thanks - Zach Burkes - Catholic Central High School, Modesto, California."

* * *

Paul returned from the restroom at about the same time as Mrs. Collins did. They sat down and Paul cleared his throat, "I want to do a story that will make many people uncomfortable. I want this story to be published, front page, in a three-piece series. I need your *best* writer to do this story. The story is about rapes in prison. It is about the production and manufacturing of rage, hatred, meanness and monsters. It is about *Blue-Eyed Blondes*! It's about reverse discrimination, retaliation and predatory behavior. In most prisons down South, Blacks outnumber Whites ten to one. And so any prison official (Black or White) will tell you that the White man runs the free world and the Black man runs the chain gang. And when you put a group of men under the same roof and deny them women, conjugal visits, etc., and cut them off from society - they group. They divide themselves as *predators* and *prey*. And by and large, the young men who are being raped in prisons, juveniles and jails across America are guys who *look like me*. They are White!

"And in many instances, there is empirical data which proves that prison administrators and guards are actually *setting* inmates up to be not only assaulted, but raped by other inmates. The lowly inmate who is incarcerated for rape, child molestation and other violent crimes is routinely set up. And even guys convicted of *non-violent* crimes. If they piss off the right prison guard, they will be set up and raped. I'm serious. In California, guards *admitted* to setting up inmates to be raped by a notorious predator named 'Booty Bandit'. If guards like Mansky, Stratton, Mayfield or Mike Todd get angry with an inmate, they purposely place him in a cell to be raped. They cover it up. They doctor up paperwork to justify their actions; i.e. transfers, ad-seg placement, SHU terms and other punitive actions.

"Who will believe the lowly convict? According to the media, he is a predator, a thug and a madman. And the last thing we should do as a free society is concern ourselves with the protestations, claims or accusations of the inmate! The system is set up so that the same guys who often abuse them, read and control their incoming and outgoing mail. These people control their access to telephone calls, etc. They get to decide whether or not this inmate can receive visits, etc. So he's helpless and defenseless and absolutely at the mercy of his keepers. And I would assume that if I held you captive in *my* house and I set you up to be raped by another slave, I would steal any letter you wrote to your family, lawyers or officials trying to expose my abuse. And I would not allow you to *call* anybody whom I knew would or could help you.

"In a sense, this is exactly how the prisons are run. The *Guards Own the Gates*! They decide who gets a visit, makes a telephone call, writes a letter, receives a letter, etc., etc., and they are sophisticated enough to create the appearance of propriety. I.e., inmate John Doe's visits have been suspended for six months for the safety and security of the institution. Who is going to question them? And, Inmate Billy Joes' telephone and mail privileges are suspended due to... Who will question them? They routinely *steal* these inmates' mail. I do mean routinely! How can a prisoner *prove* that a letter was stolen by a sworn peace officer? He can't!

"So basically when inmates are abused, beat, set up, assaulted, raped and even murdered - what happens in the house (prison), stays in the house. Ninety percent of inmate grievances, complaints and accusations against staff are also investigated by other staff. And eighty percent of America's prisons are located out in rural areas. Most of the staff in those prisons live, eat, sleep, shop and play in the same neighborhoods. So you have a lieutenant investigating a claim against his subordinate and his subordinate coaches his (the lieutenant's) son's baseball team. Another example is the nepotism. I.e., (again) in New Folsom State Prison out in Sacramento, The Chief Deputy Warden is Warden George Stratton. George's son is a first-grade prison guard who is twenty-two years old. If an inmate claim's Stratton wronged or abused him in some way or another, the final report of the investigation must be signed by Daddy Stratton. And what lieutenant is going to make a finding against his boss' (Deputy Warden Stratton) son in favor of an inmate? This kind of nepotism, hick town employment and total authority over inmates is not an anomaly in our prisons across America. It happens this way in Georgia, California, New York, Arizona and all across the nation.

"This kind of climate breeds official corruption, abuse and codes of silence. And the codes of silence amongst prison staff helps disguise and disappear the sex crimes taking place in the prisons. Now here is the clincher, ninety percent of all of the victims of rape inside prison will be released outside the prison within seven years of their initial rapes. Seventy-six percent of those raped in prison today will be released from prison within the next three years.

"And when they get out of prison with this hurt, fear, shame, confusion and rage inside of them, they often explode. And these explosions are exemplified with acts of violence. To make a long story short, the victims *of* rape find other victims to rape! Two psychiatrists have estimated that of the seven hundred thousand inmates released from prison yearly, one hundred thousand were raped! And of that one hundred thousand about forty-seven percent of them will commit rapes and molestations within three years of their release. And the psychological trauma associated with being a man in prison physically, yet incapable of preventing a rape by another man in prison, very often causes the victim to lash out at children. They prey on their innocence and they get a psychological high off of the fear in the eyes of the child. Mentally they are getting back at the people who raped them in prison!!!

"This is a threat to public safety. Pragmatically we cannot keep these people in prisons forever. Even the hardnosed, conservative republicans admit that we can't lock people up forever. It is impossible. And even the guys who devised three strikes and you're out admit behind closed doors that it is not working and it is way too expensive. They're just too arrogant and pompous to admit they were wrong. And they deceive their constituents by lying, conniving and manipulating the statistics.

"So the bottom line deal is there is absolutely no way to incarcerate our way out of crime. And the biggest kept secret of our jail system is the sheer numbers of kids being maliciously abused and sexually enslaved in our prisons. And nobody is talking about it. This results in the molestations we see in our neighborhoods everyday. We can't stop molestations in the schools or on the playgrounds unless we stop rapes in the prisons. And in order to stop rapes in the prisons, you must make prisons safe. And in order to make prisons safe, we have to bring rehabilitation, education and vocations back into prisons. We must also make prison authorities more transparent and accountable to civilians for how they run their prisons. We must also stop sending *so many* people to prisons and we must punish guard corruption severely.

"This is why I need your best writer to do this story. I want the whole story told for all the people to read. I don't want bias, yellow journalism or diluted reporting. Having seen the truth, the public will demand a change. What do you think?"

Reid Collins licked her lips, cleared her throat and said, "I'm in! You, my friend, are a genius. But let's do this right! I need all of the facts, empirical data and statistics that you can give me. I need inmates, ex-inmates, guards and ex-guards to corroborate the facts. We can use pseudonyms if necessary; we will protect the identity of any inmate or official who desires anonymity. Let's get this train rolling and be ready in three weeks. This is Pulitzer Prize winning material."

A few days later, Paul found himself at home and on the telephone with Reid Collins. "Paul, I need as much dirt as you can gather on the California Peace Officers Union; the CCPOA. From everything Mark Arax (a reporter for the LA Times) and Andy Furillo have indicated to me the CCPOA is a group of thugs. They apparently operate like the mob. They are rich, powerful, corrupt and an extremely dangerous union. They are now on my hit list. I won't run this story without mentioning their complicit, tacit approval of the rapes taking place in their thirty-three prisons."

Paul replied, "But Reid, this is not a California (only) story. This is bigger than C.D.C. This is about prisons, jails and youth detention centers all across North America. I don't wanna diminish or lessen the impact of the national impact of this story by making it about California prisons."

But Reid was a savvy, persuasive and strong-willed executive. It would be *her* way or *no* way. "It will still have national appeal. I'm giving you two of my best reporters for this damn story. It will be about what I want it to be. It will focus on how and why the CCPOA supports, defends and covers for the peace officers who engage in illegal, abusive and criminal conduct. The public won't be able to digest a story of tales of prison rapes unless they have a culprit. They will demand somebody to *blame*. And the easiest persons for us to blame will be the union. It is manipulation for the greater good. Let's be satisfied in knowing that the people we are demonizing deserve to be demonized.

"Now I have read all of the data you sent me. It is thorough, well organized and quite credible. No one will question your authenticity or the substance of your story. But my journalistic expertise dictates the need for an archenemy in this story. Society will refuse to blame themselves. You will fail if you think Black women are gonna allow you to hold Black pastors partially responsible or culpable for the conditions of their people in prisons. Catholics are still in denial as you can see. Cardinal Bernard Law should have been called *Cardinal Cover-up* for his tacit condoning of pedophile priests. Yet, his members called him a great father. And rather than the Pope (John Paul, rest in peace…may he) fire Bernard, he transferred him to the Vatican to a more prestigious job. People don't want to see the obvious. This is America, don't you know. We love our snake oil salesmen and lying politicians. We like to be lied to. We just demand that it sounds good to us.

"We recognize the fact that mayors, governors, senators, etc., don't come to our schools, churches, clubs and communities until it's election time and they want our votes. We know they will say *anything* to get elected! We know Karl Rove manipulated religion and Christians to the tune of subconsciously claiming *God is republican* but we voted for Bush anyway. We clearly understand that on Iraq and so-called weapons of mass destruction, Bush was *dead wrong*. We clearly comprehend that Bush blatantly lied and deceived us in an effort to justify going to war. We watched him say we would catch and kill the people who 'knocked those buildings down on September 11th.' We know he said he 'wanted' Osama Ben Laden 'dead or alive.' We also saw him say a few months later that 'I don't give much thought to Osama. Catching Osama is not really that important to me.' And at the debate, he clearly lied and claimed to have never made such a statement. The America public watched the split screen after the debate when CBS clearly showed Bush making the forget Osama statement he claimed he didn't make.

"We watched Dick Cheney claim to have *never* met John Edwards at the debate. We saw the footage later showing Dick Cheney and John shaking hands at a prayer breakfast two years before the debates. Dick clearly, blatantly and boldly lied to the American people. And we voted him/them back into office a few days later.

"There are a myriad of reasons why Bush won re-election, including the fact that he pushed the *God* buttons and manipulated slogans i.e., 'Kerry the flip flopper.' Bush played on our *fears* and made it appear that a vote for Bush was a vote for patriotism, God and safety. But it's important to ask why we overlooked Bush's lies on the weapons, lies on Osama *Been Forgotten* and the web of deception of his vice president. Why? At the end of the day, we believed Bush was tough, strong and a warrior. We believed that if we were attacked, he'd fight back. Ipso facto, we were able to pretend not to see the obvious. We made excuses, i.e., 'Does it really matter if Bush lied about a statement? Doesn't the President have a lot on his mind? Does it really matter that Saddam didn't have the weapons we thought he had? Isn't Saddam an evil dictator that the world is safer without?'

"Facts like - more than one hundred thousand innocent Iraqi's have been killed by our military - got lost in the footnotes of our minds. Facts such as - John Kerry was a brilliant, pragmatic and decorated war veteran got lost in the small print and back pages of our newspapers. We forgot that it took an enormous amount of patriotism, strength and fortitude for a man (John Kerry) to fight what he felt was an unjust war. We forgot there are thousands of men fighting right now in Iraq who *don't believe we should* be in Iraq. But when called to duty, they said, 'I took an oath to serve, protect and obey the orders of the Commander in Chief. So, I'm going to Iraq and I'll fight to the death.' We forgot because we wanted to be safe. And desperate, angry or frightened people don't think analytically and rationally.

"Paul, Americans will be terrified when they learn about the forceful raping, sodomizing and beating of young White males in juveniles, prisons and jails. And they will not accept that *they* did this. They won't accept that these so-called politicians and *prison crats* did this. They won't accept that if the churches to which they tithe adopted prisons, jails, juveniles, sponsored groups of inmates, taught workshops, seminars and clinics, etc. in the prisons and jails, the rapes would stop. They *can't handle the truth*!

"In schools, Paul, if parents would go to P.T.A. meetings get involved with their students etc., if parents showed up everyday in school and *sat down* in the back of classrooms, there would be no violence, bullying or fighting in schools. If parents patrolled the hallways and bathrooms of the schools, there would be no Columbines, no murders and no drugs in the schools. Theoretically and philosophically, we all know this but... It's too difficult to digest. It's much more convenient to point the finger of blame elsewhere. So we *blame* the *teachers*! But if in the process of blaming the teachers, we realize the brokenness of failed schools and we save them; it's perhaps okay to misplace the blame on to teachers.

"So Paul, you must blame somebody. And the easiest target is the CCPOA."

Paul began to see Reid's point and replied, "Well, it ain't like we're blaming saints or choir boys. I mean Professor Zimring and Attorney Davey Turner have told me that the CCPOA makes the LA Rampart Division look like Sterling characters! Let me see how much more I can come up with. I've got a lot of dirt on these bastards already."

Four days later Paul read an e-mail which sent chills up and down his spine: "Mr. Shackelford, you will leave the CCPOA out of your story. If you mention the CCPOA with regards to the data mailed to you by Max Lemon, you will suffer dire consequences. If your car explodes with you in it, your apartment burns down or your mother dies like your brother did, it will be your fault. You can consider this a joke or a scare tactic (only) if you want, but I assure you, our reach, power and influence is stronger than you think. You fuck with the CCPOA and we will send you to meet your maker."

Paul called the F.B.I. and was told by a field agent that this e-mail had been routed and rerouted and could not be traced.

Jesse McCartney (actor/singer) who was a pal of Paul's suggested this, "Dude, let's get the hackers at Defcon to trace this."

Kevin Mchaffey, Alex Bezner and two unnamed hackers (rumor has it they are U. C. Davis students) were able to trace the e-mail back to Sacramento, California. It came from a computer at the headquarters of the CA Correctional Peace Officers Association. Paul gave the trace data to Jan Sulley who was the Sacramento D.A. Jan told Paul, "We can't conduct an investigation based upon an illegal search. This case is closed."

Paul contacted the Attorney General of CA and got the same dismissal! "My life is at stake here. My mother's life has been threatened. Can't you at least call the CCPOA and let them know you're aware of the threat. Maybe just hearing from law enforcement will be enough to get them off me," Paul told Mr. Lockyer's assistant.

"We are not gonna call the CCPOA. We have no legal grounds to contact them. Idle threats are e-mailed to people all the time. If I were you, I'd just forget the CCPOA, forget your story and forget the threat," A. G. Assistant Barankin told Paul and hung up.

"Damn! I wonder if the fact that the CCPOA gave the Attorney General one hundred grand for his campaign is influencing this disregard for my safety. As a matter of fact, the CCPOA gave Jan Scully ten grand."

* * *

Back in the prison, I was reading a missive from Clay Aiken which said, "I am gay. I plan to come out of the closet and admit I'm gay on Oprah. I have come to a place where I'm happy, secure in who I am as a human. And I am not defined by my sexuality. So, Sherman, I hope you don't stop writing me simply because I'm gay."

I was flabbergasted. I got paged over the prison intercom to report to my counselor. When I got to his office, he gave me a nasty look and said, "Do you know Attorney Murray J. Janus? He wants you to call his office ASAP."

I called Murray and he said, "I'm very busy, Sherman but I got a frantic call from Paul Shackelford. The prison wouldn't deliver a message for him so he asked me to call. Paul needs you to call him ASAP."

"Hell, I figured he'd be up here to see me by now. What does he want?" I replied.

"I've absolutely no clue. Just call the man."

I hung up and called Paul.

"Thank God you called, Sherman. We have a major problem. It is the CCPOA. They are livid! They have threatened my life and my mother's."

Thirty minutes and two collect calls later, I told Paul, "Kill the story, my brother. Do not do this story. Listen to me clearly. I am not going to lose you! I feel partially responsible for Jeremy dying. If he hadn't known me, he wouldn't have been in D.C. and he wouldn't have had that car crash. The CCPOA may have killed a captain at Old Folsom Prison. I've heard many tales about them and their power. I can't take that kind of chance on *your* life. You get all your stuff back from Mrs. Collins. You get all of Jeremy's notes and anything you've ever written on these issues. You get all of my notes and you send them to Attorney Gerry Spence. Attorney Gerry Spence will get his secretary, Rosemary to type it all up as a transcript. He will then mail them to me and I will probably just write a damned book. And the book will hit so big that by the time the CCPOA knows about it, you'll be able to afford twenty-four hours a day armed guards. Now this call is recorded and they will listen to it in thirteen days. Before that time, I will have the F.O.I. at your house and your mom's house guarding you and her, I promise."

I hung up with Paul and called one of my stealth supporters. This is a person whose name I shall never reveal. And our calls are always concise, cryptic and legal. This person is a former government official. This person has logistics, intelligence and weapons training. This person is (indeed) on a first name basis with Condeleeza Rice, Bill Clinton as well as Colin Powell.

Within one hour of my four-minute call to this individual, there were no less than three armed former F.B.I. Agents trailing, watching and guarding Paul as well as his mother 24/7 and they (Paul and his mom) had no idea. I was serious. I knew the power, wrath and the corruption of the CCPOA. As for my own life, I didn't allow my fear to stop me. Quite candidly, I had/have more data in the hands of persons, in safety deposit boxes, etc., etc., than the CCPOA could ever fathom. And *if* or when they set me up (again) or have me killed, I'd have more power, influence and credibility in death than I could ever have in life anyway. I had planned for death the day I wrote my second tome.

And although I had some powerful people in my corner, i.e., Bruce Springsteen, Bono, Bon Jovi, Eminem, Simon Cowell, Geraldo Rivera, Jodie Evans, George Soros, Peter B. Lewis, Mel Bacon, John Sperling, Jeff Bezos, T. D. Jakes, Tom Hayden, John Densmore, Denzel Washington, James Earl Jones, Taylor Hackford, Jamie Foxx, Tavis Smiley, Bev Smith, Dick Gregory, John Elsmore, John O'Dell, Ashton Kutcher, Ofari Hutchison, Omar Epps, Danny Glover, Benjamin McKenzie, Adam Brody, David E. Kelly and Tom Joyner to name a few... I still knew the CCPOA could order a hit any day of the week. They could punish, transfer, ad-seg, abuse or set me up any day of any week. They sent inmates to PHU and the SHU every day as retaliation and doctored up paperwork to make it appear to be for the *safety* and *security* of the institution. I knew their power, control and wrath. So I let Jesse Jackson, Al Sharpton, Dick Scruggs, Attorney Diexler, Professor Mike Vitiello and numerous others know, "If I'm ever dead in *prison*, C.D.C. killed me. It won't be suicide or homicide. Spend whatever it takes to get the best investigators money can buy to prove it was orchestrated by the few dangerous, sophisticated and dastardly prison guards in the CCPOA."

I decided to write. I had messed around years ago and found a calling higher than me. I had stumbled upon the potency of the written word. I had learned to escape the confines of the barbed wire and concrete cages by *writing* and *reading*. I had abandoned my personal struggle for justice and opted to look outside of myself and find a purpose for my suffering. I knew there had to be a reason the Creator allowed me to go to prison.

I missed the limousines, yachts, my fine cars and all of the trappings of outside success. But away in my cold jail cell, I had begun a journey from the inside to the outside and I was bold enough to tell it like it is. I had nothing to lose. Had I been free, perhaps my integrity, boldness and candor would or could be compromised or diluted. In civilian life, the *desire for power* and political expediency and correctness has destroyed the integrity of mighty men and mighty women. There is nothing more unsightly than a compromised soul. A tongue tamed by a desire for political gain. A voice stifled or even silenced by a desire for profit. A pen censored, altered or distorted by a desire for acceptance or a need to please... But that's the *power* of the prison cell. That's perhaps the one benefit of being a convict. You're at the bottom of the barrel. There is nobody to impress. You either verify their low opinion of you by wallowing at the bottom in despair, hate or anger or you rise up and take a stand. If you are mobile, you can move no lower. You're at rock bottom. The only way you can move is to move upward. I had no election to win. I had no paparazzi to appease. I had no constituency to please. As far as most people were concerned, I was already dead. I was a prisoner. I was what the D.A. said I was! I was as all prisoners are. I was a predator! I was a thug, a thief, a rapist, a molester, and a dreg on society.

Hell, I used to wonder why they ever gave us clothes in prison! With the way most prisoners are abandoned, left out, locked out and forgotten about, I figured we would be better off declared as savages! It would show America what she truly thought of us.

"They should strip us of all clothing and just let us walk around as the savages they think we are. When they give us a set of clothing and some food and a TV, it distorts the reality of what they truly think of us. If they stopped playing games, took our clothing, took the TV and took the games, etc., society would see what her prisons were uncut. They are warehouses! They are cages. They are factories of hopelessness, rage, racism and universities of thuggery.

I want us all naked, hungry and transparent. This will show America what prison really is. And it will cause those in power to declare prison as a *last resort*! Half the guys here would be pardoned and let out immediately. America would decide hastily that the weed smoker, burglar, wrongly convicted and car thief did not belong in prison. And the one's remaining would build their lives up and thrive or kill each other off. Hell, it's a slow death machine anyway in most of these prisons." I had written in a letter to Tavis Smiley years back.

I felt God had set me up for a miracle! I felt my mission was to save lives! I knew the power of *written words*. I had watched judges wreck lives, separate families, create fatherless homes and take boys off the streets with the *stroke* of a *pen* (written words). I knew that every single man I saw in prison, every case I read about in the newspaper in which there was a conviction, i.e., a sentence of *twenty-five years to life* was the result of the *written words*.

You cannot go to prison unless the judge signs (*written word*) off on the *conviction* and he must *write in* (*stroke of the pen*) your sentence.

On any given day, a judge could, at will, sign a document which would set any man (i.e. Geronimo Pratt, Rubin "Hurricane" Carter) free! A judge could find any reason he wanted to for sending a man to prison, taking his life and freedom and yes, setting a man free. I had time to think, analyze, scrutinize, dissect and theorize. I saw the discrepancy and sinister implications of unequal justice and distorted justice.

I was angry! It angered me that a woman was locked up on fraud charges (non-violent - no weapons, no rapes, no murders) for allegedly lying and supposedly planting a finger in a cup of chili at Wendy's and this thieving woman was *held without bail* for her scam!

Yet, Michael R. Woodbury was accused of thirty-one counts of harming a child. Thirty-one counts of wrecking a boy's life! Thirty-one counts of child molestation. Thirty-one counts of being a perverted pedophile and stealing the innocence of a child's life. Yet, Mr. Woodbury walked out of jail with a fifty thousand dollar bail… I was angry. But a judge signed (*stroke of a pen*) the order for this non-violent scam artist to be *held without bail* and like when a judge (*power of the pen* and the *written word*) signs the order of release on bail for an alleged child rapist. I knew what the written word could do. It could save your soul and make you whole. It could lock you up, take your freedom, take your life, set you free and save lives. My calling was to save the lives of our young people who would end up in prison, broke, busted, disgusted, in gangs, raped or killed, if I didn't write. I had to write. *Write or die*! Yes, I had learned how important and how potent the pen could be. It began with words. Words were tools, vehicles and instruments… Words could be bombs! Words could be weapons. Words could start a war or orchestrate a peace treaty. You could use the right words to the right person and get a job, secure a promotion, make a sale or close a deal. Using the wrong words could get you stabbed, get you shot, killed and destroy a deal. I knew the importance of words spoken as well as words written.

I had seen my *grapes* of *hope* crushed into the *raisins* of *despair*. My entrance into the prison had destroyed my ability to touch human lives and psyches (en masse) through my public speaking. And I had begun working on my oratorical skills as early as five years of age. I loved public speaking. I was a student of the greatest of the great: to include but not limited to the King, Dr. Martin Luther King, Jr., John F. Kennedy, Malcolm X, Billy Graham, Zig Zigler, Jesse Jackson, the late Rev. Moses Lee Raglin and Dr. Na'im Akbar. I had come to understand how to move the masses and effect change through the gift of eloquent, articulate and fluent oratory. So, in a sense I felt that when they locked me up, they locked up my gift. Yet, I'd transitioned to the point where I learned every man and woman has at least seven streams or gifts down on the inside.

And what would have happened if they had locked up Clarence Darrow, Johnnie Cochran, Gerry Spence or Willie Gary? Quite frankly, these men depended upon their oratorical skills to often spell bind and mesmerize juries. So had their voices been rendered silent, it could have crippled them or diluted their effectiveness. They would have been taken out of their element. And lots of great trial lawyers are horrible appellate lawyers. The appeals specialist such as Ephraim Margolin, Gerald Uelmen, Dennis Riordin and Floyd Abrams were nerds, book worms and of utmost importance - *writers*. Gerry Spence often complained about how difficult it is to *write*. He agreed with me that some great, powerful and bone-chilling speeches looked like shit on paper. But if Gerry, Clarence, Barry or Johnnie had been incarcerated physically, I believe they would recognize they need not be incarcerated mentally, spiritually or emotionally. And they would have transferred the power and reach of the spoken word into an appreciation and effective utilization of the *written* hand. Ipso facto, practice often makes perfect. And the more often you do something *if* you analyze, scrutinize and objectively review what you've done, you get better at it.

I was not going to allow Paul to get hit by the CCPOA. I couldn't sleep at night knowing that his mom had lost two sons because of **me**. Nor would I have been capable of dealing with the burden of having Paul lose his mom because of his connection to me.

I had to do this! I would write this damned book. I knew how to write. I didn't need any pats on the back or compliments to write. No one needed to tell me how great I was or how wonderful I could be, etc., to get me to write. Hell, I felt like, how could I not write. I decided that the only shot I had at remaining relevant and participating in civilian activity was to write stuff on the inside, which would be perused, analyzed and scrutinized on the outside. I didn't need anybody to tell me I could write or that I should write. I didn't need any lectures on initiative, self-help or how to get started. I just sat my ass down and picked up a pen and wrote!

And it used to irk me and quite frankly, piss me off to see how few guys in prison would write. How not to write or how could you not write was my issue. It baffled my mind. I used to try to motivate guys to write. "Write a book, a song, a poem or a letter to the editor. Write your warden, mayor, senator, congressman," I'd tell them. But then I became a bit cynical. And I decided that "the poor you'll have

162

with you always," which was spoken by Jesus, could be interpreted to mean some people just ain't gonna do nothing no matter how much you tell them. True, I still believed in change, salvation, transmogrification and the ability to teach willing students how to succeed. Yet, I also knew you couldn't save anybody who didn't *want to be saved*.

Jeremy (rest in peace) had been the right person at the right time to attract the interests and intrigue, which the issues I had researched needed. In his death, he had passed the baton on to his brother, Paul. The *power of the written word* was exemplified in the fact that all of the notes, journal data and writings left behind by Jeremy had motivated and convinced Paul to *do something*. And perhaps my missives and the power of my pen also played some small role in Paul's desire, as he read what I wrote to Jeremy.

And so the CCPOA had apparently contemplated putting a hit on a young man who cared. It didn't surprise me. I had seen enough not to even be shocked by the evils, wickedness or violence of some members of the CCPOA. I had seen mailroom employees call persons whom we prisoners would try to reach out to and tell them, "If I were you I'd not write him back." Or "If I were you, I'd call the prison and say, I don't want a letter from inmate so and so." I had also personally watched them steal mail. They played games with the public. I.e., McGeorge Law Professor Mike Vitiello sent me a letter and a CCPOA member in the mailroom wrote "not without prior approval" on the envelope and returned it to Vitiello!

Professor Vitiello e-mailed my office and informed them and I filed a complaint. The response? "Professor Vitiello is either mistaken or lying." He re-mailed it to me and to date I still don't have it. We have informed Rod Hickman and the governor. They didn't want me to have the letter because it was complimentary and inspirational. It contained the words "gripping" by Professor Vitiello (Folks like David Jay, Graham Bensinger, Dan Weaver (Mt. Juliet High School), Michael Stather, Aimee Allison, Mitchell Johnson, Chris Shaull, Chris Angel, David Schankula, Aiello (Mansfield, MA), the Paola family (Carmel, NY), the Linz family (Cincinatti) and John Bradley have got to know this book is out. I.e., John Bradley is a wrongful convictions *Father Teresa*. He cares. He began *Justice on Trial* because he cares... More on *Justice on Trial* in the revised edition... I want you to let Craig Scott, David Jay, Jeff Love, Josh Askins, etc., know the book is out. Do it today...) as it related to his opinion of my book, "From the Palace to the Prison".

And *if* I read where a prominent law professor found the writings of a lowly inmate in the prison to be gripping or spellbinding, it might motivate me to write more. This is exactly how these clowns think. If I am led to believe that the public is not reading my work, doesn't like my work or is not responding to my mail, maybe I'll lose hope and give up. It has certainly worked that way before.

The prisons have cracked a lot of minds, busted dreams and arrested the development of many men and many kids.

The daily abuses, rigid programming, excessive lock downs, rapes, beatings and stabbings have driven many men to despair. I saw a guy who was razor sharp, articulate and intelligent, literally lose his mind. He went so crazy that he cut off his own penis and flushed it down the toilet.

Prisons are filled with anger, shame, hurt, fear and madness. This hurt and fear manifests itself in all kinds of ways. Fear in the prisons disguises itself as racism, bullying, fanaticism, alcoholism, drug addiction and even *comicalism*.

Prison is a cold, bitter, dank and dark place. Demons are alive and well in the prison. And prison is like a rattlesnake. It bites everything that comes into contact with it. I could see it. I could sense it. I felt it in the pit of my belly and I heard it in the air. My soul could detect it.

So I had to write. I'd go berserk if I didn't write. If I wrote hard, long and strong enough Steven Spielberg would read. Denzel, Omar Epps, Clay Aiken, Donald Trump, George Soros, Jodie Evans, President Nelson Mandela and Howard Stern all told me to write. When I would lie down and go to sleep, my angels said to write.

When Martin Luther King, Jr., Mother Teresa, Mahatma Ghandi and Christ my savior visited me in my sleep, they said "write." I could hear the right Reverend *Hosea Williams*, Andrew Young, Bev Smith, Randi Rhodes, Christine Craft and Professor Cornel West telling me to "Write Sherman, write."

It's not who *I* am but it is *what I do*. And I needed to tell my fellow inmates, guys in juveniles, troubled teens in Rancho Cordova, Citrus Heights, Oak Park, Perry Homes, Fair Street Bottoms and Watts that *you can do it too*!

And so I had to find a way to get Paul out of it and to do it my damned self.

"Sherman, I can't let go this easily. This is about my brother, Jeremy," Paul later told me in a telephone call. He said, "Trials come to make you strong. How can I quit now? After all the time, effort and money I've put in this, you just want me to fold up my tent, hold my head down and walk away like a whipped puppy? I'm not a loser, man. I can't quit."

I certainly understood Paul's strong constitution and his fervent desire to see it through to the end.

"Paul, I'm not asking you to quit, White boy. I know White folks want the credit for what Black folks do. It would be entirely out of character for you to allow me to finish this project *alone* as the ultimate author of a tome without your **name** in it."

"You're a fool," Paul said laughing. "I need to be involved. Thank you for caring about me, dude."

I interrupted, "Hey Wood, don't get all mushy on me. I have one gay friend, Clay Aiken. You know I suspect Tim Goebel of being gay also. That's enough for my gay posse. I love all God's children but you *stay*, don't go *gay* on me, Paul."

Paul laughed again. "Compromise, *Mr. Manning*. That's all I'm asking. Compromise. You'll get all the data, dude. It's already in the office of Gerry Spence. I talked to Rosemary. She is doing it up like a transcript; not a manuscript. You rush it to press under your name in tome form. But tell it all, dude. Don't redact my findings. Don't exclude my plans. Don't exclude the threats on my life by the CCPOA. And then when the book is out, I won't need Reid Collins or any newspaper. They'll do the story on their own. And regardless of how they dilute it or pollute the story, the real people who want the real answers will get the book and get the story. Then the CCPOA would be foolish to try to harm me or anyone associated with me. And of everything we know about Darchuk and the CCPOA, they are not stupid. They are methodical, professional and dangerous. But they are not stupid. When the book is out, I live. Now can we reach this compromise? Will you promise not to leave me out of the story?"

I told Paul, "White folks win again. I'm Black and the eight ball is Black. And it goes down and the game is lost. The cue ball always win. We'll do it your way. And if it is a success, White politicians like Delay, Bird, Blunt and Bush will credit **you** with exposing these evils which they knew about all the damn time. And I'll get buried in the prison system for my name being on the damn book. You'll be Seymour Hirsh and I'll be Joseph. They'll punish me for interpreting the dream for you King Pharaoh."

Paul chuckled but retorted, "But, but Joseph *got out* of the prison, my brother. He got out and became a *prince in the palace*! Don't forget *the rest of the story*. Don't act like the news media. Don't eviscerate the full story."

I told Paul, "I didn't know you knew the Bible, my brother."

"That's because I don't wave a Christian flag. I have thirty-eight videos from sermons by T. D. Jakes, Paula White and even Billy Graham. And don't forget, I went to Manpower myself. You don't have to have a flag on your car to be patriotic. Just because I don't carry a Bible in my hand doesn't mean I don't have the Lord in my heart. I know who Jesus Christ is."

On Friday evening, I read my mail with enthusiasm. I had a missive from Jason Beck of East Valley Church near Sacramento telling me that one hundred and seventy-five members of East Valley Church had come together to purchase a block of three hundred and fifty copies of my book, "*Palace to Prison*" to donate to juveniles.

I read a letter from my pal, Land Kligerman of Stamford, Connecticut. I read a missive from my good friend, Ryne DeGrave of Green Bay, Wisconsin. Sean Cashman (Sydney, Australia), Josh Davis (Salt Lake City), Matt Maloney, John Lechner, Actress Vanessa Redgrave (Boston) and Professor Scott Sandage all wrote me.

The missive from Craig Scott really, really stood out to me. Craig Scott is the son of Beth Nimmo and he resides in Littleton, Colorado. - "Dear Sherman Manning, I have read all of your books. I've also heard that you are writing a new book with Paul Shackelford."

I said, "Shit. Who told him that? Who else knows? This is supposed to be a damned secret."

Continuing on... "I will personally e-mail each and every person you name or mention (good, bad or indifferent) in your next book. I know the importance of grass root work. And I also know from experience how good it feels to see your name in a book. You mentioned me in 'American Dream/A Search for Justice' and it was a full thirteen months before I ever knew my name was in it. Somebody in France e-mailed me about the Rachel Scott Foundation and mentioned they had read of me in your book. So you don't have to worry about *mentionees* not knowing, with whatever book you all are writing now. I will take three hours per day, seven days per week, as long as it takes, to call, e-mail and text every single living person whose *name* I see in your book. I hope this helps with publicity.

Your writing impacted me in a powerful manner. You are a no-nonsense, scathing and raw writer. You don't dress it up. You just get down and dirty. It is a unique and unusual style. It wowed me in a crazy kind of way. I hope you will never stop writing. I don't know why they allow you to stay in the prison. If I were Governor, I'd have you on my payroll. Your job would be to rectify the prisons. I would

166

utilize your expertise to turn injustice on its head. They're crazy to allow you to wallow in the prison."

Craig's letter went on to stroke my ego and pump me up, but I could sense a deep integrity and an unusual authenticity within the body of his missive.

Tim Goebel's letter was quite nice.   Johnny Weir wrote a gracious missive also. Clay Aiken's missive contained a card signed by Anthony Fedorov, Bo Bice, Simon Cowell, Constantine Maroulis and Timothy Sauer. Clay was always kind, caring and generous in his writing. Regardless of his sexuality, this young man (in my opinion) was more *man* than many of *us* who are masculine and macho. Clay didn't mind telling you he cared about you and that he could feel your pain or hurt. At the end of the day, I liked Clay.

My favorite female writer (and fortunately there were lots of them, unbeknownst to my wife) was Paris Hilton. I was never really certain that Paris really (really) wrote these letters. I hoped she did but they were quite intimate and sexual. Paris knew which buttons to press. She knew the power of words. But she would not even send me pictures of her. I wanted Paris in a G-string. I really did... Queen Latifah wrote me every now and then. Jimmy Kimmel never wrote back but who cares. Uncle Frank was my real hero anyway.

Tavis Smiley wrote, "Your work deserves awards which I'm not even qualified to give you. I believe that sooner or later some of these so-called writers groups will come calling to award you for being the most prolific non-fiction author on the West Coast. Sherman, I learned from the late Mayor Tom Bradley that sometimes it takes a while for you to see the fruit of your labor. But if you are sincere and committed, the accolades will come in time. A lot of folks like Jamie Foxx, Aretha Franklin, Samuel L. Jackson and Morgan Freeman have personally told me they read your books. Taylor Hackford and Spike Lee are fans of yours. I'm not stroking your ego, bro, I'm just telling you, your *momma* should be proud of you.

"I plan to do a show about all your books. I'll bring on Willie Gary, Rubin 'Hurricane' Carter, Professor Dylan Rodriguez, George Soros, Cornel West or Professor Mike Vitiello (or somebody) to discuss your books. I can't tell you exactly when but the show is coming. Stay tuned and just *keep the faith*."

* * *

...Martha Stewart, Denzel Washington, Tavis Smiley, Rubin "Hurricane" Carter and Lisa Ling were there. Gayle King, Harvey Levin, Barry Tarlow, Chris Ochoa, Todd Bridges, Malcolm Jamal, Jamie Foxx, Omar Epps, Bev Smith, Dick Gregory, Steve Madden,

Peter Jennings (rest in peace), Dan Rather, PLN, Prisontalk.com, Tiffany Chiles, ET, MTV, American Urban Radio Network, ABC, CBS, NBC and the ACLU were there. A lot of British Reporters were there at the State Capitol in Sacramento at 9:00 a.m. as Paul Shackelford held the press conference the day the book rolled off the press. Harper Collins' CEO was there. Hugh Hefner, Larry Flynt and Dominic Dunn were also there. Paul flashed that billion dollar smile and said, "*Blue-Eyed Blonde* would not have been possible were it not for the leg work of my brother, Jeremy Schackelford. And it wouldn't be possible without the brilliance, faith, courage, concern and perseverance of my only Black brother on the planet. His name is *Joseph* and he's fifty-eight miles away from these bright lights and cameras and dignitaries. He is the brother who interpreted this dream and made the dream become a reality. With no concern for his own safety, he put pen to paper. He worked the telephone, the post office and his outside contacts. He lobbied professors, students, pastors and activists. He wrote when others slept. He fought when others wept. He should be here with you and me.

"This Joseph, of whom I speak, is Sherman Diahric Manning. He is residing in a gated community called Mule Creek State Prison. He is a good man with a great heart and we should all be thankful for his work.

"On behalf of Sherman D. Manning, Sabine Andrist Manning, Betty and James Manning, Junior, Kimberly and the A&M Enterprises, I'd like to read to you distinguished members of the press and dignitaries the following statement from Sherman D. Manning.

"It reads like this: Each one of you should kiss the crack of my Black ass. I don't give a damn who you are or how many films you've made, you can excuse my French but kiss my ass. How dare you stand there at the Capitol, smiling and laughing in the sun when you now know the plight of the *Blue-Eyed Blonde*? Here in the prisons are your brothers, sisters, babies, boys and sons. They are being penetrated, devastated and raped every minute. They're having their bowels ripped wide open and their intestines severed, with penises forced down their throats, broom handles forced up their butts, their minds damaged while you fart your way through life, eat steak, drink champagne and pretend to love America.

'How do you think they feel when they see you on TV sending billions of dollars to aid Tsunami victims in Asia, victims of tragedy in Indonesia, etc.? What do you think they feel in their belly when they see your shock and rage by the photos, which you saw depicting the sadistic treatment of the prisoners at Abu Ghraib when they know they are treated worse right here at Riker's Island, Reidsville, San Quentin and Pelican Bay? What do you think your family members in prisons, right here at home, feel when they know the abuse, violence, suffering and sorrow which fills up the jails, juveniles and prisons right here in America and *you don't* give a damn? Taylor Hackford, Mr. Rather, Hugh, Larry, ABC, CBS, NBC, I know ya'll are there with Paul and you hear these words. I don't have a long speech. Prison has taught me to say what I mean and mean what I say.

My message to you on behalf of all those in the jails and prisons here in America is this. You remember John Singleton's movie, "Boys In the Hood?" At the end of that masterpiece, Ice Cube came across the street and told Cuba Gooding, "I watched the news last night and I saw a lot about all those things going on over in Ethiopia. But my brother was murdered. A good kid, on his way to college. All this damn media and they didn't say nothing about my brother. Trey, either they don't *know*, don't *show* or just don't care bout what's going on in the hood."

So I end up where I began, all of you phony ass media and fake ass reporters who are scared to have an opinion. Those of you who are so professional that you can cover tragedies in which babies lose their parents and mother's lose their children and you don't even shed a tear. You, who are so shell shocked and sold out that you are afraid to tell the truth. You can kiss my ass.

Paul said, "That ends Mr. Manning's statement. And the only thing I'll add is you can also kiss *my* Lilly White ass."

With that Paul turned and walked away from the microphone. Harper Collins' CEO was pale. Paul marched to the waiting triple stretch Hummer limousine with the bulletproof and tinted windows. When the Marine escort opened the car door, Paul looked inside and saw **me**.

Then he turned over and caught the saliva coming out of his mouth and realized (as he opened his eyes) that it was only a *dream*. "Damn," Paul said. "I thought that shit was real. I gotta go visit Sherman anyway. Even though the plan has changed and he's doing a book, I still wanna meet the man."

Paul got up, showered and brushed his teeth. He took a crap and jumped back into the shower. This time he sang "Amazing Grace" in the shower. Out of nowhere, Paul began to sob, cry and weep like a baby. "Damn, I miss my brother," Paul said. "Damn, I wish your ass was here, my brother. Grow that gray beard and smoke that cigar, my brother. You were supposed to get older with me. On stagehands on shoulders with me. If it wasn't for the will that God hath made, I'd turn back the hands of time and take your place. Sitting here in all of this misery, thinking about what you meant to me. Even though I can't see your face, I know your ass is in a better place."

Paul had waxed poetic. He stuck his head underneath the spigot and allowed the water to wash away his tears. Paul dried off and got out of the shower. He dressed himself and picked up the newspaper. He read about a fraud trial down in Alabama. The evidence in Richard Scrushy's fraud trial made the goings on at Health South Corp. sound more like an episode of "The Dukes of Hazzard" than the operations of a damned Fortune 500 Company to Paul.

It seemed to Paul that a picture emerged of a southern-fried culture at the rehabilitation and medical services chain. Paul read where witnesses told of Scrushy hosting meetings in the middle of a sprawling Alabama Lake that was known for floating beer bashes, bass fishing and bar brawls breaking out at a going away party for a key executive who quit the company rather than get involved in the fraud, which according to prosecutors, amounted to $2.8 billion in inflated earnings over six years.

As Paul read the article in the New York Times, written by Andrew Ross Sorkin, Health South seemed a mighty long way from the starched white shirt world of Wall Street. Prosecutors said Scrushy was at the heart of a conspiracy to overstate Health South earnings from 1996 through 2001, directing subordinates to commit fraud so it would appear the company was meeting Wall Street estimates. However, Donald Watkins who was a prestigious Birmingham lawyer, claimed Scrushy was a small-town guy who cut grass and pumped gas as a teen before earning a degree in respiratory therapy - and was duped by underlings who committed fraud on their own. "This sound's like the *Ken Lay* defense," Paul mumbled.

Richard Scrushy was free on ten million dollars bail. Paul read of two garage bands fronted by Scrushy, a rock group named Proxy and a country group called Dallas County Line in homage to the Backwater where Scrushy grew up. But now the new twist, as Paul read was Pastor Scrushy. Lately Scrushy has been projecting a more churching image, singing hymns with his third wife, Leslie and even preaching in two churches. Paul thought this all reminded him of the prison system. Corrupting with a capital *C*, lies, cheating and deception. Paul's reading, research and sources had painted a picture of the American Judicial System, which reeked of scandal, i.e., the California prison system.

Paul was shocked and awed when he learned he could not send me a book, a tape, a CD or even a radio. All books at Mule Creek must come from a warehouse and the rules change everyday. All tapes and CD's must come from one company; *Access*. Paul learned that certain CCPOA members had access to kickbacks and payoffs from *Access*. This is why policy was designed to prohibit Amazon.com, Barnes and Nobel, etc. or any other company from doing business with inmates. If inmates' families were gonna buy radios, tapes, CDs and Tvs, doggonit the CCPOA would get rich in the process. This same type monopolistic empire was also being built via the inmate telephone system. C.D.C. implemented a no-bid policy and hand delivered the multimillion-dollar contract to MCI WorldCom. In exchange for the monopoly, WorldCom gave millions of dollars in kickbacks to the CCPOA, certain wardens and donated a multimillion dollar, state of the art telephone monitoring system to C.D.C.

Paul had come to believe that C.D.C. was the Enron or Health South of the prison systems. While prison guards in the Southeast struggled to make ends meet, guards in California had strong-armed and milked the public's finances to the tune of millions of dollars. California prison guards are the best paid, least qualified and worst educated in the country.

Lately, every time Paul read of a business scandal, fraud or misappropriation of funds, he immediately compared the scam to C.D.C.

"How could California citizens sit back and allow prison authorities to get away with abuse, scandal, beatings, corruption and get rich in the process?" Paul asked himself.

"These guys are pros!" Paul said to Scott in a telephone conversation. "They are specialists in their scams. They bilked Californians out of tens of millions of dollars in overtime pay last year. They were a half billion dollars over budget. They discourage education by making it nearly impossible for inmates to get *books* in prisons. They limit where they can order books, how many and how often. They discourage religion. A local pastor can't send them a recording of his church service. I'm telling you, Scott, C.D.C. is the worst I've ever seen. They run some prisons in Mexico more correctly than C.D.C."

And Scott inquired, "How do they get away with it, Paul?"

Paul sighed, "It's the union stupid. The CCPOA has nearly thirty-five thousand paying members. These members pay seventy dollars per month each. You do the math. And they buy amnesty via wining, dining, vacationing and buying politicians. I have a list of over thirty-six California politicians who have received gifts, checks and goods of fifty thousand dollars or *more* from the good ole guards'

union.   And there are some elite, powerful State senators,
assemblymen, the Attorney General, etc. who receive hundreds of
thousands of dollars each, yearly from the CCPOA. Former Governor
Gray Davis got two million dollars from the CCPOA."

Scott interjected, "So when guys like *Sherman* write, grieve and
file complaints about guard corruption, etc. those complaints are
dismissed out of hand because the people empowered to punish are
basically on payroll."

"You got it," Paul said. "And make no mistake about it, Scott,
these guys are deadly. Some of them are more obstreperous, bellicose
and volatile than the convicts whom they guard. Some of them are gun
toting, pepper spray carrying hillbillies out of the woods. Think about
it, pal, what other job do you know of where you need only a GED to
earn eighty grand a year? And to become a lieutenant you need only a
high school diploma. Some lieutenants in California earn one hundred
and twenty thousand dollars per year with overtime. If you wanna be a
warden just take a correspondence course and get or buy an Associates
Degree.   And the warden's control one hundred million dollar
budgets!"

Scott interjected, "No way!"

"Listen," Paul continued, "there is a gang in C.D.C. which is not
Bloods, Crips, AB or Skinheads. It's called *The Green Wall* or 23. It
is a prison guard gang. They are deadly. They make the Gambino
crime family look like choirboys. If there were ever an outside audit,
hidden camera investigation of the CCPOA, its money, monopoly and
the crimes perpetrated by this fraudulent union, I'm convinced half the
guards in California would be fired. And thirty percent of them would
go to Federal prison. John Grisham could not write an embellished
crime tale about the C.D.C. which would come anywhere near their
corruption. I'm telling you, my brother, they are deadly. And yet they
keep prisoners kept. Get this…Max Lemon was an Associate Warden
earning a hundred grand per year. He had twenty years in the system
when he became a whistle blower. It's on the record. He *cried* as he
testified before the senate in 2004 and begged for twenty-four hours
protection for his family. He walked the yards of the prisons for
twenty years with murderers, molesters and rapists. He inspected the
cells of convicted serial killers and fratricidal maniacs. He was not a
coward. But he was more afraid of the wrath of the CCPOA then he
was of the convicts in the prison. Need I say more?"

Scott replied with one word, "Wow!"
* * *

Back in the prison, I had gotten the transcripts from Gerry Spence and Rosemary. I had spent eighteen to twenty hours per day for nearly two weeks combing through the compilation of Jeremy's journal, missives from me to Jeremy, research data by Paul, notes to Paul from me, data from reporters, journalists, agents, professors, lawyers and sex crimes experts. I read stuff that neither Jeremy nor Paul had told me about. Brilliant computer thespian Ero Carrera of F-Secure, Inc. in San Jose had compiled numerous secret reports, which can't be mentioned herein.

Mike Farrell of Toms River, New Jersey, Ryne DeGrave of Green Bay, Land Kligerman (Stamford, CT), Peter Grossman, Jeffrey Duvall, Jennifer R. Blood, Lori Grub, Adam Morgan, Irena Medavoy, Tzvetan Chaliavski, Marcos Garza, Eric Bryant and Matt Novak all contributed to Paul's findings. Reports, critiques, opinions and essays were submitted to Paul by Malcolm Jamal Warner, Kevin Kinsella, Matthew McReynolds, Joseph Marks, Scott Merrill, Tim Krebase, Professor Scott Sandage, Dylan Rodriguez, Mike Vitiello, Clark Kelso, Josh Davis and James Emslander.

Some of this stuff was new to me. I got lost in working to put this all together in book format. I sort of felt like it wasn't the usual kinda book I was used to writing. I felt more like an editor putting together an anthology. This "*Blue-Eyed Blonde*" was unique and I guessed that perhaps it was one of a kind. I couldn't believe it when Paul sent me a picture of *Eminem* with a note from Eminem himself stating, "Yo Sherm, you can use this picture on the cover of your book, man. It's all good. Just be sure to tell all the college jocks, cheerleaders, nerds, geeks and freaks to buy my music, man. Much respect and props to you for what you're doing up in the pen. Stay up, bro."

"Paul Shackelford is bad," I said to myself. I was sometimes befuddled and bemused as I perused and re-wrote some of the stuff Paul came up with.

"How did you get Master P, Shyne, 50 Cent, The Game and P. Diddy to write essays for *my* book, man?" I asked Paul in one of our telephone calls.

"You mean *our* book?" Paul replied. Paul went on, "It wasn't that difficult, dude. Bev Smith and Doug Banks helped line up a lot of these folks. And when Eminem agreed by saying, 'Dude, you can even put my (expletive) picture on the front cover of the book. I'm down with this cause. If it's gonna save some little girl's like *Haley* and little boys from being molested - I'm down. Count me in.' That helped a lot."

There are two missives I did not wish to publicize in this book due to *my* vested interest and connections to these people. However, Paul insisted that we owed it to Jeremy to publish them. "Dear Jeremy," the missive began, "My name is Brenda Smith. I reside in Atlanta, Georgia. My biological son is in prison. He will not allow us to see him in jail."

It is unclear as to why this letter was written. Jeremy had placed it in a folder and the envelope, which it was mailed in, had been discarded.

The letter went on, "I know for a fact that my son should not be in prison. This judicial system ought to be ashamed. Our nation should be ashamed. I wonder how long we will continue to lock up innocent, wrongly convicted and brilliant men and women. I believe it is racist. My son was outspoken, opulent and a very high profile speaker. And gumption tells me there are too many pieces of evidence which points toward a tendency by law enforcement to invent a way to lock up potential revolutionaries. My son is unique. He's not just another rhetorician. He is pragmatic and was influential enough to galvanize the support of activists to advance his agenda. He thought, analyzed, strategized and vocalized his beliefs. I remember at his high school graduation he gave a speech titled, 'Where do we go from here?' He said 'Black people are told over and over that they ought to pull themselves up by their own bootstraps. You can't do that if you have no boots. What Blacks must do now is to *get ready* to *stand up*. Stand up for justice, stand up for righteousness, stand up for family and stand up for friends. Notice I said *get ready* to stand up. We can't stand until we *find our legs*. The racism, slavery, brainwashing and hatred, which we have endured here in North America, has been spiritual, mental, physical, economic and psychological torture. We've been pinned down for so long over here that our legs are numb.

'I remember one time I physically fell asleep in a squatting position. My legs were pinned or folded beneath me in an unusual position. And when I woke up, I literally could not *feel* my feet or legs. The light was out and it was dark so I couldn't see. It literally felt as if I had *no* legs. I thought I'd been amputated from the waist down. But my momma came in the room and *turned the light on*, so I could see. I found my legs and she helped me get up. But my legs were too numb and I couldn't *stand up*. Momma had to hold me til my blood began circulating and flowing again. Blacks may sometimes act lazy, look lazy and some of them may actually *be* lazy. But most Blacks in this country want to get up. They want up out of poverty, up out of jail, up out of ignorance and up out of alcoholism. But they

174

were knocked down, stolen, brought here on slave ships and enslaved. And they were held down so long that when Jim Crow and racist laws were finally overturned, they couldn't get up. Their legs and feet went to sleep. And they don't wake up instantly.

'There is a process to get the blood of economics, the blood of education, the blood of responsibility and initiative flowing again. Somebody has to literally help pick you up. And yes, it looked bad for my momma to have to help me up. I'm young, I'm strong and I'm grown.

'Now if my daddy had walked in the room and saw my momma holding and lifting me up, he might have told her to let that boy go. He's grown. He's not a baby. It's not your job to pick him up. You already raised him and took care of him as a child. He's grown now and he needs to stand up on his own! But daddy would have been wrong because daddy would have been only looking at the outside. He didn't, wouldn't and couldn't know the circumstances. Though no fault of my own, my feet were asleep. 'And we have all these outsiders looking and saying Blacks don't need reparations, they were already freed by Mr. Lincoln. But they don't analyze the circumstances. They forget that Mr. Lincoln promised reparations. He promised those freed slaves forty acres of land and a mule each. He lied. He cheated and he reneged. They got neither acres nor mules. They were and are numb. And so even though they got physical freedom they got no economic freedom. And they got no psychological freedom. They were written out of the history books and relegated to the ghettos. 'Psychologists still can't figure out how anybody could go through what we've gone through and produce Dr. Keith Blacks and Ben Carsons. But there are large pockets of poverty stricken Blacks in this country whose legs and feet are still asleep. They are numb. They're not dumb; they are numb. And we must pick them up and get them ready to stand. All they need is a chance. That's why they go to jail. That's why they commit crimes. That's why they lash out. They need a chance.'

"My son gave those kind of radical, outlandish, revolutionary, potent but pragmatic speeches. And this put him on the radar. I know it's hard to believe that somebody wanted him locked up. But the Bay of Pigs is hard to believe. Nobody expected the holocaust. Nobody wanted to believe the Geronimo Pratt story or that doctors killed off Black men by shooting syphilis in their bodies. These tragedies were *hidden in plain* sight. My son should not be in prison…"

I've redacted the final paragraph of Brenda's letter.

The final letter to Jeremy (which Paul insisted I publish) was this: "Dear Jeremy, my name is Leslie Rau. I am a White American. I am not racist and I'm not a bigot. My son (James) should not be in prison. I know a lot of Black and Brown people were set up, discriminated against and wrongly sent to prison. And this is wrong, unfair and often racist. But - I wanted you to know there are other elements involved with wrongful incarceration. My son should not be in prison.

"There are White kids who were set up, lied on and caught up also. There are thousands of Whites who were sent to prison because they (too) were poor and couldn't hire a lawyer. Some of them needed therapy and got jail. Some needed help and got prison instead. Many kids of all races, colors and creeds grew up in dysfunctional homes, foster homes or had drug addicted parents. But when they stand before a judge, none of that is considered. They are convicted of burglary or assault, etc. And the judge hauls them off to prison where they will get an education on how to become *real* criminals. I want violent predators *off the streets*. I want rapists in prison. I want murderers in prison. But I am tired of seeing decent, impressionable and vulnerable young people go off to prison for merely being poor. And I hear that if they are young and White, they get attacked and raped in prison and they'll never again be *right*. Prison ought to be a last resort, Jeremy…"

I redacted the last three sentences of the letter from Mrs. Leslie Rau.

In the meantime, I spoke with Paul a few weeks ago and we argued. He was adamant about visiting me. "I don't even want my *wife* visiting me anymore, Paul. I *hate* people *seeing me in this place*. I don't want my family or friends coming here. It breaks my spirit, diminishes my anger and I experience a variety of complex and conflicting emotions after every single visit. If it's a lawyer, that's different. But I don't want my friends, family or loved ones coming here anymore. I.e., I will never allow my kids to visit me in prison."

Paul replied, "So are you telling me I'm your *friend*? I'm flattered, bro. But I think we have business also and we need to meet."

I replied, "Then meet me in civilian life. Not here. This place is infected. It's demonic, evil and wicked."

Having said that, I methodically moved the subject to money. "How can you afford all this flying around anyway? You have not worked in a long time, Paul."

"Jeremy left a very nice nest egg as well as a two hundred fifty thousand dollar insurance policy. So, my mom is supporting me right now. Plus, I'm certain I'll get a lot of paid interviews after our book comes out."

I replied, "You know I'm not gonna discuss *business* over this telephone, Paul but Attorney Blair Berk, Mr. Barry Tarlow and Bruce Cutler represent me. David Boies also works for me on a few projects so I'm mailing all of them copies of a contract you need to sign. I suggest you get a lawyer to look over it and make adjustments if necessary. But basically, I want all the money from this book to go to a foundation in Jeremy's name and scholarships for inner city kids to go to college. Not Black kids, but *all* poor kids. I want kids in Foster Homes (Black, White, dark and light) and even kids who have been to juvenile to get a second chance. And I want us to pay for their college tuitions and books.

"I had my people at A&M to e-mail Warren Buffet, Bill Gates, George Soros, Denzel and Oprah and numerous others. We're asking them to help us fund college educations for troubled teens. It is going to take a lot of money to do it the way I want it done. I want interdiction programs, which literally removes kids from ghettos, barrios and juveniles and takes them in and puts them in homes, families and environments, which are conducive to learning and growing.

"Paul, too many kids in these broken homes don't have a chance. If they don't get help now, they'll be singing, 'All that I been giving, it's the pain that I've been living. They've got me in the system; why they got to do me like this?' Paul, I know these thirteen and fourteen-year-old boys and girls can make it if we invest in them now. I don't want them singing, 'I tried to make it my way, but got sent on up the highway.' They need us."

Paul interrupted, "Don't tell me you've been listening to Jada Kiss. I thought you were a Jazz man, Sherman!"

"I love Jazz, R&B and Rock also. But it's just that I've been *seeing* what Jada Kiss is rapping about all around me. I despise the use of the N word and I hope one day these brothers will stand up courageously enough to eliminate that word from music. But in the meantime, I've come to understand they are rapping about their lives, their pain and their reality. This is exactly what they live, what they see and feel. And in here, Paul, all I see is White boys, Mexican and Black boys who can truly say, 'I tried to make it my way and got sent on up the highway.' And I want to play a part in breaking the vicious cycle. And Paul, preachers ain't doing it. Churches are not doing it.

"Benny Hinn, Jerry Falwell, Pat Robertson and all of those guys are raising tens of millions of dollars per year. And they are not putting any large portion of that money back into the community. They are not housing the homeless, feeding the hungry or educating

177

the illiterate. I can't find any White boys in prison who are being written to, supported or taken care of by any White pastors or churches. I fail to find any Black or Mexican boys in here who can show me a check from a church. They can't show me a letter written by a pastor saying, 'We'll pay for your college education while you're in prison. We'll send you Rick Warren's book, tapes by Tony Robbins and self-help materials so you can get better while you're in prison.'

"Paul, I find no eighteen year olds or twenty-eight year olds who are being ministered to educationally and rehabilitative*ly* by any churches. What are they doing with the money, bro?

"So instead of just lambasting the churches for what they're not doing, I want *NAPS* and a *Jeremy Foundation* to do it. We can adopt one hundred kids at twelve years of age and our adoption will be educational adoptions. We will shower them with books, tapes, role models and mentors. We will have a network of college students who we pay stipends to go see these kids on weekends and tutor, mentor and inspire them. We'll take them to movie theaters, monuments and museums, etc.

"We will also adopt one hundred prisoners and pay for their college educations. We'll work with *College Beyond Bars* in Boston and also get us some professors, i.e., Mike Vitiello, Dylan Rodriguez, James Fox, Sandage, Kelso, David Coles and John Turley to sign on as mentors. And I don't want this race shit to be a factor. I love the United Negro College Fund. They are a beautiful and necessary organization…but this is the United Shackelford and Manning Fund. And it ain't race based; it's class and needs based. Jesus didn't look at skin. He looked at sin.

"We must pretend to be blind. A blind man doesn't have the blessing (or curse) of being able to separate or judge people on how they appear or the color of their skin. Blind folk have to listen to their hearts, feel the spirit and judge the content of a person's character.

"This has become my vision. The salvation of the youth. And one of our primary objectives must be to keep them out of prison by *any means necessary*. We can't let our White kids go to jail and get raped! We can't let our Black and Brown go to jail and get infected with evil, criminality and hate. And our next objective must be to provide a safe haven for those of our people who are already in prison to not get raped and not get infected. We will dramatize the issues. As Dr. King embarrassed the nation by getting cameras to document people being attacked by dogs and knocked down by water hoses, we must likewise embarrass every prison director, every governor who allows their inmates to get raped, abused and beat. We must show the

178

world what is happening in Riker's Island, LA County Jail, prisons and juveniles nationwide. Having seen the truth about what's happening *inside*, America will demand a change.

"Our third and final objective will be to rescue, assist, lead, guide, treat and employ guys when they get out of prisons. We must rescue them when they come out of the system, Paul."

Paul agreed and (boys will be boys). We concisely discussed the fact that he was leaving that night on a flight to Mexico. He was going to spend two days having sex. Initially he'd wanted to stay in Mexico only two days, fly back in and swing by to visit me. His plans were still on with the exception of the part about visiting me.

After our chat, I called Alexander and had him to call off the detail, which had been protecting Paul to his unawares. I told him, "But keep the people on his mom, Al. I think the CCPOA is satisfied that at this point there will be no *story*. And probably their thoughts of retaliation against him have subsided."

Al agreed and joked that he was sure the people would be glad they didn't have to board a flight to Mexico. "It would be rather complicated to get instant tickets for the entire team to go to Mexico, follow him and guard him without him knowing," Al told me.

Within forty minutes of our call, one Crown Victoria, a Ford LTD and a black Sedan were vacating the one-mile radius surrounding Paul Shackelford.

I placed a collect call a few days later to Jada Kiss. One of my stealth supporters had been able to obtain his telephone number and set up a time for me to call him. But before I call Jada Kiss, I had to re-read some snail mail.

I had missives from Timothy Goebel, Johnny Weir, Lacey Tomlin, Felicia Flood, Tonya Goodman, Zach Weary, Michael Cardinale, Clay Aikens, Anthony Fedorov, Michael Ciompi and Justin Daley in Tracey, California. I also had an inspiring missive from Craig Scott (brother of Rachel Scott of Columbine High School).

I want to encourage all of you reading to let your voice be heard and your face be seen. I will include many of your essays, poems and suggestions in the next book. We may even include them in the revised edition of this book. You'll have to *rush* your photo, essay, poem, lyrics, etc. to me today. And if you have a local band, etc., send us the group hook up and photo, etc., and we will give you some worldwide exposure in our tomes and publications. As you know, our books sell in Amsterdam, Sweden, Paris, Switzerland, etc.

We are picked up by blogs, podcasts, critics, lovers and haters.
* * *

"Your butt is as juicy as Anthony Fedorov's and your buns are as tight as Timothy Goebels. I want you. I wanna put on whips, chains, boots and a helmet and screw your brains out. Let's do it. Let's do it now! I want it. All of it. I'll toss your salad and lick your (expletive)," is exactly what Nicole said to Joe on *Beauty and the Geek*. At least that's what Joe told me over the telephone…

Hope Tim, Fedorov and Clay ain't offended. I'm just a journalist reporting the facts to my folks. I love America! I love my ink pen. I love all y'all…Okay…

* * *

Jada Kiss pressed *five*…"Your call is being connected," stated the automated operator. "My proud, beautiful African American Brother. What up?" Jada Kiss said. We talked. Out of respect to him and his people, I will keep the contents of our conversation private...

During the next few days I had telephonic conversations with Russell Simmons, P. Diddy, Denzel Washington and Earl Ofari Hutchison. Most of the times these talks are highly enlightening and inspirational. Mr. Earl Ofari Hutchinson, however, who is a brilliant Black columnist from LA was perturbed by what he thought was my "selling out of the brothers in prison."

"White people are gonna use the data contained in your research and books to do stories, exposés, documentaries and news specials about the plight of White boys in prison. Ipso facto, our White President, our nearly all White Senate and our majority Caucasian House are gonna jerk their knees and bring White boys home but leave Black boys alone. They will pass even more racist laws that justify unequal sentencing and unfair arrests. Sherman, there will be an unimaginable domino effect with a tome like you're discussing. They already have crack laws designed to imprison and strike out Black folks. They have methamphetamine laws designed to probate White offenders. Most of the judiciary is Lilly White. Most prosecutors are White. And with all they got going for them now, a Black man wants to do a damned book waving a White face for all the world to see, and depicting the White man as victim. I understand that a disproportionate number of Caucasians per capita are being molested and raped in prisons, but welcome to the jungle. Do you know your history? Or do you just know *his-story*? Perhaps the sins of their fathers are being visited upon them. These White masters sadistically, violated, raped and often sodomized Black women. Then thousands of Black women had their nipples cut off by these savages. And you want Black folks to feel sorry about White boys being raped in prison? It's karma!"

180

I replied, "Mr. Hutchinson, I have an in depth knowledge of authentic history. I know of what you speak. I'm cognizant of the fact that, they that know not their history, are destined to repeat it. And I also know that they who dwell on their history are destined to remain bitter, angry and stuck. Nothing justifies rape. You don't repeat illegal behavior out of retaliation.

"Something is wrong with any man who rapes another person; including a man in prison. And if I can see it, hear it, witness it or know about it and not care, then I am sick, if not complicit. I know Robert Byrd, the Tom Delay types and Trent Lott protégés will become livid and flabbergasted when they find out how many White kids have been sexually violated in prisons, jails, juveniles and got out and told *nobody* about it. And these guys may be inclined to fight to rescue Whites in prisons. But on the chance that a residual effect of this alarm being sounded in the halls of congress and the senate, will and can be a rethinking of the entire prison system, etc. I'm willing to be the fall guy. I will stand up for right because it's right. I'll speak up for victims although the vast majority of them are White. I'll do it because it's right.

"And if my radical, militant and abrasive brothers consider me soft because I fight for the justice of White America, then so be it. I don't think anybody in their right mind will accuse me of being a Clarence Thomas or Ward Connerly. The folks that *know me*, know what I'm about. I love people; I love God's people. I love folks that look like *me* and I love folks that look nothing like me.

"I don't have time to *hate* the White doctor who delivered me from my momma's belly. I want to know that White brother. I wanna commune with him, worship with him, and pray with him, teach him about me and learn about him. The more we know the more we grow. And if I mend, grow and bond with him, I'll be able to impress him and he'll impress me and our fellowship and relationship will result in more Black doctors.

"I want to know that White guy who owns my momma's bank. If I establish a bond, a friendship and a kinship with him, I can teach him, reach him and learn from him. And I can model his success and one day buy me a bank.

"I want to know the White folks who own CBS, NBC and ABC. And I want to establish genuine, authentic and wholesome bonds with them. I can teach them, reach them and learn from them. They can teach me stocks, bonds, CDs, mutual funds and how to manage money. And I can teach them how to rid themselves of bias, prejudice and even racism. If they really teach me, I'll never be broke. If I really reach them, then the next time Bill Cosby tries to buy NBC, they won't refuse to sell it to a Black man.

"Mr. Hutchinson, America is a great big house. The world is one giant big house. The nations, states, cities, buildings and houses seem to divide or partition us off into groups. Our colors, languages, dialects and even our shapes and sizes partition us all into groups. But the world is still one big house. Our divisions, the nations, the states, cities, colors and languages are all like *doors* in the house. Behind those doors are our options. I can take door number one and be a thug. I can take door number twelve and hate White people. I can take door fifteen and hate fat folks cause I'm slim, door nineteen and hate people who speak broken English, slang or other vernaculars because I'm articulate...

"But I refuse to spend the rest of my life lost in the house. I will not carry hatred, racism, bias or bitterness to the cemetery. I choose the *door of hope* and the door of *love*. I choose to genuinely love all people."

Mr. Hutchison hung up on me. You win some, lose some and some are rained out...

"I chatted with Mr. Danny Glover, Morgan Freeman, Rubin "Hurricane" Carter and Samuel Jackson numerous times over the past few weeks. *Some* of them only offered lip service and words. But I would insist on a yes or no before we hung up. "Can I expect a check from you to help put these books in the hood?" I would ask. Most of them said, yes...

* * *

Paul returned from Mexico a couple of days after we had talked. In Mexico, he had screwed one White girl and one Mexican girl. (Keep in mind the *girls* were nineteen and twenty-one, respectively).

Paul flew into Oklahoma City on a Friday evening at 11:17 p.m. After he got off the plane, he walked to the baggage claim area to claim his bags. After getting his bags, he stepped outside to a waiting Town Car and told the driver, "Rancho Cordova, please. McGregor Street."

The driver said, "Yes sir, Mr. Shackelford."

Paul did a double take and said, "You know me?"

The driver replied, "No sir, but your mother sent me. She knew your flight schedule."

Paul said, "Wow, that's a mother for you. Always taking care of us."

He decided to call mom. "Thank you for the Town Car, Mom. You shouldn't have."

His mom replied, "Well, when he offered to pick you up for free and I learned he was from St. Martin's Press, your publisher, I figured, why not."

Paul was puzzled, "St. Martin's Press is not my publisher. Unless Sherman has changed plans drastically, without telling me. Harper Collins is our publisher, *not St. Martin's Press*... Anyway, I'll take the free ride. I *love* you Mom and I'll come and see you tomorrow. Maybe I can just spend the whole day with you. Would that be cool?"

Paul's mom loved the idea. They hung up and then he saw it. Paul saw the Russian Makarov, nine-millimeter pistol as the driver pointed it at Paul and squeezed the trigger. He shot Paul four times and dumped his body and the stolen car behind an old abandoned building on the West Side of Oklahoma. The car was clean. No fingerprints, driver's license, credit cards, no nothing. The murder of Paul Shackelford was a mystery...

* * *

I took Paul's murder probably worse than anyone else on the planet other than his mother. It was unbelievable to me. I couldn't understand it. I hoped I was dreaming or having a nightmare. But I wouldn't be this lucky. As was his brother, Paul was gone.

(Editor's Note: We encourage Mr. Manning to write the details of the funeral services of Paul Shackelford. At this juncture however, he feels he can't meet that request. We respect Mr. Manning's need to grieve and in no way do we blame him for his inability to write about that painful tragedy in detail. At some point, in the future, we hope he will be able to write more about this funeral.)

Information is power and too much information can be dangerous and even deadly. I believe in candor, as well as integrity and authenticity. I cannot prove that the CCPOA killed Paul Shackelford. Thus far, there is not a shred of evidence to prove that they did. But I'm not afraid to write here in this tome that every fiber of my being believes that Lance Corcoran, Mike Jimenez, Mr. Darchuk and the power brokers who lead the CCPOA are directly responsible for the death of Paul Shackelford. It was a professional hit. It was a contract murder. They killed him for what he knew.

Ipso facto, I would not be surprised if I turn up dead in a supposed suicide or a supposed inmate killing. They are methodical, strategic and vindictive. "We transferred Mr. Manning to Pelican Bay, etc., etc., for his own safety." I am not safe, nor will I ever be safe in any prison in California. Perhaps they'll transfer me to another state and have me killed there... Many people want to know have I told Governor Schwarzenegger of my fears. The answer is yes. I like

Arnold. I respect Arnold. I really like his wife, Maria. But Arnold seems to be a typical politician. And (in general) politicians lie! Some of them cheat! And lots of them will do or say anything to get elected.

But the problem as I see it is *us*. We elect them. It seems we enjoy being lied to. It seems we enjoy hypocrisy. How else can we explain watching a politician arrive in a *Hummer* to give a speech encouraging *us* to buy hybrids?

How else can we justify electing politicians who refuse to *answer* questions at press conferences and even at debates? We watch them give sound bite, non-answers every day of the week and yet we vote for them anyway. We justify bullshit artists with little slogans like, "I chose the lesser of evils," etc. Why should we have to settle for an evil politician? Why can't we nominate credible, decent politicians? What would be wrong with getting a young man like Kevin McCarty, who is a Sacramento City Councilman and represents the 6th District well and nominate him to run for Governor? I assure you that *if* we went to Kevin McCarty (who has a Black dad and a White mother and a beautiful Mexican wife) and said, "Mr. McCarty, we want you to run for Governor. Mel Bacon, George Soros, Mr. Keenan and Sherman Manning have already raised five million dollars to kick off your campaign." I believe little Kevin would run for Governor. "Kevin, we want you to answer the questions. Don't ever answer a question with a question. Don't bullshit the people with, 'I'm not gonna say which way I'm leaning at this time.'"

That's how we energize people. We gain the energy and interest of Johnny Weir, Timothy Goebel, Richie Ripley, Steven Maher, Lewis Levron and Brittany Reading. I know Tim, Johnny, Clay Aiken, Constantine and John Ahdout personally. I know why many of them are not into politics. They don't like hypocrisy and bullshit.

They don't like listening to folk preach to them. Many of these preachers don't even *know God* themselves. You can quote scriptures and know *about God* and still not *know Him*. You can attend church every Sunday or go to mass three times per week and still not have a personal relationship with God... I've learned a lot about *me* while in the prison. And many of the young folks who write to me tell me they have no safe place to *lay their head* without being fondled. They need a *safe place*. They just need a safe bed in which to lay their heads. They need to be able to lie down and not be molested by Uncle Harry or Cousin Charlie. And when there is chaos and confusion in the home, they can't think long enough to figure out *who they are* and *why they are* on the planet.

And for many of them, even the church is no safe haven. They find predators, molesters and politics in the church. We have predators jockeying for position in the house of God. There are cliques and tricks and games in the church. And when the Boy Scout leader can't be trusted, when the priest is a pedophile, who do our young people turn to?

We need *safe beds* for our children. None of us have all the answers. All of us have issues. All of us got some junk and funk in our trunks. But what we need to do is rescue our children. We need to help provide *safe beds* in which they can think and lay their heads. We need to stop bullshitting and playing games.

"Calling on Oprah, Soros, Bill Gates, Warren Buffett, Bill Cosby, Matt Damon, Jerry Bruckheimer, all citizens and immigrants, etc. If we can't agree on shit else; can we come out of our bullshitting houses of glass and stop throwing stones long enough to find *safe beds* for our children?

For every molester who has this book in *your* hands right at this moment, I want to tell you: Get *yourself* some help. Do it *now*! In your heart of hearts, you know it is wrong. And you know you'll get caught and go to prison and they will kill you in prison. It ain't gotta be like that. Right where you are you can get help. Pick up a telephone and call a counselor, psychologist, and therapist and tell them *you need help*. Call Dr. Phil (or go to www.Dr.Phil.com) and I promise you, Dr. Phil will direct you to somebody in your area who can help you. Yield not to temptation. The very next time you think about harming a child, do *anything* else. Don't touch that boy or girl. Don't fondle them. It's not harmless. It's not innocent. It's a crime, it's a sin, and it's perverted. It may have happened to *you*. But just like it hurt you and traumatized you; why inflict that same pain, hurt and fear on somebody else? These are **children**. It may even feel good to them for a while. But it ain't good. It ruins them. It destroys them. Get help. Get help now. You can't always pray it away. You gotta get help. God walks through psychologists, counselors and therapists. You must get help *today*.

And if there are (and empirical data suggests that prison predators do *read my books*) rapists, predators, etc., reading right now, don't do it again. Don't rape that White guy in your cell! Don't rape that inmate in LA County Jail. Stop raping youngsters just because you're never gonna get out. *They* will get out and your raping them is going to create another victimizer and other victims. When they get out, they are going to the playground to rape your brother, your sister, your sons, daughters, cousins and friends.

I don't care how many times you've done it, don't do it again. Just because you *did it* does not mean you have to *be it*. You can stop it right now. I command the anointing to fall in that prison. I command the anointing of the Holy Ghost to fall in that jail cell and in that juvenile. Break that curse off of your life. Break it out of your mind and your spirit. You can stop it. You can stop it *right this very minute*.

People may not like you. Your own family may have abandoned you. Hell, I might not even like you, but who are they and who am I in the grand scheme of things?

It does not make no never mind who you are or where you are. No matter how little or much money you have in the bank, it matters not in the grand scheme. If Bill Gates is on an airplane and things go wrong on the plane, not a billion dollars will cause that engine to come back on. Not fifty billion dollars will turn the storm clouds back or stop the rain. Billions don't matter when *Dr. Keith Black* tells you, 'Mr. Cosby' or 'Mr. Soros' or 'Mrs. Stewart' or 'Mrs. Winfrey', the tumor is inoperable."

So find out who you are. Find out what your purpose is and *serve your* purpose. All those folks you see in Hollywood have the same damn problems you have in the hood. All you, who are in college, got the same problems as those in prison. The prisoner has the issues that the free man has. Mr. Gates has the same type of problems as Mrs. Wages has. The guy working in McDonald's is no worse off than the guy who owns the McDonald's. We all eat, drink, shit and sleep. We all have drug addicts, Christian fanatics, geeks, freaks, nerds, gays, straights and jailbirds in our families. Go talk to Paul Newman, Oprah, Sharon Stone, kids at the Hole in the Wall Gang in California. Call their cousins and nieces and nephews and you'll find out they have some family secrets too that would blow your mind. While you're worshipping Paris Hilton and wanting to be Nicole Kidman, Brad Pitt has moved on. While you wanted to be Jane Fonda, you didn't foresee her divorce from Ted Turner. Lots of you used to worship Michael Jackson but would you trade places with him now?

The victims of that horrible and awful tragedy on September 11th would have traded places with any juvenile, jail or prison inmate on September 10th had they known the planes were coming on the 11th. Riker's Island Prison was the safest place in New York on September 11th. And the truth of the matter is, we never know when the planes are coming. We don't know when the planes of doom, the planes of disaster, the planes of hurt or the planes of pain, the planes of divorce, the planes of cancer, the planes of a bullet or the planes of a killing are gonna come calling our name.

So I would suggest that instead of wishing and wanting to be Paris, Oprah, Nicole or Trump, we oughta thank God *we are who we are* and strive to be all that we can be right *where we are*.

So we end up where we started off. You at U. C. Davis, you at U. C. Berkeley, you at C.S.U., Carnegie Mellon, Morehouse, Spellman, UCLA, Boston, Harvard, Howard, Yale and you in prisons and jail... You are *not* alone. No man is an island unto himself. This world is one big house. It's full of doors, choices and options. Choose ye this day the God that ye shall serve! Are you gonna let Jeremy Shackelford's death be in vain? Shall you allow Paul's dream to die at the hands of the CCPOA? Will you sit on your ass and continue to ignore the cry of the children being molested at the altar? Will you waste your time farting in the wind about a rapist being paroled to your area? Or will you deal with the *safety and security* of your own home? Will you create a safe bed for your own child? Are you willing to then create a *safe bed* for the child next door? Are you willing to then create a safe bed for the kid next door when he goes down the street and moves into the prison? It's still a big house. What door will you choose? If you do nothing else as a result of perusing this tome, I could die in peace if I know each reader committed to creating *safe beds for our child...*

Lisa Ling, who hosts a show on National Geographic (as I mentioned before), sent an e-mail to Hallopeter@freesurf.ch that read simply, "Please have *Sherman Manning* call me ASAP." She left a private telephone number and I called her at about 10:00 am on a Thursday morning in April. Her first question was, "What do you think is the root cause of racism?"

I was a bit startled because I expected a question about prison, violence or wrongful convictions. Nevertheless, I gave baby girl my best shot. "Li, racism is learned behavior. It is not innate. And it has its genesis in *fear*. If you were sitting in a room as a kid at age five and you saw two Brown men speaking Spanish and it frightened you because you couldn't understand them and you had no idea what or who they were talking about, etc., you would begin with *fear*. Are they talking about you? Will they hurt you? What language are they speaking? And then that fear would *metamorphisize* into a series of emotions including anger. The anger would be birthed out of intimidation. Then you'd begin to *notice* the differences. *They* are dark and you are *light*. They're Brown and you are White. And then your parents speak ill of Brown folks. And then every time you see

Brown folks from that day on for the next ten years, it's on the news. You see them being locked up for rape, murder and assault. And you still don't understand Spanish. You would become a racist. But I submit to you, if you understood their language, vernacular and lingo, if you understood the Spanish the two guys spoke when you were five, that slang the brothers spoke when you were six, etc., etc., and you comprehended that these Brown guys were talking about you - 'What a pretty little girl Lisa is. I think she's destined for success. When she grows up she is gonna be beautiful. She's such a nice little girl.' And for the next ten years, you saw these dark-skinned people in real life or on TV as doctors, lawyers, pastors, teachers and ordinary people, etc. you would not fear them. You wouldn't notice, focus on or care that they looked different than you do.

"Lisa, none of us likes to be in the room with *strangers* speaking a language we can't understand, but there are some bilingual people in the world. Unfortunately, the bilinguals are outnumbered by those who only speak one language. If, on the other hand, in spite of your fear and interpretation at age five, sitting and listening to Brown people speak a language you didn't understand... If you never saw or rarely saw Brown people for the next few years and somebody came along when you were ten or fifteen years old and you showed them the video, 'Oh, I understand fluent Spanish, Lisa. I'll translate for you.' And that person translated into English what those two guys were saying and you discovered it was nice things, etc., you'd laugh at your own stupidity. 'I feel silly. I thought they were saying nasty things about me. Damn.' And then your translator tells you, 'I have a lot of Brown friends, let me introduce you to Maria.' And you met Maria... The key word, Lisa is *you met her*.

"If we can't understand the cultures, vernaculars and traditions of people who don't look like us or don't pronounce or enunciate their words as we do, we have options. We can fear them, hate them or learn their language. If we don't wanna take the time to learn their language, we can at least get a translator. And that translator can bring us out of our Black or White boxes, out of our rooms, out of our doors in this big old *house* that we call America. And when we meet that guy, we were taught was a Blue-Eyed devil, when we meet the guy we were told was a lazy colored dude, we will find a lot of things Green Day fans have in common with R. Kelly fans. We will discover that White boys who grew up listening to Garth Brooks are not any different than Black boys who grew up in another part of the house listening to Whitney Houston. We'll find common ground. We find it at the baseball diamond when Blacks, White, Hispanics and Asians cheer on the same team. We find that common ground at the hospital room when that White mother sheds a tear because she sees the pain, trauma, horror and sorrow in the eyes of that Black mother when the doctor tells her, 'We did the best we could ma'am, but we lost him. I'm sorry.'

"We find it in the maternity wards and in delivery rooms. I've seen big old rednecks pick up little Black infants, hold then, kiss them and melt because the innocence of that child kicks the doors of their hearts wide open. I've seen them melt... Psychologically, the implication is this: Fear needs not kick in because babies can't talk. And a *ga ga* or *goo goo* in Spanish sounds just like it does in English. How foolish would I feel preaching hatred of White people and being intimidated by that six foot tall White trucker with tobacco juice dripping from the corner of his mouth, if he said, 'Ha ha, Mr. Sherman, I remember when you was six months old and I held a bottle in your mouth. Your mommy was my momma's best friend til y'all moved out of Switzerland.'"It would interrupt my pattern and quite candidly embarrass me. Finally, Lisa, I also blame ABC, CBS and NBC for perpetuating racism. They consistently and repetitiously tell us about hate crimes, racial incidents and our differences. But they don't show us our common ground. They won't cue in on that Black soldier who is in a war zone and has to depend on the White soldier to cover for him. We don't see all the White soldiers who are covered, rescued and saved by Black and Brown soldiers. They put on their uniforms and become brothers. They become a team. They fight together. They mourn and grieve together when a platoon member gets hit. Lisa, the media thrives on hatred, racism and crime. They need to transform it. And we should demand that they do so..."

Lisa replied, "Wow, that was a mouthful. But I got it. I like your analogies. Yes, this is just what I needed. I will quote you in my story.

* * *

...*LifeHouse* was a group I'd never heard of. But I know them now. Through *Shemm* they had gotten a hold of my book "Creating Monsters" and had used it as resource data to write a couple of songs. I found that to be unique and weird all at the same time. Anyway, they sent me a letter and some photos of the group from their late night with Carson Daly appearance. It was kinda cool to see the broads with whom they took the pictures. In the meantime, I got *dissed* in a rap by *Jay Z*. Jay referred to me as soft, a sell out and whitewashed. I won't *diss* this brother in return. Instead, I will laude the brilliance of *Damon Dash*. And quite frankly some people think or believe that when you

189

withdraw from a contract, partnership or agreement with a brother, just *because*, you are a sell out! Anyway, I respect Damon Dash. D-Dog is brash, arrogant and egotistical. And it is not necessary to be arrogant in order to be successful. But he is arrogant. Yet, if you look beneath the surface and listen around the vernacular, in Damon you will hear the mind of a business genius. He calculates, strategizes and ponders in a way that is radical, unique and financially literate.

Had Mike Tyson been involved with a Damon Dash, he would not be bankrupt. If M.C. Hammer could have been hooked up with someone like Damon Dash, Hammer would not have gone broke. And I believe that if Nick Carter, Aron Carter, Fedorov and Clay Aiken will surround themselves with folk like Damon Dash, they will not go broke. And too many child stars and wonder kids like Gary Coleman get exploited by family and friends, etc. And sometimes this exploitation is not even being done *on purpose*. Often it's done just cause the folk around them don't understand that a half million dollars is five hundred thousand dollars. In other words, many people are not *financially literate*. They don't know how to save, invest, deal with or maintain money. Ipso facto, you have multi-millionaires who have never even heard of an annuity, money market certificate, etc. If you ask them what a *CD* is they'll tell you a *Compact Disc*. As a matter of fact, I am mistaken, most of them would indicate that a CD is "something ya bump music on."

And I'm not poking fun at them. It is really, really sad to see people squander riches due to a lack of financial literacy.

The Bible says a fool and his money shall soon part company. I hope that the hundreds (if not thousands) of wannabe idols, wannabe sports superstars and actors who are reading this tome will take this lesson once and for all; if you ever come into a substantial amount of money, find a good (reputable, respected and financially literate) lawyer and a great accountant. And if it's millions of dollars at stake, hire another lawyer to silently critique the primary lawyer and a silent accountant to audit the auditing of the primary accountant. And don't allow your money to change you or how you treat people. Money will improve your access and should change your circumstances but it should never change *you*. Your character and personality should remain consistent with who you are...

* * *

The California Correctional Peace Officers Association issued a written statement. The pressure was mounting. For decades these thugs had allegedly gotten away with murder, rapes, bombings, and blackmail. They bought DA's, senators, assemblymen, congress members and even governors. It turns out they even bought the media. This began to explain why we rarely got full disclosure and it explained why KOVR, KCRA and News 10, rarely covered prison guard corruption... Behind the scenes, according to Francisco Lobaco, Willie Gary and Murray Janus, there was talk of bringing in a *special* prosecutor to investigate the CCPOA and its alleged extortion, monopoly, no-bid policies, abuse of power, overtime abuse, promotions, scandals, bribery, theft of documents, fraud, conspiracy and *murder*.

And so the CCPOA which is a part (or are they) of the C.D.C. decided on a preemptive strike. They heard the rumors of a special prosecutor also. So Lance Corcoran issued the following (verbatim) statement:

"The CCPOA is a group of peace officers who serve, protect and uphold the law. Our fine officers walk the *toughest beat* in the state and they risk their lives guarding predators, rapists and murderers every day. Any rumor or speculation that our union members have been or are involved in any criminal activity is erroneous. Any past, present or future allegations claiming that any CCPOA member would condone or engage in murder is spurious and deceptive. We are in the business of dealing with vicious inmates who rape, molest, maim and murder. These are the worst of the worst. And quite often they concoct stories and feed them to the press, politicians and prosecutors. Apparently, if any charges or allegations are forthcoming, the inmates *win*. It's a sad, sad day... The CCPOA will have absolutely no further comment."

So stated Mr. Lance Corcoran in a written statement probably written by P.R. people and lawyers.

* * *

...At the Hilton Hotel in Scottsdale, Arizona at 11:30 a.m. on a Friday night in April, she walked in the room in a miniskirt. The miniskirt was short, short, short. It was tight, tight, tight. So tight that Scott thought to himself, if she sneezes she'll come out of the skirt. And Scott Coffman could see the pink, lace panties underneath the miniskirt. She was h-o-t. She looked similar to the way Brooke Shields did sixteen years ago. She could be Brooke's twin sister, Scott thought. I guess she's gonna screw my brains out. The whole set up was weird. This woman had begun e-mailing Scott three weeks ago. He'd met her in an online chat group. But she was too anxious to meet. She was - weird. I wonder if I'm a (expletive) idiot, Scott thought as he stared at her legs. What if the CCPOA planted this witch on that chat line? Is she gonna screw me and set me up in a rape

191

charge cause the CCPOA knows I did boot camp with Sherman and was a friend to Jeremy and Paul? I'm a fool for flying here.

Scott had indeed learned not to trust anyone. Especially people he met on the Internet. And via his correspondence with me and past conversations with Paul and Jeremy… Scott knew that the CCPOA was a *gang*. They were the *Green Wall*. They were *723*. They were *killers in the name of justice*. They were powerful, corrupt and rich. They had contacts with hit men. Scott felt that maybe he had walked himself right into a deadly trap or at minimum it was a *plot* to *destroy* him. All he needed was to go to jail in Scottsdale for rape! Or could it be child molestation? Even though she was standing right before him right now and she appeared to be twenty-one or twenty-two, what if she was fourteen or fifteen? Girls nowadays looked grown at twelve.

Scott was paranoid! Thank God for gadgetry, Scott switched on his recording device, which was attached to his cell phone in his pocket. "Listen, I don't want to have sex. I'm leaving," he said loudly to Lisa.

"Why, you don't like the way I look? I just got here. You have not even kissed me yet," she said.

"I'm gone," Scott said as he bolted out of the hotel room.

He'd call back later and have a concierge or bellboy to go and get his luggage. Scott jumped into a taxi and headed straight to the airport…

"Be careful. You are dealing with people who have no fear, no morals, no conscience and will do anything, *anything* to achieve their objective," Attorney Steve Fama told Scott via telephone the next day. Scott had called Attorney Fama because of Steve's connection to the *prison law office, which* had *sued* C.D.C. and won. Scott needed advice, now! Right here, right now! Scott was scared! "Other than giving a few interviews to private investigators on Sherman's behalf and that one investigator from the insurance company about Paul, I'm not involved with what Jeremy, Paul and Sherman were or are doing. Why would they hurt me?" Scott asked Fama.

    * * *

Back at the prison, I had begun receiving mail from Assembly Member Judy Chu from El Monte, CA. Mrs. Chu had a lot to say and her mail came to me sealed because it was legal and confidential. One of the letters however was stamped, "Opened in Error" by the mailroom. And I am to assume it was (indeed) *opened in error* and that the professional and fine officers, whom Lance Corcoran brags on, did not read the contents of that missive. Silly me…

This department, which promoted a man like Scarsella to Lieutenant at New Folsom. This department, which promoted Mr. Blackburn to sergeant at New Folsom. This department, which promoted R.N. Saunders to sergeant at New Folsom... Scarsella was a non-racist thug. He was just a liar and an inmate hater.

Scarsella falsified documents, beat down inmates and was finally tried in Sacramento County on attempted murder of an inmate. Saunders was the duty sergeant and he colluded after the beating and conspired to coerce his subordinates to sign fix it tickets to *cover for* Scarsella. Scarsella was convicted and finally fired by C.D.C. but the union is now fighting to get his job back... Saunders was only demoted but the CCPOA is fighting to get his *stripes* back!

...Blackburn? I'll just say I would not put anything past *Sergeant* Blackburn. If someone told me Blackburn molested a child, I would believe it. If someone told me Sergeant Blackburn raped a senior citizen, I'd believe it...

...Jeremy Shackelford was a damn good man. A young man with a bright future. I still have not gotten over his death. It was absolutely tragic. Also, Paul Shackelford was another awesome young man. I can't even use my pen (yet) to adequately describe the emotional trauma, hurt, sorrow and horror, which I feel as a result of Paul's murder.

While I still can't yet prove who killed Paul; I do believe with every fiber of my being that the CCPOA is absolutely responsible for his murder.

I will say for the record that C.D.C. does have some good officers. There are many correctional officers in every prison in America who abide by the law and who also uphold the law. Many of them are decent, professional and upstanding. They are **not all** corrupted! And *all that it takes for evil to rage is for good men to remain silent.*

By and large, even the good peace officers in this country, both correctional and police are recruited and often intimidated into an unwritten pledge of a *code of silence.* And it is this silence about abuse, silence about rape, silence about corruption, silence about Doug Pieper's death/homicide, silence about Paul Shackelford's contract murder, which needs to be busted open.

Perhaps it will take the Christine Crafts, Ed Schultz, Tavis Smileys, Bev Smiths, Randi Rhodes, Al Frankens and Oprah to tell the world about a nationally organized group of thugs and killers who wear uniforms, carry handcuffs and guns. Maybe the American trial lawyers ought to *demand* that prisons allow cameras into prisons. If prisons are not *hiding* anything and are merely enforcing the law, then why are they so adamantly opposed to allowing cameras inside the gated communities?

It's time to stop the games! Last time I checked, this was supposed to be the *United* States of *America*. We cannot ever stoop to the level of hating the underdog! We cannot ever hate, despise or neglect the least of these our brethren. We cannot allow bias, prejudice and racism to get in the way of loving our neighbor as ourselves. That neighbor may be Black, White or Mexican. But a brother is a brother. And even a racist should not support *child molestation*. What racist wants his child to be molested? Even Rush Limbaugh or Omarosa would not want their children raped. Call Omarosa and then call Rush Limbaugh and ask them would they like their children raped? Well, it is crystal clear that more than seven hundred thousand inmates *must* be released from prison every year.

Roughly speaking *two thousand* inmates will get out of prison *tomorrow*. And if they were raped in prison there is a very strong likelihood that they will commit molestation and rape when they get out tomorrow, next week or next month. Watch Out!!

It is your neighbor, your son, your Uncle, your friend's son or neighbor who made that mistake, smoked that crack, took that speed or whatever, and they have now moved to the juvenile, the jail or the prison.

And they are still *human beings*. A **few** of them actually committed horrible crimes. They deserve to be punished. And the taking of their freedom is the punishment. But the vast overwhelming majority of them are just troubled kids, who we failed to love when they were kids, got lost and made mistakes. Most of them could have been helped had we not been hoodwinked into believing that prison would help them…

They are **our** problem. They are our sons and daughters. Years ago when we held them in our arms and put pacifiers in their mouths, we felt responsible for them. But they grew up physically and we mistook that for maturity. And now they are in trouble. And sir, ma'am, Mr. President, Governor, Senator, Pastor, Preacher and John Q. Citizen: I promise you that if we don't make the keepers who keep them, keep them peacefully without abusing them, without beating them, without allowing them to be raped, sodomized and traumatized we will continue to *make monsters*, predators and molesters.

I watch people. I study human behavior. Quite frankly, this book is not about Jeremy, it's not about Paul and it damn sure ain't about **me**. I am certain about *who* I am. I *know me*. And either I'm arrogant or self-confident because I've come to a point in my life where I absolutely am not in a popularity contest. I'm not trying to win an award or get an endorsement. You either like me or you don't. But God loves me, I love me and I love you too.

But this book is absolutely a wake up call to you. I wanted you to know what CBS, ABC, NBC has failed to tell you. I wanted you to know what most prisoners won't/don't tell you. I want to tell you what ex-inmates (many of whom are ex-*victims*) *won't tell you*. I want to tell you they are raping your son in prison. Mothers, they are raping your boys. Fathers, they are raping your sons. America, they are raping, abusing, confusing, disrespecting and neglecting your family members whom you allowed to be sent to prison to get *corrected and rehabilitated*.

Your choices are simple. I don't need to write a nine hundred page theoretical, philosophical, psychological dissertation. I need not give you a voluminous, boring ass diatribe that is politically correct, etc. It is as simple as A, B, C. As a matter of fact, it's as simple as A and B…

Choice A: Every time a person commits a crime (i.e. murder, rape, burglary, theft, drug sales, drug use, fraud, assault, mutual combat, D.U.I., etc., etc.) lock them up for the *rest of their natural born* lives. Prison will be permanent. Prison will be the warehouse and cemetery or a sort of purgatory! It's as simple as that - don't let anybody get or come out - period! It will bankrupt the nation. Taxes will skyrocket to the tune of making America as poor economically as Cambodia!

Choice B: Simple - cleanup the prisons and make them a last resort. Send fewer people to prison. Send people to prison in far less instances. And when we send them to prison, make their choices simple. Yes - as simple as A & B. A. Mr. Prisoner, you may lie around and drink, drug and fight yourself to death and we will warehouse you forever! B. Mr. Prisoner, you will have a G.E.D. minimum, participate in workshops, self-help, voc-ed and reading classes and get out sooner. The more courses you complete, the better you read, the more skills or trades you learn, etc., the quicker you will get out. Reform, rehabilitate and educate yourself and we will let you out of prison. We don't want you here any longer than *you need to be here*. We want you to stop committing crimes. That is a prerequisite for your release. We would rather not support you and pay for your keep. The thirty-five to forty thousand dollars per year we are paying to keep you in prison would be better spent by investing in our children. That's our choice(s)! Plain and simple…

I called Paul Haggis (writer/director) because I'd gotten three letters from him about my books, "Creating Monsters" and "From the Palace to the Prison." Mr. Haggis was quite unique, colorful and intuitive in his approach. "I want the rights to turn those books into movies," he told me. Danny Bakewell (Chairman of the *Brotherhood Crusade* in LA) and Congresswoman Maxine Waters both sent letters encouraging me to take Mr. Haggis seriously. Rodrigo Ojeda Beck, Paul Donahue and Nez Smiley wrote. "*Focused on Equality* must be mentioned in your books, Mr. Manning." Ojeda-Beck wrote (more on that later). Wade Robson, Zachary Smilovitz of Detroit, Michigan also wrote to me. Wade wanted to promote his choreography company. Zach made a film, "A is for Auschwitz" and wanted me to know. I liked Zach and began calling him routinely.

Aaron and Alex Gobert, band members from Bloc Party in Coachella, CA wrote me. Juan Juarez, Matthew Feeley of Las Vegas, Nevada wrote... Juan is an exiting senior at Catholic High School. And Matt was a one hundred grand winner of Who Wants to be a Millionaire. Adrienne McCoy (Pittsburgh Post Gazette), Jason Vanhuksloot and Sean Taylor of Sheldon High School Fame wrote to promote their visual graphics program. "If half of y'all who write to me buy the book, it will sell well," I told Jason.

Sean Taylor was almost as enthusiastic as Zachary and Feeley. "We're gonna revolutionize the world," Sean would say. "By the time we finish inundating the media, politicians and pastors promoting your tomes, they're gonna hate that they allowed you to go to prison," Sean told me. "Every time they tell us you are a rapist, murderer, predator, robber or any other jacket they try to put on you, we will inundate the press to counter that mess. We'll leak personnel files and file pitchers motioning to force disclosure on the CCPOA!" Mr. Taylor wrote to me.

Corey Clark contacted my publisher in early April about a smut book on Paula Abdul. Corey made it clear that he was willing to say anything to make that "*B*" look bad. "I'm just a Black man trying to get in where I fit in. If I gots to say she drinks protein drinks, swallows, Simon and Ryan are gay lovers and Clay is gay; so be it. I'm tryin ta git paid," one of Corey's e-mails to me stated. (Authors note: Yes, my attorney does have the e-mail and it is authentic.)

Clay could be gay. If I knew he was/is gay I would not say. It is my belief that homosexuality is a sin. (And so are swearing, fighting, racism, grudges, lies, etc.) And I don't judge people. Clay has been respectful, kind and courteous to me. And I jokingly embellish things, i.e. Clay *came out*, etc. But I do so with his permission. And he knows he and I are friends. And I would not betray his trust. I don't know Simon. Simon does not answer my mail, etc. I can't speak on him. But Clay is my friend. I like him. My wife likes him. And he's a good-hearted country White boy. And it's desperate and low of Corey to drag people's names through the mud just to try to acquire money. And his parents are supporting him in this mess. And they *should* be telling him to sit down and shut up. *If* he really did have intimacy with Paula, a *man* doesn't *kiss* and tell. So his parents are wrong for not telling him what is right. And the media is all over it. Ludicrous!

The *Runaway Bride*? Front page news and *top story* for weeks! If Mrs. Wilbanks had been a Black woman (I'm not trying to be *Mr.* Omarosa. I'm simply calling a *spade* a *spade*. And Omarosa would call that a *racist* statement), it would not be in the news like that. In order to see feature stories on a Black woman like that it would have had to be the 1800s. And it would have been a story on a *runaway slave* not a runaway bride. Now we are glued to the TV trying to figure out her mental state and desperate to hear her statement...

On May 6, 2005 at 3:14 p.m., I called Christian Lawrence. First time we actually talked. Christian is a powerful, inspirational, intelligent, articulate and magnetic young man. First, I must applaud his parents for raising a very bright, affable and gregarious young man. His dad, Michael is a successful physician. Christian spent ten years in Trinidad on a mission with his church. He's a member of T.E.A.M. (more on that later).

I want to state (for the record) that many people compliment me on the hipness of my writing and you stroke my ego with stuff like, "You know how to write for teenagers, Sherm." I owe this writing style to young people who write to, chat with and educate me. They tell me what works and what does not. They are my teachers. Jordan Rideba (Sacto), Eric Bryant (Nashville), Jonathan Ahdout, Jacob Saul, Mike Luong, Tanvir, Uriel Ojeda, etc. These are the folks who keep me hip, current and fluid in youth lingo. To them, I say thank you.

Christian has been extremely instrumental in shedding some light on what the hell has gone wrong in our schools, communities and neighborhoods at large. My main question to Christian is always, "What the hell can we do to turn the youth around?"

Christian is methodical and pragmatic in his reply. "I can be very *idealistic* if you want. But I'd rather be realistic. We're nearing the end of times and it's hard to reach my age group."

Now I'm careful to not support a fatalistic paradigm of the world. (I don't accuse Christian of being fatalistic either). And I do know that some people get caught up in expecting Jesus to return *tomorrow* and they began to become *unrealistic*. I believe Jesus will return in the rapture. That's my personal belief. And I don't care if *you* don't believe in it. It takes all kinds to make the world go round! Anyway, Christian is very open-minded and accepting of others. He won't condone your sin, but he also won't judge you. He does not come across as phony or holier than thou. But he does believe in God. And he's not ashamed to express his faith! I'm not sure he supports or even condones the fact that I still own a modeling company which parades people on the covers of magazines in bikinis, speedos and G-strings. Yet, thirteen of my male models and thirty-seven of my female models have confessed Jesus Christ as their personal savior...

I hope Christian will continue to serve as my sounding board and to educate me. Perhaps I can teach him and Dr. Michael Lawrence a few things also. I just wish I could find ten more Christian Lawrences around the country. People I can write to and read from. People I can call and encourage and call to be encouraged. People who will *pray for me* and *pray with me*. Much of the data about youth, college students and teens in this tome reflect the things I've learned from *Christian* Lawrence. If you see him on my blogs, websites or on my homepage, etc. don't be surprised. Christian may be one of my Lazarus. And I will admit he does not support the cuss words or sexual details in the book. He'd rather I leave it out. But, I do know he's smart enough to know I'm trying to reach *Bad Boys* and *Bad Girls*. And I think Christian knows I can't reach them with three points and a poem. I can't reach them with a song or a sermon. I have to be humble enough to let God use me. I have to be pragmatic enough to use analogy, simile, allegory and graphics to pull people in. I have to write this tome in a way that the soldier in Iraq will read it. I gotta know there are guys in juvenile perusing my words today or tonight. I gotta respect their lingo, vernacular and their speaking style. I gotta go out to the cornfield, into the inner city, down in the hood, in the high rise, suburbs and in the prisons with this message of hope, healing and second chances. I love good people. And wherever Christian Lawrence, his brother and Dr. Michael Lawrence are at this very moment, I want you all to know that *I love you* with the love of God. Christian brought tears to my eyes as I listened to him that Friday evening as he said, "Can you call me back, *Sherman*?"

And if we could get more Evangelicals, Catholics and Muslims to say, "*Call me back*" to the juvenile, the prisoner or the jail inmate, etc., if we can get more of ya'll who claim to love God to quit hating your brothers, if we can get more people to embrace, educate, love and care for the *least of these*, we will make the world better. At this very moment; *right here, right now*, I want every person who is reading my words to do something for the *least of these*. Go on to some prison web site and find a guy to write! E-mail your Governor, Senator, the White House, etc. and tell them to clean up the prisons. Tell them you are reading "Blue-Eyed Blonde" and you are appalled! Tell them you are as angry about the *sodomization* of the kids of our nation as you were by the photos of torture which came out of Abu Ghraib.

Go on to http://www.house.gov and e-mail your congressman. Go to http://www.senate.gov for your senator. Call 202/225-5074 or 202/225-2761 and tell them you want a summit meeting on prisons. Call 202/225-3121 and tell them to *fix it*! If you're in California, call 916/445-2841 and/or e-mail Senator Romero@Sen.CA.gov and demand change! Snail mail the Governor and State Senators (in CA) at State Capitol, Sacramento, CA 95814-4994. Snail mail the Senate at United States Senate, Washington, DC 20510-0001 and if you want to join our efforts and exchange ideas, etc. e-mail me at Hallopeter@freesurf.ch and snail mail me at *Sherman D. Manning*, J98796, M.C.S.P., A-2-240, P. O. Box 409020, Ione, CA 95640.

I salute Christian Lawrence and I intend on including some essays and other writings by him and his pals (including some photos) in the revised edition of this book.

By the way, Christian wanted me to include mention of his youth group B.O.B. which is the acronym for *Body of Believers*. And T.E.A.M. is for The Evangelical Alliance Mission. I realized that what he wants from me is love. To love him and through him to love others. "*Sherman,* it is miraculous that you called me when you called and that you mentioned the *Life of Joseph*. I just finished studying the life of Joseph about a week ago. Had you called me before last week, I would not have been able to love you like I do. I would have thought some psycho is calling me from prison. But God got me ready for your call by leading me to study the life of Joseph. There are no coincidences in life. You were supposed to call me," is what Christian told me in our fourth telephone call on Saturday.

Paul Haggis, Danny Bakewell, Called 2 Action, Mike Luong, Nate Solov, Conrad Rupp, Jonathan Odell, John Elsmore, Willie Gary and Jonathan Rhys Meyers all signed a petition with one thousand signatures asking the Governor to release me from prison. (I hope *you* will add your name and signature to the petition, by sending an e-mail to Hallopeter@freesurf.ch and go to http:DashCash.Blogspot.com.)...

Ashton Kutcher is absolutely a fool. "Sherman, how goes it, my brother? Bernie Mac says to tell you hello. I hope you got the nude photos I sent you. I sent the wrong set. I had pictures of Paris, but sent pics of me by mistake. Keep them."

Ashton Kutcher (believe me) is one crazy White boy! Absolutely a raging idiot! I guess I should salute the legacy of Quincy Jones. Quincy is a musical impresario. He's a brilliant genius. I recall calling him in the 90s on behalf of the late Rev. Hosea Williams to raise money for our *Feed The Hungry* program in Atlanta. He was gracious and very down to earth. He understands his roots. He survived his circumstances, rose above them, yet he didn't detach himself from them. I love Q. He and Oprah both mean so much to me...

Many years ago, Phillip Coffee tried to steal Yvette Lewis from me in Pennsylvania. He befriended me and claimed to respect me and my "magnetic personality." He used the friendship game to try to steal my lady. I wonder how many Zeta frat brothers out at U. C. Berkeley, U. C. Riverside, Morehouse, Yale or Stanford, etc. have had a so-called buddy to befriend you just to try to get next to your lady? Perhaps you can drop me an e-mail and tell me about it.

...I strenuously encourage every person who is holding this book in your hands to also read "*From The Palace to the Prison*". It's a book every human in America should read. I also thank the thousands of you in Finland, Amsterdam, Britain, Switzerland and South Africa who have read and are reading my books. I encourage you to continue sending me your letters and essays. I personally read them all.

I learned a lot from Jeremy Shackelford and Paul. I learned so much from all of the letters and calls to and with Scott Coffman. And I can learn from *you*. I realize that I can't hope to please everybody. Many Christians think I ought to write just a religious book. And I should write *all about God*. They mean well. But they don't know what I'm doing. I am a missionary, a scribe and a journalist. I entertain, *edu-tain*, inspire, expose, dramatize and encourage. I am not trying to preach a sermon. People are hurting. Our children are in trouble. I see so much hurt, trauma and drama. We are moving farther and farther away from God. And farther and farther away from each other. And I can play a role in bringing us together. If I must be controversial, flamboyant and extravagant in my efforts, so be it. I will pray before I write and I will reach out with everything I have inside me. While kids kick it at Carl's Junior, Subway, Applebee's and at the skate parks, they will discuss the sex, drugs and rock and roll. I know. But at the end of the day when the smoke clears some of them will be haunted by my words and the theme of this tome. Emptiness, void, loneliness and fear can only be filled with the peace and love of God. Jesus Christ is Lord and He loves you. God really, really loves you.

Don't quit. Don't give up. Don't quit. Don't give up! Keep the faith and keep hope alive. You can make it. No matter how bad it looks, you can make it. All things don't look good. All things don't feel good. But all things *worketh* together for those that love God.

Eyes have not seen and ears have not heard and neither has it entered into the hearts of men; the things God has in store for those that love Him. "If you love me obey my commandments," says the Lord. And one commandment is to "Love thy neighbor as thyself."

I am your neighbor. Mumia Abu Jamal is your neighbor. Every troubled kid in the suburbs, barrios, ghettos and juveniles is your neighbor. We must start back caring about each other. There is no spot where God is not. No matter how wicked, evil or bad a person is, there is a small piece of the spirit of God in every human being. You must find it, honor it and talk to it. Find that love in every human being. Look beyond what they've done or where they are. Find the love of God in them and love it/him...

Jack Severson wrote me a month ago. Jack is a curly-headed dude from Virginia whose dad went on Who Wants to be a Millionaire. Won twenty-five grand. Jack (some call him Zack) wants to model. It's strange that guys like Jack, Peter Severson (actually they are *not* related) and Matthew Feeley (Las Vegas, Nevada) write me once per week begging me to force my wife to sign them. Charlie Clingan, Anthony Forte, lots of others who think they have the "look" send pictures all the time. Emily Stewart, Katie Serafin, Lillian Hughes, Jessica Stiles, Susan Hempher and Dianna West have sent me literally hundreds of amateur portfolios. Maury West turned out to actually have *that* look. The *it*-factor is hard to find but she has *it*. And she now has a two hundred grand per year contract with our modeling company. "Sherman, I know you only do swimwear, bikini and spandex modeling at A&M but I was made to model. Check out these ten pics," her first letter said.

Zack Roerig and Michael Cardelle also wrote on the same day I received Maury's first pictures.

"What am I supposed to do about lust? Are you telling me I can't ever masturbate or I'll go to hell? Are you actually telling me I'm eighteen years old and I can't ever have sex with my girlfriend until we marry? If I drink a beer, I'm evil? What's a kid to do?" Sam Neuman asked his mom, Billie, in New York, NY one Friday evening. Billie knew a person who knows me and to make a long story concise, I ended up on the telephone with Sam Neuman giving him my opinion.

I'm sure Christian Lawrence would have disagreed with a lot of my advice and comments. So be it.

Christian Lawrence is saved. He is a believer and I am certain Christian will go to heaven. I mean that. I salute and laude Christian for the *fact* that he has accepted Christ Jesus as Lord of his life and as personal savior. And I know everybody ain't Christian! And I know that God specializes in reaching down in dirty places and selecting dirty people to clean them and make *Christians* out of them.

The problem is that so many of *us* are fanatics and zealots in our own ways and we don't even recognize it. We say there is only one word, one way, etc. and we fail to realize that you can let ten people read the same book and all ten will have not only different opinions, but they will actually differ on fundamental aspects of what the book says. It's like studies on eyewitness identification which proves ten people can see the *same* man in black pants and white shirt and ten minutes later they'll all differ on how he looked and even what he was wearing. This is proven to be true. Each one will be definitive and adamant in saying, "I know what I saw." Likewise, when *millions* read the Holy Bible, we take away various meanings. And I'm tired of us dooming people to hell because they don't see what we see, understand what we understand or agree with our interpretation. I.e. a lot of us believe if you practice homosexuality you will go to hell unless you repent. Should I hate a person who believes otherwise? Should you and I not be friends because you support Bush and I do not? Or might we take lesson from Democrat James Carville and his republican wife? I do not advocate watering down the gospel. I dare not delete or attempt to alter, modify or adjust God's word! But at the same time, I won't shove my beliefs down your throat. I'll tell you the truth as I know it and respect your beliefs also. It ain't about "True For You, True For Me," which was a book Christian told me about the other day. But I do recognize your comprehension may not be mine...

But I would pray, hope and believe Christian Lawrence will continue to serve as one of my advisors, critics and supporters. I hope God will reveal to him the strategy employed herein. Since Christian is reading this - *pray for me, Chris* and drop me a line.

   * * *

Davetta was a hot, sensual and petite twenty-three-year-old young lady. Looking into her eyes reminded Marc of looking into the ocean. If there was love at first sight, Marc felt this was it. They met on P. Street in Georgetown. She had graduated from U. C. Berkeley and Marc graduated from Morehouse College in Atlanta.

Marc had a Masters Degree in Business Administration and Davetta had a degree in Anthropology. Jay Grymes, who was a professor of Musicology at U. C. Carolina, had introduced them. Jay was known throughout the South for his connections with music departments at colleges across the U.S. Jay knew Davetta's music tenure and…long story. Anyway, when they started dating, Marc and Davetta began arguing and debating because Marc had decided he was going to attend McGeorge Law School.

"I want to become a trial lawyer," Marc said one night at Mr. P's Pub in D.C. "I wanna be better than Willie Gary, Johnnie Cochran and Gerry Spence combined."

Davetta replied, "Why not become a prosecutor and do something for your country? You serve the community by putting away bad guys not by getting rich defending them. You have an M.B.A. now why all of a sudden the lawyer thing?"

Marc replied with, "I will serve my country by defending the Constitution of the United States of America. I'll make Gideon's promise come alive and well. People demonize criminal lawyers because of the right wing bias of the media. Yet, when we look at it analytically, a defense lawyer merely upholds the law.

"What of the right to a fair trial and the promise of the presumption of innocence? I'll be Clarence Darrow, Johnnie Cochran, Bobby Lee Cook, Murray J. Janus, David Boies, Gerry Spence, Floyd Abrams and Willie Gary all in one.

"Baby, I'll defend the poor and downtrodden. I'll represent the defendants who will go to prison for twenty-five years to life because of draconian laws in California, Alabama, Georgia and Arizona. I'll also sue the hell out of prison systems and police departments.

"Johnnie Cochran was the trial lawyer of the century. All of a sudden he was felled by a brain tumor that even the great Dr. Keith Black could not tame. We lost perhaps one of the greatest defenders of the people that America has seen since Thurgood Marshall. And now a White man, (me) will take up the torch.

"I'll get rich suing corporation thugs and use my wealth to siphon justice from the rich and funnel it to the poor. I'll stand up for what is right and just and fair.

"I'm sick and tired of this potent, sophisticated and biased right wing group of power brokers who identify themselves as Christians but hate any and everything or anybody that does not look like them or not like them. Some of them, Davetta, are so high-minded that they are worse than the Pharisees and Sadducees. They hate the *poor* regardless of what color they are.

"They have silenced the voice and the will of the underclass and the middle to lower class. They don't represent the Jesus Christ that I read about in the Holy Bible. They don't believe in *second* and *third chances*. They don't believe in not kicking a man when he's down they are the epitome of people who claim to love God and hate their brothers.

"Even Duane (Dog) Chapman can see through these idiots. Duane Dog is the Bounty Hunter, was a convict, an inmate; a dude convicted of murder. And a judge gave this Bounty Hunter (shout out to Leland, Lyssa, Tim and Beth Chapman) a second chance. The *words* the judge spoke helped change Duane's life. Now I don't like Duane's foul mouth, Davetta, so you don't need to mention the fact that he cusses like a sailor. I know. And that is *wrong*. But at least he believes that the prey he hunts in Honolulu, Colorado, Texas, California and all across this land deserve second changes.

"Davetta, I am gonna be that lawyer who lifts the boats stuck at the bottom. I'll force the system to change. And I'm not unmindful of the fact that I can't do it *alone*.

"I'm pragmatic enough to know it's gonna take time, skill, will, effort and perseverance. But as I employ the curiosity and interest of Anoop Ghanwani, Abace Louima, Keith Beuchamp, Matt Feeley, Jack Severson, Kevin Shelton and Craig Brewer, as I galvanize students like Kyle Love (Auburn), Vanhuksloot (Sacramento), Sean Taylor, Lisa Stokes and Brittany Young, I'll make a difference.

"Davetta, *I want to be a lawyer*! And I want to be so damned good at it that the living, the dead and the unborn will have to say, "There lived a great lawyer who practiced his job well." And as Johnnie Cochran's legacy and notoriety filled up law schools, etc., my flamboyance, eloquence and skills will cause guys and gals to attend Harvard, Howard, Morehouse and Yale instead of getting one way tickets to jail.

"Davetta, I want to become a lawyer. It is a great job with power and honor and prestige. It is a job in which the players have often been besmirched. But no one can tell me that there is any feeling better than walking out of a courtroom knowing you have obtained *justice for your clients*.

"Adrienne McCoy of Pittsburgh, Jason Vanhuksloot, Tracy Dill, Zach Smilovitz, Chat Gertach, Eric Wenzelow, Irena Medavoy, Adam Morgan, Lori Grub, Benny Moon, Zach Burkes, Brian Hawn, Matt Maloney and Jennifer Blood would love a lawyer if they were injured by a company.

"If Eric Bryant (Nashville, Tenn.) or Gayle King were falsely accused of murder, rape or assault, they too would love lawyers. I'll betcha Oprah appreciates good lawyers after she was defended by them in her beef case in Texas.

"P. Diddy, Geronimo Pratt, O. J. Simpson and William Kennedy Smith all owe their *freedom* to lawyers.

"I love lawyers! I love the lawyers who fight, care, strive and vigorously defend their clients. Davetta, just imagine how it must feel to walk out of a courtroom knowing your eloquence, your legal wit, your preparation, practice and your work has kept a man *wrongly* accused of molestation or murder from dying in prison?

"Davetta, what if Wayne Williams was innocent in Atlanta, Georgia in 1981? What if he didn't kill those *missing* and *murdered* children? The guy has spent more than two decades behind prison walls in Georgia. What would I feel like if I were the *Blue-Eyed Blonde* who walked down through the red hills of Jackson, Georgia and emerged from the prison with a wrongly convicted man set free?"

Davetta said, "You can continue your diatribe, Marc but *Wayne Williams*? Give me a break. Why are you even mentioning that *serial killer*?"

Marc took a deep breath and looked directly into Davetta's beautiful eyes and continued methodically, "My dear, I have spoken at length with Sherman Manning from Atlanta, Georgia. You'll recall he *led* the prayer vigils and marches for those murdered victims in Atlanta. Sherman made the news daily while he was a kid with Grace Davis of Atlanta Youth Against Crime, Andrew Young, Mayor Maynard Jackson, Police Chief Lee Brown, Commissioner Reginald Eaves, etc. and Sherman told me, 'None of us believed Wayne killed all those boys. There were glands and body parts missing from most of the boys. One gland is the gland which causes or affects youth. And there was much talk about a scheme to experiment with these glands to try to increase the life span of the wealthy. When I heard some of these rumors from top-level police officers, I'm not speaking of beat cops, Marc, we're talking captains, majors and higher. I discounted it all as propaganda, innuendo and *conspiracy* theory. But if these bodies were missing *glands* and other vital parts, something was up. And we missed it. The Atlanta Police Chief claimed that someone higher than him instructed them to make an arrest no matter *who it is* because our city is on fire. A reporter named Mark Picard, who was with WSB Channel 2 News told *me* that we were instructed *not* to report the fact that the murders did *not stop* when Wayne was locked up. He was told not to report the fact that the kidnappings and murders continued long after Wayne was at the Georgia Diagnostic Center in Jackson...'

"After talking with Sherman, my pals at WVEE-FM Radio in Atlanta and some retired cops I think Wayne was set up. What if I'm right? And what if I got him out? Davetta, how good would I sleep at night knowing I got a man out of prison that didn't do it?

"Davetta - I'm not being racist or biased but I must also tell you that everyday of the week guys go to juvenile, jail and prisons who *look like me* and more often than not, they get forcefully *raped* and when they get out they commit rape. They need lawyers... I hope you don't leave me because I no longer plan to become the next George Soros, Jeff Bezos or Bill Gates... You can still become Martha Stewart but I'll have to be Clarence Darrow. I want to become a lawyer!" Marc breathed, licked his lips, swallowed and repeated, "I want to be a lawyer. I wanna change the world. I want to break the cycle of despair, hatred and foolishness in America."

Davetta interrupted, "What do you mean *foolishness*, Marc?"

Marc replied, "All kinds of foolishness. Political foolishness, racial foolishness and just general *foolishness at large*."

Davetta finally laughed and smiled, "I've never heard the term general *foolish-ness at large*."

Marc went on, "We had this little girl they called Precious Doe. It took four or five years to find out her real name. Her step dad kicked her head and face and killed her. He then got a pair of hedge clippers and cut off her head. Davetta, he decapitated an innocent little girl. And it took our police and FBI nearly five years to identify a beheaded little girl. And we are worried about gay marriage or whether or not a gothic kid can wear black to school. How can we sleep at night?

"We have the audacity and unmitigated gall to go into another country claiming we are *spreading freedom*. We are building schools in Iraq and Afghanistan, but they are shutting down schools in California. We build no libraries or prep schools to teach poor folks how to get out of poverty, etc. in America, but we build schools in Iraq. That's lopsided and general foolishness.

"We have three hundred billion dollars to fight the unnecessary wars. We took it to the ass of Saddam Hussein on G.P. We can destroy and rebuild the infrastructure of Iraq and Afghanistan. But we can't fill potholes in D.C. or Atlanta or New York.

"But we build schools on foreign soil with *your tax dollars*. I talked to Bev Smith the other day and she's in her fifties. And Bev spoke at a school a few weeks ago and the school was sharing books with another school. And one of the books still had Bev Smith's *name in the book*. And Bev has not been in that school in almost forty years... Three hundred billion dollars for these wars! But *if* Ellen Tauscher, Mike Machado, Gloria Romero or the C.D.C went to the White House tomorrow and told our President, we need ten billion dollars to build state of the art schools and libraries to save the American youth, Bush would look at us like we are crazy. Actually that's not true. Bush would not even see us because we are nobodies to him. We would not make it pass the janitor.

"Davetta, we are in crisis in this country in many respects. Our failure and refusal to invest the billions of dollars in our inner cities, schools, library system and into troubled kids has cost us an entire generation of lost kids. We failed our children. I see void, hopelessness and a deadly, cold and vicious glare in the eyes of more and more kids everyday. These kids are not just in ghettos, barrios and the inner city. These are also middle class and rich children. Lost, empty and void. We think it's just low self-esteem. It's actually *no* self-esteem. You cannot have esteem for a *self* that you don't *know*. They don't know who they are. Who is the *self* we want them to have esteem for? Your self is your *purpose*, your *mission* and your *vision*. And without vision, the people *perish*.

"We want gays not to marry because we say they are a threat to our heterosexual marriages. I have a personal belief, which does *oppose* gay *marriage*. But I can't force my belief off on twenty million gays and lesbians. They are human too. And most of us marry for all the wrong damn reasons anyway. We marry to have the white picket fence and children. Those are all *wrong* reasons. You should enter into relationships to *heal*. And wherever love is, healing will prevail. We are all broken and hurt in places we don't wanna talk about.

"Davetta, I'm not an Oprah watcher and I damn sure don't watch a lot of Dr. Phil, but I did watch Brad and Kenda on May 11th on Dr. Phil. Brad and Kenda are husband and wife. Brad was molested as a kid. Kenda was also raped as a kid. And now they find out their son, Mikai is molesting his sister. What do we do when the kid you love hurts or molests the kid you love? What could Eve do when her son Cain whom she loved, killed her son Abel whom she loved?

"Davetta, the answer is to give birth to *Seth*. The name Seth means *new beginnings*. It's one - two - one. It is the *first* time after the second time. It's the ability to begin again. And for all of these troubled families like Brad and Kenda, our government should provide services like Creative Care out in California. But what raped kid in Perry Homes, Oak Park or Del Paso Heights can afford to get treatment for sexual abuse?

"What guy who was raped in Riker's Island, Pelican Bay, San Quentin, Lorton Penitentiary, Angola or juvenile can afford to get top notch therapy?

"Ninety percent of them cannot afford therapy. And they end up victimizing or having their lives destroyed. Oprah also did a show on molestation on May 11th. She had a twenty-two-year-old kid named Luis on and his mother. Luis was raped continuously by his step dad throughout his childhood. Now, on Oprah, Luis is quite effeminate and appears to be gay. If he is gay, I wanna know was this caused or influenced by his dad's abuse? I'm not *dissing* Luis. He's twenty-two and can be what he wants to be, but if his molestation led to a dysfunctional belief (by him) that he could not be with a woman shame on us as a society.

"Where were we, the church? We, the government? We, the schools and we, the parents when Luis and his mom needed us?

"We can go across the waters and build up communities and install governments, Davetta. We can send shuttles to space and install cameras on Mars...but we can't stop a man from raping a kid. We can't stop men from beating their wives. We can't keep speed, crack and heroin off our streets. This is foolishness and as an American trial lawyer, I will address this. I will sue *churches* that collect tens of millions of bucks per year but won't feed hungry people right around the corner. I'll sue companies that employ workers for twenty or thirty years but won't step up to the plate and pay for therapy and counseling when kids of their employees are in trouble or parents are in crisis.

"I will sue these prisons that won't treat drug addicts and stop rapes, violence and abuse inside the gated community.

"I'm not as concerned about marriage as I am about *Seth*. The new beginning that we need in America can teach people that people enter your life for three reasons. They enter your life for a *reason*, a *season* or a *lifetime*.

"I'll use the *law* to fight for Americans. Not Blacks, not Whites but *Americans*. I'll let Iraqi lawyers take care of Iraqi citizens... I am going to fight for Americans right here, right now. Our kids are in trouble. Our homes are being destroyed. Our America is in crisis."

Davetta interrupted, "Marc, are you swearing off sex? Please tell me you're not. I am horny. Are crusading lawyers allowed to screw?"

Marc said, "I'm being serious here, Davetta."

She replied, "Do I look like I'm joking? Listen to me. I am a good woman. I'm young, intelligent and idealistic, but I am not swearing off sex. I heard a lot of religious ideals in your impromptu speech and that's fine. But I'm not ready to give up sex. If you are then we have a problem. A major problem."

Marc stated, "I support all of the guys and gals who swear off sex. And I unfortunately believe a lot of them are lying. My mother taught me to *thine own self be true*. I will not play with me. I can front all day long and wear a façade to try to look good in the public eye, but at the end of the day, the way to peace is to respect me. And I won't love or respect me if I play games with others. So I won't claim to be a saint. I have really come to believe in the divine order of the universe. I have absolutely no doubt that God does exist. He is the King of Kings and Lord of Lords. I love Him and I want my life to honor Him on many levels. But I am still young and I am still a man. And I will continue to service you. I will tickle your fancy. I will kiss, lick and stick your vagina as often as you like. I'm still your...okay, you got the point? But there is *love* involved with our intimate exchange. It is deeper than lust. When I used to screw ladies that I didn't care about, it was empty. I was void. I didn't talk to them, eat with them and I didn't *engage* in their lives. Their families, emotions, dreams or visions were absolutely irrelevant to me. I only wanted the sex. But with you, it's different.

Way different.

"And I was afraid today you might leave me because of my career choice. You wanted me to be an entrepreneur, a Donald Trump or Richard Branson. But I changed my mind. I'm evolving, Davetta. I have transmogrified from the hairy worm, the caterpillar into a butterfly. Now I wanna try my wings as a warrior for justice."

"Will you represent child molesters and predators?" Davetta asked.

"Every man deserves a lawyer. It is the law. He or she deserves a vigorous defense by a lawyer. And so even those sick and wicked enough to rape kids deserve a lawyer. As an *officer of the court*, depending upon what city I practice in, I'll be required by law to sometimes take cases which I don't want to take. But I can tell you, I (personally) will never defend a guilty molester. I just won't do it. But those who are falsely accused of molestation, I will vigorously and strenuously fight for any person who gets wrongly accused and prosecuted for molestation.

"I will also demand justice for their victims of child molestation. I will sue systems, (such as juveniles, jails, prison, states) schools, colleges, business and even churches which are complicit and protecting molesters who lead their organizations. I'll fight to stop the victimization. I.e., that Catholic priest out in Stockton named O'Grady.

O'Grady has now admitted to molesting more than twenty-five kids. He molested altar boys and little girls. And the Bishop obviously knew this man was a pedophile. And what this Bishop did was simply the same thing the prison system does to thug cops; the Bishop simply transferred O'Grady from parish to parish. O'Grady described in graphic and sickening detail how he groomed the kids with hugs, tickles and games. And Father O'Grady was molested as a boy; yes, also by a priest. You talk about role models and victims victimizing.

"Davetta, if somebody had prevented O'Grady from being molested by a priest, he probably would not have become a priest. And I'm pretty certain; he would not have become a molester. And all those victims, like Joh Howard would never have had their innocence robbed. We ought to sue the Catholic Church in this case to the tune of tens of millions of dollars. And Bishops will begin to monitor priests more closely. And if we prevent just one child from having his/her innocence stolen, it's worth anything we can do.

"Mayor James West in Spokane, Washington used his office to lure kids. It would appear that in the 70s, the mayor volunteered to help Boy Scouts and other kids' groups and he used this as leverage to allegedly rape boys. And now he's the Mayor of Spokane. He ought to be in prison. I would sue him and take everything he has. By the time I finished with James West, he'd wish he was in prison.

"Willie Nesler was molested as a boy. You'll recall Nesler's mom shot the guy who molested Willie. Now Willie is on trial out in California for beating a man to death. Since he was molested, Willie has been in and out of juveniles on speed and in trouble.

"And methamphetamine is a highly addictive drug. It is a horrible drug to be on. Absolutely terrible. Willie would not be a drug addict or killer (I surmise) if he had never been molested. And so why didn't the village save him, Davetta? That would require a complex analysis and answer. But concisely, I'll tell you the *village*, the people of the community should always embrace crime victims. Hell, if the village patrolled the neighborhood, it would be nearly impossible for an outsider to come in and molest a child. But even after a crisis, the village is too busy nowadays to embrace, support and love a child. The nation, the state could have saved Willie. The moment molestation is reported; our government should require treatment for the offender and the offended. But Bush has *no time* to do something about treating the victims of crime or to pay to prevent crime by dealing with the underlying causes of pain. Bush is busy fighting wars and spreading freedom. And he's working hard and it's hard work.

"I wanna bring fresh minds, voices and ideas to the table. The do-it generation is you and me. We are not interested in *hearing* what you can *say*. We wanna *see* what you can *do*.

"In 2004, Doug Williams walked into *Lockheed Martin* in Meridian, Mississippi and sawed down a multitude of Black employees in a racist killing. Employees had complained for a year to both Lockheed and to the Sheriff about Doug Williams' racist comments and threatening words. They were ignored and Doug kept his job. The day after Lockheed Martin cleaned up the dead Black bodies from their factory floor, they began to clean up their own misconduct and reckless disregard for racial harmony. Lockheed covered it up by saying, 'We don't know that this killing was a racist killing.' Yet, evidence proves Doug wore a semi Klan hood to work, called Blacks the *N* word and told co-workers, 'One day I'll come to work and kill me some Black M.F.s.'

The Sheriff sat in front of a *Confederate* flag and stated, 'This killing was not racist. And I don't *recall* any complaints about Doug before this killing.' Doug killed himself also proving he was not only a racist, but also a coward. Lockheed C.E.O. and Chairman would have a lawsuit on him if I were a lawyer already. I'd sue John Stevens because he is responsible for all employees, policies, code of conduct and profits and losses. He should be sued for what he allowed to transpire. Ipso facto, I assure you he'd end up firing the other racists at the plant as well as supervisors at that plant.

"And when I find wardens, governors, etc., who allow inmates to be raped and they brush it under the rug or merely transfer officers when they are involved, I will sue their asses. (Chris Austad, David Jay, Garret Lambeta? Reading??)

"As bad as some of them will be, prisoners are human. And when we let them sit there with no hope, no love, no concern and no village, they fester, they crash and they burn. I know what goes on in these juveniles, jails and prisons. I visited LA County Jail, Dekalb County Jail, Sacramento County Jail, Alto, Chad, Reidsville, Riker's and San Quentin. They are cesspools of violence, racism, hatred and meanness.

"Davetta, a *judge*...not an advocate, not an activist but a judge said three weeks ago in San Francisco, CA, 'The problem of a highly dysfunctional, largely decrepit, overly bureaucratic and politically driven prison system... is too far gone to be *corrected* by *conventional* methods.' Those are the words of Federal Judge Thelton Henderson. Judge Henderson toured the prisons and said, 'I found horrifying conditions.'

"Judge Henderson said, 'The prison's a broken system with fundamental barriers to improvement, including budget, personnel, contracts, procurement, information systems, physical plant and space issues…prisoners continue to unnecessarily die, suffer and go unattended.' He found 'Multiple instances of incompetence, indifference, neglect and even cruelty.'

"I would sue the State of California and I would plot a strategy which would allow wardens, deputy wardens and governors to be held liable collectively as well as individually. Because I certainly don't want a void, empty, dysfunctional ex-con, fresh from a 'horrible' prison in which he was abused, mistreated, raped and neglected - moving next door to me. Moreover, I don't want a prison guard or warden who works in prison and participates in abuse and torture living next door to me either. The keeper can't keep creating monsters without becoming what and whom he keeps. If you can so much as watch a man get raped, beat or killed and do nothing about it; you are a rapist and killer and monster by default. I want to become a lawyer."

Davetta said, "It arouses me sexually when you talk like this. I love to hear that passion and fervor. But may I ask what will you do with all of your business, Internet and entrepreneurial wizardry? Will you abandon all interest in business?"

"Absolutely not," Marc replied. "I want a full service law firm. Full service, Criminal Law (i.e. Gerry Spence, Bobby Lee Cook, Murray J. Janus, Tony Serra and John Elsmore), Corporate Representation (i.e. David Boies et. al. Edwin Spencer Matthews, etc.) Civil Law (i.e. Willie Gary, David Mendolson, Norman Lippit, **me**), Family Law (i.e. Deanna Janus Cook, Lynn Gold Bikin, etc.), Free Speech Lawyers such as Floyd Abrams and the folks at the Pacific Justice Foundation in Sacramento, etc., etc.

"And I'll perhaps spend two to three hours per day dealing with business first. I gotta get through law school. I'm gonna take as many classes as I can and try to expedite my law degree. I want to get finished in rocket speed. And once I pass the bar, etc., I've got to attract the brightest legal talent in the country. I want young, good-looking and sexy lawyers. I also wanna use *Google* as a model for my law firm, i.e., I'll have an older (mature) lawyer leading and advising each division of my firm. I'll offer great salaries also. I'm gonna use the money I have in my trust fund to set up shop and guarantee first year salaries. Thank God my dad invested my trust money into Google, Amazon and Microsoft stock. My trust fund has thirty-nine million dollars in it now. And I'll use innovative, creative and abnormal techniques to get young lawyers in my firm. I'll call James Foxx, David Coles, Clark Kelso, Michael Vitiello, law school deans and staff members and ask 'Who is the brightest student in your class?' And I'll wine, dine and buy those students."

Davetta chimed in, "Can you tell me about some of your business plans?" Marc lit back up.

"Information, information and more information. Craig Newman (Founder of *Craigslists.com*) wants me to work with him. And so do numerous other Internet wizards. Caleb Sima in Atlanta, college students and even unknown bloggers. I'll narrow my involvement down to four or five of the most challenging characters and work with them. It will be fun and exciting. Keith Lantz and Caitlin McCoy are students out at Placer High in Sacramento, California. I'm gonna fund their college educations and recruit them to help the Internet company. I'll have them working with Alex Benzer and Kyern Bennett. All of them will work under Blake Ross. Blake is an Internet thespian. I wanna get Matt Funanwra and Neal Battaglia to learn from Blake. Blake is nineteen years old and he's in Stanford. He created the Firefox Web Browser in his parents' house in Miami and he's done something humongous software companies have sought to do for years - Capture market share from Microsoft Corp. Bill Gates is still my hero. But Bill had better look out. Blake Ross is coming! 'I don't think I am Bill Gates' worst nightmare, but this is a serious pride issue for Microsoft,' Blake told me a month ago.

"Firefox was released five months ago and the program has snared five percent of the market from the Microsoft Internet Explorer. Microsoft has dominated the market since surpassing *Netscape* Communications Corp. five years ago. But this Stanford sophomore (Blake) began working on Firefox two years ago while he was doing an internship at Netscape.

"Firefox, like the Linux Operating System, is distributed using a free, open source model which allows anyone to modify the program. Firefox will be a threat to Bill Gates cause it could be used for programs that bypass Microsoft's windows system, which generates more than $11.5 billion in yearly sales.

"Mike Mash is a V.P. out at Microsoft and he and his team throw darts at a dartboard with Blakes' head on it.

"Davetta, thirty-five million users have downloaded Firefox and Blake predicts the software will capture as much as fifteen percent of the browser market in the next year. Firefox has not only cloned Internet Explorer, they have done some cool things and out-innovated Internet Explorer. Last year Microsoft spent ten million dollars working on Internet Explorer. That contrasts with Netscape's prime, when Microsoft was devoting more than one hundred million dollars a year and one thousand workers to Internet Explorer. 'The fact is these bastards abandoned the browser market. We heard from customer after customer that the Internet is way too hard to use. People were tired of dealing with pop-up ads and spy ware. People were tired of the Internet experience, so we wanted to reduce these headaches for them.' Blake told me. Firefox is faster to download than Microsoft. Firefox blocks pop-up ads and allows users to quickly switch between different web pages stored as tabs on the top of the screen. Beck, the guys at GreenDay, Eminem and Justin Timberlake (as well as actor Charles O'Connell, Aaron Carter, John King, Ken Jacobson) Paris Hilton, Dr. Phil (Phil's sons *Jordan* McGraw, etc.) Oprah and even Tony Danza are using Firefox.

"Davetta, the U.S. Computer Emergency Readiness Team said in July that users could improve security by switching from Internet Explorer. My pal, Ero Carrera, concurs with that assessment. In August 1995 Netscape controlled eighty percent of the market. Microsoft hobbled Netscape by negotiating contracts with service providers, making it mandatory for them to carry the Internet Explorer instead of Netscape. This was a Don King type deal. America Online bought Netscape for $9.8 billion in 1999 and then *Time Warner* bought AOL... Blake got his beginning at age fourteen finding and fixing bugs for Netscape in the bedroom of his parents' home. Davetta, if we can bring computers to the inner city and get them in the homes of underprivileged kids, they (too) will begin to find and fix bugs. It will give them something to do, use their ingenuity and provide a bridge out of poverty. This will keep them out of these juveniles, jails and prisons, I've been preaching to you about. And we'll get Blake, Sima, Newmark and others to adopt these kids entrepreneurially. And in sponsoring or adopting them, those young entrepreneurs will provide books, programs and the educational infrastructure to lift these kids out of poverty. We can do this. We can replace their guns and bullets and drugs with the Internet, computers and programs teaching them how to discover bugs.

"And one of my pet peeves, which I know is unrelated to this segment of our discussion, is, as you know, child rape. And I want to get the brightest minds in the country including Blake Ross, F-Secure, Caleb Sima, etc. to develop a state of the art blocking system, which is continuously updated and prevents predators from inserting themselves on to the computers of anyone under eighteen years of age. Also, I want a system similar to 911, which is only for kids to report fondling, rape or molestation. We can do this with the Internet...

"Back to Blake's beginning! By age seventeen, he was in his second year at Netscape as an intern when he began to tinker with the code in the company's Mozilla Browser along with co-worker, David

Hyatt. And kids like to tinker. They love to create, to build and to recreate. And as a spin-off of my future involvement with these Internet thespians, I will get college kids like Blake to mentor teens at YMCA and in the Girls and Boys Clubs in the inner city. That's what kids need, Davetta. They don't need three points and a poem. They don't need holier than thou lectures by hypocrites. They need to know how to not make the same mistakes that their parents made. They need to have something more than boom boxes and booty dancing. And I think we can reach and teach them by utilizing the World Wide Web as a vehicle and a magnet."

Davetta said, "But if they are to find their *purpose*, you will need to do some wild shit on the Internet in addition to teaching Internet repair right?"

Marc replied, "Sweetheart, you make it sound so corny, boring and run of the mill when you say Internet repair. But I get your point and we've thought about that. And this is where our outreach will be even more impactful and powerful. We will *edu-tain* kids. We'll show videos on finding, purpose and having visions for life. Teen coping skills and how to deal with peer pressure will be shown. We will address, deal with and highlight the destructiveness of meth use and abuse. We'll blog, profile and feature how crystal meth kills people, fries the brain and creates losers. We will bring on real kids who have been on meth, speed and crack. We will let them tell their peers what it did to them and how they got off. We will show that you don't need to experiment, you can avoid it and you don't need it. And we will show the one's who are using that there is *life after* meth, life after crack. Life after this and life after that. I *gots* plans, baby girl.

"Enter Mark Pinkus of Tribe.net. He created a community-networking site in San Francisco. Davetta, we are nearly seven billion souls on the planet and we still search for ways to find each other. The sheer magnitude of our numbers seemingly makes it difficult for us to connect. Marcus Pinkus will help us create a blogging, e-mailing and *Web-eristic* (if you will) bridge across the community, bridge across America and bridge across the world. We will connect kids in the hoods with and to kids in the suburbs. We will connect kids in juvenile with kids in church, kids in jails with kids in college. So many of our babies, boys and girls have entered into the largest university in America, which is the *University of Crime*, the University of the U. S. Prison System. We must get them out of there. Many of them have no Internet access but we'll deputize correspondent agents to write to them and to serve as the glue which holds them together with their families, friends, loved ones and pastors.

"George Soros, John Sperling, Peter B. Lewis, Steve Madden, Brad Pitt, Rick Martin, Tom Hayden, Bruce Springsteen, Oprah, Duane Chapman, Dr. Phil, Bill Cosby, Tony Danza, Bev Smith, Tavis Smiley and Jamie Foxx (to name a few) have all agreed to finance this. When we put Bill Gates, Ted Turner, Marc Cuban, Harvey Levin, Matt Damon, Andy Brody, Mick Jagger, Green Day and Sharon Stone behind a project, it will catapult into the stratosphere.

"Journalism professors like Chris Burnett, Mark Burnett, Martha Stewart and Andy McDonald have all agreed to help us. All Mel Bacon, Steven Spielberg and John Marriott are waiting for is to see the plan. And we will roll out a plan that will blow their freaking minds. Mark Pinkus is also revolutionizing young people's lives and their ability to have their voices heard. Davetta, you have got to go to www.Tribe.net and www.WadeLagrone.org and set up a blog, profile or a tribe. These dudes are maximizing technology and taking our ability or potential to reach around the world and connect through the roof. Check this out: Users can spontaneously create interest groups on Tribe.net. These tribes are as diverse as imagination or visualization will take you - from people who love Hawaii to people who hate Albert Einstein. David Verrechia started his own 'Tribe' as the sole marketing tool to launch his women's apparel business, VanderKitty.com. Rubin "Hurricane" Carter, *Sherman D. Manning* and Barry Scheck are all on Tribe.net. Glenn Kohler, an aesthetician and massage therapist, used Tribe.net connections to hire people for his business. Health Arts Wellness Services in Berkeley. Glenn posted his plans to go to a motorcycle meet in LA so he could be assured of social contact when he got there. Let me tell ya what Mark told me, 'Dude, in the future, people will control their online identities. Who will host your identity will be as important as the host of your e-mail. By the end of 2006, users will be able to lodge their personal profiles on our site and deploy it anywhere across the public network.'

"Davetta, let's say you're selling on E-bay and you want to identify yourself. Your profile on Tribe.net can be linked to the online auction house. And you can have alternate profiles for different purposes - i.e. one profile for jobs and one when you're looking for dates, etc. In fact, thirty-two daily newspapers attract twelve million unique visitors per month.

I saw announcements on Craigslists.com, open site.com, Friendster.com, Myspace.com, Tickle.com, WiredReach.com and LinkedIn.com for Moveon.org, Sherman D. Manning, The Beat Within News and *The Progressive...* But nothing topped the sites and tribes I saw on Tribe.net on youth issues, juvenile inmates, prison activists, wrongful convictions, restaurants, books, music, etc.

"Davetta, I believe the Internet, Marcus Pinkus, Sergey, Blake, Benzer and the boys will figure out ways to revolutionize politics in America. By the end of 2006 youngsters will begin to take over and own issues of social justice law and order and diversity.

"Pretty soon it will become cool to wear a T-shirt that says 'We Freed Mandela, Now Let's Free Manning.' You will see teens wearing baseball caps with Sherman's 'American Dream/A Search For Justice' on them.

"Davetta, you cannot keep youth down forever. They get sick and tired of bullshit and they rise up and force change. History is replete with examples of kids discovering the truth about problems of societal impact and inserting themselves in issues of worth. It was a sixteen-year-old kid nicknamed Lazarus who spearheaded the monumental movement, which eventually exonerated Rubin 'Hurricane' Carter. It was White and Black kids who filled up the jails in Alabama to defeat Bull Connor and his racist assault tactics. In Ukraine, it was a youth movement which voided the fraudulent vote, forced a re-*vote* and elected a poisoned but powerful new president.

"Unfortunately it is our kids who are courageously fighting and dying everyday in Afghanistan and Iraq...

"Davetta, officers at many prisons in California are told they can get a quarter of their annual training by completing word search and crossword puzzles."

Davetta was red with laughter. "You're freaking lying, Marc."

"No! I'm telling you the CCPOA forced C.D.C. to allow prison guards to use word puzzles as a substitute for guard training. Finding hidden words such as 'elf', 'snow' and 'gingerbread' supposedly prepares officers to deal with so-called dangerous inmates. I called Lance Corcoran and he told me officers get fifty-two hours of training yearly in such things as use of force, firearms and transporting prisoners. Forty hours are hands on, but Lance said their union contract required the remaining twelve hours to be spent studying bulletins with policy changes, administrative directives - and puzzles."

Davetta bowled over in redness and laughter again.

"One exercise, my darling, required guards to find the names of pro football teams hidden among a jumble of letters. 'Complete the word find puzzle below and submit it to receive one hour credit. Good luck and have fun.'"

"Assemblyman Rudy Bermudez called it 'unbelievable and totally unacceptable.' I'll be you my life that the valedictorian at Davis

High School, class president at Luther Burbank High School, Kyern Bennett, Marcos Garza, Sean Taylor and Jared Yates or Kyle Love in Auburn would take one look at this elementary, preschool practice and fire the person who approved of the puzzles forthwith. But among the old, worn out and tired leaders of C.D.C. the state and even our federal government they will meet, meet, talk, hold a press conference and C.D.C. will return back to normal. Older politicians lose their vitality, idealism and energy. They drink too much, smoke too much, joke too much and lie, lie and then lie some more. But there is a hidden, methodical, technocratic and brilliant breed of young leaders rising up all across this country.

"You have boys in juveniles, kids in prisons, jails, foster homes and even kids on the streets who are getting the message that it's their time to take over. They realize that youngsters aged twelve to nineteen, spent one hundred and seventy-five billion dollars in 2003 alone. And they're telling us that two hundred billion dollars guarantees them the right to have a seat at the table of power. They are aligning themselves, strategizing and galvanizing from the bottom up. I see a movement on the horizon. These teens are savvy, sharp, idealistic and energetic. And what they are saying is 'Hey parents, we listened to you all. We trusted you to take care of us and you let *Columbine* happen. We allowed you to lead and you gave us Iraq to the tune of three hundred billion dollars and almost two thousand of our peers came back to America in body bags.

When we had slavery, you adults were in charge. When we learned about racial slurs, racism, violence, guns, drugs and hate, *you* adults taught it to us. We love, honor and respect you but we are beginning to think perhaps you don't know what the hell you are doing. Maybe you need to move out of our way and let us do the leading.'

"That's what I'm hearing, Davetta. So I want to become an attorney. I want to represent the people and fight for justice. I'll demand that these bright-eyed boys and girls who were born into a mistake because of the foolishness, addictions and failures of their parents *be given a second chance*. I will sue and utilize a legal strategy, which will *force* America to do for self and kind. It will become illegal for us to have homeless people sleeping outside the White House in D.C. while we unnecessarily spend three hundred billion dollars to fight wars and build schools in Iraq.

"It will become unconstitutional to have babies molested in America while we claim to spread freedom and civility in Afghanistan. We will stop the bullshit. We will not sit back and watch a president who *claims* to be a born again, Bible thumping Christian; yet, pass by the homeless, hungry and cold in Dupont Circle everyday of the week in his chauffeured driven, bullet proof limousine en route to the White House. "Davetta, kids are rising up and saying, 'We ain't gonna stand for it no more.' And I will represent them. I'll fight for them as a lawyer. I know Anthony Fedorov, Bo Bice, Timothy Goebel, Johnny Weir, Tanvir Kapoor, Pincus, Blake Ross, Ero Carerra, Clay Aiken, Matt Damon, Ashton Kutcher, Ben McKenzie, Brody and Zach Roerig will stand with us. They (too) see the hypocrisy perpetrating under the guise of a democracy.

"Davetta, I believe in self-reliance, self-help, initiative and all that and a bag of chips. I'm cognizant of the fact that some people are just lazy, etc. I've preached the adages and clichés that if you give a man a fish you feed him for a day, but *teach* him how to fish and you'll feed him for a lifetime and people oughta pull themselves up by their own bootstraps. But what if they have *no boots*? As a lawyer, I shall utilize my profile, status and bully pulpit to pose the question: What kind of a president can love God but hate the homeless? What kind of guy can be concerned (so he says) about citizens in Iraq and their freedom and turn his head away from the homeless sleeping outside in the *bushes* near the White House? How can Mr. Bush, Rumsfeld, Cheney and all those Jesus-loving Christians in the White House be so arrogant, blatantly hypocritical and cold as to tell us that it is okay not to remember that *Jesus Christ* himself said, 'I was hungry and you (Mr. *Oil* Bush, Mr. *Halliburton* Cheney, Mr. *Real Estate* Rumsfeld) fed me not... In prison and you (Mr. Falwell, Mr. Dobson, Mr. Pat Robertson, Ralph Reid) visited me not.' This is wrong. And the weak, scared, biased, big business and *sold out* media refuses to expose it.

"Bring me Smilovitz (Detroit), McSwane (Colorado), Craig Scott, Ojeda Beck, Kapoor, JROTC students of McClatchy, Davis Senior High School, newspaper editors, Beat Within writers, Mike Kroll, David Inocencio, Christian Dunst, Aaron Carter, Kevin Shelton, Mr. Green (Pizza King), Trey Wright (Scrabble Champion), bring me Bev's daughter Heather, Wilbert Rideau, The *Progressive* in Wisconsin, Deirig, *The Nation*, Randi Rhodes and Tom Joyner. Bring me Earl Ofari Hutchinson and the Sacramento News and Review and I will *join* a movement composed of those from the slummy side to the sunny side. The fellas from the hood like Joe Dudley and Dennis Kimbro who believed they could.

"Bring me those trapped in penal institutions who spend their mornings hoping, their days praying, their evenings reading and their nights writing... I want those who are the least likely and the left out, locked in and forgotten about and we will revolutionize and transmogrify this nation. We'll do it cell by cell, jail by jail, school by school, community by community, city by city, state by state and nation by nation. We will reach across the sea, over the waters and around the mountains and connect the youth of the world. When Bush, Cheney, those old ass senators and sold out journalists see us coming by way of newspaper, coming by song, poem, book and blog, they will shout, 'It's a bird, it's a plane; no it's Super Information Highway.' They won't know what hit them. We will take over. We will put violent, vicious and bellicose men in prison. We will create safe beds for every child. We will feed our hungry and clothe our naked. And we will get weed smokers and burglars out of prison. We will teach their asses how to read, write, work and count. We will teach diversity, leadership, marketing, sales, truth, integrity and *love*.

"I will do my part to open up (strategically) loopholes and to exploit technicalities which will guarantee *open debates* and authentic town hall meetings where politicians are required to *answer* the damned questions and stop the bullshit. I will sue politicians who sell out their constituents and excuse misconduct on the highest levels of bureaucratic government. I'll be to youth what Johnnie Cochran was to celebrity defendants. I'll handle a law book and a courtroom like Michael Jordan handled a basketball and a coliseum. I'll be to the law what Muhammed Ali was to boxing. I will take their asses to court. Lying politicians, corrupted prison staff, juvenile abusers, child molesting priests and governors who allow the innocent and wrongly convicted to languish in the funky assholes of the prison system will hate me.

"I want to become a lawyer..."

Two weeks later, through a series of e-mails, text messages and telephone calls to, fro and through talk show Queen Bev Smith, David and Lawrence (Mrs. Bev's assistant at the American Urban Radio Network) had some kind a way hooked Marc up with Scott Coffman. Scott talked for two hours with Marc during their first conversation. Scott shared all of the missives, e-mails, journals and research data, which had been retrieved from Paul (rest in peace) and his brother's personal effects. Marc maneuvered, strategically manipulated and some kind a way got all of this data to Lisa Ling. Lisa Ling shared it with Gayle King and Gayle got it to Queen Oprah Winfrey... It was June 27th when Oprah sat down with a cup of decaf at Harpo Studios and began perusing the data. One of Oprah's executive producers had reduced the voluminous data down to a twenty-seven-page report with all the appropriate footnotes, sources and subject specific indexing...

As Oprah flipped through the very last page of the report, she uttered out loud, "Wow." She then called Lisa Ling. "Lisa, I want you to go back to California and interview me ten *Blue-Eyed Blonde* Caucasian males in LA County Jail. I'm sending Gayle to do the same thing at Riker's Island and I'm gonna go to Georgia and interview young Whites at the prison in Alto. This might not happen as soon as Sherman may want it to happen, but it's gonna happen. This is horrible. I'll call Maria and get Arnold to let you in the prison up in California."

Lisa said, "We won't need Arnold if I'm going to LA County Jail. We will need the Sheriff. Now if you want me to go inside a state prison, I'll need the Governor only if I take a camera."

They chatted for twenty minutes…

* * *

Meanwhile Montel Williams was contacted about another case of injustice. This woman had been a college student. This woman was smart and idealistic. She was voted the most likely to succeed in her senior class in high school in Compton, California. In college, her one indiscretion was her love for weed. And one day, one of her friends talked her into trying a lil heroin. After that first try, *Cheryl Beridon Hayes* was hooked. She ended up like so many young girls (and guys) selling her body to support her habit. She sank lower and lower into her addiction. Yet, she found time to fall in love and move to Homer, Louisiana. She married and had a son. Her husband got a traffic ticket and she went with him to court. Damn… In court, Cheryl saw a set of hazel eyes piercing through her very being. This White man locked his eyes upon her with such enthusiasm, determination and curiosity that it almost startled Cheryl. But she was intrigued. She had heard of *love at first sight*, but she loved her husband. Even though she was a bona fide heroin addict and a part time hooker, she did love her husband. And other than her tricks, she never cheated on Bobby. But in this courtroom, this White man taught her what was *control at first sight*. He was Norval Rhodes, the most powerful District Attorney in Louisiana. This was in 1981…

One month later, the relationship between Norval Rhodes and Cheryl was in high gear. This man had a wife and kids but would be seen around town with Cheryl. He took her to lawyers' conventions. He bought her a car with D.A. money. He rented her a townhouse and put her on County D.A. payroll. He also became violent, controlling and threatening. He often told her, "no matter how often we are seen together in public, you are a Black woman and I can't ever be exposed as a *N* lover. You are to tell everybody you work for me. That's all you need to say. You do clerical or paralegal work. And if it's a close family member and they press you for details, you tell them you are a confidential informant for the D.A.s office."

After controlling, beating, screwing and abusing Cheryl for 1½ years, Cheryl decided she wanted to get off heroin. She knew that in order to get off, she'd need to stop prostituting and stop seeing the man (Norval) who was plying her with drugs, which he stole from police lockers and drug busts. "It's over, Norval," she told him one cold December evening in 1983. I'm done with drugs, prostituting and this affair. I gotta stop this now."

With the coldest and most vicious eyes she'd ever seen in her entire lifetime, Norval Rhodes told her, "I will send you to prison for the rest of your life if you try to cut this off."

* * *

Lisa Ling wrapped up her tenth interview at LA County Jail on a Tuesday evening at 3:12 p.m. "I was trained raped by three Blacks and two Mexicans. They threatened to kill me. I never hurt so bad. I bled so bad. I couldn't walk the next day, Mrs. Ling. I didn't tell nobody. I would have been labeled as a punk, faggot and a rat," Devin told her.

"Devin was twenty-two years old. Of the ten guys she interviewed, seven admitted to being raped in jail or prison. One of the three, Lisa felt was raped, but too embarrassed to admit it to her. But he knew too much, she thought, to have not been raped himself. In the seven who had been violated at various times in jail, C.Y.A. and/or prison…all of their rapists were Black or Brown. Damn! Lisa thought as she and her cameraman walked out of LA County Jail. She called Gayle on her cell and said, "Gayle? Driving while Black. Guilty of being Black. I got a new one for you, Guilty by being White! More specifically, I should say *raped for* being young, White, with blue eyes and blonde hair. This is horrible." They talked for about fifteen minutes…

"I talked to Oprah," Gayle said. "And she said the same thing you just said. And what I found at Riker's Island were very, very similar results. Six of my ten guys were raped. And all but one of the rapists was Black or Brown. And two of my guys told staff and the officers basically said, 'You should not have come to prison. Be a man. Go stab them.'"

Tavis Smiley did a show on *Desperate Prisoners' Wives*. And one of the wives told Tavis, "My husband was beat to a pulp at High Desert State Prison for cussing at a guard. We have eight eyewitnesses stating they threw more than two hundred punches after my husband was handcuffed face down on the floor. One witness was a (sic) officer himself!"

Matt Funanwra and Neal Battaglia sat in their dorm at CSU Sacramento and watched Tavis that night. "Way out, dude. I hope I never go to prison," Matt said.

"Well, you'd better leave that crank alone and get help," Neal told Matt.

"I don't use crank," Matt said.

John Goodrum also watched the same show at his college dorm at Southern Methodist University. So did Kim DeBlance. But Kim went to her computer right after the show and dedicated her entrée blog to the subject. "How can we kill in the name of justice?" she wrote. "We murder people who murder people and tell kids it's wrong to murder. If each one of you reading my blog today would go on to Myspace.com, orkut.com, Friendster.com, Friendworks.com and WiredReach.com and talk about this blog, we could organize. We need to clean up these prisons and stop manufacturing madness and *Creating Monsters* (™)," she wrote.

    * * *

Montel continued to listen to Cheryl's story. "Norval got a secret indictment by the grand jury and charged me with selling five bags of heroin. I never sold a drug in my entire lifetime. He assigned the case to one of his own prosecutors. He then included *himself* as a witness during my trial. In fact, Mr. Williams," Cheryl told Montel, "Norval was the only witness against me. The heroin came from the *evidence locker*. And he claimed *he* was out *observing* drug trafficking and he saw me sell this heroin to another confidential informant." Cheryl told Montel that this all White jury found her guilty. "I couldn't believe my ears when they said guilty. And then the judge sentenced me to *life in prison. Life*! I looked at my mother and I cried. I thought I would never see my mother and my son again. Mr. Montel, this was absolutely surreal to me. I thought I was having a nightmare. My chest started hurting. I could barely breathe. I cried. I screamed. I hurt. You don't know what it feels like to stare injustice, wrongful conviction and a railroading right in the eye when you grew up *believing* in the justice system.

"I went on to prison and for two years I barely got out of bed. I tried to commit suicide. I lost eighty-seven pounds. My mother is the only reason I'm alive. She lost three houses and went bankrupt trying to get me out of prison. I spent twenty-three years... I spent twenty-three years in prison for a crime that did not take place.

"Finally, NAACP (Parish, LA) President Jerome Boykin came to visit me. He said, 'You can pack your bags, you're coming outta here.' Mr. Boykin got a lawyer and he filed a petition for pardon and parole. The new Chairman of the Parole Board (Irv Magri) accepted my petition for a hearing. Mr. Magri called Norval personally and said, 'Listen, Mr. Rhodes, we have this woman claiming you set her up because she broke off an illicit affair with you. We have analytically reviewed the evidence in her petition. We see a lot that don't look right. This whole case doesn't pass the smell test. Now we want to be fair, just and follow the law. Ipso facto, at your convenience we'd like for you to appear before the parole board and oppose her release and answer our questions.' Mr. Montel, the D.A. *refused* to appear. And Mr. Magri tried to subpoena him to testify and the judge refused to allow the subpoena..."

Montel did the show on Cheryl a day later and he wept as they taped the show. "This woman was railroaded. *Guilty by being Black.*" And Montel said, "All these people in this town *knew* the D.A. was screwing this woman. They knew about the affair, the set up and the drugs. And yet they allowed her to sit in a prison for twenty-three years and nobody did a damned thing. This is America. The same America that will *shoot up* a *country* to the tune of eighteen hundred dead U.S. soldiers and one hundred thousand dead Iraqis to spread *freedom and democracy* in **Iraq**, but won't do a damn thing to protect the freedom, due process and constitutional rights of a woman in America. And there are thousands, literally *thousands* of set up, railroaded, overcharged and wrongly convicted men and women in Abu Ghraib like prisons right here in America. Mr. Bush ought to fight for them. *How dare we waste this life*? *How dare we* sit back and allow anybody; Black, White, Mexican, other, male or female to sit trapped in the anus of a failed prison system when they are innocent? This is sick."

Montel brought Mr. Irv Magri to the taping. Irv is a White man and he caught a lot of Black heat for paroling this woman. "We did the right thing. It don't matter that Norval was a District Attorney and he was White. What he did to this Black woman was nowhere near right. And now she has no money. No nothing. In prison, she wrote letters for women who couldn't write. She became the warden's clerk. She did everything she could to help others even though she thought she'd never get out. She was a *princess in prison* like Gloria Killian. I think my state ought to compensate her. She should find a Willie Gary, David Boies, Carl Douglas or Bert Deixler to sue. If they throw it out, keep litigating every way she can til they change the law and pay her for twenty-three years of false incarceration."

Mr. James Sandifer, another White man who is president of the *Crime Victims* Board appeared on the show also. Mr. Sandifer definitely believes in prison and in locking up criminals. But he said, "This was wrong, Montel. And I'm beginning to see cases of injustice like this are not as unusual as we think they are. I hate to admit it but there are a lot of wrongly convicted people in prison. Most are poor, many are Black and all should be set free and compensated for being wrongly convicted."

I point out that Mr. Magri and Mr. Sandifer are White for a reason. Make no mistake about it, there are still many racist people in this country. There will always be some racist people in every shade and color. Racism is a sensitive and touchy topic. Good White people don't like to talk about it. Black folks some times talk about it too much. It's divisive, hurtful and scary. But the facts are what they are. And the fact is 92.6 percent of the judges in America are White. *If* only ten percent of them (a low number) are racist what does that say to us? How many innocent minorities, will they be more proned to sentence to longer sentences in prison? 91.3 percent of all prosecutors in 2003 were White. If just five percent of them are racist, what does that say? If just ten percent are half as corrupt as Norval Rhodes was - what does that tell you?

Norval Rhodes is now a law professor in Florida and his power, corruption and venom is still infecting and controlling Homer, LA. Judges and prosecutors in Homer still refuse to talk about Cheryl's case. So this was absolutely a mixture of racism and corruption.

And the reason I still love all people. The reason I still love America. The reason I still believe in justice is because no matter how racist, biased or corrupt the George Bush's, Rush Limbaugh's and Dick Cheney's may be, there are still always human loving White people (i.e. the late Jeremy Shackelford, Paul Shackelford, Scott Coffman, C.S.U. Professor Chuck Toto, Sharon Stone, Frank Darabont, Tony Danza and Dr. Phil) who will rise to the occasion and do justice, love mercy and walk humbly with God. It was a White judge; the Honorable Judge Sarokin who signed the check at the bank of justice, which gave Rubin "Hurricane" Carter his freedom after twenty-one years in prison wrongly convicted. White lawyers such as Leon Friedman represented him pro bono. So even though a lot of good White folks still feel a bit sensitive when they hear, "It happened to him or her because he was Black." And even though some Black folks do call *every* problem a *racist* problem, I wanted to remind all of us that there are many who don't give a damn what *be* your color or what *be* your kind. They will stand up against any injustice they may find. I'll catch some heat from *some* Blacks as I stated in letters to Jeremy and Paul. There will be some Blacks who think I should keep quiet about the crimes taking place against White guys in prisons nationwide. But they can kiss my Black ass. Wrong is wrong. A crime is a crime. Rape is rape and it's wrong and a crime. All that it takes for evil to rage is for good men to *remain silent*. You. who are perusing this tome right now, have the right to remain silent. But I would hope you'll have enough dignity, altruism and just decency to spread the word about what is happening inside our broken judicial and penal system. You ought to demand that your governors get innocent men out of prison. You ought to go to Myspace.com and Tribe.net and blog about it. You ought to lobby the Congress, the Senate and even the White House and demand that these prisons let cameras inside, become transparent and stop destroying humanity. You ought to go online *today* and go to (www.cafepress.com/*creating*) www.cafepress.com/palace2prison and order copies of these books and have them mailed (cafepress will mail them directly) to your pastors, media, radio hosts, senators, congress and even to the White House. **You**, right where you are, ought to go to www.*FriendsBeyondThe Wall*.com and get the address to a few inmates and have cafepress mail them copies of this book. You ought to do something today to preserve and protect America tomorrow. *Each* (and every) of the tens of thousands of guys in juveniles and youth authority today *will* get out of juvenile one day. *Most* of the guys in prison this year will be out of prison within ten years. Seven hundred thousand inmates locked in our prisons *this* year will get out *next* year. And if they have been raped, beat, abused, frustrated and abandoned, what the hell do you think they are gonna do when they get out? Eight out of ten who get out of juvenile (California youth prisons) in California re-offend and go back. Only *one* out of ten who get out of juvenile in Missouri return or re-offend. I don't have the time to tell you *why* this is so. But I can tell you if you lock a dog in a cage and beat him for five or ten years and then wake him up one morning, give him a bone, take him to Wiltshire Blvd. in Beverly Hills and set him free, he'll be mad. He'll be crazy. And we are crazy if we think this thing that we do will get better. We are absolutely fools if we think this stuff we call punishment, this beating of prisoners, this forgetting them and denying them, this allowing hillbillies to *keep them* and *mistreat* them is ever gonna work. If we think it is going to work, we should kick our own asses.

You cannot get blood out of a turnip. You cannot produce law-abiding citizens if you correct murder with murder. If you preach love of God, but practice hatred of man. If you sing the "no child left behind" message but leave every *Blue-Eyed Blonde* child in Chad, Riker's Island, Alto, High Desert and in juveniles across the country behind. You cannot preach *democracy* abroad while you practice *hypocrisy* at home. Your child, will be molested! Your home will be burglarized! Your friends, spouse and loved ones *will be murdered.* You are not safe at the theater, in the shopping mall or even at church as long as your President and senators continue to do injustice, hate mercy, and walk arrogantly with their *god*, which is *money.* The recipe for disaster, violence and monsterism can be found in prisons, juveniles and jails. If we ain't smart enough to look at Missouri's juvenile system and *model* it in California, then we deserve the *made* gangsters, *made* molesters, *made* murderers and *made* criminals that we manufacture in our prisons.

This shit is out of control and it is off the hook. And it ain't funny...

Wilbert Rideau, Rubin "Hurricane" Carter, Barry Scheck, Eminem, Benjamin McKenzie, Adam Brody, Clay Aiken, Morgan Freeman, Denzel and Pauletta Washington, Kevin Shelton, Mr. Knedlik, Anthony Fedorov, Jamie Foxx, Sharon Stone, Thomas Dexter Jakes and Serita, Bev Smith, Rolando Cruz, Paul Wright, Tony Danza, Tom Joyner and Joe Price (along with someone whose last name is Darsie... The person's first name is indecipherable) all signed a petition, which went to every governor in America and all one hundred senators. It read: "We believe in law and order. We love America. We love our families and our friends. We have joined *NAPS* and we are extremely alarmed by the epidemic problem of rape in prisons and juveniles nationwide. We want the problem addressed and rectified immediately... We would like to send our representatives to meet with you within the next thirty days..."

The petition was mailed out on the first Monday of July. At press time, I'm still awaiting more data on what the responses were. I do know that Morgan Freeman, Montel Williams, Clay Aiken, Eminem, Timothy Goebel, Sharon Stone, Samuel L. Jackson, Jamie Foxx, Hurricane, Danny Glover and George Soros have scheduled a press conference for the first Monday in August to talk about the National Association for Public Safety. That I know for a fact, but rumor has it that Bono, Bruce Springsteen and two members of *Green Day* will also appear at the press conference...

Scott Coffman called Bill Gates and actually got through to him. Lisa Ling had gotten Oprah to get Bill to take the call. Marc had hooked Scott and Lisa up... "Bill here," Mr. Gates spoke into the receiver from his palatial estate outside of Redmond, Washington. "What can I do for you, Scott?"

Scott got a lump in his throat. He realized clearly that he was talking to the wealthiest man in the universe. Oprah is filthy rich, but Bill Gates is wealthy. He is *The Man*. Rich folks fly First Class and sporadically charter private planes. Wealthy people own *Lear Jets*. Scott felt... He was nervous, anxious and excited. His stomach was doing flip-flops.

"Mr. Gates, do you love your family?"

Bill thought this was an odd question but what the hell, he'd play along. "Yes. I love Melinda and my kids," he replied.

"Well, do you want them safe, sir?"

Bill said simply, "Yes."

Scott continued, "Well, Mr. Gates, there is a severe safety and security problem in America. Each day almost two thousand violent, un-rehabilitated, frustrated, depressed, stressed, broke, busted and disgusted inmates get out of prison. Many of them have been raped, beat, abused and mistreated in the prisons. They are..." Scott methodically explained the problem and then went into his spiel, "Friends of mine stumbled upon the *Real Life* story dubbed *Blue-Eyed Blonde* via an old Navy buddy of mine named *Sherman D. Manning*. Both guys are dead... I'm scared. I don't have the money to get twenty-four hour security for my family and me. If I proceed and in anyway involve myself in this story, I believe I'll be killed."

Mr. Gates said, "Does Oprah know all of this?"

Scott replied, "Some of it. She is doing a show but not soon enough. And I need help now!"

(Editor's Note: The remainder of the Real Life conversation between Microsoft Chairman Bill Gates and Sherman's pal, Scott, has been redacted at the request of lawyers for the Microsoft Corporation. We regret this editorial decision).

Marc and Davetta were at a hotel in Pittsburgh in preparation for *The Bev Smith Show*. "Are you gonna talk about Catholic priests today, Marc?"

He laughed and replied, "Mrs. Smith has seven million listeners and I would be remiss not to give them the full story. I think I'm duty bound to establish the parallels between the way prison authorities cover up for rogue cops and Catholic priests cover up for one another. And I know Bev mainly wants to hear about the tragedy of the White guys being raped in LA County jails, Sacramento County jails, Fulton County, in juveniles and prisons across America. And she has already indicated to me that she clearly sees a connection between victims and victimization. She is interested in the origins of rape. And there is strong data pointing to boys raped by priests growing up to abuse alcohol and drugs. They end up in prison and they either get raped in prison because of what priests did to them as children or they commit rape in prison because of what priests did to them. Bev believes any genuine attempt to stamp out rape in prison must be done with a concurrent attempt to clean up Catholic churches."

Davetta said, "Sounds good. Now can we screw right quick before we go to Avon Studios? I have a condom."

Marc unzipped his pants and Davetta began to fondle. She performed fellatio... She opened up a second condom and put it on Marc. "We can't have you going off to law school with a baby on the way," she said. "Plus we can't risk either of us getting disease. I trust you, Marc, but men will be men."

At the station, Beverly Smith, Lawrence and David were very friendly. Bev opened up the show with a powerful monologue. She talked about prisons, corruption, rehabilitation, gangs, guns, drugs and victims. She then said that we need to deal with rapes in the juveniles, jails, in the prisons, foster homes and "rapes in the Catholic church." She said, "It is absolutely sickening... Are you all familiar with the *Orange Files*? They show predator priests were shuffled around from church to church as parishioners were kept in the dark. William Lobdell and Jean Guccione did a major story on this catastrophe. For two decades, officials in the Roman Catholic Diocese of Orange California covered up for priests who molested children. They transferred predators from parish to parish and diocese to diocese protecting them from prosecution. They absolutely refused to warn parishioners of the danger. Now these documents - called the Orange Files were released by court order on May 17, 2005. More than ten thousand pages of letters, handwritten missives, memorandums and other sealed documents detailing church actions were released from the personnel files of fifteen priests and teachers as part of a court approved one hundred million dollar settlement reached in December between the diocese and ninety molestation victims. These secret files reveal, officials dumped one serial molester in Tijuana, Mexico and they welcomed a convicted child abuser from another State into their diocese even though they knew he faced three new molest allegations. They offered another serial abuser twenty thousand dollars to leave the priesthood quietly... Listen America." Bev went on...

"Even as they coddled abusive priests, church officials stonewalled and ostracized victims families...

'It is hard to believe that our spiritual leaders would knowingly sacrifice lives of innocent children to keep up the façade and live a lie,' a woman wrote in a 1986 letter to Orange Auxiliary Bishop John T. Steinbock, *now* Bishop of Fresno, after learning that Andrew Christian Anderson, a priest accused of molesting her son in 1983, had gone on to abuse three more boys... Bishops in Milwaukee; Baker, Oregon, and Tijuana helped the Orange Diocese shuffle molesting priests around, these documents state. An Archbishop from Panama intimidated and threatened an alleged victim's family into not contacting the police. The Rev. Michael P. Driscoll, *now* Bishop of Boise, Idaho who handled the allegation of clergy sexual misconduct apologized last month. 'I am deeply sorry that the way we handled cases allowed children to be victimized by permitting some priests to remain in ministry, for not disclosing their behavior to those who might be at risk.' The Boise Diocesan web site stated.

"Do we accept this apology?" Bev asked her listening audience. Marc looked on and Davetta listened attentively in the green room waiting to hear Marc speak.

Bev went on. "David Guerrero, thirty-seven, of Palm Springs, California... He was molested beginning at the age of eight by Father Siegfried Widera, who had already been convicted of molestation when he joined the Orange Diocese. David said, 'I would say Bishop Driscoll is a sick, immoral animal to allow something like this to take place. And now he's the Bishop of Boise? It's disgusting.' David received $4.5 million in a settlement.

"This culture of Catholic priests who get horny and break out in sweats at a little league game... And we're going after Michael Jackson? This culture of shielding predator priests and ignoring victim's complaints in Orange County parallels that of other diocese where church files have been made public. Now a *Senior U. S. Cardinal* is facing five hundred and forty-four lawsuits from molestation victims. I talked to Christian Robinson who did some key interviews, involved in Michael Jackson's case and he said, 'Mrs. Bev, *if* Michael Jackson is guilty of grooming and molesting seven or eight or even the one boy, he is sick. He should go to jail. But in this case, the D.A. has not *proved* the case. So by the *law*, he should be acquitted. But the case of Michael Jackson pales in comparison to the case against the Catholic Church...'

"Marc, what are the parallels between the culture in the Catholic Church and the culture in our juveniles, jails and prisons?"

Marc replied with lots of evidence from cases around the country. He mentioned Georgia, New York, Florida, Alabama, Arizona, Oregon, Washington, etc., etc. He then moved to this: "Mrs. Bev, the main reason our system is failing to stop women from being abused and raped in prison - The reason men and boys are being sadistically raped in prison is because of the caliber and lack of character of guards and administrators working in prisons. Take California for example. When you have *John Griffin* working as a prison guard while charged with extortion, theft and defrauding the workers comp. system, what else need I tell you?

"Mrs. Bev, can I tell you about Lewis Kuykendall, the Warden of Valley State Prison in California?"

Mrs. Bev said, "1-888-331-1210. Call that number and talk to us. Marc can tell us about Mr. Lewis after this break."

* * *

Wanda Sykes blared over the radio in a commercial saying, "The price of gas is sky high now. I was pumping gas the other day and the price went up four times *while I* was pumping... When I got to the cash register the cashier had the nerve to pass me a loan application."

* * *

After two or three more commercials, Bev came back. "Marc is gonna tell us about Lewis. Go ahead, Marc."

"Well, prisons are notorious for their sexual intrigue, with the strong preying on the weak. In one California Institution, the offenders weren't inmates though. Lewis Kuykendall, *Warden* at Valley State Prison for Women in Chowchilla, in the late 1990s, had more than three paramours on staff. He promoted them and bestowed other advantages.

"One of those women, in turn, formed a close personal alliance with another high-ranking woman. Together they made work intolerable for two better-qualified female officers after they threatened to complain. This mess continued for three years. Eventually, the Department of Corrections put a stop to it and the perpetrators paid for their conduct. Kuykendall retired with full pay and benefits. However, the two victims also left their jobs, following doctor's recommendations. Frances Mackey and Edna Miller turned to the courts for justice, suing the Department of Corrections for sexual harassment. The CA Supreme Court heard the case two months ago. ...Miller became aware that Kuykendall was having affairs with two women on staff. She learned of a third affair a year later between Kuykendall and Cagie Brown. About that time, Miller and Brown applied for the same promotion to a temporary captain's position.

231

Miller outranked Brown and had better work and educational credentials. Brown got the job!

"Ultimately, Mrs. Bev Brown became Associate Warden. She, along with Deputy Warden Vicki Yamamoto, with whom she had a personal relationship, regularly undermined authority in petty ways. One day Miller threatened to report Brown's affair with the warden. Brown pinned her against a file cabinet and held her captive for two hours. Corrections investigators called it an assault. Kuykendall promoted Miller in 1997, when she reported Brown's assault and confronted him about his relationship with Brown. But once Miller initiated a departmental probe, retaliation against her escalated. She lost her handicapped parking privileges, for example, and was ostracized and threatened by other staff. Mackey, a Records Manager, got similar treatment after another woman, romantically linked to the prison warden, got a promotion for which she was unqualified. The woman stripped Mackey of supervisory duties and consigned her to the mailroom.

"An internal investigation eventually concluded Kuykendall was favoring his numerous paramours in job assignments; that Brown was improperly chosen associate warden; that Brown, in addition to having sex with Kuykendall, had a personal relationship with Yamamoto. Yamamoto is currently employed at Corcoran State Prison. Mackey died and Brown is on sick leave. Attorney Barbara Lawless argued the case for the deceased and Brown."

Mrs. Bev chimed in. "You keep saying Yamamoto had a personal relationship with Brown. Was it intimate?"

Marc smiled. "Yes. It was a lesbian affair, Mrs. Bev."

Bev said, "This is absolutely reprehensible. These are the one's guarding criminals. The guards are criminals. And this woman assaulted and held another woman captive for two hours? One would wonder did she handcuff her? Did she rape her? And when the top official at the prison is a philanderer and an adulterer, will promote unqualified people to captain in exchange for sexual favors - This is akin to prostitution. This risks the safety of staff, the security of inmates and the safety of citizens. An inmate could escape because the warden is in his office doing the nasty with a captain. And this is in *Caleefornia*. The largest state prison system in the country. I see why inmates are being raped. I see why there is no rehabilitation. California is spending all of their money fighting lawsuits and shuffling corrupted wardens, captains and guards around from prison to prison like the Catholic Diocese shuffles its predator priests. And I have seen with my own brown eyes, official documents proving that the peace officers union in California is a group of thugs, gangsters, the Green Wall who maim, rape, kill and threaten. They ran Richard Polanco out of town. He was a senator who refused to accept their campaign money, which was basically bribes.

"I have a note here from an inmate in California. It has been verified and authenticated but I won't use his name. Listen Marc. 'Mrs. Bev, I was raped twice in C.Y.A. and I did not report it, but when I went to the infirmary with a torn anus, bleeding and two black eyes, not one staff member asked me what happened. In Mule Creek and New Folsom State prisons, I was a sex slave. I was raped by a prison guard and more inmates than I can count. Can you tell me how Sam Bess, Sgt. Blackburn, Billy Mayfield, Janice Mayfield, Mike Todd, C.O. Mansky and Captain Martel can work in C.D.C.? How could the state allow them to guard inmates?'

"We'll, my answer is I don't know. I don't know who these people are. After the break, however, you call me. If any of my listeners out on the West Coast have any dirt on these guys, you call and do tell. Do we need a federal investigation of the entire prison system out in California? Do we need a federal takeover? I know we need one in Philadelphia, Alabama, Georgia and New York State. We have been talking and talking for years. Talk ain't gonna cut it. We need to employ sustained and diplomatic, legal and strategic actions against the administrators of these prisons and clear em up. I know it looks dark, bleak and for those of you in these prisons, it seems like the problems are *insurmountable*. But nothing is impossible. And if we get together and fight we can win. We need lawyers like Gerry Spence, Willie Gary, John Elsmore and Tom Mesereau to sue. We need hidden camera investigations, senate hearings and the whole enchilada. I may need to also stage a radio prayer vigil for inmates. We can just take a whole day on a Friday and have you call in and tell us which inmates need prayer. David and Lawrence will get T. D. Jakes, Jesse Jackson or somebody to come on the air and pray for all those boys and men in prison. Let's talk about it. Back after this break!"

* * *

...I pause to interject my (Sherman Manning) belief in the power, potency and the *magic of reading* and the written word. Oh yes, writing and reading are extremely powerful tools for entertainment, enlightenment, fun, creativity and knowledge. J. K. Rowling does it exceptionally well. My fascination is not so much with the Harry Potter story per se. My fascination is with the J. K. Rowling story. She was a woman on *welfare*, in Edinburgh, Scotland getting

233

government assistance. But she discovered the joy of writing and now she's a billionaire with a *B*.

And what I also love is the fact that J. K. Rowling's writing has sparked a flame in the minds of other youth around the world. I read story after story of this kid and that kid who has *written* his or her own book cause they got tired of waiting on Harry Potter...

I love the fact that any writer, anywhere can write a book about any subject, which causes so many others to want to write. There is a magic, which comes from writing. Writing is a tool much more potent than any fist, any stick, knife or gun. Not only is the pen mightier than the sword, but the pen is a giant killer. The power of *words* when you write them is amazing! The power of *words* when we read them is awesome. Quite candidly, if *this tome* did/does nothing else at all, etc. if this book gives me no credibility or stature, it's okay. I'm way, way past trying to win an endorsement for me. I don't need a pat on the back, a compliment or any strokes for my ego; personally... I'm just fine. I'm not in need of any pity or sympathy votes. But if I can motivate or inspire you to write a journal, a blog, a poem, a song, essay or a book, then I'll be satisfied.

I'm so sick and tired of selfish people. I get tired of people who never think outside of their boxes. All they think about is self. They are negative, cynical, selfish and greedy. They bring your spirits down. They always look for what's *wrong* instead of what's right. They're quick to laugh at other people. They're quick to criticize other people. They are quick to anger and slow to forgiveness and understanding... The challenge at this very moment is for you not to assume, hope or to pretend this paragraph is for somebody else. Why don't you turn to yourself and deal with yourself. We all need to work on self. And I hope when my youngsters read the stories of the success of Mrs. J. K Rowling, Terri Woods, etc., which I've covered in *this* book, etc., I hope you won't do what the typical person does. I hope (instead) *you* will applaud Terri Woods, Tina, Shackelford etc., etc. And then I hope you'll decide it's *your* time. Decide it's your time to be blessed. It's your time to be creative, innovative and successful. Write! It's *right to write*. A lot of you can and should write a book! And if you just write a blog, a chapter for an anthology, an essay, an article or a poem, it's *all good*. Just do something to keep your mind employed. Even when you watch television, young people, you ought to transform *how* you watch TV. How? Enjoy it! And transform it into an educational, inspirational, entertainment and imaging tool. When you see a dude getting in a Porsche, see (also) *yourself* getting in a Porsche. When you hear a line you like or see somebody say or do something powerful on a show; see *yourself* doing it. I'll be candid, if you just watch others in awe and amazement you'll be a loser forever! You must allow entertainment to spark a flame inside of you. This is one of the reasons I give so many opportunities in this book for you to make money! A. I like being unique. B. I like giving money to young folks in school and college who need it! C. I like results... When I write that I'll pay one hundred dollars to the first person who locates (i.e. Wil Seabrooks of Charlotte, NC) so and so and send them this book. I mean it! When I tell ya'll that on July 16, 2005 Dateline (Dateline at MSNBC.com) did a special on air flights, "A Wing and a Prayer" and there was a *Marcos* on the show. Didn't get his last name. Find Marcos and get him this book. One hundred and fifty dollars to you (first person to mail verification to us).

I thrive on persuading others to do their thing. I want young people to argue, debate, discuss and contemplate the issues, which are dealt with throughout this book! I want young people to read, to study, to consider, to grow and to do. *Your* answer is not in dope, coke, beer or none of that junk! Your answer, baby boy, is in your *head* and in your *heart*. You'll notice, discover, find and observe it when your mind is clear, quiet and open. You gotta be quiet to get it, baby. There are lots of times it's cool to be noisy. When you are listening to Green Day make all the noise you want! But after you have jammed and rocked, etc., find a place to sit, stand or lay and be still. Listen to the spirit. The spirit will meet you there. It's scary at times but I promise you it's cool. Go there and see what the universe has for you.

I need some of you Internet tinkerers, bloggers, etc. to go to AskJeeves.com, Amazon's new search engine or Google and find me: Jason Fortune, Will Seabrooks, Darren Romeo, Sam Chaiton, Conrad Rupp (Brazil), Kip Conner, Robert A. Wilson, Ray Ellis (Yuba City), Mrs. Pamzich, Mgr. Of the Next Chapter in Woodland, Paul Ruditis and Becky Anderson in Naperville, IL. You tell these folks they gotta get *this* book. Tell Ashley Wilder, Brian Greene, Nate Smith (Winnsboro, Texas...Nate is a Christian and he's studying psychiatry. Tom Cruise probably does not support the dude studying psychiatry, but I do. Y'all tell Nate to get this book. *Pray for me* and tell Nate to send **me** a *snail mail*).

I need Nicholas Ficarra, Matt Feeley, Jim Haas, Ryan Gajersky (Long Beach, CA), Vern Yip, Kyle O'Conner, Randy Rutledge (in Lagrange, CA), Chris Shaffer and Ryan Landers. If *you* seek them, you'll find them. I want us to band together and raise a wall against abuse of our children. But our *wall* won't be a wall of suspicion, walls of racism, false accusation, fear or vigilantism. We won't merely *react* to the latest tale of horror or tragedy in the neighborhood. Instead, we will build up a wall to protect our children, which is pragmatic and plausible. We want a wall of hope. We want a wall, which brings *us* together in a common cause as humans. We may disagree on Bush, politic, economics, prison reform, etc., but my God, every decent human being ought to agree that our *children* deserve *not* to be *molested*. And *if* there is but a *chance* we can learn something from a gal in jail, guy in juvenile or man in prison which may lead to us catching a molester, or better still, if we can prevent a Joseph Duncan or Schwartzmiller from committing that first molestation, we ought to seek the info out.

"WANTED: Any prisoner, pervert, priest, politician, professor, etc., who might prevent one child from being molested by a sicko… Please *let us know ASAP!*"

That's the all points bulletin we oughta put out - Now! Ya'll find Ashley Smith, Amir Rahimi (Ell Grove) Jesse Riegal, Nick Davison, Nick Reineke, John Zhang, Neal Carlson and Andy Fenker and tell them I said get their asses involved; now - right now! We need them to put their names on that dotted line. Go to our blogs, petitions, etc. and sign on. Adopt a kid. Hell, adopt a school, mentor a kid, mentor a ward in juvenile etc. We need action, action, action! If you fellas are gonna get you some pussy, I can't stop you! If you gals are gonna screw around with boys before you marry, what can I do? But we don't gotta be total fools! A condom! Least we can do is know the person we're going to bed with. They might give you herpes, syphilis, AIDS. Is a nutt worth your guts? You wanna *die* for a sex *high*? You check this out; if you gonna screw, slide on a condom. Put it on! And if you choose chastity, virginity and abstinence, I applaud you! I'm rooting for you. I really am! Don't *rape* anybody! *No means - No*! I'm writing this cause I have a collective audience of frat brothers and cheerleaders, etc. and I would be *Bozo the Clown* if I thought nobody reading my words has ever committed a crime!! So *if* you contemplated rape or any kind of force, don't do it. Get help!

I want an army of young men and young ladies to write. Write, read, do, say, think, create and don't hesitate. Use *your* mind, *your* ideas, *your* skills, *your* voice and time to make the jail, the juvenile, make the school, the city, your state and your nation a safe, happier place to live. *You can do it*. Will you? I'm looking for some sons who will stand up, square their shoulders and take the country back. I need some youngsters like Alfie Dennon (www.werenotafraid.com) to connect with the guy who started www.*I'mSorry*.com and I want them to connect volunteers across the country on these college campuses and in these high schools and let's fight!

Go to FaceBook.com and tell Mark Zuckerberg that we need him! Tell Mark to link Cafepress.com/Manning up with FaceBook.com to recommend this book to his subscribers. Let's cross advertise. Go to I2hub.com and get Wayne Chang and tell him I said come here. We want Blake Ross, Markus Buckingham, Matt Wetherington and Charlie Wildman. I want my gals in sororities, group homes, women's shelters, etc. to take one hour today and get your butt online and locate some of the folks mentioned herein. I want you to know you're reading an interactive, Y-generation book. Its success depends upon **you**. Get *Michael Shackelford* in Sand Springs this book. Get it to Peter Grammatas, Neal Carson, Will Seabrooks, James Fortune and to boys all over who wanna be men.

Y'all know what turns me on? I love it when somebody like Mark Zuckerberg decides, "I'm gonna pursue my degree and my business. And I'm gonna give back by spending two hours per week corresponding with juveniles or working on prison reform, etc."

That gets me excited. It lets me know they get it. They get it. They know *service* is the price we pay for living on the planet. And it is a *joy to serve*.

Let's put it out here young people. Come by radio, cell phone, P.C., lap top, fax, text, podcast, etc. come by water, air, dirt or wind. Come on and let's change the freaking world.

I want you. You to help make this world better. Sit your posterior-anatomy down and get on the web and *push this* issue! Push! Push it, baby boy! Push it, baby girl. Push! Get your push on! Push your Senate, the Congress, the President to *change*. Change laws, bring people together! Push! Push it, Marc! Push it, Jeremy Elan Zolan, Aaron Kanter, Stephen Schultz (Marietta, GA), Mike Moss, John McKenna, Brian Ostrovsky, Michael Colen and you! Push!!...

...Adam Scott wrote to me the other week indicating that Jane Fonda is a big fan of my other books. Adam has a place in Pasadena and in Santa Cruz. "Tom Hayden gave Jane a copy of 'From the Palace to the Prison' and she loved it. So do I and my new wife. Although I play a gay role, I'm straight. And I know what it's like to have stigma attached. You're right, Sherman. Some people will always look suspiciously at you because you are in prison and when you get out you'll be an ex-con. In Hollywood, we call it being typecast. I'll always be known as gay just because of the movie. Keep the faith, *Sherman* and never stop writing. I've heard you're doing a new book called Blonde Blue? (Editors Note: *Blue-Eyed Blonde*) and that it is written by a deceased young White guy, his brother and you. So would you call it an anthology or are you co-writing it or what? They say it's sex, drugs and rock and roll. Wow... I can't wait to read it, pal..."

The most recent missive I received from Clay Aiken (in June of 2005). He wrote: "Your courage and perseverance motivates and inspires me. Sherman, I had it rough coming up. I was picked on and bullied. They would wedgie me and call me queer. In America it is so sad that so many of our kids are bullied and alienated in school. People automatically *assume* you're gay because you are effeminate. And first, it should not matter if you're gay or straight especially if you're not hitting on them and you keep your preferences private. Then, they seem to forget that many football players, so-called jocks and seeming studs are gay. It's sad. But my experiences made me better. Keep looking up, *Sherm* and I believe you will one day look back on your prison and consider it to have made you a *better person*. And please believe that *this mountain can still be moved*. Sometimes you gotta re-learn how to pray. Re-learn how to think and how to have faith. There is a great book by Professor Patricia Raybon. Prof. Rayon is at the University of Colorado in Boulder and her book is about re-learning how to pray. Actually the title of her tome is, 'I Told The Mountain To Move'. Can I send you a copy? Sherman, I spoke to Johnny ... and Timothy... and..." (redacted paragraph).

Enrique Murciano sent me a powerful missive of support. Enrique has proven to be very, very supportive of my efforts. I also got a missive from Montel Williams. I must preface any revelations or discussion of Mr. Williams' letter by stating I am not promoting casual weed smoking! As a matter of fact (preference) I don't smoke marijuana. And since I'm an adult, I would if I wanted to. It is as rampart in prisons as it is in civilian life. Montel supports the legalization of medical marijuana. It seems like a no-brainer. I believe our kids should be drug free - period. I don't wanna see kids smoking dope, drinking, doing meth or smoking tobacco. I believe it's wrong, illegal and detrimental to all teens.

And I support the rights of those, whom physicians determine, do have legitimate medicinal needs for marijuana. Renee Boje is an international fugitive wanted in the United States where she is facing a mandatory minimum of ten years in prison for allegedly watering pot plants at the home of a friend in Los Angeles who had a State License to consume and to grow cannabis. She is a dangerous criminal on the run from the long arm of the law, to the *shirts* at the Drug Enforcement Administration (DEA). To the DEA, this woman is a big-time narcotics king or queen pin who needs to be punished more severely than murderers and rapists. But to her friends, Renee is a symbol of the drug war run amok, a political victim of U.S. Government's over-the-top vendetta against medical marijuana.

Renee is petite, a beauty, thirty-five and one of several Americans seeking political asylum in Canada, because they face persecution by the U.S. Government because of their advocacy and use of medicinal hemp. When I perused the data, which Montel Williams sent me on Renee, I was mesmerized. I then compared the data from Montel with the documents sent to me from Martin A. Lee. The data jibed…

Renee notes Canada's long history of welcoming refugees from America… from Sitting Bull's Lakota Indians and Runaway slaves in the 19th century to the Vietnam-era draft dodgers who came to Canada to avoid the military. Renee told Martin, "My deepest hope is that Canada will again open its heart and help American citizens who are being abused by their own government because of their association with a healing herb."

Canada legalized medical marijuana in 2001 and if it grants refugee status to Renee Boje or any of the other U.S. drug war expatriates, it would have major political and legal ramifications. This would deliver an unprecedented, scathing and scolding rebuke to the American Criminal Justice System and to its self-image as a beacon of human rights.

In addition to sending a pointed message that Canada believes American drug policies are draconian, such a landmark decision might significantly affect U.S. - Canadian relations by providing necessary sanctuary for hundreds, perhaps thousands, of pot smoking U.S. Citizens. I asked Violinist Antonio Pontarelli, Personal Manager Michael Bruno and CBS Research Director David Poltrack what each of them thought about the possibility of Canada granting political asylum to U.S. pot smoking citizens seeking political asylum. Each of them indicated in one way or another that it might be a positive thing. Actor Warren Beatty and Robert Downey, Jr. both adamantly support pot smokers getting this type asylum. Bob Bowman, who coaches Michael Phelps, indicated to me that it is extremely important for America to stand against drug use and abuse. "But we don't need to be locking up medical marijuana users who have legitimate medical needs," he indicated.

In 1996 the State of California approved, by a wide margin, Proposition 215 (the "Compassionate User Act"), giving authorization for the possession, distribution and cultivation of marijuana for personal medical use under a physician's supervision. Eleven states have enacted such measures. These initiatives, however, conflict with U.S. Federal Legislation, which bans weed across the board, making absolutely no exception. For the deathly ill, despite compelling evidence that cannabis helps to relieve nausea and restore the appetite of cancer and AIDS patients. According to an article in *Scientific American*, weed is a versatile plant with "clear medicinal benefits". Cannabis has been used for centuries to reduce pain and improve the lives of folks with a variety of ailments, including migraines, menstrual cramps, glaucoma, epilepsy, multiple sclerosis, anorexia, insomnia, depression and post-traumatic stress disorder.

But the feds said no to medicinal marijuana and launched a massive crackdown. Renee Boje, fresh out of college, was busted in July 1997 along with eight other people in the first federal raid of a medical marijuana garden after Prop 215 became California Law. Marijuana plants were seized at the Bel Air Estate of cancer patient, Todd McCormick, who maintained he was breeding different strains of cannabis to test their effects on various symptoms. Todd had employed Renee to illustrate a tome on how to grow medical dope, her first job as a freelance artist.

DEA agents arrested Boje during the raid and brought her to the Federal Prison for Women in downtown LA. She was strip-searched repeatedly during seventy-two hours of incarceration. "Male guards watched and leered at me while I was being stripped. I could hear them making threatening and lewd comments. It was humiliating. I was in a state of shock. I felt very angry and afraid," Boje recounted.

Government officials manipulated, threatened and coerced Boje to testify against her cohorts. When she refused, they charged her with growing and conspiring to sell dope. And get this: Neither she nor her defendants would be allowed to use Prop 215 as a defense. Moreover, they could not even mention the Compassionate Use Act, Prop 215 or their medical evidence proving why they needed or used this medicine. This would be kangaroo justice; Bush/Cheney and John Ashcroft style. The defense would have to come to a gunfight carrying a stick. "A trial is supposed to be a search for truth. A search for the facts, the evidence, the pieces of the puzzle. All the facts are to be brought before a judge or jury for them to decide what is credible. They put the pieces of the puzzle together and render justice. For a system to disallow a defendant to bring credible, important and scientific facts before the jury that will judge them is inconceivable. This is when our so-called legislators, senators and governor should change the rules which governs the system so that every defendant gets a fair shot at justice." Attorney Gerry Spence told me…

240

Peter McWilliams, also a defendant, was forbidden to tell a jury he had AIDS and cancer. Deprived of his right to self-medicate with weed, McWilliams, a publisher and best-selling author, was often too nauseous to hold down food. Within a year, he would die from choking on his own vomit. "This is almost unheard of. This sounds like something the court systems in Iraq, Russia or Afghanistan might do, but not in America," states Elton John. "How can a court which is about fairness, equality and probity tell a man, who clearly began utilizing weed out of medical necessity that he can't tell the jury he has AIDS or cancer? How can they not at least put the scientific practitioners up on the stand and allow them to slug it out? This is blatant dictatorial. This is wrong," stated O. C. Producer Josh Schwartz...

Traumatized by her treatment in jail and unwilling to submit to a show trial in which she would be disallowed to present her evidence, Boje heeded the advice of an American lawyer named Anthony Brooklier and fled to British Columbia in June 1998. It has been an emotional roller coaster for her ever since she slipped across the border with only fifty dollars in her pocket and began a precarious new life on the lam. "I realized that I would probably never be able to return, but that was okay with me, because I would rather be free in Canada than in prison in America," Boje explained.

She eventually took up residence in the Vancouver area, where a flourishing ganja subculture had taken root. With its permissive ambience and city council, which favors pot legalization "Vansterdam" as it's known among the cannabis cognoscenti is probably the only urban center in North America where people ask in earnest whether a no smoking sign at a restaurant applies only to tobacco or to reefer as well. Cannabis cafes and hip strips with hemp stores are both tourist attractions and essential hangouts for local tokers. On the South end of Commercial Drive, the Compassion Club Society offers a variety of marijuana medicaments to three thousand regular clients with a doctor's note. (Patients with prescriptions for medical pot are often too ill to grow their own, hence the need for buyer's clubs).

...When U.S. Feds got wind of her whereabouts, they filed a fast track extradition warrant, a special procedure usually reserved for especially violent murderers or rapists. "They want to frighten people by making an example out of me," Boje contends.

This is when Boje challenged the authorities on both sides by launching a historic campaign for political asylum. Boje's lawyer, John Conroy warned she faced an uphill battle. Canadian officials initially ruled she was to be deported to the U.S., but a final decision is conditional on the outcome of her asylum claim, which is now before the Canadian Justice Ministry.

Conroy has argued that Boje's supposed role in McCormick's LA pot-growing operation, then permitted under California law (which did not put a ceiling on the number of plants that patients can cultivate), was peripheral at most and a mandatory ten-year prison term for Boje, who had no criminal record, constitutes outrageously cruel and unusual punishment. Conroy also cited reports by Amnesty International and other human rights organizations that document the rampant abuse of women in U.S. prisons, including frequent instances of rape and molestation by male staff. He also drew attention to the fact that the Norwegian Government had recently rejected a Federal request from Washington to extradite an American citizen charged with hashish smuggling because of "inhumane" conditions in U.S. jails.

Does this startle the reader? Does this shock and awe us? Come on now, does it really require a rocket scientist to see clearly that LA County Jail is an abomination before God? This author finds it hilarious that the Sun Times, which is owned by the notorious *Bush* supporter Rupert Murdoch, released photos of Saddam Hussein in his skivies and we find it alarming. Who took the photos? The Bush Administration, via the military *guards* took them. And we will never know how much money the prison guard photographer was paid for these pictures. *Bush* says he and his boys (Rumsfeld, Condy Rice, etc.) will investigate! This is like the pot calling the kettle black. It's like the fox investigating the henhouse. Bush, Cheney, Murdoch and others know exactly who took those pictures. Saddam is under twenty-four hour video scrutiny. There are cameras watching every single move he makes. They know when he picks his nose, when he farts, when he masturbates and when he takes a crap. And they damn sure know *who took*, stole, sold and released those pictures. But it's a game. And I am not speaking up for Saddam. It is not about Saddam. He is a violent thug, a murderer, a dictator and a cold-blooded killer. And Bush is not too far behind him. And the Geneva Convention cannot be violated. And we must require our officials to follow the law. I wish we would allow pictures to be taken inside American jails and prisons. If we allowed sneak peaks inside Fulton County jail, Riker's Island, Pelican Bay and those little rural jails in hick towns all across America, the family members of inmates would riot in the streets. If those White mommas and White daddies saw how jail officials and prison guards routinely throw their sons into cells, holding tanks and dorms to be assaulted, set up, beat up and raped by fellow convicts in America, they would demand that Congress hold a special midnight session tonight. They would see that Black prison guards work *with* White prison guards and that in most instances, those guards don't see Black or White - they see (in California) green and blue. "The inmates", they feel, "are all molesters and rapists and it's *us* against them." And in Georgia it is blue against white. Guards wear blue and inmates wear white. It's clear.

And those Black mommas and Black daddies would stop tithing to Bishop Flip Flop and Reverend Chicken Eater because they would wonder how Black preachers sit back and allow a whole generation of Black boys to be Black Balled and thrown into the Black Hole called prison. A missive from a sixteen-year-old Black kid came to me a week ago… "Mr. Manning, I think *you* are a sellout! I'm angry that most of your books are bought by White people and you don't deal with racism. *You* are an Uncle Tom. And so is Oprah, Bill Cosby, Jesse (Jackson), Al, Barack Obama, Willie Gary, etc., etc. How dare we sit back and *know* the jail and prison system was built to keep Blacks trapped in poverty, shame and hell for generations? How dare you know what you know and not write it? If Oprah, Bill, Magic Johnson, Black superstars, etc., would give ten million dollars each to Gerry Spence or Dick Scruggs to sue the U. S. Justice System, they would shut down the jail system… Mr. Manning, do you know how many Black families have been wrecked, destroyed, broken up and disbanded because they took our mommas and daddies to prisons for shit they didn't even do? And we on TV, we got Bentleys and Rolls Royces and we go to church every Sunday talking about "I'm proud to be American?" *You*, Oprah, Jesse, Bill Cosby, Tony Brown, Tavis, all ya'll can go to hell! If y'all love Black people, *give me my daddy back*!"…

…"It's very dark, what's happening in America," Boje states with some trepidation. I know a bad outcome would destroy me. But in the bigger picture, I'm blessed to be in this position to devote my life to a cause I believe in. Cannabis is a sacred herb that deserves to be respected and not demonized. Sometimes the universe will orchestrate certain situations and cause them to happen in your life in order to create a spokesman, a warrior or an activist. God bless American scribes Mumia Abu Jamal, *Sherman D. Manning* and all the others. Shame on the U. S. System for allowing Sherman to be thrown into the prison. Obviously it is clear he should not be in prison. Mumia Abu Jamal should not be in prison. But I must admit I believe *Sherman Manning* would *never, ever* have written a book on wrongful incarceration and the devastation and humiliation of the U.S. jail and prison system had he not been put in prison. So it is a blessing for

Sherman to be in jail. It does not excuse Mary Hanlon Stone, Detective Dave Winkler or Judge Robert Altman for the crooked injustice, which they meted out but in the grand scheme of things, it's a blessing..." so stated Rene Boje.

Renee felt like a torch had been passed to her. Though innately shy and soft-spoken with a fluttery voice, she embraced her role as a catalyst for transformation, a warrior for justice, a crusader for medicinal marijuana. Radiating Celtic charisma and charm, she became the poster gal of Vancouver's pro-pot movement. Renee organized rallies, gave speeches and drummed up letters of support for her legal case from the likes of actor/hemp-activist Woody Harrelson and social critic Noam Chemsky. "I say that I had an opportunity to do something really great," she continued. "I felt empowered to speak out for others who were under attack by the U.S. Government because of their commitment to medical cannabis. And guys in prisons in the U.S., i.e. Mumia Abu Jamal, James Albert Emslander and *Manning* also have the opportunity to do something for others who lack their initiative, drive, courage and determination."

Steve Kubby is also an American conscientious objector to the drug war with a strong case for winning asylum in Canada. Steve has been battling a highly aggressive and rare form of adrenal cancer. It is not an exaggeration or embellishment to say that his struggle is a matter of *life and death*. It is *do* or *die* for Steve and his wife, Michelle. Handsome and swarthy, despite his illness, Kubby always had an insatiable appetite for *living on the edge*. This tough American was a mountain climber, ski racer, deep-sea diver and a pilot with a top-secret security clearance who broke the freaking sound barrier flying a F-S Fighter Jet. But Steve saw his world crash when he discovered his body was riddled with cancer. The doctors found Steve's body had malignant tumors, which had metastasized to his stomach, liver, bladder and spleen. Steve had four major surgeries, several debilitating rounds of radiation and chemotherapy, but none of it was successful. Physicians diagnosed his condition as terminal and indicated he'd not live much longer than a year... Design specialist Jesse Garza sent me a strong message, missive and note of hope and concern. I always enjoy mail, which lifts the spirit, paints a picture and engages the imagination. "I'll design your house for you when you get out of that place Sherman unless you've hired Nate Berkus already," he said...

Barry Minkow used to be a fraud. He perpetrated financial crimes to the tune of over $330 million in the 80s. At age twenty-two, he appeared on Oprah as a young whiz kid and a financial tycoon. It turned out he and his ZZZ Best Company were an entirely fictional operation. He was a conman, a crook and a trickster. And he ended up in prison. And as he examined his surroundings, he sat next to a bank robber and looked at the locked cell door and said, "You gotta be pretty screwed up for people to snatch away your freedom and send you to a place like this." He was at Terminal Island in Los Angeles. He saw the viciousness of the system, which Renee is afraid of. But Barry was guilty. He served seven years and some months for his fraudulent storefront operation. Once he had been called on to *show* a building, which his company, had actually re-designed and he went to Sacramento, CA, he found a guard at a large office building and bribed him. He gave the security guard fifty bucks to allow him to bring his clients into the building and to pretend to know him. "Good evening, Mr. Minkow. Nice to see you again, sir," the guard nodded and bowed as Barry lied to investors claiming, "Yes, we designed this building and we put this piece over there, etc., etc."

But while he was in prison, Barry says he decided, "What if I used every skill, every con, every persuasive tactic which I know for good instead of bad! What if I employed my gifts and talents for good?" He got out of prison and says he found Christ. He is now a minister at a community Bible church in San Diego, California. He also lectures young business students on fraud detection and persuasion tactics. He also has served as a consultant for the U.S. Postal Services Fraud Detection Unit and for the F.B.I. U.S. Postal Inspector. Tim France says, "This guy is brilliant; he has brought me nine large cases in which people were being bilked out of millions of dollars. In every case, he was right."

Former Savings and Loan scandal perpetrator Mike Milken says, "Barry knows a fraud when he sees one. He now hires private detectives to bust fraudulent investment groups all over this country. And when the Feds are suspicious that some company is cooking the books, conning or defrauding folks, they call on Barry."

Barry has also written a book titled, "Cleaning Up". Barry told me in a telephone conversation, "People can change, Sherman. No matter what a person has done or how low they may sink, I still believe people can, do and will change…"

Judge Terizian concurs and has rewarded Barry by dropping his parole and probation requirements. He's free again… It would behoove the American Judicial System to look at Barry and to attempt to duplicate success stories such as Barry. The way you do it is the way the Feds are doing fraud detection. *It takes one to know one.* When the Feds wants to know if a guy is a crook, a con and a scam artist, they call on Barry! An ex-con, a crook and a master scam artist. If C.D.C., G.D.C. or any D.C. (Department of Corrections) truly wanted to know how to identify gang members, rape victims, trouble makers, staff assault prone inmates, winners and losers in an effort to clean up the prison system, etc., they would need to employ the expertise of ex-cons as well as present cons. Any so-called revamping of any prison system, which does not include extensive input from prisoners who have gone straight as well as ex-prisoners, is a sham and a fraud. And when I mention present prisoners, I am not speaking of men's activity committees, which often consists of inmates scared to be candid and afraid to ruffle feathers.

On the highest levels of state government, there needs to be a concerted effort to identify prisoners who are willing to consult with staff (not snitch or rat…but consult and advise) on how to fix the broken system. All the answers are right inside the prisons. And any answer you can't find is stepping outside the prison today or tomorrow. Catch these guys leaving and *compensate* them for advice and consultation on how to stop prison rape, abuse, violence, racism, etc.

And if we do this, we won't have to worry about an entire *nation* being embarrassed on the international scene for having the most violent, the most racist, the most abusive, sexist, *classist* and corrupted prison system on the planet.

We won't have Renee or Mr.Kubby so frightened that they run from their own *day in court* because they are afraid of being beat by guards, raped or even killed in a jail cell in Los Angeles, New York, Atlanta or Chicago. Reagan said historically, "Mr. Gorbachev, *tear down this wall*!" I say Mr. Bush *tear down these warehouses*. Tear down this corrupted, abusive, violent and vicious prison system and rebuild it. I said (wrote) that for *effect* only. If you know Bush, you'll know he ain't gonna do a damn thing. So what must happen (I reiterate) is we the people must *force change*. We cannot sit idly by and watch Steve Kubby go through this mess over prescription marijuana.

…Again, we shall interrupt our writing of this tome to reveal the contents of a recently discovered e-mail (verbatim), which the notorious Jamie Kennedy sent (a good while ago) to Paul. We are printing it here verbatim; however we have redacted his cuss words. "Dear Paul: "I'm Mr. J. Kennedy. Yes, I'm a (expletive) *Kennedy* and I'm freaking rich, brilliant, funny and cunning. How the hell are ya, Paul? I've heard from some of my co-horts that you are interested in stopping prison rapes. Why? Are you planning to go to prison soon? What illegal activities are you involved with? Inquiring minds wanna

246

know, dude?… (Expletive) Paul, on a serious note, I did hear about the possibility of you doing a story or a book of some sort. I then ordered '*American Dream A Search for Justice*'. Candidly, I didn't like it. But I did read it. Not my kinda writing! My girl bought 'Creating Monsters' and I read it. It was better! On a scale of 1 to 10, I graded it a 6 ½! My girl graded it an 8 ½! We both bought "From the Palace to the Prison". She got the book and I bought the e-book! I was wowed! *That* was totally (expletive) cool! A real ten, dude! That Sherms dude somehow learned how to write… It was hella cool!

I wanted to send my props and a shout out! If you wanna use a pic of me mooning, etc. in your book, I can send you some. They tell me I'm hella-cute with a real tighty type bun!! I have Clay Aiken tattooed on my right bun and Fedorov on my left bun and I have Paula Abdul on… (redacted expletive). Paul - the key to the success of a book like that will be youth! You'll need to reach out to the nerds: David Hankins in Minneapolis, Chris Birkett and Nate Berkus. You will need that kid at John F. Kennedy High School who loves Michael Jackson. (Editor's Note: Daniel Asare…If a J.F.K. student is reading, text Daniel *now*. You wanna reach out to all of those who supported Michael Jackson. I'd make certain the *victims* of sexual abuse by priests get copies of the book if you all write it. I suspect the priests may not like it. But thousands of victims will love the book. You'd be shedding light on a dark, dastardly and evil issue. I say do it! Set up a blog where people can talk about it *anonymously* if they want. (Editor's Note: http.SaveShastaGroene.blogspot.com. Go there and DashCash.blogspot.com… Go) And… (redacted) I gotta go now. I'm gonna share my ass cheeks. Jamie Kennedy."

Well Jamie is crazy but he has a lot to say. Awesome that we found that e-mail…Scott? Scott! Scott saw a woman who was so fine that the thought of her gave him a rise. He'd be in bed making *tents* underneath the blanket with no poles in sight. She made his mouth wet! Oooh. This girl was so fine. Scott wanted to eat her up. She looked like Angelina Jolie and Britney Spears combined. Scott met this young lady through a friend of a friend. Kate Carter (Santa Barbara, CA) has a wonderful company called *Life Chronicles* in Santa Barbara. And Kate uses volunteer students as her camera crew. A young cameraman (White dude…Brad Pitt look-a-like?) read a message Scott posted on our blog (DashCash.blogspot.com). And the cameraman told a buddy, buddy told his sister…Scott met her; Priscilla. They had safe sex. Kari Andal (Sacramento) couldn't believe her son (Patrick) put down *Harry Potter* and picked up "From the Palace to the Prison".

Cindy Coryell and Joel Coryell (Corona, CA...*Pray* for Joel's mom, Linda Coryell) both want this (*Blue-Eyed Blonde*) book. It has amazed *this writer* to see how many teens who read Harry Potter, Rainbow Party and kinds of teen speak tomes have been interested in "From the Palace to the Prison". Since experience has taught *this writer* how difficult it is to get adults, entrepreneurs, etc. to sponsor books for teens, students, juveniles and inmates, we now call on the *youth*. We ask each young man and young lady. All of you seventeen to thirty-five years old, like Chaz Wolcott, Riley Evans, Joshua Dick (the dancer) Frankie Muniz, etc., who received gratis copies of this book to now do three things. A. Go to Cafepress.com/Manning and buy at least *one* more copy of this book and have it mailed to your teacher, your professor, your parent or your friend. If you can get three or four do so and put it in your school libraries. B. Get on these message boards, discussion groups, blogs and even radio shows and spark comments about this book. Tell every high school newspaper, valedictorian, college frat, GLSA group, etc., about this book. C. Use this book as a fundraising tool. If you buy twenty copies or more you get a reasonable discount (Ask Hallopeter@freesurf.ch how much the discount is) and can sell it and make a profit. Although we are sold in bookstores and online across the world, we still love the *human touch*. Buy forty or fifty copies and take them to the suburbs and sell them door-to-door. If anyone wants to know if you're authorized to sell it...turn to this page and show them this sentence...Yes - the young man or young lady holding *this book* is authorized to *sell it to you for cash*. Buy it and you'll love it!!!

Now you can take this book to beauty shops, churches, Laundromats and sell it to the people. *Make a profit* and simultaneously you'll make a difference. Books change lives! And...I want you all to write to me and tell me of your successes and/or unique experiences. I.e. any student (high school or college) who sells one thousand copies of *this* book door to door gets a twenty-five hundred dollar cash bonus from us. Any person who sells five hundred books? One thousand dollar bonus...and to keep it interesting...the *first student* who sells one hundred copies of this book (hand to hand, via pod casts, blogs or however you sell them - the moment you place your order for one hundred books - A. You'll get a discount. B. You'll get a bonus). You'll get five hundred dollars. The *first* person to sell one hundred copies - we are crazy! We want to empower young folk to participate, represent and get paid in the process.

You can do it! You don't need me to tell you how or what or when. Y'all been wanting to be *heard*. Here is your forum! Write us!

We will print it! I want you (the reader) to e-mail Director Wes Anderson, Owen Wilson, Tom Swelling, David Lee Gallagher, Anthony Fedorov, Tim Goebbels and Paris (Hilton that is) and tell em the *book is out*. Get in with them. Go to their fan sites, e-mail B.J. Hickman in Knoxville, Tennessee, find Luke Sears in Oakland, Davis on The Scholar and mail them a copy of this book! Send it to Michael Budkie, M. McGraw at PETA in Virginia, Nathan Craft, The Aggie, funky Rush Limbaugh, the Great David E. Kelly, Roy Black, Mr. Semel (Yahoo!) and tell them to *Read This Book*. I want to prove conclusively that young folks think, read, study, matter, write and that you have an opinion!

You find John Artis in Virginia, Murray J. Janus, David Hicks, Beverly Ann Monroe, Alexander Dugdale, Gary Browning and David Quindt... The first person who can find Daniel Clay Hollifield in Richmond, Virginia and get Clay this book, gets one hundred dollars from me. Find David Joiner, Billy York, Ricky Mitchell and Eddie Cannon (Wrightsville, GA) and get them this book...One Hundred Dollars. You find Jake Reynolds or David in Chester, Virginia and send them this book and we'll send you one hundred dollars. No joke! No fiction!

You see Tim on the cover? Marshall? With permission...But I can't send everybody a damned gratis book. So the *first* person who gets Eminem this book, gets one hundred and fifty dollars. The first person who gets it to Johnny Weir, Denzel or Jamie Foxx? Two Hundred Dollars! (E-mail Hallopeter@freesurf.ch and simply ask - "Has anyone won the money for getting the book to so and so yet?" When Sabine, Peter or Lillian e-mails you back and says - "No one has won that one yet." go to work... When you *win*, you will get a check or money order. Take a photo of you and your check and send it to Sherman D. Manning, J98796, M.C.S.P. , A-2-240, P.O. Box 409020, Ione, CA 95640 and we will put it on our blog and in the revised copy of this book! Use Myspace.com, Friendster, blogs, Yahoo!, Buddypics.com and your home page as tools! Be cautious and careful. There are predators online! Anybody wanting to *meet you* or discuss sex, etc. over the Internet should be reported to police and parents.

I know what a wrongful conviction is! I know people lie and send people to prison for crap they didn't do. Barry Scheck, Larry Marshall and Gerry Spence knows. False accusations happen. But - but there are men and women who rape, molest, groom, con and are pedophiles. There are dangerous people in this world. Operate on the Internet with caution. Be very, very careful. Parents are not the enemy! They mean well! They love you! Obey your parents.

And Neal Carson? Alex Benzer, Snoop Dogg? Aron Carter? Brian Crawford (Stuntman - rides on the hood of his car - lives somewhere in Southern, CA Do you know "wanna-be stuntman", Brian Crawford in CA?) Mr. Domae? Adam Curry? Ippoder Curry? Find em and get them this book! Steven Squyres, Po Bronson, Robert Lanza, Daniel Job, Kevin Sites? Jeff Hawkins? Get them this book.

Okay, my last money offer (for the time being anyway). You find Spike Lee, Chaz Wolcott, John Singleton, Britney Spears, Tommy Lee or Tavis Smiley... Any one of them send me a letter and tells me you sent them this book and you get three hundred bucks...Three Hundred Dollars. Write an essay on this book and get it in *The Nation* or *The Progressive*? Five Hundred Dollars!! No joke! Get this book mentioned in *Wired* Magazine, Ebony or People Magazine? One Thousand Dollars. For real! No JOKE! One hundred percent guaranteed. Get to work!!

* * *

With his energy depleted and his spirits low, Steve Kubby got a visit from his former college roommate, Richard "Cheech" Marin (of the stoner comedy duo Cheech and Chong) who dropped by to cheer him up. Cheech fired up a joint for old time's sake and told his amigo, "Hey, if you're going to die, then why not die happy?" Steve took a few tokes and wow, he hadn't felt this good in a while. He started self-medicating with marijuana on a regular basis - that was thirty years ago.

A miracle of pre-modern medicine, Kubby, now fifty-eight, credits his survival to smoking an ounce of cannabis daily. Adhering to a strict dietary regimen, he supplements his THC intake with generous swabs of cholesterol-lowering hempseed oil - super-rich in protein and essential fatty acids - which he spreads on toast. "I have no medicine cabinet. I take no pharmaceutical drugs; except for an occasional rare dose of antibiotics. I drink no tea, coffee or soda," says Steve Kubby. He likens his use of medical marijuana to a diabetic taking insulin.

One of the most preeminent specialists on adrenal cancer, Dr. Vincent Dequattro, examined Kubby and concluded that marijuana stabilized his adrenal function, which is perpetually on the verge of overdrive and inhibited the growth of various tumors, which remain in Steve's body to this day. (Recent tests by scientists in Madrid conclude that THC injections destroyed malignant brain tumors in rats). If Steve is denied marijuana, according to Dr. Dequattro, his blood pressure will spike to dangerous levels, adrenaline will overwhelm his system, he'd get excruciating migraines, blindness, heart attacks, kidney failure or suffer a fatal seizure. Concisely, marijuana was keeping him alive.

Steve was living near Squaw Valley, the California Ski Resort, in 1995 when he met and married Michele Nelson, a blonde, all-American dynamo with a couple of college degrees and a job at a San Francisco securities firm. "I was a total Reaga*nite*, a young republican," Michele said, who had gotten weary with politics and business as usual. But Prop 215 was pretty much launched by this power couple and they *rocked the* world. Steve even ran for Governor of the State of California on the libertarian party ticket in 1998 to highlight the issues. "Does this aspirin, which kills more than two thousand Americans yearly need to be outlawed or this Big Bud of home grown cannabis which doesn't kill?" Steve asked at the State Capitol.

After the election twenty heavily armed swat team members battered down the Kubby's door, confiscated their two hundred and sixty-five plants and hauled them both to Placer County jail.

In a personal telephone call with Danny Glover, he told me, "Sherman, the bullshit is a set up, man. The reason they don't wanna legalize marijuana is because they are afraid they can't control enough of it to make the money they would want via taxation. Understand me, any physician will tell Bush, Harry Reid or any congressman *today* that weed is not as bad for you as alcohol. Ipso facto, half a million folks die yearly in America due to the nicotine in tobacco. But nobody is dying from weed. What is the difference? We grow tobacco here and the government makes billions off of it. Our liquor ain't shipped in from Afghanistan or Russia and the government makes billions off of it! So health ain't the concern, it is money. And at this juncture, they profit from ticketing, fining, arresting, probating and paroling weed smoking. It helps keep their jails and prisons filled. It is job security for police, judges, D.A.s, jailers, etc." Mr. Glover continued, "Sherm, ya'll gotta understand this law and order, crime and punishment thing is also about money. I take nothing away from your intelligence. In some ways *you* are brilliant. That's the truth. But let's be authentic and understand you ain't the only brother with knowledge. There are hundreds and thousands of White, Black and Brown brothers trapped in penal institutions all over this country with knowledge. There are guys who have read the Bible and the Quran backwards and forwards. They study anthropology, sociology, psychology, psychiatry, history, business and economics. And they too know what you know which is the system is designed to fail. The system is designed to create monsters. It's barbaric and belligerent, etc., and also rest assured that

Mr. Bush, Mr. Cheney, our senators and these governors are not dumb. Forty and fifty years ago some people got together and planned this mess. They planned this new slave plantation. They planned and structured it and many folks have gotten filthy rich building, designing, servicing and keeping these prisons, jails and juveniles. And I'm not racist. I love all of God's children. But let's call a spade a spade. There were no Black politicians behind the scenes making these plans. And so the plan has disrupted and crippled Black families all across the globe. And the reason youngsters don't give a flying (expletive) about politics and rhetoric is cause they see this bullshit. 'If you wanna help us, give us our daddies back. Let them out of prison.' Is what they are saying.

"And more and more everyday, phase two of the plan is kicking in. Phase two is more about *class* than it is about *race*. That's why you see more poor White guys going to prisons. They got caught up in the web of the hundred billion dollar crime machine.

"Sherman, if every Black (and I wanna say as an aside that I wish *all* people Black and White would come together as humans and work on this together. This is, after all *our* America. And Red, Yellow, Black and White, all are the same in God's sight. But for this angle of my argument, I wanna talk about Black folks), millionaire in America would descend on the White House next week and demand to see George Bush, we would get results. We done had the *Million Man March*. It's now time for the *Millionaire March*.

"If Oprah, Montel, Shaquille, Michael Jordan, Willie Gary, Bill Cosby, Russell Simmons, P. Diddy, Earl Graves, Robert Johnson, Tom Joyner, Doug Banks, etc. and every Black millionaire walked silently to the White House Monday morning and said, "I want to see the President." Then you would see some action. If you got just one hundred Black millionaires to go. Just one hundred rich Black folks to get Oprah, Montel and their cameras and go to the White House and tell Bush, we want our sons, daughters, fathers and mothers out of these prisons. We want these life sentences lifted on these three strikes cases. We want these boys who are innocent out. We want the violent, guilty ones treated and transformed. We are taking our families back! What do you think would happen?

"And I assure you that we'd see White people like Michael Milken, Tony Danza, Martha Stewart, Steve Madden etc., joining in with us and saying, 'We'll stand with you.'

"When White people saw that Martin Luther King, Jr. was serious and committed, they joined with him and stood with him.

"When John Brown and all those White, Quaker abolitionists saw how serious Harriett Tubman was, they joined with her. But they ain't gonna join a losing fight. And they will not fight the fight for you. There are millions of White people who go to bed every night and racism, hating Black people or keeping Black folks down ain't on their minds. They don't have *time* to be racist! But they will not go out of their way and stop their business, stop their lunches, brunches and golf games to concern themselves with the plight of Black America. Especially when Shaq and Kobe are on display as so-called examples, via mannequins in the shop of democracy. They wave athletes in our face and say, 'See there look, ya'll ain't doing so bad.' And Shaq and Kobe can play the hell out of some basketball but they ain't lifting a finger to do a damned thing about injustice, wrongful incarceration or the plight of the African American community. They are brainwashed. They are lost and if I were White, I would not try to make a horse drink no water either. If the horse wants to die let his ass die," said Mr. Danny Glover...

Three days in jail without reefer nearly killed Mr. Kubby. The jailers laughed at him for his requests for cannabis and went out of their way to punish him. He was forced to attend breakfast while suffering from repeated bouts of vomiting enraging other inmates who were trying to eat their meals. His wife (who also is a prescription cannabis user due to irritable bowel syndrome) believes they were arrested because they were outspoken pot advocates...

I will take a moment to digress and chitchat with *you* the person who is reading at this moment. I am absolutely concerned about our nation and our world. In a sense it seems like the world is all messed up in so many ways and on so many levels. And we are all doing time. Time in broken homes, dysfunctional families, down sized businesses, foster homes, group homes, colleges, jail cells and prison cells. As it relates to American justice and crime and punishment, it would appear that we are lost. America is behind the times. The way we approach crime is so ridiculous, I can't even write about it with a straight face. Please remember that we *punish murder* with *murder* in America. As a nation, our political leaders as well as the damned pundits remind me of Mr. Jackson, Michael Jackson that is; a damned fool. I don't know whether or not M.J. is a molester. It is not my desire to defend him, nor is it my duty to judge him. According to the *evidence* that I saw in this particular trial, I believe *reasonable doubt* existed and that jury should have returned a verdict of not guilty in that case. And I certainly believe that Tom Mesereau tried one helluva case. Tom was methodical, brilliant and he was absolutely a warrior! And again, I *don't* know if Michael is a molester. Having said that, I must also say Michael obviously is a fool! Let's *pretend* we believe he is innocent. After he was accused the very first time of molesting a kid and he settled the case, why did this adult Black man continue to camp out with White children? Even if he means well, etc., can you look me in my face and explain to me why he never found any Black boys (or for that matter, White girls) who needed his help, love, money, attention and his innocent affection? How many times must you stick your hand into a fire to believe that it burns? I think we play up *color* way too much in America. *Some* of us are obsessed with *color*. And I pray that one day more of us will overcome it and learn to love one another regardless of color or creed. Having said that, charity begins at home. Charity begins in your own tribe. I would never get angry with a Black or White (or Jewish or Asian) man who grew up in Rancho Cordova who decided to build a school for the neighborhood in which they grew up. I would not call that man a racist, colorist or neighborhood*ist* merely because he said, "I'm gonna build a school for the people in my neighborhood and then I'll build one for Del Paso Heights or Oak Park!"

Ipso facto, I ain't mad at you because you decide to put food on your family's table before you extend charity to my family. Ipso facto, it is not racist (I'd rather say colorist because it's time we realize that there is but one race and that is the human race) for people to wonder why Michael rarely, if ever, could seemingly find a Black child who needed his help! He continuously embraced White children! Why didn't he put cameras in every room of his house? Why not get twenty-four hour video or surveillance to protect him from allegations of abuse? I'm just asking.

My wife is White! I love the hell out of my White wife. I love her so much that I rarely mention her or my kids in any of my books. I protect their identity and privacy. I cherish every White inch of my White wife! She is awesome! She is a great woman, beautiful wife and a damned good mother to our children! And I am not going to support any Black (although I am Black) child or Black woman until I first support, feed and shelter my half White children and my White woman. They are my tribe, my family and as Dr. Phil says, "Families *First*."

And so why does Michael keep on repeating foolish and irrational behavior? Same thing with the justice system. We keep locking up lil White boys for the same lil stuff! They smoked some weed or took some crank and we lock em up! Black boys keep getting locked up for the same old crap! It's a damned merry go round. Build mo prisons!

Build mo juveniles! Build mo jails! Build, build, build. But we are not building libraries! We have forgotten how to build schools! We don't seem to know how to build universities! I suggest you call the governor's office in your state and ask how many high schools, libraries and colleges have we built in this state in the last year? Last five years? Last ten? Ask when was the last time they gave teachers and professors a pay raise?

But they're building jails, prisons and juveniles. And guards are getting pay raises!

Call California Senator Gloria Romero, Jackie Speier or Don Perata and ask them how much money does a C.D.C. sergeant, with a GED and ten years in the prison earn annually? Then ask how much does an educator with ten years in schools earn yearly?

Ask about the fact that a lieutenant (with a high school diploma) can earn (with overtime) one hundred and twenty-five thousand dollars per year in California! And ask how many teachers (with Masters Degrees) can earn a hundred plus grand annually.

Like Michael Jackson, we keep doing the same thing over and over. We keep jailing our kids and trying to incarcerate ourselves out of crime. We lock em up and throw away the key! But I found out it's a damned combination lock. And here are the numbers (code) to get the prisons open... When what you are doing (Michael, Mr. Bush, governors, judges, prosecutors, etc., etc.) ain't working, *Try Something Else*!

Perhaps that' not complicated enough for state senators, governors, our congress or our president, but it is what it is. We have had enough in-depth studies. We've commissioned long-winded examinations of our systems. I.e., little Hoover Commission, Urban League Reports, Amnesty International Studies, Human Rights Commission Reports, U.S. Justice Department Studies, etc., etc.

And paralysis has been born out of too much analysis. We need to turn around. We need to go another way and move in another direction. I hear Marvin Gaye echoing down the soundstage in my mind singing, "Brother, brother, there's far too many of you dying... Mother, mother, there's far too many of you crying... *War is not the answer*... Tell me what's going on?"

I hear Dr. Martin Luther King, Jr. echoing in my ears, "We've learned to swim the seas as fish, we've learned to fly the skies like birds, butstill we have not learned to love one another as brothers and sisters."

I hear the King of Kings and the Lord of Lords saying, "Love ye one another." I hear Jesus saying, "I was hungry and you fed me not. I was in prison and you visited me not."

I am well cognizant of the fact that Mr. Bush claims he is a born again Christian. I know Jerry Falwell claims to lead the moral majority. And I also know that if I died tomorrow and woke up in eternity and saw Bush, I'd be burning. I know Jerry Falwell disallowed his members to mingle with Blacks. He was and is opposed to interracial marriage. He believes Christ wanted us to love folks who look like us...

Mr. Bush? I pray for the man. And I invite each of you who are reading my words in Japan, Switzerland, New York, Georgia, Texas, Florida, Virginia, South Africa, Russia, Trinidad, etc. to pray for Bush... If he doesn't stop playing with God, he will be among that crowd which Jesus spoke clearly about... He told us many would cry out, "Lord, Lord don't you remember me." They'll describe how they went to church every Sunday, opposed gay marriage, opposed stem cell research, opposed abortion, read the Bible, sang in the choir, did this and did that, but, "I say unto you, depart from me ye workers of iniquity. I *know ye not*." When I look at the arrogance, the fraud, the deception of puffed up politicians who lie, cheat, are slow to forgiveness and quick to anger. When I look and folks who give tax breaks to millionaires and rebates to billionaires. When I watch them ignore the cry of the sparrow. When I watch them refuse to answer mail from prisoners, when I watch them abandon their own kith and kin just because they are in prison, yet they wave a Bible and claim to talk to God, I say, "King Pharaoh, the Lord told me to tell you to let my people go!"

I ask all these God-praising politicians, when will you do justice, love mercy and walk humbly with God? You can't do justice if you don't love mercy. You can't love mercy if you don't humble yourself before *God*. Second chronicles chapter seven, verse fourteen ought to be pasted up over the doors of the White House. And the church is teaching this bigotry! Many churches are leading their congregations to believe it is okay to abandon jail inmates. Ain't no Jesus in that attitude. Half of the Holy Bible was written by jail inmates, prisoners accused and falsely convicted rapists and tax evaders. Paul was a murderer while he was Saul. You can't celebrate the Paul he became if you don't appreciate the Saul he used to be.

Jacob was a crook, a conman and a manipulator. Joseph was convicted of a sex crime. David was a murderer and an adulterer. But ain't nobody protesting the book of Psalms or the story of Joseph. I say wake up America!

I got a missive from Rev. Al Sharpton. I've often excluded missives, which I felt were divisive from tomes, which I wrote. Yet I've included a redacted version of brother Al's letter…

"Sherman, America is still a racist country. They're burning crosses in Alabama and in North Carolina. Racism has become sophisticated and moved behind invisible bars. Corporate America is racist, racist, racist. And I believe a lot of the problems we see in Black America today are because we got too happy when we won a few battles. And we stop teaching our children their history. I guess we tried to protect them by attempting not to tell them of our struggle. We didn't tell them about how we were kings and queens in Africa. We were stolen and brought here on slave ships. We were forced into a country where we did not even speak the language. We didn't comprehend the culture. We were lost, trapped, enslaved, abused, beat and killed.

"Sherman, every Jewish child can tell you all about the holocaust. They are taught *their* history by their parents. But our kids don't know history. They know nothing about the promise of forty acres and a mule. They know nothing about the trillions of dollars of unpaid work, slave labor that Africans did here in America. They have no idea about what we went through just thirty and forty years ago. When we went to shoe stores, we were not allowed to try on shoes. They would make you step on a piece of white paper and trace the outline of your foot so they could get your shoe size. But Blacks in Georgia, Alabama, Mississippi, Tennessee and Virginia could not try on shoes. If we went to Dairy Queen, we had to stand outside and eat cause they would not let us inside. (All my White partners, I love y'all. I'm not a racist. I want you to call, google and e-mail Aaron Hegert, David Jay, Shawn Lundberg and Wade Williams).

"Black people were disallowed to learn how to *read* just one hundred years ago in Georgia. If you got caught reading, you went to jail or got lynched for reading. And so we have a lot of problems in America. We were fooled and tricked! *Black face* in a *high place*. We thought that if we got us some Black lawyers, judges, police officers and governors, we would get equity but we were let down. I.e., Clarence Thomas looks Black. Clarence Thomas is one of the most thoroughly brainwashed brothers not only in America but in the world. Supreme Court Justice Thomas wishes he was White. He is a hypocrite! He went to college and law school off of an affirmative action grant. Now he votes to do away with affirmative action. He

257

wants to cut down the tree from which he himself picked fruit. And in any case that has even the hint of helping Black, Brown or poor folks is a case Clarence votes against.

"Clarence Thomas and Ward Connerly would give their right arms to be White if they could. And they are cowards. They are worse than Uncle Toms and house Negroes. They refuse absolutely to engage in open dialogue. I offered fifty thousand dollars to Clarence and Ward's favorite charities if they would debate Jesse Jackson and me. They refused!

"They are worse than sellouts. They have no backbone. They are not men. They are boys. They are absolutely ashamed of their own history! *Sherman*, I don't want Clarence Thomas to let Black murderers out of jail. I want violence and criminality punished. But I also don't understand why Clarence wants to send all poor people to hell.

He is a fool. Clarence Thomas hates Black people. He is in denial. He is sick! He needs to have his ass kicked all over D.C. and then Ward Connerly needs to have the shit beat out of his no good ass. They both are terrified of other Blacks. Clarence and Ward would not go to Perry Homes, Oak Park, Del Paso Heights or Richard Allen Homes for a million dollars. They are cowards. Clarence Thomas and Mr. Connerly are absolute disgraces to the human race.

"They should move to Monterey, California and suck dill pickles with Shelby Steele. They have no problems with the reparations we gave to the Japanese or anybody else. But mention reparations for the trillions of labor and they go crazy. Mention affirmative action for college entrance and Ward's butt starts chewing bubble gum. Reparations are like workers compensation. When you get *injured* on the job, they *pay* you. If you lose a finger on the job, they pay you. IBM does not tell a man who hurt his back on the job to get over it. They pay him til he recuperates. If you think we have recuperated, you have not seen the inner cities. If you get caught up looking at Chris Webber's eight-car garage, you will *think* we have recovered. But walk with me through Compton, Nickerson Gardens, Watts, Oak Park, Fair Street Bottoms in Gainesville, Georgia and I'll show you extreme poverty. I can also show you trailer parks in Richmond, Virginia, Shade Tree Hill, Shady Grove in Charlotte, South Carolina and Tennessee, etc., etc., are full of poor White people. So there are a lot of folks who need help right here in America. And I am tired of bullshitting house boys like Ward and Clarence pretending that all is well..." So wrote Mr. Sharpton.

I will allow Mr. Sharpton's words to speak for themselves and to stand alone without comment. I believe that there is some truth in those words. I certainly do not disagree with the assessment of Ward Connerly and Clarence Thomas. These are definitely people who need help.

But I am not a prophet of doom. I am not a pessimist. I am not a person who believes everybody is racist. I am quite aware of the institutional racism and a myriad of disguised and hidden forms of an America, which still struggles with racism, denial and arrogance.

But I also know millions of *us* don't give a damn (literally) about your color or creed. And it is we who will rise up and continue to make America better. We can and we will do this. Together we will fight structural, organized and disorganized racism.

We won't allow our country to remain locked, trapped and tied up in the silliness of color or class.

Our struggle is sophisticated, strategic and pragmatic. Our struggle is a group of folks with power, wealth, status and class. And we will methodically win this war. It is a war.

Angelina Jolie, Sandra Bullock, Jessica Simpson and Vanessa Marcil are helping us...

There was a Black woman featured on Oprah a few weeks ago. Her name is Carolyn. Carolyn has been known as the woman with *no face*. And to say she has no face is a bit of an understatement quite literally. Carolyn was left for dead by her violent and jealous boyfriend in Texas. This boyfriend, whom I won't even dignify or publicize by an inclusion of his *name* in this book, killed Carolyn's mother with the violent blasts of bullets shot at point blank range. He then shot Carolyn's face off. I tremble as I write these words at this very moment. My God, this was a tragedy. This was cold. This was vicious. This was evil...When I saw Carolyn's face*lessness* on graphic display on the Oprah Show, I asked, "*How dare I ever complain?*" Words alone cannot begin to capture the extreme details, viciousness and heinousness of what this man did to Carolyn. Her face was blown off. She has no nose. She has half a mouth with no upper lip. One eyeball was blown out of the socket. Believe me, she has no face. It's hard to look at what that man did to her. Oprah brought on the paramedic who saved Carolyn's life. He explained the horror and terror of arriving at the murder scene. "It was a blood bath. Her mother was dead. And I saw no face on her. I thought Carolyn was dead too. If she had not grabbed my ankle, she would have bled to death. She had no mouth. She could not speak," the medic stated. This paramedic stood on stage on Oprah, looked Carolyn straight in her one eye and bandaged half a face... He hugged her with tears in his eyes and said, "I love you. Thank God you grabbed my ankle." The paramedic is a Caucasian man.

In light of that, I still believe America will be all right. Jesus uses his blood to cleanse our *sins*. He looks at sin not *skin*. And this White paramedic saw blood and he saved a Black woman's life. That's the love of God... When Reginald Denny (White trucker brutally beat in 1990s) was viciously beat by Black thugs. They pulled Mr. Denny from his big rig during the riots for no other reason than the fact that he was White. I can still see them surrounding him and beating him maliciously with a brick. This was a racist, thuggish and evil act. It hurt me and angered me to see this. After these evil Black men beat this White man viciously, three strangers rescued Mr. Denny. Had these three people not come to his aid, he would have died. Reginald was temporarily blinded by the cruel beating. And the people who rescued him told him, "Ill be your *eyes*," and to just hold on as they took him to the hospital. The three people who rescued Mr. Denny were Black. When Jimmy Lee Byrd (a Black man) was dragged to death by Bill King in Jasper, Texas, it was front-page news. It's racist. It sells newspapers. When Blacks kill Whites or Whites wear sheets over their heads, ABC, CBS and NBC guarantee that we are all aware of it. But when Blacks and Whites come together, get alone, rescue one another, take care of one another, laugh, live and grieve together, we never hear about it. But I believe with every fiber of my being that we will survive and overcome racism and hatred one day in this nation.

Many Black people in this country are still angry. Mad as hell about what happened. And even angrier about the manner in which Black history has been distorted, diminished and almost eliminated from American history. It is appalling to see schoolbooks, which are only one or two pages, which tell about Blacks... And when Blacks hear, "Get over it." or when Blacks hear, "That was then and this is now." It angers them. And Blacks want America to acknowledge the kidnappings, rapes, beatings, murder and inhumane treatments, which Blacks received here in North America. Some White people feign amnesia about what was done to Blacks here in America. And some Blacks are stuck on what happened and want to see everything and everybody through a prison of past slavery. It takes time to heal. It takes confession and acknowledgement to forgive. We do need to acknowledge what happened and fight the institutionalized, structural and judicial racism of today's America. And we need to overcome it. I have overcome it. I hate no man based upon the pigmentation of his skin. I don't hate anybody. I consider my White friends as dear and

260

near to me as my Black friends. I do see color. I honor it as a distinction, which serves to make life interesting and exciting. We're all in denial. We don't want to admit that many (and I do mean many) White women wonder what it would be like to screw a Black man. Duh!? We know damned well many Black women are curious as hell to know the feeling of sleeping with a White guy. We know that some of the sickest and most vile racists in America melt at the sight of a Black, White and Yellow or Brown *child*. It's very often peer pressure, fear, societal expectations and social structures that cause us to act or be racist. I know many *fake racists*. I know some folks who will say bad things about another color when they are in the presence of real racists who are their color. I wanna empower the youth and remind you to be who you are. If your momma or your daddy or your older siblings are racists, don't allow them to deprive you and don't deprive yourself. You deserve to like, love, date and marry any damn body you want to. I'm gonna say it one more time...Don't be stupid enough to limit your life by allowing older people to infect you with their racism. Rise above it. Reach across the aisle and get to know folks who don't look like you. It's exciting, fun and very interesting...

Michael Finkel is a reporter who some folks say is a fraud. But Mr. Finkel has sent me a lot of data concerning social issues and issues of injustice. Mr. Finkel knows *Wired* Magazine's Thomas Goetz, Po Bronson and Josh Davis. Davis, Goetz and Bronson were all close to *Jeremy*. So was Chris Shaffer who used to chase waterfalls at Yosemite National Park with Jeremy. Before Michael was disgraced for misreporting a story they had all told him about Jeremy. Ipso facto, Jeremy mentioned me. Michael still can't recall whether it was via a *Google* search, AskJeeves or Tribe.net that he finally came upon my address. But in his mind's eye, he still recalls seeing *Sherman D. Manning*, J98796, M.C.S.P., A-2-240, P.O. Box 409020, Ione, CA 95640 and saying, "I gotta write this dude." He did and I called him. Through him I met *Ryan Landers* of the pot movement. Ryan was adamant in his beliefs that pot must be legalized.

...The police took everything Steve Kubby and Michele owned, including all of their office equipment, which was used to run an online extreme winter sports magazine. Real estate, securities, cash and any other property allegedly linked to a marijuana offense are subject to immediate seizure under civil forfeiture statutes enacted in the mid 1980s. The Kubby's lost their company and filed for bankruptcy. Both were charged with conspiring to cultivate and sell marijuana. With another life threatening jail stint probably and tired of being haggled by G-men, they decided to get out dodge. In 2001, they took their two daughters to British Columbia and filed for asylum having a "well founded fear of persecution" by drug warriors in the United States, where there is an outstanding warrant for Steve's arrest. They now live in Sun Peaks, a mountain town four hours northeast of Vancouver. Like Boje, they hover in legal limbo while Canadian officials weigh their petitions. Michele learned the law as an erudite of sorts and developed her appreciable skills as an attorney. Backed by testimony of U.S. and Canadian doctors, she'll argue their case before the B.C. Supreme Court in the spring of 2005. If they are successful it will be a boost of titanic proportions for Renee Boje and others seeking relief from U.S. policies.

As Governor George W. Bush opined that medicinal marijuana was a state-by-state issue. But George *Dubya* flip-flopped when elected president and made med-pot a top law enforcement priority. Just a month after the 9/11 tragedy, A.G. John Ashcroft unleashed his theological police against state-mandated cannabis clubs in California, while the IRS aimed their guns at physicians who prescribed reefer. There were 755,000 pot arrests in 2003 - which incredibly surpassed the number of arrests for all violent crimes combined that year. Boje now runs the Urban Shaman on West Hastings Street, a store specializing in artifacts and information about peyote, iboga, ayahausca and other *entheogenic* (vision inducing) plants, which are copasetic in Canada. But illegal South of the Border. "I've heard from many people who want to leave the United States; they come into the store and ask for advice about how to claim refugee status in Canada," Boje says.

Boje contacted iPodder founder Adam Curry and asked how she could start a podcast for medical marijuana advocates. He set her up and mentioned her podcast on his show (The Daily Source Code) and it is doing well.

Boje is mesmerized by the fact that the podcaster allows her to record her animated monologue as an audio file. She adds a hyperlink for the show to an RSS feed on a Web server. The listener's podcast software checks RSS feeds at set intervals, downloading and adding new shows to a play list. Boje states, "I like *iPodder.org* cause it's free. This free PC/MAC/Linux program lets you subscribe to podcasts from it's directory listing or add your own. It periodically scans for and downloads new podcasts. If you use itunes, you'll find the latest shows waiting whenever you dock your iPod!"

Boje is animated and effervescent as she explains concisely how to make your own podcast. "A. Plug a USB headset with earphone and mike into your computer. B. Install the free audacity MP3 recorder for windows, MAC, or Linux. Make a recording, then save it as an MP3 file. C. Upload the MP3 file to your Website or blog. Follow the instructions on iPodder.org to create an RSS feed on your site."

Rene goes on to say, "If podcasting, blogging and the Internet had been available in the 70s and 80s there is no way Kenny Waters, Rubin "Hurricane" Carter, Rolando Cruz or Anthony Porter would have stayed in jail for decades for crimes they did not commit. This super information highway thing is awesome. And when people begin to tap into it on issues like sentencing, drug laws, wrongful convictions and governmental corruption, we will revolutionize the way we do justice in America. The new political era in America will be transmogrified by youngsters in their teens, twenties and thirties because they love the Internet. What we are gonna see happening is high school, college and foster group kids are gonna blog, podcast, e-mail and message bullshitting politicians out of office. In a few years, we won't need *vote or die* campaigns. Kids will make old school politicians wish they were dead.

"They deserve to be heard and they have so much to say. And our media (our media.org), a grassroots media project backed by the Internet archives, will provide free podcasting tools and permanent hosting for podcasts beginning July 2005. Also broadcasters such as the Canadian Broadcasting Company, BBC and NPR are currently experimenting with podcasting.

"There is also an underground Reefer Railway (an elusive network of safe houses and sympathetic contacts) that transports people further up the coast or into the British Columbia Mountains where they can lie low and, if need be, disappear. 'I've met lots of Americans coming through,' says David Malmo-Levine, a prominent Vancouver pot activist. 'Several Americans have slept on my couch. It's an act of resistance to aid and abet fleeing refugees. Canadians have a responsibility to help American dissidents if they can.' David goes on to state, 'The time has come for America to bring her secrets out of the closet. And I've heard all my life what a great country America is. And it is on many levels. But there is a segment of Americans who have been mistreated, ignored and left for dead. Many of them are in the prisons. I couldn't believe it when I read that America has nearly three million people in prisons. I wondered why people are not rioting or revolting.'

"But there is a quiet storm on the horizon. And the injustice meteorologists won't know what hit them. I see a storm coming. More and more everyday activists, unknown inmates are telling the stories of their injustice, mistreatment and abuse and we are hearing them loud and clear. The prison bosses are assuming if they don't read the stories in the New York Times or see it on TV, then there's no story. Wrong. These brilliant inmates have a built in, customized, personalized and an interactive audience. And the audience is worldwide. Monies are being lined up, pooled and channeled. There is just as much a movement for pot smokers, abused and innocent inmates in America as there is outside America."

...Back in Rancho Cordova, Oklahoma, Scott had stumbled upon a secret. Since Paul's death, Scott had called Paul's mother once or twice per week to check up on her and made himself available to do any chores she might need. He had become a handyman of sorts. One Saturday afternoon while cleaning out Jeremy's mom's garage, he stumbled upon a secret... "Did you know Jeremy did a *podcast*?" Scott asked Mrs. Shackelford.

"What in the name of luck is a podcast? She replied.

Scott thought, it's never good when a person answers a question *with* a question. He spent twenty minutes or so explaining all about a podcast - turns out Jeremy had done twelve broadcasts and they were all saved. Scott e-mailed Adam Curry and discovered Jeremy had been podcasting over iPodder for a couple of months before his car crash. Curry spoke well of him. "Dude was a Webmaster and he had a dream of revolutionizing the American Judicial System via the Internet. Initially he had only a couple hundred people downloading his podcast but then he began to go on Yahoo! and get in chats or discussion groups, etc., etc. By the time he stopped podcasting, he had five thousand faithful listeners who downloaded every podcast. These were people in their twenties and thirties. Mostly kids of wealthy and privileged people. I was amazed that he could take an issue like rape in prison, wrongful convictions, hypocrisy in politics, teen bullying and youth activism and make it relevant to college students who are the busiest people on the planet." Adam said.

"Could I do a podcast?" Scott asked. He then thought about the CCPOA. "They are dangerous. Evil. Wicked. Corrupted and violent," Scott said to himself... But if I can get a network maybe of thousands of people, I can insulate myself from the wrath or long, violent arm of the CCPOA, Scott thought. Maybe I should just leave it alone. I have sent every single document I have, all the e-mails, letters, notes, etc., every scintilla of data Jeremy and Paul had on this stuff to *Sherman*. He has enough *time* to figure out how to put a story together. Hell, he can even do a book on it. But wait, what about an anonymous podcast? The Internet can give me the kind of cover, anonymity, reach and targeted audience which I could never get on TV, in a tome, in newsprint or over the radio. I've got to call Josh Paul out in San Diego.

"We're here, we're high, we're out of the closet!" said Malmo-Levine, Founder of the School of Drug War history and Organic Cultivation. He believes weed is not just an herb or a medicine, but a political cause, a revolutionary sacrament...

Ken Hayes is another America drug war expatriate. He has tired, wistful eyes and hunched shoulders and looks older than his thirty-seven years. Yet he has always managed to stay a step ahead of U.S. law enforcement. A legend in medical marijuana lore for his copious gardens in Northern California, Hayes supplied Bay Area cannabis clubs with large amounts of high-quality organic weed. He was the Executive Director of *Cannabis Helping Alleviate Medical Problems* (CHAMP), a San Francisco med-pot dispensary, which was officially honored by the city's Board of Supervisors.

San Francisco D.A. Terence Hallinan appeared as a star witness *for* Hayes, helping Hayes beat a rap for growing nine hundred medicinal pot plants in 2001. Vindication in State Court, however, didn't stop the Feds from going after Hayes. He ran to Vancouver in January 2002 just prior to the U. S. Attorney pressing charges against him, which carried the obligatory minimum of ten years to life in prison.

"I came here because American authorities wanted to put me in jail for growing medicine for sick and dying people," said Hayes. He also applied for political asylum, but got an initial thumbs down from Canadian officials.

"There is something embarrassing and humiliating about people deciding to give up the right to live in America and fleeing to other countries just to avoid jail." HBO's Bill Maher stated on his blog. "America is a great country. People from all over the world come here to chase their dreams. But those who have spent even a couple of days in a jail cell in LA, New York, Atlanta or Sacramento will give up their American citizenship just to keep from going back to jail. What does that tell us about our prisons and jails in the U.S.A.? We raise hell and we are shocked and awed when we see photos coming out of Abu Ghraib showing the abuse there. But wait til these kids, pot activists, podcasters and bloggers get a hold of photos from prison cells in Riker's Island, Reidsville, C.Y.A., Pelican Bay and High Desert. I offer twenty-five grand to any young man or woman willing to get locked up on a minor crime and implant a hidden camera in your ass and bring us video clips or pictures. And if you're willing to get snapshots of the guards extracting and beating inmates in the prison, I'll make it fifty grand," Bill wrote on his blog in July 2005.

There is also an anonymous blog, which blatantly states, "I will pay fifty-five grand to anyone willing to become a whistleblower and expose the corruption of prison officials. If you are a lieutenant or above working in corrections and you provide video or audio evidence, which can be verified and authenticated, I'll pay a minimum of one hundred grand. Your cashier's check will be paid by the law offices of Tony Serra." (This blog was located on Yahoo! in a special anonymous flash and also streamed over E-Bay. This author has *no* idea who owns the blog.)

...Multimillionaire and Internet thespian John Gilmore of San Diego, California has a blog, which also lambastes C.D.C. and urges Stanford, Carnegie Mellon, MIT and Harvard students to get involved with inmate issues... At www.Soros.com, Billionaire George Soros offers scholarships for one high school senior on each of the fifty states (for a combined total of fifty students) who is "willing to spend one year blogging, podcasting and exposing rapes in prisons and jails." Mr. Soros' blog goes on to say, the students will receive a full four-year scholarship which includes text books, room and board - "to spend one full year utilizing the Internet to tell the world about the failure of America's In-justice System." Soros' blog goes on to state that he will "also consider granting full and partial scholarships to students willing to develop solutions and strategies to correct corrections in America."

...After the thumbs down from Canadian officials and two and a half years in British Columbia, Ken (Hayes) did not intend to wait for a warrant to send him back to America's vicious jails. "I'll only return when they decide to restore the Bill of Rights," Ken said. "I firmly believe in law and order. I also believe in pragmatic justice. It's not even sensible for America to have Federal Laws in direct conflict with State Laws nor is it sensible to assume high profile personalities such as Montel Williams would put their credibility on the line for an issue, which has no merit. And as much as I love Oprah, Dr. Phil and Rolando Watts. I wish they would be bold, courageous and candid enough to bring the cannabis issue before their viewers.

"Many people are multimillionaires and even billionaires but they are not free. They are beholden to their advertisers and backers. It's really sad. But it's a choice that they make. We would rather be free in Canada than imprisoned in America. And I'd rather be middle or working class and free to think, say and do as I choose, than a billionaire who is afraid to speak my mind. But at the end of the day, when all is said and done, perhaps I understand how it's all set up. Some of the media darlings are actually good people. They don't intend to *sell out* but they compromise. And I may not agree but I do understand. When Arsenio Hall was bodacious enough to put Louis Farrakhan on his Late Night Show, his show was cancelled! Now I believe Oprah is big enough to get away with putting Farrakhan on and not get cancelled. But how many of her sponsors are Jewish? Lots of them and who owns the networks? Jewish people do. And so she would lose ratings and money. So it's a Catch 22. But I do know that all that is changing. Thanks to Alex Benzer, Adam Curry, Kermin Fleming, Blake Ross, Marcus Pinkus, Maheesh and even Bill Gates the new citizen, the new activist, the new leader is being created. He or she is often in their teens and twenties, they are energetic, studious and they know how to operate the hell out of a laptop. And from the front seat of their cars, on the freaking toilet seats in their bathrooms, over their cell phones and via text messaging, they're turning their living rooms and bedrooms into boardrooms. They have discovered and basically they invented a new power. The power to be seen, read and heard. And when they peruse an article written by a guy named Emslander in a California prison cell in *The Beat Within*... When they see a message or a link mentioning some scribe named *Manning*, they create notoriety, celebrity and credibility. They use word of mouth, e-mails and podcasting to tell the world about the underdogs of society. And they will be the power brokers who will one day get justice for me, Kubby and Boje," stated Ken Hayes. He was getting ready to (again) skip town and head for the hills to points beyond.

But vanishing is not an option for Boje who lives in Vancouver with her Canadian husband, Chris Bennett and their four-year-old son. Chris is the Manager of Pot-TV, a Web-based video channel catering to an international pot-smoking audience.

Renee remains at the mercy of Canadian officials. One more appeal is possible if the upcoming decision goes against her...

Brian Ashcraft, Livia Corona and Jeff Howe all hosted a live chat on youth activism in June 2005. Ashcraft was mesmerized by a message from a student named Josh Goldin of Encinitas, CA who stated that, "Many people whittle their lives away on trivial matters. It is utterly ridiculous to waste the most treasured resource which none of us has enough of - *time*. There are people who were planning, strategizing and proselytizing more than fifty years ago the things, which we now enjoy in 2005. There are men and women now planning strategies, which will effectively run the world fifty years from now. The real challenge for manhood, fatherhood and adulthood is to position yourself now in ways that will benefit coming generations. I.e. generations yet unborn will enjoy the rich benefits of the space-aged studies of the 60s and the 70s. Even if I don't have biological kids of my own, I am a man if I learn something, teach something, invent or inspire something which has the potential to affect boys and girls twenty, thirty and forty years from today. I am volunteering to correspond with guys in my age group who have exchanged their bedrooms for jail cells or juveniles because I believe it helps. If the two or three letters per month I send to Steve out at C.Y.A. somehow motivates him not to fart his life away gambling, fighting and bullshitting, I may be saving a life."

Josh went on to write, "People in prisons and juveniles need help. They didn't go to jail because they were *mannerable*, well read and well adjusted. They had some problems, which obviously got them in hot water. But a tea bag ain't worth very much unless it's been in a lot of hot water. And the strongest steel comes out of the hottest fire. I tell my C.Y.A. pen pal to read something, write something, sing something, think something. I tell him to do something."

Brian Ashcraft responded, "I'm sold, Josh. You have a convert. I'm still a tough on crime republican, but I will find a prison pen pal and write to him. I promise."

Josh replied, "And don't just remind him of how bad he is. Please help him to comprehend that he is bigger than his mistakes. Let him know that some people look at the mistake and label you. And once we label you, we stop looking. But we are bigger than our mistakes. We can overcome our obstacles. If we ask the right questions, we will get the right answers. Let your pen pal know that he can't ever control what others do or say to or about him. But the one thing he has absolute control over is what he chooses to *think* about it. And he can control how and if he responds to it."

* * *

The most difficult challenge Boje faces is grappling with the possibility that Shiva, her son, might lose his mommy. "I could be fearless about it all until I had a child. Then I suddenly felt very vulnerable. I have to walk the plank. I have no choice. I'm going to fight this thing til the end. I know that if I lose, I lose big. But if I win, everybody wins," Boje states.

Her feisty spirit endeared her to alpha male multimillionaire Marc Emery, Vancouver's notorious "prince of pot", who has been a mainstay of financial and moral support for several U.S. drug war refugees. Emery, the godfather of Renee's son, runs a lucrative mail-order enterprise selling cannabis seeds to a worldwide clientele ("overgrow the government!") is his motto. An inveterate rabble-rouser, he led a "puff-in on Parliament Hill" during George Dubya Bush's diplomatic visit to Ottawa in December 2004. It was Marc Emery's way of lampooning the prohibitionist ideology, which holds just in the White House. Marc proudly sucked on a cigar-sized doob, while five hundred pot-puffing protesters gathered in front of a phalanx of Canadian cops who stood idly by. Representative of the Bush admin's desire to police the world, the DEA has set up shop to monitor local developments. A U.S. Narcotics Control emissary recently criticized Ottawa for being "soft on drugs" and threatened a slowdown in cross-border traffic if Canada resisted American demands. U.S. officials are pressuring Canadian officials to send Boje and other weed fugitives back to America.

Most Canadians favor granting refugee protection to medical weed patients. Yet, the Canadian government is reluctant to offend "its steroidal southern neighbor", as Richard Cowan, a veteran weed activist from Dubya's home state of Texas, put it. Humiliated and frustrated by the war on drugs, Cowan moved to Vancouver, where he publishes MarijuanaNews.com, which is an Internet newsletter. "Canada is a special problem for American prohibitionists because it is *too White to invade*, but too close to ignore," Cowan states.

Surveys indicate about eighty percent of U.S. physicians and about seventy-five percent of U.S. citizens support marijuana use for medical purposes, yet, die-hard Bush maniacs and prohibitionists continuously make life unlivable for sick people and many others in order to perpetuate a *forty billion dollar* a year drug control fix that ain't no where near working. Dr. Jerome Kassirer, as Editor-in-Chief of the prestigious *New England Journal of Medicine*, called federal policy on medical marijuana, "Misguided, heavy handed and inhumane. For years the DEA has habitually ignored scientific and medical data that *threatens* its *vested bureaucratic interests*, including a 1988 report by its own administrative law judge, Francis Young, who confounded expectations by concluding that cannabis, 'In its natural form is one of the safest therapeutically active substances known to man.'"

A powerful symbol of cultural conflict, cannabis rarely gets a sober appraisal from U. S. lawmakers. John Walters, President Bush's drug czar, has explicitly referred to the war on drugs as "A conservative cultural revolution." Steve Kubby and other American weed refugees also maintain that the battle against pot has long been a driving force of the culture war in the United States. "Make no mistake...this issue is no more about marijuana than the Boston Tea

Party was about tea," said Steve Kubby. Edward Zwick and Richard Solomon concur with Steve Kubby.

"I think sick people deserve anything they can get which is prescribed by a physician," says *Traffic* filmmaker, Ed Zwick. "Let us be sensible and admit that we have never and we will never, ever get rid of weed. Perhaps we should consider looking at a total legalization. At the very minimum, we should admit that any sick person can and will have access to weed. Why not trust our doctors? If they say Montel Williams has M.S. and he needs pot and they prescribe it, why not allow him to go to compassionate care stores and obtain it. Why chase him, arrest him and imprison him? Why choose to send people to the black market? It boils my blood when we do things in America that make no sense. It bothers me when we try to legislate morality and when we fatten frogs to feed snakes. We need to spend our time and efforts fighting real crime and teaching our youth how to feed the voids, which lead them to use crystal meth, to use crack and/or to involve themselves in violent crime. But I think there is indeed light at the end of the tunnel. Brian Bradt, (Lodi, CA), Nick Jones (Santa Rosa, CA), Jason Forman and Boje are galvanizing an international movement to the four corners of the universe with their podcasts, blogs and websites. Marc Emery, George Soros, Jerry Keenan, Peter B. Lewis, John Sperling, Richard J. Botto, Blaise Zeraga, Drew Schutte, S. I. Newhouse, Jr. and Charles H. Townsend are pouring tons of dough into these movements. They are providing the infrastructure, which makes it possible for these folks to organize online. And there are splinter groups of youngsters who have merged various issues of justice, rehabilitation, wrongful convictions and police brutality into and underneath one umbrella."

Zwick went on to conclude, "Young people are amazing. They are willing to put in the hours to e-mail, (this author *strongly* encourages *you* to e-mail people whose names appear in this book and let them know this book is out. Please find ten or twenty names in this book and Google them or Yahoo! or AskJeeves them. When you find out how to reach them, let them know to go to www.Cafepress.com/Manning, click on "Blue-Eyed Blonde" and get this book! We offer fifteen hundred dollars to the first *ten* people who can prove to us that *you* e-mailed, texted or called forty or more people whose names are in this book and led them to Cafepress.com/BEBlonde… We offer twenty-five hundred dollars to anyone who sets up a blog based on this book and gets at least one thousand messages on that blog. And if you get this book mentioned on a national TV show, we'll give you five thousand dollars. Even if you don't need the money, help build up the justice movement by telling everybody you know about this book. Blog, podcast, write letters to the editor, call talk shows, etc. and put the word out that *Blue-Eyed Blonde* is out...) and contact people and rally them around an issue. I salute Boje, Emery, Kubby and the Open Society Institute in New York."...

I can hear certain music and it just lifts me up. My spirit and energy just explodes and goes through the roof when I hear certain music. Country moves some people (i.e. www.StevePander.com), Rock moves some of us, Soul, Gospel and Rap moves others. Jazz excites some and the Blues moves others. But we feel certain things when we hear certain things. Also seeing certain people, places and things causes us to react, think and feel certain ways. And quite frankly, I don't know what reading this book causes *you* (the person holding this book right now) to feel, think or do. But I do know that you can't read the words of Jeremy, Paul, Scott or Boje and not feel something. I can wish and I can hope. And since the final task of bringing this data together in the format of a tome has been left up to me, I can at least wish. As a segue that calls the song, "I Wish" by R. Kelly to my mind. And I shan't conclude this book without finally imposing or exposing some of my wishes to you the reader. Yes, I *Sherman Diahric Manning* - wish! I wish we would all remember *Mattie*. Mattie had wisdom beyond his years and he wanted us all to love one another. Oprah told Mattie one Christmas season that I'll give you anything you *want* for Christmas, you name it and I'll buy it. Your *wish* is my *command*. Mattie replied, "I wish you would *pray for me* for Christmas, Ms. Winfrey." Damn...that brings tears to my eyes when I think about it. Mattie said we all have a *song in our heart*. And you know *I wish* we would sing our songs. I wish - oh how I wish. I wish those of you reading would love one another. I wish we would have integrity, charity and be kind to one another. I wish we would stop teaching our kids to worship and idolize Paris Hilton, Brad Pitt and Britney Spears. I wish we'd teach our children that TV people are just human beings with problems, difficulties, addictions and habits like all the rest of us. As silly and nasty as it may sound, I'd like to take a kid into the bathroom right after Paris (or Pitt or Paula Abdul, etc.) has just finished taking a massive crap and just let them inhale the stench. And I wouldn't tell the kid who took the dump, just allow them to get sickened by the foul odor of the defecation. It may be an *aha* moment for them just to let them know these folks crap stinks!

And so many of the guys and gals in Hollywood are hooked on drugs. It is a shame. They waste their lives, livings and savings on cocaine and crystal meth. Addictions run amok in the city of angels. And I want our children to know what living *really* is. I want them to *smile* at the boy or girl in the mirror. I wish our teens who are in trouble sitting in the juveniles would stumble upon these words and take lessons from Jeremy and Paul. I wish these humans in the juveniles, jails and adult prisons would pull themselves together and do something besides play cards. I wish they would quit running around from gang to gang, buddy to buddy, fad to fad and drug to drug trying to get a *Mr. Feel Good* high and to escape the misery of their own situation. I wish they would read, write, think, study and pray.

I wish they would turn their jail cells into classrooms and prisons into universities and figure out ways to get better. I wish inmates would stop raping inmates. I wish we'd stop the killing, stabbings, the jealously and the hatred. I've witnessed the dark, dank and dismal affects of America's prison system. I totally understand why Boje, Kubby and thousand of others are running as far away from the American jail cell as they can. I've seen what it's like to be *White* and in LA County Jail. I know what it's like to be Black or Brown in jail. I know what it looks like and I intimately understand what it feels like to be trapped in a cesspool of sin and to *know you should not be here*.

I see the void in the dead eyes of walking dead men everyday. I see the thick rage, the hurt, the hopelessness, the abuse, the arrested development, the shame, the pain and the loneliness. I wish our citizens would demand an immediate change. I wish we would not bullshit it, game it, blame it or play with it. I wish we would not become longwinded rhetoricians or engage in tautology. I wish we would stand flat-footed and transform it. I wish Bush would stop the denial and admit it. I wish Bush would care about it. I wish Bush would get down on his knees and ask God to forgive him for being a liar, a dictator, a gangster and a crook. I wish Bush would bow down and humble himself before Jehovah and declare, "I have sinned." I wish Bush would tour *his* prisons in his own country and ask himself one question after he leaves New Folsom, Reidsville, Pelican Bay or Riker's Island... "Is this working? Is this making people better? Is this humane?" That's really three questions I know but if he honestly answers the one, he'll know it ain't humane and it ain't making people better. I wish *you* (whoever you are as you *read these words*) would ask yourself what one thing can I do today to make it better? Can I e-mail the White House, call my governor, senator or mayor? Can I call the warden, the parole board, my pastor? Can I do anything *this day* to show prisoners there is a better way? Can I get out of my comfort zone, get off the couch for an hour or two and do something for the guys in the prisons? What can I do today to protect public safety?

I wish *you* would do what you can do. You can write to a prisoner. You can start a blog, open a door, hire a lawyer, send a check, write a column, call a talk show, sponsor workshop, seminar, prayer vigil or donate some money. *You can do* something. I wish that you would! I wish humans would rise to the occasion and do what we were sent to the planet to do. We must find our *purpose* and serve. And all too often what we are doing is becoming hypnotized and desensitized to the hurt, pain and the sorrow, which is all around us. Television, movies and sometimes even music numbs us up and dumbs us down. We are not only afraid of the dark, but we are also afraid of silence. We don't want to hear the nothingness. We are in a state of chaos and confusion. There is a large segment of the power brokers of this nation who see nothing wrong with a few having plenty and a lot having nothing. We think it's okay for me to live in Buckhead with millions of dollars, which I could never spend, and Lisa living in Techwood, Bankhead Court or on a park bench with little or nothing. Greed has become the norm. I'm convinced that even the few of us who think we are good, loving and giving are lost with a capital L. We justify our own perversions and greed by losing ourselves in it. We are running from humanity and technology has been utilized methodically and strategically to widen the gap on the disconnect in the family of humanity. The more *stuff* I have the more you will envy and watch me. But when you look at me, you're not seeing me. You see my gadgets, trinkets and the so-called trappings of success. I (personally) thank God for blessing my family and me with money. Money is a powerful tool. I rarely ever mention **my** money in my writing. But it is fitting for me to write here that I am a multimillionaire. I've had money all my life. And I learned from my parents that having a million bucks does *not* make you a success.

There are Hollywood actors right this minute with fifty and sixty million dollars in the bank who are lonely paranoid, addicted, afflicted and miserable. It is my belief that the curse on Hollywood actors, power brokers, etc. is karma.

Much of Hollywood has not given back. They will earn fifty million dollars in a year and give five grand to the poor and E.T. or Extra will make it seem as if they gave a million bucks.

They are cursed with a curse because they have not fed the hungry, clothed the naked and visited those in trouble. But they are living a lie and they are gonna die one day and from hell they'll lift up their eyes and regret.

What I wish, I wish, I wish is that Paris Hilton, Paula Abdul, Shaquille O'Neal and all the others would follow the lead of Oprah, Brad Pitt, Sharon Stone and others who really, really give and bless others. That's what I wish. And in the meantime, I wish you would love you. Right at this moment, find yourself and find your unique gifts and use your strengths. You are precious. You are unique. There have been over six billion people on this planet and yet there has never been another *you*.

People don't and won't always react the way you wish. They won't always give, smile or laugh when you want them to or think they should. But *you* can be good to you. I wish you would manipulate the technological advances of the computer to draw you closer to other people. We can let our blogs, podcasts, e-mails and even our cell phones bring healing, love and beauty. Let us take the time to be good to one another. We can do it. I need you. You need me. I wish we would stop pretending to be islands unto ourselves. Let's try to stand naked and tell each other what we need and what we want. Maybe you can read "Brothers and Keepers" or "God's Gym" by John Edgar Wideman. Maybe you oughta rent the DVD of "Crash" or "Shawshank Redemption" or "Mr. Hurricane" and see what's in those movies for you.

Maybe I should wish we would tell each other the truth. We are in a mess right now and we need to get it together.

Just cry. Just try. We can both cry and try. Cry your little tears out and feel sorry for yourself. Cry because you miss your momma or your daddy. Cry about the pain and the sorrows of your bad yesterdays and scary tomorrows. Get alone, cut out the lights and just cry. Let yourself hurt and allow yourself to weep. Get the pain out. I try to do it for thirty minutes every thirty days. And when the crying is over, get up. Get up, wash your face and smile. Smile about you. Smile about your divinity and your creation. Don't worship movie stars and so-called celebrities. You are the celebrity in your life. Celebrate you! You're supposed to elect *presidents* but don't worship them. Be your own president. Be the president of your household. Be the president of your jail cell. Be the president of your family or your tribe. And lead your jail cell, family or your school by example. Show Dubya Bush (or whoever is president by the time you read this book) what real president's do. As president of your family, your tribe, your club or your jail; feed your hungry, clothe your naked and care for others. Don't send a fifty million dollar bribe to Palestine while they need books in the library in Rancho Cordova.

Don't spend eight hundred billion dollars on a war in Iraq or Afghanistan when you need to *spend* it on fighting a war on poverty in New York and crime in Atlanta.

I wish you and me would open our eyes and see. Let's see the hurt in the eyes of our neighbors. Let's see the poverty and pain all around us. Tell Paris Hilton she's fine, she's foxy, she's rich and we want her to help buy Carl Jr. burgers for poor kids in the hoods. Ask Ashton Kutcher, Anita Baker, Tina Turner, our rich pastors and these colleges like Harvard who have *billions of dollars* which they don't spend; tell them to cut a check today to help kids in poverty...

Ben Bradlee is a brilliant man. He was Editor of the Washington Post. And we now need Ben to mentor Travis Riley (Nevada College student), Sheila Applebaum, prison, jail and juvenile inmates who want to become journalists. We need to get it together. We are sick, paralyzed and lost...

I said to my first wife years ago that I thought we had another bottle of champagne left. She replied, "No, we only bought three."

I said, "But I thought I saw another bottle maybe I was wrong. I just thought we had another one."

At that moment, she pulled the *other* bottle of champagne from the cabinet and said something like, "And here's the third bottle," while smiling. Now on the surface that seems like not a big deal. But it's bigger than you think. And because humans have been disconnected for *so* long and we've overlooked character defects for so long, most of us would see zero wrong with that scenario. It bothered me because A. It was rooted in deception. No, she didn't *lie* to me but she also did not say, "Oh yes - we do have another bottle of champagne left. I thought we were out." Instead, she doesn't even know *what* she did, much less *why* she did it. She repeated the fact that, "We only had three" and this is born out of a need to be *right*. She needs to convince *herself* as well as me that "See there, I'm adequate. I'm smart. I was right, it was three. Even though I thought we were out, kaput, all gone, I can't say I was wrong, mistaken or even celebrate the fact that we have more. My confidence is so *low* that I *need* to hear myself be right. Being wrong or mistaken is embarrassing... This is born out of some hurt, some shame, some pain from her past that she has not healed. It's killing her and you too.

Tens of thousands of you are reading my words and many of you have that same problem. You've *talked over* it. You've laughed or cried over it. You've ignored it or hid from it. But I tell this not to embarrass her but to help you to help yourself. You can go see Dr. Phil if you wanna or you can do what she did, read it and forget about it and keep doing what you do. Or you can tell yourself the truth and tell yourself who *hurt you*. Was it your father, mother, older sibling? Did they call you stupid or a failure? Did they whip, spank or beat you when you forgot things, made mistakes or when you were wrong? Or was it just the signals you received in school or from society about high expectations and the competitive nature of life? Did this signal of high expectations cause you to subconsciously feel people would think you were stupid or unsuccessful or were wrong about things? What was it? Something hurt you and sent you into a reactive, sensitive and defensive styled person and your feelings get hurt easily.

It don't take Dr. Phil to tell you that you must deal with this. Get to the root of the problem and you'll take the poison out of the fruit. Identify and then begin to consistently affirm to yourself that it no longer will control your life. Tell yourself, "I will not spend the rest of my life in this prison, in this pain or in the place of this hurt." Then rise above it. Lighten up and handle it. It is serious but you can change it. You begin by making up your mind that you will not spend the rest of your life doing this. You will go to your destiny. You will rise above it. The very next time you feel it coming on; the sensitivity, the need to be right, the feeling of failure, embarrassment, shame and hurt, you must smile within your soul and open your mouth and speak truth… "Wow, I was dwelling on the fact that we only got three bottles. The fact is, I thought we were out. I just did. But here is the other bottle of champagne you were looking for. Fortunately, we have one more left." That is an adult response without all the filtering and censoring.

I'm dealing with this because I see it so often. I see so many people who suffer from that hurt. People in my own tribe, family and close associates. And I am as competitive as anyone. We all like to be right… I love a debate and I enjoy winning a debate. But I can't live my *life* debating 24/7. And we must learn how to shift gears and not bring the debate to the bed. If you have etiquette, you won't tell a defecation joke at the dinner table. You are smart enough not to tell locker room jokes to your child. Ipso facto, don't come home and look at your wife, husband or lover with the same mindset or the same attitude as you look at your opponent on the basketball court. Recognize the fact that many of us are suffering from diminished human, social and communication skills. Untie and unlock your ability to communicate honestly, openly and without fear or shame. Maybe *we* all ought to slow down and celebrate self, celebrate each other and learn to love and communicate again. Look into my eyes and help me look into your eyes. Let the fear and pain dissipate. I need *you* and you need me too. Can I lean on you? Do you want to be able to trust, depend and count on me? We are all seeking the same damned thing. Let's give each other what we want. Let's begin now to *heal* our hurts, pains and sorrow. We can do it. I *wish* we would. Will we??

* * *

The air was thick with cigarette smoke. The room was about the size of the average bedroom. The walls were made of marble. The floor was carpeted with a gray carpet that was so thick that your feet felt like you were walking on pillows when you stood and stepped on it. The room had a large chandelier hanging over the lone desk in the office. Scott found it odd that this room would have a chandelier in it. He wondered why would a lawyer have a chandelier in his office? He wondered why the expensive carpet for such a small office. And what about the marbled walls? Unique and odd but Scott would never know because he'd never ask... "Have a seat, Mr. Coffman," Attorney Dennis Cunningham told him. "This is Bert Deixler, Michael Bein and John Elsmore. I asked them to sit in on our meeting. I have a general idea of what is going on with you and Manning. I read about Jeremy and Paul in the talking points you sent me. But we've got an hour, Scott, and I want you to tell me and my fellow members of the legal cloth; what is it you think a *lawyer* can do for you?" Cunningham stated.

Scott was animated. His palms were sweating. He was sitting in the room with three multimillionaires, brilliant, powerful and famous lawyers. He was pensive but decided to use humor. "I thought I was meeting with Tony Serra, Willie Gary and Murray Janus. Maybe I'm at the wrong firm," Scott said to the distinguished thespians. John Elsmore laughed awkwardly and chimed in, "But I know Willie Gary very well. I know Dennis Archer. Cunningham plays golf with Serra and Bert is close to Janus. If we decide to do this and if we need reinforcements, we can call them. Hell, we'll call Floyd Abrams, David Boies and Gerry Spence if we need them. But do we need them? Do you need us? What are you asking us to do?"

Without taking a breath or giving Bert a chance to speak, Scott said, "I need you to pick up where Johnnie Cochran left off. I have learned that Mr. Cochran (may he rest in peace) was preparing to sue the governors of twenty-eight states for allowing their prisons to be criminal organizations. He was gonna sue for the White boys being raped in LA County Jail, High Desert, Fulton County Jail, C.Y.A. juveniles, etc. He was suing for women being raped by prison guards. He was suing for the inmates who are addicted to drugs in prisons because guards smuggle them in. He was suing for abuse of power, corruption, misuse of power and for murder. I need you all to pick up the evidence and file suit. I need you to get the NAACP, ACLU, Human Rights Watch, Amnesty International, the ABA and the NACDL to file Friend of the Courts or Amicus Briefs. I need you all to leak the story to Ben Bradlee at the Washington Post, Geraldo, Dan Rather or somebody. I need you today!"

Bert chimed in, "Mr. Coffman, this is huge! This is monumental. And I want you to know you *will* need security 24/7. And we will put up the money to protect you. That is a promise. In fact, Scott, when you leave this office *today*, you will have a detail on you. This is absolutely necessary."

Scott said, "And so what I need you guys to do also is…"

* * *

…This woman looked like Paris Hilton. I mean she seriously had curves. Real curves, really nice, really, really in all the right areas. When you look at her, you actually have to do a double take. "How many times have people told you that you look like Paris Hilton?" Jacob Stone asked Pamela St. John, the twenty-six year old U.C. Riverside graduate.

"Probably about ten times everyday for the past sixteen years, seriously," She replied.

"Can I get right to the point and tell you I want… I want to eat your vagina inside out. I want to lick it up and down and round and round. I want my tongue inside you. You just turn me on so much. Yes, I know you are Scott Coffman's ex-girlfriend and Scott and I are cool. But…"

Pamela licked her lips and cut Jacob off, "There is not a *But…* and I'm not the ex. In fact, we are still seeing each other. And I don't do one-night stands in the heat of passion. I know you want me to say, 'I'm not that innocent,' like Britney. But that's *not* who I am. I am a woman. I respect myself and my body. I have sexual passions and drives like anyone else. But the few times I've done it I've been responsible. We used a condom. I believe my life is worth more than ten or fifteen minutes of pleasure. You might have AIDS, syphilis or hepatitis. And you are definitely not responsible enough to bring a child into the world. So what if I got pregnant?"

Jacob laughed and replied, "My tongue is not fertilized. You can't get pregnant by me eating you, Pam. I will stroke myself later. You don't have to let me put my penis in you. Just let me…"

Pam laughed, "You're gonna have a heat stroke. But no *thank you*. I can't do it. You may need to go take a cold, cold shower…

"Now I want to talk to you about Shawn Tallerman, Professor Jesse Schell, Dr. Keith Liang, Professor Robert Putnam, Kris Anaya, Walter Dean Myers, Markus Buckingham, Frank Tyson, Brian Hedenberg, Sam Neuman, Jerry Caperi, Greg Seaman, Josh Caulkins, Vincent Kartheiser, Zach Smilovitz, Nick Jones, Joan Felt, Luke Sears, Robby Genepri, Michael Faught, Ken Paves, Robert Downey, Jr., Dustin Maddison, Kyle Love, Kevin Mahaffey, Kevin Kinsella, Nate Solov, Anoop Ghanwani, Jason Willett, Jamie Marotte, Gary Falber, Colin Angle, Agim Kaba, Jake Turner, Barrett Lyon, Matt Feeley, Craig Brewer, Ron Droze, Ryan Salgado, Chris Salgado, Jason Goldberg, David Passrell, Bob Geidof, George Weiss, Adnan Mohamad Khashoggi, Robert Klein, John D. O'Connor, Jeff Jackson, Jay Jackson, The Kid Kwiathkowski, Ryan Landers, Chris Shaffer, Chris Abani, D. Charles Whitney, Russ Stratfull, Ben Markowitz, Peter Grammatas, Kelly Schoolmeester, Dylan Atchley, The School of Gladiotora in Rome, Joshua Truduay and Scott..."

"You are putting me to sleep with all these freaking names. What the hell are you talking about?" Jacob said.

"I am talking about taking over the world. Did you watch the two kids on Tavis Smiley June 1st?" Pam explained.

"Hell no, I don't watch Tavis," Jason said.

Pam replied, "Maybe you should. You ought to go to *LAKidsSpeakout*.com and see how the killing of Ennis Cosby moved this young kid who is en route to Stanford to get politically active. You should see the story in *Wired* Magazine written by Josh Davis on Oscar Vazquez, Luis Aranda and Cristian Arcega. They were all students at Carl Hayden High School in Phoenix. Poor kids who built an odd, three foot tall robot. They equipped it with propellers, camera, lights, a laser, depth detectors, pumps, an underwater microphone and an articulated pincer. At the top sat a black, waterproof briefcase containing a nest of hacked processors, miniscule fans and leads. It was a cheap but astonishingly operational underwater robot capable of recording sonar pings and retrieving objects fifty feet below the surface."

Jacob said, "You're shitting me."

Pam said, "No! The four teens who built it came to this country through tunnels or hidden in the back seats of cars... When the robot sprang a leak at the 3rd Annual Marine Advanced Technology Remotely Operated Vehicle Competition, Oscar decided to use absorbent *tampons* to fix the problem. It worked and they won!"

"These four high school kids who built their robot with eight hundred dollars, beat out brilliant nerds at M.I.T. who had a twelve thousand dollar budget. They were David taking on Goliath and they slayed the giants from M.I.T. and that's a perfect segue for the connection to the long list of names I just recited to you. This group represents a group of kids and students who are about to *change the freaking world.* They are using podcasts, blogs, Myspace.com, Friendster, Tribe.net and tons of other technocratic methods to shake down the jail and prison bosses! They are exposing the bullshit, crime and the sham of a justice system we have in America. You need to join us. We have Eminem, Ashton Kutcher, Paris Hilton, Drew Barrymoore, Jamie Foxx, Benjamin McKenzie, Josh Goldin, Adam Brody, Michael Cardelle, Roerig, Sean Pander, Nick Carter, Aron Carter and Frank Carter working with us. This movement is catching on like a brush fire. You'd better get on this train. Didn't you see the lawsuit? Did you see CNN last night? Do you watch Celebrity Justice? Jacob, have you been under a rock?"

Jacob swallowed and looked at Pam and replied, "Whatever the hell this is, if it is gonna help get the wrong guys out of jail, put the right guys in, if it's real and not just another bullshit group, Pam, I'm in! I'll jump on the bandwagon. Yes, I saw the news and I heard a lot about the *sick rapes* and stuff taking place *in* prison. In the freaking prison. I saw that. I was numb. *In the prison. We must do something* and..."

The End

E-mail Hallopeter@Freesurf.ch and give us *your opinion* today...

EPILOGUE

I have enjoyed writing this book tremendously. I hope and pray that y'all got it. I want people to walk away from this book changed and changing. I don't want *you* (the reader) to be like my ex-wife continuing to laugh over, joke around, talk over, ignore and deny *your* problems. I want you to dig down and find the roots of your rage, roots of your fears, roots of your anger, roots of your character defects and work to transform you. Paul said he wanted to be transformed daily "By the *renewing* of my *mind*." I hope you won't give up til you get it right. I hope you'll decide to get yourself together. Don't spend the rest of your life finding fault with others. If you decide to let our Caucasian boys all across America continue to be raped, beat, brutalized and traumatized daily in the juveniles, jails and prisons (and they are being raped somewhere this very second) that's your business. If you decide it's okay to let them get beat up, stuck up, sodomized and pulverized in our prisons, so be it. If you ignore the travesty at LA County Jail, Pelican Bay, Riker's Island, Georgia, Arizona and U.S. prisons and juveniles and focus your outrage at Abu Ghraib, that's your business. If you, my White, Mexican, Black or other brother (and mother, father and sister) find nothing wrong with the bloodshed of the *Blue-Eyed Blonde* in America's prisons; okay, so be it.

But at least sit down and work on you. Work on you like you never worked before. Get real with *you*. Some of you (and me sometimes) are in misery, woe, sorrow and fear. You are on *suicide watch* and don't even know it. You have blamed everything and everybody for your problems, your pains and your shortcomings. You are suffering from self-inflicted wounds. Wounds of disobedience, wounds of arrogance and deception. We are trapped in moral darkness and simultaneously cutting our own lights out. It is amazing to know how many of *us* actually believe we can arrive at the right destination while traveling in the wrong direction. We think we can arrive south even though we are traveling west. And we get caught up in our own perversions, lies and even anger. It's like even though we are literally driving the absolute opposite route which will lead to where we want to go, we begin to justify B.S., "Well, I am obeying the speed limit! I obey all the traffic laws. I don't drink and drive, etc., etc." But we can obey every rule on the road and that still won't get us where we wanna go if we are on the wrong route. It's like I'm sleeping with *your wife* while I gotta wife and I'm bragging to my pals "At least I don't beat Jody's wife. I'm good to her and I take her to church every Sunday."

Dr. T. D. Jakes preached "Suicide Watch" and I suggest y'all call 1-800-Bishop 2 and order "Suicide Watch" on tape, CD or DVD. Jakes mentioned how, "The Passion of the Christ" was being sold on the Black market and pointing out how some folks are so demented that they rationalize, "Well, I'm gonna get me a blessing from watching this stolen movie." I can go deeper, it's the same thing the priest, predator, Mayor West in Spokane, Washington and every molester does in their mind... They justify and rationalize foolishness (sin, crime and perversion). They tell themselves, it's okay to have sex with an eight-year-old *child* although they are twenty-eight or thirty-eight. They start thinking, "At least I didn't kill her" or him.

It's sick and this suicide mentality is killing us. It has beat us down as a nation, as a people and as a planet. We have all these people whom we looked up to because television told us they were *superstars*. But many of them are empty, void and all tied up. Tied up in methamphetamine, cocaine, alcohol, perversion and things you can't even imagine. If I could only get one thing clear to you, the reader, in this book, it would be to give yourself a check up from the neck up. Chase your own dreams and quit looking to Hollywood for your visions. Let Hollywood entertain you but don't try to imitate Chris Webber, Paris Hilton or Elizabeth Taylor. Live your own dream...

Jeremy Shackelford's mother sent me a letter late last month, which Jeremy had written to me but didn't mail... Jeremy and Paul never heard from their father. He didn't even attend their funerals. Perhaps he's in a prison somewhere. I don't know. But if by some freak of nature, coincidence or incidence, Mr. Shackelford is reading this, I must tell him, "*You lost two good young men*." I figure I'll let Jeremy have the last words. I'll see ya'll in the next book...

The following is a verbatim copy of the *undated missive,* which Jeremy wrote to me (at some point) and his mother found it and sent it to me. Thank you.

"Dear *Sherman*: I hope this missive finds you in great spirits and a positive frame of mind. At this juncture in time, I thought I'd update you in a very ambiguous manner, just to let you know I am on it. I do read each and every missive that you write to me. Contrary to your erroneous assumption, I take pleasure in receiving your post. I also enjoy speaking to you via telephonic communication. I wish you'd change your mind and allow me to visit you. But I do get it! I don't rubberstamp it, Sherman and I don't fully concur with it but I get it. A part of me would never, ever want somebody to visit/see me in prison. And I'm not certain how I'd feel when it was time for the visitor to depart. So you need not reiterate the point... I did call the three

282

people you asked me to. Two of them seem to support you (Sherman Manning) as adamantly as B. J. Hickman does Michael Jackson. The third person (the famed Mr. *Marc Emery* in Vancouver) seems to be a serious, pragmatic and determined man. Mr. Emery stated emphatically but stoically, 'Manning should not be in prison. Just as Boje and Kubby should not face prison… I read all of his books.'

"Also I checked with the *Innocence Project* at Cardoza Law School and received the most recent stats on wrongful convictions. Startling and troubling is all I can say. Amnesty International, Human Rights Watch and the Quaker Organization (Friends Committee Legislation) in Philadelphia gave me all the data they have on the *main thrust* of your argument; *rape in prison is epidemic* is all I can say I learned in those reports. It's sickening… Stop Prisoner Rape in LA fully supports and corroborates your premise that by and large, it is the young Caucasian males and females who are being raped en masse in our institutions. I can't wait to see what James McClatchy (publisher of the Sacramento Bee) will say when I show him these statistics.

"Sherman, those guys being held as suspected terrorists rarely get due process. They rarely go to *trial*. And I learned through amnesty that by and large when the very few of them do get a trial; if they are acquitted, they are returned to the same prison cells i.e. at Guantanimo Bay and *held til* the war is over. That could be decades. They get show trials, kangaroo justice and political shams. If you will be held anyway for ten or twenty years, what good is a trial? I mention this because it sort of bridges or acts as segue to your argument that many poor people in the jails never get a fair trial. And as you point out when they do get a trial, they usually lose. And if they happen to win, they are returned (not to the same cell as the guys at Guantanimo) to the cells of poverty and the inner city cells of drugs, guns, gangs and violence. So they too get show trials. And candidly, we all know that they who are guilty, imprisoned and eventually released, will get out, return to the neighborhood cell, re-offend and go back to prison. They simply leave one cell to enter another. It's like a *transfer* and the wrongly convicted; guys who should have never gone there in the first place - they'll get out and really offend. It's a sham, a show and it is destroying our country. I intend to argue this point strenuously in my pieces on the tragedy, which you've brought to my attention. It will be called "The *Blue-Eyed Blonde*." After it hits the streets, we need to do a book on the subject. It will serve as a wake up call to America. And when we do a book, *Sherman*, we'll get folk like Marc Emery, Peter B. Lewis, Willie Gary, Tony Danza, Geraldo Rivera and Montel to back it. Get them to send a copy to every senator, every legislator, judge and governor.

"And we can flood the schools and colleges with the book. Maybe you can put Eminem, your buddy Clay Aiken, Anthony Fedorov or Timothy Goebel on the cover. Maybe use Manteca High student Sam Miller on it. We'll get the Val Litwin and the fellas at Extreme Kindness (Good Karma Entertainment) and the *Surfing the Nations* ministry to get copies and pass them out.

Shavo Odadsian, Trent Reznor, Derrick Ontai, Al Young, Adam Levine, Mickey Madden, Orlando Bloom, Victor Rasuk and Stefan Eriksson will help us.

"I'll get Jesus Maldonado, Jay Pace, Scot Parsley, Theo Milonopoulos, Kris Anaya, Matt Matteucci, Joshua Schreiber - Schoonyan, Alan Stevenson, Michael Sexton, Mel Gibson, Joe Houlton, Michael Zhang, Attorney David Chu, Dealer Steve J. Jackson, Robert Downey, Jr., Tristan Imboden, Billy McNair, Sheldon Drobny, Danny Goldberg, Heath Ledger, Zach Braff, Kelly Schoolmeester, Chris Purvis, Hayden Christensen, Joey Plonsker, Aaron Funk, Jonathan Korzen, Dave Yamada and Tavis Smiley to read it and promote it. The book will reach around the world. The book will embarrass the nation as did the water hoses and dogs biting Blacks in the 60s. This will spark a new norm of the Civil Rights Movement for White boys in prisons. And the designers of our show - justice system in America will admit privately that their plan has backfired. And the wives of the power brokers will force their husbands to do something and the something that they do to save *White* America - will help *you too*. It will make prisons better all over America. And (in closing) as Martha Stewart would say... *That's a good thing*. Peace and prosperity... Jeremy Shackelford."

The friends of Harper Collins (i.e. A&M) strenuously support the active engagement of readers. Go online and visit all of the Websites, blogs and Internet links mentioned in this book. All of the Web addresses and podcasts, etc., are authentic and (to our knowledge) correct. Readers may contact the author at *Sherman D. Manning*, J98796, M.C.S.P., A-2-240, P. O. Box 409020, Ione, CA 95640, U.S.A. E-mail him c/o Hallopeter@freesurf.ch.

The data contained on the cover of this tome is fiction and sobriquet. While Mr. Manning is in contact with many of the persons who are recorded as giving comments, criticism and praise, etc., it too is mostly (with the exception of a few) fiction. Finally, the rape epidemic which is depicted in this book is factual and actual true-to-life. It is the author's prayer and hope that each person who reads this book will be compelled to take action. If you e-mail, snail mail, telephone and telegram the White House, the U.S. Senate, your governors and state representatives and demand a change in the way we investigate crime, make arrests, prosecute, sentence and incarcerate our citizens. Truly, the author believes an ounce of prevention is worth more than ten pounds of cure. The author believes if we begin today to protect, educate, love, inspire and motivate our children; we will create a crime free society and lessen the need for juveniles, jails and prisons. We invite your suggestions and comments. "From the Palace to the Prison" is in its fifth printing and is now available in soft cover. It is a must read for every Jeremy Shackelford fan.
The Publishers

Final Thoughts For My Friends
… Nobody can convince me that *together* we can't change the world. I *know that we can*. I know we can. And thanks to Marcus Pincus (www.Tribe.net), Myspace. com, Yahoo! chats and Craigslists.com, etc., the window of opportunity has broadened. I need you - right where you are - to help us do this. For the boys and girls who need a helping hand. For the girls who are being misled, misguided and misinformed. For all of the folks at the breaking point in their lives. Those who smile and carry on just like everything is all good, but inside they are on *suicide watch*. We must get this book to them. We gotta do it.

Filmmaker *Robert Rodriguez* told me, "If I ever write a book, I wanna write like you." I appreciate the compliment. And I must admit I am a man with dignity, self respect and I'm macho. I don't like asking people for squat. But when I see the state of the juveniles, youth prisons and gangs in our schools, etc. and I see how much *adults* have screwed up our youth and blamed it on them. I'm willing to beg for our youth. I am willing to get down on my hands and knees to *beg* in the name of our youth. The children are our tomorrow. They are the future as well as the present. We can't go on without them. We need them. And they have been molested, abused, raped, beat down and vilified. It is time for us to change. May I beg the owner of Tatto Revolution, George Weiss, George Soros, Bill and Melinda Gates, pastors, priests, mayors, mommas and daddies; may I beg you to get a copy of this book to some young man or woman. Get it for Ryan who just graduated from Christian Brothers High School and Heather West who just graduated from Davis Senior High School. We must be willing to log on today and buy, order and mail a copy of this here book to somebody else *today*. Have you done it yet? If not, why not? Please, please do not allow your own biases, prejudices and mediocrity to cause you to deny access to this book to our kids.

I am not writing for *my* justice. This tale is bigger than me. It's not a tome aimed at winning cheerleaders for *me*. I am just a *nobody* trying to tell *everybody* about *somebody* who can save *anybody*.

I have come to understand bias, prejudice and adult B.S. I know when we figure a man or woman to be a crook, liar, predator, rapist, thug, thief or whatever, we are stuck with that belief for **life**. But since most of us *claim* to believe in the Bible, let's be candid and straight enough to at least admit some of the most powerful folks in biblical history went to prison. And they didn't just go for believing in God. *Joseph* was convicted of a crime. Attempted rape! He served 13 ½ years in prison because folks just like you stood around and did *nothing*. You let him stay there because you claimed he *must* have done something wrong. The prosecutor and courts would not just lock him up. The judge meted out *justice* you believed.

I challenge you *adults* to really read the story of Joseph in your Bible. Our young people already know the story. They heard it from Rick Warren and T. D. Jakes. They are getting it. It's you (with your fifty-year-old self trying to play young) who need to *get it*. They still have not heard you say, "He might be innocent."

So I ask you to at least get them this book. I don't want them to end up like Mike Tyson or Michael Jackson. I want them to know *game when they see it*. I want them to be sharp enough to go on to Myspace.com and chat but to **immediately** report it when somebody asks for a nude photo or a rendezvous. I want them to know not to allow *Uncle* so and so to *touch* them inappropriately. I want them to know to follow that *gut instinct* when it says, "This is too good to be true." And they need to know they are not alone. They need a book like this. They need a project, a task such as this. If you get it to them, they will occupy their minds and challenge their own wit and skills. I can see Matt Bogart, Riley Evans, Kyle Love, Greg Sosa, Joshua Treadway, Greg Doggett, Joey Plonsker, Chris Eilerman (Kentucky), Wes Kovarik, Matt Dalio, Mr. Funk, Carly Simon's son and Cody Pitts sitting at the laptop on Craigslists, Yahoo!, Google, Tribe.net, Friendster.com sending messages, posting notes and telling folks, "You are in *Blue-Eyed Blonde*". Go to www.Cafepress.com/Blonde and get it! "They will do it but you must help me to get it to them. And for every young man and young woman reading my words right now, I thank you. I thank you for setting the record straight. Thank you for hooking up with Webligo, Storybooks.com, Yahoo!, etc. - All up in the chat rooms telling the sixty million school teens about this book. All I can say is - Go 'Head! Go 'Head!

And *I promise you* young people that if you e-mail us at Hallopeter@freesurf.ch and tell us the creative and innovative things you did to put this book on blogs, message boards and on links, etc., *we will profile* you and your creativity in the next book.

I will tell the world what you did. And we will nominate you for our cash awards, stipends, scholarships, etc. (See "From the Palace to the Prison", Chapter One for specifics on money awards for creative Internet strategies…).

We won't do you like NBC, ABC and CBS. We won't overlook your talents. No matter where you are today (or tonight). If you're in Louisiana, Massachusetts, Atlanta, New York, Redlands, Beverly Hills, Richmond, Virginia, South Africa, Switzerland, Japan or Hawaii, let us know what **you** did to promote, profile and spread the news about this book.

And if you know poets, songwriters, rappers, violinists, actors, wanna-be models, etc., tell them about this book and tell us about them. We will mention their potential, visions, goals and advertise them in the next book.

So when Bill Gates, Sergey, Wired Magazine, Peter Mandel, Jeff Bezos and all the folks in Hollywood get the book, they will *know where they are*.

And I know some connections, networks and careers will be established by these techniques. And I shall confess hands down that not all of these are my ideas. Many of these ideas were given to me by Derrick Flowers, Heather West, Theo, Lisa, Anna and Becky. (You will recall this brilliant young Caucasian female Becky from my book -

"From the Palace to the Prison". Becky played a major role in that book and has advised me for a year on how to effectively relate to our youth. Becky, you'll recall is only nineteen years old). I spoke with Becky for nearly thirty minutes a couple of weeks after *The Jackson 12* (jury) reached that sensational verdict on his child molestation case. "Are you gonna write a lot about Mike's case in your book?" Becky inquired.

"Very little, if anything," I replied.

Becky methodically persisted. "I think it would be absolutely ridiculous to not mention Michael. Don't be afraid to take a position on it, have an opinion and share it with us. Your book deals with rape, molestation and victimization. How dare you ignore the case?" Becky said.

"But I don't wanna turn my readers off, Beck. I have so many opinions of Michael. I don't wanna be divisive and controversial."

Becky launched into me with a full, frontal, verbal assault. "Then I won't read the damned book! If you don't take a position at all, I will not read it. All of the Web ideas I gave you, suggestions and input my team provided, come on, Mr. Manning. We helped you devise a plan that all of the grapevine *knows* is gonna work. We taught you about blogging, podcasting, Myspace.com and Friendster. We also explained to you how we (youth) despise weaklings and chicken politicians who will only tell you what you want to hear. And now you want to act like *Larry Elder*? Where is your courage?"

I was getting a bit perturbed... "Becky." I began softly, "What do you think about the Michael Jackson fiasco? What is it you think I so desperately need to say about it?"

Becky replied, "I think the jury got it right. He was falsely accused and tried as an act of vendetta. The vendetta was by a racist KKK member named Tom Sneddon. I know for an absolute fact that Tom Sneddon is in the KKK and as a young White lady, I am absolutely offended by the KKK as well as by *any* group of evil racists. When the first allegation was made in 93, the Child Social Services Unit in LA investigated and found nothing. No case! Los Angeles District Attorney Gil Garcetti investigated and found no credible evidence. Enter Tom Sneddon. Sneddon said that since Michael resided in Santa Maria, he wanted to see the evidence. Incredibly, Sneddon smelled a rat that the Child Services couldn't smell and a rat that Gil Garcetti couldn't smell. Sneddon was inhaling through nostrils, which are contaminated with the after effects of having smelled too many burning crosses while having his head hooded in a sheet.

"But Sneddon couldn't get the kid to testify. The kid had gotten what he wanted - a twenty million dollar settlement. And Michael did what any innocent $500 million *aire* would do; he paid to make the case go away. But once a man is labeled as a child predator, he can never get over it. And CBS, ABC and NBC will *never, ever* allow him to live down that name. And if a prosecutor goes after you to the tune of getting one hundred search warrants to search your house, you will look guilty in the *court of public media...* The man was completely, unambiguously innocent. Don't you (Sherman) agree?"

I replied, "Partially. I am not convinced that Michael is not a pedophile. I'm just not certain. I've said from the beginning, I want *any man, any woman* (no matter who you are or what your status) who has sex with children - *in prison.* I absolutely believe child predators must go to prison. And I am just put off by Michael in many respects. The man *appears* to want to be White. That ain't right. The man has never, ever lifted a finger to do a damn thing to help prisoners. He's never given Barry Scheck, Rubin "Hurricane" Carter, etc., any money. Never been there to aid a poor White boy or Black or Brown boy wrongly accused and/or wrongly convicted. I am *personally* offended by that. Just as I was offended by Kobe Bryant... Some of these superstars convince themselves that they are *above the law.* And Black one's convince themselves that they have surpassed the *color issue.* They begin to convince themselves that their Blackness does not matter. And the minute they face jail time, the first thing they holler is the race card, B.S. Even Clarence *Uncle Tom, Brainwashed* Thomas had the audacity and the unmitigated gall to claim, "This is a modern day lynching of a Black man." When Anita Hill accused him (Thomas) of sexual harassment. They wanna use their race as a crutch or a spare tire. I'm offended.

"So I don't know, Beck, but to my way of thinking, the guy could be a molester; I just *don't know.* But I do know he has absolutely no business sleeping in the bed or even *beside* the bed of young boys. Even if it's not sexual. It's just abnormal and unusual and wrong to do that. It's high-risk behavior and it's suspect. And a part of me really believes Michael actually thinks it's okay to sleep with or near kids. I think the guy thinks it's cool. Just like many moms' think it's cool to let their fourteen-year-old daughters have sex in their home. Just like some unusual parents think it's appropriate to allow thirteen and fourteen-year-old kids to have parties in the home and to drink alcohol. They let their kids drink alcohol in their homes... Unusual, wrong and actually *this* is a *crime.*

"So Michael definitely needs some psychological help. I'm very, very serious.

"Having said all of that, Becky, I believe in the law. And the law states a prosecutor must prove his case *beyond a reasonable doubt to a moral certainty*. In *this* case, Sneddon failed miserably. It was a hideous, colossal failure of titanic proportions. It did not meet the threshold. And for Tom (Silver Fox) Mesereau, it was a *thundering* victory, which echoed all around the world. More than two thousand members of the International Press reported the masterful job Tom did of dismantling the prosecutor's case. Tom Mesereau gave a *platinum* defense, which merits him a lawyer's *Oscar*. Tom beat it. Tom is *dangerous* in a courtroom...

"I believe Johnny Cochran is the greatest criminal lawyer to have walked the planet during my lifetime. Now that Johnny is gone, here comes Tom! Mesereau that is. The best of the best are Willie Gary, Gerry Spence, Thomas Mesereau, Murray J. Janus, Barry Scheck, David Boies, Barry Tarlow and a handful of others. I can't take anything away from Thomas Mesereau. In "From the Palace to the Prison", I told how I knew Tom *personally*. I won't rehash that, Becky; you know the story. But I will reiterate the fact that Arsen Serafin initially told me about Tom. Tom faithfully attends F.A.M.E. Church in LA and even directs a free law clinic for the poor. If more top notch lawyers gave back half as much as Tom does, we'd have less wrongly convicted guys in jails and prisons. 'Justice has served; the man's innocent, he always has been,' was all Tom said after he vindicated Michael's rights under the law...

"I must also salute Michael's *jury*. They shocked me and they shocked many. The pundits like Gloria Allred, Nancy Grace and that Vanity Fair Orth woman cannot accuse *this jury* of being Black and lenient. I bet my life on the fact that if there had been Blacks on the jury, the media would have accused them of freeing a Black man because he was a Black man. But not this time. This jury was thorough, fair and just. They proved that not all of us are *racist*. They proved most of us can rise above color, bias and prejudice and obey the law. Celebrity may have played a role. Money always plays a role. Johnnie Cochran even said, 'You're *innocent* til proven *indigent*.' And we must work to change that. But in this case, they tried a weird and eccentric Black man who was accused of raping mostly White kids. They tried him in a White conservative county. And a non-Black, mostly White jury rose above every single prejudice and bias and they gave a weird, strange brother undiluted justice. I wonder what the Klan thinks about that? I wonder what Blacks who claim all Whites are racist think about that? I think I'm proud to be an American! I think that jury did a service to their community and to our America. No matter what they say or do later, they did the right thing. As Mesereau told them, '*Not guilty is the only right verdict.*' I cheered. But I cheered for justice, for Mesereau and for that American jury, Becky; that's really all I have to say about Michael Jackson and the Jackson 12."

I was done with the Jackson 5 and the Jackson 12 - period. But not Becky. "Well, at least you made your opinion known. And you would have made a serious mistake had you held back. I seriously would have lost respect for you. And you should put that in your book, Mr. Manning. And you should also give props to his *fans*. Use common sense and gumption. Regardless of your obvious, partial disdain for certain portions of Michael's life, his fans are *awesome*. And you cannot be a M. J. Fan *without* being open-minded, *off the wall* and off the hook. These fans would adore seeing their names in print. So say kudos to: Sherry Hunsperger (Sacto), Daniel Asare (Sacto), Karen Mutasa (Sacto/Zimbabwe), Janet Manbrink (Sweden) Andre White (San Jose) Fariba Garmani (Mission Viejo Mortgage Consultant), Darnell Worthy (Bakersfield), Raffles Van Exel (Amsterdam), Omar Reece (Belleville, IL), Ronan Davie (Glasgow, Scotland), Jennine Elcock, Claudio Bono (Miami), B. J. Hickman (Tennessee), Cynthia D'Huart, Lacey Reinhardt (Murrieta), etc.

"Mr. Manning, put these people's names in the freaking tome and I assure you that people such as B. J., Omar, Sherry, Lacey and Ronan will inundate Web sites and chat rooms, discussing the salute you gave them in the book. And they will each want a friend and at least one family member to have a copy of the book. I think I just reeled off fifteen names to you. That's forty-five to fifty books right there. And you need only mention them and their dedication. And since you wrote so much in 'From the Palace to the Prison' and 'Creating Monsters' about people being judgmental, bias and prejudiced, I would consider you a hypocrite if you didn't mention these great people."

Can you imagine how I felt being checked and corrected by a young White lady? You can't! It turned me on!! Candidly, I enjoy fine women telling me like it is. And Becky is a brunette, hazel eyes, 118 pounds, nice breasts, great buns, pretty feet and luscious lips. And I just stared into those lips as she talked in an animated fashion giving directions.

She concluded, "You gotta remember that if you keep inserting reminders in your book about going on the Web, sending e-mails and text messages, etc., people, i.e. *Daniel Asare* will *create* a bestseller for

291

you. I.e., Daniel is a junior at John F. Kennedy High School in Sacramento. Mr. Manning, J.F.K. High has five hundred and sixty-two students who are members of *Myspace.com* and messages and comments on every member's site. Daniel can call Sara Newman at Davis High School and Sara can blog, message and text all four hundred and thirty-four Davis Senior High School members and tell them, 'Check out *The Blue-Eyed Blonde*. It's cool. Tell your parents to go to www.Cafepress.com/Blonde and get two copies. One for you and one for them.' And, Mr. Manning, I promise you this will spread like wildfire. Myspace.com, Xanga, Friendster and Yahoo! News *fuels creativity* amongst youngsters and allows worldwide connections. And your crossover appeal will be accomplished by tapping into a student like Daniel who is obviously not biased and believes a man can be wrongly accused. Ipso facto, Daniel believes a man can be wrongly convicted. Ipso facto, usually open-mindedness is a *family* trait. Ipso facto, it is safe to assume Daniel's parents and siblings are open-minded also.

"And from everything you've told me about *Blue-Eyed Blonde*, it is an awesomely cool book that every American student over sixteen needs to read. And it's also one parents ought to be glad to read. And some students will sneak online and buy a copy! And the parents will become livid. And people like Wired Safety and LA Bob Lozito will warn them against *you*. You are in prison as far as they are concerned. And Lozito and Wired Safety *mean well*. They are actually a great organization. But they don't know your books, your mind and your intellect. And teens are rebellious. And the more the media ignores you and law enforcement *hates on you*, the *cooler* you'll become to *system of a down* and Michael Jackson fans. And so I promise you this book will revolutionize the youth. It will help in so many ways. Ways you can't even imagine. It will give victims of molestation permission and coverage to tell it and get perverts off the streets. It will provide liars who have falsely made allegations with a horrific picture of prison and inspire them to recant and get the wrongly convicted *out of prison*. It will remind teenaged girls and boys that if they were actually raped, *they* are not evil. They don't need to be *ashamed*. It's not their fault. They can get help. If they call Dr. Frank Lawlis, Dr. Phil McGraw, Montel Williams and then hot lines, they can get help.

"Mr. Manning, you were bold and courageous to dare scribe a tome that even mentions the fact that thousands of White youngsters are being traumatized and victimized mostly by Blacks and Browns in America's jails, juvies and prisons. A. This will inspire young men to make damned certain they don't drink and drive, don't use drugs, don't follow the clique and commit some stupid crime so they won't end up in prison. Ipso Facto, *Blue-Eyed Blonde* will be a *deterrent* to youth criminal activity. B. The universe will *bless you indeed* for doing this. C. Everybody is entitled to their own opinion, but they're not entitled to their own *set of facts*. And no media pundit or hater will be able to dispute what is inside your book. It's the bomb.

"As an exit statement, Mr. Manning, I want to reiterate to you that if you *tap* into the Michael Jackson fans, use them as a segue or junction into their parents, friends and siblings, etc., you will have a *run away book*. This I promise you. And don't forget to tell the youngsters in the book to select twenty-five or thirty names randomly that they see in the book; and to inundate the Internet with messages, texts, comments, etc., in order to notify the people you name that, 'Hey, you are in the book!' And Mr. Manning, if you mention Craigslists, Tribe.net, Yahoo!, Google, AskJeeves, and Myspace.com half as much as I've told you to, this is free advertising for these businesses. Tell them to quid pro quo your link, your book to their home pages. Guys like Marcus Pincus, Craig Newmark and even *Visual Therapy* will at least give you a link. And you want each of the Myspace.com members to mention your books on their blogs. That's eighteen million sales for ya. And remember these students are geniuses. I.e., Josh Walker in Temecula, Rene in Santa Barbara, Daniel at J. F. K. Any *one* of them could see the name *Jarod Miller* in your book and if you state he's a zoologist (he is), they'll search the Internet and find him in fifteen minutes and Jarod will receive two or three hundred e-mails telling him, 'I don't know you but I'm in Folsom (or Temecula, Sac-Town or Davis, etc.) and I'm reading a book called *Blue-Eyed Blonde* and you are in it. Just wanted to let you know. TTYL.

"And you remember you and I were laughing about the guys on David Letterman that night called the *Piedmont Bird Callers*?"

Finally I got to utter a word. "Yes," I said...

Becky continued, "I guarantee you that Michael Jackson fan, Daniel, will Google, AskJeeves and even contact the David Letterman Show until he finds the Bird Callers and get their names and e-mail them to say, 'I was ROTFL when I read your name in the Blue-Eyed Blonde. Go the Amazon.com, your bookstore, etc. and be sure to get it. Write to Sherman D. Manning at S.D.M., J98796, A-2-240, P.O. Box 409020, Ione, CA 95640 and tell him you've ordered it. GTG.'

"Mr. Manning, all those students you bragged on in 'From the Palace to the Prison', the student contests you launched in that book which are still *open*, the youth money giveaways, stipends and scholarships you offer, etc., Daniel, Kelly and Sara, etc., will find them and put the word out. How else are you gonna let Justin Cardinale, Jeffrey Bramell, Joshua Griffin, Kyle Fletcher, Jess Di Girolama, Elmer Kulp and Riley Evans know they are in the book if you don't employ the brilliance of the *teens online* to connect with them?

"Listen, Mr. Manning, my parents may not like you, they may actually believe your B.S. Rap Sheet...but I know my dad would *much* rather me spending two hours per day *online* connecting and bringing together students and stars mentioned in your book than me out smoking weed. My daddy would rather me locate Zach Roerig and Scott Kinworthy in LA about your book than me chatting it up with some dude online seeking kiddy porn or nude photos of *me*. If you are absolutely serious about putting this message out, tapping into a powerhouse called YOL (Youth Online) and you wanna get into the hearts, minds and soul of the worldwide youth; you will do it if you do as I say. Adrian Holovaty (www.Chicagocrime.org) will tinker with search engines, etc., til he finds Clay Hollifield in Richmond, Virginia, Sean Farmer in Texas (?), Sheila Flood, Sonya Tucker, Chris Eilerman (Kentucky) and David Passrell in Santa Rosa. They'll find Kyle Love in Auburn, etc. And within a month or two, you'll be inundated with e-mails, tired of the snail mails and photos, etc. And they'll be on your *American Dream* site buying your caps, t-shirts and coffee mugs. People as far away as Zimbabwe will be reading the *Blue-Eyed Blonde*. Mr. Manning, you can do this."

Wow! I must say that the above data is pretty much a verbatim transcript of Beck's words. So mission accomplished. She said it all for me. And I will repeat the fact that I humbly accept her advice. And I do accept the innovative efforts of any/all Michael Jackson fans, YOL, youth groups, frats, sororities, surfers, skaters, etc. to use your brilliance to put this tome out there. I also repeat that cash prizes are waiting to be claimed (as well as stipends, plaques, certificates and iPods) by any special people, i.e, the Daniel of J. F. K. whom Becky mentioned. I.e., if Daniel will do a cool blog, message or e-mail to every Myspace.com member in Sacramento, get *this* book himself and get "From the Palace to the Prison"... The minute Daniel finishes reading both books, we'll send him five hundred dollars for his creative action.

If Josh Walker will send a thousand e-mails or text one hundred of the persons he sees named *in this book*, etc., the minute Josh finishes reading this book and "From the Palace to the Prison" (Publisher's Note: Any participants who want to claim awards, prizes, money, etc., must provide verification of their tinkering, texting, blogging, etc.)

we'll send Josh or whoever five hundred dollars. That *ain't* true-to-life fiction, etc., that's serious. We need young college students, high school seniors, etc., to sit down and find via Google, Craigslists, etc., Nicholas Eilerman, Tom Massimo, Ryan Janousek, Chris Purvis, Joshua Goldin, Kevin Olivero and all the others in this book and inform them that...you know what to tell them. Let us hear from you at *Hallopeter@freesurf.ch* via e-mail.

And I don't need to repeat all the stuff Becky said, but I do salute each and every Michael Jackson fan. I don't call you freaks and clowns. I call you dedicated and loyal. Your loyalty to justice is not unnoticed. Every time you look at *this tome*, you can know that I honor and salute you. And I can't wait to see what folks like Cynthia D'Huart and Lacey Reinhardt think of this book. Lacey is an aspiring journalist. Perhaps she can pick up where *Jeremy* and *Paul* left off. Cynthia is a student at Mount Jacinto College. They are both extremely attractive, young ladies. They both say they learned a lot about the judicial system by attending the Jackson trial. D'Huart had to write an argumentative essay for class about the trial. She got an *A*.

Lacey and Cynthia are my kind of people. They understand media bias and they are not the kind to wait for Nancy Grace or Diane Diamond to tell them to read a book. They use their own minds, judgment and thinking tools. One of the girl's moms (Tracey D'Huart) said, "I think it's great she's going beyond what she hears on TV and gossip. She's trying to get her own opinion about it. She's reaching *out beyond her little world* here in Murrieta. She's *growing up*." I love that! And no greater words could be spoken to promote *Liberty and Justice For All*.

May I tell every youngster all up in the suburbs, in ghettos, in juveniles, jails, prisons, on drugs, off drugs, in high school, college or whoever you are, to listen to Tracey. We all gotta *reach beyond our little worlds* (in Antioch, Birmingham, Tennessee, Temecula, Buckhead, Shrewsbury, Pennsylvania...) and grow up. I command you to make up your own minds. Base your opinions on **facts** - not fiction, rumor and gossip. Don't believe it just because the media or the police said it. And don't think that because the media did not tell you about *Blue-Eyed Blonde* that he/she does not exist. The epidemic described in this book is real. It is alive! And I don't think Lacey, Cynthia, Daniel or Scott will sit back and let it continue. I believe the moment they read this, something will *click*. I believe Lacey and Cynthia and many of you will immediately go to Yahoo! LiveJournal.com, Tribe.net, etc., etc., and begin posting, podcasting and texting and telling Jackson/Justice fans in America, Switzerland,

Scotland, Brazil, England, London and China about this book and this issue.

And when seventeen and eighteen year olds in China, twenty and twenty-five year olds in Amsterdam start reading this book our American leaders will start getting e-mails worldwide and these senators and congressmen will have to do the same damn thing Tom Sneddon did when Tom Mesereau, Susan Yu and Scott Ross delivered justice and kicked his butt... As did *Tom Sneddon*, our leaders will have to hold their heads down in shame and defeat. And I'll remind every Daniel Asare, etc., who is reading this right now that your name is forever in this book. And you deserve to be proud of it! And now I want us to come together, *get out of our boxes*, our little worlds and reach out and connect with others. We're all on the same planet and at the end of the day; little Mattie (Heartsongs) still brings tears to all of our *eyes*. Y'all - can we come together? Can we *please* not allow another young White man to be raped in LA County Jail, the prisons, juveniles and the Catholic Church? Yes, Black and Brown men (and women) are also raped and molested.

But in these prisons, the victims are more often than not - *White*. And in the Catholic churches all over America and *all over the world*; most of the victims of child exploitation, molestation, etc., are *White*.

We need to stop it! We need to shout on every rooftop til it stops. I want bloggers to tell the world what's happening to our Caucasian kids in prisons. I want the *youth* to raise hell about what's happening to our kids in church.

All these protesters rioting and raising hell about a molester getting out of prison and moving to your neighborhood, etc., you're farting in the wind and wasting your damn time. Get a life and get the facts. The civilian molesters are *in the family*, in your *church* and coaching little league. Some of them are police officers, judges and prosecutors by day - pedophiles by night. "Spiritual wickedness in high places." Most *molestation* occurs at the hands of a family member, priest, or someone who has official capacity over your children. Go get your child's *innocence* back! We need to look our children and our teens in the eyes and listen to them. We need to let them know that we *love them*. This will loose their trust and loose their *secrets*. The reason they won't tell us who raped, who molested and who betrayed them is because they can't *trust us* to love them anyway. They have heard us berate and belittle gays, lesbians and others, etc. So when the young man is raped, he feels shame. The shame is *worse* than the sex. And even our girls feel shamed. And they are conditioned to believe we won't love them if we find out what

296

happened to them. It becomes the *big secret* and secrets fester into illness, anger, crime, rage, drug abuse, etc. Hell, it would help if we open up and tell them the *truth about us*. We need to become transparent and admit to them that we have been hurt and shamed. Tell em what happened to *us*. If we admit our pain and our secrets, it will release their trust. *We* were raped!

Some of us were raped by a judicial system (like Joseph) that falsely convicted us of rape. And our alleged victim was far less credible than Gavin Aviso and his lying mom. But we are in prison. Or we were falsely convicted of murder, drug dealing or hate crimes and we are hurt. We must release that hurt by telling it. Don't allow it to fester. It can kill you. It can influence you to kill others. I want adults to do our job and to become agents of change. And true change will come when we conquer the fear to open ourselves up to, with and for our youth and tell them the truth. Now, if you are still waiting on the book to end, we did that a while ago. But the Bible says *they that are led by the spirit* are the sons of God. And I tried to stop writing weeks ago. I was finished, done and through with this. But the spirit led me to pick the pen back up and write. "You are the *Damon Dash* of *writers*. Do your thing man and don't let nobody stop you," stated Quincy Jones. And so *Damon Dash* would do it his way. And being led by the power of the spirit, I gotta do this my way. I can't wait, hesitate or assume what anybody else is going to do. History is replete with situations in which people did not do what they should have and could have done. And there are a few of you who will just peruse this tome in scanning fashion. Some of you are not excited about books like Damon Dash is. But you can't start out selling CDs from the trunk of your car and end up the CEO of the Damon Dash music group unless you are willing to love information and to try, try and try again. And one can never rise to one's full potential unless one is willing to never take *no* for an answer. And you learn how to have a strong personal constitution, to fight, to excel and to *create* by reading and studying. And Jeff Bezos, Donald Trump, Montel Williams, Tom Mesereau, Mel Bacon, Mel Gibson as well as Ted Turner are *readers*. They visualize, think, pray and believe.

And this book can help somebody on their way to the crack house. This book can help some young man being bullied at PS 76, Davis Senior High or in some college in San Diego to turn around. This book can go where my body may never go. Thousands of kids who wanna be like Ashton Kutcher, Eminem or Damon Dash will pick this book up and get the point. In those lonely, violent, vicious and bellicose juveniles out in California, some little Reggie, a James, a

John, a Paul or a Josh will sit in that concrete cell and read, re-read and read (again) this book and begin again. Some gangsta in Harlem, in Riker's Island, in Reidsville State Prison or Pelican Bay will take this book to the *SHU yard* and find something in this that will cause them to take another look at the *man in the mirror*. That's why I write. To be true it ain't for me. It's not necessarily for you but there is a *you* who needs this tome. He's a geek, a freak, a monster, a gothic, a predator, a victim of sexual abuse, a lonely child who is bored to death. It may be a kid whose been chatting online with some predator who is grooming them for sex. They can read this book and say, "Aha!" or "Wait a minute!" They can decide to adopt a strategy, employ a technique and utilize their time to do something positive... If I am the *Damon Dash* of writers, I say to the folks who need (read) this book to *wake up and live*. Write your own poetry, make your own youth group and be your own president. You are the *CEO* of your own *mind*. You are the *president* of **you**.

I don't want to hear what you can say but I wanna *see* what you can *do*. I want to see *you* design jewelry, write a blog, start a podcast, read the dictionary, study the encyclopedia, read the Bible, become fascinated about the difference you can make with the Internet. Jam up the computers at the White House with e-mails telling Mr. Bush (or whoever is the president in your country at this time), "You gotta read, *The Blue-Eyed Blonde*." In your jail cell, prison, juvenile, classroom, frat house or bedroom, write e-mails or snail mails to Montel Williams, Jeff Bezos, George Soros, *Coronado Stone Products* in Fontana, CA and ask the movers and shakers to donate this book to libraries, group homes and book clubs. Get your butt online and go to Storybooks.com, Amazon.com, Tribe.net and write a book review on *this book*. There are a lot of things you can do if you'll just think. We are the *people* and the people must take our *power* back.

Get out of the box. Do what Cynthia and Lacey did. Get out of the confines of your little world in Murrieta, Dalton, Georgia, Wilton, Sand Springs, Davis, Encino or Orange County and see some things you've never seen. Think some thoughts you've never thought. Try something new. Put your opinion out there so we can evaluate it. If you are seventeen years old or twenty-seven years old, etc., let us know that you *matter*. You have a mind, an opinion and a thought process.

We'll never know it if you don't show it. And that is the reason I'm trying to empower people. I want to publish your essays, your comments, your ideas in our books and put them out there for all the world to see. You may wanna sell them out of the trunk of your car. Sell them at the basketball games or football games. Hell, give them away; I don't care but get your butt back in the *game*. Let the world see your name. I'll fight (write) with you. Where are you? I'm looking for *your* letter, your poem, your idea and your strategy. I'm looking to have my agents or some of the college students whom I'm in contact with to tell me, "I saw something on Yahoo! News from a student at John F. Kennedy High School" or "I read a letter to the Editor in the N.Y. Times by a student at U. C. Davis (or Carnegie Mellon, Boston University, Santa Monica Community College, an alternative high school etc.) who was moved to take action by *Jeremy Shackelford*." I'm not writing to *quitters*. You can't **win** it if you're not *in* it. Everything that has given me strength and character has been painful, hurtful and challenging.

It's even painful sitting here on the edge of my bed in a prison cell *writing to the world*. But I promised my momma I wouldn't come here and die. I promised myself I wouldn't come here and give up. I promised my maker that I would be extraordinary, unusual and unique. I would challenge every ounce of faith, courage, motivation, belief and vision that I have inside of me. I'm pulling out all the stops. I'm finding some stuff in me that I didn't even know I had in me. I can make it. And so can you. I want to leave the world just a little bit better than I found it. And so should you. We must come together and work to make the world better. There is something strange and unusual about some of the things, which we allow to transpire in this great country. And if we want to leave it better than we found it we must be willing to challenge the status quo - we need to read and look beneath the headlines and find more facts that the A.P. and perhaps NBC forgot to inform us about...

I recall Becky and Matthew Feeley (N.V.) along with Shawn O'Connor (son of U.C.L.A. music teacher Brian O'Connor) all telling me in a conference call - "Sherman, we need to exploit the Internet as a news source. And I don't say 'exploit' with a negative connotation. I mean we must utilize it to bring real issues to the people which the mainstream press ignores," stated Matt Feeley. And Becky chimed in and Shawn concurred.

Becky said, "Mr. Manning, this is indeed a fabulous country. I am patriotic. I'm proud to be an American. But we must struggle to get better on the social front. *Greed* is controlling the nation. Ask Paris Hilton, Donald Trump or even Michael Jordan did they know we have more *animal shelters* than we do women or youth shelters to care for victims of sexual or drug abuse in America? Mr. Manning, we do more for our animals than we do for women; just ask Paris."

Becky was a brilliant, unique and candid young gal. When you look at her it's difficult to be offended by anything, which comes out of her pretty mouth. Becky's ass would make Paris a brand new face. But this was a teleconference; I couldn't *see* Beck and I was a bit perturbed... "Why are you always bringing up Paris Hilton to me? I'm not a big Paris fan. All you White women look alike to me."

Matt and Shawn were laughing but Becky didn't miss a beat, "Oh, is that why you married a White gal, pal?"

I retorted, "Come on young lady, all I'm saying is you'll never hear me saying *I wanna be a Hilton*. I'm proud to be a human first, Christian, Manning and a Black man. I take pride in who the *creator* made me. I'm too busy living my life, dreaming, hoping, yearning, visualizing, writing, praying, thinking and caring to spend a whole lot of time worried about Miss Hilton. She'll grow up. But I understand clearly what you guys are speaking of. I remember telling James a few weeks ago, 'I can't believe the national media ain't covering that thirteen-year-old boy in Florida who was beat down, on camera, by a cop. The boy had stolen a Public Work's truck. Five or six cops had him face down, cuffed and this big ole corn fed dude ran up, looked around and began beating him in the back. His cell phone rang and he jumped off the boy and stopped. I think somebody called him to say he was on camera.'

"Becky, I'm always surprised at the stuff they don't cover. But the *Runaway Bride* just sold her story for a half million bucks in advance. *We* love salaciousness. We love bullshit. What is the story? She got cold feet and stood a man up. She stood up six hundred good people. She lied and claimed she was kidnapped. And it's so important that Katie Couric had to interview her. Neither Katie, nor Matt, nor ABC or CBS will think multi-dimensionally and tackle the story from a unique angle. It's the same old biz. We should feel sorry for Jennifer. But why not tackle the story from the angle of false accusations! I.e., let's examine how close Jennifer came to causing the Albuquerque Police Department to launch an investigation looking for her kidnappers. And if that *good cop* hadn't used his hunch to tell this sister that he didn't believe her story, she would have proceeded. And some bad cops who maybe meant well would have went out and found some suspects to fit the profile of her description. And those suspects would have been arrested, prosecuted and convicted.

"And the chances of those defendants being able to afford a Gerry Spence, Blair Berk or a Thomas Mesereau, Jr. to methodically dismantle her story would have been slim to none. They would have ended up with a Scott Hess, Donald Dorman or some other sellout lawyers and they'd be sitting in prison trying to find some of y'all to believe in them. But nobody in the media sees this as a story. I get sick, Becky, by what I see as stories in the media. The bias, prejudices and the weakness of most of those who are calling themselves reporters. But I wanna know what can we do about it, Becky?"

Becky gave me a twenty-minute lecture on the solutions…

… "I took a trip to a prison cell in Greene County today… I had wanted to meet this man for so long," Bev Smith said on Friday June 17th. "I went to visit Mumia Abu Jamal. Amnesty International says Mumia is innocent. He got an unfair trial. When I walked into the room he was shackled. There was a glass between us and he stood there smiling. I wondered *how* could a wrongly convicted man be smiling. I didn't want him to smile. I wanted him to be *angry* by the injustice of which he is a recipient. I asked him, have you heard from Al Sharpton, Jesse Jackson. Where are the civil rights leaders? Mumia deserves a new trial and the *church is silent*. According to Amnesty International and The Innocence Project, tens of thousands of innocent, wrongly convicted men and women are rotting in our prisons. And we run to church every Sunday morning. We sing in the choir. We serve on the deacon board and we preach in the pulpit but we never speak out on issues of innocence, justice, prisons and jails. *God* is not pleased. America. I am not pleased. I am glad that Michael Jackson got justice this week. I believe Michael Jackson was totally innocent. But Michael got justice due to a powerful fan base and a great lawyer. What about Mumia? What about the thousands who pled their cases out because their lawyers sold them out," Bev said.

I will repeat that I am not certain that Michael was innocent. I just don't know. I do *know* he had no business sleeping with boys. I do know it was *foolish* (at best) to sleep on the floor while boys were in his bed after all the crap he's been accused of. But I love Bev and I love Andrea Augusta, Lacey, Cynthia and their pal Cody. (Cody works at the Mulligan Family Fun Center with Lacey and Cynthia. And Cody was extremely cordial, respectful and considerate to me when I called.) And I do believe Mumia Abu Jamal is innocent…

"Have you ever heard Mumia speak?" Bev asked her audience. "We, who are captive in America's new slave ships which are ships on dry ground, which they call prisons; we were not surprised to see the photos of the abuse at Abu Ghraib. The main *star* of the story of abuse was *Mr. Graner*."

"Mr. Graner was a prison guard at this prison where I am housed," Mumia stated.

"Where did Graner learn this hate, violence and abuse?"

"He honed his skills here as an American prison guard practicing on American inmates. Yet, no one in the mainstream media made that connection. We must organize, organize, organize," Mumia spoke.

I have no idea when, where or how sister Bev got this recording. But I was moved. Bev got to see the man. I got to *hear him speak.* He sounded like Malcolm. I see why they wanna keep him in prison. He is a revolutionary. I have a question. I'll preface this question with a comment. I love the *Potter's House.* I love the preaching, teaching and ministry God delivers through T. D. Jakes. But I shall admit that I wonder what would happen if T. D. Jakes got the sixty-five thousand plus people who will attend the Megafest in my hometown at the Georgia Dome to march on the Pennsylvania Supreme Court shouting, "Give Mumia a new trial!" Damn. And it's unfair for me to single out my favorite preacher. To be fair, Rick Warren, Eddie Long, Noel Jones, Creflo Dollar, Fred Price, etc., all have a lot of members. What if each member sent an e-mail to the Pennsylvania Governor saying, "Free Mumia or give him a new trial?"

Don't hold your breath. But I know what I know. And I know something is wrong, when we pay more attention to the Runaway Bride than we do to Mr. Schwartzmiller in San Jose, who has apparently molested thousands of young, White males. He reportedly has molested mostly blue-eyed blondes on every coast and as far away as Asia. But he has been free for years. Free to buy ice cream, cookies, cake and candy for your kids while he grooms them for molestation. While he steals their innocence, he buys them gifts. He smiles at them. He tickles them. He wrestles with them. And finally, he *destroys them.* And while we were sleeping on the *game of life* - while we were out picketing because we didn't want a convicted child molester to be released to our neighborhood - while we were trying to figure out when Paris was gonna marry Paris - while we were arguing over Tom Cruise and Katie Holmes - while we were concerned about Brad Pitt and Jennifer Anniston... the kings of molesters infiltrated our synagogues, churches, temples, schools and communities.

The media did not tell us that most molesters are *family members.* The media never featured the fact that only one percent of *molesters were ever convicted* of molestation. The media did not tell us that in fourteen states including California and New York, you get less punishment for molestation if you are a *family member* than you do if you're a stranger. The implication is that as a society we understand a father raping his twelve-year-old daughter or fourteen-year-old niece because it's *sex* and she would eventually have sex anyway. But if you are a man and you get caught molesting a *boy,* we'll take it more seriously because we consider the sex act unnatural and because you are not a family member. We absolutely refuse to take molestation seriously in America.

America has become the king of molestation. Yet, we are also the king of incarceration. But our prisons are filled with dope smokers, burglars and folks convicted on testimony (i.e. Ricardo Calvario) by folks who are even less credible than the Janet Aviso/Jackson who testified in Michael's case.

Where are the preventative measures? When are we gonna take child molestation seriously enough in America that we begin to treat people with these strange proclivities? Can you (the reader) point to *one single program* that you know of off hand in which a man can call right now and say, "My name is Matthew and I feel an attraction to children. I noticed it a month ago. I want help before I act on it. Can somebody help me *now*?"

I challenge you to call your police department today and ask them what could/would they do for a man who called with that i.e. *today*?

Be careful... knowing a lot of cops, what they will do is make an arrest on "suspicion of child molestation". And if you're in Kern County, DA (Ed Jagels) etc., they will assemble a case against you. They will coerce kids into lying and saying you already molested them. *When* will we take child molestation seriously? When will we ask the tough questions and effectively deal with this *epidemic*? If we hesitate, procrastinate or wait on the congress or senate to effectively rectify the problems, we're in trouble. Perhaps we need to begin with the person in our house. Perhaps we need to begin by taking a peek at the *person in the mirror*. I would suggest each of us ask *self* the question, "Have I done anything to create a *safe bed* in my city or my neighborhood? Maybe that teacher, coach or pastor needs to pay closer attention to that student, athlete or youth member and begin to let that child know, "I'm here for you. You can talk to me. I'll help you." And perhaps we need to begin to call on our counselors, social workers, psychologists and sex therapists and insist upon developing programs, which identify, treat, prevent and rectify a man or woman who has a proclivity toward molesting children.

Perhaps we need to come out of our shells and discontinue the name calling and/or simply throwing words at the issues. Calling a man evil won't change him. Yelling, screaming and picketing won't *smoke a molester* out of the *closet*. But if we open up and admit our failures as a society to deal adequately with the issue - change begins. We must never, ever attempt to justify the fondling, molesting or raping of a child. We must, however, admit that our norms of today were abnormal yesterday. Let's remember in some parts of the world children are marrying at twelve years old. Can we be real? Ipso facto, if a person reared in that type culture comes to America and has consensual sex with a thirteen year old, he or she has committed a crime. Should we forgive him/her? Should we allow it? I think not. But we should not pretend that we don't understand it.

Let us also not forget that right here in America, a few decades ago there was nothing unusual about a twenty-year-old man marrying a twelve, thirteen or fourteen-year-old girl. We allowed it. We also disallowed interracial marriage. So we don't suggest that America should legalize (again) kids marrying just as we don't suggest that America re-illegalize interracial marriage. What we do suggest is that we have some degree of understanding when a few persons still frown upon interracial marriage. We should not allow the person or persons to harass, bother or harm those who do marry interracially. But by the same token if we create an atmosphere of scandalization, the person will hide their bias. And as long as they are afraid to tell us *why* they oppose interracial marriage, we won't be able to talk about it. And where there is no discussing, no dialogue, etc., there can be no counseling, no therapy and no healing. And they will more often than not hide their bias. And secrets fester into sickness. Also, if we create an atmosphere of scandalization around the issues of child molesting and molesters there will be no dialogue, no discussion and no healing. And even though the Schwartzmillers of society may be a lost societal case...we created Schwartzmiller. We failed to prevent him from becoming a molester. We missed all the cues. We missed all the clues. And not only did he apparently get away with molesting for years, but we allowed child after child to be perhaps ruined and devastated.

But *if* Schwartzmiller had called *you* (or *me*) ten years ago and said, "I have a problem. I'm attracted to children. I have this dysfunction. I can't get excited by the norms." What would you have done or said? Some of us would have kicked his butt. Some of us would have shot him. Some of us would have called the police. But would any of that stop the problem or deal with the roots? Will we ever realize that many of the *molested* go on to molest. Their molestation as victims is the umbilical cord which ties them to their past and hinders them from a normal future.

It's sad to say that many of the same little boys and girls who we look at today with so much sympathy, care, love and guilt because we know they were molested last year, last month or last night, etc., those same little victims whom we love and feel sorry for today, those will be the ones society hates, despises and want to put away forever tomorrow. They will become molesters.

I apologize for my graphic descriptions and depictions. But I'm not writing for babies. This book is not milk and cookies or a snack before naptime. This is real. And our lopsided media has lulled us to sleep for too long. They don't have time to really deal with cause and effect. And to ABC, NBC and CBS prevention is out of the question! When you see a victim of molestation today; you are more than likely looking at the *molester* tomorrow. It would behoove us to begin now to intervene as psychiatrists, psychologists, writers and pastors. We need (as parents) to begin getting immediate help for *children while they are children* (victims)...

I want Daniel Asare, bloggers and tinkerers to inundate pastors, politicians and the press with this issue today. If as a result of this tome, I get no award, fine. If I get no mainline press - great. (Most mainstream media won't mention a prison scribe anyway without attaching scandal, innuendo or evil. It's (to them) the only *right approach*. But if **one** little twelve-year-old boy doesn't get molested by a coach or uncle. If *one* little girl does not lose her virginity or chastity to some perverted adult as a result of a blog, message, e-mail and this book; then the book is a remarkable success. Just one human life being saved is worth me writing this entire book. Just one life.

May I pose one question to one parent? If you knew that your eleven-year-old son would not be molested because of something he *read in this book* would it be worth him reading?

May I pose a question to the youngsters? If you knew some molester would not molest because he or she read this book would it be worth you telling others about it? I admit to you young folk hands down that we adults *failed you*. We have failed you miserably. We have allowed you to be vulnerable, hurt and tampered with. I am sorry. I apologize. Please charge it to our head and not to our heart.

But Michael Grillone, Chris Egar (LA), Jodie Evans, Roberta Franklin, Oprah, Gayle King and I don't mind admitting that we have failed. But if Thomas Foster, Rick and Drew Baker, Dimitri Hamlin, Andrea Casiragm, Sherry, Farmani and I know about your pain, we'll try to help you. If we will get together, e-mail by e-mail, telephone call by telephone call, text by text, blog by blog, podcast by podcast and book by book and deliver this information to the people, we can make it better.

We must not surrender. We must never underestimate the power of standing up. Those students out at Center High School got their

305

coach (J. Beily) back. Students and parents put marching feet in the street. They inundated the superintendent of schools with e-mails and telephone calls, etc., they attended the meetings and expressed their outrage and they got their coach back on the football field.

When students and parents, pastors and teachers, judges and lawyers, citizens of the world start locally and go globally, we can stop child exploitation. We can prevent prison rape. Once we acknowledge the umbilical cord which ties the raping of the eighteen or nineteen-year-old guy in the prison, up with the victimization of the child on the streets and then ties that back to the perpetrator who committed molestation in the church and...so forth and so on.

There is a root to the rage. There is a root to rape. And when we control and stop the rapes in prison, we will prevent rape and molestation in civilian life. When we stop molestation in our homes, schools, churches and around the neighborhoods, we will prevent men from growing up to commit rape in the prison. And when the one who had a *safe bed at home* is thrown into the dungeon, the juvenile or the prison and then gets unlucky and is raped in prison. Then all of a sudden the youngster who was merely sentenced to a few years in prison for burglary or theft comes out of prison as a rape victim. And now he's full of hurt, shame, rage and anger. He is a predator.

And very often, he's not looking for an unknown victim. He goes to his kinfolk's house. And he begins to groom a child for molestation. And/or he rapes his own kith and kin.

I want you to go to www.Ironworksmusic.com and tell *Life House* to sing about it. Tell Cillian Murphy and Attorney Tom Goldstein (D.C.) that I gave them a shout out and we need them to get on board and help us.

Tell Private Greg Smith (Dublin, GA), Montel and Ed Schultz that I said we need them. The very day (or hour or second) *you decide* that we will no longer accept molestation in the home, rape in the prison or rape in the college dorm...that's the day of empowerment. That's the day we begin to win...

If I only think in terms of outrage and anger, etc. I will only frustrate me and I'll never create change. Tony Robbins and even Dr. Phil routinely talk about how we must change our perspective or changing the manner in which we view a problem in order to solve it. And *if* I am allowed the liberty of playing make believe for a moment then I'll be able to demonstrate and ipso facto - elucidate my point... If somebody asked me to spend one hundred dollars on a known child molester to buy him a television, I would refuse. I'd like to be able to write that I'd think about it, etc., but candidly my reply would be *no*.

And if the *universe* communicated to me with certainty that my daughter was gonna meet with a child molester in one year. In one year (for sure) my little girl would come in contact with a molester for thirty minutes, alone. And there was/is absolutely **nothing** I could do to prevent the rendezvous and then Dr. Phil or Tony Robbins or Dr. Frank Lawlis called me and stated, "Sherman, we'll need one million dollars to diagnose, treat and counsel this child molester for one year. There are no guarantees! No full proof system. But for one million dollars, we will do everything we know to try to get this craving for kids out of the molester." I would pay the one million dollars in order to try to (at a minimum) lessen the chances of this molester, molesting my child when they meet. Do y'all feel me? And simultaneously, I would teach and train my child. I'd teach the child to know the signals of a molester. Know how to yell, scream, shout, run, kick, bite, etc. I'd equip the child with a cell phone and teach the child to call 911 the moment they feel uncomfortable, etc., etc.

If we are gonna begin to do some things proactive to stop child abuse, etc., we need an immediate paradigm shift. We need to focus like a laser beam on the innocence of *our* children.

And we must be willing to pay whatever it takes to prevent child molesters from molesting, etc.. so forth and so on. *We the people,* must do as the kids and parents did out at Center High School. Take *our power* back! Now! May I remind us all that just a few years ago we felt sorry for Willie Nesler. He was a fourteen-year-old victim of a child predator. His mother, Ellie Nesler went to the courthouse and killed Willie's molester. Most of us said of the murder, "Good for her. That's what that Chester (aka molester) deserved. I'm glad she shot him." And (again) we all felt sorry for lil Willie. He was the victim. Let us fast forward to June 2005 and now Willie the former victim has been transmogrified into a predator. He was convicted and sentenced to life for beating a man to death with his bare hands.

Now we are angry with Willie. The guy he killed was not a molester! This was no pervert. Just a domestic dispute. And where were we when Willie was victimized and traumatized? Where were we when he began abusing drugs due to no self-esteem? Have we any idea what it feels like to be a fourteen or fifteen-year-old boy and have the *world knowing* you were sodomized by a man? What damage does that do to the psyche of a boy? Is it not to be expected that he may abuse drugs to anesthetize his shame? Might it be possible that he might lift a lot of weights, take drugs and steroids and try to make a name for himself as a kick-butt guy because of his shame, hurt and anger at what happened to him?

We lost Willie. He is a killer and a predator but we made him. We need to counsel, treat, help, heal and support victims of rape, molestation and abuse.

While Paris Hilton is pampering her puppy and Chris Webber is buying another car, our kids were in *trouble*. We can change this right now. I don't have time for a *sermon* and Brother Falwell and Pat Robertson can save their prayers. I believe in prayer but not one which claims God is a republican or God hates people.

What I'm looking for and the people I'm writing to are those sixteen and seventeen-year-old boys on the basketball or football team out at Cordova High School. I'm writing to those girls who are cheerleaders or in the pep squad out at Davis Senior High, Archer High School, Ralph Bunche Middle School, PS 96, etc. I'm writing to college freshmen on the debate team and in the frats. I'm writing to valedictorians and class presidents at Stanford, Yale, Moorehouse, Carnegie Mellon, Harvard and Howard University. I'm telling *you* to go on to Yahoo! News and on to your blogs, etc., etc., and organize, organize, organize. Do it now!

...This fellow is not the lone White brother in a trench coat, stalking kids on the playground. He's not the *known* child molester being released into our community tomorrow. I wish it were that easy. Seeing the folks pictured on the registered sex offender Website can assist us. But by and large, those are not the main threats. The guy we need to fear is not usually showing us as we think he'd appear.

He's not a thug! He's not a gangster. He sometimes is not even stalking online. We hear tales of on-line molesters using the Internet as a ploy to steal the innocence of our children. And we must be watchful, vigilant and cautious. But the main threat against *safe beds* is not the idiot in the trench coat... The man who we must fear is...the serial molester who allegedly kept meticulous notes about the molestations of thousands of boys. Repeatedly, he slipped away and avoided long prison terms despite abusing children in at least five states for more than thirty-five years.

This White man often defended himself in court, he got two convictions overturned and was twice exonerated on appeal, although the Idaho Supreme Court labeled him a repeat offender who "uses his *intelligence* to take advantage of the *weak* and *oppressed* and those who are in need."

Charismatic, wily and "smarter than heck" is the way James Kevan, one of his lawyers in the mid 70s, described him. "He could write up legal documents better than most lawyers."

This gentleman is now sixty-three years old and has been arrested *nine times* and spent twelve years in prison. But police say, in his out of jail time, he's become perhaps the nation's most *prolific* serial child molester.

A search of his San Jose home turned up computers and notebooks with lists of more than thirty-six thousand entries that include children's names and codes indicating what sex acts he did with them.

Kevan, later disbarred after drug problems, said he knew this man as *Tim Miller*, one of his dozens of aliases. At the time they both lived in Idaho.

"He brought several suits against the sheriff here and against the state and against anybody and everybody," states Mountain Home Police Captain Dave Pursell.

In 1970 he was convicted in Alaska of lewd and lascivious conduct with three teen boys, two of whom he brought with him from Kentucky. He got only two years probation and was indicted two years later for molesting another boy, but fled the state... The very first time he got probation is when Jerry Falwell, Pat Robertson, Crisis Intervention and perhaps in-patient treatment programs should have gotten his butt. We should have diagnosed, treated, treated, treated and treated this man. We should have found out when *he* got molested. And we should have spent every dime necessary to try to help him *fix* himself thirty-five years ago and this would and could have saved the lives of the two boys he's accused of molesting in San Jose in 2005...

Instead (pay close attention youngsters) he wound up *coaching* youth football. And parents thought he was great. I'm sorry to tell us that *parents* don't always know what to look for. They thought he was a *great man* and a *great coach*. Period! And I will repeat that most twelve, thirteen and fourteen-year-old boys never admit to being molested. And *no* child under the age of sixteen or seventeen has the mental apparatus or maturity to *consent to sex*. And so there is not any justification (ever) for a grown man having any kind of sex with any kind of kid under seventeen years of age; period!

"No one suspected a thing. He was an excellent coach," stated a Mountain Home, Idaho parent. In 1974 he was locked up again. Why? Raping two thirteen-year-old boys. He bailed out and fled to Brazil! Interpol caught him and extradited him. He spent *only* two years in prison in Idaho. This youth coach, intelligent White man got out of prison... He was arrested again in Idaho and fled to Oregon. In Oregon he was accused of bringing a boy from little Rock, Arkansas to San Francisco in June 1980.

The U. S. Attorney deferred prosecution to the local D.A. in Idaho. He was convicted of molesting two boys and the coach spent six years in prison. By this time, the *youth coach* had hired Attorney Lance Churchill.

"Coach was famous as one of the best prison lawyers in Idaho. He knew how to type and write briefs. He could do it all. He was respected because if an inmate needed help in a legal case, he would help them out," Churchill said. This *youth coach*, intelligent, charming and nice *predator, molester* and child *abuser* also helped himself. He appealed his case to the Idaho Supreme Court and won in 1976. He tried again in 1983, arguing "vague" legal definitions of illegal sexual acts. He lost this time but the justices did recommend that the legislature should *clarify* the law.

After the coach was released from Idaho in 1987, he was arrested at least five more times for molesting kids. He served three more years in Oregon, got out, was repeatedly arrested for violating parole and allegedly abusing other children, won an acquittal in Washington State and fled instead of facing arrest on another warrant in Oregon. Every time, this coach avoided stiffer punishment and each time the government, justice system, the church and the community failed to spend their money to treat him. His name is *Dean Schwartzmiller*. His name is also irrelevant. He's coaching, teaching, policing, etc., in schools and cities nationwide. "He could have become a lawyer," stated James Albert (Leslie's son)... And I submit that just as easily as he could have become a lawyer, etc., many molesters are lawyers and judges and police. We miss them because we are looking for him. Him the lone White stalker in the *trench coat* with a candy sack in his hand. I submit that we taxpayers spent 2.3 million dollars chasing arresting, prosecuting, extraditing and re-trying coach Dean. But if somebody had suggested back in 1970 in Alaska when he got probation, that "Your Honor, we need $2.3 million now to put Coach Dean in a state of the art, *lock down* treatment facility. This facility is only for adults convicted of sexual abuse of kids under sixteen. Dr. Lawlis, Dr. Phil McGraw, Tony Robbins, David Israel and a team of sexual experts will treat this guy and do everything they can to prevent him from harming anymore kids." That judge would have said something eloquent i .e., "This court does not have the power to allocate those kind of funds or expenditures for treatment." But they can slowly screw the public out of $2.3 million while simultaneously allowing hundreds and thousands of kids to be molested over and over again. And these victims will more often than not become victimizers. So (again) *when you look into the eyes* of a victim of molestation *today* and feel that sympathy and sorrow, etc…just know that in a few years, you'll look into those eyes with anger, outrage and shock. We have but one way out and I believe that Chris McClendon (*Straight Edge* Youth Group - Reno), Mike Silver (Barber), Lisa Scottoline and Ben Bish would be willing to help transform the system if we seek them out. Scott Parsely (New Freedom, Pennsylvania), Jeremy, (Westminster, CA) Dave Walker, Lois Hart and Queen Latifah would help spread the word *if we* contact them. I believe that if you tinkerers will text and e-mail Shawn Abbott, (Ivy League Admissions) Professor Adam Wassen, Professor James Fox, Mike Vitiello, Scott Kinworthy, (LA) Davis (Political Activist…Memphis, Tennessee) and tell them about the Coach, etc., they will help us to *create safe beds* for our children. We need to get this book to the teens out at Casey's Coffee Place in Chester, New Jersey and let them help put the word out…

I called Becky just last week and she was at the *Coffee Beanery* in Torrance, CA. She was animated and said, "Don't you dare forget to mention the *Coffee Beanery* (shameless free plug…I may never hear from the owners but *Becky knows best*) out here in Torrance, CA and need I remind you to insert the names of some students, scholars, podcasters and bloggers in the book. Mr. Manning, I know what I'm doing. Just *one* popular teen is all you need to get a hold of *the book* when it is published. And just one teen will use blogging, bulletins and postings to cause it to spread like wildfire. Caleb Kerby, Phil at New Opportunity TV, Heidi Fugeman, Photographer Mark Brown, Designer Eric Shore, Garza, Berkus and Cunningham must get the word that your book is out.

"Mr. Manning: I *promise* you that this book will *rock the world*. It will rock the colleges, the churches, the schools, the homes and it will explode over the Internet. Be candid. All my age group wants is candor, truth and frankness. Let's put it out there," stated Becky the Boss!

I don't ever recall a time when Becky, James, Lisa, Amanda or any of my advisers *under* the age of thirty-two years old have ill-advised me…"

I trust them and their suggestions have served me well! And I suggest you (the reader) contact Dr. Thane Hancock, Dr. Leeser in Maryland and Kermin Fleming etc., blog, e-mail and text every member of your youth group, church group, frat, band, orchestra and association and tell them to help us to create *safe beds* for our children.

From what James, Becky, Lisa, Scott and my other youth posse members are telling me, the answer *ain't* in our present day politicians. I.e., Becky pointed out to me that "Mr. Manning, two weeks ago Vice

President Dick Cheney made a statement about decreasing insurgency in Iraq, etc." She continued with "Last week a general in Iraq stated the opposite of what Cheney said. And today (6/20/05) when asked about the conflicting statements, Mr. Bush (the President) ignored the question. That's why the youth don't want any part of this type of a sham. It's not real. It's hypocritical."

Sheila Thompson is a bright, articulate and classy young lady. Sheila is twenty-four years of age. She is a redhead; naturally. Sheila stands 4 ft 11 in. tall and weighs in at one hundred and fourteen pounds. Sheila has hazel eyes and is as cute as all outdoors. Sheila is perhaps one of the best-dressed young ladies to hail from Shrewsbury, Pennsylvania. For a time, she dated Scot Parsley of the Scholar fame. She then dated Davis from that same show. Her romance with Davis never blossomed. But she and Scot were quite serious for about seven months. Sheila has a degree in advertising and she now works with Gabriel Afana out of Moreno Valley, California. One day Gabe went on to www.scriptlance.com and Sheila responded to a message. Three months later, Sheila had moved from Shrewsbury to Moreno Valley. She is a wizard with public relations, advertising in unusual ways to unique groups of people. I heard about Sheila through Gabe. Gabriel was introduced to me by my pals, Eric Bulrice and Michael Noble. Eric and Michael were both or *are* both on my think tank and they attend Idyllwild Arts Academy in Idyllwild, CA.

Fast-forward to June 2005 and I teleconferenced with Eric, Noble, Gabriel Afana and Sheila Thompson. It was interesting. Subject or theme? "How to spread the word about the sexual assaults in prisons and make the issue relevant to young people." To say the least, Sheila led the discussion and was the *point lady* during most of the fifty-nine minute long teleconference...

"Greetings, my friends," I began the call. "I wanna thank Eric, Gabe, Mike and you, Sheila, for the time and effort which y'all have put into this assignment. I am in receipt of all of the research, polls and surveys, which you all have mailed to me. It was quite interesting. I really, really want each of you to know that I don't take your courage, commitment or expertise for granted. I value your opinions. I cherish your vision, optimism and your energy. Thank you so very much. Your efforts mean the world to me.

"And I want you to know that I will utilize your ideas, communicate your suggestions and demonstrate your ideals in the tome which we plan to rush to press. Now I wanna hear from you all. Who wants to go first?"

Upon clearing his throat, Gabriel indicated that, "I think Sheila should lead us off."

Sheila didn't wait for a seconding of the suggestion. She rushed in beginning with, "I believe you make the issues relevant by tapping into the nerd and geeks in high school and college. You tap into youth ministers and young college professors. And you also tap into the religious conservative base by proving the need for *safe beds* for kids. *Mr. Manning*, we must admit there is very little data available on sexual offenders in this country. What we do know is that folks A. don't like to adequately discuss it and B. few are capable of intelligently discussing it. We generalize and group people all together. A child predator/pedophile is distinctively different from an adult who rapes adults. Both are horrible crimes. And any adult who molests *children* is the worst of the worst. A recent study out of Canada's solicitor's office states an adult who rapes adults can be cured. A combination of punishment and therapy very often prevents these people from re-offending.

"However, studies show adults *over* eighteen who molest children under fourteen rarely, very rarely ever stop. So any discussion, which groups rapists with molesters, is a foolish discussion. Any discussion generalizing some *non-existent* connection between pedophiles and rapists is a non-productive discussion. And so I think your book must spark an authentic discussion on blogs, podcasts, college campuses etc., much like the discussion of civil rights, which began on college campuses in the mid 60s and 70s. Real debate leads to transformation.

"Young people enjoy real discussions. We love anything unique and…"

Sheila and all the crew had much input which is reflected throughout this tome. I really appreciate the lessons I've learned from my team as well as from folks, i.e. Adam Getchell and Professor Bob Ono (Bob and Adam teach Anti-hacking at U. C. Davis), Antonio Pontarelli, Matt Trainor, Luke Sears (Oakland, CA) and many others. *Some* of the above-mentioned heroes don't even know how or when they helped or influenced me. Some of them don't even know about this book. (Editor's Note: But they will if you e-mail them and tell them about it).

And I need bloggers, script kidders, crackers and podcasters to inundate the Internet with comments about this book. If *you* will link this book to your blog or podcast, etc., liberals, conservatives, nerds, gothics and student political activists will snap up copies of this book like snow cones on a hot summer day. Peter Severson (Sioux Falls, S. Dakota), Ryan Salgado (S. Lake City, Utah), Chris Quick (Frankford,

W. VA) and Trevor Gordon (Medford, Oregon) will get this book *if you let* them know about it.

Eric Shores (brilliant, fabulously successful home designer) will buy a few hundred copies of this book and donate them to *Oprah's Angel Network*, the Montel Williams Show or the Boys and Girls Club of America if/when you let them know... Do *your* part.

I am not afraid to tell you the student, professor, yuppies, stud, prep, dude, sista, etc., etc.) right now that *I need you*. There you have it. I need you. I cannot and I will not be able to do this thing without you. My attempt is monumental. I'm like David attempting to take on Goliath. I don't wanna be like Johnathon. I don't want to try to stay with *Saul* simply because it seems *natural*. I want to cleave to David because it's spiritual. (You Bible readers know of what I speak). I know I may *look like a fool*. I know I'm out on a limb talking about a subject that most of the politicians simply throw a law at. I know I'm not gonna get a civil rights award for telling the world about a rape epidemic in which our *Caucasian* brothers are the victims. I will anger some Black activists who may feel I should utilize my power as a scribe to *only* talk about driving while Black or Brown, etc. And I understand clearly that many want to marginalize me. I'm in prison. You knew that right? But I will tell you for the billionth time that if **you**...right in your high school computer class, right in your youth group, in GLSA in Tracy, CA in your church, college dorm, at the Gothic Fest, at the Club House or where ever you are... If you will give our babies, boys and girls just *one hour* of your time today - You give them at least *one hour* right here, right now by cutting on your computer, e-mailing folks i.e. your pals, your pastor, band members, newspapers, Bev Smith, Ed Schultz, Doug Banks, fraternity, sorority, etc., etc., and tell them about this book. Once they get the book, they will know what *you and I* know. And having seen and read the truth, they can't ignore it or deny our children.

And if you have not sent an e-mail, text or done a blog on this book yet; just imagine what happens if every other reader does or doesn't do; what you've done or not done. If you don't, who will? You get the point. I am asking y-o-u to **please** make *Blue-Eyed Blonde* an issue they cannot ignore for another day. You do your part. This book is mine. Prayer!? Come on y'all I pray. I believe in the power of prayer. And faith is urgent. And *faith* without works is *dead*. I want ya'll to pray if you believe in the divine creator, the universe or God. But that's between you and *God*. But what I am called to do is to get some work out of *you*. I need you to put those fingertips to the mouse pad and keyboard and don't stop til you've done something to help create *safe beds*. Believe me safe beds create safe homes, create safe neighborhoods, create safe schools, safe cities, safe nations and a safer world.

I understand, as I said, that my challenge is humongous. But I believe we can. I may not ever get you to *believe in me*. That's all good. I can handle that. I am not seeking an endorsement on **me**. If you consider this entire book to be a manipulation - you're right. It is a manipulation to create an intelligent conversation, which creates safety for kids and prevents sexual molestation. It is a manipulation to get you to look in the mirror and decide the person in *your* mirror must get involved today.

Have you ever looked at a *child* (a child, a kid...) and gotten any kind of sexual arousal? If so - go get help *today*. That is a signal of a severe problem and if you don't kill it, it will kill you. Don't try to laugh it away or deny it. Call Dr. Phil, Montel Williams, a therapist, a pastor or somebody and get that stuff *out of you*. It's a problem. Don't deny it...Call 1-800-Bishop2 and tell Bishop T. D. Jakes you want help. Go rent "Woman Thou Art Loosed" on DVD and it will help you. *Please*, please deal with it before you act on it. Do it *Now*! It is Urgent!

If you have already molested a child, you can still get help. I wanna tell you to turn yourself in to the police. And that *sounds* good and it is the right thing to do. But pragmatically, I don't expect most to do that. So since you're probably (wish you would, you can and you should) not gonna do that, I'll tell you to at least tell a therapist, "I need help."

Invent a scenario (if you refuse to do the total right thing) and just tell somebody, "I need help before I do something sinister." If all my writing saves - one - child... Just one - I'll be totally satisfied! If one father walks into his child's room and shakes his head and says, "Not tonight. I'm not gonna do this again." This book is an awesome success. If one, o-n-e child sleeps tonight without being molested, threatened or hurt, then I've done what God called me to do. I can't force you to like me or believe I mean well. You may suspect all kinds of ulterior motives for my writing this book. I relate well to mistrust, distrust, abuse of power and B.S. I know many so-called writers, prisoners, journalists and Christians who *talk east* and *walk west*.

Don't worry about me. Put your eyes on *you*. Look around in your house, your school, community, church and city. Do your part where you are, with what you have. I must account to God for *me*. You are only responsible for *your* actions. There is something every lawyer, student, professor, parent and even prisoner can do to *create safe beds*.

You can write a letter, sing a song, do a dance, write a play, draft a plan, organize, strategize and galvanize to make a *safe bed* for some child today. How dare we discount the psychological, physical and spiritual value of *one* life? That *one* child we save, protect and deliver from abuse could grow up to become a Mattie, a Martin Luther King, Jr., a Mother Teresa, a teacher or preacher.

We don't know *who* that child is supposed to become. But we can imagine (today) what if it was *me*? What if it was *my child*? I want you to do something about all the stuff you've read in this book. I want every head to bow, heart to mourn and every tongue to speak to *create safe beds* in our world for our children.

The power of *one* life. I could be wrong but I believe that if fifty million dollars would have (for certain) saved the life of little Mattie - Oprah would have paid it. The Angel Network would have paid it. Bill Gates, Jeff Bezos and George Soros would have paid it.

How much would *you* pay to save the life of your child? People pay millions of dollars everyday in ransom money. At some point, we need to collectively comprehend that when a child is raped, his or her life ends as they know it. They lose their innocence. Their shame can kill them.

There was a guy in California convicted of raping a twelve-year-old boy. This defendant ended up winning an appeal. Rather than testifying against him again, the kid committed suicide. Kids commit suicide everyday. They abuse drugs, run away from home and get involved with violence etc. Very often, due to the trouble, hurt and harm they endured because of the un-safety of their bed.

We need Ryan Gajersky (Long Beach, CA), Tim Robbins, Tony Serra and Attorney Dennis Cunningham to fight with us. Laurence J. Lichter and Mrs. N. Ruiz can fight with us.

Being a criminal trial lawyer is a complex and a difficult occupation. Many folks scandalize lawyers til they need one. But a lawyer operates within an adversarial system of rules put in place by our founding fathers. And a real lawyer often defends a man or woman accused of molestation. And each defendant is presumed innocent by law. And it is clear that folks like Nancy Grace want us to assume that defendants get away with murder, molestation and rape all the time. Yet, statistically speaking, we are persuaded to believe the opposite. O. J. Simpson, Robert Blake and Michael Jackson's cases as well as their outcomes are *not* the norm. Prosecutors usually *win*. Rarely does a defendant get a not guilty verdict. More than seventy-six percent of the cases brought to trial are won by the prosecution. Most defendants are not wealthy. Most defendants have public defenders. And public defenders don't get even twenty-five percent of the funding, which the prosecutor's office does.

So, regardless of what Court TV tries to tell us etc., it is a fact that prosecutors rarely lose a trial. But no lawyer wants a child molested. And even the lawyers who represent the accused, as well as accusers, want children protected. I know it is difficult to believe. But I will submit most of *us,* lawyers, cops, judges and everyday citizens want our children protected.

So this book is a beacon call to every judge, lawyer, cop, robber and citizen to get involved today. We need to join hands and form a wall of protection around our sons and daughters. We must pay any price to defend them. They are our hope. They are defenseless. They are important. They have bright futures and visions.

It is our job to make sure they have a chance to live their lives in peace, hope and joy.

I want their joy restored. I want their laughter restored. There is something exciting, hopeful and amazing about the noise and laughter filled rooms of our kids. They ought never need to worry about being hurt, violated, beat or molested.

And it is time for us to rise up, speak out and take action. I know it's difficult to discuss. We are pained and outraged by crimes against our children. But *silence* is not the answer. All that it takes for evil to rage is for good men to remain silent...

It was July 2005 and I had just been released. Some combination of prayer, fasting, belief and lawyers had gotten me out early. One of my main goals now was to get James out early. I won't rest til he's free. And there are others who don't belong in prison that we will combine our efforts to try to get free...

On July 24th at exactly 2:06 p.m. I boarded my dad's private plane. It is a rather flamboyant and extravagant plane with the name "*Manning*" emblazoned in gold letters across the sides. All of the hardware accents, including doorknobs, cup holders and the towel bar in the bathroom, are plated with gold. The woodworking throughout the craft is a rich mahogany, set against elegant furnishings and silk-brocade wall covering. The plane can accommodate up to eighteen passengers, who can kick back on the plane's two ivory-colored leather couches, which line the first third of the plane's thirty-four foot long cabin...

We taxied down the runway from the small airport outside of Fulton Industrial Parkway. It was a far better option than flying out of

Jackson/Hartsfield. I sat there with my shoes off. I was wearing an old (very old) jogging suit which I'd purchased back in Valdosta, Georgia before I ever saw the inside of a jail cell. I looked out the window and saw the buildings, moving faster, faster and faster. And then I was leaning back with my nose in the air. I could feel the wheels stand, which the plane was doing as the front lifted. A few moments later and we were indeed, fully airborne. I saw the clouds hitting the windows as we moved on up a little higher every second. Other than the pilots, I'm flying solo. Sabine, my kids, Peter and Katrin were already in Washington, D.C. They had all flown in from Switzerland and were meeting me there. Outside of some sporadic, minor turbulence, my flight was uneventful. My idea about getting some sleep on the plane was wishful thinking. No sooner had I shut my eyes, after being told, "Mr. Manning, we're now thirty-five thousand feet airborne," my phones began ringing. And I do mean cell phones - plural. On one phone, Attorney Tony Serra called. Mr. Serra and Mrs. Ruiz were working on an early release petition for James. "I think we can shave at least ten months off of his sentence." On the other phone was Montel Williams asking if I could do his show the first week of September. "I want you, Wilbert Rideau and Scott Ross," Montel stated.

After explaining to Montel that I would be in Reuthal in September, I then took a call from Mr. Dick Gregory. Mr. Gregory wanted me to teleconference with Bev Smith and Earl Ofari Hutchinson in October. I agreed to do it. This teleconference would be special in that we would strategize and discuss ways to bring together pastors, lawyers, professors, students and activists on issues of prison violence, prison rape and alternatives to prison...

I was grown. My prison experience has caused me to grow. Sometimes God allows you to be put into a situation so you can *change the situation*. There are also times he allows you into situations so that the *situation* will *change you*. And *God* is a *God* of *changes*. Sometimes there is a *shift* in the process and if you don't recognize the time for the shift, you'll miss your blessing!

I knew I was not prison material. Everything about the prison system turned me off. It was a mess. Many of my fellow inmates were so evil, so phony, so wicked, so weak, so ignorant and so fickle. Many of the guards were likewise, all of the aforementioned, and sometimes worse. It was a lonely and desperate place. I.e. a Mexican inmate at Mule Creek died of an apparent drug overdose in 2005. I heard his (they called him Angel) own comrades, buddies and his pals joking about his death the day after he died. How sick have you become and how low have you gone when you make fun of the death of any human? Much less your own friend? Something hit me when I wrote about how they made fun of Angel's overdose and that is how staff deals with it. If an officer dies in C.D.C. they locked us down for forty-eight hours so staff can grieve. If an inmate dies, they don't skip a beat. They bring in no grief counselors, etc., etc., and they wonder how people in prison get so perverted, mad and abnormal.

When you treat humans as animals long enough, they adapt. They begin to react like animals. That's one of the *main* reasons I decided to write this book. It is why I've linked it up to "The Law Firm", "Boston Legal" and "Law and Order".

David E. Kelly is brilliant and his shows i.e., "The Practice" and *Boston Legal* definitely are reflected in *From the Palace to the Prison*, *Creating Monsters* and **this** book. I employed all of these various strategies, etc. because (more than anything) I want this book to inspire, motivate and teach those young people in schools and colleges to avoid any/all habits and behaviors which lead to incarceration. I am pragmatic and I believe in being extremely realistic. I get in trouble with some church folks because I won't play games in my writings. But I am not stupid. I know some teenagers are gonna have sex! Some of them are gonna drink. I can't pretend to my readers that I have never done wrong, but I can tell youngsters who are experimenting with this and that to get out of it. It's a losing battle.

Hollywood, the music industry and the celebrity roles are replete with names like Bobby Brown, Whitney, Richard Pryor (God bless Mr. Pryor) and others who *had it all*. They had cars, money, bling bling and penthouses. But some lost a lot and some lost it all because of *drugs* and *alcohol*. I tell young folks to tune in to Bishop T. D. Jakes, Billy Graham and Rick Warren and get some *word in their lives*.

It's now the last week of September and I'm on the move. I am livin' large and some would say I'm *havin it my way*. But really I'm doing what I am supposed to do. I am living the life God chose for me to live. I kept looking around me and being haunted by memories of the prison. I came to understand that I would never forget. I was like a former *prisoner of war*. I had nightmares about the White guys being raped sadistically, in LA County Jail. I saw the sexual abuse of boys in juveniles and prisons nationwide. The staff abuse and corruption was of titanic proportions in the in-justice system. I could never forget...

I won the support of Attorney Susan Yu, Debra Opri, Gerry Spence, Floyd Abrams, John Turley and Michael Vitiello. Susan and Debra were key members of NAPS (National Association of Public Safety...to create *safe beds* via creating a safe society) who worked on our *justice* committee. The job of the justice committee is to weed out wrongly convicted prisoners especially those incarcerated for violent crimes.

"Anytime the wrong person is in jail or prison for rape, molestation or murder, we jeopardize the safety of citizens in society. If the actual perpetrators are roaming the streets, they will commit more crimes," stated Attorney Johnny Griffin, III who is also on the committee. This team of powerful civil corporate and criminal lawyers work for free. Each of them commits to spending at least ninety-six hours per year pro bono looking at cases, which NAPS student leaders (and scholars) have identified as possibly wrongly convicted. Student leaders in fraternities, sororities, college clubs, mentoring programs, junior achievement, etc. and journalism courses locate the cases for consideration. *NAPS* has become my pet project. I absolutely love the idea of getting the wrong guys out of jail and putting the right guys in jail. It causes me to tremble when I think about it. Wow! What a life. To me, this is *living*. Helping others as they fight for justice.

I can't thank (seriously) Gabriel Afana for all of Gabe's help. College students are extremely busy. Especially those majoring in marketing and business. And so many folks are so skeptical of incarcerated humans. Nevertheless, I reached out to Gabriel while I was in the prison. He received my call in a gregarious, affable and cordial manner. He immediately went to my Web site and began offering criticisms, critiques and suggestions. We took his advice... Gabriel is a master advertiser and is also creating software to protect against spam. (I suggest you look up Atomi and/or Gabriel Afana in Moreno, CA). I hope that many other marketing, journalism and law students, etc., shall stumble upon this book and immediately *Pay It Forward...*

In latter November, I met with Jarod Miller (zoologist), Carlos Smith (he appeared on Fear Factor on 6/27/05), Jeremy Petty (Sacto Tagger), Michael Krog, Jr. (Sacto, CA...Mike's sister, Marissa was viciously murdered in Sacramento, CA in 2004. I hope and pray the killer will be found out), Michael Levine (Hollywood Publicist), Dave Lieberman, Heath Ledger, Hayden Christensen, Matt Damon, Daven Yamada, Matt Matteucci (Fair Oaks, CA) and Tony Danza. Peter Wentz and Patrick Stump of the group *Fallout Boy* were also at the meeting in Richmond, Virginia. We all discussed efforts to get *"Creating Monsters"* and *this* book into every high school and college. After the meeting, I called Mel Gibson and Michael Moore and candidly asked each of them to sponsor five thousand copies of *From the Palace to the Prison* as well as *Blue-Eyed Blonde* and send them to Oprah's Angel Network.

D.C. Lawyer Todd Goldstein gave a presentation to a *NAPS* workshop on California Supreme Court's rulings upholding state sentencing guidelines, etc., as well as on the U.S. Supreme Court's ruling concerning racially *diverse* juries...Johanna Botta from Riverside, California called me to tell me that "Rachel, Wes (Kansas City) Danny (Billerica, Mass.) all talked about *Blue-Eyed Blonde* every day in "The Real World" house. Eric Cabrera (Georgia State University Junior) e-mailed me to say, "*Blue-Eyed Blonde* was awesome. I got an advance copy and I was spellbound. It should be required reading for every White male aged sixteen to thirty."

Lawyer, law professor and author Kermit Roosevelt (Law Professor at University of Pennsylvania) e-mailed me, "If half the youth reading your book goes online and does half the things you request of them, your book will break records. I thoroughly enjoyed it. A splendid read. I think a lot of criminal justice, English and law professors will make this book a part of their curriculum."

Author Jamie Reidy wrote, "I got lost in that damn book. It was great."

On a cold November evening, I met Serena Williams at the Jefferson Sheraton Hotel in Richmond, Virginia. Becky had arranged the meeting. Serena was *bad*. That big butt and those thighs. She had on all white and she said, "I'm impressed with your work, Sherman and your ability to survive through all of that mess. Blogger Bob Fesmire and his wife, Gina (Sunnyvale, CA - www.downingstreetmemo.com) are friends of my coach and they think you're brilliant. 'The media took a pass on the story but Sherman is getting it out there,' they said. What can I do to help NAPS?"

I was humbled by Serena's inquiry. Ethan Watters, Po Bronson and Ethan Canin invited me to join *The Grotto* in San Francisco, CA. "You can share office space with us and it will *free* your creativity," Ethan suggested in a cell call while I was with Serena.

Pierre-Luc Gagnon, Geoff Rowley and Brandon Turner offered to do a skating demonstration at a *NAPS* fundraiser on call. I assigned that proposal to Gabriel to handle.

Adrian Holovaty and Ero were fabulous at recruiting Caleb Sima, Tim Robbins and the guys at Defcon to volunteer to teach computer classes in urban pockets of poverty for NAPS. We held a Dream Jamboree for teens in Oak Park, Del Paso Heights and Techword Court teaching computers... Gabriel carved out a mentoring program to teach at-risk youth advertising and marketing. "If we teach kids how to become successful ad salesmen, car salesmen, computer and software salesmen, we won't keep losing them to juveniles and prisons for drug sales," Mr. Afan told me in a late night meeting.

Dr. Hyung Chun, Marcus Pincus, Matt Fununwra, Neal Battaglia, Author David Sadaris and Kevin Henkes taught strategy sessions for our staff sporadically.

Kirsten Daniels (Summa Cum Laude Graduate from Seattle University School of Law), Jon D. Markman (investment manager), Brad Pitt, Mark Wahlberg and Morgan Freeman all donated their time and expertise to our staff. Chris Vomund (University of Missouri-Columbia) and Mike Sweeney (Director of ARC) offered to touch the hearts and lives of NAPS members by staging a bicycle ride across America for the youth.

"Push America's sixty-one members of the Pi Kappa Phi Fraternity want to help people with disabilities. And people in prisons, juveniles and in poverty are disabled. We want to help them, Mr. Manning," stated University of Michigan graduate Chris Kozak.

And Walter Pape (a junior at Colorado State University) said, "Mr. Manning, we prove that young people do care. And we want people to go to www.PushAmerica.org and help us. We are the Journey of Hope Riders."

Becky said, "They're all young and good looking and they do a lot of good." I salute the Journey of Hope Riders and I encourage all to contribute money to help them do what they do. Becky wants to give them copies of this book to pass out to the people as they journey across the nation. I concur…

On the last night in November, I had a late, late night meeting with Becky, Cody and Gabriel Afana. "We need to do small conferences and workshops to help men improve their lives. Rev. Lacy Sykes, Pastor of Crossword Christian Church in Moreno Valley will help us. Sykes has done Rev. Dr. Martin Luther King, Jr. Men's Deliverance Summits, which are very successful. Let's get with Sykes, Pastor Ron Woods, John Harris, Rev. Phil Murray and James Baylark and begin organizing these men's summits for high school seniors, college students and teens in juveniles."

(God is working… Remember Dwayne McKinney? Told y'all the brother served twenty years in a California prison for a rape he did not commit. Rape… Twenty years… He was proven innocent and received a $1.7 million settlement. Now he's in Honolulu and he owns an ATM Company. My Lord. I want some of my readers to go to IslandATM@Yahoo.com and tell that brother to pray for me. I salute him… Attorney Willie Jay in Churchville, Maryland? Call W. Jay and tell him he's in this book... Neal Carlson (Long Island, NY), David Jay, Joel Risberg, Drew Allison, Mrs. Lydia Allison, Jeff Wadlow, Jesse Dobbie, Tom Boak, Robin Lorifice, Isaac Cotton, etc. ought to know I saluted them... On September 14, 2005 on Oprah, there was a Jesse on the show. No last name. Find Jesse and if he writes me, I'll give *you* one hundred and fifty dollars. Brian Foskuhl of Richmond, VA? Anyone know him? Alexander Dugdale? Lorenzo di Bonaventura, Craig Brewer, Ron Samuel, Todd Cole, Anthony Hingle, Anthony Nata, Roy Campanella, Dr. Mark Sapir, John L. Sullivan?? Mr. Ralph White? How dare we not salute former Stockton City Councilman White? He's a great man. And if I ever get this book to Mr. White, David Perez (Oilman in San Diego, CA), Brian Pards, etc., they won't let me die here... Keith Chandler, Mandy Brazell, Jesse Lee Soffer, Daniel Pintauro, Travis Isreal (Cape Girardeau, Missouri), Dr. Keith Ablow, Robert Klein, Dennis Prince, Judson Rosebush, Neal Shapiro, Mike Hudson (Edmunds.com), Douglas Wood (Alamo, CA), Eric Bulrice, Al Green, Ben Taylor, Gary Holland, William Villarreal (Mystrength.org)... Craig (my friend) Scott... Y'all think I put their names here for nothing? If so, you missed it. I love Craig Scott, Beth Nimmo and all the folks I've named here... Albert Hayes in New York, etc., etc. Hector Hoyos? Agim Kaba? Tyler Hudson? Wil Seabrooks? Trevor Loflin, Wil Whetton, Jesse Garza, Stuart Pfeifer, Aaron Marchand? Jason Costa at Emory Law School in Atlanta? The Jamie Kennedy Show? Seqib Keval, Seamus, Seamus, Seamus Farrow, Scissors Sisters, Daniel Cummings, Gerard Wax? Douglas Pieper, Luke Klipp, Michael Colen and Tristan Imboden?

I need *you* to let them know they are in this book. Contact William Blackwell or Underground Books store in Sacramento High School and put the word out... Go to *ShermanManning.blogspot.com*...or e-mail me at *Hallopeter.manning@blogger.com*... One more time... *Hallopeter.manning@blogger.com* is where y'all can e-mail me... And do look at *ShermanManning.blogspot.com*, SaveShastaGroene.blogspot.com, *TheLawFirmTV.blogspot.com*, JusticeonTrial.com and The Innocence Project.org... Pray for me... Tell everybody you know about "*The Blue-Eyed Blonde*"...)

Gabriel said, "We will keep them small. Our goal will be five hundred men. We can be interactive. Have *you* to speak to the entire group. Then we break up into small groups of fifty."

"Beauty and the Geek" host Brian McFayden was also at the meeting. "Fabulous idea, but how well does Sherman speak publicly?" he asked.

Becky said, "Try Martin Luther King, Jr., Jesse Jackson, Tony Robbins and T. D. Jakes combined. That's how Sherman speaks. He's bad. If he can do *nothing else*, I know three things he has mastered. A. Public speaking/preaching. B. The modeling business. C. Writing books." Becky continued...

December 1, 2005, I boarded a jet (chartered) headed for Chicago, Illinois. I had Becky, Sheila, Gabriel, Chris Eilerman, Michael Krog, Jr., Fununwra and Spike Lee with me. We were headed to a convention on crime and punishment. "We need to buy a tour bus and just take this movement en tour," Michael Krog stated. We all laughed but I began to visualize and I saw a brown tour bus with gold trimming in my mind. I thought it would cost two to three hundred grand to get the kind of bus I'd want.

We got to Chicago and checked in at The Palmer House Hotel. We brunched in the Palmer's restaurant and then hustled off to Mercy Seat Baptist Church auditorium on Roosevelt Highway. I gave the keynote address: The Chicago Tribune gave us front-page coverage. "Ex-con Blames Society for Criminal Behavior," read the headline. Not exactly the coverage we would have hoped for. But I was not surprised. The large media house in this nation are controlled by corporations. And they are biased to say the least. Very, very biased. But thanks be to God for bloggers, the Internet, podcasters and Yahoo! News...

The Tribune mostly wrote about my jail record and all of the negative things former prison guards had to say about me. I was manipulative, controversial, vicious and ruthless. The normal adjectives prison officials used to describe all prisoners who don't tap dance and buck dance for them. But smokinggun.com, ourmedia.org, the American Urban Radio Network, the Progressive News, The Nation and Air America were kind to us.

Randi Rhodes stated, "No ex-con has been able to bring together Phi Delta Theta, Kappa Alpha Psi, Pi Kappa Phi and many other college frats and sororities in the way Sherman Manning has. This dude has used the Internet to electrify students in high schools and on college campuses all across America. They are standing up for justice. They are standing up against the war. They are standing up against the domestic poverty, racism and child molestation transpiring right here in America. Damn, this guy amazes me. Sherman Manning has his books on E-bay, Google, Yahoo! Cafepress, Barnes and Noble, in libraries, churches and juveniles all across the world. If you have not read *From the Palace to the Prison,* you must get it." Randi then said, "Sherman has done more for social justice, the fight against poverty and the least of these our brothers and sisters, in a couple of months of freedom than most of the big name churches have done in decades. Where are the pastors? *Bishop T. D. Jakes* is driving a *Bentley* and living in a *mansion*! Benny Hinn is filthy rich! Creflo Dollar makes money hand over fist! Why don't these crooks help prisoners, rape victims and the homeless?"

I was extremely humbled and thankful that Randi Rhodes was complimenting *our* efforts. And my mind told me to leave it alone. But I had to call.

Tim says, "We have Sherman D. Manning on the telephone."

"Hi Sherman." Randi stated.

"...But I must disagree on the Jakes issue. Randi, there are crooks in every field. I know many, but I don't include Jakes in that group. Often when you pastor a large church, you have some members who are filthy rich. And they will buy you a Bentley. They will buy you a mansion. And I see *no* problem with a pastor owning a Rolls Royce, etc. as long as he is not *stealing church money* - period. I.e. Joel Olsteen's Church took in fifty-five million dollars last year. Fifty-five million dollars! What *if* we found out Joel received a two million dollar salary last year? To hear a pastor got two million dollars from a church per se *sounds* fishy. It sounds crooked! But if we discover he got only two million dollars out of fifty-five million and that his church knew about it; we get a different picture. My problem with some preachers is that all they preach about is money. And they turn poor people off. But Jakes preaches messages, which leads back to the cross and back to the word. His sermons are dealing with real issues for real people. He does not keep waving a dollar bill in your face. He waves Jesus. And I sense an anointing on that man's life, which is awesome.

Job was rich. Solomon was rich and so was David. And it's not logical to think *any* pastor of twenty or thirty thousand people will be broke. Now having said all of that, Randi, I do understand how it can turn some people off! I get that. I really do. But in closing, Randi, let me say this - I don't care what Jakes drives or where he lives. If (and I doubt it but) *if* Jakes is a crook, if his Bentley sends him to hell, it's okay with me. The gospel messages that he preaches check out with the word. They lead me *back to the Bible*. And that's what matters to me. I love the gift he has. And there are (indeed) many gifted men and women who get *caught up* in the things of this world. But I leave it to God to deal with them. But if the head of Enron can drive a Rolls, why not be head of the church. I hear nobody complaining about the fact that Rev. Billy Graham's (and I love Rev. Graham) ministry in 2003 was worth $880 million. And the Catholic Church is worth billions. At the end of the day, I don't care what you drive, where you live or even how you live. Preach Jesus crucified and resurrected to me and I'll hear it."

Randi didn't buy it but we talked for thirty minutes or so. For the record, I am a fairly wealthy dude. And I offer *no* apology! I own a business. I am in business to make *money*. I own a legitimate company and it affords me a lavish lifestyle. And I drive nice cars and sometimes I am driven by chauffeurs. And *NAPS* is raising a lot of money. My salary from NAPS is one dollar per year!! That's all I earn from NAPS! A buck per year. NAPS can withstand any audit any day of the week. My money comes from my company, my books, videos and public speaking honorariums. I get one hundred thousand dollars per speech in some instances. And *if* I speak for a church, I usually don't *charge* anything. I allow an offering. I do pay my NAPS employees extremely well! You can't recruit college kids and top-level youth if you don't pay them well. We also give a lot of money to prison funds, self-help videos to prisons, juveniles, Boy Scouts, etc. We provide stipends for high school seniors (seriously) nationwide, etc., etc. So NAPS goes through a lot of money. Matt Damon, Damon Dash, Russell Simmons, George Soros, Peter Mandel, George Weiss (Connecticut) and numerous others help us give this kind of money away.

You cannot show up for a gunfight with a stick or a knife. If you wanna impact the masses, you must have money. It takes millions of dollars to do what we do. We are not a *prison group*. We are not a group for prisoners. We are instead, a group of high school seniors, Boy Scouts, junior achievement students, college kids, professors, professionals, pastors, bloggers, podcasters, wizards, nerds, geeks, gothics, studs, jocks, gays, straights, Americans, Europeans and Canadians serving humanity. Our mission is to leave the world better than we found it. To protect our citizens and streets. To *create safe beds* for our children. To create safe communities, schools, colleges, churches and cities.

Kids can't *learn* if they are scared of a bullet coming through the school window. They can't study if they are being molested at home, at church or at school. When we fight to rehabilitate prisoners, it's because we know they *will get out*. And if they only fought, drank, slammed and killed in prison, they will come out of prison in *worse* condition than they went in. We simply want to *protect our* citizens. My posse of college volunteers keep me pragmatic. The folks like Chris Vomund (University of Missouri - Columbia), Chris Kozak, Walter Pape (University at Colorado State), and Bryan Eichler are great people with sharp minds. They *care* about people. People with disabilities and people who are hurting, etc. These youngsters care. And they are open-minded enough to get in where they fit in. We may not always agree but you can't tell these youngsters what or how to *believe*. They know what I know and even *more* than I know. They are aware of the fact that the *BTK* killer was a Boy Scout official in Kansas. He has a degree in criminal justice. This means he went to college with somebody and sat right next to them and they *never* suspected him. They thought all the killers were in prison!

The BTK killer also was a law enforcement official. He was also a deacon in his *church* and president of one of the men's groups in the church. Are y'all reading this? The *binding and torturing* killer who raped, suffocated, asphyxiated, beat, sodomized, traumatized and killed people, wore a uniform everyday and attended church every Sunday for decades until about six months ago.

But y'all tell seventeen and eighteen year olds to stay away from ex-cons or don't correspond with inmates in the prisons. And while you're looking down your nose on the fella in the jail or the fella who just got out, the man who is molesting, binding, torturing, stalking, tolling and killing is in school with our children. He is a scout leader. He's a deacon. He's in the choir or he wears a collar...

What *my* college volunteers are taught is to be open-minded, careful, watchful and prayerful. I teach them that if it looks, sounds or seems too good to be true, it probably is. I teach them to believe very little of what they hear. I teach them to trust their instincts. I teach them to believe that little voice inside which says, "Get out of here" or "Call 911" or "Tell mom or dad", etc. I teach them to be sensible and practical but not prejudiced and biased. And they get excited by corresponding with youth in juveniles and group homes. They enjoy teaching reading to underprivileged kids. They enjoy our food outreach programs in which we feed the hungry, clothe the naked and restore those in our prisons. They love going to senior citizen's homes and caring for the elderly. They love freeing innocent and wrongly convicted prisoners. They also love our picnics, excursions and the rock concerts we take them to.

Christina Zhao, Andrew Almeda, Matt (Piedmont Birdcallers at Piedmont High School...Piedmont, CA - as well as last year's Piedmont Birdcallers. See *From the Palace to the Prison*), George

Derieg, Dan Taylor and Kathleen Ridolfi are all deeply involved with NAPS and our coalition with the Innocence Projects at Cardoza Law School, Santa Clara, San Diego Law School and the other Innocence Projects across America... We could not do what we do without them.

And I invite (again) every high school senior and every college student (as well as professors, teachers, physicians, etc.) to join with us at *NAPS* today! For more info send an e-mail to *Hallopeter@freesurf.ch*. We can use your expertise, voice, poetry, lyrics, mind, talent and time today. (Editor's Note: The first thing you can do today is to write a book review on *this* book on Amazon.com. Also mention this book on blogs, podcasts, etc. And if you received this book gratis - share it with somebody else. Also go to www.Cafepress.com/Manning and get coffee mugs, caps, t-shirts as well as other books by *Sherman D. Manning*).

If you are a true Eminem fan, you ought to be down with the cause. If you are a fan of *System of a Down,* where are you? If you watched *The Practice*, you should join with us. If you are a fan of Boston Legal, The Law Firm, Court TV or Just Legal, you should join us. This is *Reality Books* at its best. And *Jeremy* set it up for us, then Paul, Scott, etc., etc., etc. Now it's on *you and me*. You, Kevin Olivero, you, Phil Waterford, you, Brittani Johnson, Justin Cardinale, Jeff Bramell, Donna Hobbs, Charlotte Griswold, Kyle Fletcher, Jesse DiGirolam, Professor Kristal Brent Zook and your friends. I need you to grab hold of that baton which the *Shackelford* brothers left for us. I want each of you to do what you can do to put the word out.

There are billionaires in every corner of this earth looking for a cause to join, a scholarship to fund, a way to be involved. With this book, we can reach them and form a kind of universal coalition of hope for our children. I can't stop til we get them all. We *must* get Bill Gates. Ya'll call brother Bill at *Microsoft* and tell him I'm coming for him. Send him and Melinda a copy of this book (and don't assume somebody else already sent it; you send it too!) If he's already read it, I got him. If he does not have it yet, you send it to (Microsoft Way in Redmond, Washington. Put a note inside and tell him if he already has it, to *give* away the copy you sent him. One by one, book by book we can reach Bill, George Soros, Sergey Larry Page, Terry Semel and every entrepreneur in this country and other parts of the world) today. When you talk about *Blue-Eyed Blonde* on your blog, admit that I'm *crazy*. You tell the world of Blogosphere and tell the members of the Dukes of Hazzards Fan Club, tell all the Michael Jackson fans, Nancy Grace enemies, war activists, thugs, pimps, prostitutes, rockers, musicians, cheerleaders, band members and your student government class that *I* am a crazy writer. Tell them I am stupid enough to still believe in transformation, unity and the power of the written word. You tell them I still believe in telling it like it is. You tell them I don't believe in failure. I believe in knocking on the door. I will keep knocking and if they don't let me in, I'll kick down the door. I believe if God does not open up the door, He'll open a window. I believe there is a way where there is a will. I am crazy enough to believe there is still hope for you and me too. There is life after this, life after that, life after cocaine and life after crack. I believe you can be down but not out.

I believe there is a young man right this minute (you?) who is sitting up at 2:00 a.m. reading these words. You feel like a failure. You feel empty and there is a void. Life seems all messed up and confusing right now. And I know *you are exactly where you* are supposed to be at this moment. And when you learn what you are supposed to learn; then you will move on. I want you to come stand with us. I want you to play a role in the on goings of our city, our state, our nation and our world. I want you to be crazy. Crazy enough to send e-mails to folk you never even thought about contacting. Crazy enough to call your church and leave a message for your pastor and ask, "What are we going to do about *Blue-Eyed Blonde*?" I want you crazy enough to think creatively and innovatively. All I need is a few *good men* and a few *good women*.

If I can get you in Sacramento, Los Angeles, New York City, White Plaines, New York, etc., you in your high school, you on your cell phone, you in your office and you in your school newspaper to tell others to tell others about the *Blue-Eyed Blonde,* we will accomplish a remarkable task. Come stand with us today.

Wherever you are, whatever you are doing, I need you to get on this train with us. I lost some of you sixty pages ago, but for the rest of you who are still reading and for those of you who picked up this book just to scan it and landed on *this* page, you e-mail us and tell us your story. *You* read the entire book and tell your friends to get it. Give it to your local library, the bridge club and to your pals on the football team. When coach so and so, Bishop Flip Flop, Deacon Willie Wonder and the folks out at college, Beyond Bars find out about us, the rest is history. We must kick the door down. "Mr. Bush, *tear down* this wall. This wall of shame, this wall of assault on the very fabric of society. This wall which divides us. We can come together. People read books (you are reading now). Movers and shakers read. Make damn sure that all the deans at your college, chairmen at the

English Department, vice principal at your school, doctors in your hospital, D.J.s at your radio station, etc. discuss *Blue-Eyed Blonde.*

If only one hundred of you literally call or e-mail the Damon Dash Music Group, I'll get em! Damon is a bibliophile. He loves to read books. P. Diddy, Zach Roerig and frat brothers read. There are millions; millions of college students who do more than binge drink...they read. How will they know if you don't tell them? I call on you to tell somebody about it...

Listen to Mattie. Mattie just wanted peace, safety and happiness. That's all we want. Let us connect and find joy in helping others. Let's stop playing games and get this thing together. We can't win a war over poverty if we don't fight it. We won't conquer racism if we don't practice diversity. We also *must* tell the stories of all those students at U. C. Davis, U. C. Berkeley, Cal State Bernadino, Chico, CSU, Morehouse, Stanford, Independence High School, J. F. Kennedy High, Christian Brothers High School who date, lunch, brunch, prom and live interracially. I will wave *your* story, *your* life and *your* success all in their face. I'll put it in the book and let folks in Sweden, Switzerland, Canada and Africa read about you. Do tell! Send me a photo and I might use your picture also. Let's do this...

Sheila was happy. Sheila was ecstatic and ebullient. "Cool," she told me when I gave her a junior Rolex two weeks before Christmas. Sheila had breakfast with Becky and me. Just me and the two young ladies at Lone Star Steak House in Baltimore, Maryland.

We were there to teach a clinic for the Varsity Football Team at Baltimore High School. Breakfast for me was two scrambled eggs, bacon, biscuits, orange juice, milk and coffee. Becky had an egg omelet over easy and toast. And Sheila ate only two pieces of toast with a small piece of ham. Neither of the two ladies drank coffee.

The next day, I was in a limo as we turned onto Mamaroneck Avenue in White Plaines, New York. As we pulled up outside of the building and stopped at 197, the driver let Becky, Sheila and I out. We were at the Big Apple Smoothie Shop. Gustavo waited on us and made some of the best smoothies we'd ever had. I engaged Gustavo in dialogue and convinced him to come to the youth rally we were having at 5:00 p.m. "I'll be there, I promise," he said while eyeballing Becky.

"You better because if you don't show up, I'll skip our flight tonight and come hunt you down tomorrow, dude," Becky stated and we left.

The next day, I was back at my house in Atlanta, Georgia. I had been crisscrossing the country, building up the troops. Traveling, speaking, listening, answering and asking questions were the norm for me. At home now, I received a call from America's dad - Dr. Bill Cosby. Mr. Cosby was riotously funny. He said, "Am I now speaking to America's richest ex-con?"

I replied, "I don't know how rich I am compared to Martha Stewart and a few others, sir, but I am an ex-con."

Mr. Cosby stated, "I'm glad to see you doing what you are doing. I want you to keep pushing forward. They will criticize you severely, Sherman but keep going. They claim I'm doing a tour against the poor or I shouldn't be speaking out because of the spurious accusation against me but I'll never shut up. People can use the accusations as an excuse not to hear me but they'll regret it. It will be a dangerous thing not to hear me. And some of them will use your criminal background as a reason not to hear. But whoever disqualifies you because of your prison experience will regret it. You can tell our kids what prison is like. They need to hear you. Look at our neighborhoods. In the projects, we all *love Jesus*. You have Christians in the projects who go to church every Sunday. And then they come home and see drug dealers and gang bangers in their hoods. And the Christians *keep walking* they ought to stand still, stand up and run the damn drug dealers out. They ought to have *manpower* and *woman thou art loosed* right in the ghettos."

Mr. Cosby basically lectured me for thirty minutes and when he was finished, all I needed to say was "*Amen*."

He was right about a lot of things and I needed to hear that. I was accustomed to criticism. You're damned if you do and damned if you don't. You can never, ever please everybody.

I always try to teach people close to me to develop tough skin and learn to overcome *criticism*. If you don't learn how to accept criticism without losing your belief in yourself, you will fail. You will fail in school, business, relationships and in life.

I was taught by my parents how to let compliments as well as criticisms roll off my back. If you give me a compliment, "Thank you" and I keep walking. If you hate me, hate what I do, hate my work or writing, etc., I'll listen, figure out if it's true or not and keep walking.

Mentioning criticism, I remember a prestigious, powerful and brilliant law professor who sent me a criticism about one of my books, which I sent him gratis. I read it and kept writing. To be fair, ninety-five percent of it is complimentary and positive. And he is a *law professor* not a creative writing professor. And it helps to consider the paradigm and mindset of the person(s) who give you compliments or criticism. Read - "My biggest frustration with Manning's writing is that he needs greater discipline." He goes on to say, "*From the Palace to the Prison* does not sustain the same level of humor throughout and often slips into a lecturing tone - not evident in its best sections."

I could reply by saying, "Fool, I ain't writing comedy. These are real life/death issues. And as Bill Cosby will tell you, we need some lecturing." Or I could be glad some of the book frustrates him. And I assure you, if the press got a hold of this letter, they would *only* publish that *one* paragraph. That's three sentences out of a twenty-four-sentence letter. But I was not offended. I get e-mails from folk who *love* the book, a few who hate it and some in between. And some say, I should not ever use humor when dealing with issues of justice. But I accept the professor's criticisms and maybe he'll like this one better. For the record, here is a verbatim copy of the missive from McGeorge Law School Professor Mike Vitiello:

"*Dear Reader: I have never met Sherman Manning, but we have exchanged numerous letters. He is an avid correspondent, interested in sharing his life's story and learning about other people's stories. He tells his story in numerous books, most recently, in 'From the Palace to the Prison.' Parts of 'From the Palace to the Prison' are gripping. For example, his satire of Ken Lay is scathing. I could not tell whether I should laugh or cry when I read it. Imagine the cynicism that state criminal prisoners must feel when they watch a man like Lay, accused of cheating millions of people out of hundreds of millions of dollars, while he avoids or at least delays for years his day in court. They must ask themselves how they might have done with resources and well connected friends.*"

Then Professor Vitiello writes the three sentences about his biggest frustration, which you read a few moments ago. And he closes with this:

"At the end of the day, however, *From the Palace to the Prison* offers those of us who live staid lives insight into the challenges faced by a person facing a long prison sentence, a person with a unique point of view. Sincerely, Michael Vitiello, Professor of Law: University of the Pacific - McGeorge in Sacramento, California."

Now I kinda think it was a pretty positive endorsement. A few errors, i.e. a *long prison sentence.* I ain't got that much time left in prison or at least at the time, back when he sent me that letter, I didn't have much time remaining in prison. Perhaps he referred to the decade I served. Also, *From the Palace to the Prison* does not tell **my** *story.* If you combine every book I've written, you'd be lucky to find a total of *fifty* pages in all of them combined which deal with *my* story. I tell the stories of others.

But I thank Professor Vitiello from my heart for this mostly complimentary missive. And I will share parts of it with others. To be fair to him, I included the entire letter in this book. I also encourage all the other professors, students and readers (I know a lot of you all send me e-mails, etc. Keep them coming. But some of you all should follow the lead of Professor Vitiello and snail mail me your comments. I will use them as you can see) to write me letters telling me how you feel about my writing. At a minimum, you get to have my readers know *who* you are and what you *think*...

...Back in November, I could not believe what I laid my eyes upon. Rather, I could not believe who I saw and where. I gave a *NAPS* (National Association for Public Safety) rally at *The Potter's House* of Dallas, Texas. Attending the rally to my utter surprise was the one and only *Ashton Kutcher*. I half thought I was about to be punk'd, mooned or wedgied. You never know what is coming from Ashton. He brought along Jamie Kennedy. These guys gave riotously funny stand up comedy. They began with Ashton stating, "I came here to Dallas because I believe in *Sherman* Diahric Manning. I don't care what the police, prisons or whoever thinks of this young man. Sherman Manning is one of the most brilliant persons I know of. I've read all of his books. I read his books while he was in prison. No matter how they tried to scandalize him and heap gross vilification upon his name, he would never *quit*. He never gave up. He kept writing like O'Henry. He kept writing like Shakespeare. I think the biggest mistake the injustice system made was allowing him to go to prison. He *found himself*. He found his calling..." And then Ashton began his comedy. For fifteen minutes, he rocked the auditorium. Jamie also had me rolling.

Jake Theil (Davis, CA) Matt Kester (Hollister, MO), Dr. Chris Kaliakan and Tanuir Kapoor were there. I was glad to see Rodrigo Ojeda Beck, George Derieg, Shemm and Chris Dawes there. Tom Rundle was there with a stunning brunette. My pal, Jeffrey Frieders (Sacramento, actor), Karl Roberts and his girlfriend from Fairfax, VA, Charles Wildman (Prattville, AL), James Sooy (Dallas), Gloria Sherman, Martha Conley, Felicia Gordon, Enita Holmes and Renae Simpson were all there. I could not believe the red and white shoes that Matthew Wetherington (Climax, Georgia) had on. We had computer recruiters, i.e. John Herring, Caleb Sima and Dan Leierwood there. Jai Breish and Lisa Nielson were there... I was glad to see Zach Roerig and Michael Cardele. Mikko Hughes and Dan Parkinson, etc., Brad Lyon (Hollywood, FL), Anthony Forte and Anoop Ghanwani were in the house. Ari Zlotkin and David Hankins were there.

I gave a pep talk. I talked about child predators and how we must begin to take it seriously. I explained that folks should actually take classes on what to look for. We should get educated on how to recognize the signals and traits, etc., which suggest a child is being abused. I explained we must stop allowing our children to be afraid to tell us they are being touched and abused. Jake Phelps (Thrasher Magazine Editor) sat spellbound as I explained that we must take our kids' *beds* back. Jennifer R. Blood, Jeffrey Duvall and Irena Medavoy nodded in agreement. Kevin Agee looked perturbed as I gave the statistical data about molesters re-offending. Scott from Uncrowned.com and the bass player (my good friend…go to Uncrowned.com and take a look) were there. Dr. Bill Dorfman and Ray Krone were on the edges of their seats as I explained that the answer is *us*.

"We must take our kids back. Make them safe and protect their innocence," I stated. Dmitry Tursunov seemed to agree. Kevin Kinsella and Rick Serna applauded. "It's impossible not to see this epidemic hidden in plain sight."

I said, "We need runners like Scott Cleland, musicians like Brian Lane, Andrew Saxena, Jesse Riegal and my dear friend Eminem to sing about this epidemic. We need computer programmers like Adam Greene, Christians like Nate Smith (Winnsboro), pro bowlers like Chris Barnes, Nick Ficarra, Jason with *Life House* (www.Ironworks.com), etc. We need Ted Alexandro, Kenneth Depagter (Chicago, IL) to stand with us. My dear buddy, Chris Austad (Bellhower, CA) was there and seemed to be appalled by some of the facts. (I've no idea how to reach most of these guys, so your bloggers and crackers should let them know)."

It was actually a tough speech for me to deliver. It is extremely taxing on the emotions and stressful on the spirit to discuss an issue, which has been swept under the rug for hundreds of years in America.

But I felt that I had *to tell the truth*. I told the crowd of six thousand that, "This room should be full! This auditorium holds eight thousand people. Where are the other two thousand? We all say we love our children. We ought to be representing. We loved Willie Nesler when he was fourteen and the victim of molestation. We felt sorry for him. But that's all we did - feel. And we never thought to find out how Willie felt. Hurt, shame and pain transformed into rage. We didn't counsel him or treat him. And so he exploded and killed a man. The victim became a victimizer. Now we hate Willie!" I went on to explain, "We can't incarcerate our way out of this. We gotta deal pragmatically. *Some* pedophiles or molesters will never get cured. We must lock them up! And the seventy percent who can be helped, we must *treat* them. It may have a high price tag. But the cost won't be as high as it would if we let their perversion fester. We need to support SNAP (Survivors Network of Those Abused by Priests) and Barbara Blaine. And we need to raise awareness. I have some help... Floyd Landis, Fred Rodriguez, Dave Zabriskie, Dr. Max Testa, Levi Leipheimer, Scott Jurek and Tony Hawk are gonna do running and skateboarding workshops for NAPS. Danny Way also. At these workshops we will have counselors, psychologists and psychiatrists on hand to talk to the children and help them..."

It was a pretty good speech. I got back to my hotel at the Marriott in Dallas at 11:37 p.m. that night. I wondered what the morning newspaper would say about the event. But fortunately, I knew what http.*DashCash.Blogspot*.com and other blogs would say. They would tell the truth. The event was awesome. And my team did a terrific job of bringing so many sixteen to thirty-five year olds out to the meeting.

Chris Austad sent me an e-mail describing a modeling agency out in Bellflower, which was for sale. "Lots of people don't know you own a modeling company, Mr. Manning. But my cousin told me about it years ago. Since I know you and respect you, I thought it'd be great for you to buy this company. I..." I gave the e-mail to Gabriel Afana and asked him to send it to Peter. I was finding *little* time at that time to really be involved with my companies. I did go in to our offices twice per week whenever I was in town to read the *profit* and *loss* statements.

I told Gabriel, "I want to e-mail every pastor who has a church with more than three thousand members. I wanna send it to Joel Olsteen at Lakeshore, T. D. Jakes, Eddie Long, Creflo, Noel Jones, Bishop Charles Blake, Ulmer, Floyd Flake, Paula White and others."

Gabriel interjected, "Why pastors? Are you gonna try to steal some of their women and get them to work for your modeling company? I heard churchwomen got some good (expletive). You were down (in prison) a while so you wanna get your money (sex)."

I laughed. Wanna-be rock star Neal Carlson called and interrupted. I brushed him off with, "I'll call you back later, dude." I felt bad afterward. I knew that many powerful people get so busy, so materialistic and so caught up that we come off as arrogant. It's like we get to or near the top and develop amnesia about how we got there. We have degrees galore. Some of us got so many degrees, we forgot what they are but we *dis* people and in the process, we miss our blessing. People are important. All of us...

"Gabriel, I read an article in Ebony about the new Black spirituality and mega churches. One of the churches seats 17,505 people. Another 10,000 etc. *Five* of the mega churches seat nearly 70,000 people combined. Gabriel, why should any man in prison go months without a visit? Without so much as a letter? If these pastors preached, 'I was in prison and you visited me not' half as much as they preach Malachi and the need for tithing, we would transform prisons. Every church member ought to at least write a prisoner once per month." I told Gabe, "I don't have any problem with what kind of car the pastor drives or how much he paid for his suits. What I do care about is, does that church, which took in fifty-five million dollars in collections last year, etc., do they send books, Bibles or free tapes to prisoners? Are they reaching inside the jails, prisons and juveniles with educational grants and assistance for the least of these our brethren? The family members of inmates go to church, pay tithes and give offerings every Sunday. The family members of inmates want to ask the chairman of the deacon board and the pastors to do something for prisoners. Gabriel, if you called ninety percent of these churches and say, 'Can you help me get a lawyer. I'm innocent.' They will hang up on you.

"I'm wondering can these preachers hear and recognize the voice of God? God told Abraham to slay his first born. And Abraham was about to kill him but there was an updated memo from the CEO of Heaven. He decided not to require Abraham to kill him. He called out 'Abraham'. If Abraham didn't recognize the voice of God, he would have gone on and killed his son.

"Gabriel, I believe we are killing a lot of brothers that God does not want killed. We are killing them by neglect, by default and because we have not gotten the updated memo from Heaven. We are like the Pharisees who wanted to kill the woman in the New Testament. They wanted to stone her due to the old law, rules and traditions. But Jesus Christ of Nazareth updated the memo and said, 'He that is without sin, cast the first stone.' He did not approve of her adultery. He did not condone sin. Sin is sin and wrong is wrong. And God hates sin but he loves sinners. We still have the death penalty in this God loving country. Mr. Bush presided over more executions in Texas than any other Governor in America. We selectively read the Bible and say we believe in Thou Shall Not Kill. Yet, we do our own update and transform it to read, 'Thou shall not kill and if thou killeth, we shall (forget the commandment) kill!' We overlook all the credible statistics, which lead all penologist and criminologist to conclude that the death penalty is not a deterrent to crime. And out of our feel good politics, sound bite toughness, etc., we choose to fight murder with murder.

"Gabe, I want every pastor and parishioner to send an e-mail to the president and ask him and the senate, did they get the update from Jesus which talked about how you qualify to cast the *first* stone. Ask Mr. President how many men has he killed that didn't need to die. And I wanna know also how many people we the church, we society and we the people are killing (figuratively speaking) who didn't need to die. Are we killing them because they are a freak, a geek, a nerd, a gay, a lesbian, a square, a junky or a gang banger? Do we have a sign above our parishes, edifices and church houses saying, 'some people are welcome at the House of God' or do we say 'Everyone's welcome at the Potter's House?' If you won't let the dude in your church because he has green hair or an earring in his nose, you must not have gotten the update. Jesus said, '*Whosoever* will let him come.' Gabriel, I'm despondent about the church. Where is the church when that boy is abused, confused and has no one to talk to? Where are we now that Shasta Groene has been violated by Joseph Duncan? Will we embrace her, love her and counsel her? Or are we just gonna shout all day Sunday and forget the people's needs all day Monday?

"I wanna ask pastors to help us intervene in the penal system. I want them to get their members to write senators, congressmen and governors and demand a change. I want church folks to stop killing people who don't need to die...

"The problem with Mr. Bush, many in our senate, church members and even some preachers is that unlike Abraham, they don't recognize the voice of God. Many of them know the Bible, but even Lucifer knows the word. But Jesus said, 'My sheep know my *voice* and a stranger they will not follow.'

"You can't know his voice unless you develop a relationship with *Him*. How many brothers are we killing that don't need to die? Gabriel, I want to e-mail or text these pastors and ask them to match their members to a prisoner. To mentor them and minister to them would be ideal.

"But even if they won't visit them, at least write to them. For decades, I know personally that pastors in churches have been complaining about the lack of *men* in church. There are some churches in which the pastor is the only man in the church. But overall, women outnumber men twelve to two in church. And preachers have tried to devise failed strategies to get more men to come to church.

"Gabriel, in our e-mail I want to let pastors know that *one* of the main reasons men don't come to church is because the church does not come to them. Jesus went out and met Peter and His would-be disciples where they were. He found them fishing and said, 'Follow me are I'll make you fishers of men.'

"Look at the two million men in prisons, jails and juveniles, Gabe. Big shot preachers could reach them. If I'm in prison and you write to me consistently. If you reach out to me right in the place I'm broken, busted and disgusted. If you reach me while I'm down and out and do the work of a minister or missionary, etc., I guarantee you the minute I get out of prison, I'll be in your church.

"Gabriel, I'm telling you what I know. I just left the prison. I saw how pastors don't write to inmates. I saw hurt, void, pain and hopelessness. I saw shuffling, shiftless and angry boys trying to be men.

"I saw drunken stupor, disaster, shame and an enormous amount of pain. I was there. I know of what I speak. And I know most of those men would run straight to the doors of the church if the church would write them in the prison.

"Gabriel, since you've taken notes on what I want to say, I need you to get with Becky and Sheila... Y'all reduce my message into two hundred words or less and bring it back to me so I can approve it, please."

Back when I was still in prison, I remember the first time I made contact with Damon Dash. Some details I won't write here because you can't tell *everything*. But I will write that Damon Dash has some good people working with him and L. A. Reid. I salute John Bartleson who is his vice president of digital sales and media. John is bright, gregarious, down to earth, a scholar and a gentleman. To John, I say *thank you...*

DiGol J'Beily and those students at Center High School proved the potency, which can be garnered, channeled and directed when students, parents, teachers and preachers join together the fingers of diversity and work together for a cause. DiGol J'Beily would not be coaching football again at Center if those good folks had not come together...

I lost Jeremy Shackelford and Lord knows that hurts. I then lost Paul Shackelford to perhaps the wrath and corruption of the CCPOA. But I won't despair or quit.

Every three seconds a child dies in Africa from poverty, HIV-AIDS and hunger. Mahatma Ghandi said, "poverty is the worst kind of violence." So I commend Brad Pitt, Ricky Martin, Heidi Fugames and Oprah for what they are doing for the hurting across the waters. I also commend Bon Jovi, Bono, Bob Geldof, Stevie Wonder and all the other Live 8 Performers.

As an aside, I also salute Oprah for what the Angel Network does right here on the bullet-ridden streets of America. I.e., "Never in Your Wildest Dreams." Did ya'll see that woman (Bernadette) in Chicago who rose early and worked late at Starbucks in Chicago trying to provide for nine children? Bernadette represents millions of mothers all across America who struggle to make ends meet. Oprah bought her kids fifteen thousand dollars in toys. Oprah (and my pal, Nate Berkus...may his partner rest in peace) bought her a house full of furniture. Oprah bought her a house!! Oprah... (just go to Oprah.com and check out "Never in Your Wildest Dreams" episode).

It's time for us to fight for the protection of our children. I need Andrew Davis, my pal, Garitt Mathews (Fair Oaks, CA) and Matt Matteucci to come together and help save young America. I need *Push America* and every college club, fraternity and sorority to help us *create safe beds* for our children.

We can do this. I'm more convinced than ever that we can. Will you commit today? Where there is a will there is a way. We don't have a child to lose - no not one. I hope to God I've done Jeremy (rest in peace) and Paul proud. I gave it my best and my all in all. No better way to climax than with the real life words of judge (pseudonym by request) Robert Altman in Minnesota...

"I'm the Honorable Judge Robert Altman and Mr. *Joseph Edward Duncan*, III, you've been charged with molesting a six-year-old boy on March 16, 2005. How do you plead?"

Mr. Duncan stated, "Not guilty, Your Honor."

The judge asked, "What's the people's position on bail?"

Prosecutor Gloria Allred stated, "No bail, Your Honor."

Judge Altman stated, "I'm going to grant bail in the amount of fifteen thousand dollars. Next case."

Gloria Allred was livid. But she's always livid.

Just 2 ½ months later in Coeur d'Alene, Idaho, there was an entire family bludgeoned to death. It was a quadruple homicide too graphic to describe. But there were two kids missing from the scene of the crime. "I wonder what happened to nine-year-old Shasta Groene and her brother Dylan," Detective Roberto said to himself as he stepped on a lit cigarette. He turned his foot in a half spin to extinguish the Marlboro as he trotted back to his Crown Victoria. For six weeks the authorities had nothing. Pictures of little Shasta and Dylan were plastered all over the country. For six weeks there were no strong leads. And then over the Fourth of July weekend, a 911 call was placed in Coeur d'Alene. "I'm Linda at Denny's Restaurant and there is a tall gentleman in our restaurant with a little girl who looks just like Shasta."

Two hours later, Shasta Groene was in the hospital being examined and Joseph Edward Duncan, III was in the county jail. Why he chose to bring Shasta to a Denny's in her hometown nobody knows. Perhaps a part of him wanted to be caught.

Earl Ofari Hutchinson wrote a scathing column on the case. So did Pulitzer Prize winning columnist Leon Pitts. Montel Williams stated, "How and why was this man out of jail? Duncan did fifteen years in prison for molesting a child at gunpoint. When Judge Altman gave him a fifteen thousand dollar bail, he committed murder and molestation; the Judge did. That woman out in San Jose who faked finding a finger in her chili? When they locked her up for fraud, they gave her no bail. *No Bail*! A few weeks later a judge granted bail in the amount of half a million dollars. She had *no* criminal record whatsoever. And she was not accused of any violent crime. Why give her a half a million-dollar bail, yet Altman let Duncan out on a fifteen thousand dollars bail.

"I am lost. I don't get it. If that judge had done his job, we would not be here today. Shasta would not have been raped. Her family would not have been tied up and killed like cattle. The judge dropped the damned ball, I'm telling you. And society also dropped the damned ball. We can't stand for this any longer. Joseph apparently killed the rest of the family and kept Shasta and Dylan so he could abuse and molest them. Took them to a campsite and repeatedly molested little Dylan and Shasta. What did we do for this animal for fifteen years in the prison? Let's pull his prison record and see how much sex therapy he received in prison? How much therapy while he served this sentence. The answer is *none*; zero. We keep thinking that if we just lock them up, they'll get better. It's preposterous. He got worse. He saved kiddie porn in prison and he would masturbate to commercials showing babies with no pamper on. He got worse. And nobody said anything and nobody did a damned thing. I want to call Judge Robert Altman and tell him he is guilty of being an accessory to murders and molestation. Back after this commercial." As they went to a commercial break, Montel broke down and cried. He was angry and sad.

After the break, he said, "And we have with us today, Professor Karen J. Terry who is an Associate Professor at John Jay College of criminal justice here in New York City. She wrote the National Report on the scope of child sexual abuse in the Catholic Church as well as the book, 'Sexual Offenses and Offenders: Theory, Practice and Policy.'

"Professor Terry, we are all outraged, angry, livid, concerned and disturbed but none of those emotions create change or help stop child molestation. What has America been doing wrong? Tell us what we need to know."

Professor K. J. Terry replied, "Thank you, Montel. Hatred of child molesters is inevitable when we hear about victims like Jessica Lunsford, the nine-year-old Florida girl sexually abused and buried alive by a convicted sex offender. Cases like Lunsford generate such outrage that we cry for justice, Montel. Citizens tell politicians to pass stricter laws and this is how we get so many new and diverse laws.

"These laws fail miserably at protecting our children. Education is required in order to develop informed policy. As it relates to child molesters, most politicians don't have a clue. They write and implement laws based on hype, media coverage, raw emotions and unfortunately, to get re-elected.

"Sex offenders constitute a heterogeneous population of people. Sex offenders encompass people as disparate as an exhibitionist, a violent rapist, and a nineteen-year-old high school senior who has sex with his fifteen-year-old girlfriend, a sports coach who abuses hundreds of kids in his care and a mom who sexually abuses her son.

"Montel, most convicted sex offenders don't attack strangers. More than seventy-five percent of adult victims know their attackers and more than ninety percent of child victims know or are related to those who molest them. By and large, sex offenders reside in the community, not jail, not prison, and (*most field agents in charge of supervising them have little or no specialized knowledge about this population and few resources to monitor them thoroughly. Sex offender treatment can and does reduce recidivism for most sexual offenders.*) Blanket policies implemented after a high profile case don't work."

Montel interjected, "I hear you and pragmatically what you're saying makes a lot of sense. So some of these laws we are passing are basically backfiring and driving offenders underground. And if you're a homeless molester, you can't register any way right?"

Professor Terry replied, "Exactly. Treatment is where we need to be leaning. And we must stop just reacting to a horrible tragedy in the news, i.e., you could use Joseph Duncan to argue that treatment does *not* work. But on closer scrutiny you'd find that A. He *dropped* out of treatment. If cops and courts had done their jobs, he would have been re-incarcerated the very second he dropped out. B. The treatment program he was attending was *shut down* because it proved to be an ineffective program. And many programs work. Many offenders stop offending. Montel, this may get me in trouble, but I stand by this statement: Most effective programs are too expensive for the average poor offender. And the states are unwilling to pay for real expert treatment. Therefore, the true story is that the biggest kept secret is the fact that thousands of potential molesters, molesters, potential pedophiles and pedophiles get successful treatment each and every year.

"These people are physicians and their children, judges, lawyers and even CEOs. Their treatment is top notch, well guarded, private and secretive. You never hear about it in the press. Perhaps bloggers will begin to dig up the client and patient rolls of some of these expensive sex experts such as Dr. David Israel. You'd be surprised. You would be floored. There is a White House employee presently undergoing sexual offender treatment."

Montel said, "You're kidding me."

Professor Terry said, "I'm not... treatment is not a panacea; it doesn't cure sex offenders anymore than alcoholic anonymous cures alcoholism. And some alcoholics get in cars and drive recklessly and kill people. We don't argue that the alcoholics anonymous program is ineffective. We rather recognize that not all are committed to the program. But treatment does give offenders tools to address the root of their problems, identify high-risk situations and better manage their behavior."

Montel stated, "We have got to do something about this. As far as I'm concerned, the blood of four people, including Dylan Groene is on that judge's hands who gave this predator a fifteen thousand dollar bail. That is sickening. That judge should be thrown in jail. And Professor Terry, I understand exactly what you are saying. It's time for us to come out of *denial*. None of us wants to admit that anyone who rapes a child is *sick*. It's a disease. It's like we feel that if we use terminology like *sickness*, it implies it's not a criminal act. We are afraid people are gonna think we are soft on crime, etc. I still think child molesters ought to be put away for a long time and I believe we *must*, we must pay the price to treat them for their sickness and perversion while we punish them.

"But the availability of top notch treatment must be inclusive and not exclusive. It must be universally available. And the more we learn how to identify the signals of a potential pedophile, the more we can move in and treat them *before* they molest a child. The more we learn to counsel the victims of abuse, the more we will be able to stop the

342

vicious cycle in its tracks. We have got to break the cycle. Shasta Groene needs our help. Our rage, anger, hurt and reactionary law making won't save Shasta. What will save this beautiful little girl is if we, the taxpayers, rally around her. She must be counseled. And we must pay for it. She may look alright and act alright for a long time. I'm already seeing interviews where they say she's *strong* and she's handling it well and all that, but that's crap. That little girl is traumatized. Her mother is dead and her brothers are dead. You can't watch three members of your family murdered and tied up. You can't be driven to Montana and watch your only surviving sibling, Dylan, get molested over and over and then killed. And get molested yourself and be okay. She's not okay. And she is worth saving. Whatever the cost, we need to make certain she is in treatment.

And if that judge who gave this monster that fifteen thousand dollar bail is watching," Montel looked directly into the camera with tears rolling down his cheeks. His right hand was balled into a fist. He was shaking. "Judge, you are a murderer. Judge, the Groene family's blood is on *your* hands. Shasta's trauma is on *your* hands, judge. If you're any kind of man with any kind of dignity, respect and a conscience, you should *resign*. If you don't resign, I hope they start a petition to recall your butt. Put it up on the Internet and let millions sign it. We've held up picket signs protesting the release of molesters coming out of prison. We protect their moving into our neighborhoods. I say we should protest *Your Honor* for contributing to the murder of four people and the molestation of at least two..."

* * *

...Thanks to C.D.C. and their inadequate, abusive staff, we're able to include a few more pages. After years of prison, this author (*Sherman D. Manning*) has received over twenty thousand dollars in bank (cashier's) checks from my (Sherman's) account in Switzerland. Yet, staff continues to play games with my money and mail. Perhaps they want me to insert thousands of dollars in lump sums into my prison account (as I used to) so they can draw interest on my money. My last check was mailed to the prison on 6/13/05. C.D.C. did not put it into my account until 7/6/05. It will be held for twenty days before I can spend it. Ipso facto, the money can't be used by me until 7/26/05. It's 7/20/05 and rather than being fair and pragmatic and charging against my bank check for postage, they rejected *this* manuscript and refused to mail it. I must wait six days. Foolish? Unfair? I agree. But on further contemplation, I'll consider it a blessing. *God* sent it back to me so I could inform you about it. And I can reiterate some issues with you. These few pages which I'm adding due to the foolishness of petty staff may save a life, change a mind, lift some spirits or help somebody to get it together.

Perhaps the dates, etc., shall confuse you. And you'll recall I'm *not* a typical writer. I have some Teri Woods, Tina, Patricia Cornwell and James Patterson down inside of me.

I write like an idiot, madman and a fool. But it's Generation Y and Generation X, I'm writing to and for. And *we* don't look for structure, set forms and antiquated composition. We look for power, conviction and realism. Damn, I'm glad they sent this *back to me*.

Perhaps a hundred readers should call Mule Creek State Prison or e-mail them and tell the mailroom, "Thank you." I'll send a shout out to Mr. Hoang (L.A., CA), Renae Gonzalez in Hollywood and (again) to *Neal Carlson*. Neal Carlson did not make the INXS cut but he's okay. I want you all to send text messages to Craig's List and tell Neal Carlson we have a job for him at A&M. He should e-mail us at once. (On the spinoff of American Idol? The Dancing Show, which appeared on 7/20/05... Craig? Craig wearing *no shirt*...y'all tell Craig to e-mail us). Go to Rockstar.msn.com and find Neal Carlson today... and find Dominic Sophia, The Hip Hop Dancer) send your shout.

I hope Doug Pieper (Folsom, CA) gets this book. I believe in cross promotions and shout to Joshua Bandez who owns *Easy Bands*. We thank Tim Farriss and Conrad Riggs for all of their input and help. I'm looking for some sons and daughters, who will stand up, square their shoulders and fight for our children. I'm looking for a gathering together of geeks, freaks, nerds, weirdoes and ex-cons who wanna make a difference. I need some people in my corner who will stand with me as I stand up against pedophilia, rape, murder and the victimization of our younger generation. I need some positive minded, optimistic thinking folks in schools, colleges and prisons who want to make a difference. I want people who will look up and stand up and pick somebody else up.

The time has come. I'm ready to *take action.* I wanna kick ass and take names later. I wanna throw down, baby boy and baby girl. I need Dan Crane, Wil Seabrooks, Neal Carlson, Anthony Fedorov, Zach Weary, Michael Cardinale, Mr. Roerig (L.A.) and Steven Cozza to stand with us. I need U. C. Fresno student leaders like Roberto Vaca, John Welty, Chancellor Charles B. Reed and Asim Hussain (Leeds - England) to stand with us. I'm calling Matt Cedero (Moses Village Washington) to get on the good foot... Former Appeals Court Judge John Fitzgerald Malloy, wrote a new book... "The Fraternity" that all y'all need to read. I want Farah Joy (Sacramento), Douglas

Hicks, Little Jacob Monroe (Oakdale, CA) and Nathan Craft to join with us. If we don't/won't do it, who will?

Read the newspaper and look on the Internet... *Jeremy Shackelford*, Paul and Scott were not embellishing the story. Our children are being molested daily. Every three minutes in America a child is molested. Must I repeat? I'm sorry it's uncomfortable to talk, write and read about. I'd rather be writing about William Hung or Shemm or somebody. It takes a lot to write about such a horrible subject. But I'm inviting my mentors and pals - James Patterson, John Grisham, Lisa Scottoline, Robert James Waller, Kevin Henkes, Walter Dean Meyers and *you* to write (DashCash.blogspot.com) some suggestions for solutions to these problems.

I want us to solve this mess together. We must be open, receptive and pragmatic. It's not about lock em up and throw away the key. *That* can only happen *after* the crime. The cameras flash and the presses roll and we all applaud having arrested another molester. But we forget this means *another* victim. And we can't think long term and realize that the *victim* will more than likely become a victimizer. If we want to change the *fruit*, we must get to the root. We can't get corn out of a tomato seed. We must look at the seeds of rape, molesters and pedophiles. And once we understand pedophiles, perversion, diseased sexuality, etc., we can prevent it. In order to stop producing Willie Neslers, we must stop allowing Joseph Duncans. We must *stop child molestation*. Pastors, teachers, lawyers and doctors gotta come together and deal *with the root*. I want you to bombard the switchboard at the White House, the senate, talk shows and your legislators and demand a *change*. Tell them we want prevention... Again - thank my captors *for this input*...

And I also thank Tony Moxham. Tony Moxham (Interview Magazine) has been really cool in getting me connected to all of my readers worldwide. Jonathan Farley, Anthony Harkin, Ryan Adams and Jonathan Safran Foer were all introduced to my writing by Moxham. Tony took his own time and wrote e-mails to these guys and went on Zabasearin.com and told thirty of them, "You are in Sherman's book, *From the Palace to the Prison*." I hope Garitt Matthews, Matt Matteucci and Stefan Wolpert hear about this (tome) beacon call. I want all the students at the John's Hopkins University Center for talented youth to hear about this tome.

Nicholas Eilerman called my *NAPS* assistant a week ago and said, "I wanna get involved with *NAPS*." Tom Massimo sent me a letter encouraging me to keep *NAPS* going and growing.

Erin Runnion was livid on Friday, July 22nd when her daughter's (Samantha's) murderer received the death penalty. Unless you have lost a child you can't even begin to understand her pain. She said a lot. I didn't agree with her saying she hopes *no one* will pray for this guy. That statement does not line up with the word of God. Having written that, I still send my thoughts, prayers, hopes, condolences and regards to Erin and her family. The media had forgotten Erin. We tend to forget about pain and tragedy as we move on to the next story. But I know Erin will never ever forget what this monster did to her child. There was a line in what she said, which I thought was awesome, powerful and deserves to be heard and acted upon. (But knowing the weak kneed media, i.e., Matt (Bush loving) Lauer and Rush Limbaugh, the drug addict... They will gloss over Erin's words). Erin said she wanted her daughter's killer to spend the rest of his life in prison and *think.* Think about what he did to little Samantha and "Write it down." She wants him to write it down so *we can study monsters like you and Stop*...people from doing such evil as that.

To that, I should only add, *Amen*, Hallelujah and I agree. That is why I support all kids, prisoners, juveniles, crooks, cons, etc., being able to write. This is why I stood firmly against the *Son of Sam* Law until the State Supreme Court in California overturned it. Because I want to hear what all people have to say, and if Jeffrey Dahmer had had a blog, podcast or a book out three or four years before he killed and ate seventeen boys and men, we might have been able to stop him. If that bastard, Justin Weinberger, had a blog telling us his peculiarities, perhaps we could have prevented him from molesting and murdering twelve-year-old Courtney Sconce...so I reiterate (here and now) the fact that I believe forcefully and adamantly in free speech and artistic expression. And I want all pragmatic thinking citizens to encourage folks to write. If they are sinister, wicked and evil like Justin, Joseph Duncan, etc., etc., we will feel it, see it, read it and have a shot at maybe being able to prevent it. There is a great young lady named Jamie Miller in Rancho Cordova (second opinion) who does a podcast, which is great. And if Jamie Miller (Casey Ryle...an iPod/skateboarding owner in Rancho Cordova) knew about Justin's proclivities, she could have alerted us and perhaps prevented a murder.

I love free speech and I love technology. And the more technologically savvy we become the more of us like Jeremy Hunt, Casey Ryle, James Doan (great man in Davis, CA), Dr. Firpo Carr, Larry Pozner, Ross Kelles, Robert Dreyfuss, Abdullah Higazy, Jorge Hernandez, Chris Hillman (Chris is a student at Arizona State University), college (Sacto...CSU?) student Jason Wong and actor

Luke McFarlane will hear, read, take note and pay attention. I encourage Barry Diller (IAC/AskJeeves CEO) billionaire to continue to be innovative, daring and to visualize the success of technological advances and developments. And I encourage Chris Hillman, Wil Seabrooks, Gerard Way and *you* to help us create *safe beds* for kids by logging on and participating in discussions and surveys on how to make our kids safe.

May I remind *you*, I would not have been able to include this writing had not it been for the pettiness and foolishness of my captors - C.D.C.

They are like cow *manure* around my feet. They stink and they are low but they help me to *grow*. I hate the way they (the manure) smell but I love the way they cause me to excel. They propel me into my destiny. They are vicious and malicious. And they keep me praying and prayer changes things. Yes, it really, really does. So I encourage Riley Evans, Anthony Fedorov, Chris Hillman, Zach Weary and *you* to continue to fully utilize and completely exercise your right to free speech and artistic expression.

The very reason I insert unusual, unique and unheard of interactive suggestions and challenges in this book is simple. I wanna Rock the World! I wanna be heard! I wanna *hear you*! I wanna reach, honor, help, represent and connect with people who never thought they would hear from me. I want folks who never, ever expected to see their name in a book to stumble upon their name herein and to be proud. I wanna hear stories like - "I was getting ready to go screw and Daniel Asare sent me an e-mail saying, dude you're in a new book, *Blue-Eyed Blonde*. You can get the E-book immediately if you go to www.Cafepress.com/Manning. I went and it was hella cool to see my name in the book."

Yes, yes, I salute George Hincapie, Danny Way, Robin Roberts, Jamie Foxx, Denzel and all y'all who are already doing something to help. And I don't want none of y'all to *trust me*. It is not about you *elevating* me on some type of platform or giving me *status*. That I don't deserve. Use me like you use your car or the bus. When you are on the bus, you don't even think about the damned bus. You don't spend time engaged in useless discussions about the bus. You *use* it. Use the bus to get where you are going. You need not call anybody and brag about what a great bus you're on. You don't spend time analyzing the bus, you just ride it. My books? Just read it, baby boy! Get what you can use out of it and keep the line moving. Don't give me a second thought. I am not the issue, problem, solution or concern. Let **me** be the bus. If I start going somewhere you don't wanna be or go to, just don't get off at that location *or* get off the bus. No pun intended.

But don't waste one single minute of your valuable time discussing this author... *If, if* somebody in the traditional media begins to discuss me negatively, tell em to kiss my ass and *you* (the reader) move on. If we find out James Patterson picks his nose while he writes his books, it won't affect *us* reading it. I'll still enjoy Detective Alex Cross. *If* we find out Oprah farts twice before every commercial, it won't stop me. I still love Oprah. Rush Limbaugh? Rush (allegedly) is a freak! Rush is (supposedly - I'm not certain) a fat, lying, dope smoking, pill popping, undercover homosexual. Rumor has it Rush Limbaugh literally came on to Larry King. Rumor has it Rush and Sean Hannity are sexually active. Now if Rush decides to slam me on his show, don't y'all defend *me*. Defend the book.

The *book* not the author. I don't need defending and I assure you if the media brings me up, it will be sensational, false, innuendo and it will be shit the D.A. (supposedly District Attorney, but D.A. stands for Dumb Ass - ask Tom Sneddon) had told them.

They never wrote or said positive things about Rubin "Hurricane" Carter while he was in prison, not *before*, *during* or even *after* he wrote his book, "The Sixteenth Round". They don't do that. They can't write or speak about us unless we are the *rapist*, the *murderer*, the *predator*, the bad man... So don't even think Matt Lauer or Katie Couric, etc., etc., are gonna jump on TV and say something *nice* about me. Forget it. But I ain't writing for their biased, fickle or corporate sponsored asses. I'm writing for wards of the state, victims of rape, movers, shakers and those who wanna make a difference. And I've given all y'all (tinkerers, podcasters, bloggers, etc., etc.) your props and recognition in *this* book. Now you get on your blog or podcast Mr. Curry, Jonah Perati, Jamie Miller, etc. and quid pro quo it. Give it up (not for me) for the freaking tome *Blue-Eyed Blonde*.

Traci McCarthy does care about our children. I'll betcha if Anthony Fedorov, Tim Goebel or Johnny Weir *knew* they could save the life, innocence or chastity of a child by something they learned in a book, they would *read the book*. So I treasure this opportunity to bring to you the words of Jeremy, Paul, Scott and others, which can make a difference. I don't give a flying flip about what Limbaugh, Karl Rove or Pat Buchanon may think of me as a person. I want to stand up and put my *mind* on the dotted line to help make the world safe.

I've been walking by myself for quite a while. I've been dipping, dodging and surviving amongst dysfunctional and failing humans for a good while now. I have observed the characteristics, traits and behaviors of the sick and perverted dregs who prey on our children. I've watched up close and uncomfortably, the walk, talk, swagger, strut and the body language of abusive and violent persons trapped in the university of crime. I've noticed some common threads which are A-typical to vicious persons. Some of what I've learned is scientific and systemic. Some is not black and white but gray. And I'm still learning. But what I do know is we are in *Code-Red*. What I do know is the *house of cards* is falling. What I do know is that while you've been reading this page and contemplating these words there is a *priest* molesting an altar boy. There is a *man* online this very moment trying to seduce a twelve-year-old little girl as a paramour in some type sexual tryst.

It is abnormal. It is evil. It is wicked and just flat wrong. And we won't prevent it if we don't acknowledge it. We can't acknowledge it unless we talk, blog, podcast, write and think about it.

So I am looking for boys and girls who know somebody who weirds you out. I want that kid to go to mommy or daddy and talk about it. I'm looking for that sixteen or seventeen-year-old boy or girl who was touched inappropriately or molested a couple of years ago by a teacher, coach, pastor, uncle, aunt or whoever, to report it. I want you to come out from under your fear, shame, hurt and confusion and talk about it therapeutically. Talk to a counselor, officer, parent or to your homeroom teacher.

I want citizens of all stripes, persuasions, colors and ages to go on to *Dashcash.blogspot.com* and write suggestions on what we can do as a society to prevent the next Dylan Groene, Samantha Runnion, Courtney Sconce, etc., etc. I want to know what you feel we must do to embrace, console and counsel Elizabeth Smart and Shasta Groene to keep them out of denial, shame, hurt and pain. I want solutions. We'll be racist, biased, bigoted and petty later on. But for now, we must save our children. We must rise up and *take our children back*. For this moment in time, for this day, we're got to find, discover and to invent a way out of no way. We can't let Shasta sit around and act like she's okay while we fart in the wind. We've got to come out of our denial and deal with the fact that there is more than *meets the eyes*.

We looked into the eyes of that Catholic priest and thought he was a holy father, but never suspected him of being a prolific child molester. We heard the booming voice of Rush *fat ass* Limbaugh and never imagined this conservative pundit was coming into our homes over live radio while high, low or sedated on drugs.

We watched denial upon denial, upon denial from the White House about the Big Leak (*the big lie*) of the name of CIA operative

349

Valerie P... Joe Wilson's wife and found out later the denials were orchestrated by the architect himself, Karl Rove. We have lost too many boys and girls to scout leaders who were civic leaders by day and child predators by night. We could not see it *in their eyes*. Had it been that easy, we would have treated them before their first victim. We would have kept Dylan, his mom, her boyfriend and others alive. We don't *know* them by their eyes. So we must learn to read, identify and prevent them by *our* actions.

We must utilize the information superhighway, *Big Brother* and even little sister to *stop* child abuse. And no matter how much disdain we like to have concerning those trapped in our prisons, we must admit that they are a part of the solution.

The priest molesting the altar boy now (while you are reading this) is not an ex-con. So prisoners are not the immediate problem. On the flip side of that very same issue, the teenaged boy we send to prison for some petty offense, will get raped, abused and beat in prison. So by the time he gets out he will have been transmogrified from a weed smoker, conman, dope seller or burglar into a pervert, rapist or molester... When we *place non-violent* or semi-violent offenders in the prisons, on the yards and in the cells with rapists, molesters and killers - it rubs off. Association does (quite often) bring about assimilation. Bring a sixteen, seventeen or eighteen-year-old thief, burglar or armed robber to a California prison and give him five years, I guarantee you that more than eighty percent of them will be violent, perverted and wicked when they get out. And they do get out to the tune of seven hundred thousand per year...

Solution? Transform the way we sentence people to prison, where we send them and what we do to them when they get there.

Solution? Get your ass on to Dashcash.blogspot.com and download it and send it to your governor.

Solution? Send your elected officials copies of this book!

Solution? Organize a *NAPS* Chapter in your neighborhood.

Solution? Start a *safe beds* program or neighborhood watch in your city.

Solution? Get your ass off the sidewalk and step *away* from the door of that registered sex offender who just moved to your neighborhood. Redirect that energy in to teaching your child how to survive in a dangerous world. Redirect that energy into watching that molester. Help the fool get a job. Drive him to his treatment program. Give him a lift to his probation appointment and never leave him *alone* with your child.

How about that?...

350

Are you sitting on a chair? Couch? Bed? Until or before I mentioned it (be honest) how much time did you spend thinking about the chair (or couch, etc.) you're sitting on! Probably none recently. You just *use* the seat to sit on in order to get what you need. It's a tool or stool which you're using to do what you're doing, i.e. read this book. If it's comfortable (and according to Becky it is very comfortable if you're Timothy Goebel, Johnny Weir, Fedorov, Carlson, Aiken or Seabrooks cause, "They got major buns!") and if you're J. Lo or Destiny's Child, we know you're quite cushiony; the chair is an afterthought. The chair is irrelevant... Again use **me** as the chair. I'm just a tool, stool or vehicle leading to information, discussion, dialogue and hopefully change. Don't endorse *me*. Find something in this book, which *you* can join, do, start, hone, create or develop which may save a child. And if it works, give God the praise and keep doing it. Don't nominate *me* for a humanitarian award. Let *me* be an after thought. Give Jeremy, Paul, Scott, etc., the credit for the greatness of this book. I'm just an editor of sorts.

I hope R. Kelly is not a rapist. I really hope it's all a big mistake. And if R. Kelly or even S. Kelly is a rapist, he needs treatment, therapy and he needs to go to prison; period! And guess what? When I listen to R. Kelly sing, "I Wish", I use it. It sounds good to me. I like it. It brings back memories and visions. And if R. Kelly was doing life in prison, I'd still like the song and his music. And how many folk's music do ya'll listen to who are dead? Their status, aliveness or death, etc., doesn't really affect how good or bad they sing.

Ipso facto, *if* I'm in prison when you read this. If I'm dead, alive and in Switzerland, on a yacht, singing a song, preaching a sermon or giving a speech, it don't matter. What does matter is what happens *inside you* while you read it...

If your pastor is a crook don't worry. Be not deceived, God *ain't* mocked; your pastor will *reap* what he sows. And if his sermon sends you back to the Word or God, back on your knees to pray to God, you'll get blessed. If you make the mistake of worshiping *man*, you'll get wrecked. You gotta learn how to *lift up your eyes* to the hills from whence cometh your help. And if Bono, Marilyn Manson, Carrie Underwood or Fantasia sings a song, which leads you to *look up to the hills* and see *God* and not man - you'll succeed.

So I'm not certain *what* Oprah, Montel, Tavis Smiley or Tony Danza will do, say or think about me. They're probably unwilling to rubberstamp me. I don't *blame* them. I really don't. But Lord have mercy if they endorse some of the stuff in this book... Good God if Oprah says, "Y'all oughta read *Blue-Eyed Blonde*. A. It would be unprecedented and surreal. B. It would motivate other prisoners, teens and unknowns to write. C. It would accomplish what Erin Runnion wanted.

Some molesters, killers and thugs would start writing and we'd be able to figure them out. Some will *claim* they're innocent. Some will *be* innocent. But that goes with the territory. But overall, when we profile, examine, dissect and analyze their writing, we will gain...

They won't outsmart us all. I say *write on - right on*! Forget the chair per se. Just sit down and rest your legs... while you read and take heed... Tell y'all again, the good Lord works in mysterious ways and His mercy endures forever. I don't know why you are reading this book. You may have never ever heard of me. Why are you reading it? Why? Perhaps you think you know why you're sitting there holding your Capuccino, Expresso, Coca Cola or glass of Scotch reading this. You may just be reading it for the monetary offers and contests which you heard about online. Perhaps a Michael Jackson fan, a Green Day, Nine Inch Nails or Maroon 5 fan club Website mentioned this book and that's why you picked it up. But nothing just happens. Iyanla Vanzant was right when she said, "You are exactly where you're supposed to be and when you learn what you're supposed to learn, you'll move on."

Little Lesra Martin was only sixteen years old when he *learned how to read*. And the *first book* he read was by Rubin "Hurricane" Carter. "That book *chose me*," Lesra said. And Lesra and those Canadians moved to America, moved to the damned town where the prison was, to *get* Rubin out... After seeing a Black man wrongly convicted of killing three White people and spending twenty years in prison, you might think Lesra would wanna be a defense lawyer. Instead he became a prosecutor. We need good prosecutors and there are many. Lesra did what he was supposed to do. And at this very moment, *this book* is what you're supposed to do. If *Interscope* wants to sue me (they know what I mean) so be it but I am *supposed* to do this! And I get tired of dealing with people who think life just *happens*. They don't understand the universe has a *plan* for your life. Nothing just happens. There is a reason you're here and you can *save* lives. But you gotta believe, work, study, pray and take action. You are all up in this book because there is something *here* for *you*. It is not *me*. It's your role, your job, your input, your place, etc., that you will find as you read this... I'm tired of traditional people doing traditional bullshit. I'm worn out and fed up with soothsayers, prophets of doom and critics. Obviously, what we have been doing is not working. My friend's listen to me; *read* closely: *We* have locked up an entire generation of people. *We* have come to a point where we will lock up eight, nine, ten and eleven-year-old girls for throwing a rock. *We* arrest and handcuff seven-year-old girls for being unruly in school. We take babies' fathers and wives' husbands away from them for twenty-five years to *life* for stealing a loaf of bread under our three strikes laws. And although we have more people in juveniles, jails and prisons in America than any other country on the planet, we still have not seen a major decrease in violent crimes. We still have not protected the children. We still leave them behind to get molested, abused and denied. We spent three hundred billion dollars fighting dual wars in Afghanistan and Iraq and still have not found Osama...

But we won't spend the money to *fix* our prisons, *fix* our jails, *fix* our juveniles and *fix* our neighborhoods. Why do we see *homeless* people dying in Phoenix because of heat exhaustion? Why do we have sweltering poverty and crime-ridden streets? Why are we trying to stop terrorist from being bred and trained in Iraq but we allow terrorists to be trained in jails and prisons everyday in America? Racism is terrorism. Poverty is terrorism. When you molest a child, that is terrorism. It wrecks lives and begins a cycle of dysfunction! When you commit rape, murder and randomly just drive along and kill somebody because they are wearing a certain color; that is terrorism! But we let George Bush look us in the face and never mention it.

We allowed three or four presidential debates in 2004 which never mentioned prisons, jails, youth crime, poverty or education.

So I think it's *safe* to say George Bush is not going to save the children. I need to find some weirdoes who are not traditional. I need to discover a freaking team of frat brothers, sorority gals, teens and seniors, convicts, ex-convicts, lawyers, law students, physicians and citizens who are willing to take up their cause with fire in their belly and fight. I want some ordinary people with extraordinary ideas who are willing to *step into the light* and be heard. I want some teens willing to start their own reading club, poetry team, think tank, newspaper, action coalition and *do something* for others.

I want some survivors with unusual ideas and great faith to get online and blog about it. Did you know there are two billion (yes with a B) text messages sent every month in America? I'd like to see two hundred million of those become motivational, educational and inspirational. As we stated, our traditional stuff ain't working. If we continue to trust our fate to Mr. Bush, Karl Rove, Slick Tricky Dick Cheney and others, we will continue to fail miserably on the social and domestic front. So I say forget traditions, customs and the norms. We gotta try any and everything to save our children. We need you. We need him, her, them and all of us who care, to put the pedal to the metal and accelerate our efforts to change.

I told you that *nothing* just happens. I met the late Rev. Hosea Williams when I was supposed to meet him. I met former Ambassador Andrew Young when it was time for me to meet him. I met Jesse Jackson when I was supposed to meet him.

I met James Emslander, Leroy Elliott, Jasper Williams, Thomas Dexter Jakes, Debbie and Marva when I was supposed to meet them. People come into your life for a reason, a season or a lifetime. There is a reason for every season. And even though it sounds like a cliché, baby girl, God really, really, really does know what is best for you and for me.

Mike Doyle promised to do a story on one of my tomes months ago. To date, to my knowledge he has not done it. *Craig Dogface* Bone Boy at 98 Rock interviewed me telephonically numerous times before he got the tome. He has not followed up. Why? I don't know. Frankly, *I don't care*. I have learned to trust the universe. Maybe, I could be wrong, but maybe God knew I was not ready.

Had I gotten tons of attention and accolades, I wouldn't be writing this and you wouldn't be reading this. I won't ever try to explain it in more details but for the two or three hundred folks who were supposed to comprehend it; *you* got it. This book needed to be written. I had to write it for Lydia Rupp (I hope she's okay) and her mother… At the time of this writing there is an *Amber* Alert for Lydia. Apparently her mother's roommate has kidnapped her. Damn! Lydia has a good mother and this writing does not seek to scandalize her mother. It does seek to educate *us*.

Lydia's mom *met* this dude at a *church*. A church service a few months ago. Fernando P. Aguerro is a sex offender. But perverts go to church also. Perverts sing in the choir, serve on the deacon board, pastor churches, lead synagogues, teach schools preside over courtrooms and wear badges also. Perverts are mayors in big cities, etc., also. And so when she met Fernando at church, she thought it was appropriate to let him move in with her. And she let him baby-sit eight-year-old Lydia. I hope you got the message. Just as I told you not to trust *me*; don't trust the judge or the priest either. To stop child molestation, you must stop trusting people - period.

I'm sorry but that is where we are. And you can only trust **God**. I trust Him and the proof of Him deserving my full faith is in the pudding of the *tome* you're holding in your little White, pale, Black or Brown hands right now. I would not have been able to use Lydia and point out her mom's mistake had C.D.C. not been petty last week (as I told you earlier) and returned this manuscript to me. I told you petty staff in the prisons are the *wind* beneath my wings or the damned manure beneath my feet. They may stink! They may be corrupt, mean and evil upon me but God will take everything, which your enemies try to use against you and make it work *for* you. Paul said all things worketh together for good for them that love God. And even though you're sitting in that prison, even though you are sitting in that classroom, juvenile, library, café, lunchroom or wherever you are, it didn't say all things look good, feel good or seem good. But they work out for good. When you are working out, your muscles ache but it's working to strengthen you. And y'all fellas at Howard, U. C. Davis, CSU, Morehouse, Notre Dame or Stanford on the basketball or football team, you are quick to say no pain, no gain as it pertains to your physical workouts. And we need also to know if there's *no pain* in high school, college, life, marriage or relationships, etc., there is *no* gain. And in this microwave generation, the reason we *divorce* so much in America is because somebody forgot to teach us how to handle our midnights. We saw a soap opera or a fairy tale on TV and we thought we would live happily ever after. No one taught us life coping skills. Nobody told us that if you stay married long enough, you'll have certain seasons where it seems *stale*. Your wife might not be as bootilicious at fifty-eight as she was at twenty-eight but if you hang on in there, it can be exciting!

It's happening for a reason. You have this book for a _____ - you fill in the blank. I want unusual people like Dan Cummings in Florida. When Dan's son, Daniel got hooked on drugs and stole, and then sold a gun, he ended up in prison with a twenty-year sentence. Dan Cummings did the almighty though it was unlikely. He entered the drug world. He investigated until he found the drug dealer who bought the gun from his son. He got the gun back and took it to the damned judge. The judge released Dan's son from the twenty-year sentence... Now Daniel is working with his daddy, Dan in the family bait and tackle shop. That's who I'm looking for. I'm searching for some sons who'll go get their daddies out of the crack house. I'm looking for some parents who will go get their children out the crystal meth house. I am looking for some sons and daughters who are ready and willing to *stand up* for justice. Stand up for righteousness and fairness. When we see a Rolando Cruz in prison for molesting and killing a little girl in Illinois and he's *wrongly* convicted; let's do what Rubin "Hurricane" Carter did. Let's stand up and fight. Rubin went and got Rolando *out of* prison. He fought against public opinion, politicians and even the police. And he proved Rolando was innocent.

And when we see innocent folk in prison, we gotta pull out all the stops and get them out. I tell y'all if we *recalled* our governors in Georgia, Illinois, New York, Florida or wherever, the way they did in California, we could get the innocent *out*. Tell your governor you will kick his ass out of office if he does not get the wrongly convicted, innocent and unjustly incarcerated out of prison and he'll clean up the prisons. We need to align ourselves with George Soros, Peter B. Lewis, Jerry Keenan and David E. Kelly and put muscle behind our political threats. Tell our governors we want prisons to be humane, fair, un-cruel, usual and rehabilitative. Let's get this thing together today. We can do it...

Do y'all think it is coincidental that James Emslander called me about three weeks before this book was due out to indicate that *Bev Smith* did a show all about sex offenders? I think it was divine order and perfect timing. Bev was doing exactly what she was supposed to be doing. The universe, I tell y'all, will always open up windows of opportunities to get you exactly where you are supposed to be. And you shall arrive on time if you are prepared. It requires sacrifices and faith, hope and readiness. You can't be unwilling to *step out* on your dreams and beliefs.

And sometimes you won't have the support or backing of even your closest friends and family. Sometimes people won't or don't understand your dream, your hope or goal. They can't understand what is happening or where God is trying to take you to. And you cannot allow them to get in your way. At some point, you must be willing to pull out all the stops, press forward and do whatever it takes to obey the universe.

For all of my youngsters who are perusing this tome, if I can't get you to see anything else, please see this... I want you to see that true fulfillment comes from the willingness to separate yourself, live your own life, set goals and go for it.

I'm cognizant of the fact that some of you are going to smoke weed. Some of you will drink. Some of you will experiment with this or that. And there is zero, which I can say or write, which will stop you. But I would hope you would not overdo it. I don't want you trying any of that crap. But for those who do, I feel for you. I hope you don't get too far gone before you turn it around. And it's not easy to turn it around...

Find something (anything) you like to do which is legal. Find something you like to do and *master* it. Do it in your sleep, your dreams, your mind, soul and spirit. And when you master it, you will succeed. That, I promise.

Daniel Yoder and Casey Ryle called me in late, late November. Daniel told me how sick he felt about what happened to Shasta. He told me he was sickened by what that man did to Dylan, Dylan's mom and her boyfriend. "What can we do, Mr. Manning?" he asked. "Calling them perverts, yelling, screaming and talking about how much we despise them won't stop it. What can we in our teens do to stop it?" he asked me.

Two days later, Daniel, Casey, podcast thespian Jamie Miller (from Rancho Cordova), David Foster's two sons, Jamie Kennedy and Timothy Goebel all joined me in a press conference at Center High School in Antelope. Jeremy Hunt introduced me... I told the teens how important it is to learn to *listen*. "I just left the prisons," I told them. "And I can tell you one of the most severe problems which I saw in people in prison, especially youngsters was bad listening habits. If you don't *listen* well, you miss out. Your comprehension is incomplete. You will miss out on job promotions, special connections, information and educational development, etc., if you don't learn to develop your listening skills. I saw hopelessness and helplessness. I saw humans in their twenties physically but twelve years old mentally. I saw laziness, anger, hurt and pain.

"But if we are ever to get to the root of any problem, we must learn the power of listening. Your doctor can't diagnose you properly if he does not *listen* to you describe your symptoms. He must listen to your heartbeat, etc. If you go to a mechanic, he needs to *listen* to you describe the car's problems. He can't catch the tail end or cut you off. He needs to get all the information he can. Go to an auto body shop or auto detailing shop and the people working need to *hear* what you want. Learn to listen. It will trap you, hinder your success and delay your destiny. All brilliant people are great listeners. I want a team of youngsters to *listen*. We can solve this travesty of child molestation if we learn to listen. Think with me; one of the main reasons most children don't tell their parents or other adults when they are molested is they are ashamed, afraid and they are so accustomed to us cutting them off mid-sentence. Shut up! Be quiet and listen. It will not kill you to remain silent for seven or eight seconds to be sure the talker is finished before you open your mouth and tell everything you know.

"Kids need our ears. And if I were a kid with a big secret, the last person I'd wanna tell would be some dude who I knew would *cut me off*! Be quiet. Listen... Develop those skills now. It is not too late to learn. I want a team of listeners in every school and in Boy Scout clubs, etc.

"I am setting up a new Website, interactive blog and telephone bank tomorrow specifically so kids can call in and be heard. Join with us... Let's get this thing together." I said.

After the press conference, I shook a few hands then Daniel, Becky, Casey, Jamie Miller and I went to the Lone Star Steakhouse for lunch and a meeting.

At our meeting, we ran into Renae Gonzales and Fatima Hoang from Hollywood, CA. Seamus Farrow also joined our table. I could not believe Seamus' story. I shan't even mention Seamus' famous parents. Seamus is eighteen and most brilliant eighteen year olds want to stand on their *own*. This may be the first time Seamus has been mentioned in a book on his own merit. I respect Seamus so much. He told me he entered Yale Law School at fourteen years of age. (More on Seamus in the next book and on our blog at *Dashcash.blogspot*.com). Seamus wants to change the world. I thank God for the Seamus Farrows of the world. And at the meeting, he immediately began firing off questions. He wanted the specifics about how/what and when *NAPS* would tackle problems facing young people in trouble? How and when we would set up phone banks. Who would man them? Who would train them, etc.?

I hope all of the youngsters out at *Jesuit* High School, Folsom, Center High in Antelope, etc., will do as Seamus Farrow and be energetic, positive and excited about the world. Steve Madden (Atlanta, GA), Elton Bailey (Okay Magazine), David Rolfson, Daniel Rudolf and Mr. Seamus need this book. I hope you all get it to them. Use Craig's List, Find Anyone type search engines, Zabasearch.com etc. and mail them this book. It's difficult to get some folks to understand the monumental task of putting a book like this together. Then I get a lot of notes and e-mails asking, "What did Seamus think of your tome?" And I have to reply, "I don't know. Did you send Seamus a copy?" And they'll reply, "No, I don't know where to reach him." And I'll reply, "I didn't know where to reach you but I found *you* and sent you a gratis copy of this book - *Pay it Forward*."

So, if you really want lil Aaron Peckham, Kate Carter (Santa Barbara, CA), Kari Andal, Patrick Andal, Actor Tim Robbins, Susan Sarandon, Luke Klipp, Elias Ravin, Ryan Sheehy, Alex Hurst, Jack Rosenfeld, Cass McCombs, Tyson Ritter, Ray Toro, Frank Lero, Mikey Way, Steve Valentino (Davis) Jo Chandler and Zechariah Diamond at Street Breeze Newspaper, etc. teens at the Wind Youth Center etc., etc. If *you* want them to have this book - *Send it*. What better way to make a statement as a parishioner than to send *your pastor* this book. What better fan statement than to send Brad Pitt, Angelina Jolie, Paris and Paris Hilton this book? Albert Zakes, Kyle Bruce (Natomis, CA), Ryan Pearson (Sacto, CA), Brandon Biggs, Adam Daniels, Chad Gunderson, Farah Joy (Sacto, CA), Brian McInnes, Brett Sestric, Luke, Kyle and Carl Abbott (San Jose), David Hankins, Craig Yarenko, Cody Alcott, Chris Ciompi, Ivan Ganchev, Victor Mercado, Joe Chan (River City High School), Travis Thum, Matt Maloney, Sheila Barry, Ken Jacobson, Floyd Landis, Fred Rodriguez, Dave Zabriskie, Dr. Max Testa, Levi Leipheimer, Stephen Susco, Dmitry Tursunov, Jonah Peretti, Jimmy Wayne, Todd Swank, George Derieg, Dan Taylor, Peter Wertz, Patrick Stump (Fallout Boy), Andrew Rauscher need this book. Y'all can use Zabasearch.com (call Zaba and tell the owner he owes me some quid pro quo for all the hits I send em)… And find these folks. Do it? Good!

I could not believe the fabulous dancing skills of Giovanny Martinez (Vista, CA), Nick Lazzarini (Bay Area), Nick McGough (Las Vegas, Nevada), Geronimo "Timo" Nunez (Santa Barbara) and Rodrigo Guzman (Van Nuys, CA)… What a group.

Gabriel and Michael Scott Sellers got Richard Greenfield (North Ridge, CA), Ryan Conferidi (Downey, CA), Giselle Peacock and her husband Artem to lead the dancing team for NAPS. Joshua Dick (Illinois) also was on the team. They danced for justice twice per month on our NAPS dancing tours. We had come up with numerous ways to get youth active in non-boring ways, which exerted their energy and showcased their talents while shining a light on justice, safety and the protection of our citizens.

We tried to find Carly Simon because we knew she knew how often the justice system is unjust. Mrs. Simon had struggled for years to try to free John Forte who was a man unjustly incarcerated due to harsh, cruel and unusual mandatory minimums. (I encourage all readers to e-mail senators and tell them to let John Forte out of prison). We wanted to get Carly's son involved with NAPS. (If Carly or her son is reading - Go to http://SaveShastaGroene.blogspot.com). We employed the talent and appeal of Peter Wentz, Patrick Stump (Fallout Boy Band), Walter Smith (Ohio), John Artis (Virginia - of "The Hurricane" Fame), surfing the nations, seeds of peace, Jarod Miller, Doug Pieper (Folsom, CA), Attorney (fmr. Judge) John Fitzgerald Malloy, John Elsmore, Josh Bandez (Easy Bands), Conrad Riggs, Kevin Shelton, Alexander Dugdale (Richmond, VA), Dominic Sophia, Plan B Productions, Brody Darvin, Brandon Gibson (Knoxville, Tenn.) Bradley Jacobs, J. D. Roth, Travis Perryman, Steve Schumbauer, Drew

Z. Greenberg, David Lee Gallagher, Luke and Kyle Abbott, David Hankins (Minn., Minnesota), Steve Sachs, Matt Dalio, Seamus Farrow, Daniel Cummings, Andrew Rauscher (Harry Potter fan), Emma Jacobsen, Stephen Schultz (Atlanta, GA), Shemm, Prof. Kareem Crayton (U.S.C. Law School), Joey Gluveri, D. J. Hublen (Rocklin High School), Aaron Muller (MO), Jeffrey Frieders (Sacto), Chris McClendon (Reno - Straight Edge), Mike Silver (Inside Edition), Judge Richard A. Howard (Florida), Frank Feltes, Jr., Buford Turwilleger, Kate Carter, Seqib Keval, Daniel Yoder (Sacto), Casey Ryle (Rancho Cordova), Steve Peak (Sacto), Brad Pitt, etc...

Kate Carter had motivated *me* when I saw she was doing Life Chronicles. She records messages (on camera) for family members, etc. so that when a person dies, etc., the family can go back and review the video over and over. A young man working with Mrs. Carter (young college student) touched my heart when he explained how much he grew from *volunteering* to film for Life Chronicles. Teens will volunteer if they feel it is important and a worthy cause.

James, my mom and I had all been moved to tears when Ted Koppell interrupted Nightline's regular programming to tell the world about the suffering and starvation in *Niger*. There is a tragedy, a horrific catastrophe of Tsunami-like proportions taking place in Niger right now. A few months ago just ten million dollars would have prevented an enormous amount of this starvation. They showed families eating rats for dinner. My God... And we eat rats for fun on the *Fear Factor* trying to win fifty thousand dollars. It's hard to look at those kids in Niger. I would strongly, strongly, encourage every person reading my words to help feed the starving and hurting people in Niger. They need immediate help. I want you to pray for Niger. Prayer really does change things. But baby boy, baby girl, when you get through praying, write a check to feed those people. They need help now. They really, really need our help. This is an emergency!! Yes it is!!

At the end of the day, my friend, James Emslander is still in prison. Carly Simon's friend John Forte is still in prison. And there are molesters on the streets. People who are raping babies. Mr. J. Benson was in charge of the Sacramento *Youth* Symphony! A position of authority, trust, esteem and he had little boys and girls under his auspices. Guess what he did? He molested little boys! While you and I were picketing the ex-con getting out and demanding he not live in our neighborhood, etc., the man and woman whom we trusted, respected and believed in, etc., the Catholic priest, the Baptist pastor, school teachers, coaches, symphony directors, Boy Scout leaders, politicians, police officers and even judges were downloading kiddie porn and seducing our children into their webs of deception, disease, pedophilia and porn. We will never stop it unless we come out of our denial and quit pretending we don't know what the statistics are. The statistics are what they are; by and large, more than likely in more cases than not... the pedophile is a professional White male. No wonder the media does not tell us. Blacks and Browns rape also. And I, of all people, don't wanna racially profile anyone. But if statistics tell us that eight out of ten suicide bombers are of a certain color or religion, etc., we *must look at it*. We won't ever stop robberies if we are busy fighting speeding violations only! The police won't stop cocaine distribution if they only focus on weed smokers.

America won't stop or even curtail child molestation if they don't go after the judge, police, firemen, priests and other Caucasian professionals who are committing most of these crimes and when we do catch them we must stop *slapping them on the wrist*. The punishment must fit the crime and if you do the crime you must do the time. And give me a kid like James who made a silly mistake and got locked up for a non-violent crime. I'll also accept a John Forte busted for drugs. They deserve a *chance*. But we must change how we approach, treat, arrest, sentence, correct and punish violent sexual predators. Most especially child predators. We must protect the innocence of every American child!

We must call on Jack Ritter, Zach Weary, Angelina Jolie and Nate Berkus and ask them to help us! Call the *White House* switchboard and inundate the President's telephone with calls about pedophiles. Tell our government we demand a change and we want it *now*!

Ashton Kutcher said, "I know what it's like to eat government cheese and to be on welfare... I know what it's like to be laughed at in school because you're on the free lunch program." And Ashton has never forgotten what it was like to be poor. He got his big break modeling! (All my sista girl readers want a pic of Ashton in the revised edition of this book modeling his Speedos back in the day...Ashton? The pictures? Can we use them?) And when we reach out to people in Hollywood, Paris, New York and in power, we must remember that many of them have been poor. Many of them have not forgotten. Our job is to *reach out* to them and say, "Help." Tell em, "We go to your movies, buy your CDs and DVDs and we need you to help us to help our children." Reach out to them via their fan clubs, agents and Websites...

My bloggers must demand that America's polit*r*icians and I did say polit*r*icians, do something different to *create safe beds*. The media ain't gonna do it because it is their colleagues and folks who look like them (mainly Caucasians) committing these evil acts against children.

I'm cognizant of the fact that I'm striking a *nerve* by pointing out the color of the pedophile. Get over it. If you have no problem with me pointing out the fact that Black folks consume more greasy foods and crack than Whites… if you ain't got no problem with me pointing out that most of the *victims* of *rapes* in prison are young and White and most of the *perpetrators* of *rapes* in prisons are Brown and Black… Then don't have a problem with the picture of a pedophile. Crime is crime and wrong is wrong and we need to change it. Soul by soul, heart by heart, person by person and human by human, we must come out of the closet of silence, rise up as humans who care and prevent another Dylan Groene. We must stop rapes *in* prisons, out of prison, in Catholic churches, in homes, in America and in the world.

It must begin in *your* household, on your street, in your school and city. Begin locally and it will grow globally. I know it will. America is ready for a miracle and ripe for change. Children believe in miracles - how about you??

We need a miracle. And I will reiterate the fact that the church needs to be involved. All these mega churches with five, ten and fifteen thousand members ought to step up to the plate. The top ten churches in America took up about a half billion dollars last year alone… Joel Olsteen's church took up fifty-five million dollars. How much of that half billion went towards educating members on how to *create safe beds*, feeding the hungry, clothing the naked and visiting (restoring) those in our prisons?

I'm sorry the *Blue-Eyed Blonde* had to come from Jeremy Shackelford, Paul, Scott and me. I know some of y'all still think I may want your *endorsement* for *me*. But I'll tell y'all like Paul that I am the chief of sinners. Don't trust *me*. Don't trust *me*. Just educate yourself, analyze the data and then accept the *prescription*. If your doctor examines you and prescribes a treatment i.e. penicillin; you may get a second opinion. Then look on the Internet and in medical journals and compare your symptoms to his prescription. If the prescription is correct - take it! It will save your life. Now if that same doctor on the other hand (physician heal thyself?) has *your* symptoms and refuses to take his own medicine, i.e. the penicillin he prescribed you, he may die but if you take it, you'll live! If your pastor preaches it and does not *live it*; get your Bible out and examine the sermon (prescription). I.e., if the prescription is right, the pastor may go to hell, but if you confess Jesus, you'll live and have life eternal.

That's why I'm in your home right now! That's why you're reading this book. It is a dramatic description, which includes a prescription for saving the children, doing justice, loving mercy and walking humbly with our God.

Check out the prescription. Call Snaps, sex experts, professors and psychologists and ask the questions about the data in this book. It's the *data* I offer you to save the children.

If you trust *me*, Bishop Flip Flop, Joe Bloe or coach so and so with your child, just cause he wrote a book, you are a fool. You didn't get the point of this whole book. If I come to your house and you leave me *alone* with your child, you missed the whole point. Re-read the book from page one. Trust nobody, nobody with your child!

We have all of these young, energetic and healthy Black boys in the neighborhoods being recruited into the gangs now at eight, nine, ten and eleven years of age. And they shoot up the damned neighborhood and kill up other brothers over bullshit. They cut down human life as if they were simply stepping on roaches or ants. And we have our White brothers who are Hell's Angels riding across country on their Harleys etc. It's time now for us to go to the neighborhoods and recruit eight, nine, ten and eleven year olds to join NAPS and any real public safety groups in which we can occupy their minds, utilize their creativity, sponsor them, feed them, expose them to life and tutor them. We need to go out to the suburbs and get some bikers who are kid *likers* and organize the *Heaven's Angels* bikers club. Let's get White folks to take off their shirts, tie a bandana around their foreheads and ride for child safety, *safe beds* and find programs to teach kids how to effectively avoid child predators.

I'm calling Nick Lazzarini, Geronimo "Timo" Nunez (Santa Barbara, CA), Nick McGough, Ryan Conferidi, Giselle (and Artem) Peacock, Timothy Goebel, Ashton Kutcher, Mark Hughes (author) and Kevin Henkes to *help*!

All ya'll Fallout Boy, Metallica, My Chemical Romance, Green Day and Scissors Sisters fans get busy. Let on your Websites, message boards and in discussion groups and let's make history together while saving the lives of our children.

I'm looking for those willing to organize Heaven's Angels Bikers Boyz in the Hood 4 Good gangs and groups to establish some troops for safe beds. Where are you? Come out, come out *wherever* you are...

Those cunning, confused, racist and addicted little thieves, gang bangers and bikers are *seeds*. They are seeds and a seed cannot grow unless it has been underground, in dirt and in darkness. And if we motivate them to (come out, come out wherever you are) come out of that mess, junk, dirt, danger, darkness and evil; they are qualified, ripe and ready to grow. If we inspire them to come up out of the darkness and into the light, they will. Right. They will kick ass and take names later. You can't convince me that those big ole (so-called) pecker woods won't stand up for the safety, protection and innocence of our children. Not White children but *all* children. You can't convince me that those Black and Brown thugs out in Nickerson Gardens, Watts, Harlem and Fair Street Bottoms are unwilling to gather up the troops and *bust some* heads for the safety of our boys and girls... All children.

And we must tackle this issue without *emotion*. It's difficult, I know. It's emotional, angering and troubling to *think* about people raping babies. It's sicker than sick. It's like we wish they had a separate *cemetery* for baby rapers. But we cannot solve this tragedy with our emotions. Emotions are not solutions unless they emote us into action. We have to stand away from our temper and rage and go to a place of pragmatism and creatively develop strategy. It's a war. And the war must be fought with sane, sober and sensible minds.

We can use all the tools which predators use to get our children (I.e. the Internet) to get *them*. Expose predatory priests and coaches and police, etc.

Don't you dare read this as just another good book. I'm not writing to *play* with you. I know there is a lot of humor, drama, comedy and sobriquet in this book. Paul and Jeremy designed it that way. They are the brilliant folks! They (Jeremy and Paul Shackelford) are White. And I just did what a Black man supposed ta do! I obeyed them and composed this tome to include sex, drugs, rock and roll.

We refused absolutely to preach to the damned choir! If the choir ain't saved yet, let em go to hell! But we wrote this book to go all down in the high schools, colleges, frat houses, book clubs, Boy Scout troops, Girls and Boys Clubs, etc. and we couldn't write it without zap, pizzazz and energy. We had to put it out there and put it down... I thank Kate Carter for what she is doing with *Life Chronicles*. Yes, I mentioned Mrs. Carter earlier. But thanks to an expert journalistic effort by James Emslander, I was able to speak with the folks at Life Chronicles and hook up. They are covering NAPS. Thank God for concerned student volunteers like *Brian Glover*...

Brian Glover is volunteering to do the filming for Mrs. Carter. I salute Brian Glover, Ryan Conferidi, Brian Lane, Jesse Riegal, Ray Toro, Andy Fenkner, Clayson Whitney, Scott Reed, Janousek, Eric Shore, Casey Ryle, Christopher Hillman, Chaz Wolcott, Joshua Dick, Dr. Terry Thomas, Isotalent, Luke Klipp, Straight Edge, Michelle Tinnes, Daniel Yoder, The Nation News, Roy Black, Jay Renfroe, David Garfinkle, Ron Yates, Michael Colen, Geraldo Rivera, Calvin Langford (River City High School Sacto), Buford Terwilleger, Chad Gunderson, Terrence Howard, John Singleton, Adam Daniels, Timothy Goebel, Johnny Weir, Ashton, Damon Dash, Marshall Mathers, William Hung and *you*. None of this would have been possible without the patience, speed and expertise of Ms. Patricia Lee, Peter Andrist, Katryn, Brenda Smith, Betty and James Manning, Almighty **God**, Michael Shackelford (Sand Springs), Justin Dill, Scott Cozza and Michael Phelps. I salute Brad Pitt, Michael Moore, Mel Gibson, Angelina, Sharon Stone and Swiss producer Mark Forester...

    * * *

They snatched the eleven-year-old boy. They drugged him. They beat him. They put him in girl's underwear. They were about to sodomize him. But a White guy in a new group called Heaven's Angels and a Black guy in a gang called Boy'z in Da Hood 4 Good and Michael Colen showed up and *stopped it*. You can stop it too. What will you do?

    * * *

"If there is any molester watching our show right now or if you have ever been sexually aroused by thinking about a child, *get help now*. Don't ruin a child's life. Get help *now*. If you can't find any help, you call my show and I will personally get somebody to help you. Stop *molesting* our babies! Stop it! Join us on the next *Montel Williams Show...*"

...Bob Woodward let me down. How dare he be so selfish. I don't have time to go into details but I'll say it was entirely manipulative, selfish and wrong for him to go on NBC and play a tape from a 2000 interview so he could make sure we knew W. Mark Felt was suffering from dementia and has no memory of Watergate! Message? "Buy *my* book, 'The *Secret* Man' and get the facts. Any book allegedly written by W. Mark Felt is fiction cause you just heard, he didn't remember any details."

Self-serving interview from a man (Woodward) I used to *respect*. But I hope Nick Jones and his mom can see through Bob and I hope they continue to take care of that *great man*, W. Mark Felt.

Speaking of self-serving reporters brings me back to Nancy Grace. *L.A. Times* writer and author Tim Ruttin wrote an article in which he mentioned Mrs. Grace. "If you watched this week's coverage of the watch on the Jackson jury, you must have lost count of the number of times Nancy Grace - Court TV's harpy in chief and the dark star of Headline News - looked into the camera and, with swimming eyes and a quivering lower lip, began a sentence by saying, 'As a crime victim myself, I...'" Ruttin goes on to write, "Once you obliterate the boundaries that used to delineate journalism from advocacy, all sorts of other irritating barriers fall as well... The customary prohibition against, using your position in the news media to promote personal interests. All last week, Grace has been using her shows to promote her new book, 'Objection', published this week."

Tim goes on to point out that "Every one of her shows ended with some sort of plug for it, but the apogee was reached Wednesday. That was the day the book hit the stores and Grace not only discussed her book on both her Court TV and Headline News shows, but also for a full hour on CNN's top rated show, 'Larry King Live.' You can't buy that kind of publicity - unless, of course, you're engaged in the media equivalent of self-dealing." Tim Ruttin also points out that Nancy Grace hates all defense lawyers. Nancy writes that "the founding fathers set up our constitution in a way that allows defense attorneys and defendants to literally get away with murder..."

It is absolutely horrible and tragic that Americans have allowed the so-called media to dictate and to control how, what, why and when we think. We figure out how we're gonna think or who we are gonna believe, etc., based upon how it is presented in the media. If Fox News, the O'Reilly's, Hannity's or Limbaugh's get a hold of us first, they hypnotize us into believing whatever they say.

This is why I absolutely love Generation *Y*. I love these technocratic, idealistic and energetic youth who have the infrastructure to tell the world where they stand.

I support the rights of folks like Sacramentian Aaron Peckham who founded urbandictionary.com. "I've always been *fascinated* by *words*. Regular dictionaries try to be authoritative and *neutral*, but there's nothing neutral that's written by a *human*. Urbandictionary.com puts that power back in the hands of the people who use language," the twenty-four-year-old Aaron said. This wonder kid started his Website with a list of fifty to sixty slang words. Today, he has more than 600,000 entries... I.e. do you know the meaning of any of the following? Podestrian, Ear Worm, Icescapee, Maplash, Emaelstrom, Parentnoia, Bis Cas Fri or Death Star?

"When I started it, it was totally random, with no particular reason for being. But now it's gained purpose and a ton of people come and document pop culture and explain the world," he says.

I love the idea that a kid in jeans and t-shirt can sit down and start a Website, blog or podcast without even a clearly designed purpose. And then watch that dream, idea or vision bloom.

People such as Aaron are the biggest threat to the Rupert Murdoch controlled media which has ever been seen. When I think of Aaron's words, about the power of words and think of how he points out that *no* writing is *neutral*. It reinforces my belief that perhaps I should try to be to publishing what Damon Dash is to music.

I think all of us deserve to have our voices heard. I wanna lift them up for all the world to see and hear.

I want the world to know how much I have in common with one of my writing mentors; Mr. *Norman Mailer*. Mr. Mailer is eighty-two now and he's still writing. I salute him… Lisa Bloom and her mom, Gloria Allred will continue to tell us how bad men are. They will continue to tell their half of the story. Maureen Orth and Dominick Dunne will continue to tell us about private jets and Martha's Vineyard type prison walls. They'll tell us their right-winged views of celebrity justice and ask us to weep for Peter Bocanavic because he's doing *five* months in a federal country club. They will tell us how bad the poor are and good the wealthy are.

They'll explain the evil genius of Karl Rove and how the public has no right to know about Rush Limbaugh's kinky medical procedures and addiction to drugs.

But if we are ever gonna know about Rolando Cruz, David Quindt, Anthony Porter, Kenny Waters or Marcus Dixon and how often prosecutors abuse their powers and trample upon justice. If we will ever know about the boys being raped in prison and transformed into monsters. If we will ever know about the hypocrisy our youth sees and feels about us. The voices of the gothics, Y Generation and college frats who log on to Myspace.com and Friendster… The only way we will hear from them is if people like Aaron Peckham, Norman Mailer, Geraldo Rivera, Eric Bulrice, you and me, continue to tell the story. That's what *Jeremy Shackelford* would have done. That's what Eminem, *System of a Down* and *The Killers* (Murder Inc.) do.

We tell it and sell it however we must. If it means selling books, tapes or CDs out of a car trunk, at a bake sell or door to door.

If it means podcasting, blogging or telephone calling, we are here and we're here to stay. It will be a cold day in hell before we go away.

We will tell the story of the left out, locked in and forgotten about. They can't stop us. We are savvy, sharp, methodical and strategic enough to invent ways to be read and heard. We will tell our story without Rupert Murdoch. We have Morgan Freeman (clickstar), Geraldo Rivera, George Soros and Damon Dash.

We gots Russell Simmons, you, her, him and me. We will rock the very foundation of traditional media outlets. With books such as this one, we will fashion a new order, carve out our own destiny, be recognized and see our visions realized right here, right now.

We know clearly that you'll never know about Jose Rogelio Ibarra in Riverside... You won't be inclined to look up Attorney Stephen Bedrick, in Oakland and find out how Stephen got Jay Johnson's case overturned due to the fact that Jay should not have had an all White jury. No White American should be tried before all Blacks. Maybe I should call Mr. Bedrick (bloggers feel free to let him know). You won't be made aware that the U. S. Supreme Court has recently held it is unconstitutional on its face to strike jurors based upon race unless we (Mr. Mailer, Peckham, Abu Jamal, Afana, Holavaty, etc) tell you about it. We will tell you! Yes, we will! We are pragmatic, transparent and clear thinking. We heard sex offender Jake Goldenflame loud and clear... "If you just start locking child molesters up for ages, with no chance to get out, they'll start *killing* their victims," he says. Ipso facto, we fight for prevention, prevention and more prevention. Also, when a person is a molester, we do believe in tough sentencing and treatment while they do time. And the Atascadera bullshit ain't it. We want real treatment and prevention for offenders...

Have you heard Rush Limbaugh, Sean Hannity or Bill O'Reilly mention anything about Death Row inmates funding scholarships? No? Well, if you went to DashCash.blogspot.com, you'd know about it. Death Row inmates from around the country were responsible for presenting a college kid whose younger sister was murdered a decade ago with a five thousand dollar scholarship. Zach Osborne, nineteen, got the scholarship from a group who solicited the money through their bimonthly publication "Compassion." They've given seven scholarships to the tune of twenty-seven thousand dollars. "We would like to help him in realizing his dream," wrote Dennis Skillicorn, a death row inmate in Missouri who is the newsletter's editor.

Osborne is studying at East Carolina University where he'll be a sophomore this fall. His father and grandparents attended the scholarship ceremony. Stephen Dear, Executive Director of the Carrboro based People of Faith Against the Death Penalty, presented the scholarship. "He has wisdom beyond his years, gained the hardest way - a wisdom that victims need healing and that victims can come to forgive even those who have caused the greatest pain," Dear said. Death Row prisoners contribute artwork, essays and poetry to "Compassion", a project of the Roman Catholic Church's Peace and Justice Committee. Money from subscriptions pays for publishing and funds the scholarships. To win his scholarship, Zach Osborne wrote an essay about the crime and the effect it had on him... Brandon Biggs, whose father was hit by a car in Fort Worth, Texas, in 2001, also has received the scholarship. Osborne, however, still wants the perpetrator executed. I hope, he'll mature and grow to the point where he no longer supports killing people, i.e. the death penalty. Bloggers, frats, brats, computer nerds, etc. will make sure you know about stories such as this...

Javier Ovando was just awarded $6.2 million for his public defender's negligence after being set up, falsely arrested and shot by corrupted police. He was paralyzed from the waist down and had a gun planted on him by the LAPD. A jury had sentenced him to twenty-three years in prison. Later, the case was overturned and he was awarded fifteen million dollars for the wrongful conviction. Attorney Tamar Toister was the public *pretender*. Why didn't you know this?

Attorney David Kendall, Gerry Spence, Leo Terrell and Carl Douglas would have told you, if you asked. Richard Smith (Journalism student at Cornwall College in Camborne, England) and Luke Bateman, Michael Noble, Tim Noble, Eric Bulrice (Big Bear Lake, Technical Theater student at Idyllwild) would tell you, if you asked. Since we won't learn about wrongful convictions, police and prosecutorial misconduct or the thousands of men who are like Javier Ovando from Gloria Allred, Nancy Grace or Mr. Dunne, we write, we write and we write. We gotta keep on writing til we get the word to Scott Perri of Pleasanton, California. We wanna reach Franz and Annelies Leuthardt. Annelies Leuthardt (Smithville, Missouri) and Franz are from Switzerland. And Annelies has a law degree. Perhaps we can motivate Annelies to put that law degree to use here in America with NAPS, our frats or our scholarship programs.

Margaret De Barraicua, the McClatchy High School teacher charged with having sex in the back seat of her car with a sixteen-year-old boy, while her two year old looked on? She had twenty-four college professors, teachers, long time friends, neighbors, a pastor and family members say a prison sentence is too harsh for De Barraicua. Margaret is thirty years old. Marcos Garcia wrote that she "has a stream of qualities that many of us only hope to mirror." I disagree. This kid was not only a student but sixteen. Not only sixteen, but a special education student. If Margaret was Melvin and the student was a girl, we'd be outraged. Let's be fair and deliver equal justice under the law. She was wrong. And if she was a he and he was a she would we argue that we should "mirror" her? I think not. Bloggers believe in justice. Scott Sellers, Mike Jiminez, Clark Domae (Rancho Cucamonga) Dimitri Hamlin, Danny Way and Matt Taylor, Zach Weary, you, tinkerers and me will put it out there. We want the world to know.

Political junkies like Elizabeth Newell and Eli Pariser want us to push forward. We will win Ryan Sheehy, Elias Ravin, Casey Gray, Jack Rosenfeld, Alex Hurst, Austin Cregg, Aaron Richter and Samantha Dellos if we push forward. Gerard Way, Billie Joe Armstrong, Rufus Wainwright, Ronnie Vannucci and Brandon Flowers will come on board. Brian McFayden, Jose Escoto, Bloc Party and Rufio will join us if we continue to write, blog, chat, tinker, think, pray, give and podcast.

At some point in our lives we should try to become *caretakers* of the universe and of each other. I heard a singer on Tavis Smiley say that the other night. And at the end of the day, we are either *caring* or we're *taking*. The people who moved the universe forward, the Dr. Martin Luther King, Jr.s , John F. Kennedys, Mother Teresas, etc. were willing to care for others. I don't believe all of the negative, the mainstream media has to say about young people. I believe deep within that senior at John F. Kennedy High, Christian Brothers High, Sheldon High School in Elk Grove and Davis or Pittsburgh High, etc., that freshman at U. C. Davis, Boston University, U. C. Berkeley and New York University, etc., etc., I believe our students care. Expressing those feelings while being judged, suspected or indicted is what proves to be a deterrent for that expression...

Joshua Dennis (Willis, Michigan), Chris Eschbach, Mike Pierce (Meredith College, Raleigh, NC), Alan Hopkins (scientist in L.A.) David Hopkins (L.A.), John Gilmore, Randi Rhodes and Jodie Evans will stand with us if we reach them. There are students at El Camino High like Bryn Wolf, Dani Sousa and John Cleveland, etc., who are radio hosts on campus, etc., who have a passion for liberty and justice. They are the folks we need to reach. Riley Evans (Davis), Tanvir Kapoor and all those students who participate in the First Amendment education programs sponsored by the ACLU are our people.

David Yalof and all the constitutional law professors at the University of Connecticut and at McGeorge School of Law need to know about the findings of Jeremy Shackelford. Peter Liu at the Sacramento Country Day newspaper and Don Winters need to be recruited. When we get Riley, Andrew Solorio, Patricia Fels, Jennifer Vogel, Meredith Bennett-Smith, Nobbs Nzima and Kiran Savage-Sanguan, we will win. KYDS (El Camino Radio Station) Aurn, Reach Media, The Aggie News and activist, James Henderson/Riley Evans Tyre students are the folks we must reach. When we get Riley Evans, Wes Kovarik, Nzima and David Hankins on Myspace.com telling it like it is, dropping science, blogging, entertaining and explaining, we will run predators off line and send sexual miscreants off these sites.

I believe that the information contained in this nonfiction novel (of sorts) represents the best of our youth. It represents Riley Evans, Liu, Solorio, Kapoor, Kovarik, Severson, Bulrice, Noble and Nzima. I wrote it for, with and to them. It will take off through them. They have the power. And the success of this book will be a testament to the powers of the First Amendment, artistic expression and freedom of speech. Some of the folks who peruse this tome will question me, my motives and my status. So be it. But they will never be able to question the *facts*. We are entitled to our own *opinions*... But not our own set of facts. To the skeptics and critics, I say just give me the facts. Just the facts. How many kids will be molested tonight? Not by guys doing time in jail for burglary. Not by guys in jail who used drugs. Not by anybody who is incarcerated. But by priests, judges, coaches, teachers, etc. How many children will sleep tonight in unsafe beds? Millions! That's a fact! And the more we allow our boys and youngsters to go to juveniles, jails and prisons and get raped, the more they will learn to rape. And the beat goes on and the cycle continues. The facts, just the facts. We can stop it... to be continued... October 2005.

Sherman D. Manning
Author
With contributions by *Jeremy Shackelford* and *Paul Shackelford.*

Publisher's Note: Honoring *Harper Collins*... This tome in no way purports to be a comprehensive or exhaustive study on the epidemic of child molestation or pedophilia. It is rather a culmination of data, which has been researched by the author and based upon what we feel is sound, solid and credible information. It is a continuing work in progress, which this company feels is time sensitive. We believe that when reader's blog, chat, text, podcast and continue the dialogue in a constructive manner - change will come. No child deserves to be molested. No human deserves to be raped. And any person who actually commits such an atrocity upon another, is a *sick* person in need of serious treatment, therapy and punishment.

We concur with this author (*Sherman D. Manning*) in his conclusion that merely throwing outrage, anger and laws at the problem, will not solve the problem. We also conclude that this tome is a gem; a diamond in the rough. And when it sends teens, parents, teachers and professors back to prevention, back to pragmatic solutions and back to intervention, then the book has done its job.

We encourage readers to demand that your library, bookstore and school carry copies of this book. We applaud Brad Pitt, Andrea Casiragm, Alex Ebert, Astor, Thomas Foster, Volunteermatch.org, Teach for America, Rick and Drew Baker, Timothy Goebel, Eminem, Tyler Hoechlin, Chris Egan, Jordan McGraw, Jason Fortune, Aaron Peckham, *Joyfulchild*.org, the Joyful Child Foundation, Robin Power, Bryan Powell, Matt Dunbar, Mando Diao, Noren, Carl-JoHan Fogelkou, Dixgard Samuel Giers, Ashton Kutcher, David E. Kelly, Jamie Kennedy, Gardner Rich & Co., Tyler Perry, Serj Tankian, Wade Robson, Macaulay Culkin, Patrick McCarthy, Fairchild Publications, Abercrombie & Fitch, John Ewing, Kevin Mahaffey, Soroptimist Int., *Damon Dash* Music Group, Scott Ross, Atty. Bedrick, Atty. Leo Terrell, Tom Mesereau, Susan Yu, Tom Goldstein, Gerry Spence, Dijol J. Beilly, Dr. Keith Liang, Dr. David Leeser, Jesse Schell, Rodrigo Ojeda Beck, Adam Getchell, Stephen Susco, Ron Droze, Barrett Lyon (Hollywood, FL), Ken Sunshine, Mike Lathan, Visual Therapy, Michael Phelps and Andy Roddick.

And we respect Marshal and Tim for the photos and will try to use even more photos in the next book. We encourage all high school seniors, valedictorians, football players, cheerleaders, college students, frats, brats and fan club members to write. Write a poem, essay, blog or comment(s). Send your work to newspapers, blogs, participate in chats, etc., etc., and spark the debate today. Tell all of your friends as well as enemies about *Blue-Eyed Blonde*. Go to Myspace.com, Friendster.com, LiveJournal.com, FaceBook.com, Craigslist.com, Tribenet.com, www.*SaveShastaGroene*.blogspot.com, www.*DashCash*.blogspot.com, www.werenotafraid.com, www.I'm sorry.com, and to Web logs nationwide and worldwide and tell others about this book. Just do it. We want great men like Peter B. Lewis, Bill Gates, George Soros, Damon Dash, Russell Simmons, Willie Gary, Gerry Spence, Sergey and Larry, etc., to go to www.Cafepress.com/Manning and order one thousand, two or three thousand copies of *Blue-Eyed Blonde* and (you can give Cafepress any address you'd like them sent to or we can send them to Oprah's Angel

Network, FMI, YMCA, public libraries, etc.) today. Order today so we can get this to the people. And each of you who received a gratis copy...what are you waiting on? We should not need to mention it but we will. Please order at least one more copy of this book today. Not tomorrow...Today!

Your comments, profile and biographical data, photos etc., will be publicized in the next book. Rush it, via snail mail to the *author* of *this* book.

Every financial and monetary offer mentioned in this book is backed by *this publisher*. You may participate in the interactive offers by following the author's instructions.

All financial rewards and awards are simply termed as such by the author. Legally, they are not a contest, lottery or raffle. They are unique and creative ways to give money to college students. Books are more powerful than bombs. They transform lives...

The Publishers

Editor's Note: The following is a *prelude* to *Sherman D. Manning's* next tome... Due out in January 2006. Let's peek in on a conversation and excerpt from Sherman's next book. It is *not untitled*. It is, however, unnamed herein. Read now...

It was clear that Teri Woods wanted *me*. Teri Woods wanted me from the very moment she laid her eyes upon me. I could feel her undressing me. No other woman made me feel this wayexcept Oprah. I can't write a lot about it here. It was a hot summer night and this White gal was in bed with me. She was hotter than the sun itself. We screwed for hours. It was real good. I turned around and Mark Zuckerberg was standing there nude. "I want some too," Mark said. I was hoping against hope he was speaking of Lisa. He was. Mark got in bed and I got out.

Wil Seabrooks called me. "I wanna be a model, dude. I think I can get rich. Mr. Manning, *please help me*," he said... (No disrespect to Wil Seabrooks but Neal Carlson and Craig Scott are my real... Tyler Hudson? Jesse Lee Soffer? Seamus Farrow? Jack Taylor??)

I got a call from Peter Grammatas about doing some cross cultural, cross-entrepreneurial and social advertising. Peter has a flower shop in the New York area. He promised to introduce me to Carly Simon and her son, a musician out at Martha's Vineyard. Carly's son was brilliant. I listened to Sean Hannity ranting and raving about Jodie Evans, Randi Rhodes, Christine Craft and Mike Malloy. Then he went on a diatribe and a vicious, ruthless and scathing rampage about a prison scribe!

"This convict is a predator, a rapist, a manipulator and a scam artist who writes books and cons high school teachers into reading them," Sean said.

"This bullshit artist, named *Marc Rice,* hails from Savannah, Georgia. He is a rapist. Why should anybody read his books? He even used Marshall and Timothy's pictures without proper permission on one of his tomes? If he were sincere, he would have given five percent of the profits from that book to Eminem's Foundation in Detroit. He has not given Eminem a dime. Why doesn't he set up a scholarship in Tim Goebel's name if he's really this wrongly convicted, Rubin 'Hurricane' Carter?" Sean asked. Marc called the show. "Thank you for taking my call, Mr. Hannity. Foremost and first, if Marshal was/is offended by any photo I've used as a form of artistic expression, all he would need to do is contact me, sir. Next, if he wanted even *ten percent* of profits to go to his foundation, I'd do it today. So far as scholarships are concerned, if Tim wanted one in his name I'd do that also. Now having said all of that, sir, my books are not about *me*. I passed trying to get people to believe in me long time ago. I know I am absolutely wrongly convicted. I challenge *you* or any lawyer, retired judge, etc., to get my trial transcripts from Santa Monica Superior Court in Robert Altman's court and read it. When you finish reading the transcript, you tell me if you think I did the crime. And you tell me if it was fair for me to have an all White jury. You tell me if Mary Hanlon Stone, Dave Winkler and Robert Altman gave me justice or injustice... I am no saint! But with everything inside me, I know what I know. I committed no crime there."

Sean Hannity interjected, "They denied your appeal. You're in jail. You had to do something. Why should we believe you?"

Marc replied, "Mr. Hannity, I don't give a damn whether you believe me or not. It's really irrelevant. Your endorsement, your vote of approval or belief in me would not get me out of prison. Thousands believed in Rubin 'Hurricane' Carter's innocence, but their belief didn't get him or John Artis out. It took twenty years, lawyers and God to get him out, sir. In the Bible, the one you say you believe in, Sean, Brother Joseph was convicted of a sex crime. Folk endorsing him didn't help him. It took 13 ½ years and a needy King Pharaoh to get him out. Now we love, celebrate and honor Joseph. Great tomes of encouragement i.e., '*God meant it for good*' by R. K. Kendall have been written, as a result of Joseph's wrongly conviction of attempted rape. So **God** got glory out of Joseph's story.

"My trials and pain have made me better. If you really read *Blue-Eyed Blonde* you'd see I don't ask any reader to endorse *me*. I ask readers to report child molestation. I tell kids to report online, predators. I tell kids that if anybody touches them inappropriately, to report it. I tell moms and dads not to turn their kids over to priests, family or friends but to check people out. I explain how molesters groom and con children. I explain how parents should learn to listen to children. Really listen. Sean, I know what it feels like to be wrongly convicted of an *adult* crime. It's horrible. It's wrong and it is a crime against humanity.

"But I write very, very little about *me*. I write more about the fact that only *one percent* of child molesters will ever be convicted of molesting a child. I talk about how society fails to deal with preventing molestation, treating molesters, treating the victims of molestation and watching for traits, signs or identifying characteristics of a potential molester. I talk about a subject painful for us to discuss.

"I put it out there in such a way as to appeal to seventeen to thirty-five year olds. And if a fifteen or sixteen year old gets a hold of *Blue-Eyed Blonde* so be it. They get a hold of pornography! They find the Playboys and Hustlers parents hid underneath the mattress. They see sex on TV and read about sorcery and witchcraft.

"So it's not a bad thing if they get a hold of my book and learn what to look for. If it encourages **one** fifteen-year-old kid to report molestation it's worth it to me.

"Sean - you damned right I'll use manipulation, controversy and sensationalism to spark a debate which will end up in action. At the end of the day, when you all finish scandalizing me... some young man i.e., Robert Zapeta, Brian Fernandez, Ricky Gill, Kevin Long or Fatima Hoang will (I promise you) decide, 'Well, even if Marc Rice is a thief, murderer, rapist or whatever, that book is compelling. If I put a piece of tape over the author's name and read *Blue-Eyed Blonde*, it is haunting. We gotta do something,' they'll say. Jason Knight (reporter for KCRA TV), Mr. Eli Broad (The Broad Foundation does great work helping young people go to the college of their dreams), Rob Nelson, Melissa, Jeremy at Harvard, Scot Parsley at Dartmouth and I know Davis at University of Southern California will do something to help."

Sean Hannity replied, "I still don't like the idea of prisoners writing, Mr. Rice. *You* are a criminal."

I replied, "I am a human being! I am innocent. If I escaped and were walking down the street in New York City, Sean, and saw you dying, would you want me to give you CPR and perhaps save your life? Or would yo ass want me to keep on walking and let you die because I was a prisoner, ex-con or escapee?"

I didn't allow Sean to reply, I continued on, "At some point, Mr. Hannity, you, Rush Limbaugh, Karl Rove and all of you undercover bigots need to get out of your prejudices and understand what is happening. Babies are being molested this very second while you try to discredit a convict with a potion. I have no panacea or magic potion but the danger in delay is tragic and not magic.

"If I'm dying, I want CPR from anybody who knows CPR. We'll discredit you later on. We'll find something to debate about later on. But for now - *save my life* if you can. If a convicted murderer could have saved Dylan Groene, Steve would have been happy. Sean - this is not about me. Our children are dying. Our children are dying. Analyze that. What are you, Rush, Karl Rove or any other pundits gonna contribute to saving the children? A man in a burning house wants to be rescued! *Blue-Eyed Blonde* is a rescue. That book is a rescue for youth not a resume for me."

I hung up...

I thank God I hooked up with Clay Aiken, Justin Daley in Tracy, CA, Maneesh Seth, Chani Suri, Jeannette Vaghozzi (2hands.blogspot.com), Damon (DashCash.blogspot.com) Dennis Depagter, Chris Austad, Cindy Coryell, Joel Coryell, J. D. Roth, Steve Schwabauer and Chad Vannucci. They helped give me courage, hope and faith that our efforts were not in vain.

I got a lot of pussy. I drank Heineken. I ran the streets quite often. But at the end of the day, there was this desire to change the freaking world. There was this hope. Letter came...

"Dear Marc Rice... Thank *you*, Mr. Shackelford (rest in peace), Mr. Kutcher and Harper Collins for your great work, hip hop writing for the Millenials (Generation Y) as well as Gen X - your true to life fiction told a controversial story which is literally *saving* lives. How - I enjoyed the input from *Sherman Manning* also. Thank God ya'll had the balls to put it down. We have started a *NAPS* Chapter here in Iowa. Evan McGregor, Kate Carter (Santa Barbara, CA), Dudley Benton (Knoxville, TN), Brian Lee Crawford (Pittsburgh), Kari and Patrick Andal, Clark Domae, Fatima Hoang, Todd Reyes (Sacto, CA), Dr. Andrew Salner (Light One Little Candle Foundation...West Hartford, CT), Darren Romeo, Mickey Madden, James Valentine, Jerry Saetern, Alex Benson, Georges Malbrunot, Anita Khandpur (Starwood Mont. School in Frisco, Texas), Chris Eschbach, David Holmes, Mike Pierce (Meredith College in Raleigh, NC), Robert Corea (Riverside Friday Night Live), Mr. Barry Diller, Cindy Christianson, Evan Strano, Keith Gardner, Lara Fox, Hilary Frankel, Zach Rich (Swept Away TV), Richard Cohn, Jeremy Petty, Erin Moriarity, Leslie Morgenstein (www.alloy.com), Tom Welling, Parag Sanghrajka (UCR Bio Major), Phil Hendrie (Sherman Oaks Radio Shock Jock), Gareth Newfield, Alex Wilson, Chuck Miller (art curator), Brad Garlinghouse, Jeff Mattenley, Jerry Dean Martin, Linda Worth, Tyson Madsen, Michael Colen, Tristan Imboden, Walter Dean Myers, David Reynolds, Michael Zhang (http://blog.MichaelZhang.com), Robert Downey, Jr., Jordan McGraw, Charles Best, Trent Reznor, Heath Ledger, Danny Way, Chris Wing, Chris Zeleny, Trevor Gordon, Dr. Chris Kaliakin, Alan Nierob, Atty. Mayorga, Brad Warren, Grayson Holmes, Chris Dawes, Sharon Stone, Kevin Shelton, Prof. Patricia Raybon, Wade Lagrone, Matt Funanwra, Neal Battaglia, Matt Damon, Kermit Roosevelt, Jeffrey Frieders, Tony Danza, Chris Purvis (Sacto), Jarod Miller, Andrew Rauscher (Harry Potter fan), Emma Jacobsen, Matt Dalio, Ken Gushi, Chris Jones, Rainer Hosch, Stephen Elliott, Matt Nie, Todd Eberle, Adam Nadler, Chris Mueller, David Fenner, David Friend, David Harris, Stephen Hua, Agim Kaba, Dr. Thane Hancock, Roger Westrup, Paul Nassif, Matt Christy, John Artis and Rubin Carter have all signed our *NAPS* support letter. We love you, bro.

I ask you to please publicize the *names* of all of these people. We are doing blogs, podcasts, newsletters, bake and cake sales, etc. to raise money for a Blue Ribbon Emergency Task Force on stopping child molesters, molestation and victims. We..."

As I hopped into my Rolls Royce Phantom and drove down Broadway, I was pumped. I pulled in to Uncle Charlies. There I met with Timothy Goebel, Burke Anderson, Andrew Rauscher, Craig Scott, Michael Shackelford, Steven Cozza, Chad Vannulli, James Patterson, Lisa Scottoline, Blake Ross, Tina, Terri Woods, Montel, Damon Dash, Jodie Evans and her twenty-year-old son.

I told them, "The American media can kiss my butt. Quite frankly, Rush Limbaugh, Karl Rove, Armstrong and Getty, The EIB Network and Sinclair Broadcasting can suck my 10 ½ inch (expletive)." There was riotous laughter.

"These people who head ABC, NBC and CBS are the triple demons of deception. They thrive on negativity. They let *Bush* get away with taking America to war on false information. They let me languish in jail for a crime I did not commit. Were it not for Damon Dash, Russell Simmons, George Soros, Peter B. Lewis, Peter Andrist, Sabine, Rubin, Tony Serra and Almighty God, I'd *still be in jail*.

All of them can go to hell. If you are dying and you need life saving measures... If you need CPR, I assure you it won't matter to you if the person giving you mouth to mouth is a convicted felon, pot smoker or liquor drinker... All you will want is CPR so you can live.

If the convict, pervert or ex-con saves your life, you will be thankful. You may even pay or reward him or her. But - that does not mean you'll move the person in your house or allow them to befriend your children.

My book *Blue-Eyed Blonde* was life support, emergency life preserving measures or CPR for Shasta Groene, and the millions of victims of child molestation rapes in prisons, rapings because of prisons and the shame the victims have to endure alone. I wrote the book as CPR for victims. Just because I wrote it does not mean people will or even should invite me to dinner or move me into their homes. Just take the CPR, the medicine in that book and leave it at that... The little boy said, "My priest has been molesting me. It started to feel good but I think it's wrong. I can't tell my mommy because she loves the father and she would not believe me." The little twelve year old said, "Mayor James West molested me. I could report it but the Chief of Police is the Mayor's lover." The little girl said, "My high school music teacher touched my vagina..." CBS, NBC, ABC didn't report the stories. They were too busy telling America how great Karl Rove was... I had to give CPR, will *You*?

* * * *

shermanmanning.blogspot.com
saveshastagroene.blogspot.com
dashcash.blogspot.com
hallopeter@freesurf.ch
www.cafepress.com/manning